THE WEREWOLF OF LISBON

CHICO KIDD

Dragon Moon Press

Copyright © 2015 Chico Kidd

Edited by Kathryn Halpern

This is a work of fiction. Names, characters, places, brands, media, and incidents are either the product of the author's imagination or are used fictitiously. Any resemblance to similarly named places or to persons living or deceased is unintentional.

PRINT ISBN 978-1-988256-51-1
EPUB ISBN 978-1-988256-52-8

Library of Congress Control Number: 2013916182

www.dragonmoonpress.com

As always, for my father
Kenneth Charles Kidd 1921-1994
And, with thanks, to Rosemary Pardoe

"In the year that is a hundred years after the bear's victory the
    wounded king may be reborn.
"Yet to regain his domination over the land he must receive again
    the dolorous blow and be healed of the unhealable wound.
"By the coming together of the four hallows may he be made whole.
"By the broken sword.
"By the silver platter.
"By the chalice.
"And by the bleeding lance.
"And the key to the hallows lies with the child in the city of Ulysses
    who is the child of no man, and whose mother is no woman,
    and who shall be born in the year that is a hundred years after the
    triumph of the bear."

—FROM THE *PROPHECIES*
OF JOHANNA KUNDRIE

PROLOGUE

IT'S NOT EASY TO SHOCK A WEREWOLF.

Of course, a werewolf doesn't last long if he's easily shocked. And usually the worst thing he ever sees is himself. Until he encounters a gun with a silver bullet in it, that is.

He smelt it first, or perhaps tasted would be a better word, although the two senses are so dependent on each other that they are difficult to separate. Blood, quantities of it, freshly spilled, rich and appetising, tainted with the stench of viscera. It was, however, human blood, and though it made the wolf salivate he would never follow that appetite through.

On wolf-nights, though, he did like to hunt when he got the opportunity, when *Isabella* was in port. But rats were the only things he killed. Edward Harris detested the taste of rat in his mouth when he woke up in the morning, but Harris-wolf was less fastidious. By now he knew the city fairly well, its many more than seven hills, its descents, alleys and back ways. Its shadows and secrets. The high Bairro Alto, the depths of the Baixa. Even, in part, the maze that is the Alfama, where when he was in human shape he sometimes felt his shoulders wouldn't fit between some of the houses and where some of the houses never see the sun. He kept to the dark places mostly, relying for the rest on a talent for going unobserved that seemed to have come to him with the nature of the beast.

The night was waning, and so soon would the moon as well: this would be his last wolf-night of the month. Harris was heading home when his expanded senses discovered this extravagance of blood. It was easy to locate, the olfactory equivalent of a scream, the kind of scream that stops you in your tracks and makes you clap your hands over your ears. It emanated from a flat roof halfway down this flight of steps, he could jump that quite easily.

As wolf, eyesight was not his strongest suit. A wolf doesn't see in the same way a man does. So he didn't exactly *see* the chiaroscuro of moonlight and gore, and that was lucky in a way since it saved him the trouble of losing his supper over the remains.

You couldn't tell at first glance, whether it had been a man or a woman, although the small size of the corpse suggested the latter. The throat had been torn out, and so had the entire chest cavity and abdomen. Something had apparently taken an enormous bite out of the body. Harris did *not* want to meet anything with jaws that size. But that wasn't really the worst part. It looked as if the attacker had then scooped out the rest of the flesh with a giant spoon. The ribcage looked like meat hanging in a butcher's shop. There was an extraordinary amount of blood around the savaged cadaver, gouts and splashes and slippery clots of it. Difficult to imagine that a human body could contain so much, especially such a small one.

Nervously, Harris licked his lips. Changed, he did not think as he did in man-shape, that is to say, he didn't subvocalize. However he was aware of an anomaly.

Something unhuman had savaged this woman and devoured soft tissues from the remains. But the only scents he could detect on the rooftop were human.

And Harris, belatedly, realized something else, and his heart began to pound. If anyone happened to see him anywhere near these pathetic gory rags of flesh that had not long ago been a human being, they'd be reaching for the silver bullets first and asking questions later. Or maybe not even bothering with asking the questions. Half-eaten corpse, one. Werewolf, dead, one. QED. He whirled round, too hastily as it turned out, to spring back down to the steps. And found himself scrabbling frantically for a foothold.

It wasn't shock that made him fall, and not panic either, not really. It was just that there was so much blood spilled around that he lost his footing and plummeted off the rooftop into the alley below.

But it was sheer bad luck that he fell onto a dustbin and broke his leg.

1

JUST A ROUTINE VOYAGE TO LONDON. Murky weather, but you expect that in January. Running *Isabella* without a second mate isn't a problem since you really only need two of 'em. I missed having Harris to talk to, though. Strange as it may seem. He's not the most talkative fellow I ever met, and he gives a whole new dimension to lugubriousness. Ashley's too stiff and formal and English for a proper conversation, and Yeoh can be disconcerting. Though in his case it could have something to do with being around a hundred and eighty years old.

If Harris hadn't ended up with his leg splinted to a board I might've suspected he'd done it on purpose. Somewhat to my surprise, he's acquired a lady friend. Since turning into a wolf each full moon must make any kind of relationship difficult even if you don't have to spend most of your time at sea.

Who it is, is even more astonishing. However, being a 'prentice witch and the daughter of a witch presumably makes a girl more adaptable to the idea of a beau who turns furry every month. But it's a brave man who pays court to Paciência Verdinho's daughter. I never knew a woman less appropriately named. Though if you ask me it's tempting fate to christen a child with a name like that. Call her Linda and she'll grow up with a face like the back of a tram. The only Bianca I ever knew had red hair and a moustache.

Still, Harris and Luzia know perfectly well that Paciência'd skin him alive, furry or not, if she thought they were up to anything. Which I'm quite sure they are, when they get the chance. Human nature being what it is. You can probably accomplish quite a lot with a broken leg, if you put your mind to it.

London was its usual grimy self, something a thin coating of dirty snow did little to disguise. The Thames was full of filth and garbage and the oily sheen of the muck the steamships vomit out. I remember the days when the Port of London — and any other port you care to mention, come to that — was a forest of masts. And a steamship was something the 'prentices rushed to the rail to gawp at. Yes, I did that in my day.

In my day. Good God, listen to yourself, da Silva. You're forty-four, not ninety-four. Not ready for the scrap-heap just yet.

But I suppose, new century, new order. Barques like my beautiful *Isabella*, their days're numbered, and I know it. So it's all the nicer to have a regular contract, shipping wine for a man who likes the idea of using a sailing vessel. Likes it so much, in fact, that there's a portrait of *Isabella* on the label of every bottle that travels aboard her.

And as for me, I'm visiting London so regularly that I'm beginning to recognize the ghosts on the wharf.

Should be used to it by now. Five years I've been seeing ghosts. Five years, almost to the day, since I lost my left eye in a fight with a demon. No, I didn't come off second best. As Harris might say, you should've seen the other fellow. And I may have lost an eye, but I gained my freedom. After nineteen years of what was slavery in all but name.

Still, it takes a lot longer to get used to seeing ghosts than it does to missing an eye. I spent months trying to avoid the damned things before I realized they aren't aware. Not in any real sense. If one seems sentient on occasion, it's usually me that's doing it. But it's quite difficult to convince yourself that something that looks like a human being, even if it's transparent, can't see or hear or feel you. Thinking of them like magic lantern projections helps. Or nickelodeon films, since they move.

Anyway the two officers I do have this trip are perfectly capable of dealing with customs and all the rest of it. I left them to it and went in search of a cab. Jorge Coelho had wired me that he had a cargo for *Isabella* to take back to Lisbon, and that's always better than returning with an empty hold. As long as it doesn't involve any more side trips to Egypt. I still haven't quite forgiven him for his last effort. Not that he could've known it'd involve me with a three-thousand-year-old sorceress who tried to fry me. But I'm irrational that way. Call me fussy if you like.

Coelho and I go further back than I like to count. Once you get in the habit of saying *Meu Deus was it really almost twenty-five years ago, that's a quarter of a century,* you might as well call for the embalmer. Though meu Deus, if I drank as much these days as I used to when the pair of us were out on the town I'd probably drop dead. And not *need* the embalmer. Now he's a shipping agent. Quite rich, quite fat and quite bald. I'm none of those things. But I own my ship, and I'm my own master. So I think we're about even.

It was bitterly cold. The wind sliced straight through my clothes and chilled me to the bone in about two minutes flat. It made the scar on my face ache, something that hasn't happened for a long time. I rubbed it, glad of my eyepatch for once.

What was left of the snow was frozen solid. I rediscovered something I'd forgotten, that sea-boots aren't designed for walking on ice. I skidded about like a vaudeville act, just about managing to keep my feet. Luck, as much as anything else. Good thing I don't spend my time trying to dodge the ghosts any more, or I'd have been flat on my back on the pavement half a dozen times before I found a cab.

Couldn't see much of the driver between the scarves he was bundled in and the steam coming off the horse, so I hopped in quickly out of the wind. I was momentarily startled to find I was sharing with a ghost, a sad-looking woman who huddled on the seat next to me and looked at me so intently I could almost swear she did see me. I rapped on the roof and called out the address to the driver.

"Right you are, guv," he said, cheerfully enough for a man who had to be freezing his backside off. I sat back against the chilly leather seat. Pulled out a cheroot and lit it, then consulted my watch, hoping eleven in the morning wasn't too early for Coelho to break out the aguardente. My fingers were frozen already, and the cab wasn't a very effective barrier to the wind. But it rattled along briskly and deposited me outside Coelho's office in twenty minutes or so.

The office was warm and stuffy. Which is a great improvement on cold and draughty. I started to thaw, though my feet'd probably take a bit longer to catch up with the rest of me. A gust of wind rattled the window, just to let me know it was waiting there till I came out again.

Coelho got to his feet as I came in, and so did his other visitors. Who I eyed with a certain amount of bemusement, because I'd met them both before. One, a couple of years ago. The other, probably nearer fifteen. I remember him in a bar in Hong Kong, I think it was. Or Macau, it might've been. Spinning a yarn about a sea-serpent in the middle of the Australian outback. Which naturally nobody believed. Even though sailors are notoriously superstitious folk. But now, I suppose it might well have been true. Though in fact I'm almost sure I met him some ten years before that, as well.

"I think you know Mister Arkright?" Coelho said, in English, and I couldn't read anything at all from his tone. Though there was something in his face that was almost mischievous. Or would've been if he didn't look deadly serious as well. I know that sounds odd, but it's the best I can come up with.

I nodded to Arkright. Exchanged the usual pleasantries, good to meet you again, trust you're well, and so on. Like I said, it's nearly two years since a box he was accompanying to Portuguese Guinea aboard *Isabella* turned out to have unexpected contents. And I ended up in the Englishman's debt for a piece of quick thinking.

"This is Thomas Carnacki," he said. "Carnacki, Captain da Silva."

He hadn't changed very much. A medium-sized fellow, mid to late thirties. Athletic looking, which made me want to smile. From what Arkright told me, his brand of ghost-finding doesn't involve much in the way of action. I'm the one who ends up fighting demons. He keeps them under control with pentagrams. The English and their siege mentality. Not that I haven't tried the same thing. But that was a mistake. One born out of desperation, to be sure. But a mistake nonetheless.

We shook hands. "I've wanted to have the chance of a chat ever since Arkright told me about you," he said. People discussing me. Gives me an odd feeling. "We *have* met before."

"I'm not really surprised you don't remember me," I said, tapping my eyepatch. He stared at it curiously for a moment, but made no comment. Points to him. Most people fixate on it. You can see them thinking, *I wonder how that happened.* And *I wonder what the scar looks like.* Ghouls. "Ninety-eight or nine. You were second mate, I think, on a ship called the *Port Moresby*. Macau or Hong Kong, I'm not sure."

"Would've been Hong Kong," he said thoughtfully, stroking his chin. "But I didn't ask for this meeting in order to reminisce."

Now, I wasn't particularly surprised that two shipping agents based in the same city should know each other. But what the one was doing in the other's office I had no idea, let alone why a man they call the ghost-finder was there as well. Although I had more than a sneaking suspicion that the reason wasn't going to prove pleasant for Luís da Silva. A conclusion that wasn't particularly difficult to reach, mind you. Given the way things happen around me these days.

"You mustn't blame Mr. Coelho," Arkright said, looking a little embarrassed (something Coelho himself didn't have the grace to do). He took a cigarette-case out of his vest. More for something to occupy his hands than because he wanted a smoke, if the ashtray on the desk was any guide. "I asked him if he could put us in touch with you. Since we've both had reason to be grateful for your... uncanny abilities."

Not sure I liked the idea of the pair of them sitting there discussing said abilities. Although I could imagine the conversation quite easily. *Do you happen to know a compatriot of yours, fellow with one eye, sees ghosts, As a matter of fact I do, why do you ask.* And there I stuck. I shook myself. Sitting there inventing dialogue, who do you think you are, Eça de Queirós? I took out a cheroot and frowned at Arkright.

"Why?" I asked bluntly. Struck a match and lit up. Offered it to him for his cigarette. He bent his head to the flame.

Arkright glanced at Coelho, who shrugged minutely. You're on your own here, *senhores*, it said. I smiled. Looked at the two Englishmen expectantly. Carnacki glanced down at his hands, then back in my direction. Always try and discomfort people if you think they're going to ask you for a favor. Though he was uncomfortable enough without any help from me. English diffidence, but don't let it fool you. You don't get an empire that size by being bashful. Speaking from the Portuguese point of view, you understand.

He produced a pipe and began to stuff tobacco into it. "The fact is, Captain da Silva," he said, "I find I'm out of my league for the first time in a good many years. But from what Arkright told me, you might be able to help."

All right. Now I'm interested. Damn it. I scratched my cheekbone.

"Perhaps," I said. Rising inflection: go on. He stared at me for a moment.

"I don't know how much you know about my business," he said, frowning a little. "Some people call me a ghost-finder, but that's almost entirely inaccurate. I don't find 'em, they're already there. And for the most part they aren't ghosts either." I nodded encouragingly. "Things I deal with aren't man-made. Mostly. They may have had human origins once upon a time but — I'm not explaining this very well, am I?"

I raised my eyebrows, feeling the scar on the left side stretch. "Take your time," I said.

He struck a match and applied it to his pipe. After a minute he found a phrase that satisfied him. "Things made with malicious intent," he said. "I don't actually know how to deal with them."

"Actually I know quite a bit about magic," Arkright interrupted, "but only academically, you understand. And I haven't read very deeply in some of the, ah, source material."

No, it's not a good idea to read grimoires very closely. Unless you want to go down a path I'd rather avoid. I took a few steps on it once, quite unknowingly. The consequences were, very nearly, appalling. I still go cold when I think about it.

Então, Arkright couldn't know the direction of my thoughts. I blew out a long breath and said noncommitally, "No." He stubbed out his cigarette with a quick, nervous movement.

"Fellow called Sutherland called me in," said Carnacki. "I expect you understand how people are when they have problems with the ab-natural." I glanced at Coelho, who'd been busy denying it all the time it was chewing his leg off. Ah, not literally. He narrowed his eyes at me, and I grinned.

"I know how it is," I agreed.

"So it was a little difficult to understand what he was getting at, at first. But what it boiled down to was that the man was being blackmailed over an… indiscretion." Trust an Englishman to find a euphemism like that. But what it could have to do with me I couldn't imagine. Or Carnacki, for that matter. He went on, "And he was convinced that the lady in question wasn't real. Was in some way artificial."

That stopped me in my tracks. I mean it literally stopped me. I sat there frozen for an instant, cheroot halfway to my mouth. Too surprised to swear.

Because I know someone in London who'd made an artificial man. Who wouldn't be above a spot of blackmail. And Coelho knows her too.

Tatiana Dimitrovna, the Russian witch. Who'd constructed a golem and brought it to life to save Coelho's wife from creatures she called soul-eaters. Who'd blackmailed me into helping animate it. And who'd given the damned thing my face.

Coelho, having anticipated my reaction, pushed a glass across the desk to me. I ground out the end of my cheroot and took a mouthful of his good aguardente.

"You are thinking what I'm thinking?" he said to me.

"I'm thinking I ought to shoot you," I said sourly. Springing that on me. Or getting Carnacki to do it.

Who looked from me to Coelho and back again as if we'd suddenly lapsed into Portuguese. Which of course we hadn't.

"It means something to you, then," he said slowly, comprehension dawning.

I nodded slowly. I could go straight to the source. Or the cause, call it what you like. Despite never wanting to set eyes on the bloody woman ever again. Should know by now that you don't ever get what you want. Or else you get too much of it. Don't know which is worse, to be honest. Always assuming, of course, that she was still living in the same place. Which, come to think of it, was unlikely.

"Yes," I said, and sighed. "I know someone who… made an artificial man. She might listen to me."

After I've hunted her down.

And what will you do when you find her, da Silva? I asked myself.

"That's not all," said Carnacki, his attention apparently on his pipe. "Sutherland consulted me because he was convinced the woman was a… construct of some sort. But he's not the first man to be targeted in this way."

Doesn't surprise me. If she was blackmailing one man, she wouldn't stop at that. "How many others are there?"

Carnacki didn't reply at once, but got to his feet. Took his pipe to the window and stared out. There wasn't much to see in the wintry street below. So he must have a problem with what he's going to tell me. Some English embarrassment at a delicate topic, perhaps. Take your pick from a hundred or so. Cynical, da Silva?

"This is in confidence," he said at last, still facing the window. "It mustn't go further than this room."

If it'll make you happy. "Of course," I replied.

"So far she has caused a suicide, at least two broken marriages, three or four bankruptcies... She chooses wealthy men, powerful men." He lowered his voice. "I understand her latest victim is a member of the government. A highly-placed member."

So politicians cheat on their wives. What a surprise. They're also venal, self-seeking, and power-obsessed. I shrugged.

"Feet of clay," I remarked. Feet, limbs, body, head. But he seemed to think the fellow was worthy of some respect. Perhaps a country that still has a king sees matters a little differently. But pardon me, I can't get worked up about a president.

Carnacki may not have sensed all this, but he noticed my indifference. Well, he'd have to be blind not to. Being English, however, he's too polite to do anything other than frown slightly. When he spoke again, his voice was cool and professional once more.

"Do you think you can find her?"

If I'd been in Lisbon I could've got Paciência to do me a finding spell. As I wasn't, it looked as if I'd have to resort to ghosts again. Because the bankrupts and the divorcés might not talk to me. The politician certainly wouldn't even if I could bring myself to talk to him. But the dead man would, because he had no choice. Damn it.

"If I hunt down this witch, Sr. Carnacki, what will you do with her?"

"Have her arrested, of course," he said, puffing on his pipe. "There'll be barriers powerful enough to confine her."

Visions of him trying to draw a pentagram around Tatiana Dimitrovna had me trying not to smile. I didn't share his confidence. She had more power than Paciência. And I don't think there's a jail built that would hold Paciência. Still, arresting the witch wasn't my problem.

"I'll need to know the name of the man who committed suicide. And where he's buried," I said, scratching my eyebrow. He looked at me curiously. I didn't feel like explaining.

Unfortunately, that wasn't an option.

"Why?" he asked bluntly.

Equally abrupt, I said, "So I can ask him where to find her." But he was nodding his head eagerly.

"Yes," he exclaimed. "Arkright said you could see ghosts."

Arkright and Coelho, it seems, have been singing like a pair of bloody nightingales. I stared at them, exasperated.

"Does the whole of London know about that?" I asked, sourly.

"Good heavens, no," exclaimed Carnacki. "Nothing we discuss ever goes any further." Except, it seems, in this case.

I ground out the end of my cheroot in the ashtray. "The man's name?"

"Francis Arkright," said the English shipping agent quietly. "He was my brother."

* * *

Under a flat gray sky, Lisbon appears leached of color, a monochrome city. The roof of clouds reflects in puddles lying in streets and on pavements, but not in the swollen river, which is dyed a sullen mud color. And yet yesterday the sun was shining, how changeable the weather is — it is our nearness to the vast Atlantic that does it, we hear Great Britain has the same problem, and what a difference the sun makes.

The orphanage is quiet in mid-morning, all the children at their lessons. Day-dreaming out the window isn't nearly as appealing in dull weather, so maybe the children are all paying attention to their teachers, although this may be a flight of fancy.

In the infirmary, Doctor Inácio Bosque listened to the fetal heartbeat through his stethoscope. He felt like frowning, wanted to share his puzzlement with someone, but didn't want to alarm the mother-to-be. Yet there were just too many odd things about this confinement.

He was not, strictly speaking, a gynecologist. Or, as director of the orphanage, a man who had much time these days for general practice. But in sixteen years of running a clinic in Mozambique he had coped with everything from birth to death and all that lies between, all the ills that flesh is heir to. And he was attending to this case as a favor.

His patient, Ana Sobral, peered at him over her hugely distorted abdomen. She was not one of those women whose beauty increases with pregnancy. Her blonde hair lay lank on her head, her face was pinched and thin and pale. She was tired all the time, had constant backache and the beastly baby spent most of its time kicking her. The thing she wanted most of all was for it to be over and done with.

"Is everything all right, doctor?" she asked.

"Yes, my dear, fine," he lied.

But when she had gone, gravid and slow, he walked through to the outer office and flung himself down into the spare chair with an explosive sigh.

"How is she?" Teresa asked. The doctor shook his head.

"She's fine, the baby's fine. Lively little fellow. Or not so little." He fiddled with the green stone on his watch-fob, scarcely aware he was doing it. It was supposed to be a charm against blindness. Dr Bosque was a pragmatist. His years in Africa had left him more open to the possibility of magic than most of his contemporaries. And to the efficacy of folk remedies. Privately he put more faith in the eye-drops Sra.Verdinho had given him than in the charm. He was convinced his sight, blighted by cataracts and macular degeneration, had improved since he'd started using them. The stone, though, he wore because Teresa had given it to him. "But it's too well advanced for seven months. I'd say she's due any day."

Neither of them mentioned the fact that though Ana had been raped the previous June she still appeared to be a virgin.

Teresa kept her worries to herself. Open-minded about sorcery Inácio might be, but she was pretty sure he'd baulk at being asked to believe that Ana had been impregnated by a demon. What that meant she had no real idea. But she couldn't help entertaining a lot of extremely unpleasant suspicions.

Since her late father had been a *mandingueiro* himself, and had been, towards the end, in the habit of summoning demons almost on a daily basis, she was a little ambivalent on the subject of religion. But her early schooling had been at the hands of the Sisters of Mercy in Rio de Janeiro, and her mind persisted in making connections that made the blood chill in her veins.

One word in particular kept on bobbing to the surface: *Antichrist*.

She pushed the hair out of her eyes and got to her feet. Dr. Bosque looked up at her, his spectacles magnifying his weak eyes, and smiled. Teresa went round behind him and began to massage the tension out of his shoulders with her strong fingers.

They had been lovers for a little over eight months.

* * *

In a cheerless office in another part of the city, Inspector Ricardo Corvo stared glumly out of the window. The view consisted solely of the building opposite, which in fine weather boasted the exciting embellishment of the residents' laundry hanging from it. On this damp dank January day there wasn't even any Lisbon bunting there to relieve the façade.

His office smelt of stale tobacco and damp overcoat. The offending garment was draped over the radiator, steaming gently and cutting off most of the warmth it gave out — which wasn't much — making the room stuffy without actually heating it. Corvo didn't hold out much hope of the coat drying out, since the downpour that had apparently singled him out that morning had drenched him so thoroughly that the shoulders of his jacket were damp as well. The rain had waited, cunningly, until he got off the tram, bucketed down until he was indoors, and then stopped. Inspector Corvo believed devoutly in meterolological malice.

On his desk was evidence of malice much more visceral. Which didn't get any better, however many times he read it. Words like exsanguinated, part-eaten, mutilated, and eviscerated, kept jumping off the page into his tired brain.

There had been three murders now, and the gutter part of the press was enjoying not only prurient delight in what gory details it could glean but also lively debate as to whether the perpetrator should be dubbed João the Ripper or simply the Werewolf of Lisbon.

London's Ripper murders, twenty-five or so years ago, had never been solved. And from the amount of evidence he had, Ricardo Corvo doubted whether these would be, either. In which case his own twenty-year career would be down the pan.

The dead women's names had been María, Mercedes, Rita. María had been a seamstress, Mercedes a housemaid, Rita a prostitute. María was from the Alentejo, Mercedes from Badajoz, Rita from Lisbon. The first body had been dumped on a rooftop in the Alfama, the second in a back street in the Bairro Alto, the third down by the docks. They had nothing in common, not even their ages, forty, twenty-two, thirty-five, respectively. María had been the only one who was married, snatched off the streets on her way back from visiting her sister. Mercedes had been walking out, as the euphemism went, with a soldier, whom the police were unable to suspect as he had been in the company of around a hundred and twenty of his comrades for twelve hours before the still-warm body was found. Rita had a four-year-old son, father unknown.

Three women, taken at random off the street, murdered and mutilated beyond reason, their bodies partially eaten. Only a madman would — *could* — perpetrate such atrocities. And you would think someone as barking mad as that would've been noticed. By his foaming at the mouth, if not the blood all over his clothing.

One every week. But not even on the same day of the week. Was the lack of a pattern itself a pattern? Corvo didn't know. But he did know one thing.

Until the murderer was caught, no one was safe. Because given the lack of pattern, the next victim might be a man. Or a child. Anyone at all.

Even a policeman.

He tipped the overflowing ashtray into the bin, checking first that all the dog-ends were truly extinguished. One of his colleagues was still known as The Arsonist for setting his trash alight more than eight years ago.

That done, he found to his irritation that he was out of cigarettes.

For a moment he toyed with the thought of sending Santos out to buy some, but then the idea of coffee came into his mind and he decided to venture out, malicious weather or no, and drink a *bica* in the café as well as replenishing his supply of gaspers.

Inspector Corvo picked up his hat and his damp but warm overcoat, and marched down the stairs and into the street beyond, not without suspicious glances at the sky.

* * *

She wasn't there, of course. I should've known it wouldn't be that easy. It's been three years, after all, and no sensible sorceress would stay in the same place as long as that. I'd asked a ghost to find her then. But once she knew that was possible you can be sure she's done something to hide herself from them. And I don't want to call ghosts from their graves unless I have to. Unlike the faint shades I see all the time, a summoned ghost has form and intelligence and a kind of substance. It's also bound to my will. Which makes me profoundly uncomfortable, given my experience of being bound to the Venetian. Any form of slavery does.

It also, of course, makes me a necromancer, which is something else I'm not very keen on being. But I've got no choice about that. If I have to use the talent, I will. Just don't expect me to jump up and down with joy at the prospect.

Raising ghosts is easy. Luckily it seems to be an uncommon talent. Otherwise the world and his wife would be at it, because the one thing everyone seems to know about ghosts is that they know secrets. The most difficult thing about calling Francis Arkright's ghost was dissuading his brother from tagging along. I don't appreciate having an audience.

The ghost surged out of the frozen ground in response to a sprinkling of holy water and the sound of his name. He looked, as they all do, sturdy and solid. No trace of fuzziness around the edges, as a few have. And he was in a towering temper.

"What—?" he said irritably, looking down at himself, feeling his neck with one hand. He'd hanged himself, but his ghost wouldn't know that. I think they're not allowed to. But some instinct made him touch his throat. "Who the deuce are you?"

"Who I am isn't important," I replied. Wanting to get this over and done with so I could go somewhere warm where I could feel my toes. Now *that's* important.

"Damn it, I'm dead, aren't I?" He patted himself down, his face petulant. "I don't think I like this. Send me back."

I stuffed my freezing hands into my pockets, searching for warmth. "Tell me where the witch is, and you can go."

Francis's ghost gawped at me. "What the devil are you talking about?"

All right, a new response. What fun. A ghost that can't answer questions.

"The Russian witch, Tatiana Dimitrovna," I said. He shrugged.

"Never heard of her."

Now what? Perhaps it wasn't her, after all. But making golems isn't something your average hedge-witch can do. Besides, the ghost's irascibility was making me bad-tempered as well, so I spoke his name again, a little spitefully. His head snapped to attention, and he glowered at me at the reminder of the geas. I was instantly ashamed. Nice work, da Silva.

"Your mistress, then," I suggested, wondering if my fingers would get frostbite if I took them out of my pockets for long enough to have a smoke.

"That bitch," he spat. "I'll tell you where she lives, all right."

"What's her name?"

"Sarah Turner, may she burn in hell," growled the ghost. He didn't sound like someone who'd been driven to kill himself. Not that I've met that many suicides, you understand. But you expect them to be miserable, not angry. Still, what do I know? "I suppose it's too much to hope that you're going to put a bullet in her brain," he added.

I decided to risk the frostbite, and took out my cheroots and matches. "Not exactly," I said. "Do you remember telling your brother you didn't think she was real?"

He frowned. "No, I don't recall that. What on earth d'you mean, not real?"

"It doesn't really matter," I said, and lit a cheroot, grateful for the tiny heat of the match. "But if she's what I think she is, I can destroy her." I think. But it begs the question, who created her? Would she tell me? Not in a million years. I rubbed my nose. Couldn't feel it any more. As for my ears, they'd gone numb ten minutes ago.

"She has a flat in Belgravia," the ghost supplied. "I wondered how the damned woman could afford it."

My feet felt like blocks of ice. The wind crept inside all my clothes as if they were tissue. I stamped, futilely.

"What exactly did she do?" I asked. He looked at me sourly.

"Threatened to tell my wife if I didn't pay her, what d'you think, man?"

It takes two to have an affair, that's what I think. And sometimes you forget all caution and say to hell with it. I've never cheated on Emilia. But I wasn't guiltless before we got married, and that nearly got me worse than killed. So I know that thinking with your groin is never a good idea. Just as I know that sometimes you can't help it.

The ghost didn't need to hear me say that, though. He knew it all too well.

"Just tell me her address, and I'll let you go," I said, blowing out smoke. Suddenly sick of the whole business.

"The address," he repeated, looking embarrassed. "I've forgotten how to say the address." Common enough. The dead forget things. Different things. But they learn others. Never been able to work that one out.

"Take me there, then," I suggested, and he brightened.

"Yes," said Francis Arkright. "Yes, I can do that."

* * *

Sarah Turner, whoever, or whatever, she was, inhabited the swankiest apartment block I've ever seen. Calling them mansion flats is like calling the Palácio da Ajuda in Lisbon a town house. Not at all the sort of place to admit a disheveled, one-eyed sea-captain. The concièrge would've laughed himself silly.

On the other hand, having inside knowledge helped. The ghost had told me about the back stair. And the hidden key.

I waited until the concièrge was busy with another visitor, then slipped in through the side door and marched purposefully to the servants' entrance. As long as you look as though you know where you're going, anyone who sees you will assume you have a right to be there. Which, strictly speaking, I did. Francis Arkright had given it to me. Only Sarah Turner didn't know it yet. She'll find out, though.

Four flights of stairs later I was a little out of breath and my legs were asking me what they'd done to deserve this. But at least I was warm. Always look on the bright side. Yes, and what's the bright side of calling on a golem, da Silva? You saw what Tatiana Dimitrovna's creation was capable of.

That thought made me realize I'd already accepted that the Russian witch wasn't the blackmailer. I hadn't liked the idea from the beginning. Not her style, however much I dislike the woman. No, be honest: dislike isn't really the word. I am, however, afraid of her. Not of her powers. Afraid of what I might do.

Anyway, if she didn't make this one, I won't have to see her.

The key was where Francis Arkright had promised. I slipped it into my pocket and opened the service stairway door cautiously. No one in the corridor. The carpet was red-patterned and thick enough to muffle my footsteps. I paused outside the door of her apartment. Pretty sure there was nobody in there, either. Nobody human, at any rate. Whether I could detect an artificial person was another matter. If you can call her a person.

Ha. Prevaricating. Must be nervous. I stared round again, took a deep breath and put the key in the lock.

And the door slammed back out of my hand, crashing open against the wall and overbalancing me. I staggered forward and felt my coat-collar seized from behind. Hell. Of course she'd have some kind of a guard. Should've thought of that. *Idiota.* I ducked swiftly out of the coat and pivoted, putting my back to the wall inside the door. Didn't want to draw my knife unless I had to. Until I knew what I was up against.

It was big, and for a fleeting moment I thought it was human. Then I saw the eyes, red as embers, and smelt its charnel breath. I lashed out with my foot, kicking it solidly in the crotch before it occurred to me to wonder whether it'd have the same equipment as a human. But the creature doubled over most satisfactorily with a thin gasping whistle of pain, and I followed the kick with a punch in its descending face. Heard a crunch. Blood started to dribble out of its nose — almost black, and it smoked when it hit the floor, but still blood. At this rate I won't even need the knife. But I drew it anyway, the solid weight reassuring in my left hand.

Just as well I did, too. The creature reared up again, snarling. I'd hurt it, but it hadn't had much of an effect. Except to make it mad. Damn it.

I thrust the knife towards it, and it backed off with a hiss. Sensing the silver in the alloy, I expect. It's very effective against things like these. Of course having a fourteen-inch razor-sharp blade helps, too.

Or does in most cases. The creature grabbed hold of the blade and tried to wrench it out of my hand. It was bloody strong, too. And I couldn't understand why its severed fingers weren't littering the floor, until I saw that its hands were made of metal. I switched the knife to my right hand and punched it as hard as I could below the ribcage. Which should take its breath away for the moment. Yes, that did the trick. I wrestled the knife out of its relaxing grip, and got a kick in the shin that made me gasp and brought tears to my eyes. It sent me reeling backwards. Felt like the thing had iron feet as well.

Swearing at the pain, I drew the knife back and spitted the thing up under its chin. More black blood sizzled on the floor, and it swiped a hand at my head. I tried to dodge, but it caught me a glancing blow on the temple which made me see stars.

Bloody hell, what do I have to do to kill this thing? I backed away, panting, and it stared at me murderously with its red eyes, blood dripping from its nose and chin. That'll be the devil to get out of the carpet.

It swayed in place for a moment, and then fell forward onto the floor, as if it'd just not wanted to acknowledge that it was dead. I knelt and wiped the knife-blade clean on its clothes. Don't know what it was. Not a demon. Not, apparently, a golem. But it wasn't showing any sign of vanishing, as most of these things do when you kill them. Oh *merda*, perhaps it wasn't really dead then.

But what I couldn't understand was why the noise of the fight hadn't brought someone running to investigate. Ah well. If they hadn't heard that — I pulled the revolver out of my pocket and shot the thing through the head. It twitched once. Shriveled slowly into a papery husk. Then dissolved into dust, leaving only the bloodstains on the carpet.

Wonderful things, silver bullets.

Silence. Sudden and shocking. Am I the only person aware of the contrast? Does a golem hear the same way I do? Did the thing I just disposed of?

I replaced the gun in my pocket and the knife in its sheath. Which is concealed down my back, in case you're wondering. Saved my hide more than once, that has. Then I retrieved my overcoat from the floor and hung it on a rack together with a man's ulster and a lady's coat with a big fur collar. Put my cap there too while I was at it. By then I'd got my breath back, though I was still sweating.

Checked my reflection in the mirror. Bit red in the face, but otherwise fairly normal. Rumpled is how I always look. I ran a hand through my hair, which had no effect at all. Rubbed my face, cleared sweat from the eyebrows, adjusted the eyepatch. Nervous, da Silva? You can bet on it.

Do it. I sighed. There was a door to my right, one at a right angle to it, another next to that, and a corridor leading off to the left. Pick a door, any door. I took the first one, limping. My leg felt as if I'd been kicked by a horse.

The instant I put my hand on the doorknob, I heard a movement behind it. So that's it. Callers only reach the inner sanctum if they've passed the door-guard. And she doesn't need to move, or wake, or whatever you'd call it, until then. Economical, if nothing else.

My hand was sweating. Or the doorknob was slippery. I turned it, and walked in.

Not quite sure what I was expecting even then. But it wasn't a woman in a negligée. Who rose languidly from the sofa, apparently oblivious of the way it was gaping open, and said, "Charles, how nice to see you again."

That steadied me, strangely enough. I shut my mouth. Gaping like a codfish. Swallowed, and fixed my gaze on her face. Remember, she's not flesh and blood. But my God, what a facsimile. Even though I knew she was made of clay, I still wanted to touch her. Mentally I apologized to Francis Arkright.

"You were expecting someone else?" I asked, amazed at how level my voice sounded. And it was only then that she seemed to realize she was looking at someone she wasn't conditioned to recognize.

Another spell took over then, as best as I can tell. It was like that fellow Pavlov's dogs, responding to a stimulus. She shifted to another personality, and put up a hand to draw her robe together.

"Who are you?" she asked harshly. "What do you want?"

Well, that's the question, isn't it? Except that the answer isn't something I can bring myself to say. I've got to destroy you.

But I couldn't say it, and I couldn't do it. Any more than I could the Russian witch's construct three years ago. It wasn't her fault. She'd been created to do what she did. She had no free will at all.

And she sensed my hesitation. Her expression changed slightly as she realized I'd stopped being a threat. I stared at her, amazed at the realism.

Sarah Turner, the imitation woman, reached out a hand to my face. Touched it with fingertips that were warm and soft and lifelike. I heard her breathing, and put my hand on hers. Felt skin, flesh over bones. She isn't real. I found I was trembling. What's happening? I'm going to kiss her fingers. And she isn't real.

I moved her hand, and then there was a frantic banging at the door of the apartment. I jumped, drew in a rasping breath and backed away from her. She blinked rapidly. Moistened her lips with her tongue. I stared at her mouth in confusion.

"Open the door, if you please, madam, this is the police," came a shout from outside. The knocking resumed. Sarah Turner didn't move. But her gaze held me transfixed. Her eyes had green flecks in them.

A thunderous crash on the door, and then another. Splintering noises. And in came the constabulary. Or was that the cavalry?

"Miss Turner?" asked one of them, a vulture-faced man in a bowler hat. "Constable, fetch the lady's coat. Inspector Radford, Scotland Yard. I'm afraid I have to ask you to come with us, madam, if you please." She didn't reply. I don't know whether she could. The policeman turned to me. "May I ask your name, sir? And your business here?"

The constable returned, holding the coats from the hall. He was followed by Arkright, who took one look at Sarah Turner and muttered "Good Lord."

"Sir?" the inspector said again.

"Luís da Silva," I said, swallowing. Still staring at her. "Mr. Arkright can tell you why I'm here," I added. Couldn't come up with the words to explain, myself. Couldn't figure out how Arkright had gotten there, either. Something in the brain's not functioning properly.

Radford turned to Arkright, who was gazing at Sarah Turner as if he thought she might bite. And who's to say she won't? And then the tall constable moved to drape her coat round her shoulders, and cut off my view of her.

Awareness came back to me in a rush, and I swore, realizing I had to've been under a spell myself. "What are you doing here, Sr. Arkright?"

"I followed you," he said. And I suppose I was glad he did. Because her glamor, or whatever you want to call it, had nearly done for me. I grimaced, wanting to spit. To get rid of the taste in my mouth. I settled for a cheroot instead.

Pretty good going there, da Silva. For a man who's seen off demons and werewolves, not to mention vengeful ghosts and vampire spirits, I do a good imitation of a twenty-year-old with a bad case of lust. Over a woman who's not even real. Impressive stuff.

Damn it.

* * *

Disgruntled and frustrated, Harris maneuvered his crutches to hoist himself out of the chair. He grew uncomfortable sitting anywhere for more than fifteen minutes, but sitting was more or less all he could do at the moment.

In the three weeks since he'd limped to the captain's house on three legs he had dwelt on little other than what he'd found on the rooftop. Annoyingly, if he'd had one more wolf-night, the bone would have knit much faster. As it was, he had to heal at human speed until the next full moon. Which left him, by turns, bored, aching, and bad-tempered.

He worried at the problem, like a dog with a bone.

Goddamit can't you let it alone? Been over it a coupla hundred times. Yeah, I know. I know. But something *et that woman. And I ain't saying it couldn't have been something like me, but I sure as hell didn't smell wolf up there. And if anyone knows what wolf smells like, it's Mrs. Harris's little boy. Trouble is, I didn't smell anything else up there, either. Which just leaves one thing, don't it? Cause ghosts can't tear bodies up like that. And everything else smells like what it is. Demon smells like demon. Wolf like wolf.*

And something with a bite that big sure didn't oughta smell like human.

Denied even the roof-terrace by the intermittent rain, and denied the relief of prowling by his leg, he stared out of the window into the glistening street and watched a bedraggled yellow dog negotiating the puddles.

Thing like that ain't gonna stop.

And there was nothing in the wide world he could do about it.

Harris heard the door open, and turned awkwardly to see the captain's wife. His saturnine face relaxed into a smile. Emilia had that effect on most people.

She leaned her walking-stick against a chair, and sat down in it. *House fulla gimps,* thought Harris, not that he would ever say anything like that out loud. Nothing like having a pin out of action to make you sympathize with a real cripple. *Least I know* my *leg's gonna get better.*

"*Olá,* Sr. Harris, *como está?*" she asked.

Aw Jesus. Portuguese lessons. Da Silva had given up on him well over a year ago, but Emilia had apparently determined to take advantage of Harris's enforced immobility. It hadn't mattered too much to him before, as the lingua franca aboard *Isabella* was English, but he had to admit he had more motivation this time around, since Luzia's English was rather fragmentary. Charming, but sometimes incomprehensible.

He was making progress, of a sort.

"*Não muito bem,*" he said now, which he knew meant "not very well". One of the first things he'd managed to commit to memory. *Falou português mas não muito bem.*

Perhaps it don't mean the same thing when applied to health. Can't remember. Anyhow that's spreading it thin. Hurts like a son of a bitch might cover it. Como um filho da puto? *Wouldn't even try to say that in front of a lady even if I thought it was right.*

"It's all right," said Emilia in English without correcting him, "I haven't come to torture you. Quite the opposite. Luzia just telephoned to say she's coming to town this afternoon."

Harris's day suddenly grew brighter.

And how did that happen? Sure don't know what she sees in me. Not that I'm complaining. No sir. Not me.

But that was for later. "You can torture me if you like," he said resignedly. "I ain't going nowhere. Mind if I smoke?" He took his cigarettes out.

"You don't really need to ask me every time," she smiled. "I don't even notice the smell of those things Luís smokes, so a cigarette isn't going to bother me."

"Yeah, I suppose," said Harris, needing no further encouragement to light up. "But I know I ain't big on being polite, so I guess I'm trying to make up for it."

Emilia could have discerned his exact emotions if she'd let herself, but she refused to use her new-found talent on her friends. And she thought of the American as a friend. She said simply, "You have a polite soul, Sr. Harris."

I got a wolf's soul, according to John Yeoh, if I couldn'ta figured that out for myself. And I damn near lost it, at that.

Harris was glad he wasn't sleeping in Zé's room this time round. Too many memories of that confusing, nauseating few days. But Zé's bedroom was right at the top of the house, a slope-ceilinged room with a view over red rooftops, and impossible to climb to for a werewolf with a gimpy leg. So the office of what Emilia jokingly referred to as the Da Silva Line had been turned into a werewolf hospital and Emilia was dealing with ship's business temporarily from her jewelry workroom. With the desk shoved up against the window and the chairs removed, there was just enough space for a mattress on the floor.

"You find time to go to the library again?" he asked, depositing his used match carefully in an ashtray.

She brushed an errant strand of hair off her forehead, and sighed. "Yes, I did," she replied. "Sr. Zacuto hasn't found anything yet. Pity no one seems to've thought of compiling a supernatural bestiary."

"Yeah, you'd think there oughta be some kinda encyclopedia or something, wouldn't you?" complained Harris. Emilia smiled.

"Nothing's ever so simple."

"You sound just like the skipper." *We need to know. So's we can tell him when he gets back. Cause you can bet your ass he's the one's gonna have to deal with it. And we're gonna have to tell him that. Shoot, won't that be more fun than going over Niagara Falls on a tea-tray.*

*   *   *

Ever since his mysterious illness last year, he'd been having the most extraordinary dreams. It was almost as if the days he'd spent in a coma had admitted him to a whole new level of dreams, visions more intense and vivid than any he'd ever experienced before.

Sometimes they seemed more vivid than real life, although he wasn't going to make the mistake of thinking that they were more real. Even if they did sometimes build to an almost unbearable pitch of reality. But he had an outlet, a safety valve, for that pressure. One that the other victims of the mystery malady didn't have, always supposing that they too were dreaming with this same intense clarity. And they might not be, he might be the only one.

He could paint his dreams.

In his studio there were currently some thirty canvases with their faces to the wall. He didn't really want anyone to see them, was, to tell the truth, slightly embarrassed by some of them. Not that there was anything obscene or even vulgar about them, it was just that they were, on the whole, so utterly bizarre that he didn't want to try and explain them.

No one was likely to see them, anyway. The visitors who came to sit for portraits were usually rather in awe of him, as if they thought him a magus rather than a painter, someone with power that it was best not to cross, and wouldn't have dared to turn any of the canvases round to face the day. And of those, there weren't many. He painted whom he liked, because he didn't really need to work. It was just that he couldn't stop. Painting was too much a part of him. And at last he was able to paint things he enjoyed putting on canvas.

And maybe that was why he painted his dreams. And maybe there was another reason. Maybe he wanted to take his mind off reality. Or some aspects of it. Or one aspect of it.

So you've finally narrowed it down to that, have you, after all that? he said to himself, contemplating his current canvas with his eyes slightly narrowed. Finally admitted that you can't talk to your son. That it's not his fault. It's yours.

Part of him knew that he wasn't being entirely fair to himself, but he seemed incapable of accepting the lifeline, even as he was unable to admit that it had been his wife who had not only driven Luís away thirty years ago but also blighted his own life and ruined whatever chance he might have had of being a serious artist with her obsession with religion. Her religious mania.

He had, he knew, squandered his talent in a vain attempt to please her. On altarpieces and devotional pictures, saints and prophets and miracles. And now the chance for miracles was long past, even though her death had at least freed him from the tyranny of religion and allowed him to find pleasure in portraiture. And, the last seven months, half-guilty release in painting his dreams.

The painting in front of him now was a composite picture, showing, like Botticelli's *Primavera*, several aspects of a myth. What the myth was, or if it even existed anywhere outside his own head, Sebastião da Silva didn't know. It showed a daylit townscape with the hard shadows of a desert sun, under a night sky of unfamiliar constellations. No Orion here, no Ursae Major and Minor. No Lyre or Swan or Hunting Dogs. The street, though it would become crowded, was now utterly deserted except for a figure reminiscent of Goya's painting of the Titan Saturn devouring his father. Through the windows of the houses various things could be glimpsed, and would be glimpsed. A woman without a face. A child. Others he hadn't yet painted.

Perhaps, he thought humorlessly, I'll end up being remembered as the heir to Fuseli and Doré... or Hieronymus Bosch.

If, that is, I don't burn the damned things first. But he knew even before the thought formed that he'd never be able to bring himself to do that.

* * *

The problem now is, of course, that if Tatiana Dimitrovna didn't manufacture Sarah Turner, who did?

And the other problem is that sooner or later I'm going to have to find the Russian witch after all. To ask her how to destroy the artificial woman.

Unfortunately I get the distinct impression that she doesn't want to be found. And what makes you think that, da Silva? Well, the fact that I couldn't find her. *I could find you in hell itself,* she'd once said to me. But the opposite doesn't apply. Apparently.

But I've got to set sail for Lisbon tomorrow, so everything will have to wait for a while. At least with Sarah Turner behind bars, it might cramp her creator's style a little. Depends on how long she stayed behind bars, of course.

I wasted time I couldn't really afford with the police. Had been tempted, just for a moment, to try the "no speaka da English" approach. But that would've wasted a lot more time and given me only limited amusement. So I did a combination of Ignorant Damn Foreigner and Bluff Sea-Dog instead. Have to say it worked a treat.

Although it was only four o'clock when I finally headed *Isabella*-wards so we could catch the morning tide, the sky was almost pitch-black. Thick clouds had rolled in while I was helping the police with their enquiries. Raised the temperature a degree or two, but felt like more snow on the way. It was still bloody cold. Next time some idiot tells you it's too cold to snow, by the way, just ask him what the hell he thinks happens at the Poles.

My feet were like blocks of ice, and the cold was making my leg ache. So I decided I had time to stop for a drink, and limped into the first public-house I came to. It had an open fire, so I finally got my feet warm. Smoked three cheroots. And drank two glasses of execrable brandy, but then the English don't know what good brandy is like. Or anything else, for that matter. No, not quite true. Some of their beer isn't bad.

When I left I found I'd been right about the weather. Which didn't cheer me. Being right isn't always the best option. Because now it was, indeed, snowing. Fat, thick flakes of the stuff. It wasted no time covering my shoulders and cap with a white crust. I muttered an imprecation, and lit another cheroot before getting on my way again.

Snow always reminds me of Venice. Though of course I've been to snowier places. Happily, not many. While I'm not fond of extreme heat, especially when it's humid as well, I'd rather be too warm than wondering whether my toes are going to fall off when I remove my socks. Call me fussy if you like.

For nearly twenty years I lived in, or that should probably be returned to, Venice. A city that taught me all about snow. That it can lie on water, for instance. I've seen the lagoon covered in white, boats cutting black trails through it. But I also found that it's quite easy to ignore it completely when you get back two days early from a voyage to find your fiancée's father is out for the entire afternoon.

It didn't teach me that snow can form into lumpy animated things that come whirling out of nowhere howling like a blizzard and try to smother you.

Thinking about Emilia'd nearly made me miss them. I had time to think: what the devil's that? and then the first one caught me in the chest like a huge wet snowball and nearly knocked me off my feet. I skidded backwards and whipped out my knife, not knowing whether it'd be any use. A second later there were a dozen more, and I couldn't tell whether they were forming from the snow as it fell or came from somewhere else.

Couldn't see them clearly. Teeth and claws of ice glinted in the gaslight, imagine the deadly cold if they sank into your flesh. Not sure they stayed the same shape all the time, didn't really care. As long as the silver in the knife cuts whatever magic holds the things together, that's fine by me. I swiped it around at random, and the nearest one disintegrated into snowflakes and the surrounding storm. Good.

There are so many of them, though. They just kept on coming. I kept on slashing at them. They kept on disintegrating. Where the hell are they coming from?

As soon as I thought that, I realized that they *were* all coming from the same direction. And that there was a mound of snow lying on the ground there. It was just the right size to be a body. What had they been doing to it?

Slashing from side to side, turning my head to see all round, I battled towards the mound. They definitely didn't want me to investigate. I found myself dodging slashing talons as well as buffeting blows now. Which made me all the more determined.

But I knew they weren't going to ease up. I wondered what to do, though *wondered* makes it sound as if I had time to consider it. I had to keep my eye on the snow-things, and my arm was getting tired.

Lacking a left eye when you're also left-handed puts you at a disadvantage in a fight. Still I was hardly needing any finesse here. All I needed to do was swing the blade and keep hoping that they didn't overwhelm me with sheer numbers. So I switched the knife to my right hand and knelt in the snow by the huddled figure. Started clearing snow off it by feel.

Icicle fangs snapped together inches from my eye, and I jerked my head back. Sliced the knife through them, swearing at the jolt of panic that shot through me, hearing them snap. Now I could feel a face under my hand, chill flesh, slack eyelids, but warm moist breath from the chapped lips. Still fighting off the snow-creatures with one hand, never looking down, I slapped the cold cheeks with the other.

"Wake up, damn you, whoever you are," I muttered urgently. Fended off the snowball things with increasing desperation. I found a shoulder and shook it, hard. Was rewarded by a groan. Movement. The body rolled over and started coughing.

I jumped to my feet, my bruised shin protesting. Switched the knife back to my left hand. Carried on swiping the creatures away with renewed vigor, thanks to the brief rest my arm'd just had.

Then a voice I knew said something hoarsely in Russian that made my hair stand on end. The snow-things melted away. I whirled round.

And Tatiana Dimitrovna was standing there, her hair and clothes crusted with snow. I suppose I looked much the same. Breathing heavily, I ran a hand through my hair. I'd lost my cap at some stage.

"We have to hurry, Luís," she said as if we'd been together all the time. "They'll be back, and I need your help. Is your ship close by?"

Like I always say, there are no such things as coincidences.

2

THE FIRST TIME I MET TATIANA DIMITROVNA ANDROPOVA, SHE TRIED TO KILL ME. The second time, she tried to seduce me. She's tried to do one or the other every other time we've run into each other. Hasn't succeeded in either.

Must be my charm.

Right now, however, she's as near panic as I've ever seen her. And I've never seen her anywhere near panic at all.

Never found her lying unconscious in the street before, either. Though to be honest, when I first met her, it was my crew who were likely to be unconscious in the street. For different reasons, of course.

Your mind's wandering, da Silva. Get it back to the matter in hand.

She stumbled against me, and almost fell over again. I put an arm round her waist to support her. Not that I felt that steady myself.

"Are you all right?" I asked. Stupid question. Idiocy often descends at times of stress. When least needed.

Any other time she would've taken advantage of the arm. Somehow or other. Now all she said was, "I need to get out of London. Will you help me?"

I stared at her, appalled. That's all I need. I shifted my grip more firmly round her waist and said, "You've got some explaining to do first."

"Yes, I know, and I promise I will. But can we get on board, where he can't reach me?" The words tumbled out in a rush. She was at the end of her courage. And that was even more appalling. I didn't even ask who "he" was, just helped her hurry through the deepening snow.

"Not far now," I said encouragingly. Though who I was trying to encourage, I'm not sure.

I got her to my cabin and gave her a brandy. Had one myself for good measure. The ones I'd drunk earlier had worn off long ago. Remembering the taste, thank God. She was shivering, I hoped from the cold. Never seen her like this. Not natural. And therefore frightening. I made her take off her soaked overcoat and gave her my spare one. Which smelt of mothballs. Better than mildew, I suppose.

At least it was warm in the cabin. If a little pungent from the heater. I shed my own coat and sat down opposite her. Lit a cheroot. All of a sudden I felt desperately tired.

"Now for God's sake tell me," I said,

She tossed down the drink as if it was vodka. My good aguardente. Never even touched the sides. I raised an eyebrow ruefully and poured her another. Guess she needs it.

"Do you know who Sir Robert Munro is?" she asked. I shook my head. "He's in the government, the British government, a cabinet minister." I grimaced automatically. Wondered if it was the one Carnacki mentioned. Scratched my cheekbone.

"And?"

Tatiana Dimitrovna shot me a critical glance over the rim of her glass. "He's an influential man, Luís, that means he has power," she said sharply. "And he's also a sorcerer." Well, that's nice. Another damned sorcerer. What do they do, crawl out of the woodwork and hold a convention when they see me coming?

"Did he make the golem?" I asked. "Sarah Turner?"

"Yes," she said, sounding a little surprised. I hid a smile. Oneupmanship, da Silva. "How did you know about her?"

"Never mind that now," I said, knocking ash off the end of my cheroot. Suppressed a desire to yawn. "You go on."

We were interrupted by a knock on the door, and Zé came in. My son is junior 'prentice aboard *Isabella*. Given a choice between him running away to sea and giving him a job, what would you do?

"You wanted me?" he asked, hopefully, eyeing the witch.

"You're supposed to call me sir," I pointed out. I am, after all, the captain.

"Sorry, *papai*, sir," he said unrepentantly. Brat. "You wanted me, *sir?*"

"Take a heater to Sr. Harris's cabin and get the bunk aired," I told him, restraining myself from giving him a swipe round the head. "We've got a passenger."

The Russian witch gave me a relieved smile, and lifted her glass to me. Zé looked at her curiously, then back at me. I raised my eyebrows at him. He knew he wouldn't get an answer then, so he grinned and said, "Aye, aye, sir."

"Your son," she remarked at the closing door. "He doesn't look much like you."

"Takes after his mother," I said shortly.

"Ah yes," said Tatiana Dimitrovna with a hint of her old malicious fire. "Emilia, to whom you are ever faithful." She closed her eyes. Pressed two fingers to the center of her brow. "I'm sorry," she added, and that was a first as well. Seriously worried, now.

"You were telling me about this Munro," I said, neutrally. She nodded, and took a mouthful of brandy.

"We were lovers for a few months. A year or more ago. He wasn't that powerful a warlock, then." She glanced at me, eyes narrowed. A warning look? Her hands twined in her lap. "I was a fool. I showed him how golems are made. Thought no more about it. Thought he was only curious. He certainly wasn't powerful enough to animate one then. But he's changed. He's gotten power from somewhere. More than I have."

My back crawled. More power than Tatiana Dimitrovna? Don't like the sound of that. Not at all. I ground out the end of my cheroot in the ashtray.

"Did he send those snow-creatures after you?"

She pulled a face. Picked up her glass and drank some more brandy. I followed suit. The drink, not the grimace, that is. "He sent a searcher. A killing one. It takes whatever form suits the moment, or the circumstances. I can destroy it, if I have time and protection." A sigh of relief. "Which I have here. Thank you, Luís."

I never, incidentally, invited her to call me by my first name. But it hardly matters now.

"Why does he want to kill you?" I asked, leaning back in my chair. Bad move. My eyelid drooped. I sat forward again.

"I threatened to go tell the police about him when I found out about Sarah Turner." Oh, yes. And I'm the poet Camões.

"You, go to the police?" I said incredulously. She gave a bitter laugh.

"Yes, me," she replied. "I can't fight him. He's much too powerful. He broke my golem, destroyed my watcher. *Connard.*"

So you're running away. That's not the Tatiana Dimitrovna I know. But neither is the one who considers calling the police. Not without getting something out of it herself. Well, I'll have to worry about that later. Right now I have to get word to Carnacki. I drained my glass, put my hands on my knees, and stood up.

"Do you think leaving London will satisfy him?"

"I don't know," she said. "I hope so. Where are you going?"

"There's someone who needs to know." She reached out and took hold of my arm. Her palm was hot.

"He'll try and stop you."

Looking into her face. Once I'd thought it was dangerous to let those deep dark eyes capture my gaze. Well, it still is. But not in that way. "What — that searcher?"

"No, you're in no danger from that. It's after me. Is there somewhere quiet I can go to prepare a counterspell?"

"Of course," I said. Took her to Harris's cabin. Bad timing. Zé was on his way out. He gave her another curious glance, then took a look at me and made himself scarce. Smart boy.

Tatiana Dimitrovna stopped just inside the door and her eyes went wide. "There's been a werewolf in here," she whispered.

"Yes, I know, he's my second mate," I said impatiently, scratching my cheekbone. "Is it a problem?" Shouldn't forget that most werewolves like to eat people, da Silva. After all, one tried it on me.

She shook herself. "A problem, no. No, this will do very well."

"I'll leave you to it, then."

Outside I almost ran over Zé, loitering shamelessly. "Are you looking for a good hiding?" I asked him. He did a little dance of impatience.

"Who *is* she?" he asked. "She looks like a Russian countess or something." Zé's preferred reading matter consists of shilling shockers. Full of mysterious Slavic adventuresses. Or so I imagine. Never having read one. But I've seen the covers.

"That's because she is," I said, a little irritably, and frowned. " Isn't there something you should be doing?"

"What, a *countess?*" he breathed, ignoring me completely. Well, I'm only his father. Good God, I'm only the captain. No competition.

"No, you twit, Russian." I tried a menacing stare, which succeeds with everyone else. But of course it's wasted on him. "And since you're so interested, you can be her steward till we get home. In addition to your usual duty," I added firmly.

He looked a little crestfallen. Anything that means more work blights his life. Or so you'd think. But he perked up again almost at once, no doubt concluding that it might prove more interesting than just his normal duties. Though if she teaches him words like *connard* there'll be trouble. He scampered off quite happily. He's a cheerful lad. Probably gets that from Emilia, too.

I retrieved my coat and cap from my cabin and went up on deck. The snow had stopped, somewhat to my surprise. Half a dozen crew members were busy clearing it away, grumbling the while. Not that I blame 'em. Damned stuff. I nodded to Yeoh on the poop and saw him nod in reply. The wind was still bloody cold, and I stuffed my hands into my pockets, searching for warmth.

No time to call on Carnacki. Chelsea is miles away. And his business card didn't have a telephone number. But I know Jorge Coelho's, and if someone I knew was on duty in the customs office, I might persuade him to let me use their instrument.

And I was in luck. The man who was warming his hands round a mug of tea was an old acquaintance.

"Oh, Captain da Silva," he said as I came in. I shut the door quickly behind me to keep the wind out.

"Good evening, Mr. Davison, how are you?"

"Damned cold, if you'll pardon the expression. I was hoping to have a word with you," he added. "You're off in the morning, aren't you?"

"First thing," I said, nodding. "What did you want to talk about?"

Davison put down his tea, blew on his hands, then fumbled in a desk drawer. "Funny note shoved under the door." He broke off with that expression people get when talking to foreigners: Did he understand that? "Odd, I should say," he amended. "Here it is."

A folded piece of writing paper. I took it from him and read, in neat copperplate script, "*Barque* Isabella. *Portuguese registry (Lisbon). Master, L J da Silva. This vessel is believed to be engaged in smuggling. Search of captain's quarters advisable.*"

My jaw dropped. I shut it with a snap. Looked across at Davison, who shrugged and rubbed the faint stubble on his chin.

"Don't know who delivered it. Looks like a bit of malice. Been treading on someone's toes? Anyone you know got it in for you?"

Sir Robert Munro? I shook my head. "Not that I know of."

"Well, you're not smuggling, I take it?"

"No," I said, "I'm not."

"Then I'll just bin this," said Davison, and dropped it into his wastebasket. It bounced straight out again. As if made of rubber. He'd turned his attention back to his tea, and didn't notice. "Good thing it didn't come while Vaughan was on duty," he went on. "He'd've had your entire cargo on the quay and your crew strip-searched if he'd read it."

"When's he on?" I asked idly, determinedly not looking at the paper lying on the floor. Just making conversation. Nothing to see here, people.

"Oh, not till tomorrow. What was it you wanted, anyway?" he said.

I'd almost forgotten. Nice going, da Silva.

"Could I use your telephone?"

"Help yourself." He pushed it towards me. "The exchange is usually half-asleep this time of day, so don't worry if you have to wait."

"Thanks," I said absently. He was right about the exchange. I began to suspect Sir Robert Munro of being capable of all sorts of machinations. Shut up, he's not omnipotent.

"This is Coelho and Associates, shipping agents," came the clerk's tinny voice at last, making me jump. The line was bad.

"Mr. Coelho, please, this is Captain da Silva."

"Please wait a moment." Hisses and crackles and screeches. Must be the weather. A snowstorm on the line.

Finally, the man himself. "Luis. *Como estás?* Aren't you sailing in the morning? What can I do for you?"

"In order, fine, yes, and can you get a message to Mr. Carnacki."

Coelho laughed. "I expect so. Have you solved his problem for him?" Well, not exactly. Presented him with a bigger one, perhaps.

"Tell him the man he wants is Sir Robert Munro." I noticed Davison, who'd lost interest once I lapsed into Portuguese, prick up his ears at the name.

"The cabinet minister? Is that the man Carnacki went all secretive about?"

"No," I said. "He's the one responsible for the, er, woman."

"Are you sure? I thought it was that Russian witch of yours."

"Of course I'm sure," I said, irritated. "And tell him to be careful, he could be dangerous." More so than most politicians, it seems. Most of them are only after one kind of power.

"Didn't catch that," said Coelho. "This is a terrible line."

"He's dangerous," I said again. "Jorge?" But I was talking to a dead telephone.

The operator tried to connect me again, but without success. Too bad. Just have to hope that Coelho got the gist of the message.

And warned Carnacki that politicians don't deserve respect, unless it's for the damage they're capable of.

When I left the office, the wind was like a razor. I huddled in my coat, swearing. Set off briskly across the snow, already compacted by hundreds of footprints.

That note. I should've taken it. Should've asked what time in the morning the suspicious Vaughan was expected. Sloppy, da Silva.

The cold was making my face ache. I walked faster, head down through wind and ghosts alike. I was pretty sure I was being followed. You get a feeling about these things. But I was equally sure I wasn't in any danger. Which makes a nice change.

So who's following me? Or what, I suppose I should say. Since it's usually a what rather than a who, these days.

Then someone came up on my left side and fell into step with me. I whipped my head round to see who it was so quickly I nearly sprained my neck. Jumpy, aren't we?

It was like the ghosts I see all the time, but it wasn't one of them. Semi-transparent, but it was aware. And watching me in a distinctly unfriendly fashion. A man, my height. Late fifties, maybe early sixties. Well-groomed. Sleek, even. Broad, fleshy face, arrogant expression. Instant antipathy from da Silva.

"Sir Robert Munro, I presume," I said. The eyes narrowed. Nostrils flared. It could hear, then. But could it speak, or was it just sent to spy? I kept on walking. Whatever it wanted, I wasn't going to wait for it. Too bloody cold.

A whisper in my ear. Made me jump even though I was expecting it. "Accidents happen to people who don't mind their own business."

"Are you threatening me?" I asked. Conversationally, you understand.

"If you care to take it that way," came the whisper. "Just make sure you remember."

"As long as you remember something too," I said, wondering whether my knife would have any effect on it. It doesn't on the pale shades this phantom resembled. But this was, I presumed, a magical sending, a construct of some sort. It had more substance. Though not, admittedly, the physical sort.

"And what might that be?" it asked contemptuously.

"Everyone has a weakness," I replied, drew my knife, and shoved the blade straight through its body.

The sneer vanished from its face. It looked down incredulously at the knife. Seemed about to speak. Then faded away entirely.

Grinning, I pulled out a cheroot and struck a match to light it.

* * *

Time passes at different speeds. In the library of São Rafael, in a hidden square in Lisbon, it hardly seems to pass at all, but this is because, in a sense, it does not. In a sense, the library has always been here. It exists, not outside of time, but through time. Its roots go down a very long way, past Spanish kings and Moorish occupiers, past Visigoths and barbarians, past Felicitas Julia, Lusitania and Olissipo and even Ulysses. Neither invaders nor earthquakes have any effect on places like this — although the great earthquake destroyed the church from which the library took its name — because they are the anchors of the world, and if they fall, then so too does the world.

Every city has places like this, and so do places that have no cities. The library of São Rafael is more useful than many, though who can measure usefulness across all cultures? But as a repository for knowledge, it would be hard to surpass. In such a place, what scholar would not wish for more hours in the day than he is granted by God, or by the earth's orbit around the sun, depending on your point of view?

The library has its fair share of ghosts, but the ghosts of scholars would be peaceful things if they were sentient. At present it has only one ghost who is capable of using its facilities, and he has learnt more here in seven months as the living reckon time than he did in fifty years of study during his life.

Which had ended in the year 1506, at the hands of a mob which then threw his body onto a pyre in the Rossio. Along with many others, not all of whom were dead.

His name was Isaac Zacuto, and in life he had been an apothecary. Like his namesake Abraham the astronomer he came from Salamanca. He could not remember whether they had been related. The first things that ghosts forget are those to do with their lives. Otherwise the pain of a loss might be unbearable, and how could a ghost relieve it, not being corporeal.

Unlike most summoned ghosts, Zacuto had no desire to return to nothingness. He had acquired a staggering amount of knowledge, from the circulation of the blood to how Bartolomeu de Gusmão made his Passarola fly. Seven months earlier, he had helped counteract one of the Great Spells of making and unmaking, something that mortals really shouldn't be allowed to play with, but sometimes things get written down in books despite all the safeguards.

And he had made, to his very great surprise, a friend. Two, in fact, though one was more of a sparring partner. In the philosophical sense, of course.

It had been the library of São Rafael that had convinced Montague Pierce to move his antiquarian bookshop from Rio de Janeiro to Lisbon. He didn't regret the move. His reputation among scholars for being able to find rare books was solid enough to survive relocation to Alice Springs or Alaska. And in many ways being based in Europe was actually better for business. He was nearer to many of his sources, and a lot of his customers lived this side of the Atlantic too. And for those who didn't, well, there were fast ocean liners, weren't there?

Not that Pierce was spending a great deal of time in his shop. Which housed, apart from his stock, thirty-two clocks left by the previous owner, John

Yeoh, currently third mate of the *Isabella*. Pierce found himself a little tyrannized by them, their relentless ticking, their orchestra of chimes, their insistence on being wound. He sought refuge in the library, and paid a small deaf man with the unlikely name of Caracol to sit in the shop.

At the moment, the Englishman was a willing enough recruit to Emilia and Harris's company. Though neither he nor Zacuto had any ideas to add.

With an explosive sigh of annoyance, Pierce looked up at the ghost and snapped shut the book he'd been skimming. It was called *Necrophagy and Cannibalism in Mediæval Europe*, and it had told him precisely nothing.

"I can't get hold of this at all," he said crossly, removing his spectacles and rubbing the lenses on his sleeve. "Have you had any more thoughts, Professor?"

Inasmuch as a ghost could experience emotion, Zacuto rather liked being called *Professor*. It wasn't quite *Rabbi*, but it would do.

"Every avenue leads back to the same conclusion," he said. "It feels like the work of a demon. And yet the wolf detected nothing."

"We need more information," Pierce muttered, rearranging the pile of books in front of him with a sort of febrile compulsion, moving them to and fro on the table. "Where the other victims were found, for instance."

The ghost shot him an accusing look. "I hope you are not intending to try and follow this creature's footsteps?"

"How can I, when I don't know where to look?" retorted the antiquarian, waving his spectacles at Zacuto in frustration. Not that he would have gone charging off in hot pursuit of something that took very large bites out of people. He was happy to leave that sort of thing to Captain da Silva and his long knife.

"I fear we will have to wait until Sr. Harris is mobile again," said the ghost, for about the twentieth time since they began their research.

"Or until someone else gets eaten," grumbled Pierce, putting his spectacles back on and bending his head to the pile of books he'd just rearranged, possibly in the hope that something useful might have materialized since he last looked.

Zacuto sighed. Of course he didn't breathe, but he was very accomplished at making the sounds and gestures of a living man.

"Now what have we here?" he said to himself, turning his attention to the book in front of him, intrigued by the star of David on the cover.

If the library had a fault it was one it shared with every other, that of autocentricity. The books it contained were predominantly European, predominantly Western, and where they touched on religion, predominantly Catholic. They were in Latin, Portuguese, Spanish, English, Greek, a smattering of other languages. Only a few in Hebrew. Given the Moorish occupation, a number were Arabic. But most of the treatises on matters from further afield were written from a western perspective.

He held his hand over the book, and it opened obediently. Riffling his fingers caused the pages to turn. Zacuto couldn't touch anything material any more than a man could touch him, but he found ways round this handicap, both for convenience and artistic verisimilitude. For instance, he gave the appearance, for Pierce's benefit, of sitting on a chair, whereas in fact he was hovering a little way above it. He stopped the pages moving at random, and began to read.

Pierce, glancing up, saw him suddenly grow very still. Stiller than anyone alive, as if he'd forgotten to keep up his normal semblance of breathing. The old scholar was frozen in place, motionless as a statue.

"What is it?" Pierce asked. "What've you found?"

It seemed like minutes before Zacuto raised his head, but his eyes seemed alight with inspiration. "What if it were a constructed creature?" he said. "A golem? Do you suppose that would smell of anything a werewolf could detect?"

"My God," breathed the antiquarian, staring at him open-mouthed. "My God, professor, perhaps that's the answer."

That would be an interesting theory to try on the police, he thought at the same time, and was unable to control the smile that came to his lips.

*   *   *

Time passes at varying speeds.

Ed Harris, currently awaiting the arrival of his inamorata, could attest to that.

Can't decide whether it goes slower while I'm sitting on my ass with my leg on a stool, or while I'm sitting on my ass with my leg on a stool trying to learn Portuguese.

But when Luzia arrived he didn't want time to go quickly, though it did.

He'd first seen her on the quayside, waiting for Ortigão. *Except it wasn't her then, it was that demon pretending to be her.* He'd still been attracted to her, even as the demon's aura repulsed him.

The real thing was infinitely better.

Goddamn, even if'n everything was normal it's purely nice to have a girlfriend that don't look like she'd gonna break if I give her a hug. Course that Teresa woman's even taller, but I'd rather cuddle a wolverine.

As Emilia was still in the room, he kissed Luzia on the cheek. *Though the way those two carry on I don't reckon she'd bat an eyelid if I gave her a proper smacker on the lips.* Harris would never have admitted it, but he was mildly scandalized that the captain and his wife apparently couldn't keep their hands off each other.

Cuts both ways, though. She don't mind leaving us alone when my girl's mother thinks she's acting the chaperone. So I ain't complaining.

Unfortunately for any hopes Harris and Luzia were harboring of serious hanky-panky, though, Montague Pierce chose that moment to arrive at the front door.

"Sr. Pierce," Joana announced resignedly a few moments later, obviously wondering whether his advent in such a flustered state would mean a repeat of last year's upheavals, up and down like a jack-in-the-box answering the door all day long.

Pierce's head came round the door and blurted out Zacuto's idea before being followed into the room by the rest of him.

Huh, even I gotta admit I'da wanted to hear that sooner rather'n later. He squeezed Luzia's hand, and she shot him a brilliant smile.

Luzia had changed a lot since her part in unmaking the Great Spell, the Eidolon, that the sorcerer Batista had constructed. Mostly it had taught her self-confidence. How to value herself. How to stand up to her mother. And when to speak up.

"*Em Português, se faz favor,*" she said now, and Pierce obligingly translated for her. "A golem, that's a clay man, isn't it?" she asked when he'd finished.

"That's right," said the antiquarian, adjusting his spectacles, which had slipped down his nose. They immediately started to descend again.

Wish I'da paid attention to the skipper after all. Harris felt like growling. *What'd she say? Um homem — what?*

"Man of what?" he muttered to Emilia.

"Clay," she murmured back. But Luzia was still chattering away to Pierce.

"So it's sterile, isn't it? It has to be baked — fired."

Harris looked helplessly at Emilia, who whispered reassuringly to him, "I'll translate when she's done."

The antiquarian was nodding excitedly. "I know what you're going to say. If there's nothing, er, living, in it, you wouldn't be able to smell it."

"Yes," said Luzia, equally excited. "It'd be inert. But if there was any trace of — I don't know, a drop of sweat fell on it, maybe, or if you need blood to animate it?" Pierce shook his head.

"The Prof didn't say anything about that."

Before Emilia had a chance to translate, Luzia turned to Harris with her eyes shining and asked in English, "Ed, can you smell — earth?"

"Clay," amended Pierce. "Fired clay. Does a flowerpot have a smell you can distinguish?"

This bilingual chat's doing my head in. I think I got it, though. "Yeah, I guess," he said. "It'd smell like a flowerpot. Uh, but if a dog p — I mean, relieved itself on it, then it'd smell like dog."

"And if someone spit on it?" Pierce asked.

Shit. That's what they're getting at.

"It'd smell like human," said Harris slowly.

*   *   *

Time and tide wait for no man, they say. So I have time and tide to thank for not having to worry about over-zealous customs officers. *Isabella*'s well on her way by two bells in the morning watch. And for once I'm glad to have to set off in darkness, even in this dead cold.

Why do I have the feeling I haven't escaped from anything?

There are rules governing these things. The supernatural, I mean, though that isn't a word I like. Maybe Carnacki's word *ab-natural* fits better, I don't know. More rules, anyway, than the ones that govern the physical world. And as I understand it, nothing can board my ship unless I invite it on board. I myself. The skipper. Not Ashley, or Harris, or Yeoh.

Of course, whenever you get a set of rules, people start inventing ways of getting round them. I've done it often enough myself. And not only people... That's how the thing in Arkright's box came on board. The box was a Trojan horse.

Search of captain's quarters advisable.

I flung the remains of the cheroot I was smoking into the sea and headed to my cabin at a dead run. What could I have inadvertently brought on board? Who could've slipped something into my pocket?

Sarah Turner could've.

Wait, da Silva, wait. There might be something with a nasty little delayed reaction. You need Tatiana Dimitrovna to check it for you first.

But can I wait that long? I could see, very vividly, the drowned crew that sorcerer called out of the sea. How their eyes gleamed in their water-shriveled faces. How they'd held my crew captive while I had to fight their master. The dead gleaned from centuries of seafarers. Pirates, buccaneers, press-ganged men. Their rotted clothes dripping and salt-stained. Dead white skin glistening. A strange and terrible sight.

Also, I remembered Tatiana Dimitrovna. Not so much the last time I'd seen her. When the golem with my face had destroyed the things she called soul-eaters. But the first time we'd met, when I'd only just seen the stiletto in time. And the second, when she was in my arms, and the world narrowed down to lips and tongues and teeth. I winced.

Like I said, she didn't succeed. But it'd been a near thing.

Between smoking and pacing the deck, I held out till five bells sounded. I heard the timekeeper strike, and the lookout answer. It was Benjamin, a man I know is quite well-informed about *vaudun*. But these waters don't know that pantheon, and I didn't say anything.

He let go the bell lanyard and nodded to me. I nodded back. Something unspoken passed between us.

I paused outside Harris's cabin, with an awful sense of something impending. But you know that anyway, go ahead and knock. How deeply does she sleep? I pictured myself shaking her naked shoulder. Though why I thought it would be naked I don't know, well — I do know, of course. But she'd gotten a message to her maidservant last night, and a neatly packed trunk had duly arrived. So she presumably had nightwear. And here am I standing outside her door wondering about it. Brilliant timing, da Silva.

Academic speculation, of course. I knocked and a moment later she opened the door wearing what looked like a man's dressing gown. Very sensible, given the temperature. I gave a mental, rueful, grin at myself.

"Good morning," I said. She raised her eyebrows.

"You may be in the habit of getting up at half past six, Luís," she replied a bit tartly, "but you might have let me sleep in after yesterday."

I raised an eyebrow of my own. "I got up at quarter to four, if you want to know," I told her. Which wasn't what I meant to say. Damn. I shook myself in irritation. "I need your help." No, I wasn't going to apologize.

Tatiana Dimitrovna pursed her lips. "What is it?"

"Something occurred to me," I said, rubbing my chin. I hadn't shaved. Bad idea, that. Made me feel grubby. "Could Sarah Turner have planted anything on me?"

"On you?" The witch's eyes narrowed, and she looked me up and down so closely that I grew embarrassed. "There's no trace... What were you wearing when you were with her?" I looked down at myself.

"This, more or less. Changed my shirt," I said. Underwear and socks as well, but we'll take that as a given.

"Did you have an overcoat?"

"Yes, but I—" I broke off. Frowned. Scratched my cheekbone. The constable had brought all the coats from the hall. And I'd been too busy being bemused by Sarah Turner's spell that I hadn't noticed what she was doing.

She stared at me quizzically. "You've thought of something?" I nodded. "Then I'd better come and take a look. Did you notice anything last night?"

"No." But I'd had other things to occupy my attention.

Pulling the robe more securely round her — more for warmth than modesty, knowing her — she stepped through the door and pulled it shut behind her. I led the way to my cabin. She halted me outside with a hand on my arm.

"Wait," she said peremptorily. "Let me go first." I stood back and she turned the doorknob with great care, muffling her hand inside her sleeve. She opened the door and peered round. Drew in a sharp breath. *"Boizhe moi,"* I heard her say. Since I know she usually curses in French, there must be something really startling in there.

"What is it?" She was blocking my view. Moving to one side to let me pass, she pointed to my desk. Not that she needed to point. At all.

There was a tree growing out of the top of it. Not a large tree, you understand. No more than a foot tall. It looked like one of those little Japanese bonsai things, all gnarled and contorted. But though it was shaped like a tree, it didn't feel like a tree. It gave off a sort of — I don't know, aura? A feeling of something soiled. The sort of thing that makes you want to spit to get the taste out of your mouth and rub your hands down the sides of your pants, to get rid of the feel of it. It was disgusting, in all sorts of ways I can't even describe, but in a small-minded, sly, petty kind of way, if that makes sense.

I stared at this impossibility for a moment. "What in the name of—"

"It's a Judas tree," she said. "She must've put a seed in your pocket."

Which told me everything, and nothing. I took out my cheroots, and lit one. Reflex. "What does it do?"

"Anything spiteful, malicious. If your customs man had come in, he'd have found... something incriminating, contraband. If you'd come in unawares it might've blown up in your face. They're... very adaptable."

Adaptable. That's one way of putting it, I suppose. I rubbed my eyebrow. "How do we get rid of it?"

Tatiana Dimitrovna smiled grimly. "Fortunately, it's very easy." I raised my eyebrows at her questioningly. "Salt water."

Couldn't help it. I started to laugh. "No shortage of that." Since we're in the middle of the *Canal da Mancha*.

"Well, seawater won't really do," she said. "There's too much… other matter in it. The best thing would be distilled water."

"How about holy water?" I asked, and she gave me an odd look.

"Yes, that would be acceptable."

Eyeing the tree suspiciously, I sidled round the desk and slid the drawer open. Took out my silver liquor flask and handed it to her.

"How much d'you need? It's nearly full."

She took the flask and shook it. "All of it, I would think. Why do you keep holy water in your desk?"

Deadpan, I said, "You never know when it might come in handy." She shot me a minatory look. "I'll get you some salt." Didn't want anyone coming in and seeing that thing. Least of all Zé.

The holy water? It works like antiseptic, if you get bitten or clawed or otherwise damaged by any kind of supernatural nasty. Even their touch'll bring you out in a rash. And the stuff I have is blessed by a priest who I suspect has a direct line to God. So you could call it the premier cru of holy water.

The witch poured half the salt into the holy water in a clockwise spiral, muttering in Russian all the while. Then mixed it vigorously.

"Now, we have to be very careful to get every single root," she said seriously. "If even one tiny bit gets left behind, you'll have another tree tomorrow." I grimaced. Who the hell thought that one up? She looked at me sharply. "Clear your desk, Luís. Unless you want everything soaked."

I did as I was told. Which consisted, admittedly, of moving everything to a chair. There's not really very much. You can't afford to be untidy on a ship. For one thing, as soon as you get a bit of a blow, everything ends up on the deck. I'm not the world's most orderly man, but even I see the sense of that. She watched me impatiently. I heard six bells sounding. It seemed a very long way off.

Very slowly and carefully, she began to pour the salt water over the desk. Starting closest to the strange tree and working outwards. The air in the room began to take on a breathless curdled quality I recognized. The feel of magic being worked.

After a while, steam began to rise from the desk, and hovered about four inches above it like mist over the sea.

The cabin was chilly, but the witch's face was wet with perspiration. I knew how she felt, and scratched my cheekbone reflexively. No sweat to clear away, da Silva. I could hear myself breathing harshly. Tension stretched the atmosphere until it felt as if it had to break.

Which it did, suddenly and explosively. A burst of air like a leviathan exhaling, draining the tightness from the cabin. A brief scent of roses. Then the salt smell of the sea. The mist cleared away, leaving the desktop glistening wet. The witch nodded to me. Pointed to the tree. I moved to join her beside it.

Together we picked up the smaller of the two pieces of sailcloth I'd brought and wrapped it round the wrinkled trunk of the Judas tree. Under the cloth it gave slightly, like flesh. An unpleasant sensation. Then we started to pull. Gently. Firmly. Most important of all, carefully.

It seemed immensely heavy for its size. But it slid out smooth and easily, a dozen big roots as fat as my thumb branching and dividing into a hundred smaller ones, tapering to hair-fine tendrils. My arms were at full stretch above my head before the last tiny one cleared the surface of the desk. The tree seemed to wriggle and shudder as that happened.

We put the thing down on top of the other piece of sailcloth, and Tatiana Dimitrovna sprinkled the rest of the salt over it. It writhed and whimpered, a thin keening that set my teeth on edge. But gradually it started to desiccate until it dwindled down to a tiny shriveled dry thing like a mummified spider.

Now I was sweating as well. When I struck a match, my hand shook slightly. The phosphorus flared. I dropped it onto the remains of the Judas tree, and there was a brief intense burst of greeny-blue flame. So bright I had to close my eye. When I opened it again, there wasn't even a trace of ash on the cloth.

I struck another match, hands still unsteady, and lit a cheroot with it. Drew the smoke in gratefully.

"Just what the hell was that thing?" I asked. My voice sounded strange even to me. Impressive. Da Silva, who kills demons, gets the willies from a bush.

"What the hell, is right," said the witch, as seven bells struck somewhere very far away. "The Judas tree. The only plant indigenous to hell that can also grow in our world. Be thankful for that. It can take root in anything but fire."

Her face was very white. Eyes like two pieces of jet. Cheekbones sharp as rocks, pushing against the thin covering of skin and flesh. She looked like a memento mori.

"What is it?" I said, feeling a fresh surge of alarm.

"You can only collect seeds from a Judas tree in person," she answered, and her voice was as stark as her face. "Which means I know where Robert got his power, now. He didn't make any metaphorical, metaphysical pilgrimage."

Yes, I knew what she was going to say. "Don't," I began, but she said it anyway.

"He's been to hell, Luís," she whispered. "Been there, and come back."

My God, da Silva, don't you just know how to pick 'em.

*   *   *

Today a pale winter sun shines over the city, transforming it from a dull and dripping place in shadowy layers of gray to a potential of its summer clothes. If the bougainvillaea vines are quiescent, there are still a few geraniums bravely flowering, pink and scarlet and orange. If the canaries in their cages are still within doors, at least we know they are there and their owners will let them enjoy the fresh air soon, that is if the poor little creatures in their prisons ever enjoy anything. Still, they sing nonetheless, and if all the song means is a lament it sits well enough in Lisbon where humans sing fado with its melodies of loss and longing, *saudade* given voice.

The painter watched his subject leaving the house with barely-concealed impatience. It wasn't that he'd grown tired of portraiture, not after barely a year of freedom, but he was eager to return to his other painting.

Now he was free of the constraints his wife had put on his work, it was as if a dam had burst. No longer did each reluctant brushstroke remind him of wasted time: now they were celebrations and necessities as well. In his studio a kind of wonderful compulsion overwhelmed him as the pictures grew under his brush. He rarely ventured out, sometimes forgot to eat. As long as there was daylight, he painted.

Never enough daylight, these winter months. January begrudged him light, but not as much as December, imperceptibly the days were lengthening.

A small surge of excitement burst inside him as he uncovered the canvas. He had been moved to add another building to the street of the town in the desert, a severe churchlike edifice that somehow reminded him of India, though it was no temple. He'd never been to India, of course, the nearest connection he had to the subcontinent was that his wife had been born there, his father-in-law having been, despite his title, only some kind of minor civil servant in India. The old man had died not long after he and his wife were married, but he remembered him as a fearsome old Jesuit with all the zeal of St Francis Xavier. And all the warmth of the saint's cold and uncorrupted corpse, in its catafalque in Old Goa.

He thought about his own parents, something he rarely did, long dead as they were. We never really imagine our parents dying, he thought, it's bad enough witnessing them grow old, nonetheless when they do die the hole it leaves never truly fills in, whether or not we actually liked them. We never get over the surprise of their deaths.

Sebastião da Silva's father had been a soldier, his mother an Englishwoman from whom he had inherited a pair of incongruously blue eyes, which he in turn had handed on to his son. But there's only one left now, he remembered with regret. Perhaps it's even more difficult to accept the aging of our children than of our parents.

Certainly he found little of the son he remembered in the man of forty-four he'd only met again last summer after thirty years. His grandson, though, except that José took after Emilia in appearance, could have been Luís at fourteen.

A little guiltily, he realized he hadn't been to visit Emilia in over a week. This afternoon, he decided, it could easily be remedied, all he had to do was get on a tram. He was still more mobile than his daughter-in-law, for all that she got around surprisingly well with her walking-stick or her crutch.

But on this occasion he was interrupted. There came a knock on his studio door, and he looked up and smiled. They were random, these visits, unpredictable, whirlwind too, but never, never unwelcome.

"Come in." he called, and Alegria opened the door and stepped in. She was well-named, he thought, Joy, although it had been no prophetic parent who had christened her that, the name had come to him spontaneously as soon as he finished her face.

He had painted her into being nine weeks ago.

*   *   *

Seven months before, seven demons were summoned to collect souls. Most had departed when their errands had been completed, probably impatient to return to the proper business of demonic existence, perhaps annoyed at being called so peremptorily from what they were doing for such a petty purpose. Two, though, were dead, even if a part of one survived, and had a purpose it moved towards. If slowly and impotently in comparison with its former powers.

And one had never left at all.

She had been fascinated by the brightness of the soul she'd had temporary care of. Had not possessed it, that hadn't been in her remit, and so had no access to it, it was barred to her. But its feverish, fervid imagination, lush as a rainforest, unpredictable as the weather, that she had feasted on. It had been clamped down, though, locked in a cupboard of convention and swamped by enforced mediocrity that was wholly alien to its nature.

The demon called Belphegor, a patron of discoveries and inventions who had it in her power to bestow riches, had bestowed the richness of freedom to that imagination, set it loose to roam where it would. Such vividness might drive a man insane, if kept at such a pitch for any length of time without a safety valve. But she was, after all, a demon, knew little of the capacity of humans, and had no care or compassion for such matters.

So she gloried in its dreams, night after night, as he traveled lands never even created before, and met the people who lived there.

*　*　*

Ricardo Corvo, who looked very little like Poe's raven — but who would dearly have liked to croak "Nevermore" over his current caseload — drained his coffee cup and lit a cigarette. He cast a jaundiced glance around the café, which being situated where it was, was full of policemen. As if he didn't see enough of them at work.

But here was a stranger, a tall thin fair man with a beard and small round spectacles, and unless Corvo was much mistaken, he was headed towards him. In the seconds remaining he speculated on the man's occupation — schoolteacher? poet? — and then a polite voice was asking him if he was Inspector Corvo.

He lifted his rear briefly from the chair and inclined his head politely.

"My name's Montague Pierce," the newcomer said, an outlandish name, thought the inspector, but it explained the man's accent. "May I join you?"

Corvo waved his hand at the other chair. "Go ahead."

"Chá," Pierce said to the hovering waiter, then took off his hat and sat down. Then turned back to the inspector. "I understand you're the man in charge of these recent, ah, murders."

"Yes," said Corvo guardedly, thinking, meu Deus, not another damned idiot come to confess. But the Englishman didn't look insane. Just embarrassed, for some unknown reason. He drew on his cigarette and tried to look inscrutable. The inspector looked down at the other hands. From the look of them, he was older than he seemed at first sight. Yes, much of the blond hair, and the beard too, was white.

"Can I ask if you have any theories about the, er, perpetrator?" Pierce asked diffidently, and Corvo almost laughed at the nerve of the man.

"You can ask all you like, but I'm quite sure you never held out any hope that I'd tell you anything," he said. "What are you, a journalist?"

The Englishman looked horrified at this suggestion. "Good heavens, no," he exclaimed. "Nothing like that at all. I'm an antiquarian."

And why, Corvo wondered, should an antiquarian be interested in a series of exceptionally gruesome murders?

"Do you know something about these crimes?" he asked stiffly, narrowing his eyes and staring at the other man.

"Not directly, no," said Pierce hastily, looking almost as scandalised as he had when accused of being a journalist. "But have you considered he possibility that they weren't committed by, er, by a human agent?"

Corvo eyed him levelly and refused to rise to the bait. If that was what it was. "You mean, do I believe in the Werewolf of Lisbon? In a word, no."

"That wasn't exactly what I meant," said Pierce, adding "Obrigado," to the waiter who had just brought his tea to the table. Corvo took the opportunity to order another coffee. He stubbed out his cigarette, looking ruefully at the nicotine stains on his fingers as he waited for Pierce to explain himself. But he lost the waiting game: Pierce was apparently too intent on his tea. The cup rattled as he picked it up.

"Well?" the inspector said at length. The other looked over the rim of his tea-cup with a nervous smile, then put the cup down, took off his spectacles and began to polish them.

"Am I right in thinking you didn't find any, er, fingerprints, Inspector?" he asked after a moment.

"Why should I tell you—" began Corvo, frowning, then had second thoughts. "Yes, that's correct."

Pierce regarded his spectacles critically, apparently decided they passed muster, and replaced them. "And you would've expected to find some, I take it?"

"Yes," Corvo said shortly, thinking, *certainly given the amount of blood.* He took out his cigarette case and extracted another smoke from it.

"Then I think those women might have been killed by a, er, an artificial contrivance." Pierce picked up his cup again.

Cigarette in mid-air, the inspector gaped at him. "You mean some kind of an *engine?* An automaton?"

The Englishman shook his head. His spectacles slid down his nose, and he peered over them myopically. "I don't really know what I mean." He sighed. "Are you familiar with the work of the English detective, Sr. Holmes?"

Corvo nodded, though he was still frowning. "I had occasion to correspond with the gentleman some years ago." He lit his cigarette without elaborating, though he had actually found the exchange of letters most enlightening.

"Then you probably know what he says about eliminating the

impossible," said Pierce, pushing his spectacles back to the bridge of his nose.

"*Whatever remains, however improbable, must be the truth,*" Corvo quoted, rising to the cue with a small smile. The antiquarian inclined his head in acknowledgment.

"And do you think it's, er, impossible for anyone human to have killed the victims?" he asked.

"We found no physical evidence at the crime scenes," said the inspector, reluctantly.

"Then think about it, Inspector." The Englishman's voice was deadly serious.

Corvo contemplated the tail of ash on his cigarette, then knocked it deliberately into the tin ashtray on the table with a long sigh. "Sr. Pierce," he said at last, "either you're completely insane, or I am, or the world is."

"Try the last one," suggested Pierce, and drained his cup.

"I always do," said Ricardo Corvo. "I always do."

*　*　*

In the Channel, *Isabella* ran into fog. Which meant the wind dropped almost to nothing. Irritating and nerve-wracking in equal parts. Her sails flapped limp and unhappily, not making much way. I hadn't shortened sail when we lost the wind, and there wasn't really any point in all that canvas. But I wanted to be ready for the first sign of a breeze.

I can't explain the urgency I'm feeling. Surely Munro couldn't send anything after us so far over salt water? But who knew what he could do. Having been to Hell, and all that. I had no idea what that might mean, and neither did Tatiana Dimitrovna. But it was about power. It always is. Some people are never satisfied with what they have. The Venetian was like that, though God knows he didn't turn out to be a very competent sorcerer in the end. But it was trying to get more power that killed him in the end. All right, I cut his throat. But he'd been dead for fifteen minutes when I finally did.

The creaking of the gear was getting on my nerves. "Come on, wind," I muttered, throwing another cheroot butt into the sea. I'd smoked so much my mouth felt like a doormat. And at this rate Munro'd be able to walk after us on a sort of raft of the things I'd chucked into the ocean since the mist came down. Damned stupid weather. I stuffed my hands in my pockets. The damp cold was debilitating. Gazed morosely into the white dimness. Visibility was fifty yards or so.

Yeoh came to stand by me at the rail. "Something is odd," he observed, in his soft voice. Yes. Thank you for that, Sr. Yeoh. Stating the obvious, then, isn't a monopoly of the English. Unless he really could sense something. Since he isn't anchored in time like most people.

"What can you see?" I asked.

But he shook his head. "Nothing to see, senhor capitão. Until this mist breaks up."

I stared into the vapor, angry and frustrated, and scratched my eyebrow. I didn't even know what I expected. Is the fog hiding something, or is it just my imagination? Come on, da Silva. This is your environment. Your territory. Your *ship*. Take control.

And then, unexpectedly, a breath of wind. I let out a sigh of relief. "At last," I said.

The breeze freshened. Tore into the mist. Ripped it to shreds and blew them away. *Isabella* started to move, her sails filling with taut noise. My hands itched to take the wheel, but Angelotti, who had the helm, is perfectly competent. I restrained myself. Bad enough having me breathing down his neck.

Pretty soon we were making six or seven knots. The sky was still overcast, the day murky and miserable and cold. But what the hell, we were moving at last.

Yet I'm still apprehensive.

Towards the end of the forenoon watch — coming up onto midday — I spotted what looked like another barque on our trail. I frowned at it. That was unusual enough for me to take a closer look. There are still plenty of sailing ships around, and they tend to stick to the coastal routes mainly these days, but you're much more likely to run into a vessel under steam.

Anyway, I wanted to see whether I knew her. But I wasn't prepared for what I did see.

Because it was *Isabella*. Her exact twin. Identical in every respect. My back crawled. What was going on? For a moment I wondered it was some kind of mirage or optical illusion. She looked much too solid for that, though. Bad. Very bad.

Looking round for someone to send for Tatiana Dimitrovna, I spotted Felipe, the senior 'prentice, hurrying by on some errand. Or maybe just hurrying because I was watching him. Too preoccupied to care, I told him to fetch the Russian witch. Not in so many words, of course. Ever tactful, da Silva.

A few minutes later she joined me at the rail. The other ship was plain to see now. And most of the crew had seen her, too. I yelled at them to get their butts back to what they were supposed to be doing, and most of them went. But not without backward glances and muttering.

"*Putain,*" whispered Tatiana Dimitrovna, arriving at my side. I turned to look at her. Her face was white as ice. Which alarmed me even more. She put a hand to her mouth.

"What is it?" I demanded.

"*Isabella,*" replied the witch, making it sound like another oath.

"I can see that," I said irritably. "What the hell's going on now?" I didn't need to ask *who*. I am really, truly fed up with every damned sorcerer I run across deciding I'm a threat. Então. I will be one, now. But maybe I'd be less of one if they didn't persist in making it personal all the time.

Tatiana Dimitrovna didn't answer my question at once. When she did, it wasn't really an answer. And the answer wasn't anything I wanted to hear.

"Are you familiar with the term *doppelganger?*"

"I don't speak much German," I said, rubbing the scar on my cheekbone. "A double, is it?" She nodded slowly.

"Yes, but it's more than that." And why doesn't that surprise me? "If you see your double, your doppelganger, it means you're going to die."

I got out my cheroots again. Lit one, and pointed it at the other *Isabella*. She was nearing us steadily, if slowly. Would overhaul us eventually. "It's a warning?"

"That isn't," she said. "At least only in the sense that it could be the end of all of us." And that differs from a warning in what respect? "He created that ship, Luís, that... anti-*Isabella*, using the sea as a speculum. And if it gets too close—" She broke off. We both looked at the other ship. I swallowed. Above us, the wind hummed tightly in the sails and rattled the rigging—familiar sounds — while she told me terrible things.

"What?" I said. The witch shook her head slightly and sighed. She looked infinitely tired. And I knew exactly how she felt.

"Well, I'm not precisely sure. I've never seen it done with anything the size of a ship before. But the two things, the object and its mirror-image, they can't exist at the same time, in the same place. If they're brought together... At best... at best *Isabella* could become like the Flying Dutchman."

My scalp prickled. A cold fist seemed to grip my heart. If that was the best, I didn't want to find out the worst. I took a ragged mouthful of smoke.

"Not with my ship, they don't," I growled. "Tell me how to get rid of it."

"You can evade it," she said. "Your seamanship... It's not crewed, at least not in any real sense." Whatever than means. "If you can outsail it, it can't harm us."

Well, compared to some of the things I've had to do since I became Sr.

Knight-in-shining-armor, that'll be a piece of cake.

If, of course, that's all there is to it.

"What is it, captain?" said John Yeoh's voice. I hadn't seen him come up on my blind side.

"I wish I could say it's a mirage," I said, turning to him. "But it's been sent to get rid of us."

Or of me. Of the Russian witch. He's condemned an entire crew for the sake of removing two inconvenient people.

Not even if hell freezes over.

"Luís," the witch began. I interrupted her.

"Sr. Yeoh, get some more canvas on her. I want every inch of sail we've got," I bellowed. "Angelotti, get your helm over. I want us closer to the wind than you've ever been with that little Spanish *puta*. The rest of you for Christ's sake get your fingers out. This old girl needs to go faster than she's ever sailed in her life. Get moving!"

3

SIR ROBERT MUNRO, BARONET, GLOWERED SO FIERCELY AT HIS FAMILIAR THAT THE CREATURE CRINGED. Although it was a demon, it was a minor one, and although its master was human, he was more powerful than his infernal servant. And, perhaps, more than human — or maybe a better expression would be *other* than human — since his chthonic pilgrimage.

The familiar was currently wearing the shape of a small street urchin, only so that it could speak properly to him. Of course, being a demon, it could talk to him whatever form it took, but the forms always seemed to come with constraints. So as a cat, it found itself growing indolent and thinking about mice; as an owl, confusing the uses of its limbs and thinking about mice.

Inasmuch as so minor a demon could have an opinion, it didn't think very much of being assigned to Munro.

"What was the point," the baronet snarled, "of going to hell in the first place when the best I could get was you?"

"I translated the prophecy," said the demon sulkily, adding, "Your mortal friends couldn't." Which was true. Neither the legitimate scholars he had consulted nor the likes of Morgan Karswell and Aleister Crowley had been able to decipher the mysterious scroll that Munro had acquired a year ago from the antiquarian in Rio de Janeiro.

Since it had been, as it transpired, written in no human language.

"Much good that did," Munro grumbled. "I'd have done just as well visiting Gypsy Rose Lee and crossing her palm with silver."

"Don't you realize how much power the Fisher King could have," the demon implored, "especially a *healed* Fisher King?"

Munro didn't reply. He was looking at the image of two identical ships, one pursuing the other. Their shadows were passing across the floor of the room.

"Why can't the fetch-vessel catch her?" he asked angrily. The demon was silent. "Answer me!" Munro snapped.

"The captain," said his familiar reluctantly.

"The captain," mimicked Munro. Savagely. Understanding at last why the lower orders used spitting to express an opinion. "Why are you so afraid of him? You? Afraid of a human?"

They watched the ships, and even a landlubber like the politician could see that it was superior seamanship that gave the one in front an edge.

"He kills demons," the urchin-shaped demon said nervously. "He killed Alastor, hell's executioner. And Malphas the cunning."

"He's a man," said Munro contemptuously. "*You're* more powerful than he is. He's only a mortal."

With the baronet in this mood, the demon knew better than to try and contradict him. But privately it intended to heed the warnings of the demonic grapevine and keep well out of the way of this Captain da Silva.

Unless, of course, Munro got lucky and his phantom ship worked. But, somehow, the familiar didn't think so.

Ignoring the demon, Munro paced the room, the ship-images almost forgotten. Suddenly coincidences were multiplying, and he didn't like coincidences. The antiquarian in Rio had relocated to Lisbon, for some unknown reason. This troublesome sea-captain came from that city, and he shipped wine for Munro's own brother-in-law.

And, he suddenly realized, the reference in the scroll to "the city of Ulysses" could also refer to Lisbon and not Ithaca.

A number of ideas fell into place in his mind.

* * *

Isabella's a fast ship. I generally reckon on a week between London and Lisbon. But a week of this I can't take. Even supposing I could get twenty knots out of her and cut another day or so off the voyage. And what if the wind drops?

I stared over the gunmetal-gray sea at the other ship, smoking morosely. We were pulling away from her, making better speed. For now, anyway. But she still had the potential to go as fast as *Isabella*.

She'd been created, the witch had said, using the sea as a speculum. Well, that just means *mirror*. Yes, the same way doppelganger just means *double*. Wonder why they do that. Sorcerers, I mean. Why should translating a word suddenly make it magical. Maybe that's what spells are. Maybe if I told the wind to blow in Latin instead of Portuguese or English, it might listen to me. Of course it would, and I'm the Admiral of the Fleet. Come on, da Silva, your mind's wandering. Think, man, think.

And then an idea struck me.

Tatiana Dimitrovna hadn't gone below. Like me, she was standing by the rail watching the ghost-ship. As was a good portion of the crew, it seemed. I walked over to her. The wind plucked at my hair.

"You said that was made by some kind of mirror-spell," I said without preamble.

"Essentially, yes," she answered, not turning her head. I rubbed my cheekbone. Had to test this theory on her.

"Then what would happen if we weren't here?"

Now she did turn to stare at me, her face flushed from the wind. "We can't go that much faster than she can," she said. "We're too... intimately linked." Did she narrow her eyes when she said the word *intimately?* Never mind that now.

"No, I mean if we literally weren't here." The witch frowned. I took a final drag on my cheroot, and threw the remains into the sea.

"She'd cease to exist, I should think." What I hoped she'd say. I gave what I suppose was a wolfish grin. That is, I bared my teeth, but there wasn't any humor in it. It wasn't a laugh. Not of amusement anyway. "Luís," she said, "what are you thinking of doing? Don't forget *all* magic is double-edged."

Ups and bites you in the ass, is Harris's way of putting it. But this time I did laugh. In disbelief. Raised my eyebrow, too. *"You're* telling *me* that?"

"I just mean, be careful," she snapped.

"Oh, I'm always careful," I assured her. Not entirely accurate, of course. Sometimes you've got to take risks. Like now, for instance. I scratched my cheekbone again, sticking my finger under the eyepatch. Turned away from the witch. "Sr. Yeoh," I called.

Never know why people describe the Chinese as inscrutable. Yeoh's face is very expressive. Right now it was telling me he didn't much like Tatiana Dimitrovna. Well, that makes two of us. I stuffed my hands in my pockets to get them out of the wind.

Yeoh's papers give the year of his birth as 1720. He took himself out of time when his wife and son were lost at sea. To wait for them. And now he can move in and out of time. Can he move a ship? Only one way to find out.

He didn't blow me out of the water.

"Not alone, captain," he said. "But perhaps — with help." He was looking at the witch. Did I mention he also sees the shape of a person's soul? I've never asked him what mine is. But I bet he spotted Tatiana Dimitrovna for a witch the instant he clapped eyes on her.

She was staring at him just as intently. Though when she spoke it was to me.

"Should I wonder why you have such strange shipmates, Luís? A werewolf for a second mate... Mr. Yeoh here..." You don't know the half of it, *bruxa*.

"Serpent," said Yeoh to me, in Cantonese, taking me by surprise. Then I nodded, realizing he meant the witch. Slow on the uptake there, da Silva. Better wake your ideas up. I rubbed a hand over my chin.

"*Isabella?*" I said, taking out my cheroots. Yeoh nodded. I shielded a match from the wind and lit up.

"Madam," he said politely to Tatiana Dimitrovna, switching to English. "Can you make a power triad?"

"I do not know that word," she said slowly, her Russian accent more pronounced, and my heart sank. Yeoh merely looked irritated with himself, and tried again.

"Linking three people to work magic. One with the knowledge, one with the power, one for an anchor." Ah, like Paciência did last year. Guess who the anchor will be. I blew out smoke, and the wind snatched it away.

"Oh, yes, of course," she said. "Can you really displace us in time? Or out of time?" She frowned in confusion, then shook her head.

"A year ago I would have said it was impossible," answered Yeoh. "But as I am sure you know, everything gets better with practice."

Another time I might've found that amusing.

So here we are on the foc's'l head. As far from our pursuer as we can get. Though Tatiana Dimitrovna assures me that what passes for crew on that phantom ship is not, precisely, sentient. I didn't press for details about that, however. Suspect I wouldn't like the answer.

Afternoon watch. Six bells just gone. Getting dark already. January. The Russian witch's technique is different from Paciência's. Though why I'm focusing on irrelevant details like that I can't imagine. Well no, admit it, I know exactly why. To take my mind off — off what might happen if this goes wrong.

She instructed us to stand round the capstan (Witch's translation: *this round thing*), our hands on the top. Touching like people at a séance. Not that I've ever been to one. Don't need any help to talk to ghosts, thanks very much. Then she started to speak in Russian.

After a while the air grew tight, took on a dangerous brightness. It became a little difficult to breathe. The wind, which was strong in my face and making my eye water, suddenly seemed to surge *through* me and chilled ten degrees. I had to squint my eye almost completely shut. Would've closed it but I wanted to see what was going on. Something tugged inside me, an uncomfortable feeling. The sensation of a gale blowing traveled down both my arms at once, then instantly reversed itself with a force that made me gasp.

Tatiana Dimitrovna stopped speaking. Drew a deep breath.

"Now," she said.

Last time Yeoh took me out of time I felt as if I'd been turned inside out. This was infinitely worse. The gray sea and sky went black, the scene like a negative plate for a photograph, and the sensation shifted into my ears. The rush and rattle of the wind, the noise of the sea, changed to a screeching squealing shriek that set my teeth on edge and replaced the air's salty tang with the smell or taste of something sour and decaying. And that in turn became the tramping of a thousand insects over my skin.

For a split second that seemed to last an eternity I felt not just weightless, but without existence. I tried to open my mouth to breathe. Tried to move my hands from the capstan. Tried to turn my head. Couldn't move, couldn't breathe, didn't exist. Everything hung in the balance, suspended in time.

Then I heard a noise, but it was inside my head, and it was like the crack of doom. I flinched away from it, and had substance again. I could move again, and breathe. All was normal. Except that I was suddenly so tired I could hardly stand, and the others looked the same.

One thing we had to know, though. I staggered aft, yawning uncontrollably. Didn't need to go very far. Half the crew was at the starboard rail, shouting in a confused mixture of languages. The gist of which was the same, whether Portuguese, English, Italian, Spanish or any of the other tongues represented on board.

"Where did she go?"

And, to my surprise, a decisive: "Skipper, he get rid of her." I didn't need to look to see who'd said it. But I did anyway. Turned to see Benjamin at the wheel, Ashley's scandalized face behind. No doubt as horrified by Benjamin speaking out of turn as he was by the rabble at the rail. His mouth was working, but nothing came out.

Zé came elbowing out of the pandemonium, yelling "You did it, you did it," at the top of his voice.

I took a lungful of air and bellowed "Quiet," a couple of times before it made an impression. But all that happened was that they all turned to me and started to ask questions, all at the same time. "Shut up!" I shouted. They subsided, and I scowled at them. "Whatever it was, it's gone now. You lot get your butts back to wherever you're supposed to be. If it's not your watch, make yourselves scarce. Jump to it!"

"But sir—" There's always one.

"That means you too, Kirby."

He subsided. "Aye, aye, sir."

Kirby trotted off. I leaned against the rail and closed my eye. Knew I wasn't alone. Predictably, Zé'd interpreted my orders as not applying to him. But his voice sounds so concerned I can't be cross.

"Papai?" I opened my eye again, raising the brow. Dragged a hand over my face. Rubbed the back of my neck.

"What is it, Zé?"

"Are you all right?"

"Yes, I'm all right," I told him with a weary smile. Took out my cheroots. Covered a yawn. "Just a bit tired." A bit tired. I'll fall asleep on my feet if I don't get myself below soon.

"You look awful," he said. Tactful child. I lit the cheroot.

"It's a prerogative of being forty-four," I said, blowing out smoke, and he grinned.

"Just thought I'd tell you."

"Oh, thanks. I'll do the same for you one day." I shut my eye once more. When I opened it he was still standing next to me. "You still here?"

"What was that ship?" Thought he'd caught me at a weak moment, did he?

"Not now, Zé."

He looked mulish. "You never tell me anything." And that took my breath away as much as shifting *Isabella* outside time. I raised my eyebrows, and he backtracked hastily. "All right, you do. Will you tell me about it some time?"

If it'll get you out of my hair now. "Maybe." I took another drag at the cheroot. "Did you see where Sr. Yeoh went?"

"No, shall I go and look for him?" Meu Deus, he's volunteering to do something. Put out the flags and fire all the cannons. Yes, and we all know why he's volunteering. No reason to waste a good opportunity, though.

"Yes, but don't wake him if he's asleep. And the same with our passenger."

Zé scampered off. I don't know where he gets all that energy. Still I suppose I was just the same at his age and some miserable old sod was muttering *I don't know where he gets all that energy.* Though right now I feel about a hundred and two.

I leaned against the rail, not entirely sure I was capable of movement. The motion of the ship was soothing. *Isabella* skimmed over the darkening sea. Overhead, the cloud cover was unbroken. It'll be a starless night.

Seven bells. I jerked awake. This won't do. *Get yourself below, da Silva, or you'll fall over the side.* Never live that down. Having to fish the Old Man out of the drink.

"They're both asleep," Zé said, startling me again. His eyes glinted with amusement. "Snoring their heads off, both of 'em," he added.

"And that's where I'm going," I said, pushing myself off the rail. Not to be woken even if Neptune himself rises out of the ocean.

Before I fell onto my bunk I caught sight of my reflection in the glass door of the cabinet. Zé was right. I did look terrible.

* * *

Something jerked me out of sleep. The night was pitch black. And I was wide awake, all of a sudden. But not feeling threatened, which was a nice change. On the other hand, it would've been even nicer to've been left to sleep.

No idea of the time. The time doesn't matter. Can't hear anything unusual. Ship sounds. Breathing. Mine? I held my breath. The noise went on. Someone in my cabin.

All that went through my head in a split second, then I had a box of matches in my hand and was fumbling to light the lamp. The flame sputtered. Dazzled me for a moment. Then it steadied, and showed me Tatiana Dimitrovna. As I'd half-expected.

Damn.

I sat up stiffly. "What's the matter?" I said irritably, finding I'd fallen asleep fully-dressed apart from my coat, and my knife had dug a trench in my back.

Not the most brilliant opener. Now she'll tell me she can't sleep.

"I didn't want to be alone," she whispered. Wrong again. Worse, much worse.

Still, at least she had a dressing-gown on. I rubbed my hands over my face, pushing the fingers of my left hand under my eyepatch. I hate sleeping in that thing. Wish I could take it off. I don't normally subject the public to my scar. It's not a pleasant sight. But then, she's come barging in here in the middle of the night, and normally I wouldn't have it on. Normally I wouldn't have all my clothes on, either. Don't go down that road, da Silva.

So I pushed the eyepatch up onto my forehead and gave the scar a scratch.

"Go back to your cabin and go to sleep," I said, stifling a yawn. "If you don't need to sleep, I do."

Or I swear to God I'll tie you up with Harris's leash. Ha. Trouble with that is, she'd probably enjoy it.

She sat in the chair in front of my desk. So she took a hell of a lot of notice of what I just said to her, didn't she?

"I mean it," she said. "I'm tired too, God knows. But I'm awake, and I'm worrying too much to sleep." So you thought you'd come and make sure I can't sleep either. Thanks very much, Tatiana Dimitrovna.

I sighed. Got wearily to my feet and rid myself of the knife, rubbing my back rather ruefully. Don't usually even wear the thing on board. But Munro's phantom ship had spooked me. I stretched a bit. Didn't do much good. Old age creeping up.

"If I'd known you were coming, I'd've stocked up with vodka," I said. Took down the decanter, poured two glasses of brandy and handed one to her. She took it with a small smile. Glad one of us was amused.

"Not all Russians drink vodka," she remarked, tartly.

"You used to drink vodka." I searched for a cheroot. Lit one, hoping the smoke would pep me up a bit. Fat chance.

"I *used* to be the most powerful sorcerer in London," she retorted. In the lamplight her face had grown dark shadows. The chiaroscuro aged her. So God knows what I look like.

"What do you think Munro will do?" I asked. She shrugged.

"I don't know, Luís. I ask myself what I should do in his place, and I don't know. I am out of my depth."

Which was, I recalled uneasily, exactly what Carnacki'd said in Coelho's office. Why do these people think I can succeed when they don't even know what to do? I tapped ash into the ashtray irritably.

"I'm even more in the dark than you are," I pointed out, and she shot me an annoyed glance over the rim of her glass.

"It's about time you stopped denying it, you know."

Not expecting to be told off, I raised my eyebrows in surprise. "What?"

"Oh, wake up, Luís," the witch said impatiently. "You've been given these powers for a reason, even if you won't admit it."

To be honest, I've suspected something of the sort. Even had it hinted at before. More than once. I scratched my cheekbone, rubbing the smooth scar. What I don't understand is, why me? Why a man — as I was then—whose job included doing things that were, shall we say, morally ambivalent? The Venetian didn't have any scruples at all. So if I'd shown any sign of growing some on his business, *adeus* da Silva. Besides, the man who killed his brother didn't have any justification for taking the moral high ground. Even though mad Aldo had shot me just before I put the knife in him. I winced at the memory, still fresh after all these years. Why was I singled out to be some kind of champion against evil? More to the point, who picked me? I'd like a word with him. I didn't ask to be chosen.

The witch was staring at me curiously. I shook myself to rid my mind of these thoughts, and took a drag from my cheroot.

"What reason, Tatiana Dimitrovna?" I asked her. "And how do you know what... powers I have?"

Still irritated, she banged down her glass and snapped, "Everyone in this line of business knows when someone like you comes on the scene. It resonates. As you would know if you'd admit what you are."

And what am I? That's the question. That *is* the question. I looked at her. Took a deep breath. "I am — Luís da Silva," I said finally. "Everything else is incidental."

The witch sighed, but accepted it. "I don't know the reason, Luís." She took a sip from her glass. "One thing I do know, though," she added, and laughed grimly.

"What?"

"By now he knows the doppelganger is gone."

Of course he does. I scratched my eyebrow. "Will he follow us?"

She was staring at my face. Not, I don't think, at the scar. "Eventually. It depends on how much of a threat he thinks we are. Or you are."

If he caught a train, he could beat us to Lisbon by days.

"How much of a threat are we?" I asked. I think it was a rhetorical question. Certainly Tatiana Dimitrovna chose not to answer it.

Instead she said, "You never did tell me how you lost your eye."

"No," I agreed, "I didn't." And I'm not going to.

"You—" she began, but I never knew what she was going to say, because at that moment there was a knock on the door.

I exchanged a surprised glance with her, then hurriedly put the eyepatch back into place. "Come in."

Felipe put his head round the door, and blinked at the sight of his captain drinking brandy in the middle of the night with a witch in a dressing-gown. He recovered himself admirably, though, I must say.

"Sr. Ashley's compliments, sir, but could you come?" he said. "There's something you need to see."

My God, what now? I drained my glass and stubbed out my cheroot. Got wearily to my feet, surprised I didn't creak. Resumed coat, picked up knife. And followed Felipe to find out the latest interesting development.

Interesting, in the sense of the old Chinese curse: May you live in interesting times.

I wonder who put that one on me?

*   *   *

Demons can die. They are, in that sense, not immortal. But the demon Malphas, which da Silva had killed seven months before, had left a legacy, and that legacy was called Mouffi, and Mouffi remembered who had killed Malphas.

Mouffi was a fragment of its parent, although parent is not a very accurate word to use as it implies creation, and that is one thing that demons are not able to do. One day, it might grow into a new demon, but it would be new only in the sense of having grown through new experiences. To all intents and purposes, it would be Malphas, a demon with certain immutable powers and attributes. But since Malphas was dead, it would not be Malphas, but Mouffi. Unless it was given another name by its master.

For the moment, though, Mouffi was having to be patient, and patience does not come easily to a demon. It had to wait for growth to take place, and growth could be hastened, but only to a certain extent. At first it had permeated the fabric of a house in the Bairro Alto, until it grew tired of the paltry poltergeist activity which was all it could produce, and which was largely ignored by the house's inhabitants.

Inhabiting a human child as it grew inside its mother, too, had afforded little amusement and much tedium. Though the potential of having a human host was vastly attractive to Mouffi — who badly wanted a body again but had been unable to find anyone else stupid or ignorant or careless enough to let a demon in — floating in darkness in warm fluid lost its attraction very quickly. Accelerating the infant's growth was easy, if not particularly interesting, but all it achieved was a two-month reduction in the pregnancy. Mouffi had toyed with the idea of giving the baby horns or a tail, but acknowledged that this would probably be counter-productive in the end, however amusing it might be at first.

Mostly, Mouffi spent its time in the shape the demon Malphas had shaped the fragment when splitting it off, as a mouse. It was delightful to tempt a cat that thought it was getting a meal into sinking its teeth into something which could blow its head off. Mouffi enjoyed the thought of a mouse that toyed with a cat before destroying it, and the feline population of Lisbon was undergoing considerable depredations for its entertainment.

But compared to its former powers this was tame stuff, and infinitely frustrating for the remnant of a powerful demon.

Now, however, a ginger cat Mouffi had been stalking for a day or so was granted a stay of execution, because the demon-fragment became aware that its new host was very close to being born. The mouse-form vanished; it had acquired enough power to move bodilessly now, and not have to rely on stowing away on a passing carrier.

Mouffi could not truly possess the child, since no one can be possessed without consenting to the possession, and neither an infant in the womb nor a newborn baby can do that. Before we grow aware, we are protected. But it could occupy, it could share.

And so the child had a chance of growing up free. A very small chance, given that it would take exceptional strength of will for a personality to survive sharing a body with even a fragment of a demon. But a chance, nonetheless.

Ana Sobral, bent over with the pain of the contraction, squeezed her eyes shut and never noticed the mouse which ran over her foot and disappeared.

* * *

Teresa Batista, whose father had called the demon Malphas in the first place for purposes of his own, stepped out of the bath, wrapped a towel round herself, and sat on the edge of the tub to dry her hair vigorously. The only thing she missed now he was dead was having him as a fencing partner. It was proving incredibly difficult to find a replacement; most of the masters she'd approached were too scandalized at the very idea of her wanting to fence at all, let alone go up against her with a saber. The workouts she'd devised to replace a real bout were unsatisfactory, but at least they kept her fit. She had no intention of losing either her strength or her agility, and one day she'd find someone to hone her skills against once more.

Having finished her early-morning workout, the leisurely bath was both a necessity and an indulgence. But one that was cut short, on this occasion.

She heard Ana scream.

"*Merda*," she muttered, let the towel fall, grabbed her robe and headed for the stairs to the maidservant's room. As she passed the door of the bedroom she shared with Inácio Bosque, the doctor's sleep-rumpled head emerged.

If he was surprised at the sight of Teresa galloping by still shrugging into her robe, he didn't show it. Or maybe he didn't notice her state of undress, though he was of course wearing his spectacles, the first thing he does every morning is put them on, or sometimes the second thing. But

Teresa calls out Ana's name as she passes, and his professional instincts take over.

So, he thinks as he puts on his own robe and collects his medical bag, it's time for the virgin birth, it's lucky that Inácio Bosque is not a subscriber to the Christian myth, otherwise the whole of Lisbon would be waiting with bated breath for the miracle, we would have shepherds and sages banging on the door, followed shortly after no doubt by the slaughter of the firstborn.

As it is, fewer than a dozen people know about Ana's condition and the article he has begun with the medical journals in mind may never see the light of day, although doctors are no more immune from vanity than the rest of the human race so who knows what the future may hold, even Inácio Bosque may one day succumb to the seductive lure of seeing his name in print and forget prudence for a moment.

But now he has a patient to attend to, and banishes such fantasies and speculations to the back of his mind.

*   *   *

As I came up on deck, six bells sounded. Three A.M., then. Thank you, Tatiana Dimitrovna. *Isabella* was forging steadily along with the comforting sound of taut canvas from aloft. The night was chilly but had lost that dead cold. Maybe that had been part of Munro's magic as well. Ha. Take that as a given.

I gazed around suspiciously. Everything seems in order. No demons, sea-serpents, phantom ships, Flying Dutchmen, or great white whales in the offing.

So why has Ashley, of all people, sent Felipe to wake the skipper in the moribund hours of the morning watch?

And then I looked up, and knew the answer.

"Mother of God," I exclaimed, involuntarily.

"Captain?" asked Ashley in his English drawl, and he sounded as tentative as I've ever heard him.

"I see it, Sr. Ashley," I said.

"The wind backed about ten minutes ago," he told me flatly. "Backed, and dropped to force three."

Yet *Isabella*'s sails were full of wind, keeping us swift and steady on our course. I stared up at them, open-mouthed. Had the Russian witch called the wind for us?

Finally I realized I was standing there gaping like an idiot, and shut my mouth. *Not the time for codfish impressions, da Silva.* I took out my cheroots and said, "Well, whatever's causing that, it's nice to have it on our side, for a change."

Laughter from behind me. I turned, matches in hand, to see that Tatiana Dimitrovna had followed me on deck. The dressing-gown was covered up by a set of oilskins that almost swamped her. Harris's.

"Madam—" began Ashley, but I waved him to be quiet.

"What's so funny?" I asked her. She gestured up at the canvas and smiled in what looked like honest delight.

"It must be you." Now one thing I don't want at three o'clock in the morning is cryptic utterances. I raised an eyebrow at her.

"What," I enquired, suppressing a yawn, "do you mean?" I lit the cheroot I'd been holding. The end glowed red.

"You must have called the wind," the witch explained, eyes wide. Seeing my expression, she added, "Come, Luís, you must know the metaphysics of this by now. You're the master of the ship, symbolically you *are* the ship. Did you say anything that might sound as if you were summoning a wind?"

Remembering, I took the cheroot out of my mouth. "Yes," I said slowly, "I said, come on wind, or something like that."

"Well then," she remarked tartly, "I suggest you don't ask for it to drop any time soon. And don't say anything about rain, either."

As soon as one mystery gets resolved, another takes its place. Story of my life. I leaned against the rail.

"You heard the lady, Sr. Ashley," I said. "Carry on."

"Sir," he said stiffly, and moved away. Meu Deus. Even Ashley's so used to bizarre things happening on board that he didn't bat an eyelid at the witch's explanation.

She moved to join me at the rail. I blew out smoke. "Why didn't I have to say a spell?" I asked her. Under the stink of the oilskins she smelled of soap, and I wondered when she'd had time to have a wash.

"You did, but instinctively," she said, "not like that Englishman, what is his name, Carnacki, with his structured magics and his diagrams and his organized routines. You called for a wind, and it answered you."

I sucked in a lungful of smoke. "But I didn't say it in Latin, or anything." Not even sure what the Latin is. Veni, vento? Sounds catchy, anyway.

"Spells don't need to be in Latin, that's a common misconception." She reached out her hand and touched the scar on my cheekbone. I moved my head back, but she kept her finger there. "The power and the need, is all."

Congratulations, da Silva. You win the jackpot. "So will I be able to do that any time now?" I asked.

"That I don't know," she said. "It may be that this time it truly was the only answer. And so the wind came when you called it."

Well, I'll be damned.

*   *   *

The chilly rain that had draped the city in melancholy curtains is just a memory now, or not even that, for when the sun shines we never think about bad weather, we leave that to the meteorologists and poets. But it is pleasant not to have to pick up an umbrella every time we go out, even without the strong possibility of leaving the thing on a tram it is such an awkward drippy nuisance to cart about.

Harris, for whom that wasn't a consideration at the moment, looked away from Luzia's apparently sleeping face and scowled out of the window.

Funny, ain't it? Mostly changing's purely torture, and I hate it anyway, but this month I'm looking forward to it. Amazing how one gimpy leg changes your point of view. But I can't wait for this week to end.

Since his metamorphosis always felt as if his bones were snapping, he considered, or rather hoped, that it might have the opposite effect on a really broken bone. Failing that, any wounds he acquired healed pretty fast when he was in wolf-shape. *Even that silver bullet last year.* He grinned ruefully, and shot another glance at Luzia. *Bad enough turning into a wolf without getting shot in the ass. But Jesus, better'n getting shot in the head.*

He stared down at a piece of paper on the table. *Skipper's wife sure has a sense of humor.* In an attempt to illustrate the difference between *ser* and *estar*, Emilia had written: *O senhor Harris é um homem*, But sometimes, *Ele está um lobo*. Harris shook his head. Even the thought of a language that had two ways of saying "is" made his brain hurt.

May as well admit it. I sure wish Luzia hadn't gotten that cat idea into her head. I got a real bad feeling about that. If he'd been wolf, he would've growled. *But I reckon it's more than half my fault, at that. Goddamnit.*

Their conversation, when it moved away from the words all lovers speak in one variation or another, always came back to his frustration at his immobility.

"Jesus, I sure wish I could go take another look at that rooftop," Harris said for about the fiftieth time.

And this time Luzia squeezed his hand and said, "Ed, I will go."

Huh? Can't see her shinning up a drainpipe. "You can't go," he exclaimed in alarm. "How could you get up there?"

"I will go with a cat," she answered, which baffled him completely.

"A cat?" he repeated.

Luzia made a face. "I learned 'ow to..." She clicked her tongue in annoyance, and muttered some Portuguese, then, "Share 'is mind. *O senhor gato* goes on the roof, I see what 'e sees, smell with 'is nose."

Christ up the mainmast with a frock on, she's talking about possession. He tried in vain to think of a counter-argument.

"Ain't that dangerous?" he asked lamely.

She waggled the fingers of her free hand and made a dismissive "pff!" noise through her lips. "Not when I am careful."

"I don't think—" he began in alarm, then changed his mind. *She'll do it for sure if'n I try and talk her out of it.* "Did your ma teach you to do that?"

That earned him a sly but delighted smile and a kiss on the forehead. "No," she said smugly. "I, I... made it up?"

"Figured it out," he supplied, and she nodded. *Smart. But* shitfire! *how in hell's name do I stop her?*

The answer, of course, was that he couldn't. *Gave it my best shot. But she's as stubborn as her ma.*

Lot better-looking, of course.

"You must watch me," she said seriously.

"Sure," he agreed, beaten.

* * *

The ginger cat was quite oblivious of its escape from mouse-Mouffi, but now it felt something insinuating into its mind. It tried to react mentally as it would do to a physical threat, but had never learnt to use the claws of its mind, and Luzia slipped in. The cat hissed furiously, but she soothed it, and after a moment it accepted its temporary tenant.

Cathood overwhelmed her, sounds, smells, sensations, a kaleidoscope of senses, multi-layered, confusing. *Is this what Ed feels?* she wondered, but there was no time to pursue the thought.

She knew where to direct her feline steed, but not, for a moment, how. Obviously she had to let the cat walk by itself, if she tried to propel something with four legs she'd mess its motor control to kingdom come. And then she caught the trick of it, it was so simple, all she had to was imagine food in the direction she wanted to go, and her feline host padded along obediently.

Luzia was momentarily dismayed at the distance the cat would have to jump to reach the roof, she had forgotten the disparity in size between cat and werewolf. But she had also forgotten the agility of cats. It sprang across at her urging, and she let its senses absorb the rooftop.

Despite the days of rain the residue of blood was still very plain, and though quiescent in the cat mind she was horrified at the amount there had been. There had been mice up here, delicious, and birds, thousands of buzzy things feasting on the blood, rats — ah! wolf too! humans of course, nothing here now but blood smell.

Nothing to eat *now*, came a disgruntled impression from the cat, which was losing interest, but Luzia made it stay and sniff around for a while longer. She found nothing, though, except pigeon droppings, a crusty deposit by a drain, some flakes of paint, an empty wine bottle, and a small unidentifiable pile of rust.

And that was it. Luzia's control began to tire, the cat-mind squirmed, trying to break free. She recognized that she'd seen all there was to see, not that see was quite the right word, released it and flew back to herself, in the da Silvas' parlor.

Her eyes jerked open, making Harris jump, jarring his leg sharply, making him swear under his breath at the stab of pain. Though mostly it was no more than a dull ache now.

Luzia's cheeks were flushed and she had a big grin plastered on her face. And Harris, smiling in return and relief, was amazed at just how worried he'd been. *Got it bad, ain'tcha?*

And even that thought was strangely comforting.

"I did it, Ed!" she exclaimed.

* * *

There might've been circumstances that would've let me enjoy this voyage. But I can't think of any. The wind I'd called held steady in *Isabella*'s sails. The clouds blew away on the world's winds. A pale winter sun came out and shone on us. And everyone on board cheered up. Ghost-ship gone, all's well with the world.

Do I believe that? Not for a moment.

I wish I knew what kind of power Sir Robert Munro's journey to hell had given him. I spent a lot of time pacing the deck, expecting Adamastor the Titan to rise from the deep. Or the sea itself to transform into fire.

Neither of those things happened. But the skipper has to think of everything.

Could do with Harris to talk to, as well. What I had was Tatiana

Dimitrovna.

We'd talked all round Munro. Up, down and round. Talked to a standstill. Come to no conclusions. Except that whatever powers he picked up in hell probably means that all bets are off, as Harris would say.

"I'm sure he must still be bound by the rules," the witch said, "but if we ever start to think *He can't do that*, we must stop ourselves." I stared at the choppy sea, a color between pewter and blue, and *Isabella's* creamy wake dragging behind us.

"The rules," I repeated.

"You know there are rules, Luís." She put her hand on mine. I was so preoccupied I didn't even move it away. "He can't come on board without an invitation. Or send anything without a channel for it."

"You just said *He can't*," I pointed out, rubbing my eyebrow absently.

"It's a fundamental rule," she said. "Evil can't come in without an invitation."

Rules. Make a rule and someone'll figure out a way to get round it.

"He got that Judas tree on board," I reminded her.

"He got you to bring the seed." I suppose the only thing to do is empty all my pockets before I embark. Yes, and frisk the entire crew. *Practical, da Silva.* Perhaps I could borrow the zealous Sr. Vaughan from Customs in London.

A sudden rattling roar made me leap away from the rail, looking up in alarm. If I'd been smoking I'd probably have swallowed my cheroot.

"What—" I began, and then saw what was making the noise. Flying low, only about a hundred feet above the sea, an airplane. A monoplane, like the Frenchman Blériot's. It neared us rapidly. Now I could see the pilot waving. I waved back. We must make a strange contrast. A machine of the twentieth century and a wooden ship of the nineteenth. The one at the beginning of its career, the other nearing the end.

It was a noisy beast, though. This century's going to founder under the noise as the world abandons silent transport. Steamships, motor cars, airplanes, trains. Who knows what else.

And I was so busy watching the future of transport that I nearly missed what was following it. I turned to watch the monoplane's dwindling shape to starboard. Then Tatiana Dimitrovna shouted my name in a panicked scream so unlike her normal voice that made me whirl round with my hand instinctively going to my knife.

Birds. Damn it, of course. Something that flew didn't need to be invited *on* board.

There were four of them. I don't know whether the airplane guided them or whether they'd just taken advantage of it to sneak up on us. They weren't birds, of course. Though they had that general shape, and they had feathers. Any resemblance ended there. Their wingspans had to be ten feet across, bodies big in proportion. Great taloned scaly feet, claws gleaming in the pallid sunlight. Nightmarish heads, naked like a plucked chicken's, bone-white beaks three feet long and full of shark's teeth, snapping and clacking and dribbling saliva. And they stank, a foul stench unlike anything I've ever encountered.

Swooping, they screeched, a howling banshee yell that was almost as tangible as their stink. Down they came, claws outstretched, and I ducked one and spitted the second with my knife, ripping the blade swiftly out of its body. It screamed once, and fell to the deck with a thud. As it hit the boards, it vanished. I couldn't spare time on it. Couldn't see what the witch was doing. Couldn't worry about her. I am, after all, missing one eye. And it's a bloody nuisance at times like these. I swung round to meet the next bird-thing.

Claws flew past an inch from my face. I yelled out in reflex and smashed out with the blade, severing the taloned foot. Black blood fountained out. And Tatiana Dimitrovna came from nowhere and brought a belaying-pin down on its head with a very satisfying crunch.

Two down, two to go. But they were both after me, even though the witch had just killed one. These two were smarter, as well. Or just more cautious. One of them hovered in the air, slashing at me with its claws. The other was angling round to my blind side, hampered by the witch and her belaying-pin.

Stalemate. Can't stay that way for long. I'm getting tired, never a good idea in a fight. But I've been exhausted ever since we took *Isabella* out of time. The anchor, I'd been. Don't entirely know what that means. But I've got a good idea. Sweat was running down my face, and my arm was beginning to tremble with holding the knife aloft.

The creature the witch was fending off suddenly shot straight up in the air, reversed, folded its wings and stooped like a falcon. Tatiana Dimitrovna, reacting almost as fast, threw her belaying-pin at the one I was fighting, striking it squarely amidships. It tumbled backwards through the air, shrieking. I wrapped both hands round the hilt of the knife and rammed it upwards, catching the descending bird-thing. Which came straight down on it, the blade striking up through its body. Screaming in anguish, it fell, and I jerked the blade out and jumped back before its steaming black blood could pour down on me.

Pivoting on one foot to meet the other creature, I ducked under its outstretched talons and punched the knife upwards with the intention of doing the same thing to it as I'd just done to its fellow. But it was too fast. It seized my arm in its fanged beak, wrist to shoulder nearly, and I felt the jagged teeth slide into my flesh. The pain came an instant later, breathtaking and tearing. I fought frantically. I don't want to end up losing an arm as well as an eye. It leered at me, and there was such an awful knowing look in its gaze that it warned me, and I looked downwards.

It drew its huge taloned foot back to eviscerate me. I saw the claws flex, and grabbed the leg in my right hand and wrenched it backwards, trying to twist it off like a chicken drumstick. The beak chewed on my arm, and it keened viciously.

And then the witch threw a handful of salt into its eyes. The beak's grip relaxed. I wrenched my arm free, feeling the blood running down it, and cut off the bird-thing's hideous head with what felt like the last of my strength.

I dropped my knife and collapsed against the rail, clutching my savaged arm. Blood dripped onto the deck. My vision blurred and splintered. Tatiana Dimitrovna, white-faced, hitched her skirts up and ran to help me.

"Holy water," I gasped. The pain was murderous.

"We used it," she said bleakly.

"Refilled it," I got out. Think I don't travel with a reserve supply?

John Yeoh appeared, his face flaring and fragmenting in my sight. I knew I was on the point of passing out.

"Get his head down," I heard the witch say.

"What were you fighting?" Yeoh asked. "I couldn't see it at all." I felt hands on my arm, round my waist, supporting me. Nausea in my throat. Vision sparkling, breath shallow. Cold sweat on my face.

"Later. We need to get him below."

Maybe I lost consciousness. I'm not sure. They got me to my cabin, somehow. Not to the ship's doctor. Yeoh knows I'd rather cross the Atlantic in an open boat than let O'Rourke anywhere near me with something sharp.

Someone wiped my face with a damp cloth. I was too dizzy to see.

"Brandy?" suggested Yeoh.

"Afterwards," said Tatiana Dimitrovna. "Luís, can you hear me?"

"Yes," I mumbled.

"Hold on," she said. And then I think I did pass out for a moment, because the next thing I knew I was flat on my back with my shirt off. Felt the soothing chill of the holy water bathing my arm. Breathed more easily. The nausea began to retreat.

"How did these wounds morbidify so fast?" Yeoh asked, sounding amazed. Has he not seen it before?

"We can't stand their touch, Mr. Yeoh," the witch replied. "But the speed of the infection, it has to do with how potent the wounded person is. Against evil."

"Ah yes," said Yeoh. A wealth of meaning in the word. "That makes sense. I have seen the shape of the captain's soul."

I opened my eye. Didn't want to eavesdrop any more on *that* conversation, thank you very much. "Excuse me," I interrupted, and started to cough. "It's not very polite to talk about me as if I'm not here."

"Good," said Tatiana Dimitrovna briskly. "How do you feel?"

"Better," I told her, pushing myself up to a sitting position. I felt more than a bit lightheaded. But that would soon go. "Where's that brandy you promised me?"

Yeoh handed me a glass, and I drank gratefully. Then looked at my arm. It looked nasty enough even with the suppuration cleared, a dozen or more deep punctures, ragged and torn where the fangs had ripped out. I clenched my fist against the pain, then flexed my arm. It made me grit my teeth and draw in breath sharply through them.

"Well, don't do it if it hurts," said the witch, sharply. I grinned at her, and she rolled her eyes heavenwards.

"Here, captain," Yeoh offered, and made me hold dressings in place while he bandaged me up, quickly and efficiently. Doesn't really surprise me that Tatiana Dimitrovna's skills don't extend to nursing.

When he'd gone, I pushed myself shakily to my feet. Not too bad. Head's stopped spinning. I rubbed a hand over my face, scratched my eyebrow, and went to look for a clean shirt. The one I'd been wearing, and my coat, lay in a bloody heap on the floor. Damnation. I made a face at it.

"I suppose," said the witch from behind me, "this is as near as I'll ever come to getting you naked in a bed."

She put her hand on my back. The palm felt burning hot. I straightened. Turned to face her. She is exactly the same height as I am. Her hand slid to my waist.

"You never give up, do you?" I said, torn between amusement and arousal.

"I've always been attracted to you, Luís." She put her other hand on my side. "Ever since I first met you."

"What, when you tried to stab me?"

"Especially then," she whispered. I resisted the urge to put my arms around her. "I'm not used to being refused, you know."

"I know." The witch slid her hands round to the small of my back. Our bodies were almost touching. Her lips were slightly parted. She moistened them with her tongue.

If you kiss her, da Silva, what then?

I put my hands on her shoulders and pushed her away. Not without regret. She laughed.

"Your loss, you know, Luís." I don't think so.

"Can't let you take advantage of a casualty," I said lightly.

"Take advantage?" she repeated. "Don't you ever lose control?" I almost laughed. Although it wasn't funny.

If she thinks I only do things because I want to, she doesn't know me half as well as she thinks she does.

*   *   *

Lisbon in the morning, thank God. If that's who I should be thanking. These days I'm never really sure.

The wind I'd called was still driving us smoothly southwards. Should I dismiss it yet? Or wait until we reached the mouth of the Tagus? Normal seamanship doesn't cover what to do with winds from — well, wherever this one came from.

So now, the glass is falling. Which usually means a blow. Would the world's wind and the ship's wind conflict? I shortened sail a bit. We're so close to home that I don't need to worry about our speed anymore.

I chewed at the end of my cheroot, wondering what to do. Angry at myself for this indecision. Pull yourself together, da Silva, and stop dithering around like a maiden auntie.

We'll keep the wind. I can always dismiss it if I need to. Decision made. I felt happier. I checked the glass and the weather again. The one had fallen a little more, the other turned to light rain. I brought the log up to date and went to bed.

Only to be jolted awake in the middle of the night by a noise like the explosion of Krakatoa. Which I remember, by the way. Not the eruption itself, of course. Otherwise I probably wouldn't be here now. But certainly the extravagant sunsets the dust it spewed out caused for two years and more afterwards.

At the same time the ship canted sideways so violently I nearly fell out of bed. Meu Deus, she's almost lying on her side. She righted herself an instant later, flinging me in the other direction with teeth-jarring violence and banging my injured arm on the bulkhead. Damn it, that hurt.

I staggered out of my bunk. Flung my oilskins over my nightshirt and hunted for my boots in the darkness. Around *Isabella* the wind shrieked wildly.

"Go, wind, go away!" I said out loud. Found my boots. Slid my bare feet into their clammy depths. No time for socks. We had to've lost sails. I pictured them ragged and flapping. Swore violently. Dashed up on board in the wake of the creak and rustle of oilskins, the slap of bootsoles and the muffled curses of half-awake seamen. Ashley'd called all hands to shorten sail, and I hoped like hell he wasn't too late.

The wind I'd called was gone. This was a wind of the world hammering us. I felt it veer lightly, heard Ashley shout "Stand east," and something inside me said *No!* but my voice blew away in the rain-filled darkness. The binnacle lights swung madly, haloed through the rain. Water ran down my face, trickled under my eyepatch. I hate that sensation.

Isabella started to come round, and then a tremendous blast of wind came from nowhere with a howling booming explosion, solid as a rock, and the next instant we were flat aback, sails straining and groaning.

Get the canvas off her, I wanted to yell, but everyone was already aloft. The fore and main t'gallants had gone, which was probably just as well, and they were flapping and thundering in tatters overhead. Rain teemed down, the wind shrieked. And just to be creative, both binnacle lights blew out at once, leaving us in pitch darkness.

"Mr. Ashley, get her before the wind!" I bellowed. Huge gouts of spray broke over the deck, but I was so wet I didn't care. Wet was the least of my worries. If we don't get her round, we're done for. Masts and yards aren't made to take the wind from the front. Obviously. And you can't use the rudder in case the sea's weight smashes it off its pintles. You have to work with the elements, not against 'em.

I could only watch once I'd given the orders. Get the spanker off her, square the mizzen yards, leave the fore and main aback. Not that I had any wish to be up there. Done enough of that when I was younger. Not that I could've done anything any faster if I was. But it all seemed to take such a time.

Isabella knew what I wanted, though. She canted herself without the helm, backing gradually into the screaming wind. Come on, old girl. Get those afteryards filled. *Ah… Don't call anything you can't handle, da Silva.*

Slowly she turned. Agonizingly slowly. And then the after-sails began to fill, followed by the fore and main. Now we can use the helm again. I let out a long breath of relief, got her shortened right down, and we ran before the wind in the rain and darkness.

We got off lightly. No damage to the masts. None to the rigging. Though the fore and main t'gallants were rags, and there were splits in a couple of the others. But changing the blown-out sails can wait till morning.

It kept on raining. Dawn came gray and murky late in the morning watch. The wind lightened as we turned to approach the mouth of the Tagus, and I sent some of the crew up to replace the damaged sails.

Tatiana Dimitrovna joined me at the rail. Wearing her own rain-gear this time, not Harris's oilskins. Suits her better, I must say.

"Is everything all right?" she asked, watching the activity aloft. I took the cheroot I was smoking out of my mouth.

"It is now," I answered. "Bit of a blow last night." And that's all it was. A bit of a blow. All right, it caught us by surprise and it shouldn't've done. But it was fairly paltry compared with some of the winds I've met. Can't even compare it with a hurricane.

She smiled, not knowing this. "Yes," she said drily. "Is that the river-mouth?" I nodded. I was looking at a low black cloud that had appeared from nowhere and appeared to hovering directly in front of us. Barring our way.

"What d'you make of that?" I asked the witch, but she didn't get a chance to reply. Because the cloud suddenly funneled downwards and sucked up a column of the ocean just like a waterspout. The pillar of water writhed and flowed, thrashing to and fro directly ahead. It changed shape, shivering between strange sea-creatures and something almost human in form, the black cloud its hair. A mouth opened, and it gave out a huge and anguished cry that made me want to stop my ears. It sounded as if it came from the depths of the ocean.

"You cannot pass," it bellowed. Oh, what now? I've had enough of this. I threw the butt of my cheroot at it. It fell well short, of course, but made me feel better.

"Why not?" I shouted back angrily.

"What are you?" called Tatiana Dimitrovna at the same time.

"*O espirito do Tejo*," came the mighty voice. Why should the spirit of the Tagus bar my way? "What you bring cannot be permitted to pass."

Well, damn it, on this trip I've called the wind, evaded the ship's death, fought off a flock of harpies or whatever the hell they were, and wrestled *Isabella* through a storm. One blasted talking waterspout isn't going to stop me now.

"This ship makes landfall in Lisbon today," I yelled at it.

"Your ship is tainted," it howled. "It bears the mark of Gaziel, stormbringer, which loosed the earthquake on us."

And that was a name I knew. "Look at me, spirit," I shouted hoarsely. My throat's getting sore with all this yelling. "I have the key of Solomon," the invisible mark I acquired when that particular demon was exorcised from me, "and I am the master of this ship. Let us pass."

A long finger of water extruded from the waterspout toward me. I stood still, although the back of my neck was prickling.

"What?" Tatiana Dimitrovna whispered, not having understood anything I said. Though she'd heard, she told me later, the Tagus-spirit's words in her native tongue. To me it seemed to be speaking Portuguese, and I'd replied automatically in the same language.

"I think it's checking my credentials," I muttered back in English.

The watery tentacle touched me over the heart, where the mark lies that only Emilia can feel. There is a matching one on her own breast, and only I can see that. I felt a thin cold touch under my clothes, tracing the outline of the five-pointed star. It chilled me, that touch of the ocean. It would any sailor. There were too many drowned men in it.

It withdrew, and I drew a deep shaky breath and lit a fresh cheroot. It felt strange, somehow. But the taste of the smoke anchored me once more in reality.

"And so you do," said the Tagus-spirit in a muted roar, and sank back into the sea.

4

HE'D BEEN KNOWN AS ARANHO, SPIDER. ARANHO ALVES. But Ricardo Corvo had always thought of him as being more like a cockroach. Something malicious and sneaky, contaminating whatever he touched, creeping in where he had no right to be. Aranho had been a thorn in the inspector's side for some time, mainly because although, like a cockroach, he left clues to his presence, they were never enough to nail the little low-life. If that wasn't enough, his wretched wife — not that Corvo had any illusions that their marriage had enjoyed the benefit of clergy — would give him an alibi for just about anything. And frequently had.

Well, the wretched Nina was now sleeping off a severe bout of hysteria with the help of a copious amount of laudanum, and Corvo was reflecting that the cockroach, or the Spider, had now been well and truly crushed.

If crushed was the word for it. Smashed might be more accurate, as if the man had been thrown, say, from the top of the Sé. This corpse had only been cursorily gnawed, unlike Mercedes, whose face had been eaten, Rita, who'd been almost entirely devoured above the waist, and María, which had been the worst.

In fact, if it hadn't been for these few bites, Corvo would've been tempted to assume, or hope, that some of Aranho's associates had thrown him off a roof.

But that would mean that there was more than one killer on the loose with a penchant for munching on dead bodies. Which was not a pleasant thought.

Corvo lit a cigarette to help kill the smell of blood and bowels, and knelt by the shrouded corpse, careful of his pants. Someone had thoughtfully placed an extra piece of tarpaulin on the ground for this purpose. He folded back the other sheet, which covered the body.

The late Aranho Alves lay on his back, his head smashed like a watermelon, though bizarrely the features of his face were intact save for a trickle of congealed blood from one nostril. He was wearing only a pair of pajama pants. His arms and legs were twisted and distorted, almost as if they'd been arranged on purpose to show how many pieces the bones had been broken into. The bites were confined to his arms and torso, the right arm being the most damaged and the right hand missing altogether.

Although he couldn't possibly have sustained such injuries by falling from the roof of a two-story building, that was where the body lay. Behind the house where he and Nina lodged. The blood and other matter on the ground all around him, and presumably under him (though Corvo had no intention of moving the corpse to check, he would leave that for the blood-wagon) indicated that it was unlikely he'd met his death anywhere else.

There wasn't anything to be gained by staring at the body. It wasn't going to speak to him. Corvo got to his feet, careful not to drop ash on Aranho's remains, and wished that the dead *could* speak. It would make his job so much easier.

He thought of the Englishman Pierce's theory. Something mechanical. On the one hand it seemed completely mad, but on the other, Aranho did look as if he could've been crushed by some monstrous engine.

Inspector Corvo didn't even begin to think about the fact that yet another body had turned up which fit no pattern at all.

A voice interrupted his reverie. "Sir? Inspector Corvo?"

"What is it, Santos?" asked Corvo, mildly surprised that his corpulent and indolent subordinate had actually approached him rather that have to be asked several times to do it. Initiative was not a word that featured in his vocabulary. The inspector looked round and observed that, on the other hand, the verb *to pick one's nose* obviously did. He was glad he never had occasion to shake hands with the man.

"The fellow who found him, sir? Wants to talk to you. Says he saw what happened."

"Mother of God," exclaimed Corvo, his heart starting to pound. "Where is he?"

Santos, having excavated his nostrils to his satisfaction, indicated a bewildered-looking man standing a little way off. "Lives right here, sir."

He looked like a clerk rather than the standard low-life Corvo would have expected to be Aranho's neighbor. The inspector finished his cigarette and pinched it to extinguish the butt, not wanting some over-zealous foot-soldier to commandeer it as evidence.

"Wheel him on, then."

The witness approached nervously when Santos beckoned, and Corvo gave him a reassuring smile. But you can't ever hope to make the general public enjoy dealing with the police, however affable you seem to them.

"I understand you saw what happened, senhor," said the inspector conversationally. The man nodded jerkily. "I'm Inspector Corvo. May I have your name?"

"It's Branco," Santos put in, and Corvo shot him an irritated glance.

"Sr. Branco, then," he amended. "Could you tell me what exactly you saw?" The witness, Branco, fiddled nervously with his necktie.

"Yes, Inspector," he said unhappily. "But it didn't make any sense at all to me." Corvo's heart sank. He shouldn't have got his hopes up.

"Suppose you just tell me," he suggested.

"Very well," said Branco. "I was putting out the trash before I went to work — I'm a clerk at the Ministry of the Interior — I'd just opened the door when—" He gulped. His Adam's apple was prominent and it looked as though he was swallowing a hardboiled egg. "— he just came *plummeting* down out of the sky and landed on the ground there. The noise—" He shuddered.

"Did you see where he came from?"

Branco looked, if possible, even more miserable. "I looked up, of course. But I, I don't think he came from the roof. I know it sounds mad. I thought he might have fallen from one of those airplane things, but I know they make a noise and I didn't hear a thing. And there was nothing. Just... him." He swallowed again, without looking at the body, although it was covered.

"What did you do?"

"I, I'm afraid I was sick." A small pool of vomit not far away bore witness to this statement. "Then I sent the boy to fetch you lot."

Fell from the sky, thought Corvo. Just about as likely as the Englishman's infernal engines. Am I surrounded by lunatics, or is it just me?

* * *

The sky over London was a uniform steely gray, giving the city itself the grim formality of a steel etching. A thin icy wind was blowing relentlessly, carving the snow which lingered on inaccessible places like rooftops into fanciful curves and waves. None of the snow stayed white very long. Even high above the ground it is thickly peppered with soot from the dirty air that the citizens are obliged to breathe day in, day out. Breathe in, hack out. But the citizens must heat their homes somehow, the businessmen their offices, the tradesmen their shops. The trains must run to convey all those people to wherever they need to be. All kinds of engines, infernal or not, must be fed with fuel to keep the wheels of the city turning, and so the capital's citizens must put up with smog and soot and the thousand unnatural stinks that the

Londoner is heir to.

Scowling darkly, Sir Robert Munro let himself into the mansion flat which the construct he'd called Sarah Turner had been using. He had two purposes there, neither of which could wait until the police had finished with the place.

Not that the presence of a stolid and bored constable outside the door was any hindrance to him. A simple charm of Look-over-there, the sort that any hedge-witch could do in her sleep, mutated in his hands to a spell of great potency. So he had no fear of being noticed, let alone discovered. He had no fear of anything, any more. But that didn't mean he couldn't recognize a potential threat when he saw one.

Munro usually prided himself on his control, but he felt a surge of almost overwhelming anger as he saw the bloodstains on the carpet and sensed the fading residue of the guardian demon. Regaining control with something of an effort, the sorcerer chalked up another score he had to settle. Did that bloody man even think before destroying his work?

In the parlor, he seated himself on a ridiculously spindly ottoman and opened the carpet-bag he had brought with him. From this he lifted, with great care, something wrapped in damp cloth, which he placed on the table before beginning to unwrap it.

Several layers later he had revealed a clay model of a woman's head. The face was Sarah Turner's. He contemplated it for a few moments, and then, without looking up, made a beckoning gesture with one hand.

His familiar appeared with an implosion of air. It was wearing its urchin shape.

"I want all her residue," said Munro without preamble.

The demon, relieved to be given a mundane task for a change, set about its work. Being a lowly creature it floundered when Munro tried to hold a conversation with it. Since it was unable to answer most of his questions: Demons, for the most part, not having very much in the way of imagination.

When it was done, Munro smoothed the dusty detritus over the clay head and re-wrapped it. Now all he had to do was fire the thing, and smash it, and Sarah Turner would be no more. He smiled nastily at the thought of her jailers' bafflement.

And then he went to do the other thing he had come to her apartment for.

In the bedroom, he directed the familiar to move the wardrobe, a huge heavy oaken thing. Behind it, a closet. Munro pulled a curiously-warded key from his pocket, a key which was made from no metal found on earth, and unlocked the door.

A clay figure, his exact likeness, stood inside, mute, unmoving, waiting to be animated. Munro smiled.

If he had to go to Lisbon, he needed a stand-in. And an artificial cabinet minister required no more complicated instructions than the regular sort of whore. Each, after all, was only required to go through a series of motions and reflexes.

If no one had noticed with Sarah Turner, some of whose lovers had been intelligent men, no one at all would notice a false Sir Robert Munro in the empty charade of Parliament.

* * *

Tatiana Dimitrovna's perfectly capable of finding somewhere to stay. But Zé seemed to want to carry on being her steward. So I left her in his hands. Or vice versa. She may have her own interpretation of morals but she's not going to seduce a fourteen-year-old boy.

I've got plenty of other things on my mind, anyway. Well, that's not strictly true. I have one thing on my mind, and his name's Sir Robert Munro. Ship's business, I don't need to think about. It's automatic.

On the quay, the usual noise and bustle. The usual routine. The usual ghosts. And one unexpected face. Sr. Montague Pierce, the antiquarian. I disembarked and strolled over to him. Wondering what the hell was up. Since it'd normally take another earthquake to prise him loose from São Rafael.

Didn't let him see any of that, though. Poker face, da Silva. I shook hands with him, saying, "Pierce. *Por aqui?*" He adjusted his spectacles. One of life's little certainties. If the Four Horsemen of the Apocalypse came galloping into the Rossio, Pierce'd be pushing his spectacles back to the bridge of his nose. Yes, I know. And I'd be scratching the scar on my face. We all have our irritating little ways.

"Skipper," he replied, not that I'm his captain. His pale eyes looked worried. I don't know how old Pierce is, possibly fifty-five. But right now he looks all of it, and more.

"What's up?" I asked, lighting a cheroot. The Englishman grimaced, and kicked at a stone. It flipped abruptly into the air, passing through the ghost of a man so small he was almost a dwarf. Pierce sighed, puffing out a cloud of vapor. The rain had stopped, leaving the air chilly and bleached.

"People being eaten," he said in an undertone. I blinked. Do you call it a blink when you only have one eye to do it with?

Well, hell. Thought *I* had something to tell *him*. "People," I repeated. "Plural." He nodded unhappily. "Go on."

Three that he knew of. "And the inspector was so baffled he even agreed it might be, er, a golem." I nearly dropped my cheroot. That's not a coincidence.

"How the hell did you come up with that theory?"

"Wasn't me," said the antiquarian. "Was the Professor." He likes labeling people, Pierce. I tried to picture him selling the idea of a golem, suggested to him by a ghost, to a policeman. But my imagination wasn't up to it.

A fat seagull sauntered too close, and I lashed out with my foot. The knowing look in its round black eye was entirely too much like the bird-things that Munro'd sent to Isabella. My arm ached suddenly. The gull flapped off, blundering through drifting ghosts.

"Golems," I said with distaste. "Met one in London."

Pierce's eyebrows shot up. It's no fun baiting him. He's too transparent.

"Good God," he exclaimed. "D'you know who made it?" I blew out smoke and grinned mirthlessly at him.

"Yes. Someone we might expect a visit from soon. Fellow called Sir Robert Munro — what?" The Englishman had gone so white in the face I thought he was going to pass out.

"*Bosta,*" he muttered. Obviously he's lived too long in Brazil. "He's, er, he's one of my customers."

"He's what?" I said stupidly. *Full marks for trenchant questions, da Silva.*

"He's the man who offered me two and a half thousand American dollars for the *Book of Souls,*" Pierce replied. But, luckily, the antiquarian hadn't been able to deliver that time.

"Pierce, what the hell *did* you sell him?" I asked. He took off his spectacles and waved them around in an agitated sort of way.

"A scroll," he said. "The Prophecies of Johanna Kundrie. A mish-mash of gibberish. No one's ever been able to translate it."

"And?" I prompted him.

"And nothing," he answered. "Though there's, er, a story that once a man went to hell to try and get it translated, but of course he was never seen again."

I took the cheroot out of my mouth and contemplated it. I could top that. But there was no pleasure to be had out of it. None at all.

"Sir Robert Munro's been to hell," I informed him. "But he *did* come back."

Pierce got a sick look on his face. Like a man who looks down at his feet to find he's being slowly swallowed by a boa-constrictor. "And now he's coming here?"

Pretty much a given, I'd say. "I wouldn't be surprised. He certainly didn't want us to get back to Lisbon."

The Englishman hunched his shoulders. Should imagine he's forgotten what cold weather was like, and doesn't think much of it. Don't like it much myself.

"He send something after you?" Yes, you could say that. I nodded. "So he thinks you're, er, a threat to him?"

"Well, it looks like it." Don't get too ratty with him, da Silva, he's only asking the obvious questions. And you're not exactly being forthcoming. I sighed. "Do you know anything about him, Pierce?"

Apparently he hadn't noticed my flash of ill-temper. "Not much." He pushed his spectacles up again. "He was married to your wine-merchant's sister."

Give me full marks for not blurting out *He was what?* like an idiot. Although saying dumbly "Sr. Williams?" isn't much of an improvement. Which was what I actually came out with. Pierce nodded.

"Yes. She died, though. Er, I think it was a good many years ago." I scratched my cheekbone. Have to pump Williams on that. What kind of terms was he on with his brother-in-law, I wondered? Depends on whether Munro'd ever tried to hex him, I suppose.

"Any children?"

"Don't think so."

There are no such things as coincidences. I turned and stared at *Isabella* for a few moments. It made a change from watching ghosts.

It's happening again, isn't it? And why in God's name am I surprised?

None of this was worth saying out loud. I raised an eyebrow at Pierce, and said, "Maybe you ought to be more careful when you choose your customers."

"I can't really—" he began, and then smiled thinly and a bit self-deprecatingly. "Sorry. Bit, er, slow on the uptake there, skipper."

"How long have you been selling books to him?"

My hand was cold, but I'd finished my cheroot. I threw the end into the harbor. The water was pretty filthy, as usual. But at least in winter it doesn't stink. At least not as badly as it does in summer. In summer you can cut the stench with a knife. And probably the water, too, come to that.

"Hurt your arm, skipper?" I flexed it, and winced. Still hurt like the devil. That bloody bird-thing had had some serious teeth.

"Something Munro sent tried to chew it off," I said. The antiquarian grimaced, and fiddled with his spectacles.

"Er, I've been selling Munro books for about fifteen years," he said before I could prompt him. "Firstly it was just the sort of stuff an interested dabbler would want, harmless material. Then he obviously got, er, a bit more serious, but... didn't really know what he was talking about. D'you know what I mean? Then after that, about two years ago, he started asking me for seriously powerful stuff. Grimoires."

I stuck my finger absently under my eyepatch, but withdrew it when I noticed him staring. I haven't told him the story, not even the expurgated version. Took out my cheroots instead. "Did you sell him any?" I asked. "Grimoires."

The antiquarian's face went pink. An improvement on chalk-white, I suppose.

"I wasn't in the business of passing judgment," he said defensively. Whoa, back off, da Silva. I held my hands up placatingly. My past is hardly blameless. We've all done things we regret. Though killing mad Aldo isn't one of them.

"It's all right," I reassured him. "I'm not trying to blame you for anything." I lit the cheroot I was holding.

Still pink in the face, he admitted, "I sold him a couple of, er, minor ones. Nothing special, not the *Grand Grimoire* or anything like that."

Just the prophecies of Johanna whatever-her-name-was.

"So," I said, "how d'you feel about contacting him and telling him you've got photographs of the *Book of Souls?*"

Pierce's jaw dropped. He took off his spectacles and rubbed them with his handkerchief. After a moment he looked up, eyes bright, and said, "Bait?"

"Bait," I agreed. Beats the hell out of using da Silva as bait.

I want to see Emilia. Go home and put my feet up. Forget about everything, even if it's only for a couple of hours. But you don't always get what you want. And even if you do, it always comes with strings attached.

What I have to do first of all is head up to the library of São Rafael and have a chat with Sr. Zacuto.

If it was just a question of finding out whether he knows anything about these prophecies, I'd delegate to Pierce. But I have to fetch the ghost I summoned down to *Isabella*, because Zacuto can't do that on his own.

In theory, since I summoned him, he has to do what I tell him. *Has* to. In practice — apart from detesting the idea of it — he's the least biddable ghost

I've ever called. And that includes the Venetian himself and the three-thousand-year-old Egyptian sorceress.

When Father Pereira first showed me the way to the library of São Rafael I had difficulty in finding it. It didn't quite trust me, I think. Although you'd have thought it'd be more likely to be suspicious of an antiquarian. A book collector.

Now, however, I don't have any trouble at all. Pierce and I found Zacuto deep in conversation with Fr Pereira, who may or may not be his I-don't-know-how-many-greats-grandson. Since the scholar changed his name to Pereira when the Inquisition forced him to convert. But obviously, he didn't change the name of his soul.

The pair of them reacted predictably when I walked in. I think they both see me as some kind of protegé. Fr Pereira wants me to lapse back to his church. Which isn't going to happen. I'm not quite sure what Zacuto wants. To let him be my mentor, perhaps. And that's not going to happen, either. I'm too old to need a mentor. Not to mention too stubborn. At the moment I'm my own man after nineteen years of being someone else's, and I intend to keep it that way.

So who do you kill demons for, da Silva?

"Gentlemen," I said, interrupting, but with a smile. "Good to see you both again, but we have a problem."

"Another one," remarked Zacuto, sounding completely unsurprised.

Fr Pereira got to his feet and nodded affably to the ghost. "Until later, Sr. Zacuto." He shook my hand enthusiastically and gave me a wink. "Good hunting, Luís."

Now you may think this is an unusual way for a priest to behave. But this is an unusual sort of priest. He's somehow managed to come through all that training and indoctrination with a completely open mind. Amazing, really. I watched his rotund form waddle to the door, scratching my eyebrow idly. Then turned back to the ghost.

Who said, "And so, senhor capitão, what do you bring in your wake this time?"

"Will you come to my ship?" I asked.

"Do you know the *Prophecies* of Johanna Kundrie?" enquired Pierce, at the same time.

Zacuto looked from one of us to the other, eyebrows raised. "Which?" he said.

"Sorry," said Pierce, being English. I explained about the Tagus-spirit. Then backtracked on the topic of Munro. The ghost looked unsurprised. And why should he be? I'm not. Good God, now I'm even getting blasé about it.

"I believe a clue lies in the name, Johanna Kundrie," Zacuto said as we walked. Pierce, for some reason, had elected to come back with us. Perhaps for company, who knows? Probably not for the fresh air. There's a noticeable lack of it in Lisbon. Not as bad as London, though. No wonder the English call their fogs pea-soupers. *Pull yourself together, da Silva, your mind's wandering.* I dragged my attention back to Zacuto, who was saying, "Kundry, in legend, was the Grail Messenger and a sorceress—"

"Oh, good grief," exclaimed the Englishman in disgust. I wondered at the mildness of the oath, if you can even call it that. Until I realized he was toning it down for Zacuto's benefit. As you would with your father. I smiled to myself, and went for a smoke. *"Parsifal."* Pierce added, and glanced at me expectantly. Don't ask me why. Do I look like a Wagner enthusiast? But somehow it doesn't surprise me that *he* is. Not that there's anything Teutonic about him. He just looks the type.

"Wait a moment," I said to Zacuto, ignoring him. "The Holy Grail is just a Christian legend, isn't it?"

The ghost stared down his long nose at me. "You know better than to call anything 'just' a legend, senhor capitão," he said severely. "Don't make the mistake of denying everything to do with the religion you've renounced." I raised my eyebrows, taken a little aback. "But in fact," he went on in a milder tone, "it is much older. Just like many other traditions, the Christians took over the legend and absorbed it into their mythology. That they claim it does not invalidate the fact of its existence."

"You're saying the Holy Grail actually exists?" said the antiquarian excitedly, walking straight through a closely-grouped bunch of ghosts. Probably earthquake victims. That's usually the case when they're clustered together like that.

"All the so-called Grail Hallows exist," Zacuto said, still in didactic mode. He'd lost me, though. But I let him go on. The antiquarian was hanging on his words. Let him get some fun out of it. Ha. I've noticed this suspicious evidence of altruism before. The ghost went on, "The sword, the spear, the chalice, the dish. Things of great power."

"What sort of power?" Pierce asked. "Spiritual, magical, symbolic?"

Zacuto glanced in my direction with a slight frown. I bet he knew I wasn't totally with him. "All of those things. If the prophecies deal with the Grail Hallows, and this man Munro has translated them, he will go in search of that power."

Pierce took off his spectacles and squinted through them critically. "Then would the *Book of Souls* tempt him?"

That was a question I could answer.

"Oh yes," I said. "People like that, they can never get enough power."

* * *

It's not true that nothing supernatural can cross water. It is true that Zacuto can't come on board *Isabella* without an invitation. A ship is as much a dwelling as a house is. And it's subject to the same rules.

He paced the deck. Or appeared to. His feet didn't make contact, because they couldn't. But he draws curious glances because of his robes, not because anyone realizes he's a ghost. He does a damn good imitation of being alive.

Unless, of course, someone dropped something on him from aloft. Because one thing he can't do is an imitation of being dead. Ironic, no?

"This ship reminds me of the past," he said thoughtfully. It resonates, unlike those..." He gestured distastefully around. "Iron things." I smiled. He sounds just like — well, just like me. Of course there are sailing ships made of iron, and older ones than *Isabella*, at that. I've sailed in more than one. But *resonates*? My ship's younger than I am.

"Does she need — ?" I asked. He frowned a little, and didn't reply at once.

"I think not," he said after a moment. "I cannot detect anything so dire as to perturb the spirit of the river itself. Strange. I wonder what alarmed it." Him and me both.

I wondered where Pierce had got to. But then I spotted him, deep in conversation with Yeoh. Not difficult to guess what those two are talking about, not to mention that Yeoh's the biggest gossip between here and Hong Kong. The Englishman's chronic seasickness seems to've disappeared, though. Normally he turns green the instant he sets foot on a ship. Maybe Paciência gave him something, although you'd hardly call them the best of pals.

"What about the Judas tree?" I enquired.

The ghost pursed his lips. "This is not something of which I have any knowledge. For something to be capable of being brought out of the infernal regions — It goes against all reason. Perhaps if I were to see where it grew?"

Well, I only had Tatiana Dimitrovna's word for where it came from. But I think I trust her on that, at least. I took Zacuto below to my cabin. He looked round with interest, spending some time examining the portrait of Emilia that my father'd painted.

"It was on the desk," I told him.

"One tends to forget that you have another life," the ghost mused.

"This is my life," I said, a bit sharply. I've spent thirty years on ships like this. I know how they work. I know how this life works. I never asked to see ghosts, or raise them. Or be a part of the world that Zacuto inhabits. Damn it.

"Like it or not, Captain da Silva," he snapped back, "You walk in another world as well, now." As if he'd heard my thought. And who knows, he might've.

I lit a cheroot morosely. He's right, of course. But I don't have to like it. As if liking has anything to do with it. Live with it, da Silva.

"The desk?" I reminded him. That digression was his fault.

"Yes indeed," he murmured, and went over to it. Walked all round it. Though I suppose he could've walked through it if he'd felt like it. Then he put his hand out flat, and sank it maybe half an inch into the surface of the desk. Strange. Even though I know he's a ghost it still looks odd when he behaves like one. I tapped ash into the ashtray.

"Anything?"

"There is a… faint trace, a taint, but nothing that I can feel needs to be exorcized."

"Then what the hell," I asked, scratching my eyebrow in exasperation, "did the Tagus-spirit mean?"

"I can only assume," replied Zacuto, with a shrug, "that it was more mischief by this man Munro."

Sir Robert Munro. I scowled. When I get hold of him, he really is going to know it. "What are you smiling at?"

"I am sorry, captain. Just the thought of you offering physical violence to a sorcerer this powerful… might even take him by surprise, since he probably considers himself invulnerable."

I grinned at him. "Just one chance, that's all I need, " I said, and then, "Wait. You did it again. Are you reading my mind?"

"No, not precisely," replied the ghost. "But being what I am, I can hear thoughts as clearly as words."

God. Just as well I hadn't let my mind wander back to Emilia, then. Something made me look up at Zacuto, then. His hand was still embedded in the desk. And he had a very peculiar look about him. Used-up. Two-dimensional.

"What's the matter?" I asked sharply.

The ghost shuddered, and gave a horrible moan. It chilled my blood. It sounded like the noises ghosts are supposed to make. The malevolent, rattling-chains-at-midnight type. Or like a damned soul.

"Captain da Silva!" he gasped, reaching out his other hand. His voice was thin. Tight. "I have —My soul is caught!"

"What—?" I took a step forward, heart suddenly pounding. He was fading as I watched. "What is it?"

"Help... me..."

"How?" I can't lose Zacuto — "Tell me how!"

He turned his face towards me. My heart almost stopped. His features were blurring, melting. He looked as though he was burning. Again.

"You have to let me in," he whispered. "Or I'm lost..." My God, he's asking me to let him possess me. But such terror in his voice. He's being dragged down to hell. It's caught him like a quicksand.

Oh *merda*.

This is no time for squeamishness, da Silva. "Do it," I said harshly.

"Closer..." groaned the ghost, smoke on smoke. I could smell sulfur. I stepped up to him. Into him. Shut my eye instinctively. And felt myself stagger backwards until I hit the bulkhead with a crash that almost winded me.

Brightness filled my mind. Brightness, and incredible heat. Roaring in my ears, the smell and crackle of roasting flesh and fat, acrid tang of burning hair. I lifted my arm, and felt his hand tear loose from the desk. Every single nerve-ending was on fire. My head felt bloated, throbbed like a drum. The scholar's mind sluiced through mine, and the pain was unbelievable. Memories, knowledge, faces, secrets, I didn't want them. I refused to look at them. Momentarily, a completely different body, unfamiliar proportions, old, weakened, circumcized, two short-sighted eyes, bearded, arthritic. Two bodies, two minds. Vertigo surged through me. I opened my eye to see, in front of me, the desk glowing with rottenness, like a shining fungus: A portal into hell. I knew it without having to be told. Knew it for a fact.

And then Zacuto, having passed right through me, burst out the other side. I fell to my knees, sick and gasping for breath, trying to stop myself from throwing up. Put my hand on the cheroot I'd obviously dropped. Luckily for me it had gone out.

I became aware that the ghost was leaning over me, concern on his long face. But at least he had a face. Don't ever ask me to do that again.

"I suppose," I began, and was caught by a coughing fit. My throat tasted of foul smoke. "I suppose I'll have to buy myself a new desk now."

Zacuto looked down at me. I think there was a trace of a smile hiding somewhere in his beard. But it's always difficult to be sure, with him.

"You think me intransigent, sometimes," he said. That's one word for it. Stiff-necked. Judgmental. There are others. But at least I understand why, now. "But I thank you. I know how hard it must have been for you."

And he did, too. I hauled myself to my feet. Using a chair, not the desk, you can be sure of that. I don't know whether it could trap someone alive, and I'm not going to try to find out. I poured myself a hefty brandy. Amazing thing, didn't spill any. My hands were shaking like an old drunk's. I took a long swallow, enjoying the warming of the neat spirit on the way down.

"Well," I said unsteadily, sinking into the chair. "At least now we know what upset the Tagus-spirit." Or as Harris might've said, given it a hissy fit. Or even got its underclothes in an uproar. Good man with the telling phrase, the werewolf.

*   *   *

Teresa stared at Ana's slumbering face. Then she looked at the baby, also asleep. Ana looked quite peaceful now, except for a certain hollowness around the eyes, but not long ago she'd been screaming the place down. Teresa had expected neighbors to come banging on the door demanding to know who was being murdered.

The whole process of childbirth had completely horrified her. She'd seen foals being born, and calves, at her cousins' farm when she was a little girl, and the animals had it so easy compared with humans. Heavens above, she thought, if I'd ever wanted children that would've put me right off. For life. Poor Ana. And all because — She broke off the thought, and glanced back at the infant instead. A small red person, fast asleep. Rather scaly-looking. No hair. But no horns or tail, either. Be thankful for small mercies, she thought with a slight smile.

"I want to call her Susana," Ana had said, looking blearily at her daughter before falling into an exhausted sleep.

Somehow it was a great relief to Teresa that the baby had turned out to be a little girl.

*   *   *

The studio is very silent. Afternoon light falls through the window in the precise way it always does at this time of year when the sun is shining, and even if it is a pale winter sun and a shadow of its summer self, still it provides ample and luminous light for painterly activities. You would not, perhaps, call it lemon-colored, but it is nonetheless a pale yellow, maybe the color of straw or even blonde hair. Yes, blonde light is a good description of it. The blonde light falls on the canvas, and the canvas depicts another kind of light altogether, the harsh brilliance of a tropical sun shining on a quiet street. Thus, under a night sky, the winter sun inflames that of the desert, and is greater than it, and the desert sun is contained by it.

This canvas is more crowded now. The cathedral-like building dominates the silent street. A strange arthropod-creature lies in front of it, seemingly crushed by an enormous foot. Sebastião da Silva contemplated it thoughtfully and wondered which of the images crowding his brain to put into pain next.

His dreams have returned night after night to this desert city, an extensive metropolis but sparsely populated and that by strange creatures. There is a kind of peace here, though, none of the dread you might expect to feel, given the nightmare quality of some of the images that flood in. But he is the one who has the power over it, he creates its inhabitants, unconsciously maybe but he is still its god, or the nearest thing this place has to one.

He let his thoughts idle while contemplating the rush of images, let them parade by like a bizarre carnival procession, perhaps they are celebrating a saint's day. Yet for a festival they are all strangely muted, their gaiety a doubtful thing. Maybe they are all on their way to a public execution or a political rally or some other enterprise of mixed entertainment value.

Finally he decides, or something impels him, to paint not an inhabitant of the city but a flying creature in the sky, a fantastic bird like a roc or a phoenix, or it may be mechanical like the Passarola. Yes, on closer inspection it seems to possess struts and wires, and the texture is more like canvas than flesh or feathers or anything living. How strange to think that men can fly again, when the secret was lost for so long.

Sebastião da Silva, without benefit of charcoal or pencil to draw an outline, begins to rough in the shape of a great bird in the sky above the city in the desert, and the blonde light strikes the canvas at just the right angle, just the right intensity.

* * *

Home. Finally. Unless something jumps me on the doorstep. I stifled another yawn. Meu Deus, I'm tired. Could sleep for three days, the way I feel at the moment. Ha. I might think it's creeping old age. If it wasn't for the fact that I've got several damn good reasons to be exhausted. Few good years left in you, then, da Silva. With a bit of luck.

Never asked Pierce how Harris is. Então, I'll find out in a moment. I opened the door. Let the familiar missed smell of home sink in. Rubbed a hand over my face. Then walked wearily towards Emilia's workroom.

Found Harris in there, leg propped up on a chair, eyes glazed. Emilia was apparently still trying, with little success that I could see, to teach him Portuguese. Now I don't want to see Harris at this particular moment. He's pleased to see me, though. His glance lit on me like the proverbial drowning man spotting a floating spar. Everything about him was saying *now maybe she'll forget the lessons. Please.*

I grinned at him mirthlessly and helped him out by putting my arms round my wife, lifting her out of her chair, and kissing her thoroughly. She kissed me back with enthusiasm. I heard her walking-stick clatter to the floor. It always does that. Took no notice, caught in the moment and the scent and the taste of her. So long since I've felt her in my arms. Too long. Even though I try not to undertake lengthy voyages these days.

Yes, I know this sort of thing embarrasses Harris. But he was the one who wanted her distracted. His problem, then.

And having distracted her, I let her sit down again.

"And welcome home, Luís," she said, a little breathlessly.

Moving an escapee tendril of hair off her forehead, I asked without looking round, "How's the leg, Harris?"

"Taking its goddamn time," he grumbled. Then brightened slightly. "Night before full moon tonight. Here's hoping that'll help."

"And how's Luzia?" I enquired innocently. Emilia hid a smile.

"She's fine," said Harris, shifting uncomfortably in his chair, and not with the healing leg. He sounded somewhere between guilt, miffed at being teased, and outrage. Outraged innocence, of course.

Had to let him off the hook, though. Too much going on.

They say talking helps you solve problems. Take it from me, it doesn't always work. There ought to be connections, but we can't make the pieces fit together. They're like bits from two different jigsaws. Munro making golems in London, fine. Someone *else* making them in Lisbon, who? No such thing as coincidence. But if not a golem, what? And above all, why? Why kill and eat people at random? If it is random. And if it isn't, what links these people?

"We need to talk to Sr. Williams," said Emilia. The most practical suggestion yet. She amended it. "*I* should talk to him."

Since she can, to a certain extent, read people's minds. Zacuto, our expert in such things, thinks it was something she always had, and it was woken when she got the mark, the Key of Solomon, from me. Although reading minds isn't quite what she does. Feeling people's emotions is a better description.

Então, she doesn't like it. Any more than I like seeing ghosts.

"I'm seeing him in the morning," I told her. Which she knows, of course. "Why don't you come with me, he's used to dealing with you." As she's so much better at financial stuff than I am.

She nodded slowly. Something else was worrying her. I put out a hand to touch her face. She put her hand over mine.

"Luís—"

"What is it, love?"

"I'm worried about your father."

He visits about once a week, I know. He gets on well with Emilia. It seems to be mutual. And Caterina appears to like him, too. Me, I haven't got used to the idea yet. He's still a stranger to me. A pleasant enough stranger, but still a stranger. I was away too long. Thirty years. I can barely remember what it was like to be fourteen. Though Zé helps with that. But we have a different relationship, Zé and I. When I was his age I hardly knew my father, hardly saw him. Never without my mother as in intermediary. *He's busy, Luís. Doing God's work. You mustn't distract him from God's work.* God's work, my backside. Not even the bloody faithful look at the paintings in the church, so I'm damned sure God doesn't.

But my father was the one who made the effort, after she died. I'm not sure I would've done. What would I have said to him? I'm still not sure what to say to him. Making excuses, da Silva. Yes, I know.

I lit a cheroot one-handed and asked, "What's worrying you?"

Emilia made a face. "It's probably nothing. Absent-mindedness. He's seventy-seven, after all. But he hasn't been to call in over ten days."

My father doesn't possess a telephone. Not may people do, I suppose. Though I expect one day everyone will. If they can make the things more reliable, that is. But I can just picture my mother's long pinched face scowling, and her refined aristocratic voice saying scornfully, *Inventions of the devil.* God knows what she made of the motor-car, let alone the airplane.

God knows what she'd make of me, now.

"I'll go and see him," I promised. Emilia closed her eyes for a second, and smiled.

"Thank you," she said.

* * *

Tatiana Dimitrovna wasn't usually so indecisive, but her defeat at Munro's hands had rattled her badly. She wasn't accustomed to setbacks, let alone a rout, any less than she was used to being rejected. What had happened to the powerful sorceress who could've had any man she wanted? Pull yourself together, she told herself, your power isn't any less than it was, and Luís da Silva has always been able to resist you.

Her coat smelled of his horrible cheroots.

Stroking the coat absently, the witch stared out of the window at the street below. Her trunk stood in the corner of the room. She hadn't unpacked it, and didn't intend to, since she didn't intend to stay here for very long. It wasn't a question of money, it was a question of visibility. Munro wouldn't give up, she knew that, and staying in a hotel was a good way of presenting him with a sitting target.

Yet she knew, with uncomfortable certainty, that she couldn't hide from him forever. Or for very long at all.

This feeling of impotence was frightening in itself. Not since she'd fled the man who had murdered her father had she met anyone powerful enough to defeat her. And she'd taken his power from him, in the end, before she killed him in return.

She saw her father's face rise in her mind's eye. He'd been a sorcerer, too. One too powerful for his own good. Dimitri Sergeivitch Andropov had been exiled by the Tsar for his pains, had spent the rest of his life wandering the remoter parts of the world. He'd met her mother in a part of China so remote that Tatiana Dimitrovna couldn't point it out on a map. Neither did she know her mother's real name. She had been a shaman, an adept in ancient animalistic magics, and belonged to a cult whose members never told their names to any living soul. Dimitri Sergeivitch had always referred to her simply as "your mother".

But Tatiana Dimitrovna had spent her childhood traveling with her father. Had ridden the steppes with the horse nomads. Flown through empty skies in an eagle's mind. Stood on the roof of the world. Of her mother, she had no memory at all. Only the legacy of her power.

And her daughter had no intention of tamely giving in to Sir Robert Munro. And if that meant taking a trip to hell to match *his* power, that was what she would do.

There were things about the Judas tree that she hadn't told Luís. That it wasn't simply a tree that only grew from a seed fetched from hell. That it was, in fact, a demon in the form of a tree. That, combined with fire, it could open a portal to hell. She wasn't putting him at risk, or so she told herself. She lifted the coat and sniffed it. Being corporeal, he couldn't be dragged down by the

Judas tree's influence.

Of course, it meant that she couldn't get to hell that simply, either. But for the child of a shaman, separating the soul from the body posed no great problem.

Now all she had to do was sneak back aboard *Isabella*. A simple story of a lost trinket, or some such, would do the trick.

The witch stared out the window, still holding her smoke-smelling coat, hugging her arms tightly round her body. Why was she so reluctant, she wondered, why this strange disquiet in the pit of her stomach.

It dawned on her slowly, although the answer was obvious: She was afraid.

Once she identified the feeling as fear, however, she shook herself and set about busying it away. She unlocked her trunk then and took out a small oval of smoky glass. You might have thought it a paperweight, except that when she placed it on the hotel blotter she did not touch the hotel notepaper or the pen thoughtfully provided beside it.

Instead she sat down and focused her mind on it. Tatiana Dimitrovna put no trust in instruments like the telephone, which is both easily eavesdropped upon and likely to lose your connection at a crucial moment.

After a few seconds, the face of her maid appeared in the glass. The little woman looked relieved to see her mistress.

"You're well, then, mistress," she said, her Russian betraying the slightest trace of a Georgian accent.

"Yes," replied the witch, simply. "What is he doing?"

"Preparing for a trip," Masha told her. "He has made a substitute so no one will know he is gone. So he will be up to no good. Again."

"Hold fast," Tatiana Dimitrovna said. "I will defeat him in the end."

"I know, little mother," said Masha. "Be careful."

"I will."

She broke the connection, and stared unseeing at the glass for some time. It was, after all, a momentous step she was considering, and an irrevocable one.

It could also mean her death, and much worse than death. If her strength failed, or her will, or her power, or if any one of these was not up to the task, she was lost. Her soul would remain in hell. Forever.

Ironic, she thought, before Munro defeated her she would've had no doubts that she could do it. She was stronger than she had ever been. Stronger than anyone she had ever met. But thanks to Munro, now, she really had no choice.

And it was that which decided her. She got to her feet, put the glass away, donned her hat and coat and went out into the corridor, locking the door behind her. The smell of smoke that clung to the garment steadied her. She drew a deep breath, then hurried down the stairs and out into the Rua do Alecrim. It would not take very long to walk to *Isabella*'s berth.

The afternoon sun was already low in the sky, elongating her shadow in the street. Clouds were creeping in from the north-east, dragging weather from the bitter Russian plain perhaps, and she remembered wolves running through the snow under a white moon. Which thought reminded her of something. Why would Luís employ a werewolf?

Tatiana Dimitrovna had encountered werewolves, of course, and even were-bears. And without exception they had been savage creatures, unable to control their beasts. In her experience, once a man changed into an animal he had that animal's nature. Bears and wolves are predators, and she couldn't imagine either being held back by any scruples.

Nor could she imagine a were-creature that retained its humanity after changing. How was such a thing possible?

Her certain world was crumbling round her. Even, she thought mordantly, to the extent of ending up in a city where she didn't speak a word of the language.

As she approached *Isabella*, she was startled to see what looked like da Silva's desk sitting on the quay. Her heart began to pound. How had he found out? What had he found out? She drew a shaky breath and hailed a sailor she recognized, a black-bearded Englishman, at least she could talk to him, and enquired about the desk.

"Told us to get rid of it, ma'am," he said. "Dunno why."

"May I buy it?" she said, thinking fast. "If the captain's not here, could I speak to Mr. Ashley?" She took out her purse, it still held English money of course, and selected a half-sovereign. The sailor's eyes lit up.

"I'll get him," he volunteered, and she permitted herself a small smile as he turned and hurried away.

Fifteen minutes later, Tatiana Dimitrovna was the owner of a mahogany desk and a portal into hell. The former, the visible part of her purchase, caused a small stir among the hotel staff until she offered to pay for its storage as if it were a wooden guest, at which all the protestations about lack of space suddenly evaporated.

And presently she was examining the desk in a mildewy-smelling room in the hotel basement. It was sharing space with a pile of wooden chairs, a threadbare couch with horsehair stuffing poking out of various tears in its upholstery so that it looked like some sad bedraggled animal, and a wardrobe with a broken door. No one would come in here. Good.

Tatiana Dimitrovna made herself comfortable on the ratty horsehair couch and stared fixedly at the desk, fixing its reality in her mind. If she knew it thoroughly, every scuff and scratch, every repair, every detail, she wouldn't need to be close to it when she set her soul free.

Once she had a picture of its physical shape, she relaxed her mind still further and studied the portal into hell.

Then she went up to her room.

Outside in the street, Zé grew tired of waiting. Besides, it was cold. And people were starting to give him funny looks.

He stuffed his hands in his pockets and headed back towards the quay.

The witch, closing the curtains, saw him leave, her mouth set in a narrow line, then smiled grimly. It was too late for anyone to stop her now. Even Luís da Silva, with his new powers. Or even his old ones.

I could find you in hell itself, she'd once said to him. Now the words came back to haunt her, hard and bitter. Yes, she was going to hell, but out of necessity, and not to find a lover.

To find the way to kill one.

She knew that was the most likely outcome. Munro would let nothing rest, and so he had to be stopped. Tatiana Dimitrovna found the idea that she would have to fight on the side of the angels a little incongruous, given where she was headed, given her past. Oh, she'd never come down wholly on the other side, that was true, but she used dark magics when she needed to, and she used her powers with impunity for personal gain and for convenience. *So I'm not exactly what you'd call a white witch,* she thought wryly.

Sighing, she began her preparations. First she stripped down to her shift; she would have preferred to be naked, but wasn't sure how long her physical body would lie here untenanted. The last thing she wanted was to scandalize the hotel staff. Besides, the room was none too warm, though that at least would improve when the heating creaked into action.

Then she lay down on the bed and emptied her mind of thought, slipping with the ease of long practice into a light trance. From there, she began to free her spirit, slipping it from its moorings one by one.

Time ceased to matter, but eventually she rose out of her unconscious body, looked down at it dispassionately for a second, and then dove down toward the portal. She could see, or sense, it gleaming evilly through the incorporeal fabric of the hotel. It seemed the only solid thing in the universe.

Drawn down ever more swiftly, she paused above the way into hell for the barest second before plunging into it like a diver.

And fell, screaming, as her hair caught fire and a great mocking laughter filled her senses and possessed her entirely.

*   *   *

The last time I went to my father's house at Emilia's request, he'd just had his soul stolen by a demon.

I'm pretty sure *that* won't happen again. Although it's all rot, you know, about lightning never striking twice in the same place.

This house, once so familiar, is now an alien place, but still full of memories. I remember it as being bigger than it really is. Perhaps memory always exaggerates. Oh, yes, and perhaps my mother wasn't really so cold as I recall. Ha. No chance. The house seems smaller now because I was fourteen when I left it for good. And the memories that stay with me are of a smaller boy than that. Long ago and far away. As they say.

Stop wool-gathering, da Silva. Ring the damn doorbell.

My father's housekeeper, Sra. Reinaldo, opened the door. A small neat cheerful woman who seems fonder of him than my mother ever was. Not that I'm suggesting any impropriety. Impropriety. There's a word. See, I can use euphemisms as well as any Englishman.

Today, though, Sra. Reinaldo looks like a woman who's been sucking lemons. Although she brightened on seeing me.

"Senhor capitão, how nice to see you," she said. "Please come in." I followed her, wiping my feet on the mat. Gave her my hat and coat. "Although he's got That Woman with him," she went on. You have to put capital letters on those words.

That Woman? I rubbed my cheekbone and tried not to smile. Has he found himself a lady friend? And made Sra. Reinaldo jealous? "Who, senhora?"

She sniffed. The lemons were back. "Alegria, he calls her." She dropped her voice. "I'll give her Joy if she does anything to make him unhappy." He's suffered enough, she didn't say, and I wondered, not for the first time, what was between the two of them. If anything.

"Who is she?" I asked.

"I don't know, senhor capitão," she said unhappily. "She turned up about two months ago. Brazen, she is."

Somehow I couldn't frame the words *Is she a whore*. But then my father emerged, rubbing his head, from what used to be the parlor. It's now his studio. He seemed distracted. Or maybe distressed is the better word.

"Luís," he said in surprise, holding out his hand. "What brings you here?" I was suddenly cross with him. He'd been the one who wanted to re-enter my life. Now he drops my family the instant this Alegria shows up. I rubbed my eyebrow. Don't be too hard on him, da Silva. He's seventy-seven. As Emilia had reminded me earlier. But I ignored his hand.

"Emilia was worried about you," I said mildly. He looked shocked.

"Oh, dear Lord," he said, "don't tell me I forgot."

"She says she hasn't seen you for ten days. May I come in?"

I wanted to meet Alegria. I advanced to the door and pushed it gently. I'm not taking no for an answer this time. He backed into the studio, protesting.

"The place is a mess."

It wasn't, particularly. Today's newspaper was carelessly thrown on the couch, true. I caught a headline — *Mysterious Death, Man Crushed in Twelve-Foot Fall.* But even though Sra. Reinaldo isn't allowed into the studio, the place wasn't full of moldy cups and unwashed glasses. There was a dirty painty rag on the floor. A big canvas, uncovered, by the window, though the light was nearly gone now.

And also a woman.

Exotic. That's the only word. Elegantly dressed. Perfectly conventional clothes. But beside even Tatiana Dimitrovna she'd be different. Like a bird of paradise next to a falcon. Or even a phoenix. Somehow there was a hint of the fabulous about her. She appeared to be Emilia's age, or a little older. But it was difficult to tell.

"Aren't you going to introduce us?" I asked.

My father's eyes slid from side to side. Like a trapped animal's, I thought, and raised an eyebrow interrogatively.

"Alegria," he said quickly. "My son, Luís."

She inclined her head regally, but didn't speak. Perhaps she couldn't.

"Pleased to meet you," I said, extending my hand to her. After a moment's hesitation, Alegria took it slowly. I was hard-pressed not to recoil in shock. Her hand felt like nothing alive. Not warm, not cold. Yielding to my touch in a way quite unlike the way flesh yields. Her skin was like paper, dry and smooth. I dropped her hand quickly. Oh, very nice, da Silva. Spooked by — by what, though?

"What is she?" I blurted out, resisting an urge to wipe my palm down my pants leg. My father tugged unhappily at his beard.

"I painted her," he said. "Two months ago, or a bit more, I dreamed of her. I've been painting my dreams." I glanced at the easel, uncomprehending. "I painted her. And there she was."

"Sebastião. Do you want me to go away?" Alegria asked in a low voice, making me jump. I thought she couldn't speak. My father turned to her hurriedly, and took the hand I'd dropped. He didn't seem to feel anything unusual about it.

"No, no," he exclaimed. "Don't do that."

"You created her," I said.

Still holding her hand, he looked at me rather guiltily. "But she's not real, I know that. She's harmless, Luís. A fantasy. Not like—" He gestured convulsively with his other hand, indicating the large canvas on the easel.

I would've killed for a smoke. I rubbed my scar instead. "Not like what?"

"That," he said. I moved to look at the painting. It was seriously strange, a landscape of impossible things. A city in a desert. Night sky, day's light. What the hell was he dreaming about? Has he started smoking opium?

"Tell me about your dreams," I suggested.

5

STILL HOLDING ALEGRIA'S HAND, MY FATHER SIGHED. His face looked drawn and aged. I have to keep reminding myself how old he is. How deep the lines on his face. His hair is white, his beard is white. His eyebrows have gone tufty, and there's hair in his ears. He looks too ancient to be my father. Because I still don't feel anything like forty-four. Except sometimes. Like now, for instance.

"They started after I was ill last year." I felt a stab of guilt. He hadn't been ill, he'd had his soul stolen. But I haven't told him that. Mainly because I can't think of any way to make him believe it. Some of the things that happen to me, I sometimes have trouble believing myself.

"The dreams," I said, scratching half-unconsciously at my eyebrow, still looking at the painting. It was disturbing. I've never seen anything remotely like it. Why a night sky? Why a desert?

"Yes." Alegria's voice. I turned round. He was staring into her face. Just how real was she? More so than a ghost. But also in some way, less. "He dreamed me," she murmured.

"Vivid, extraordinary dreams," he said. "So intense. So much... I don't know, more *vibrant* than reality." And I see ghosts. Is there much difference? I shook myself.

"What—" I began, and had to clear my throat. "What about this painting?"

"Did you see the newspaper?" he asked suddenly, and, apparently, irrelevantly.

I raised my eyebrows. "What?" Glancing across at the couch.

"The paper." He sounded agitated. Alegria patted his hand, and he looked gratefully at her. "The man who was crushed. I'm responsible. Those women who were killed, the papers have been talking about werewolves. The Werewolf of Lisbon, they call it. It's not. I painted it, and it happened."

And having delivered that, he gazed at me imploringly as if he thought I could fix it. I stared at him, appalled. Stared at the painting. I couldn't see anything like that in it. Even supposing he's right. That he can paint things into existence. And Alegria is proof of that, isn't she?

What can you say to something like that? That he's imagining it? "I don't see the connections," I said slowly. Am I being really stupid here? My father gestured at the painting with his free hand.

"Look, this is the first figure I painted." He pointed to a sort of ogre eating a vaguely human-shaped thing, though to me it looked more like a pastry man. I glanced at Alegria. She had her head on one side as if listening carefully, but I wasn't sure she was. That she actually needed to listen. That there was anyone at home. Of course there's nobody at home, da Silva, she's not real.

"What's it supposed to be?" I enquired. Still stunned by his claims. Not thinking straight.

"I don't know, Luís, I dreamed it," he said impatiently. "And then there's a half-eaten body found. Then there's this," a child peering out of the window of a house.

But I still don't get it. "A child was killed?"

"No, a mother was killed. Leaving the child on its own, don't you see?" I frowned. It seemed a tenuous connection. But he seemed determined to make something out of it. "And this," he pointed again, this time at a woman with her hair falling round a smooth featureless expanse of skin where her face should be.

"I give up," I said.

"Damn it, Luís, don't be so dense. Some poor woman had her face eaten. How do you think I feel?" I spread my hands. How to reassure him?

"You don't know it's you. You might be seeing it happening in your dreams, somehow, painting something you're witnessing…"

"I wish I could believe that," he said wistfully.

"Why did you go on with the painting when you realized?" I asked.

"I only realized today! You can see for yourself they're metaphors, symbols. Look what it says in the paper."

I crossed to the couch and picked up the newspaper. Skimmed the piece: a man had apparently fallen from a two-story building but his body was smashed up as if he'd fallen from an enormous height. A man known as Spider. My father pointed out the squashed spiderish thing on the canvas, and looked at me imploringly. And Alegria watched with her strange luminous uncomprehending eyes. I shook my head again, still not convinced of any connection.

"What do you want me—" I began. And the air in the room was suddenly tight. The way it goes when someone's working magic. I felt the back of my neck prickling, and moistened my lips. Turned round slowly. Three hundred and sixty degrees. Nada. I touched my cheekbone. What was going on? I wish Harris was here. He can smell demons.

And then I realized. It wasn't magic. Or not primarily.

We were being watched. I reached over my shoulder and drew my knife. Things always feel better with the reassuring weight of its hilt in my hand.

My father goggled at the blade, but Alegria didn't seem afraid of the silver in it. And why should she? She doesn't exist.

"That's a fearsome great thing to carry around," he observed, and his voice was very calm. As if he thinks *I'm* a threat, and he's humoring me. "But what's the occasion? Where's the... enemy?"

"Something's watching us," I said, ignoring his expression. Something, or someone. I went to the window and peered out. Nothing.

"How can that be? What are you talking about?" I looked at my reflection in the window, and his. And Alegria's. She was that real, then. I scratched at my scar in frustration. Then the thought struck me. He's just told me something impossible, hasn't he?

"Listen," I said to him, turning round again. "Last year, just before you were taken ill. Do you remember what happened?"

He stared at me in bafflement. Have I grown an extra head? But he was also, obviously, making an effort to remember. None of the others recalled what had happened when their souls were gathered. Except for Harris, of course.

"A girl," he said after a while, with an effort. "She was in here. And there was a coin. She said her name was on it, and it was in my pocket. That's all I remember."

A girl and a coin. "Have you still got the coin?"

"I don't know," he said. "Maybe it's in the desk."

That desk I remember. I used to think it was full of secrets, with all its little drawers and cubby-holes hidden away until you rolled the top down. Which I did now. After carefully laying my knife on the top of the bureau.

A spill of papers, letters, photographs. A cigar box without a top, full of junk. Penknife, stick of sealing-wax, dried-up tubes of paint, plenty of coins but they were small change and foreign coins with holes in the centers. A piece of string. The blade of a palette-knife. A large carved ivory bead. I rummaged.

My father came and peered over my shoulder at what I was doing. Alegria was still attached to his hand.

"Is it in this box?" I asked. He poked a finger in the collection of rubbish and stirred the contents around.

"Ah yes, that's it, that one there." And he indicated a large coin with indecipherable writing on it. Bronze, it looked like.

"Don't pick it up," I warned. Took out the penknife and opened it. Picked up the palette-knife blade. Maneuvered the thing out of the box. Wondered what to do with it. Got no intention of picking it up. Or taking it anywhere.

"What's my being ill last year got to do with anything, anyway?" he asked me. I looked round at him.

"You weren't ill," I said. "Your soul was stolen by a demon." The girl must've been the demon, and she'd slipped the coin in his pocket when he wasn't looking. And there you are, instant entry to your victim's home. Trojan horses again.

He gaped at me "My *soul* was stolen? I don't understand." Alegria rubbed his arm sympathetically.

"You've been creating things by painting them," I pointed out, looking at her. "And you know I see ghosts. So why is that so difficult to believe?"

"I — don't know," he admitted, fiddling with his beard. "But how is that possible? How did I get it back?"

"By magic, of course," I said impatiently. "And it was Emilia who got it back for you, so you can thank her properly the next time you see her."

"Now I'm even more confused," he complained.

I stared down at the coin. So there must be a demon still around somewhere. Watching. Well, I think I'd guessed that. What does it want? Same as they always want. Cause mayhem. Steal souls. Drive my father insane?

Alegria's no demon. But it must've been the demon that gave my father the power to create her. Doesn't necessarily mean she's evil, though. And what about the painting? I wish I could remember the name of the demon that took his soul. And precisely why, da Silva? You're not going to summon it. You know where that kind of hubris nearly got you.

It's watching us. Or watching me. It wants to see what I'm going to do. Perhaps it's a little afraid of me. If it knows I've already killed two of its kind. Important demons. Princes of hell, according to Pierce and Zacuto. And they do know these things, apparently. Some kind of demon bush telegraph.

Which is very nice for them to get the latest news. But not much fun for me if they decide I'm a threat.

I decided not to be a threat. Picked up my knife and sheathed it. Turned to my father, standing forlornly hand in hand with the woman of paint.

"You'd better come home with me," I said. Zé'll have to give up his room again. That'll make me popular. "If you let a demon into the house, it's not going to go away on its own."

"What about Alegria?" he asked. I shrugged.

"That's up to you." And it is, too. I'm not going to force him to make a choice he doesn't want. He had enough of that from my mother.

"I'll stay here," he said. "We'll stay here. I won't add any more to this canvas. That'll stop it." Not force him to make a choice, da Silva? I felt like shaking him. It'll only find another way to get to him.

"I'll keep him safe," said Alegria unexpectedly, and my father smiled at her.

"You see?" he said.

Do I trust her? I'm not sure. Does he? Apparently. So that'll have to be enough for me. I suppose I trust my father, then. That's good, no?

"Pay Emilia a visit, then," I said, and he nodded.

Though how long he remembers that promise is anybody's guess.

* * *

"What did it feel like?" enquired Pierce, curiously.

"What did what feel like?" asked Zacuto.

"Well, er, you possessed him, didn't you? Just for a second."

Zacuto levitated the book called *Mappa Mundi* from its home on the second-story shelves. It drifted down as gently as a falling leaf to the table in front of him. Pierce watched its descent. The ghost's skills always fascinated him.

Not looking at the antiquarian, he gave a very natural-sounding sigh.

"Yes, Sr. Pierce, I did," he said. "And it was extremely strange, rather unpleasant, and very, very tempting."

Pierce took off his spectacles and hunted in various pockets for his handkerchief, blinking at the suddenly-blurry figure in front of him. "How would it be unpleasant?"

The ghost sighed again. "Being incorporeal has its advantages." He gestured at the book, which opened obediently, awaiting further instructions. "A body feels like... a prison of flesh. Heavy, earth-bound. When it's not the body you remember, you feel like an intruder. The shape of it is wrong in fundamental ways. And the whole business of living seems... too much trouble. The needs of a physical body — distractions. Yet I wanted all that, Sr. Pierce, I desired very much to possess Captain da Silva."

"Would you have—?"

"No," said Zacuto. "He has a horror of it, and with good reason. I learnt
— his memories. And that is one thing I shall not be telling him. A man must
keep his own secrets." He looked at Pierce, who had a strange avid look on
his face. "What, you expect me to give away confidences I was never
intended to receive?"

"No," said Pierce mendaciously, since he had rather hoped that Zacuto
would dish the dirt. Which phrase he recognized as a Harris-ism the minute
it popped into his head. He finished polishing his spectacles and put them
back on, a little embarrassed. He cleared his throat. "Do you think the *Mappa
Mundi* will tell us about the prophecies?"

"Since the book was published sixty-seven years after my death, Sr.
Pierce, you probably know it better than I do, but it has proven itself useful in
my studies here where the source materials are missing. Or indecipherable."

He moved his fingers, and the pages of the book moved swiftly. Despite
its name the *Mappa Mundi* was not an atlas, but a map of human knowledge
in the year 1572, a time when human knowledge was other than it is today,
different but not necessarily inferior, who knows what has been lost in three
hundred and thirty-odd years.

"A prophecy isn't really the sort of thing I'd expect to find in there,"
Pierce objected, having apparently decided to play devil's advocate. He
stared round at the three stories of books lining the walls. Not that he really
expected to find a volume entitled *Obscure Prophecies Down The Ages
Deciphered,* but the library of São Rafael constantly proved itself capable of
surprising him.

"It depends on the remit of the author," said Zacuto, his attention on the
book in front of him. "Whether he found prophecies worthy of serious
consideration as a source of future knowledge."

"I suppose so," said Pierce. "What do you think?"

"I think that fellow Nostradamus talked a lot of utter nonsense,"
answered Zacuto. "But that does not mean that all prophecies are, de facto,
worthless."

The antiquarian shoved his spectacles back up to the bridge of his nose
again. "They are if nobody can read them," he said sourly.

"Just because no one today can read them does not mean that they were
never capable of being read," the ghost pointed out. "Observe, for example,
the case of the Egyptian hieroglyphs and the Rosetta stone."

Obviously, Pierce thought without surprise but with considerable
amusement, Zacuto's reading in the library had been more comprehensive than
even he had imagined.

"Failing that we could always ask the captain to call up a ghost who could decipher it," he said.

"If we had a copy of the prophecies, yes," agreed Zacuto.

"Oh yes." The antiquarian had forgotten, for the moment, that they didn't. That he had sold it to Sir Robert Munro over a year ago. *How was I to know he was going to turn into some kind of super-sorcerer?* he thought indignantly.

"You couldn't," Zacuto said, startling Pierce. Although the ghost did occasionally answer his unspoken thoughts. He should be used to it by now. He spent enough time with the old scholar's spirit, and Zacuto sometimes forgot to pretend he couldn't hear what people were thinking when he was preoccupied.

"Any luck?" he asked.

"Not so far. Bear with me, it is a long book even to flick through."

This time next week, thought Pierce, then looked at Zacuto. The ghost was smiling into his beard. The Englishman smiled back, and riffled the pages of the book on top of the pile beside him. It was one he'd been hunting for weeks, but his mind wasn't on it at all now.

"Professor—" he began, but Zacuto held up his hand. "Have you got something?"

"There is, apparently, a demon of prophecy and speaking in tongues," said Zacuto slowly, looking down at the closely-printed, blurred type without apparent difficulty; another advantage of being a ghost appeared to be a complete lack of age-related longsightedness. "His name is... Alazadir. Do not worry," he added at Pierce's horrified expression, "I certainly am not capable of calling him up by speaking his name."

Pierce moved round the table quickly to look over the ghost's shoulder. "Is there more?" he asked eagerly. "*To summon the demon Alazadir to speak prophecy,*" he read, "*the* Rituel de Sept Douleurs *is employed. Prophets who have performed this rite and obtained enlightenment include Edward Vance, Arrigo Montevecchi, the so-called Johanna Kundrie,*" he skipped the rest of the list, his heart thumping madly, and then swore silently as he found himself reading the summoning ritual. He broke off quickly and crossed himself in reflex.

"Wait." Zacuto turned the page. But the *Mappa Mundi*'s author, having noted the rite, was off on another tack.

"Any footnotes?" asked Pierce plaintively, reaching out a hand in an attempt to find the end of the chapter.

If Zacuto had been able to, he would probably have slapped the antiquarian's hand aside. "Sr. Pierce, be patient," he said testily.

"Sometimes he puts notes at the end of the chapter," Pierce insisted, too excited to apologize. He took out his handkerchief and rubbed vigorously at one of his lenses without taking his spectacles off.

"Yes, I know," replied the ghost, still turning pages.

Then he reached the end of the chapter. "Eureka," said the antiquarian softly. Just think, he said to himself, if Munro had a copy of the *Mappa Mundi* he wouldn't have needed to go to hell. But then, maybe he would've anyway.

"*In the year that is a hundred years after the bear's victory the wounded king may be reborn.*

"*Yet to regain his domination over the land he must receive again the dolorous blow and be healed of the unhealable wound.*

"*By the coming together of the four hallows may he be made whole.*

"*And the key to the hallows lies with the child in the city of Ulysses who is the child of no man, and whose mother is no woman, and who shall be born in the year that is a hundred years after the triumph of the bear.*"

The antiquarian read the prophecy and smiled to himself, imagining da Silva's response. *Oh God not another bloody riddle.* Zacuto nodded, not bothering to hide his own amusement.

"Fortunately, though gnomic, it is not indecipherable."

"It's not complete, either," Pierce pointed out, indicating the page header, which read "Extracts".

"No, but for the time being I think it is sufficient," said Zacuto. "And you will need to warn Senhorita Teresa that the child will be in danger when this Munro arrives."

Because the child of no man was the child of a demon, and the child of no woman was the child of a virgin. Apparently.

Pierce would have been frantic with self-recriminations if he hadn't known that Munro was on his way to Lisbon anyway.

* * *

The telegram had arrived minutes before the cab had arrived to take him to the boat-train. Munro chose to take it as auspicious.

GOOD CLEAR PHOTOGRAPHS OF BOOK YOU REQUESTED AVAILABLE STOP ADVISE IF INTERESTED STOP MONTAGUE PIERCE.

Oh yes. He was interested, all right.

"No," he said to the boy. "No reply. I'm on my way to see the gentleman who sent it."

"Very good, sir," answered the lad, and bicycled off through the snow. Sir Robert Munro looked at the telegram in his hand.

Everything was falling into place.

*   *   *

Inventions, despite what the pious would have us believe, are not necessarily the work of the devil. It all depends on how they are used. And by whom.

The demon Belphegor, for instance, preferred to see the mischief that human inventiveness can cause rather than its benefits. But, like all demons, she was incapable, herself, of creating anything original.

She could, however, corrupt things. Invert them. And copy them.

Once she had seen the fecund combination of loneliness, imagination and unfettered creativity that had created Alegria, she could imitate it, fashion a homunculus, as it were, from her own desires grafted onto a borrowed imagination. The difference being, of course, that a demon's desires do not bear any relation or even resemblance to a man's, and she had to batten onto the physical reality of the painting in order to find a purpose. Find it, and twist it. And so a spider could represent a man called Aranho, and a painted ogre's appetite break through into reality.

It is a thing of air and darkness, her construct, incorporeal, as it has to be when Alegria is made from paint and light and longing, which as everyone knows who has experienced it is the heaviest of all emotions. You might be able to perceive this thing as an *absence*, a distortion in the air, perhaps, more likely you would not perceive it at all until it ate your heart or lifted you two, three hundred feet in the air to throw you down to shatter on the ground.

Now it withdraws from the abandoned painting, leaving behind a taint of hell like a snail's glistening trail, and moves through the darkened studio, tasting canvases. Sebastião da Silva's burgeoning imagination has ranged from the simple, like Alegria herself, to the bizarre, like this seascape in which a ship (it is a three-masted barque) made out of water sails an archipelago of clouds like those you see at sunset which make you yearn towards unreachable countries in the twilight sky.

Like a man in a gallery, Belphegor's creation savors the pictures. A mountain that is an eagle. A sleepwalking girl lighting candles in a deserted street. The head of a statue, lying on its side, observed by a man shorter than the length of its nose and by a curious raven. A man removing a mask to reveal emptiness, the sky behind his face framed by his hair.

Having surveyed the art on show, it returns to the painting of the statue's head.

* * *

Harris was looking more apprehensive than I've ever seen him when I got home for the second time. God knows what I look like in terms of being apprehensive myself. I don't believe — I can't believe, or I can't let myself believe, that my father's responsible for those deaths. And if he knew anything about demons, he wouldn't believe it either. But, meu Deus, there's always a remote possibility. I know that. Good intentions aren't enough. Look how close I came to letting one possess me, and all I wanted to do was keep my family safe.

And I can't shake the feeling that things are coming apart around me. I'm watching the glass plummet. There's a hurricane on the way. It's not just the thought of Munro — I think I believe, in the back of my mind, that I can handle him, and if that's hubris, well, too bad. I prefer to call it optimism. And when were you ever an optimist, da Silva?

In spite of all that's happened to me, all that I've seen, can see, I don't have Harris's instinct for these things. He can smell, or sense, demons. And not just when they're close by.

Which still leaves us with the question. If a demon is responsible for those murders, the body on the rooftop and the others, why couldn't he feel it?

"Moon's nearly up," he said tightly when I put my head round the door. And how do you tell a werewolf to stop fretting?

I didn't try. I took the cheroot out of my mouth and asked, "Is that demon-sense of yours working?"

He stared at me as if I'd asked him to sing opera. I suppose he had all his energy concentrated on the wolf-change.

"Skipper?" he said, and his eyes seemed yellow in the gaslight.

"It's important."

Harris took a few deep breaths. Not looking at me, staring at his splinted leg. After a moment he raised his eyes. "They're around," he said slowly, "but there's always some around. Y'know, lurking, I guess."

"Nothing specific?" I pressed him. "Nothing on me?" He shook his head.

"What's up, skipper?" he asked. Finally noticing that something was. Well spotted, that werewolf. I blew out smoke and sighed.

"I think one of 'em's after my father," I said. He grunted. Fidgeted, and shifted his leg around.

"What, same one that got to him last time?"

I nodded. "Most likely. I suppose."

"You tell him its name?"

Yes, should've done that at least. Except that I couldn't remember it. I said as much to Harris, who looked about to reply — not even Harris would call his skipper an idiot, although come to think of it he probably would, at that — but a spasm of agony passed over his face.

"Harris?"

"Mind getting the hell outta here, skipper?" he ground out between his teeth, his face white with strain. I nodded, and shut the door on him. Leaned against the wall outside. Everything just caught up with me again. Even the bitter acrid smoke of my cheroot wasn't helping. Did I say I don't feel my age? Lying a bit there, da Silva, aren't we? Well, more than a bit. I stubbed the cheroot out in an ashtray and shut my eye.

And I must have dozed for a second, because the next thing I heard was the sound of Emilia's stick right beside me. I looked round to see her staring at me anxiously.

"Are you all right?"

I ran a hand through my hair. Stifled a yawn. "Tired," I admitted.

She put her arms round me, and I reciprocated. "But you're still going to go out with Sr. Harris?"

"I need to take him to my father's," I said.

"Be careful," she whispered, and slid one hand round to touch the mark over my heart, the key of Solomon. A jolt went through me. The usual, familiar, missed burst of brightness. Made me suck in a breath.

"Emilia—" I said into her hair, and put my fingers on her own mark. She gave a gasp.

"You're asleep on your feet." She outlined the sign with her finger, and I felt a tingling surge of energy, apparently from her. I traced the mark on her breast through her blouse, tempted to undo a few buttons while I was at it.

"But that's helping," I murmured, in some surprise. Though why I should be surprised I don't know. Emilia put her palm flat on my chest. A moment later I did the same to her, covering her mark with my hand. I took a deep breath, and so did she. We breathed in unison for a few moments, and then she took her hand away with a gasp.

"Oh..." she exhaled. "I've given you—"

"Are you—" I asked at the same moment. A bit anxiously. I don't want to drain all her energies away, if that's what's happening.

"Yes," she said breathlessly, and touched my cheek with her fingertips. "We really are linked, aren't we? Husband and wife are one flesh."

"We don't need the key of Solomon to tell us that," I replied, kissing her hair, and then her face. Though I'm quite sure sharing energy isn't meant for this, right now.

Anyway, Harris's wolf-howl interrupted us. Damn it. I released her.

Gave her a quick kiss. And pushed the door open. Harris put his wolf's head through the gap.

He can't speak very well in this shape. Wolves not having been designed to hold conversations. Então, I don't suppose many of them want to. But he didn't need to speak. He was walking on all four legs, and his relief was obvious. If you can imagine a wolf that comes up to my waist looking relieved.

"It worked," said Emilia unnecessarily. Bent down and, to my astonishment, planted a kiss on the lupine head. I felt my eyebrows shoot up. But from the expression on my wife's face, she was as surprised as I was. So I won't have to have words with Harris in the morning. Just as well. How *do* you tell off a werewolf?

The wolf lolled his big tongue out and said, "'Es."

I scratched my cheekbone, more for punctuation than anything else, and said, "Let's go and check up on my father, then."

Kissed Emilia on the lips, and went out into the night with the werewolf.

First time I did this, I was jumpy as a virgin in a whorehouse. Worried sick that we'd be seen. I don't exactly look like a man walking his dog. But I didn't entirely understand how these things work. For one thing, people see what they want to see. For another, werewolves seem to have some sort of built-in "look somewhere else" power that makes it easy for them to go unnoticed. Hell, he doesn't even seem to worry the horses. Short of doing something completely stupid like trying to catch a tram, we can pass through these moonlit streets without attracting attention. As long as we're careful. And you can bet anything you like we'll be careful. Caution. Da Silva's middle name.

Of course, since I only have half the number of legs, I hold him up. Half the number of eyes, too, come to that. He wants to chase ahead, investigate smells, range around. Hunt.

Since that's what werewolves do.

Tonight, we're hunting a demon. And I've remembered its name, though nothing would induce me to speak it. Yet that knowledge will protect us.

Belphegor.

Last time I was abroad in the night with Harris, it was June. Early summer heated to boiling point by the presence of seven demons, by the working of a Great Spell of making. Now, in winter, the weather seems equally uncertain. Veering from teeming rain to unaccustomed frost. Tonight, the moon full and round and white as a pearl. Stars hard and bright. One of the latter. Though not as cold as London, thank God.

When I was a child I knew these ghost-filled streets. Not that I knew they were ghost-filled then. At least, I couldn't see the ghosts then. And when I came back I thought I'd forgotten the city entirely. I was wrong about that, but I'll never regain that easy familiarity. Though Zé acquired it himself in just a couple of years before he joined *Isabella*. And Harris seems to navigate by instinct. Of course you're not much use at sea unless you have that instinct.

It didn't take us very long to reach my father's house. Despite not being able to take a tram. Lisbon isn't a big city. How odd the house looks by moonlight. But of course, at fourteen, nobody's seen his home by night that many times. And at fourteen, I couldn't see the ghosts drifting round it. Somewhere inside there, now, is my mother's shade. And that's one spirit I *won't* be raising from its grave.

"Anything?" I whispered to Harris. He shook his big wolf-head

"No' 'ere," he growled in an undertone, casting around. Then his muzzle came up, and I heard him sniffing.

"What is it?"

"No 'emons." I can't imitate his wolf-speech exactly. He swallows the *n* and *m* sounds in a way you can't copy. Unless, I suppose, you're another wolf. "So'thin' h—" a sharp exhalation of breath, "—unts."

Something hunting.

"Go," I said. And he sprang off into the night. Leaving me to follow as well as I could. Cursing in his wake.

* * *

Freed from the need to let da Silva keep up, Harris-wolf went hunting. He didn't know what he was in pursuit of, just that he could sense a desire for the chase almost as strong as his own, though differently motivated.

He had never hunted in the wild. Even his initiation in snowbound Riga had not let him leave the port for fear of the local werewolves that had already killed him once. So city streets held no mysteries for him. He had roamed them from New York to India.

But he had never, in all that time, killed a human. He did not know what made him different from other werewolves, though perhaps John Yeoh, who saw souls, could have made a suggestion: he'd had a wolf's soul before he gained the ability to take a wolf's shape, and so turning into a wolf did not drive him insane. Since he was embracing his true self.

To be fair, Yeoh had not shared this conclusion with Harris. In his experience, people who eventually grew into the shapes of their souls would fulfil their destiny; those who never achieved it, would not.

As Harris himself might have said, though, he wouldn't have known his destiny if it up and bit him in the ass.

Harris found his quarry before he found the pursuer. To be more exact, he found the quarry, but was quite unable to detect the pursuer.

The man was half-running, terrified of something, though there was nothing to be seen. Nothing at all. But Harris felt his fear, the sort of solid desperate dread that demons love, that would make any normal werewolf salivate with delight. He was a man in good condition, not too old, which would make the chase more interesting… A surge of bloodlust washed through Harris, momentarily powerful enough to make him lose sight of Harrisdom, of humanity, red before his eyes, red in his brain, how delicious it would be…

No. Harris shook his head, not the determined shake of a man's denial but the baffled movement of a bewildered animal, yet it was enough to make him stop in his tracks. What was happening to him?

As wolf, he did not think in words, any more than he saw with his eyes in the same way as he did when he was in human shape. But his denial of the intrusion was as unequivocal as the human word, No.

And the disappointment he sensed was as tangible as the desire had been. And as alien.

The wolf sneezed. He had no intellectual comprehension of the term possession at the moment, but he resisted it instinctively.

Why he kept on in pursuit of the quarry he wasn't sure, not really remembering his purpose. His first headlong rush had long slowed, cautious stalking was the order of the day. Or, as it happened, night.

*   *   *

Ricardo Corvo, having been a policeman for fifteen years, knew when he was being followed. Had much experience of it, from both sides. He'd been a target before too, when he'd refused bribes, tried to root out corruption. But being stalked by a thug with a bludgeon, or even a firearm, was something he knew he could deal with.

This was different. And even as he acknowledged this fact he was berating himself for a credulous fool, cowed by the ridiculous rubbish the newspapers and the gossips and even the police informers were peddling. He could believe in murderous mechanical contrivances more readily than werewolves, but what other than the atavistic fear of nightmares was frightening him so, now? He gritted his teeth, and increased his pace.

He'd first become aware of his pursuer some fifteen minutes before, and had gone from mild amusement to annoyance to anger to fear. To a sudden terror of the unknown more intense than anything he'd felt since being a child afraid of the dark.

But what could possibly frighten a police inspector so much he was in danger of losing, not the veneer of civilization, which is not so important as most of us imagine because it *is* only a veneer and thus easily re-applied, all it takes is a bit of spiritual french-polishing, which is something quite easy to self-administer, but the layers and layers of adulthood? Which, being built up from within, are bastions that, if they fall, are much more difficult to rebuild. What is a madman, after all, but someone in whom that stronghold has fallen, or, for some reason, was never properly constructed in the first place?

The stealthy pursuit was quite noiseless, but he was as certain of its presence as he was of the passage of time, the silent march of the hours, which stalk us to our death more surely than any assassin. He would almost have preferred the great soft tread of unseen horrors, or even fangs in the darkness, to this huge overreaching unknown. Corvo was armed with his police revolver, but he hadn't drawn it. He knew it would be useless.

Though the thought had crossed his mind that he might do better to use it on himself.

As I might well have to, he thought bitterly, turning a corner, his breath ragged — and realizing that he hadn't known his surroundings quite as well as he'd thought.

He was in a blind alley. No way out.

* * *

When Harris loped off, leaving me standing, for a moment, like an idiot, I didn't think I stood any chance of catching him. But I followed in his wake all the same. God only knows what I'm letting myself in for now. But when did that ever stop you, da Silva? As the English say, fools rush in where angels fear to tread.

And in this case, my foolish feet seemed to know which way to go. As long as I didn't think too closely about it.

I didn't draw my knife. Without Harris, people can see me. And a man wandering seedy back-streets and alleys holding a fourteen-inch blade is, you might say, looking for trouble. Especially a villainous-looking character with an eyepatch.

On the other hand, it's perfectly natural to keep your hands in your pockets in this sort of weather. And if one pocket holds a revolver loaded with silver bullets, what better reason to keep a hand close to it.

How do I get into these things, anyway?

It didn't take me very long to catch up with Harris. I found him loitering at a corner, sniffing and casting round. A couple of ghosts were wavering round him. He couldn't see them. They couldn't see him. But it looked as though they were having a conversation about him. Funny the way things seem sometimes. The wolf, however, looked so wary that now I did draw my knife. But there was also intense frustration in his stance. Don't ask me how I find it so easy to read a werewolf's body language.

There wasn't really much point in asking him what he'd found, since he gets extremely frustrated at not being able to answer me properly. But I asked him anyway. Being human. That's what humans do. Ask questions.

"What is it?" I whispered.

"D'no. Man — 'fraid," growled Harris-wolf quietly. I put my back to the wall and sidled round the corner, knife held loosely downwards, right hand in the pocket where my revolver was. I had to learn to shoot right-handed. It's just too damn complicated trying to sight with the opposite eye. And anyway I'm not trying to be a marksman.

There was something impending. A sense of — I don't know what, some sudden dreadful thing in the night. Stalking. It made me catch my breath, the groin-shriveling awfulness of it. My mouth was suddenly dry, my heart pounding. Run, it said. Run faster than you've ever run in your life. The hilt of my knife was slippery in my hand. I swallowed.

"Who's there?" I called softly. The alley's not lit, of course, but by now the moon's high and bright enough to cast shadows. I made out a man's shape in a deep doorway before he jumped out and pointed a gun at me. His hand was trembling. Never a good sign.

"Drop the knife," he snapped, his voice tight with strain. Behind me, Harris growled, a deep basso rumble in his chest, and the weapon moved to point at the wolf.

"Don't shoot," I said quickly. "—Either of us."

"What the hell is that?" exclaimed the man, eyes widening.

"Not what you're afraid of," I said, looking round for some visible sign of whatever was making me shake with terror like a child in the dark. "Harris, find it!" My own voice was rising to panic. I swung round, sweeping the knife in an arc. Sweat was running into my eye, but I couldn't spare the time to wipe it away.

"Find what?" The man was close to losing it. He wasn't the only one.

The moon silvered something — curve of a great back, perhaps — and then it was gone. My back prickled. I whirled round. Then Harris leapt into the air, clear over my head. I ducked. Heard his jaws snap. A shadow whirled past me, making me stagger with the wind of its movement. The next moment I heard a gun go off, the explosion deafening in that narrow place, and something hit me sharply in the temple. I reeled back into the wall with a yell of pain and a jarring thump.

For a moment I thought my other eye was blind, but it was only the blast of the gun.

"*Filho de puta!*" I bellowed. "Stop that!" I couldn't understand why I wasn't dead, either, if he'd shot me in the head. I put my hand up to my temple, found a lot of blood running down, what felt like a cut. *Merda*, that hurt. Ricochet?

No time to speculate about that now. I flicked blood off my face with my palm before it ran into my eye. The drops hit something close with a horrible wet hungry noise, and abruptly it faded into visibility.

"Jesus," gasped the man, and fell to his knees.

Now I know what's been taking bites out of people, and it sure as hell wasn't anything my father had painted.

It looked like something made from spare body parts. But it wasn't anything like that other construct in St Petersburg. Mainly because not all the parts were human. Well, most of them weren't. The torso and the feet were human-looking, and female, but it stood on legs like a bird's without the feathers. Its arms were mismatched. One might've been a man's. It had muscles like a stevedore's. The other was long, hairy, maybe an ape's. Both hands had long black nails, more like talons really.

But the worst thing of all was the head. It was a woman's head, but about twice life-size. A face that would've been beautiful. On a human body. The great eyes were kind and brown, the huge mouth very red, scarlet as a whore's. The long black hair loose about the face.

And then it opened its mouth, and it wasn't beautiful at all. The bright red lips drew back from its enormous pointed teeth, and it lunged at me. I skipped back, swinging the knife at it. It didn't seem afraid, even when the blade sliced the massive face from cheek to chin. No blood came out. It wasn't real.

So how do you kill something that isn't real?

Harris pounced at it again, and this time I saw it stagger back. He obviously had enough unreality in him to do some damage. He went for its throat, but it put its arm in the way, the human one. The wolf savaged it, snarling viciously. I know how he felt. I worked my way round behind it, skidding in my own blood, and aimed a blow at its neck. The blade passed right through with little resistance, but the head stayed put.

Except that it turned to look at me. All the way round. And smiled. And the look in its eyes was so terrible that I took a step backwards. Not even demons have looked at me like that. There was a promise of something in those big brown eyes that terrified me. Right down to my soul. I lifted the knife and pointed the blade at it, breathing heavily.

"Belphegor?" I asked. The smile wavered slightly. Or that might've been wishful thinking on my part. It shook Harris-wolf off with a casual flick of its arm, never taking its eyes off me. I heard him land with a solid thud and a startled *whoof!* of breath.

"We will meet again," it said, and the thought of that scared me worse than almost anything I could remember. And then it disappeared, with a shock like a slamming door.

I sagged back against the wall, breathing hard. Then pushed myself unsteadily away and sheathed the knife. My hand was shaking so badly it took me two goes. My head was pounding in agony. I found a handkerchief and pressed it to the wound. Could I please just go for a few days without something trying to do me damage?

Harris, panting, got to his feet and looked at me yellowly. "Stay," I told him. He'll pull my leg about that. If he remembers. I walked over to the other man and held out my hand. Pulled him up from the ground. He was a bit younger than me, a couple of inches taller. Very dark, the kind of beard that needs two shaves a day. "You all right?" I enquired.

He dusted himself down convulsively. Not that he was a snappy dresser. His clothes were more rumpled than mine.

"What in God's name—?" He cleared his throat. "What was that?" I took out my cheroots and lit one. My hands were steadier now. Good. As for his question, I wanted to know the answer, too. I flipped the dead match away.

"I've no idea," I admitted.

"You seemed prepared for it." I mopped blood off my face and gave a mirthless laugh. "Ah, I'm sorry about that," he added. Sorry. He nearly puts a bullet in my brain, and he's sorry. He held out his hand, somewhat incongruously. "Ricardo Corvo. Inspector of police."

I looked at the blood-soaked handkerchief in my right hand and then at him. Quizzically. He coughed, and withdrew the hand. I nodded to him.

"Muito prazer," I said, politely. "Luís da Silva, ship's captain. And I believe you just encountered the thing the newspapers are calling the Werewolf of Lisbon." He shot a wary glance at Harris. "No, *that's a real*

werewolf," I told him. "He doesn't eat people. He's on our side."

The inspector stared round wildly, the whites of his eyes visible. Good thing he can't see the ghost that's practically on top of him. Especially since she'd obviously been a prostitute and *on top of him* is probably the wrong expression to use here, da Silva.

"Captain—" he began, then looked at me helplessly.

"Da Silva," I supplied.

"Captain da Silva. Perhaps we could continue this discussion somewhere more comfortable." Now he sounds like a policeman.

"I'd rather not continue it tonight," I remarked, "unless you fancy explaining to your colleagues how you came to shoot me." God, it was painful. I took a drag on my cheroot. Didn't take my mind off it. Still hurt.

Inspector Corvo took out a packet of cigarettes and fished one out. "I wasn't referring to the police station," he said. "But you can't leave me like this." Oh no? Just try me. "I might die of curiosity, and you wouldn't like that on your conscience, would you?"

God help me. A policeman with a sense of humor.

"All right," I sighed, offering matches. "As long as you don't decide to arrest me."

"For withholding information," he asked dryly, "or for that damned great knife you're carrying?" He doesn't know how close I'd come to adding "assaulting an officer" to that list.

"Well, I'm not withholding information," I retorted. "I just told you what killed those people. And you saw it for yourself."

"Much good it does me," he grumbled, and struck a match.

Harris gave a short attention-getting growl. His equivalent of clearing the throat. I turned to him and said in English, or rather Harrisian, "Amscray," so that even if Corvo speaks regular English he won't know what I'd said.

The wolf turned and trotted off into the night.

"Where's he going?" asked the inspector. The end of his cigarette glowed as he inhaled.

"Don't ask me," I said. "Come on, damn it." My head hurt like the devil, and the energy I'd borrowed from Emilia was almost gone. Plus, I now have another problem on my plate apart from an imminent Munro. That thing may not have been real, but the threat it posed was. And how do you kill something that isn't real? I think I've got the answer. I hope I have.

You set a ghost on it.

* * *

I put my key in the lock, Joana having long gone home, only to have the door pulled open for me. Enter da Silva, falling over his own doorstep. Good way to impress the police inspector.

"Zé, what the hell are you playing at?" I said irritably. But he was staring at me, wide-eyed with shock.

"What happened to you?" he blurted out in a squeaky voice that made him turn pink in the face with embarrassment.

For a second I was tempted to tell him, "the inspector here shot me," but that was probably a bit too much for him. Instead I said, "Make yourself useful and keep your mother away till I've washed it. This is Inspector Corvo. Inspector, my son José. I'll leave you in his hands for a moment."

The pair of them looked as bemused as each other, but I left them to it. Emilia's had to mop blood off me enough times. I'd like to give her a rest from it for once.

When I looked at myself I was glad I hadn't had to barge in on her. I'd never describe her as squeamish. Or prone to fits of the vapors. Whatever they are. But I knew why Zé'd reacted like that. My God, I look a fright. I know scalp wounds always bleed a lot, but you could've painted a wall with my head.

Who would've thought the old man had so much blood in him, I said to myself in English. It's a quote from something. I've no idea what. The things that stick in your mind.

Muttering curses, I washed away the blood and examined the wound. Which turned out to be a rather pathetic-looking cut about two inches long that had already sealed itself, more or less. Still hurt like bloody murder, though. And another shirt ruined. I'm too tired to change it, and what's the point at this time of night, anyway? I pulled out my watch and was somewhat surprised to discover it was only just past nine o'clock.

My wonderful Emilia, bless her, had not only gotten rid of an inquisitive Zé —a feat in itself — but also plied Inspector Corvo with wine. He was sitting smoking, and seemed more or less recovered. Wish I could say the same for myself. I feel as if I've been put through a mangle. I *hope* she's thought of reading him.

"Oh, Luís, you might've changed your shirt," she said as I came in. I stifled a yawn and poured myself a glass of wine.

"Seemed like too much effort," I said, shrugging.

Emilia sighed, obviously finding me hopeless. "Come here and let me see the damage."

"I've said I'm sorry," the inspector interrupted.

"I don't even know what the devil you thought you were shooting at." I sat down next to Emilia, and she touched my temple with cool fingers.

"Are you saying Inspector Corvo did this?"

I grinned at him. "Over to you," I said. He narrowed his eyes and turned to Emilia.

"Your husband, senhora," he explained politely, "was hit by a chip of brick from a wall. It was dark, I thought I saw a movement, and fired at it."

"I suppose we'll have to forgive you then," said Emilia judiciously. "What was it?"

"That," replied the inspector, blowing out smoke, "not even the senhor capitão could tell me, and he was looking for it."

She picked up her wineglass and took a sip. Then she turned to look at me.

"You found it, then?" I made a face and took a cheroot out.

"In a manner of speaking," I said sourly, striking a match and lighting up. "It's still out there."

"You couldn't get rid of it?" she asked in surprise. Good God. My wife thinks I'm infallible. Get swollen-headed at this rate, da Silva.

"Knife just went through it," I told her. Fingered the wound on my temple gingerly, wincing at the pain. She picked my hand away.

"Don't fiddle with it," she scolded. "Or I'll put a bandage round your head and you'll look like Sr. Singh."

"Sr. Singh is six feet four inches tall and doesn't wear an eyepatch," I pointed out.

Corvo was watching us with a slightly bemused expression on his face. He cleared his throat when I caught his eye, and looked down at his cigarette.

"Would you happen to be acquainted with an Englishman called Sr. Montague Pierce, by any chance?"

I could've strung him out for a few more minutes, but this time I took pity on him and gave him a straight answer.

"I know the senhor, yes."

"And he knows about all this?" I nodded. "Werewolves and so on?"

"Yes, he does."

"Was he right, then? Was that thing — constructed, somehow?"

As much as Alegria is. I fought down the urge to yawn again, and said, "I think so. But I don't know who," or what, "constructed it." Though I wonder about Belphegor. Can demons make? Or only destroy? I took a mouthful of smoke and exhaled slowly. "I do, however, have an idea about how to get rid of it."

Corvo looked startled. "You do?" I nodded again. "How?"

"If I told you, Inspector," I said, "you wouldn't believe me."

* * *

Much later, Emilia said to me, "You really don't know why this Tatiana woman is attracted to you?"

I brushed hair away from her face and replied, "No. Not really."

"Then you're the least vain man I've ever met." I laughed. Not much cause for vanity. "No, Luís, I'm serious. You're not a captain just because you passed your examinations and served your time on however many ships."

"I'm not?"

"Don't be dense, love. You're an attractive person. In the sense of attracting people to you. They want to follow you. Your crew stays the same year after year. They don't sign on other ships."

"Costa did," I pointed out.

"He got a First's ticket. That's not what I mean. And look at Sr. Harris, and Sr. Yeoh, and Sr. Pierce, and Sr. Zacuto—"

"All right," I said, "I get the picture."

"Do you, though," she said softly. I looked at her face in the gaslight. So serious. She touched my new cut, than moved her fingers to my old scar. Five years old, now. "You spend a lot of time now doing what's right. Fighting for it," she went on. "Did you know I asked Sr. Yeoh what shape your soul is?"

"No," I said, adding quickly, "Don't tell me." Her fingers slid down to my lips.

"I think I should. Or you might go on hoping all this will go away." She pressed my mouth shut on a protest. I shook my head. "What are you afraid of?" she whispered.

That's a question. "Knowing too much."

Emilia took my face between both her hands. "A paladin," she said. "He says you have the soul of a paladin." No, I definitely didn't want to know that.

But, on reflection, I suppose I needed to. Live with it, da Silva. But then again, I don't have to like it. I don't want to be anyone's champion.

I put my left hand over her right, and closed my fingers round it. She dropped her other hand. "I don't understand it," I muttered, and I really don't, "I spent nineteen years with the Venetian. You know the sort of things I had to do for him. I'm not the kind of man who—"

"But you are," she insisted, putting fingers back over my mouth. "The first time we ever met, you did something completely selfless. Ssh, love, let me finish. I don't often talk about this, but I've thought about it a lot. If you hadn't killed Aldo, I — I don't know where I'd be now. Dead bones in the lagoon, I expect. Not living a life I enjoy, with someone I love. But you had to pay for that, not for what you did, but for what Aldo was. I know you had to break the law for della Quercia. But you did all that for me. And if that's not what a paladin does, well, they can go and stick it, as Sr. Harris says, where the monkey put the nuts."

Ashamed, I brought her hand to my mouth, and kissed her palm. "I don't deserve you," I said.

"No," she whispered, "wrong way round. *I* don't deserve *you.*"

We could go on like this all night.

"I suppose I was being a bit selfish," I said, releasing her hand.

"You were. A bit. But I do know why." Yes. She doesn't want the sight, or perhaps you'd call it insight, that acquiring the key of Solomon woke in her. Which reminded me. I put a finger on the mark, very lightly, but she still drew in her breath sharply.

"Did you—" I still don't know what verb to use. "Read... look at Inspector Corvo?"

She wrinkled her nose. It made me want to smile. Well, it made me want to kiss her, to be truthful. But that could wait. For a minute, at least.

"Yes, *I* know," she said. "But I haven't gotten used to it yet. Ah... he was worried, ashamed at being scared, annoyed you got hurt," I wasn't too keen on that myself, "wanting to deny what he saw but he couldn't, a bit skeptical, couldn't really believe it was that thing that's going round eating people, had a million questions, shocked that you let a delicate female know about such topics," I gave a snort of laughter, and she hit me, "but mostly appalled that the world isn't the way he thought it was." She exhaled sharply.

"Is that all?" I asked, and she hit me again. I grabbed her wrist. "Delicate females aren't supposed to beat their husbands, you know."

"Oh, and what are you going to do about it?" she said, laughing. Cue for that kiss.

For some strange reason, my last thought before falling asleep was, I must remember to ask Zé if he got Tatiana Dimitrovna settled in her hotel.

* * *

The house was silent, only the susurration of four humans breathing sighed quietly through it. That was another annoying thing about babies, Mouffi considered, they spent most of their time asleep. And waking Susana up soon palled as entertainment. The demon-fragment wanted a little more variety than feeding and nappy-changing. Which wouldn't cease any time soon. Mouffi was nowhere near powerful enough to accelerate her growth that much, though it was doing all it could. Which wasn't a very great deal, considering that the best of all its efforts had only knocked two months off Ana's pregnancy. Which Ana, for one, was delighted about.

Out of spite, Mouffi woke Susana anyway, and her insistent unignorable screams broke the peaceful silence in pieces.

They intruded into Teresa's dreams as well, until the noise woke her up.

She lay looking at the darkness and swearing silently. Inácio said some babies were just like that, there wasn't anything you could do about it, and he should know. Teresa yawned, picturing Ana, still drunk on lack of sleep, staggering out of bed to see what was wrong with the little menace now. At least Ana seemed to like her baby. Though Teresa was still quite baffled as to how she managed it, given the rape, an appallingly uncomfortable pregnancy (Ana had spent most of it throwing up) and a labor that went on for the best part of five hours.

If the poor mother had to get up every five minutes, her daughter appeared to be thriving, putting on weight daily and growing at a rate of knots.

Eventually the squalling quieted, and Teresa closed her eyes again and settled back to sleep, only to have Inácio roll onto his back and start snoring.

Teresa cursed, and poked him until he turned over.

*   *   *

And in a street near the castle, someone banging on the door of a shop.

Shutters open, sleep-tousled heads peer out in annoyance, perhaps wishing they had thought to bring a chamberpot to toss at the disturber of the peace, who on earth is that, and what does he want at this time of night, making enough noise to wake the dead.

"People trying to sleep here," complains a voice.

"Do you know what *time* it is?" demands another.

"Shut the noise or we'll fetch a policeman," a third threatens.

Sir Robert Munro, who did not take the boat-train after all but traveled by quicker means, takes no notice, he speaks neither Portuguese nor any other damned dago tongue but even if he did he would not be swayed by the protests of lesser beings. However, the shop is dark and shuttered and though the owner lives on the premises he is obviously not at home, the dirty dog.

Munro turned and stalked off, shutters slamming shut as he left, that'll teach him to come knocking on people's doors in the middle of the night and waking up honest citizens who have to work tomorrow, but what do you expect from an Englishman, how do you know he was an Englishman, didn't you see his clothes? Words, strong words, will be had with the other Englishman, the bookseller whose shop it is, in the morning.

Who slept undisturbed, not far away as crows fly but an enormous distance in terms of time and accessibility, his head pillowed on a book where he had fallen asleep as he read, in the library of São Rafael.

6

DAMAGE ALWAYS FEELS WORSE THE DAY AFTER IT HAPPENS. In the morning I felt as if I'd been wrestling with a bear. And the bear had won, and hit me over the head with a brick wall. I know why that damned cut hurt so much now. It was the center of a bruise as black as my boots. Good thing Williams knows me, I thought sourly as I examined the results of last night's encounter. Or he wouldn't let me anywhere near his office. I look like a citizen of the seedier side of Lisbon's underworld. No, even a seedier citizen wouldn't want to talk to me.

Zé was stuffing his face, as usual. He crammed the remains of the bread into his mouth when I came in and tried to swallow the whole lot. Obviously he thought I was going to get away. I can tell. But I decided to let him off the hook for once.

"Don't give yourself a seizure," I said. "I'm not going anywhere for the moment. Did you get Tatiana Dimitrovna settled all right?"

He swallowed, nodded. Sprayed a few crumbs around for good measure. "Yes, but she came back a bit later."

"Why?"

"I don't know." he said, "But she bought your desk."

I stopped dead. Hand halfway to a plate. Mouth open in shock. "She did *what?*" I exclaimed before thought caught up with reaction. Apparently oblivious, Zé picked up another bread roll and stared hungrily at it.

"Gave Sr. Ashley cash for your desk. Why did you want to get rid of it?" He took a bite out of the roll.

She knew about the portal. I was certain of it. Oh God. She must've used it. Chasing after power. Sorcerers are all the same. I could find you in hell itself, she once said to me. What if I have to go there and fetch her instead?

"Zé, do me a favor and go and see if she's all right."

"But—" He looked at me imploringly.

"I'll tell you all about it later," I promised.

"That's what you always say," he complained, darkly, adding, "And I'm supposed to be off duty at the moment."

Oh, so he wants to play it like that, does he? He should know better by now.

"Sorry, Zé. Haven't relieved you from steward's duty yet." I grinned at him. "And guess what? I'm the skipper."

He scowled, but I'd cornered him and he knew it.

"Can I finish my breakfast first?" I surveyed the debris on the table, eyebrows raised.

"Yes, if you promise to leave a crumb or a crust for the Old Man."

"I'm a growing lad, I need feeding," he said.

"I'd like to know what you're growing into," I remarked, eyeing him. Although I suppose I must've been the same when I was fourteen. Eating for king and country. Yes, we still had a king in those days, and no, it wasn't Manuel the First.

Emilia put her head round the door and *tsk'd* sternly at my unshaven state.

"Remember we have to see Sr. Williams in an hour," she reminded me.

"I know," I said soothingly. "I refuse to put that collar on until I have to." Or the eyepatch. Though the stiff collar is worse. Luckily a collar and tie isn't the kind of get-up I have to wear all the time.

"I'm going," Zé announced. Seized a last roll and went out eating it.

"Where's he off to?" Emilia asked.

I explained. Her eyes widened as the implications hit her. Then she crossed herself. Automatically, apparently.

"Dio mio," she breathed. And then a question I'd like to know the answer to myself, "What does it mean, though? Is hell a physical place?"

"I don't know," I admitted. "I shouldn't think so. I think Zé's going to find her sound asleep in her bed." Sound asleep, and not waking.

She took my hand. Hers looked very small and pale, but it's stronger than you'd think. All those years of using a walking-stick.

"What will you do?"

"Nothing I can do, at the moment," I said. Except wait. And see what happens.

* * *

Edwin Williams is the spitting image of the king of England, but he's the least stuffy Englishman I ever met. Though Pierce isn't really what you might call formal, but then he lived in Brazil most of his life. Most of them, however, seem to be like Ashley, *Isabella*'s First. I don't know whether Williams was always like the way he is or whether it's the result of marrying a foreigner. Latter's unlikely, since his wife is a pretty miserable sort of woman. Emilia calls her a crybaby. Anyway, Sra. Williams is irrelevant at the moment.

So here are the da Silvas for their appointment. Emilia the business manager, neat in blue. Accompanied by one more-than-usually ruffianly-looking captain. Rumpled and decidedly second-hand. And I won't mention the stiff collar again.

Williams's clerk, one of the stuffy kind of Englishman, is used to seeing Emilia by now. Though he makes it clear he disapproves of women in business. The first time we went to see Williams the man nearly had a seizure. You'd think he'd never even seen a woman before. Tough. I can't add up a column of figures to save my life — damn good thing demons don't come after me brandishing account books. So, far as I'm concerned you use the best person for a job. Doesn't matter if it's a man or a woman. Or, come to that, a werewolf. Well, maybe I'm prejudiced. But not as much as this fellow Nicholson.

"He's got someone with him at the moment, Captain da Silva," the clerk said, ignoring Emilia completely. "Though I don't suppose they'll be very much longer."

Since I hurried breakfast and put on that damned collar — all right, I lied about not mentioning it again — to come here, I can't say I'm happy to hear that. But, not much I can do about it. Have a little patience, da Silva.

However I hadn't even had time to light up when the rumbling voices in the inner office started to make unmistakable goodbye noises. You can tell in any language. And a moment later, silhouettes behind the frosted glass.

The handle turned, the door opened and Sir Robert Munro came out, followed closely by Williams.

I don't know when I've had a nastier shock. And I've confronted everything from succubi to murderous ghosts to demons. However, usually I'm more or less expecting them. Not in this case. *Merda*.

Bad situation. I'm unarmed, of course. Can hardly bring my knife to a business meeting. Not the done thing, you know.

What I did, all I could do. Got to my feet and moved in front of Emilia. The clerk can take his chances. My only consolation was that I hoped he wouldn't do anything in front of witnesses. That he was still human enough to consider innocent bystanders.

Behind me, I heard Emilia draw in a breath. Knew what'd happened. She'd recognized why I'd got up to shield her, and had read... sensed

Munro. Really must decide how to describe it, but even she can't find the right word.

"Ah, Captain da Silva," said Williams, beaming, in English, and even then part of my mind was glad to be spared his version of Portuguese. "My brother-in-law, Sir Robert Munro. Big noise in the House of Commons. Ah, British government, don't you know."

Munro stared at me impassively, and I met his eyes. Hoping my face was just as expressionless. Since the last time he'd seen me I'd stuck a knife into his sending, or whatever you call it, perhaps I found it easier than he did. Seems normal enough, for a politician. Meu Deus, what did you expect, da Silva, that the man'd reek of brimstone? Well, yes, something like that.

He didn't offer me his hand. For which I was grateful. I really didn't want to have to touch him, even without any discernible souvenir or taint from his trip to hell. Just gave a chilly little bow, which I returned.

"Da Silva," he said, rudely I thought. So I replied in kind, trusting he'll think I'm an ignorant foreigner who doesn't know any better. Anyway I'm damned if I'll call him Sir Robert, as if he's somehow better than me.

"Munro." I turned back to Williams, went on, still in English, "Is it still convenient for our meeting?"

"Oh yes," said Williams affably. "Sir Robert's just leaving." He emphasized the words "Sir Robert" slightly, but there was a twinkle in his eye. Like I said, he's not stuffy, and he recognized Munro's rudeness better than I did.

"Indeed," Munro agreed. "I'll speak with you again soon, Williams." He turned to me, and bared his teeth in something most unlike a smile. "Perhaps we'll meet again."

Not if I see you first. "Perhaps," I murmured. Williams was apparently oblivious to this byplay. He waved at his clerk.

"Will you show Sir Robert out, Nicholson?"

The clerk stood up. Williams turned his attention to Emilia. Bowed deeply over her hand. "Senhora."

"Sr. Williams," she said with a smile. He helped her politely to her feet.

"Won't you both come in?"

Once inside his office he scowled genially at me and took out his pipe. Started the usual pipe-smoker's ritual.

"What did your brother-in-law want?" I asked idly, lighting the cheroot I hadn't got round to earlier and taking a welcome drag.

"Pompous ass," observed Williams, fiddling with his tobacco-pouch. "Says he's here on business, though God knows what that could be. Must think I'm stupid. He's nothing to do with the Foreign Office. Or the Board of

Trade." He got the pipe stuffed to his satisfaction and put the pouch down on his desk. "And since he's in Lisbon he feels duty-bound to call on me. He says. Haven't clapped eyes on the man for six years."

I heard Emilia stifle a giggle. Williams translates his English idioms literally into Portuguese. Sometimes with very bizarre results.

"So what d'you think he did want?" I asked, exhaling smoke.

"Up to no good, what d'*you* think? He's a government minister." Obviously not all Englishmen think politicians are a good thing. I smiled, amused, and raised an eyebrow at him.

"*Claro,*" I said. Williams smiled back, and started the laborious business of trying to set light to his pipe. "Any idea what?"

"No idea," he said. "Don't much care, either. Just have to make sure I watch my back for a while."

Well, now we know the answer to the question we wanted to ask him. But I thought I was going to have some time to get ready for Munro. To do what, da Silva? Quite frankly, I've no idea. Though God knows it would've been nice to have a breathing space after that last voyage.

So what next? Wait for Tatiana Dimitrovna to come back, I suppose. And hope he doesn't act too soon. But he's here in Lisbon sooner than I thought was possible. Sort of implies he's not going to wait to do anything.

Not a nice thought.

*   *   *

Every time he woke during the night, and it was several times, he saw Alegria standing silent and still by the shuttered window. The shutters were slightly warped by the passage of years, and not all their slats matched perfectly any more. The moonlight fell through them, the opaline light of a winter moon, and patterned her in light and dark, a different angle, a different painting, each time he woke.

He knew she had no need of sleep. Understood at the fundamental level that she did not really exist. But, at a more fundamental level, she did. She had been created to fill his gaps, like this chiaroscuro of moonlight, positive and negative, yin and yang. And so, though she could never be flesh and never have a soul, she did have an existence, because she was needed.

And because she was guarding him, he rested more easily.

But because she was guarding him, he kept on waking up. To watch her. To enjoy the simple fact of her presence.

After all, he had no way of knowing how long she would last.

When the moon set and the light went away, he fell into a sounder sleep, through the sullen gray winter dawn, and never woke until full daylight. Though today thick clouds had rolled in again and covered up the sun, at least it was up there somewhere. He knew nothing of demons, they had not featured in his wife's religious passions — to her, sin was to be found only on earth — but daylight diminished the thought of them; even such dull daylight as this, that made him want to light the gas before noon.

Finally he padded downstairs in slippers and robe, but with his hair neatly combed, Alegria a step or two in front of him. He didn't know quite when she'd appointed herself his guardian, but he was, he thought, glad of it.

Still without speaking, for since she completed him they had little need of it, they went into the studio together.

Sebastião da Silva made a bee-line for the big canvas he had ceased to work on, and uncovered it silently, only to stare in astonishment and growing dread at the painted scene. Another of the houses was now inhabited. No, two of them were. In one, he could see through the window a black-haired woman looking anxiously over her shoulder.

And several doors away, something frightful looked out of a window, something with horns and fangs, and he knew it was hunting her.

His calm evaporated, and fear seeped in. The painting no longer needed him, and what poor wretched woman was now bleeding in a gutter somewhere?

"I should've gone with Luís," he said sadly. Alegria squeezed his shoulder, and he put his hand over hers.

*   *   *

His eyelids were gummed together. His mouth tasted of rat. *Jesus. Can't I go one stinking night without munching on the goddamned things?* All his joints ached. And his head felt like the world's biggest hangover. Even his hair hurt. *And that's the bummest deal of all, seeing as Mrs. Harris's little boy hasn't touched a drop of alcohol in nearly four years.*

Harris rubbed his eyes vigorously, and the glue came loose. He reached for the water carafe, removed the glass from the top, drank all the water straight down. That was good for the shitty taste, but he knew from bitter experience that he'd just have to wait for the headache to go away of its own accord.

But damn! He looked down at his legs, and a smile came to his face. *Didn't that do the trick and then some? Someone oughta bottle it as a cure for broken bones. Make a fortune outa the medical profession. Still and all, better get some clothes on. Not much point sitting round buck naked like a red Indian. 'Sides, it's cold.*

He pulled on his clothes without too much thought — he was about as interested in sartorial matters as the captain, mainly because he considered he looked like a bear in coat and pants when he was dressed — and examined his face in the shaving mirror. Scowled at the luxuriant growth of beard a wolf-night always gave him, swore vividly, and set about shaving. He was too hungry to wait for luxuries like hot water before appearing in human company.

That done, and considering himself as presentable as he ever was, he went in search of something to eat.

And coffee, for Godsakes. Can't function till I've downed some coffee.

The house, however, was deserted, though he supposed Joana was in the kitchen. Harris checked the time and found to his surprise that it was after ten. Nearly half past, in fact.

Musta slept like a stone. He yawned. *Least there's some breakfast left. Even if it's only bread. My fault. Got Zé's leavings. Boy eats like a horse. Me, I could eat a horse.*

There was coffee, too, still faintly warm. Harris had no objection to cold coffee, and filled a cup happily.

When he'd cleared the table and taken the edge off his appetite, though he deplored the lack of bacon (there were enough Englishmen in *Isabella*'s crew for more substantial breakfasts to be a regular feature on board), he sat down by the window and lit a cigarette.

What in hell's own name was *that thing, anyway? Shouldn't be surprised at anything the skipper turns up, I guess. But Christ on a camel, that was something else.* He blew smoke out through his nose. *Looked real enough. But didn't taste of anything at all. Like biting water. No, that ain't quite right. Had a bit more to it than that. And something like a taste. Smoke, ash, dust... Coulda been dust. Stale, it tasted stale. Cold, too. I got a hold of it, but couldn't hang on. No substance to bite into.*

He remembered another thing. *Huh. I'll give him "stay". Woof, woof.*

*   *   *

Zé, half-annoyed with himself at letting his father outmaneuver him — again — trotted Tatiana-wards with alacrity all the same. As a serving sailor he didn't get to meet many women, certainly no girls of his own age, and recently he'd realized that he'd quite like to. Felipe, who was eight months older than he was and whose voice had, in fact, broken (although you wouldn't know it from listening to him, in Zé's opinion), had to have the same problem. But at least he didn't have his father breathing down his neck every five minutes. Not that Zé believed a great deal of what Fil' said about anything, especially girls. And Fil' had spots, too. Zé pulled a face at the idea of getting acne.

So Tatiana Dimitrovna had been an interesting novelty. She was quite old, of course, Zé had no idea how old, younger than his mother probably, but he wasn't sure and he wasn't interested enough to speculate.

He loitered outside the hotel for a few minutes, slouching with his hands in his pockets and wondering how to tackle his enquiry. It was all very well for his father to tell him to check that the Russian woman was all right, but it would've been handy to have had some sort of clue as to how to go about it. No self-respecting hotel clerk is going to tell a fourteen-year-old he doesn't know from Adam anything about any of the guests. And he didn't think anyone would believe him if he said she was his sister.

The answer to Zé's problem came furtively out of the hotel then and lit a cigarette. Smiling to himself, Zé sidled up to him.

"Hey," he said. The bellhop looked up in alarm, then his expression cleared as he recognized Zé from the previous day.

"Hey yourself," he replied. He was about sixteen, with a fine crop of pimples. They beat Fil's hands down for repulsiveness.

"What's your name?" asked Zé, trying for affability.

"Who's asking?" said the other suspiciously. Zé grinned.

"Someone who wants to pay you money." He got a prompt reply, accompanied by a smoke-ring and a sly expression.

"Miguel."

"Right. Miguel. I'm Zé. Listen, you remember the lady from yesterday?"

"Yeah," said Miguel enthusiastically. "A looker, huh, *pá?*" Zé nodded, wondering how to frame his questions.

"Anybody said anything about her today?"

"Said anything?" Miguel took another drag from his cigarette, flicked ash off the end. "Like what?"

"Oh, I don't know," said Zé. He scratched his cheekbone in unconscious imitation of his father. "Then she's not been taken ill, or anything?"

Miguel shrugged. "I wouldn't hear about anything like that, *pá.*"

"I need to see her."

The bellhop leered at Zé, and he felt his face heat up. He hated it when it did that. "Oh yeah? Bit old for you, ain't she?"

"None of your business," he muttered. The other sniggered.

"What's it worth?" he asked, a calculating look in his eye.

Zé pulled out half the cash he had in his pockets, and the bellhop peered at it critically. They haggled cheerfully for a while, and eventually arrived at a satisfactory figure. By then Miguel had finished his cigarette, and threw the dog-end into the gutter. This earned him a disapproving look from a passer-by, which he ignored.

"All right?" Zé asked.

"Come on," the bellhop urged, leading him round the side of the hotel. "I'll get shot if anyone sees us."

"Nobody's looking," Zé said, with a confidence that wasn't entirely real.

"That's all you know," said Miguel darkly, looking up and down swiftly before opening a side door. They slipped through into a linoleum-floored corridor that smelt of garlic, slightly rancid oil, and disinfectant. Zé followed the bellhop, and presently he opened another door to reveal a narrow uncarpeted flight of stairs.

"What's her room number?" whispered Zé.

"Hundred and ten. Hurry up, before someone comes looking for me."

Outside Tatiana Dimitrovna's room, which had a "Do Not Disturb" sign hanging from the doorknob, he paused, suddenly apprehensive. What would he do if something *was* wrong? He drew a deep breath.

Beside him, Miguel made an impatient noise. Zé rapped softly on the door. No reply. He repeated the knock, harder this time.

"Can you open the door?"

"You must be joking, *pá*," said Miguel. "I'll get the sack for sure." But his eyes were gleaming avariciously.

"Nobody'll know," Zé insisted. "*I'm* not going to tell. Here." He offered the bellhop the rest of his money. His father had better stump up a refund, too.

Miguel snatched the coins, produced a key, and unlocked the door. Then he said, "I never saw you," and bolted off down the corridor.

Better off without him, thought Zé, pushing the door open nervously. He only hoped the bellhop wouldn't decide to double-cross him and spill the beans to the management. But no, he was in the room now, wasn't he? Miguel hadn't struck him as stupid enough to incriminate himself by shopping Zé after he'd been the one to let Zé in.

The door creaked, making him jump. He slipped into the room and closed it carefully"Hello?" he called softly, in English.

The room was dim with the shutters closed and curtains drawn. Zé tiptoed carefully in, hoping for a lack of obstacles on the floor. Falling over something would only make a row, and that was the last thing he wanted.

Tatiana Dimitrovna lay on her back on the bed, breathing softly. She was wearing only a shift. Zé gulped as this fact registered, and peered through the dim twilight at her sleeping face, which was safer.

"Ma'am?" he whispered. No movement. No change in her deep regular breath sounds. Unhappily, he reached out one hand and touched her bare shoulder. Her skin was very warm and smooth under his fingers. He was acutely embarrassed, and not at all sure he wanted her to wake up right now.

She didn't. And of course that was worse. Zé took his hand away, dread beginning to rise, like a cold fist clutching his heart. He took a step back.

And then she drew in a terrible shuddering breath, and sat up in the bed. Zé jumped backwards with an involuntary squawk of alarm, his heart hammering, knocking over a chair with a noise like the crack of doom. He overbalanced, caught the side of the desk, stopped himself, with difficulty, from bolting, and opened his mouth to speak.

The Russian woman's eyes snapped open, and they were white, the pupils rolled up out of sight. She wrenched in another rattling breath, then fell back on the bed once more.

After a moment, Zé took a few nervous steps towards the bed. His legs were shaking, something he hadn't believed possible, he'd thought it an invention of dime-novel writers.

He watched her until his own breathing slowed and his heart calmed down, then lifted her robe from its hook on the back of the door and draped it carefully over her before fleeing the hotel, using the route Miguel had shown him earlier.

* * *

Emilia walked out of Willams's office under her own steam. But it was touch and go. Ever since she'd read Munro her face had been white, her eyes wide. What did she see, for God's sake?

The door closed behind us and I caught her before her knees gave way. Her stick clattered to the floor, and I swore under my breath. Holding her upright with one arm, I lifted her hand to the Key of Solomon. Hoping I could give her back some energy this time.

It worked. I felt a jolt, then a sustained tingling. And then a pulse like a heartbeat through her fingertips. She sucked in a long gasp of air.

"I'm all right," she said breathlessly. I picked up her stick. Walked her to the elevator with one arm round her. She didn't object. The bored elevator operator didn't spare us a glance.

Once in the street, she took several more deep breaths of the cold damp air.

"Munro?" I asked. She shook her head.

"Coffee first," she replied. "Maybe a brandy."

Cursing Munro, I steered her to the nearest café. It turned out to be rather more genteel than I'm used to, but what the hell. I'm wearing a suit. Looks like an old sack on me, but it's still a suit. The waiter looked at me down his nose as though he was thinking about asking to see the color of my money. But I glared at him and he thought better of it. Staring people down is easy. Looking anything else in the eye, that's more of a challenge.

And the same, apparently, goes for Emilia and Sir Robert Munro.

"Are you sure you're all right?" I asked.

She nodded. A little more color in her cheeks now. Though not much. I lit a cheroot. Let her take her time. When the waiter brought the drinks she poured the brandy straight into her coffee and drank half of it down.

"Sorry to be so wet," she said at last. "But oh! that was disgusting. He's not human." Emilia shuddered. "I don't know what he is, but... It was like reaching out to pick up something harmless, maybe a stick, and finding you're holding a piece of—" she lowered her voice — "of dogshit. And you couldn't put it down, and then you realized that it was alive, and looking at you, and it knew what you were doing." She swallowed the other half of her caffè corretto. "He's... I think he's dead, Luís. He may be walking around, but he's not alive any more. Not in any sense we understand. It's a hollow shell that looks like a man, with something vile inside."

There was such a sick look in her eyes that I wanted to put my arm round her. Not possible. Not here. We'd get thrown out for lewd behavior. So I scratched my scar. Drank coffee. Tapped ash off the end of my cheroot. The waiter appeared and exchanged the ashtray for a clean one. "What was he — could you tell what he was thinking?"

Emilia shook her head. "I don't 'hear' thoughts, as such. Emotions, yes, and they sometimes *imply* what people are thinking. But he was just a jumble of hate, fear, lust, greed—" She broke off with a gasp of laughter, but there wasn't much humor in it. "The seven deadly sins, walking. Be careful, Luís. I don't know what he's up to, but he thinks you're in his way."

Óptimo. That's good news. Even though I know it already. I gave a humorless snort of my own and said, "Well, I am, you know." She looked at me with a tight, worried smile. And there's that strand of hair falling across her face again. The one that always escapes. The one I always want to stroke away. "I have to be. You said it yourself, *querida.*" A paladin.

Ironic, really. Here's da Silva laboring under the pleasant delusion that being free of the Venetian means being free. When I'm really just as much of a slave as ever. Might've known there'd be a catch. Just changed one master for another. Does the master's purpose make a difference to the man he owns? Or is freedom always an illusion? Perhaps it isn't possible to be human and not be owned by something. Father Pereira would say God. And maybe Zacuto would as well. Although it means something different to each of them. But this is hardly the time for theological speculation. Let the pair of them spar it out. I've got things to do.

Trouble is, I'm not entirely sure what they are.

"Shall we go?" said Emilia.

"Your wish is my command," I replied, flippantly. All right. I know. But this is willing submission. Always has been.

Now there's one more call I want to make. Have to make. I've got to visit my father. Harris is right, I should've let him know the demon's name. For protection at least. Though it doesn't seem to mean him physical harm. At least not at the moment. But I can't get into a demon's mind. I don't know what it wants. And Munro or no Munro, my father deserves any protection I can give him. *Filial obligation, da Silva? Whatever next?*

Still, ultimately it was my fault that the demon stole his soul in the first place. Although when I said that to Emilia, she scolded me.

"Don't beat yourself over that," she said sternly. "If you want to wallow in guilt, go to confession." Something I haven't done for twenty-five years. "It wasn't your fault. Batista was the one who did the summoning. It's on his head."

But Batista's dead, and guess who has to clean up the mess? Right first time.

It started to rain again, but lightly. I think I'm pretty waterproof by now, but there's no reason why Emilia should get wet. So I hailed a cab. By the time it deposited us at my father's house, the rain was bucketing down.

To my surprise, my father opened the door himself. He looked tired. A bit pinched around the eyes. "Luís," he said, blinking rapidly. "Emilia. How nice to see you. Come in out of the rain, both of you."

"Saving on housekeeper's wages, are you?" I asked him with a raised eyebrow, letting Emilia go first.

"Sra. Reinaldo's got the flu," he said, and I thought, an attack of nose out of joint, more likely. He turned to fuss over Emilia in his old-fashioned, gallant way. She endured it stoically, though she hates being treated like a piece of porcelain. I could see a twinkle in her eye. There's genuine affection there, I recognized with a twinge almost of jealousy. "Come into the studio," he went on. "There's something I want to show you." His eyes were bright and urgent, but he offered her his arm as if escorting her to a grand dinner.

Alegria was standing by the window, gray watery light coloring her face. I found myself examining it for brushstrokes. My father introduced her as though she was real. And Emilia shook her hand politely. Was there anything there for her to sense? I was intensely curious about that. Since I can't explain Alegria at all. She baffles me.

The big canvas that my father'd been working on was covered up. He beckoned me over, and took the cover off. Alegria moved to join us.

"Have they moved again?" she asked.

"Yes," said my father. Then he turned to me. "I haven't touched this thing since you were last here. But this morning there were two new figures in the picture. They were here, and here." He indicated two of the empty houses. "When we looked again, they'd moved. And now, they've moved again. Look."

The scene was dominated by a building that reminded me of a cathedral. Although you got the feeling that whatever was worshipped in there wasn't something that humans would find a good idea to revere. At its door was a horned, demonic figure, its back to us. It was black in color, yet seemed to be burning. It gave off a pitchy glow, like hot tar. I couldn't tell whether it was trying to get in or not. It might even have been a sentry.

Scratching my eyebrow thoughtfully, I looked up, following my father's pointing finger. At the top of the tower, which might or might not have been a campanile, a woman was looking over the parapet. Her long black hair was loose, and streamed back from her face in an unseen wind. I knew that face very well.

It was Tatiana Dimitrovna.

"Meu Deus," I said.

He's painted a city in hell. And how am I going to explain *that* to him?

Rain hammered on the window, water sluicing down the glass. In the painting, the desert street seemed to glow with an inner light. I stared at it, wondering whether Zé had found her asleep, or what. Tried to figure out just what was going on. Was she fleeing the demon? Had she been looking for sanctuary in the cathedral that wasn't a cathedral?

Had she found it?

"What is it?" asked Emilia, joining me in front of the painting. I put my arm round her. Glad to feel her, here and solid and alive. A woman with a heartbeat, not a soul in hell. Or a thing of paint and air. She slipped her arm round my waist, and squeezed back. Distractions, da Silva.

"Don't ask me how, or why." I pointed to the woman on the tower. "But that's Tatiana Dimitrovna."

"She's waiting for the flying machine," said Alegria suddenly. We all looked at her, then back to the painting.

"Mother of God, yes," exclaimed my father. "That's moved, too."

"She did it, then," Emilia blurted out. "And she's found a way to get back."

Half of me was elated. Half appalled. If Tatiana Dimitrovna's succeeded, is it good news or bad? Will she come back able to help and wanting to, or with a soul turned to something rotten and slimy and stinking?

My father was looking at us with a quizzical expression on his face.

"Are you going to let me in on the secret?" he asked.

Oh well, why not. He created a woman out of paint, after all. He hardly batted an eyelid when I told him about the demon — *still haven't told him its name. Must remember to do that.* —The idea of someone paying a visit to hell shouldn't faze him.

I explained, a little impatiently. Not sure why I was impatient. He watched me thoughtfully. His gaze was so intent it was starting to make me uncomfortable.

"We should leave the room," said Alegria when I'd finished. "Give her a chance to escape." I turned to her, glad of the relief. She smiled, and opened her eyes wide. "I know a little about paintings, you see," she added, and I blinked. Was that a joke? You don't expect an artificial woman to make a joke. Never met an artificial man who could.

"Can you paint something to help her?" Emilia asked my father, but it was Alegria who replied, shaking her head slowly.

"No," she said. "I think she has to use what is already there."

We all trooped out of the studio.

"Did you get anything from her?" I whispered to Emilia, almost side-tracked by the smell of her hair. It was slightly damp from the rain.

"Later," she muttered back. Which wasn't very illuminating. I'd been after a *Yes.* Or, come to that, a *No.* Neither would've surprised me, to be honest.

When I was a child, the house always seemed to have a damp chill about it. Today, even in January rain, it felt warm and comfortable. I glanced at the staircase. Had no wish to go upstairs. None at all. Too many memories. I rubbed my cheekbone and looked back at my father. He was scratching his beard in a perplexed sort of way.

"Why did you come?" he asked abruptly, catching me unawares even though I was looking at him.

"To warn you," I said shortly. My head was aching fiercely. I put my fingers to the cut on my temple, very carefully, and winced. Glanced guiltily at Emilia, who mouthed, *Leave it alone.* I tried not to smile.

"Isn't that a little late?" my father retorted. I blinked at him.

"Late?"

"How long has it been since this demon business started? I think—"

"Don't," said Emilia, cutting him off. I looked down at her, startled by her tone. "They like to set people against each other, don't they? I bet that's what making you argue."

Or it might just be a cantankerous old man, what do you think? And by that I mean da Silva senior. In case you're wondering.

Sighing, I delved in my pocket and pulled out the paper with Belphegor's name on it. I'd forgotten it again. But unfolding the paper reminded me.

"That's its name," I said, adding hastily, "Don't read it aloud." Gave my cheekbone a scratch. God knows I could do with a smoke.

"So what do I *do* with it?" he grumped.

"You can use it to tell the demon to go away," I told him. "It won't banish it for good. But it should get rid of it for a while." He still looked mulish.

"Why didn't you tell me yesterday?"

I pulled a face. "Because the demon managed to make me forget it until I was too far away from here to come back."

He unfolded the paper and stared at the name as if it might bite him. Which I suppose it might, at that. "This isn't what's written on the coin," he objected. I groaned silently. Damn it. Do I have to beat it into him?

"You can't read what's on the coin," I said, holding onto my temper with difficulty. "Or so you told me." And I couldn't read it, either.

"Have we left enough time?" Emilia interrupted. "For the picture to change again? Should we go and see?" I turned to my father, eyebrow raised.

"Have we?"

"*I* don't know," he said, sounding sour. "You tell me. You seem to know what you're doing." He thinks so, does he? Well, that was what Inspector Corvo had said, too. Both of them are wrong, though. I haven't any grand strategy in these affairs. Good God, I don't ever know what's going to happen next. You want an overall strategy, find a general. Not a da Silva. I may be fighting a war here, but *I* never volunteered for it. All right, I know. Everyone who's ever been drafted, volunteered, or press-ganged says that. And I'm no different.

"It might need no time at all. So why don't we go and look?" suggested Alegria, mildly enough. She was smiling.

For a woman made of paint she has a knack for getting to the heart of the matter. So we all traipsed back into the studio, and my father took the cover off the painting again.

And it was back as it had been before. Except for one thing.

The flying machine had flown. Now the sky held only strange constellations, and a waning moon.

Alegria clapped her hands, and my father cleared his throat and said, "Well, I'll be damned." Which was either a highly inappropriate remark. Or the most apt you could imagine. Given the circumstances.

Now I have to get to Tatiana Dimitrovna, and fast. But I really don't want to have to take Emilia with me, much as I'd like to have her by my side. I don't want to endanger her.

"Will you be all right here for a while?" I asked her.

She decided to dig her heels in. "I'm going with you." I scratched my eyebrow ruefully. Knew I couldn't argue with her. "You *are* going to see how she is, aren't you?"

"Yes, but—"

"Stop arguing, love, you aren't going to win this one."

I gave in. I know when to do that, most of the time. The last thing I want is a rift. Much less a silly quarrel over nothing. But she *has* been on her feet all morning. And I do worry, although I don't tell her so. She knows anyway. That's how it works.

"All right," I said. Turned to my father.

Who just told me, "Go."

The rain's stopped, for now. Great big bulging clouds above holding lots more to come, though. Streets full of puddles reflecting back the sullen sky. Emilia grumbled under her breath, holding her skirt up out of the wet and maneuvering herself deftly with the help of her stick. Something she's very good at, naturally, having lived in Venice for thirty years. I mean, of course, that it rains a lot in Venice. Since that conjured up an image of her going along the surface of a canal, at least in my mind. Stop wandering, da Silva.

We found another cab without her getting splashed too much, which was lucky, because the next minute the skies opened again and within seconds the rain was teeming down once more. I listened to the horse's hooves rather smugly, peering through the steamy window at people who hadn't been so lucky.

In the hotel lobby I shook rain off my hat. I was about to make a probably doomed attempt to persuade Emilia to stay downstairs, when Zé emerged from behind a pillar.

"Thank goodness you came," he blurted out. Half-exalted, half-anxious. No, anxious doesn't come close. Frantic is a better word. His voice cracked in the middle, and all he did was give a small frown.

Emilia looked from him to me, raised her eyebrows slightly, and smiled. Then she lowered herself, with a small sigh, onto an uncomfortable-looking couch. One of those hard overstuffed things with the spindly legs. I lit a cheroot.

"How was she?" I asked Zé, who was hopping up and down with impatience. Or, as it turned out, excitement. He was bursting to tell me how he'd bribed his way into her room. I do call that using his initiative. But we had to hear the whole story.

"And then she flopped back down again," he finished in a breathless whisper. "And that bellhop cleaned me out, by the way, so you owe me—"

"I'll refund your money, you extortionist," I said, going to finger the cut on my head and changing direction when I caught Emilia's eye. Rubbed my cheekbone instead. "Right now we need to check again. She might've woken up."

Zé bounced on his heels, eyes alight with interest. "Really? How? What's the matter with her, anyway? You said you were going to tell me."

"I will," I promised, knocking ash off the end of my cheroot. "That was well done, by the way." He wasn't to be put off, though.

"You're trying to put me off," he said accusingly, and I grinned. He's getting to know me too well. Have to change strategy, da Silva.

But later. "You may be right, but you'll still have to wait. What's her room number?"

"Hundred and ten."

"Then go up and knock on the door again." I took off my overcoat and draped it over the back of Emilia's seat, then sat down carefully next to her, half-expecting the couch to collapse. Ninety pounds of Emilia, yes. Hundred and sixty of me, risky. But it held.

She turned to me, and I wanted to kiss her. Or at least put my arms round her. Couldn't even do that.

"You must be careful," she said starkly, eyes open wide. "Promise me, Luís, we don't have any idea what—"

"Ssh," I said, putting a finger to her lips. "I wouldn't have sent Zé up there if I thought he'd come to any harm."

"I know," she whispered.

I took a drag on my cheroot. Take her mind off it, da Silva. As if she won't see through anything I say. Have to try, though. "What d'you make of Alegria?"

Emilia played along, with a small smile that said she appreciated the effort. Even if it didn't work. "Oh, now, that was a strange thing. I've met real live people with less depth than Alegria." She paused. "Let me see now. Affection, gratitude, fear—"

"Fear?" I echoed. "Of what?"

"Of not being there any more. Isn't that strange, she's afraid of death, like any human. She's afraid that if that demon is banished, she'll cease to exist."

The elevator went *ping* before I could contemplate this, and Zé emerged from the cage. I stubbed my cheroot out and got to my feet, looking a question at him. He shook his head. I squeezed Emilia's shoulder, and her fingers brushed mine as I moved off to meet him halfway.

"No answer," he said. I nodded and turned away, but he caught my sleeve. "Wait." He looked round furtively, then quickly took something out of his pocket and slipped it into mine. I didn't recognize the heavy weight until I put my hand in to investigate.

And found my revolver. I raised my eyebrows. "What the hell were you doing with that?" Zé gave an unrepentant shrug.

"She's a witch, and you told me you don't trust her," he explained in an undertone. I should tan his hide. But I can't fault his logic. And to tell the truth, I'm glad to have it.

Knowing my son, he read all those thoughts. So I ruffled his hair in retaliation, making him scowl and duck away, and said, "Thanks."

I examined myself briefly in an ornate mirror with a baroque gilded frame. Ran a hand over my damp and rumpled hair. Tugged impotently at the collar and tie. Couldn't do anything about my face. Turned away, pulling down my shirt-cuffs and hoped I looked enough like a respectable businessman — well, a businessman at any rate — to get past the ogre at the door. Or, to put it another way, the hotel receptionist.

Who was a small weedy man with a face like an overbred rabbit. He ignored me until I rang the bell, then looked up with a smirk that grew rather fixed as he took in my appearance. So much for power games.

"Can I help you, senhor?"

"Lady in room hundred and ten," I said. "I think she might be unwell. She missed an appointment."

"I'll see if there's a message. What name, senhor?"

"Da Silva," I said. "Captain da Silva."

He turned and rummaged, coming up with nothing, of course. "I'm sorry, senhor." Not that he sounded it in the least. They never do.

"Then I'll need someone with a passkey." The receptionist looked scandalized. As if I'd asked him to organize a whore for me. This is a *respectable* establishment, senhor.

"Oh, I can't authorize—"

"The manager?" I suggested, giving him the benefit of the da Silva stare. The one that says, I'm not going away, so ignoring me isn't an option. Neither is fobbing me off with anything less than what I want. Hell, I look like a thug at the moment. Might as well capitalize on it. Rabbit-face blinked, and dropped his gaze.

"Just a moment, please." He snapped his fingers, and a pimply bellhop appeared. I wondered if it was Zé's friend. If friend is the right word. Still young enough to be fascinated by an eyepatch. Or, come to that, a battered face. You can't wink when you've only got one eye, but I raised an eyebrow and grinned conspiratorially at him. Bet he's had the sharp side of the receptionist's tongue more than once.

This time he satisfied himself with telling the boy shortly to fetch Sr. Marques. I presumed this was the manager. The bellhop winked at me, cheeky brat, and sauntered off. I leaned on the counter and lit a cheroot.

Rabbit-face looked as if he'd have liked to tell me where to stick it, but didn't have the nerve. At length a sweating fat man, who turned out to be the manager, appeared from an inner office and started to quiz me. I cut him short.

"I don't have any time to waste standing round here, Sr. Marques. If the lady's ill, we need to do something about it."

He tried to outstare me, but that contest was lost before it began.

"Very well," he said. "I'll take you up myself."

"Fine. Lead on, then." I caught Emilia's eye. She waved her hand slightly, *You go on.* I nodded, and smiled. Followed Marques to the elevator. For one floor. No wonder he's got a backside the size of the island of Madeira.

Sharing the elevator, even for one floor, with the scent of the hotel manager's hair pomade, made me feel slightly nauseous. I shot a glance at the elevator operator, a wizened little man who looked like a shaved monkey. Decided his nose had probably been desensitized over years of sharing a space the size of a cupboard with variously perfumed humanity.

There was no reply to Marques's rap at the door of room one hundred and ten. So he made a ceremony out of producing his passkey. Which made me want to plant a boot on his ample backside. The click of the key turning in the lock gave me a twinge of apprehension. More than a twinge, to be quite honest. I thought that if she'd been all right, she would've answered Zé's knock. But she hadn't. And she was still silent.

What would I find? Had she succeeded? And if she has, what is she now?

"Senhora?" the manager called, tentatively, pushing the door open a crack. "Are you all right?" No answer. He turned to me unhappily. "Shall I call a doctor, senhor capitão?" No, damn it, just get your fat backside out of here.

"Let me see how she is first," I said. He loitered. "It's all right, Sr. Marques. You can leave everything to me now."

"Very well, senhor capitão." I pushed the door open. Looked after Marques as an afterthought. He scuttled ponderously towards the elevator and pressed the button.

I waited until the operator had closed the gates behind him, then walked into Tatiana Dimitrovna's room, shutting the door quietly. All was deathly silent. The room was dim, like twilight. It smelt warm and slightly stale. No hint of brimstone, then.

She was silhouetted against the window, but there was no light to silhouette her. I turned on the electric light.

"Tatiana Dimitrovna?" I said softly. She whirled round, and in that instant her face showed what it would be like when she was a hundred years dead. The shape of the skull stark and under a mummy's paper-thin leather skin, flesh eaten away. The eyesockets hollow as the grave. The lips shrunk back over long yellow teeth. It was only a moment's vision, but my heart came into my mouth and I heard a ragged gasp drag out of my throat.

And she came at me, hands outstretched like claws, black hair loose about her face, screaming in a high inhuman voice that made me want to stop my ears.

Revolver forgotten — it never even occurred to me — I grabbed her wrists. Had to keep her nails out of my face. It was like holding a couple of steel hawsers, no softness of flesh there. And meu Deus, she was strong. She wrestled me with the frenzy of a cornered beast. Her face was inches from mine, eyes now flat and black, now spinning with sparks like fireworks. Mouth open, stretched with her keening scream, spittle flying. The sound alone made the nape of my neck crawl.

Her momentum carried me backwards to crash solidly against the wall.

The impact made me swear. But I could bounce off it and get some momentum of my own. Which is what I did. I pushed her violently back as far as the bed and hooked one foot round behind her ankle to unbalance her. At the same time she tried to knee me in the groin. Missed, luckily. With the result that we both fell on the bed, with me on top.

At least I could pin her with my weight. I hoped. She was so insanely strong I wasn't even sure of that. She wrestled her left wrist out of my hand and caught me a resounding thump on the side of the head. The side that was bruised already, of course. I would've sworn if I'd had any breath left. I pinned her other hand down and caught her wrist again. Flinging her head from side to side, she tried to bite me. I heard her teeth snap shut, again and again. She bucked on the bed, nearly throwing me off.

Hell, at this rate she was going to wear me out before I got her under control. I dragged her hands over her head and caught both wrists together, freeing my left hand. This seemed to be a cue to struggle even harder. I punched her hard in the jaw. Couldn't think of anything else to do.

Her head snapped to the side and she went limp under me. Breathing heavily, I collapsed across her.

Suddenly realized where I was. In a hotel bedroom, lying across a woman wearing nothing but a thin nightgown. And having a totally inappropriate reaction, considering the circumstances. I pushed myself up hastily, cursing under my breath. Now I was only straddling her. Not a great improvement, da Silva.

Tatiana Dimitrovna opened her eyes and looked up at me. Then down at herself. Her nightdress was rucked up over her thighs. I stayed, frozen, where I was.

"This is a fine time to pick to have your wicked way with me," she said huskily, and laughed. I released her wrists. That's the Russian witch I know, all right.

Then she grabbed me by the hair and pulled my head down, opening her mouth under mine. I tasted salt. Disentangled her hand and broke loose, rolled off her rapidly, and sat up. Not going to try standing yet, thank you. I leaned forward, elbows on knees.

"Tatiana," I said, not trusting myself to say any more. Except that it came out imploring, rather than admonitory. I felt her hand slide up my back, inside my shirt, and shivered.

"You do want me, don't you," she whispered. Damn it, I've never denied that. Just, will never act on it. I reached to my right and pulled her nightgown down to cover her thighs. She laughed again. I shut my eye, took a deep breath, and opened it again.

"I would say, go to hell," I said, turning my head to look at her over my shoulder, "but you've already been there."

She thought that was immensely funny.

All that took, I should think, no more than five minutes. If that. After a moment, Tatiana Dimitrovna stopped laughing and sat up. She reached out her hand. Turned my head to face hers. Her warm fingers trailed across my scar, my cheek, my chin.

"I'm glad it was you," she said, quiet and seriously. "I knew it would be bad — coming back. I just hoped you'd find out about the desk in time."

"Damn the desk," I retorted. "I thought I was going to have to come after you."

She touched my lips. "Don't ever try and go," she said. "You don't have enough... darkness in you, not any more." What does she mean, not any more? She paused, and I heard her swallow. "Even I had barely enough."

"Did you get what you went for?" I asked bitterly.

"I think I can deal with Munro now," she replied, her eyes glittering. "I can even command a demon as a familiar and not end up in its thrall, so I'm told. Although I don't think I'll put that to the test. But it seems I didn't come back with my heart's desire. *Boizhe moi,* even hell cheats you in the end." Shouldn't that be *especially* hell?

I don't want to go any further down that route. Or am I flattering myself about her heart's desire? Vanity, after all, da Silva. I merely said, "Munro's here. Already." It didn't surprise her. But then, would anything, now?

She held me with her gaze. "Do you know what he wants?" As if I'd know. Who does she think I am, a mind-reader? I raised my eyebrows.

"Don't you?"

"We could assume it's just to finish what he started with us, but I have the feeling it's more than that." Oh, good. And I suppose this one wants to rule the world. Well, slight improvement there. The last sorcerer I went up against wanted to *end* it. I rubbed a hand over my face. Touched the bruise gingerly. My head was throbbing like a steam-hammer.

"Well, I've no idea," I said irritably. "What gives you that impression?"

"They gave me something to say to you." To me, specifically? I don't like the sound of that. "Well, not by name! You understand that it's not that specific," she added, perhaps reading my face. Or my mind.

"Don't tell me, there are no such things as coincidences," I retorted. But then perhaps I've not said that to her before. She frowned slightly. Touched my face again.

"No, there aren't," she agreed, and fell silent. I didn't say anything. She'll get round to it in her own time, I expect. Whatever *it* is. I sighed, suddenly exhausted. And stale, and let down, and frustrated. Could do with a smoke, too.

After a moment, I said, "Tatiana—" but she cut me off with a hand on my leg.

"There's more than one power at work here," she said slowly. "Everything is muddy. I'm sure this has some significance, though, so I'll tell you. *'The child is born knowing four words.'* That's all. Does it mean anything to you?"

The child. Only one child I'm aware of. Ana Sobral's daughter, Susana. But what Tatiana Dimitrovna's prophecy means, I haven't a clue.

"There is a child," I told her. "Last year—" No, it'd take too long to tell the full story. "The mother was… was raped. The father was possessed at the time."

"Possessed," she repeated. "By what?"

"It called itself Mouffi," I said.

The witch shook her head, and hugged her arms around herself as if suddenly cold. Then she got up from the bed and bent to retrieve her dressing-gown from the floor.

"Not the name of any demon I know."

"How many do you know?" I enquired.

She tied the sash of her robe and looked down at me with an expression that didn't have much humanity in it. Or much amusement. "Enough," she said flatly. What did she go through, in Hell? Do I really want to know? Always supposing she'd tell me. I scratched at my scar and wished, again, for a smoke. Decided it was time to leave. Past time. I got to my feet.

"What now?" I asked her.

"You tell me," she replied, softly. "I take it you want my help?" Not if it means being in her debt. Who knows what she'll ask in return.

"Dealing with Munro's as much in your interests as mine," I said, taking a quick look at myself in the mirror. Tidied myself up quickly. As well as I could, anyway. Some things you just can't remedy instantly.

"Of course it is. I meant with the other matters." And what other matters would those be? I've only told her about the father of Ana's child.

"It might not be me needing your help." Thinking about last night's encounter. And maybe it is me asking for help. Since I can't see the police calling her in.

"We need to discuss it more," she said. "But not here, not now. Why don't you wait downstairs, and I'll join you when I've gotten dressed?"

She's right, of course. I can't turn down an offer of help out of fear. Because that's all it is. But I've always been afraid of her, one way or another.

7

RAIN SLUICED DOWN THE WINDOW, AND THE THIN WIND MADE IT RATTLE IN ITS FRAME. There was no space in the room to pace, even though now Harris's makeshift bed was gone from the floor. Pierce was making up for it, getting up from his chair every five minutes and staring at the rain from a different angle.

"Where the devil is he?" he demanded for the twentieth time. Harris, smoking placidly, decided — as he had the previous fifteen or so times — to treat the question as rhetorical, and didn't bother to reply.

Zacuto, being a ghost, had more patience than the antiquarian, but even he gave off a sort of aura of urgency.

"Surely the captain should be back by now?" he said mildly.

Jesus, now they're both at it. The American sighed. "They went to see the wine fellow, Williams. And sure, I'd'a thought they shoulda been back. But hell, I'm only manning the telephone." *Or wolfing it, if you like.*

Which hadn't rung, not that even the skipper had thought it would. But as Emilia pointed out, we should at least look as if we're running a business. Harris knocked a long tail of ash off his cigarette, and stubbed it out.

"What if Munro's turned up?" worried Pierce, turning from the window and fiddling with his spectacles.

If he takes those goddamned things off again, I swear I'll take 'em and jump on 'em.

"Did Captain da Silva say he was going anywhere else?" Zacuto asked, and Harris felt like biting something.

"Not to me," he ground out, between his teeth.

Pierce sat down again, took off his spectacles, and began to polish them with his handkerchief. Harris rolled his eyes.

"He really needs to know what we've found," the Englishman said worriedly. Again for about the twentieth time.

Jesus Christ on a bicycle crossing Brooklyn Bridge, don't they ever stop? It's like that Chinese water torture. Drip, drip, drip.

"Sr. Harris," Zacuto said, breaking into his exasperated thoughts.

"Yeah?"

The ghost paused for a moment as if trying out the shape of a phrase. "Do your... wolf-senses remain with you while you are in human shape?"

Nice of him to remind me that I ain't human anymore. Still, no skin off my nose — he ain't, either. Harris nodded cautiously, being as wary of volunteering for anything as the next man. Or wolf. "Why?"

"Could you track the captain?"

Aw Jesus. Shoulda seen that coming, goddamn it. "Guess I could," he said. "But I promised to stay here."

"Damn it, I can answer a telephone," Pierce burst out. "Will you go and find him?"

"And tell him what?" asked Harris, taking out another cigarette and lighting it. Pierce and Zacuto exchanged glances. *And what's that about?*

"That we think we know what this Munro is up to," said Zacuto patiently.

"Yeah, and then what? He needs to talk to the organ-grinder, not the monkey."

"Well, he will," snapped Pierce, "if you bring him back here."

Still seems like adding in a middle-man when you don't need one. "So tell me the plot already," said Harris irritably.

"It is a little complicated," Zacuto said, and Harris ran his hands through his bushy red hair in exasperation. *Shitfire, there's nothing wrong with my brain. Except for not getting itself to grips with Portuguese, a'course.*

"What isn't complicated, when the skipper's involved?" he asked with a short barking laugh. "Try me."

Ghost and antiquarian exchanged another look, which was beginning to annoy Harris a great deal. Then Zacuto gave a very human-sounding sigh.

"Very well," he said, and went into what Harris called teacher mode. "Do you know the legend of the Fisher King, Sr. Harris?"

*   *   *

Ana watched Dr Bosque without thinking much about what he was doing, all that prodding and measuring and weighing business little Susana has to go through at regular intervals holds little interest for her. She is not stupid by any means, she knows that delivering an apparently full-term infant after seven months makes both her and the baby objects of interest, and supposes that she is thankful it is only Dr Bosque who is doing the poking and prying.

"She's putting on weight a little faster than I'd expect," the doctor said to her with a reassuring smile. "And I *think* she's progressing more quickly in general." But it might not be abnormal, for every slow developer there's one like this, it's really to early to tell if there's any abnormality. Logic told him this.

Instinct, however, told him otherwise. And he was sure baby Susana was looking at him with far more awareness than she should have had at her age.

He wondered about possession. He certainly didn't discount it. The evangelists may have been as zealous in Mozambique, where he'd lived for sixteen years, as in every other Portuguese colony, but local religions have a habit of surviving. His patients, even the ones who called themselves Catholics, had evolved a rich mixture of tribal beliefs, folk traditions, and whatever bits of Christianity they thought fitted in. As far as he could make out, Christ had ended up as part of the pantheon, but not necessarily a terribly important god among many. Which was a view he could sympathize with. Why should the great god Pan be dead, anyway? But the point was, he'd seen cases of possession, and not all of them could be explained away as medical conditions, mental illness, or an over-active imagination.

What if Susana *is* possessed? Dr Bosque wasn't inclined to entrust her to an exorcism, no matter what religion. Bell, book and candle or witch-doctor, with a child that tiny it would be a bit like using a sledgehammer to crack a nut. He fell into a common trap in thinking this, that of assuming that an infant's soul is proportionately small; but Mouffi was not truly possessing her, so his instincts were right.

Susana, obviously fed up with his attentions, began to cry.

"All right, *pequena*, all right," he said, relinquishing control to her mother, who cuddled her dutifully enough, but he still thought she was only going through the motions.

When they'd gone, he put his head round the door and said to Teresa, "I'm going out for a while. Just thought of something. Can you hold the fort?"

Teresa, bored, looked up from the novel she was reading and nodded. She almost wished something would happen. That little Susana *had* been born with horns and a tail. She has, herself, no talent for magic, but she knows a great deal about it, given her upbringing. It would have been — she caught herself before she framed the word *fun* and substituted *interesting*.

Last year wasn't fun, she admonished herself, remembering with a wince of disgust her transformation into the armored guardian of the first amulet. Her father had used her, and if he'd still been alive, she would never have forgiven him. But he was dead, and she had killed him herself, so she supposed forgiveness was pretty much mandatory. He'd been so much a tool of the demons that he'd thought were his servants, in the end, that she hardly felt she'd killed a man, let alone her own father. She still missed him, though.

She looked at the rain again, sighed, and returned to her book.

Dr Bosque, meanwhile, under an umbrella which failed to shelter anything lower than his chest from the driving rain, was beginning to regret the impulse which had prompted him to head for an address near the docks. Surely he could have waited until tomorrow, or at least for the rain to stop, not that it looks as if it is going to stop any time soon. His wet pants-legs molded to his shins, and inside his shoes and soggy socks his feet squelched. If Teresa missed Rio constantly, he missed Mozambique when the weather was like this. Although he had known bad floods there, at least the water that falls out of the sky in the tropics is warm.

He had to pause and get his bearings more than once. Though he has visited this address before, it is hidden in a maze of streets as intricate, in its way, as the Alfama. Not out of any particular wish the occupant has for concealment, even though some of the narrower inhabitants of the city might be worth hiding from; and he has reason enough to hide, though not from them, but simply because of the nature of the area.

The man he had come to see was called Leão, though there was nothing particularly leonine about him, and he was a witch-doctor. Inácio Bosque always made it his habit to contact the local shaman wherever he went, and Lisbon was no exception.

In consulting Leão, he didn't feel he was going behind Teresa's back. He knew what her father had been, of course, and knew that she was at least acquainted with some of the local practitioners. But he'd been only peripherally involved with the events of the previous June, to the extent that he didn't actually know that he himself had been the guardian of an amulet for a time. What he wanted, in this case, was a fresh perspective.

Having arrived at his destination after not too many wrong turns, he knocked at the door. After a few moments a woman's voice called out huskily, "Who is it?"

"Dr Bosque," he replied. Presently he heard a key turn in the lock, and the door opened to let him in. He remembered the woman, who was very tall and thin with aquiline features and skin so dark it was almost the color of coal. She was wrapped in yellow cotton that contrasted with her like sun and earth.

"He expecting you?" she asked, looking him up and down as if she were a lioness and he some gazelle she fancied for lunch. He shook his head. "Wait here, then. You can leave your coat and things."

The place, even under that sullen sky, smelled of remembered spices, an odor that took him back instantly and nostalgically, though it lacked one ingredient: the particular tang that a cow-dung fire would have added to it — such things are not easily come by in the metropolis. But there was nothing in the room to show that someone from an entirely different culture lived there. The furniture was all second-hand, though not ancient; no pictures hung on the walls. Dr Bosque knew better than to expect animal-skin décor and spears adorning the place, but he was aware of a vague feeling of disappointment all the same.

That inchoate sense of a thing missing or missed, even if it was only an opportunity, was compounded by the witch-doctor's appearance. He hadn't exactly westernized himself so far as to wear a business suit, but he was wearing shirt and pants. His feet were, however, bare.

Leão was the sort of man you would pass in the street without a second glance. Even though they'd met before, Dr Bosque found himself regretting something unidentifiable. No reason why a shaman should look impressive, after all.

"I remember you," he said. His voice was deep and resonant, with only the merest trace of an accent. "You have a mind like a sponge, it absorbs everything and believes nothing."

The doctor didn't know whether this was a compliment or an insult.

"Better than a mind in blinkers," he countered. The tall woman snorted. Leão turned to her with a smile.

"You remember Julia," he said. Dr Bosque inclined his head politely. He found her fascinating, a human frame stripped to its essentials, with a statuesque beauty that transcended her angular scowl. You saw women like her infrequently, and they stayed in the mind a long time. "Why are you here?" Leão asked him, and he pulled his mind back to the present.

"I wanted to ask your opinion about something."

The shaman laughed. His upper left incisor was made of gold. "The doctor wants a second opinion? About what?"

Dr Bosque adjusted his spectacles. The thick lenses were heavy and they tended to travel down his nose. They had also steamed up again, though he'd wiped them when he came in. "Possession," he said.

Leão narrowed his eyes and subjected his visitor to a long raking stare that seemed to bore through the bones of the doctor's skull. "Possession," he repeated. "What can I tell you that the sorcerers of Europe cannot?"

"I don't know the sorcerers of Europe," said Dr Bosque sharply. "I know you. I know Africa… better than Europe."

Julia made a disbelieving noise, but said nothing. He watched her bony gracefulness as she lit a cigarette.

"You have seen people who are possessed? You believe in possession?" asked Leão. Dr Bosque nodded in reply to both questions. "Then what is it you want to ask me?"

"It's a child, less than a month old."

"So," said the witch-doctor, taking the lighted cigarette from Julia. His brown skin, next to hers, looked almost pale. His hands were small for a man's, hers large for a woman; they were almost the same size. "Cannot be possessed. Possession requires consent. Little baby like that can't say yes or no."

"Good," Dr Bosque said shortly, wishing his feet were drier.

"Might be something waiting, though," Leão added, thoughtfully. "You're sensing something, else you wouldn't be here." He eyed the other man shrewdly. "Who do you not trust?"

The doctor looked back, startled. Trust? He trusted Teresa, and she is the only person close enough for him to mistrust, but he hadn't told her he was coming here, had he, and is that what Leão means? "What do you mean?"

After blowing a smoke-ring, Leão smiled, but the smile didn't reach his eyes. "Doctor, maybe you lived a long time in Africa, but you're still a white man. Takes a lot of fear to come so far outside your own people."

With a short, irritated sigh, Dr Bosque got to his feet. "I'm sorry," he said stiffly. "I made a mistake."

"Sit down," the shaman told him, peremptorily. He did as he was told, a little surprised at himself. "Do you think you are the only person to have sensed what has been happening? What happened last year?"

"Last year?" echoed the doctor uncomfortably. He didn't like the feeling that he'd somehow lost the initiative, but can you ever have the upper hand when talking to a sorcerer?

"Demons, doctor," Leão said. "Too many of them. Some are gone. Some remain. You're afraid for this child, you make damn sure you guard her."

He breathed a sigh of relief. "How?" he asked.

"Well, since you ask, I can give you something to help," said the witch-doctor judiciously. "If you can pay. If you are willing to pay."

Now we come to it, he thought, a little sad that this man turned out to be as venal as the rest of humanity. "What is the price?"

"Ah, the price." Leão opened his eyes very wide, and took a long drag from his cigarette. "I think — a promise."

Regretting the impulse that had brought him here, Dr Bosque stared at the other man, who returned the gaze with a slight smile. "A promise?"

"When I need you, I'll call you," said the shaman. "You promise to come. That's all. I may never even need to do it."

It is not sixteen years in Africa that makes him reluctant to agree to this, but the knowledge that no one who seeks power is to be trusted. He hesitated.

The woman, Julia, said contemptuously, "He won't make the pledge." But her sculpted face was unreadable.

"Why would you want me under an obligation?" Dr Bosque asked, but the word he wanted to use was *geas*.

"Because everyone of good intent may be needed soon, doctor," said Leão. "Hear me, I say I may never need to call you. But if I do, it means you *are* needed. War is coming. And not just the kind of war the German Kaiser wants."

"I don't understand." He felt sweat break out along his hairline, as at a threat identified, the sense of a predator nearby. The shaman ground out his cigarette, crossed his legs, and leant back in his chair.

"The land is falling apart," he said. "It needs... a king. A father. You don't have a word for this. Someone linked to it, someone who is responsible for its well-being. Sorcerers come, they weave their magics, whether they succeed or fail it leaves scars and echoes. Sooner or later, there will come a crisis. And then, goodwill may just save the day. It may be, doctor, that you are part of our final hope."

Well, that's pleasant, thought Dr Bosque, his scalp prickling. I came here to find out if little Susana might be in trouble and I get a warning about the apocalypse.

*　*　*

I admit I was a bit worried about the thought of introducing Tatiana Dimitrovna to Emilia. I'd never thought the pair of them were ever likely to meet. But it just goes to show you shouldn't take anything for granted. And you ought to've known that, da Silva.

Guilt is a peculiar thing. I don't really think I ought to feel guilty over the Russian witch, but I do. Damn it.

Emilia, in my absence, had charmed the hotel staff into bringing her coffee. I stood for a moment looking at her. Something I never get tired of doing, even after nearly twenty years of being married. Meu Deus, where does the time go?

Quick check in the mirror, again. Guilt, again. What did I expect? Look exactly the same as the last time I checked. Of course. Still no writing on my forehead. I lit a cheroot, and went to join Emilia and Zé.

And saw Harris push his way out of the revolving doors into the lobby. What the devil is he doing here? Come to that, how did he find me, assuming it is me he's looking for and he hasn't come for an assignation. Which, given the way he looks at Luzia, is unlikely. Werewolf in love. Ha. *Quem diria.*

He caught my eye and nodded in a satisfied sort of way. Must've tracked me. I gestured towards Emilia, who saw the movement and looked round. Her eyebrows went up when she spotted Harris. Zé shot me a glance full of intense curiosity. And I'm going to have to tell him *something*. Can't put it off much longer.

We converged on them, Harris and I. Be a jolly little party when Tatiana Dimitrovna turns up. With da Silva in the middle. What fun.

Putting a hand on Emilia's shoulder, which she covered briefly with her own, I said, "And what brings Sr. Harris here?"

"Got a message from the Professor," he said, touching his cap to Emilia.

"*Bom dia,* Sr. Harris," she said mischievously.

Harris gave an embarrassed cough, and muttered, "*Bom dia.*" Then he turned back to me and said, "It's 'bout young Ana's kid."

The child is born knowing four words…

Oh *merda.*

Zé glared murderously at Harris. Another interruption. I lifted an eyebrow at him, and said, "Better pull up a chair, Harris. Looks like we're going to be here for a while." Though whether one of those spindly chairs'll hold him, I'm not at all sure. "And bring another while you're at it. Tatiana Dimitrovna'll be joining us at some stage."

"Been busy, skipper?" he asked dryly. I grinned at him.

"Something like that," I said. Yes, *busy* could just about cover it.

"Senhor capitão," said a voice behind me, and I turned to see Marques, the manager. "The lady, is she well?"

Almost tempted to say, *as well as you could expect after a trip to Hell.* Instead, I just nodded. "Thank you, yes." He loitered, like a waiter hoping for a tip. I ignored him and lit a cheroot. "How's the leg, Harris?" I asked.

"Dandy," he replied. Whatever that means. Harrisian is a dialect all its own. I'm willing to bet not everyone from Boston talks like he does. But I had no time to ponder about linguistics, because Tatiana Dimitrovna was coming down the stairs.

She looked severe and professional, like a lady ambassador, if you can imagine such a thing. Wearing a sharply tailored outfit. If the oleaginous Marques had got the impression, from my talk of missed appointments, that the guest in room hundred and ten was a whore, that alone must've persuaded him otherwise. I got to my feet and gave her a bow. Da Silva, being polite. Well, it's been known.

"Captain da Silva," she said, haughty and formal.

"Tatiana Dimitrovna," I replied. Tried to match the tone. "My wife, Emilia. Sr. Harris, *Isabella*'s second mate." Her eyes narrowed slightly. She knew what he was. "My son you already know." She smiled warmly at Zé and inclined her head to Emilia politely. Ignored Harris completely.

*   *   *

So this is the woman, thought Emilia. *Should I be jealous? I think perhaps I am, a little.* Exotic-looking. A mixture of Slavic and Chinese. She let her still-new sense probe the Russian witch, cautiously, the memory of the raw stinking rottenness that was Munro still sore and aching in her mind. But there was nothing like that here.

There was a potential for darkness, real darkness, it was true, but an unexpected sense of humor was keeping it at bay. Maybe the trip to hell has heightened her emotions, they are fierce things, lust that almost makes Emilia blush, white-hot delight in her strength, incandescent hatred of Munro, and intense curiosity. This last directed at her, at Emilia.

Who withdrew quickly, exhilarated and surprised by the mind she'd encountered, and saw Tatiana Dimitrovna smiling coolly, hiding the furnaces within.

*   *   *

"Forgive my bluntness," said the Russian witch. "We are all on the same side." She glanced suspiciously at Harris, who looked miffed. "We all have one purpose. Sir Robert Munro must be stopped. Whatever it is he's up to."

Harris leaned forward, scowling. Looking rather like a bear that had decided to perch on a child's chair. He's not that enormous. Six feet tall, heavy build. But hell, Marques the hotel manager probably weighs more than he does.

"Believe I can shed some light on that one," he growled. That got her attention. "There's this prophecy." I looked up, startled. Though why, I don't know.

"The one that Pierce—" I began.

"That's the pup." He nodded his head. "They managed to track some of it down, those two." He dug in his pocket and pulled out a piece of paper. Handed it to me with a wolfish grin. "You're gonna love it, skipper."

I raised an eyebrow at him, took a drag on my cheroot, and unfolded the page. Read the first line. *"In the year that is a hundred years after the bear's victory the wounded king may be reborn."* Glared at Harris. "Óptimo," I said, sourly. "Do they have any idea what it means, or is working it out all part of the fun?"

"Hey, this is Pierce and the Professor we're talking about here, skipper," he reminded me. "Those two think this kinda thing *is* fun. Day ain't worthwhile less'n they've figured out three mysterious riddles before breakfast. But yeah, they come up with the goods. You ever hear of a fellow called the Fisher King?"

"No," I said. Looked round at the others. Only the witch looked as if she might, but she didn't say anything. I gave my eyebrow a scratch, more out of habit than because it was itching or anything.

Harris cleared his throat. "Okay. Lemme see if I can get this thing straight. This is old, old stuff, right? Pagan, the Professor says. All that Holy Grail stuff, that came later. This is the real McCoy. The original." Accept no substitutes, I thought, irrelevantly. "So. Fisher King, wounded king, same fellow. Linked to the land, somehow. Not clear how that works, but it makes him a pretty powerful customer. Except that while he ain't well, the land's sick too. With me so far?"

"Go on," I said.

"What the Professor thinks is, Munro wants to be the new one. That year of the bear stuff is this year, he says. Something to do with Napoleon, according to Pierce." Tatiana Dimitrovna was nodding.

"The Russian bear," she said, almost to herself. I looked back down at the paper I was holding in my hand.

"By the coming together of the four hallows may he be made whole." Zacuto had said something about hallows. I raised my head and frowned at Harris. "Hallows?"

"Jesus, what were they?" he muttered. "Cup, plate — oh yeah. Spear and broken sword. He gets his hands on 'em, it cures the wound and gives him the power."

There's always a kind of logic to these things. Even if the rules are mad, they always follow their own rules. They drive me berserk sometimes. Should be thankful for it, da Silva. I got rid of the remains of my cheroot in a plant-pot.

"And all this stuff at the end makes Zacuto and Pierce think the child is Ana's baby?" Harris nodded. I looked at Tatiana Dimitrovna. "Tell 'em what you told me."

"They told me something as I was leaving," she said slowly. I don't even want to know who *they* are. "They said, *the child is born knowing four words.*"

Four words, four hallows. I rubbed my cheekbone. "Teresa Batista needs to know this."

"Who is Teresa Batista?" asked the Russian witch. I groaned inwardly. Ran a hand though my hair. Oh God. How many more things do I have to do? And how the hell do I sort out which to do first?

Delegate, da Silva. You're the damn captain. Give some orders.

"Zé," I said. "Go to Dr Bosque's and tell Teresa that Susana's in danger."

"And what else can I tell her?" he enquired. "I don't know what's going on. You said you'd tell me, and you haven't."

True enough. "You heard what Sr. Harris said," I told him. "That's all you need, for now. Munro's bound to track her down." I turned to Tatiana Dimitrovna. "Can you do anything to protect the child?"

Her eyes flashed. "Not from here." Zé brightened.

"You could come with me," he suggested. The witch looked at me narrowly.

"So you are asking for my help?" She really does want me to owe her a debt. Well, she's not going to get it from this. I took out a cheroot and pointed it at her.

"You don't want Munro to get that kind of power, do you?" She shook her head. "Then you'd better make sure he doesn't get his hands on that baby."

"Very well," she said after a pause, while I lit the cheroot. "I see the sense in that." Got to her feet. "Come along, young man, we have an errand to run."

He leapt up. "Will *you* tell me what's going on?" he asked, with a triumphant glance in my direction. I tried not to smile. Appreciated his persistence. It reminds me of me. And you have to admit, he's consistent.

"If your father says I can," she replied, raising her eyebrows at me. I nodded. She turned to go. I called her name, and she looked back at me.

"When you've done that," I said, holding out one of my father's cards, "there's something you ought to see." Well, two things, really. If you can call Alegria a thing. And I don't think I can. "Meet me at this address."

She took the card. "Sebastian da Silva?" she asked curiously, ending the name with a hard *n* sound.

"My father," I explained. Her eyes widened. But I'm not telling her anything just now. Leave her guessing.

"All right," she said, when she realized she wasn't getting anything more out of me. "I will see you there. In two hours."

"She's not at all what I expected," said Emilia when Zé and the witch had gone. I blew out smoke and fingered the cut on my head gingerly.

"What *were* you expecting, a broomstick and a warty nose?" I asked.

"No, otherwise I'd be really worried about your taste in women," she shot back. Harris gave a short bark of laughter, and I raised an eyebrow at him. "You never said what she looked like. I suppose I was expecting someone less... exotic."

"She knows what it's like to be a wolf," said Harris suddenly.

"What?"

He gave an embarrassed cough, and shrugged. "Don't ask me how I know, skipper. But she's a shape-shifter."

Well, you never know when that'll come in handy.

Emilia finished off her coffee and put the cup back in the saucer with a clink. Took hold of the handle of her stick. "I'd better be getting home. Rescue the Da Silva Shipping Line from the tender mercies of Sr. Pierce's caretaking."

Harris colored. "I didn't mean—"

"It's all right, Harris," I said, moving to give Emilia my hand. "She's teasing you. Is Zacuto with Pierce?" He nodded.

"Couldn't prize 'em apart with a crowbar."

Then home's the next port of call. And it's not even lunchtime yet.

* * *

Ricardo Corvo wished fervently that the nausea in his belly and the pain in his head had been caused by a hangover, and the events imprinted in his brain were the memory of a drunken dream. But neither of those things was true, and he knew it. His world-view had just undergone a sea-change, and he was sick with it.

He sat in his poky office and stared out at the rain, smoking morosely. On his desk the piles of paperwork gave a comforting illusion of industry and productivity, and indeed there was no shortage of casework to engage his attention. But his mind was full of other things.

What in God's name had it been? Captain da Silva, who seemed to know something at least, if it was only how to move through this new world, hadn't been able to enlighten him. He didn't quite know what to make of the captain. Or the fact that — had he really said his companion was a werewolf? It was too big to've been a dog. Wasn't it?

Corvo groaned silently and put his head in his hands. This was one report he wasn't going to be able to write. On the plus side, though, it seemed there hadn't been another murder last night.

No, he thought, but there damned nearly was, and the memory of the dreadful fear he'd felt came back to haunt him. Not the fear itself, for luckily we can never bring our minds to imagine terror, but the fact that he had felt it at all. He removed a strand of tobacco from his lower lip, mashed out the end of his cigarette, and took out another without thinking. Reached a conclusion as he lit it, one he should have acted on last night.

I need the full story, he thought. If the world really is full of goblins and werewolves — and ghosts and vampires and bloody pixies, for all he knew — he needed to know more. To know how to stand against them, even fight them. He was a policeman, after all. He was supposed to uphold law and order.

Absorbed in his thoughts, a knock startled him. "Come in," he called, and Santos's face and all its wobbling chins came round the door.

"Boss wants you, sir," he said. Corvo sighed.

"Tell him I'm on my way."

His superior was the last person in the world he wanted to see right now. He'd want to know the same three things he asked Corvo every day. *How is the investigation progressing, Have you got any suspects, When can we expect an arrest.* To which the inspector would give the same three replies as all the other times. *Slowly. No. And I haven't the remotest idea,* though in fact this last usually came out as *I'm afraid I don't know, sir.*

Inspector Corvo pushed himself up out of his chair and was greeted once more by all the aches he'd woken up with that morning. He muttered an oath under his breath, hitched up his pants, put on his jacket, and headed off to beard his boss in his lair.

*   *   *

At Tatiana Dimitrovna's bidding, Zé hailed a cab. Without her asking, he handed her into it. She smiled at him in a way that made him optimistic about getting more of the low-down than his father would ever tell him.

For the moment the rain had stopped, but a glance at the sky would tell any landsman that more was on the way, let alone a sailor. Zé squinted at the clouds, though, and said sagely to the cabby, "More where that lot came from."

The cabby eyed him in a jaundiced sort of way from beneath his dripping headgear, spat in the gutter, and replied, "Don't need you to tell me that, *rapaz.*"

Unabashed, Zé hopped on board and grinned at the Russian witch. *"Were* you ill?" he asked her curiously.

"Not really," said Tatiana Dimitrovna, looking at him from under straight black brows. "My spirit was… elsewhere. I think you came into the room, no?" Zé went pink and suddenly appeared to find his boots fascinating. "And covered me with my robe. That was kind."

"Thought you might get cold," he mumbled.

"Your father said I could tell you what's going on. Would you like me to?"

"Yes, please," exclaimed Zé, embarrassment forgotten at once. "He never tells me anything." This was not strictly true, and Zé knew it. "Even though I made him a silver bullet when I was only twelve, *and* he killed a werewolf with it."

The witch looked interested. "Where was this?"

"In Goa… Portuguese India. Where Sr. Harris joined *Isabella.*"

She took a moment to work this out. "There were two werewolves, then?" she said finally.

"Yes, and one of 'em tried to eat us, but Sr. Harris stopped him."

"Fascinating," remarked Tatiana Dimitrovna. "A werewolf with some… awareness. Usually they are ravenous beasts, did you know that? Ruled only by the hunger, as a vampire is."

Zé's eyes nearly popped out of his head. "Then there *are* such things as vampires?" He nearly said *shitfire*, which was a word he'd heard Harris use and thought a very fine exclamation, but perhaps a lady wouldn't agree. He stopped himself in time.

"Of course," replied the witch. "You doubted it?"

"Well, I've never seen one," said Zé reasonably, "and I've seen a lot of things since—" He broke off.

"Since what?" she asked. "Since Luís… your father lost his eye?"

"Yes," said Zé, a bit reluctantly.

Tatiana Dimitrovna laughed, but kindly. "It's all right. You are not betraying a confidence."

"Did he tell you?"

"No, I worked it out," she told him, smiling. "It wasn't very difficult. Do you know how he lost the eye?" Zé shook his head.

"He never tells anyone that," he said. "Except my mother."

"Ah, your mother," repeated the witch in a peculiar tone of voice. "A lady with her own... talents."

"What do you mean?" he asked breathlessly, but she shook her head.

"Not my secret to tell," she said, but not without regret. Zé decided not to push his luck, though he would've loved to know what she meant.

*   *   *

Finding Pierce's shop open at last, Munro pushed the door open and strutted in. To look at him, though he is not tall, you would say there is something bull-like about the man, more than arrogance in the way he moves, he looks as if he might paw the ground and snort down mighty nostrils before charging, brushing aside your cape, goring you, trampling you into the dirt for good measure. This is the minotaur, perhaps, or some other unnatural creature, that will rend you limb from limb if the fancy takes it.

Clocks, why was the shop full of damned clocks? Pierce was supposed to be a bookseller. By the time Munro reached the counter and its somnolent custodian he was ready to kill someone. His temper, always uncertain, was stretched too tight for anyone in the vicinity to survive.

And the person in the vicinity, unfortunately for him, was Caracol. A wizened gnome of a man, deaf as a stone, who could read the penciled price inside a book's cover and give the customer the correct change. Who had never, himself, read a book in his life. And who could ignore the telephone with a clear conscience, because he could no more hear it than fly to the moon.

"Who the devil are you?" roared Munro, shaking him awake. And, "Where's Pierce?" And, "Answer me, you stinking peasant."

None of which the hapless Caracol understood. Even though he could lipread quite effectively, that didn't stretch to English. He shrugged his shoulders helplessly. What does this madman want, coming in here with his face of thunder and mouthing gibberish? This is a bookstore, for the Holy Virgin's sake.

Fury boiled over in Munro, and he struck out at the old man. His fist did not connect, but Caracol, with a hoarse, startled cry, was flung backwards across the shop, crashing into the wall. The impact broke his back. He felt an instant's incandescent pain, a hot wetness as his bladder let go, and then numbness.

Munro hit the air again, and something burst in Caracol's brain, killing him instantly. Anger relieved somewhat, the sorcerer left the shop. The thought of burning it to the ground crossed his mind, but he decided against it. Spite like that might deny him something useful, like the book he had come for.

But he needed Pierce for that.

* * *

"No one telephoned," said Pierce without looking up. I have to say he's not that convincing in the role of a secretary. Seated behind a desk, true. Dressed as neatly as ever. Did he wear a collar and tie every single day he lived in Brazil? But you can tell his heart's not in it. The preoccupied air's a giveaway. Not to mention the musty tome he's reading. Harris eyed him with some amusement, and raised an eyebrow at me.

By the window, Zacuto at least turned round and examined my bruised face critically, but made no comment. Good. I touched the cut carefully. It still hurt. *Well, what did you expect, da Silva?* It's so long since I sustained any damage that can't be helped by holy water that I've forgotten what it's like.

"I've got another riddle for you," I told them. That made Pierce raise his head. He took off his spectacles and pinched the bridge of his nose.

"Life is never dull around you, skipper, is it?" I think it was a rhetorical question. I didn't answer it, anyway. What answer is there? Just like an Englishman, stating the bloody obvious. I took out my cheroots. Only one left. Must've been smoking a lot.

"The child is born knowing four words," I said, and lit the cheroot. Zacuto's head snapped up. Pierce blinked and replaced his spectacles, which I suppose was his equivalent. Harris borrowed my match to light a cigarette.

"What?" exclaimed Pierce. I repeated Tatiana Dimitrovna's contribution to the prophecy, and then had to explain where it came from.

"That source cannot be trusted," the ghost said severely, shaking his head. With you on that, old man.

"Count me in on that too," added Harris.

"Maybe," I said, "but I think Tatiana Dimitrovna can." Emilia made me fairly confident about that. If embarrassed. Harris, it seemed, was less sure. Think he was just annoyed at being ignored. Well, not exactly ignored. But not trusted, certainly. The Russian witch can't seem to believe in his good intentions. It seems to be mutual.

"What four words might they be?" wondered Pierce.

Zacuto pursed his lips. "Clues to the whereabouts of the hallows, possibly.

We must wait for the child to say the four words."

Pierce looked down at his book again. Pushed his spectacles back to their proper position. They promptly slid down his nose again. I raised my eyebrows at the ghost and the scholar, and blew out smoke.

"She's less than a month old," I pointed out, tapping ash into the ashtray. "She's not going to start talking any time soon."

And that's not stating the obvious, da Silva?

"We do not know that, senhor capitão," said Zacuto thoughtfully. "Remember, this is magic and prophecy."

"You think she might have been born with just the ability to speak those four words?" speculated Pierce.

It's almost a pity to interrupt them. They can turn anything into an academic debate. Quite entertaining, in its way. Mind you, you should hear Zacuto and Fr Pereira when they get going. They lose me after about ten words. But then, they do mainly concentrate on theology. Not a favorite topic of mine.

However, right now I've got something else to discuss with Zacuto. The thing that stalked Inspector Corvo last night. The one that doesn't exist. And I suppose I'd better mention Alegria as well. Though presumably we don't want to destroy her.

To my surprise, though, Zacuto didn't bat an eyelid at the thought of my father creating her. Not that he has any real eyelids to bat, of course. But you know what I mean.

"Thought, rendered visible," he said. "Or, in this case, tangible. Consider, senhor capitão: your father's imagination created Alegria *in potentia*. He then painted her image, the image of someone who did not exist before he visualized her. It is but a short step from there to make her one degree more real."

I scratched my cheekbone. "Did the demon give him that power? Or—" I remembered what he's said about Emilia's new sense "—did he always have it, potentially?"

"That I do not know," said the ghost, shaking his head. "Any more than I know if the same thing is true of you, since a demon took out your eye."

That made *me* bat an eyelid. How the devil did he know that? I'm sure I never told him. And then I remembered his soul in me as I dragged him from the hell-portal. I stared at him. Couldn't think of anything to say. Da Silva, speechless. Doesn't happen very often.

"Demon?" Harris repeated. "What, another one? Goddamn things can't leave you alone, can they."

"Is that how it happened?" enquired Pierce, with interest.

"Yes," I said shortly. "And that's all I'm going to say." I looked at the ghost accusingly. "And I'd be obliged if you'd keep your mouth shut on that, senhor *fantasma*."

Of course he's obliged to do anything I say. In theory. He smiled into his beard, not at all contrite. I finished my cheroot, and stubbed it out.

"Rest assured, your secrets are safe with me," he said. Which doesn't sound much like a vow of silence, if you ask me.

"They'd better be," I muttered.

"What about that other thing, though?" asked Harris, and blew a smoke-ring. I don't know whether it was deliberate. He was pulling a face, presumably at the memory of trying to bite its arm off. My own arm twinged in sympathy. The bird-creatures' attack seems such a long time ago, now.

"Wonder who thought that one up?" Pierce added.

Zacuto gazed thoughtfully into the middle distance. "That, I believe," he said, "was the demon." I raised my eyebrow. Felt it pull at the scar.

"I thought they couldn't create anything," I objected. The ghost transferred his stare to me. Shifted into didactic mode.

"Strictly speaking, you are correct," he said, "they cannot. But it is very like demon-logic to argue that neither Alegria nor this creature exist, therefore they have not been created."

"Ha," I said. Demon-logic sounds a lot like lawyers to me. But then, they have a lot in common with each other, no?

"However," Zacuto went on, "even the process of imagination is not normal for a demon. I believe Belphegor learned how to do it by watching your father, senhor capitão. Or maybe even from having his soul in its care, if only for a little while. But, being a demon and unable to create anything, it was just not very good at it. Hence its grotesque appearance."

Pierce took off his spectacles and gave them a polish. Long-overdue. He hadn't wiped them since I came in. "Wouldn't a demon *want* to create something grotesque, if it found it could?" he asked pensively.

"Not necessarily," replied Zacuto, steepling his fingers, still in schoolteacher mode. "They are as capable as mortals of perceiving beauty, though it may be that they appreciate it in a different way. But remember that many exist only to corrupt the good and pure, so they must be able to recognize it in the first place."

I didn't ask for a discussion on demon esthetics. What I want is the answer to one question. "So how do we destroy it?"

Harris nodded in agreement. "Add me to that, in spades."

The ghost smiled sadly. As if the thought of destroying anything created pained him. Even something as hideous and homicidal as that. "You seem forever fated to ask me that question, senhor capitão," he sighed. "But I suppose it is your task." Paladin. Ha.

"Congratulations, Sr. Zacuto, you're fated to provide the answer," I said tartly. "Could *you* destroy it?"

"No," he replied. "I should imagine that to destroy a thing created by Belphegor, you must kill Belphegor."

Oh, thanks very much. I might've known it'd come to that. Doesn't it always? I leaned my head back and closed my eye for a second in resignation.

But wait a moment. "Where does that leave Alegria? Emilia said she was afraid that *banishing* the demon would destroy her. Never mind killing it."

"No, no," said Zacuto, shaking his grizzled head. "Your father created Alegria. While he lives, or while he needs her, she will survive."

Well, I suppose that's good. I'm still not sure how I feel about Alegria. But I'll have to leave it until I get some leisure to work it out. I really haven't got the time right now.

On the subject of killing Belphegor. "All right," I said resignedly, scratching my cheekbone. "Can we summon it?"

Zacuto knows why I'm asking. Last year I summoned a demon to try to protect my family, and damned near ended up possessed by it. That's what happens when you mess with 'em. Anyway, the old scholar's ghost was the one who exorcised me. And the thought of that still brings me out in a cold sweat.

"You cannot, without endangering your soul once more," the ghost replied. "Nor can any living thing."

Pierce coughed. I'm less inclined to be delicate. Tact, what's that? "Any living thing," I said. "Do you mean you could do it?"

"Not without help."

"What sort of help?" interrupted Pierce, peering at Zacuto and polishing his spectacles in an excited sort of way. Saved me asking. I felt for my cheroots, but I'd finished them. Forgot that. I settled for fingering my scabby bruise instead. Then changed my mind and begged a cigarette from Harris. Won't be able to taste the thing, but it's better than nothing.

The ghost looked at us. "Demons must be summoned by someone, or something, with physical substance. I would need… some sort of amulet, or charm."

I felt my mouth stretch in a humorless grin. "It gave my father a coin. With its name written on it. That's how it got into his house last year."

No such things as coincidences. As I keep on saying.

Zacuto smiled back at me, and his expression had even less humor in it than mine. "Then I suggest we go there without delay, senhor capitão."

Hard to fault his logic on that one.

* * *

The rain had returned with even more vigor by the time Zé and Tatiana Dimitrovna reached their destination, and he eyed the sullen bulging clouds crossly, wondering how much more was up there. At this rate Lisbon was going to end up like Venice.

This vision was sufficiently entertaining to divert him for a few moments, visualizing a kind of floating funicular arrangement to drag transport up waterfalls, and trams careening down sloping waterways.

You wouldn't know the place was an orphanage if it wasn't for the sign on the door, he thought. It was utterly silent under the teeming rain, no trace of children's voices could be heard, perhaps they'd all been struck dumb. Probably, though, they were all still at their lessons, since it wasn't yet lunchtime.

At the thought of lunch, Zé's stomach growled. It seemed an awfully long time since breakfast, and a lot had happened to burn up what he'd eaten. He considered that he should've at least been offered a snack in return for his efforts while they were all sitting round in the hotel. His mother had wangled coffee, after all.

Tatiana Dimitrovna, apparently not noticing the rain, rang the bell with a gloved hand, and Zé suddenly realized that she was literally not noticing the rain. Or it wasn't noticing her. She wasn't even damp, the drops weren't reaching her. He goggled at this interesting phenomenon for an instant, but anything he might have said was cut short by the door opening.

Zé didn't recognize the servant who answered the door, it wasn't the sour one who always looked as if she'd been sucking lemons. This one was a little more cheerful than her predecessor, at least, but about a hundred years older by the look of her.

"Yes, how may I help, senhora?" she asked politely, ushering them in out of the rain. Zé dripped on the mat, enough for both of them, in his opinion. But the prune-faced maid appeared not to notice the witch's lack of damp. She cast a sideways glance at Zé as if considering him a potential inmate. He scowled at her.

"Is Senhorita Batista here?" he asked. The woman frowned, presumably at some perceived lack of protocol. Zé felt obliged to explain. "The senhora doesn't speak Portuguese."

"Oh," said the maid, not noticeably advancing the conversation. "Yes. What names shall I give her?"

"José da Silva," he told her, feeling rather important. "She knows me, she doesn't know the senhora."

The servant's mouth thinned. "I'll still need a name." She stared at the Russian witch disapprovingly. Tatiana Dimitrovna was obviously too exotic to be acceptable.

Recognizing the tone if not the words, she said haughtily, "Countess Tatiana Dimitrovna Andropova," and Zé thought, startled, *Countess?* It was true, then… But he translated it smugly to the maidservant, *senhora condessa*, and was meanly pleased to see her become servile in a second.

"Please wait here, I'll go and see," she mumbled. Zé grinned at the witch as the woman scuttled away.

"That told her," he said with satisfaction, adding curiously, "Are you really a countess? I thought I made that up."

"My father had a title," she replied, looking at herself critically in a plain mirror that hung on the wall, and making a minute adjustment to her hat. "But the Tsar exiled him, so I'm not sure whether I'm really supposed to use it."

"Well, it did the trick, didn't it?" remarked Zé happily.

*   *   *

Teresa Batista, who had just finished teaching and was damp and sweaty and looking forward to a bath, muttered an imprecation under her breath. She was, subversively, teaching some of the older girls to fence. Boys, too, but that wasn't controversial, apart from the fact that it was a woman teaching them, of course. But no one was going to come and censure her. Dr Bosque had a free hand to run the orphanage as long as he stayed well away from its account books, a state of affairs he was more than happy to maintain.

And Teresa, having shown an aptitude for teaching that astonished her, taught English, fencing, and the theory of sorcery. Practical witchcraft was tackled by Luzia Verdinho. Without her mother's knowledge, naturally. *("A minha mãe,"* she'd said to Harris, with a nice mixture of advancing his Portuguese lessons and borrowing his own turn of phrase, "would 'ave a cat.")

Now, though annoyed at the interruption, Teresa felt a pang at discovering it was Zé. Which meant his father must need her help in something. Her feelings about Luís da Silva were ambivalent. She'd spent so long in her father's thrall, planning revenge on the captain for events twenty years in the past, that she still occasionally forgot that he was now, in a way, her friend.

And who in God's name might this Countess Tatiana be, who had poor Sra. Flores in such a tizzy?

Draping a towel round her neck, she hurried to meet her visitors. At least she was dressed in a skirt and blouse. Thumbing her nose at convention did not go quite so far as letting her young ladies wear pants, although she would've if she thought she could get away with it. And so she, too, wore a skirt, though it hampered her movements more than a little. But still, if they could learn to fight with that disadvantage, she thought, it would only increase their skills.

One thing was certain about her visitors, though. They'd come unannounced. And that meant trouble.

They were in the entrance hall, where the flustered maid had left them. Teresa looked over the banister, curious to observe briefly before they caught sight of her, and her breath suddenly got stuck in her throat.

The woman seemed to be burning with a dark flame. Just for an instant the whole hallway was illuminated so fiercely by a black incandescence that her vision inverted, turning it into the image on a negative photographic plate. And then everything was back to normal, and the woman was looking up at her. Teresa didn't trust herself to speak, so she just smiled, and started to descend the stairs on legs that were all of a sudden inclined to be wobbly.

From below, Zé called out a cheerful greeting, and she gave him a wave. He appeared to be on good terms with the woman, whoever she was.

Whatever she was.

Zé was an observant boy, but the tension between the two women would have been obvious to the most obtuse. He looked from one to the other in sudden concern, tall Teresa, flushed and sweaty with her hair in damp tendrils round her face, the Russian witch, her expression inscrutable and distant, and belatedly realized he needed to make introductions. He did it in English, which he knew Teresa spoke, but not how fluently, though he needn't have worried on that score. And he felt something like ozone crackling in the air between them.

"What do you want here?" asked Teresa, hostile as a hawk defending her territory, wiping a trickle of sweat from her face with the towel but never taking her eyes off the other woman.

"She's here to help," Zé interrupted nervously, wondering how — or if — he could defuse the tension. "It's about Dona Ana's baby, she could be in danger."

Tatiana Dimitrovna's black eyes glinted. She was as bristly as Teresa. Who topped her by six inches, and was an athlete, and strong, yet it was clear to Zé that the Russian witch was by far the more powerful of the two. And that, he understood suddenly, was why she was so hostile. This was Teresa's home ground. She was used to being in control.

"Someone got here first," Tatiana Dimitrovna said to him. "There's a protection spell at work within these walls. But it is the wrong sort."

"The wrong sort?" Zé echoed. At the same time, Teresa was shaking her head and frowning at them.

"What spell?" she enquired. "I can't sense anything." Her voice was indignant.

The Russian witch laughed. "You haven't the power," she said coldly. "But any sorcerer will sense it. Munro will know it at once, it is like a beacon. It will alert him. It is as if someone in this place has mobilized an army to defend it. You cannot hide an army, nor conceal the fact that it is arming itself for war. Oh, it will give protection from demons — that is its purpose — but it will be no defense against the likes of him. I could break it myself without a thought."

Teresa put her hands on her hips. "Who would work magic here without my knowing it?" she demanded. "None of the students has that kind of power. Luzia wouldn't do it unless I asked her. And who is… Munro?"

Zé interrupted again, in a vain attempt to deflect them from each other. He felt as if he was trying to separate two fighting wildcats. Except for the lack of scratches and bites, of course. "He's a sorcerer. He thinks Dona Ana's baby is in a prophecy. That she can help him get something he wants."

"What prophecy?" asked Teresa, bemused. She toweled her hair absently, apparently not noticing that she was doing it. "You can't just spring things on me like this. Let's go into the office and talk about it."

"There is no time to talk," said Tatiana Dimitrovna impatiently. "Didn't you hear what I said? He will detect the child through this ill-judged spell, and we are not prepared for him."

"Is Dona Ana here?" broke in Zé, desperately. "Maybe she asked someone for a charm, or something." Teresa looked down at him. He refused to be cowed, and met her eyes. Then she gave a small smile.

"She's helping in the kitchen today," she said. "Let's go ask her."

And she turned on her heel and strode away down the corridor, shoes tapping on the linoleum. Zé exchanged a glance with the Russian witch, and then they followed her. The smell of cooking reminded Zé again that he was starving. He wondered whether there was any chance of scrounging some lunch. He'd eaten here before, and the cook was not only an artist but also understood the fueling needs of fourteen-year-old boys.

The kitchen was welcomingly warm on a cold and rainy day, and the three of them sidled in cautiously in the furtive attitude of all kitchen invaders; whether clandestine or legitimate, the wrath of cooks is not to be risked lightly.

Ana was chopping vegetables, apparently this menial task was something she could accomplish unsupervised, and the cook's attention was elsewhere. Zé watched her covertly for a moment. He thought she was very pretty, and though nineteen made an impossibly large gap between them, she was nearer his age than any other girl he knew. Her fair hair was tucked under a kerchief, and her face was flushed. She had nice hands, with long fingers.

She became conscious she was being watched, and looked up. Teresa smiled encouragingly at her.

"How are you today, Ana? And how's Susana doing?"

"Oh, well enough, thank you, senhora," said the blonde girl, raising one arm so she could mop her brow with the sleeve of her blouse. "She wakes up so often, and—" Ana flushed and lowered her voice — "she *bites.*"

It was the first Zé had heard of this. But then, he'd hardly been in a position to learn that the baby was developing somewhat faster than normal, or that she'd been born with a full set of teeth. For a split second he wondered what Susana had been biting, and then he realized, and went pink himself at the picture that came into his mind. He looked away from Ana hastily, turning to Tatiana Dimitrovna, who couldn't understand the conversation.

"The baby keeps her awake, she says," he gave as a free translation, and the witch nodded, looking past him in Ana's direction.

"Did you get a charm for her, Ana?" Teresa asked carelessly. "Did someone give you something?" Ana blinked, seemingly in surprise at her ignorance.

"Yes of course, the doctor gave us a little magic bag, he said to tuck it in her cot and it might stop her waking so often."

Zé repeated this information to the witch, noting as he did so that Ana had said *might* and not *would.* Tatiana Dimitrovna muttered under her breath. Then she said quietly to him, "It may do that as well, but that is not its main purpose."

Teresa was frowning. "Did the doctor tell you where he got this charm?" But Ana shook her head. Teresa patted her arm, then turned to Zé and the witch. "Come along," she said in English.

The orphanage is a rambling building, in fact it is not strictly *a* building, being several houses with connecting doors and the odd demolished wall here and there. Most of the children find it fascinating, they are allowed to explore within reason since Dr Bosque does not believe in the kind of regime that likes to regulate people, be they large or small. True, the children wear a uniform, because it is expected. but their minds are not regimented.

One of the older girls — she was about fifteen — rounded a corner and nearly bumped into Teresa, who put out a hand and touched her arm.

"Sílvia, is Dr Bosque in the nursery?" she asked. The girl nodded, but she was looking at Zé with frank curiosity. He stared back. She was that rare creature in his life, someone close to his age. She had curly black hair and rather thick eyebrows like two tilde signs.

"Hallo," she said. "My name's Sílvia Meiro."

"I'm Zé," he replied, still staring at her. "José da Silva."

Tatiana Dimitrovna cleared her throat, pointedly. Zé ignored her, but Teresa gave Sílvia her marching orders and she trotted off. Not without a backward glance and a little wave, though. Which Zé returned.

Unexpectedly warmed, he followed the two women with something of a swagger. The three of them, Teresa leading, climbed yet another staircase and came up into what must once have been a dark and cobwebby attic but was now a nicely light and pleasant room with skylights all along one sloping wall. Even with the rain slashing down them, the nursery was airy and bright.

It seemed full of babies to Zé, who had blocked out memories of his sister until she became a person. They resolved themselves into five crawlers in a playpen and three infants in cots. Tatiana Dimitrovna marched up to one of these and said, in a voice that brooked no denial, "This charm must be destroyed."

Dr Inácio Bosque, who was examining one of the other children who was coughing in a painful phlegmy way, turned round indignantly and exclaimed "What!"

And Susana looked up at Teresa with bright intelligent eyes and said, *"Kealba."*

8

TERESA'S MOUTH DROPPED OPEN. THE WORD MEANT NOTHING TO
HER, nor to any of the others, but it was unmistakably a word and not a baby-
sound. She'd been around babies enough now, since she'd been with Inácio,
to know that.

Then everyone started talking at once.

"Boizhe moi," muttered Tatiana Dimitrovna.

"Was that one of the words?" asked Zé excitedly.

"What words?" Teresa demanded.

"Who *are* you?" said Dr Bosque to the witch.

And Susana, still looking up and obviously feeling neglected, let loose a
heartfelt wail that was so precisely the noise you would expect a baby to
make that all four of them suddenly doubted what they'd heard a moment
before.

Frowning, Tatiana Dimitrovna asked, *"Kealba,* was it not?" Zé nodded,
and fished in his pockets. He wasn't going to sacrifice a page of his
sketchbook for something so small. Eventually he came up with half a sheet
of paper with the address of the hotel in the Rua do Alecrim scrawled on it in
his father's untidy handwriting, and wrote Susana's word down
phonetically.

"Now we won't forget it," he said.

"Would someone like to tell me what's going on?" enquired Dr Bosque,
a bit plaintively. Teresa gave the other woman and Zé a minatory look.

"I wish I knew," she said tartly.

All three adults stared at Zé, who suddenly knew one of the reasons his
father smoked. He would have loved to have something to do with his hands
at that moment. Sticking them in his pockets was the best he could manage.

"Er... what about the charm?" he asked, deftly deflecting their attention
onto Tatiana Dimitrovna.

Who blinked, and then cleared her throat. "The charm, yes." She looked at Dr Bosque. "This little one is safe from demons, but the magic that protects her shouts her presence to the man who means her harm."

"Why would a man want to harm her?" the doctor demanded. "And who are you, anyway? José, is she with you?" Zé nodded, swallowing nervously.

"Yes, senhor doutor," he answered, and performed another introduction, remembering to call her *countess*.

"You know about such things, then?" said Dr Bosque skeptically, and Zé grinned, only to be quelled by a frown from Teresa. If only they knew!

But all Tatiana Dimitrovna said was "Yes. And one day I'd like to meet whoever made this charm. It's a... very unusual piece of work. And very nicely done."

She put her hand into the cot, delving underneath the covers, and drew out a small bag of brightly-colored cloth. To Zé it seemed to sparkle slightly.

Dr Bosque looked at it with regret. "Do you have to destroy it?"

The witch examined the bag. "It does seem a pity," she agreed. "I'll look after it for you. And you can tell me why you think this child needs such powerful protection from demons, after we've dealt with our present problem."

"How are you going to hide her from Munro?" asked Zé, curiously. "Can you take her out of time, like Sr. Yeoh did with Isabella?"

"No," said Tatiana Dimitrovna, shaking her head. "Taking a child so small out of time would mean she'd never have an anchor *in* time."

Zé thought this sounded like rather a good idea. He would've liked to be able to do what Sr. Yeoh did, step in and out of time at will. But he kept quiet on that one. "Take her to the library," he suggested, forgetting that she was unaware of its special attributes.

And having dug a hole for himself, he found them all looking at him again. There was no escape this time.

He drew a deep breath, and began to explain.

* * *

I don't like this one little bit. It's not that I haven't done it before. Summoned them or killed them. But when I did the summoning, the demon was safe inside a pentagram. I was safe from it, and it was safe from me. The idea of calling one, loose without any safeguards, that's a different thing altogether. For one thing, there's no guarantee I can kill it. And somehow I don't like the thought of summoning anything just to kill it. Seems like cheating. Yes, I know a demon would do it in a heartbeat if the positions were reversed. That's what demons are.

On the other hand, I'm quite happy — well, happy's not the right word, but you know what I mean — to kill them if they attack me. But, apparently, get squeamish about setting them up. Heaven help me, sympathy for the hosts of hell. Getting soft in your old age, da Silva. Ha. Soft in the head, more like.

Zacuto's illusion of solidity doesn't go far enough to use public transport. One impatient jostle on a tram and the cat would be well and truly out of the bag. Or the ghost, in this case. Taking a cab was out as well, because he spooks the horses. Mind you, walking through the rain without getting wet is a dead giveaway too. And I don't possess an umbrella.

So, we walked. At least I did. He pretended. Nobody gave him a second glance. In a city that's a port and crammed to bursting with people from all the Portuguese corners of the earth, not to mention the rest of the globe as well, an old man in sixteenth-century robes blends in fairly well. At least, he doesn't stand out too much.

Ghosts, the other sort, I mean, the faint shades that throng the streets, they always seem much less substantial in the rain. Well, they never look exactly substantial, being more like magic-lantern images at the best of times. But when it's raining they always look as though they're about to melt into it.

As we walked, I tried to explain to Zacuto. Feeling like a bit of a fool. Well, more than a bit, to be honest. To my surprise, he seemed sympathetic.

"Your concern is perfectly natural," he said, "because you are making, as all men do, the mistake of anthropomorphism. You have forgotten what demons are really like, because our minds were not designed to cope with such thoughts for very long. So you feel that because this thing is sentient it is worthy of your concern. But it is not, senhor capitão. It is a native of Hell. It is inimical to mankind."

"I do know it, really," I nodded.

"Remember, you do not have feelings of this kind when you confront a demon. You know them for what they are. Believe me, we will not be placing it at any disadvantage by summoning it — would that we were! We are merely calling its name, as when you call your enemy's name on a battlefield."

Having never been on a battlefield, I wouldn't know. Still, I took his point. "Maybe it's just cowardice, then," I said lightly, and took out my cheroots. The rain had almost stopped.

He answered me with deadly seriousness. Should've remembered he has no sense of humor. "Never accuse yourself of that, Captain da Silva."

I grimaced, and struck a match. "Sometimes everyone's a coward."

"Not when the better part of valor is discretion," he retorted. "Do not confuse it with prudence. Even generals have to know when to retreat."

Since when did he get all military? Must've been reading von Clausewitz. Obviously sitting in a library gives even a ghost cabin fever after too long.

"All right," I said, letting it go. Blew out some smoke at a passing ghost. "Tell me about the Fisher King... the wounded king. Harris wasn't being very clear how it works."

Zacuto smiled into his beard. "Sr. Harris is an admirable man in many ways, and intelligent. But one would never call him an intellectual."

Goes for me too. At least, I think I'm fairly intelligent. "He'd probably feel insulted if you did."

"Very likely," agreed Zacuto, gravely. "What is it you want to know?"

Where do I start? I scratched my cheekbone. "The name, I think. Why Fisher King? You said it's nothing to do with Christianity." But that sounds suspiciously like it, to me.

I know I was running the risk — hell, the certainty — of sending him into his professor role. Better than getting metaphysical, though. I think.

"You must understand, senhor capitão, that this tradition predates all modern religions. Any similarities you see, were also seen by Christian scholars, and exaggerated in order to incorporate it more legitimately into their mythos." I must've looked impatient. He made a throat-clearing noise, and went on, "As for the name, it depends on whether one considers the fishing or the kingship to be more important. I am sure you—" he looked at me from under his bushy brows — "will be more comfortable using the name wounded king. *Roi mehaigné*... maimed. The wound being symbolic as well as physical."

He walked through a ghost. Didn't appear to notice it. An interesting effect, since he's no more substantial than the wraith itself.

"And what's that all about?" I asked, rather sourly. All this symbolism is giving me a headache. Nothing's ever straightforward in this business. It's always one thing standing for another. Riddles instead of facts. Mysteries wrapped up in enigmas.

I wouldn't mind so much, except that the usual result is that da Silva ends up having to fight something.

"Believe me, senhor capitão, it is a concept I find almost as outlandish as you do." I doubt that, somehow. "The king and the land bound together. The health of one a hostage for the well-being of the other. None of the sources we have consulted allows for a *healed* Fisher King. All assume that the land suffers as a matter of course. Perhaps the land *has* to suffer, metaphysically speaking. Perhaps the king must be healed by the hallows as a... cyclical requirement." And so we get the metaphysics as well as the didacticism. Nice.

Far as I can see, all this begs one question. At least one. "If Munro wants to be the next one, who's the king now? And where is he?"

The ghost looked put out, like a teacher asked an awkward question by a pupil. "The short answer to that is that I do not know." Well, at least he's honest about it. "One tradition puts the Grail Castle — his home — in Spain. But it is somewhat difficult to sift the stories since the Christianization of the tradition. No doubt every country would like to claim the seat of the land's symbolic ruler for its own."

"When you say the land, what does that mean?" I asked, skirting a puddle that was almost a miniature lake. "The world? The continent of Europe? The Roman Empire?"

"The last is most likely, I should think," said Zacuto. "But again, I do not know. My feeling would be that if this is indeed an archetype, then each people should have some kind of equivalent tradition, one that sits in with their own belief patterns."

He's floundering, if you ask me. I took another drag from my cheroot. "You mean that in the western world, the Christians absorbed it into their creed, but the same thing happened in — in Africa, and China, and the Mohammedan countries, and so on?" It seemed a democratic sort of solution. The ghost nodded thoughtfully.

"Just so."

"And the wound?" I pointed the cheroot at him. "Who wounded the king?"

"Unclear," he said. I couldn't help grinning. He doesn't really know very much, for all his erudition. For all the books in São Rafael. Being an intellectual isn't all people like Zacuto crack it up to be. "The wound itself, of course, is symbolic."

Of course. It would be. "Yes," I agreed, since he seemed to expect some reaction. Sorry, can't make it any more intelligent than that.

"The sources agree that it is in the leg or the groin." I winced involuntarily. Talk of maimed groins does that. "The generative area. It ties in with the symbolism of the land being sick. In the purely literal sense."

I finished my cheroot and threw the end away. Looked up to see where we'd got to, and found to my surprise that we were nearly there.

It still feels a little strange, getting used to the route to my father's house after all these years. I don't mean I'd forgotten it. You don't. But I honestly hadn't thought I'd ever make it part of my life again. People say you shouldn't go back, though it's not as simple as that. Anyway, I didn't. My father came to find me. *Figure that one out, da Silva.*

And all the same ghosts used to throng this street thirty years ago, and I didn't even know. The dead of Lisbon.

As I thought that, I realized something else, and it made my back creep. The ghosts were disturbed. And that's never a good sign. It takes a lot to make a shade sit up and take notice. They don't have much more consciousness than a photograph.

However, they do seem to know when there's a demon in the offing. I looked quickly up and down the street — we'd just turned into the Rua do Pornar where my father lives. Saw nothing apart from the wraiths. Turned to Zacuto and asked, "Do you feel anything?"

The ghost frowned. "Such as what?"

"Such as, are you able to sense demons?" I explained.

"What makes you ask?" he said, narrowing his eyes.

"The shades are restless," I replied. Scratched my eyebrow. Wondered about lighting another cheroot. "Something's stirred 'em up. Usually it takes a demon to do that. Or something pretty dire, anyway."

Zacuto looked round, much as I'd done. Shook his head somewhat irritably. Probably wondering why feeble shades that aren't much more than memories of people can sense something he can't. Well, I can't, either. Wish I'd brought Harris. Not sure why I didn't, to be honest. I'm taking a ghost to my father's house, so why not a werewolf?

"You have more experience in these matters, senhor capitão," he said worriedly. "What do you advise?"

I almost laughed. I did grin. Well, showed my teeth, anyway. "What you said earlier," I told him, drawing my knife. "When it comes, I'll kill it." And the whole summoning question wouldn't even arise. Sounds easy, doesn't it? So do a lot of things. In theory, anyway. That's why they're called theories.

Around us, the shades floated, tugged this way and that like weed in a current. Zacuto eyed my knife suspiciously. Well, it's supposed to make him nervous. Silver is poisonous to supernatural creatures. It's nice to have one advantage. Just happens this particular ghost is on my side. Whatever that is.

Of course I expected the demon to come bursting out of the air, since they seem to favor the melodramatic entrance, and I've seen them do it before. I also expected something armed and hideous that stank of the grave. Obviously learnt nothing about demons, then, da Silva.

Not even that they like to do the unexpected, for instance.

This one waited until I was stretching out my hand to ring my father's doorbell. I turned half-round to say something to Zacuto. And then there was a young girl between me and the door.

Who smiled up at me and said, "Surprise."

She looked about sixteen years old. Only a little taller than Emilia, and just as slight. Tiny little hands. Dirty bare feet. Tangled black hair. A gypsy, I thought for a split second before I realized otherwise. Before Zacuto shouted a warning.

Before she shot out a hard little fist and thumped my jaw so hard it took my breath away. I backed away, shocked, not nearly quick enough. Still not quite understanding. She jumped straight up into the air and kicked me in the chest, sending me staggering with a triumphant laugh.

Even then I was reluctant to use my knife. Demon it may have been. It looked like a little girl. I'm too conditioned. By my sex. My age. By society. By instinct. By all sorts of things. I ducked under a flying foot and gasped its name, "Belphegor."

The demon sniggered, and lashed out at me again. I blocked its wrist this time, and it jarred all the way up my arm. She was solid all the way through. Too damned solid for something from hell. Aren't they supposed to be elemental, or something? They fade soon enough when they're dead.

"You cannot bind me," she taunted. "You are too afraid."

Well, maybe so. But with good reason, I know. I backed away, raising the knife threateningly in front of me. Or I hoped it looked threatening.

"Kill it," urged Zacuto, from behind me. All very well for him to talk.

"My name will not bind me without more than you are prepared to give," said the demon, launching herself into the air again and almost landing another kick. I dodged it. Angrily, but still only half-heartedly, I thrust the knife in her direction, but she swayed out of the way. She was much too fast. It was like trying to cut water.

"Can you ring the doorbell?" I asked Zacuto breathlessly, without looking round. If he could get the medallion... But he had to be invited into the house first. *Bad idea, da Silva.*

The demon giggled. "You know better than to ask a ghost," she said, and sprang at me. I tried to dodge, but her foot shot out again like a piston, caught me on the thigh as I turned. It felt like the kick of a mule. I grunted in pain, but managed to pivot on the other leg and raised the knife in pure reflex. She launched herself into the air again and somersaulted over my head like an acrobat. Half exasperated, half terrified, I whirled round, only to come to a dead stop when I saw her face.

Now she looked like Emilia. Though not as she is now, but how she was at fifteen, the first time I saw her, frightened and vulnerable. And although I knew what this thing was, knew she meant to kill me if she could, and worse than kill me, knew what she was doing and why she was doing it, I couldn't follow through with the stroke. I let the knife drop.

And the demon smiled, and raised her hands with a merry little laugh, and I saw hell in her eyes.

"Da Silva!" shouted Zacuto, and threw himself between us. Insubstantial as he was, the demon could strike at him, and he took some of the force aimed at me. It saved us both, his being a ghost. Her blow was for a mortal, and would've killed me. Zacuto was already dead. But she hurt him, as probably nothing else could.

Furious, mainly with myself, I stabbed the blade at her. She dodged awkwardly, still hampered by Zacuto, and stumbled. The knife caught her a glancing blow across the back.

She hadn't expected that. Hadn't expected that either of us would be able to resist her. She shrieked, a harsh off-key keening that set my teeth on edge. Her back split open like a chrysalis, and the demon's true form came boiling out at appalling speed. And it just went on and on, rising up from the fallen husk of its girl-form.

It looked more than half mechanical. Huge metal hands with fingers that tapered to wicked points. A long muzzle full of glinting razor teeth. Eyes like a fly's, faceted, made up of mirrors. So close I suddenly saw, shockingly and just for an instant, myself, reflected a thousand times before I jumped back, knife outstretched at arm's length in front of me. Out of the corner of my eye I noticed Zacuto struggle to his feet.

I was already off-balance from its Emilia illusion, and my leg was aching like the devil where it had kicked me. And now this great damned thing screeching like a bloody banshee and slashing at me with its blade-fingers.

My temper snapped and I charged it. Zacuto must've thought I'd gone completely mad. I raised the knife. Brought it down as hard as I could on one of the wrists, where metal appeared to be fused to flesh. The impact jarred me to the bone. Sparks flew. The blade bounced up, stinging my fingers, and I used its momentum to bring it down again. This time I got the angle right, the knife sliced through the arm, the severed hand flew through the air and landed with a crash. The demon dodged away, screaming. *Ha. It's not laughing now.*

Dimly aware that Zacuto was shouting something I couldn't make out, I went after the thing. Then there was a huge tearing noise, and great black metal-ribbed wings burst out from the demon's shoulders. They unfurled like monstrous umbrellas. It rose into the air, wings pumping. Its legs and feet were like an enormous bird's, iron talons as long as my forearm. Gasping for breath, I ducked under the swipe of a clawing foot, belatedly realizing that it could spit me with ease. Could have spitted me at any time.

So why hadn't it? Because it'd been lying to me, of course. I lifted my knife, pointed the blade upwards. Sweat ran into my eye, but I couldn't spare the time to wipe it away. The knife weighed about two tons by now.

"Belphegor," I panted, and the demon hissed and swiveled its faceted eyes at me. I knew its name. It couldn't get past that. It's a fundamental rule. I laughed breathlessly, and said its name for a third time. Behind the demon, Zacuto shouted something else, also incomprehensible. It made me wonder vaguely whether he was talking Hebrew or whether I'd forgotten how to speak Portuguese. Witless, da Silva.

Chanting now, the ghost spread his arms wide. I felt the mark over my heart, the Key of Solomon that had appeared when he exorcised me, blaze suddenly with excruciating pain.

At the same moment, the demon wailed and disappeared. Air rushed in with a hollow boom like a sail backing to fill up the space it had occupied.

Vision flaring like a star, I suddenly found myself lying flat on my back with no idea of how I'd got there. Or what I was doing there. I stared up at Zacuto. Asked him, trying to enunciate clearly, "Have I forgotten how to speak?" Thought I saw Tatiana Dimitrovna behind him.

And passed out.

I don't think I was unconscious for very long. Since I was still lying in the road when I came round, with a taste in my mouth as if something had crawled in and died there. And my chest felt burned. I could feel the outline of the mark like fire.

Tatiana Dimitrovna was kneeling beside me, apparently unconcerned for her elegant costume on the wet cobblestones. She put her hand on my forehead. Her long fingers were cool.

"It looks as if I can't turn my back on you for five minutes and you're off fighting demons," she murmured. Which is a bit rich, coming from her.

"Better than gallivanting off to hell the minute *my* back's turned," I croaked. She put an arm under my shoulders.

"Can you sit up?" I thought about it.

"Think my head might come off if I do," I said. She smiled grimly.

"Let's try it," she suggested, and pulled me up. My head stayed put. That was a bonus. I was feeling as sick as a dog.

"Zacuto," I said, looking round too fast. Everything spun dangerously, and the witch steadied me with her hand. When my vision cleared, I was relieved to see him standing watching us. "Are you all right?"

He nodded, urbanely. "I am recovered, thank you, captain."

Leaning on Tatiana Dimitrovna, I got to my feet. Took a few deep unsteady breaths. Reached automatically for my cheroots. She pushed my hand away.

"Give your lungs a rest," she said irritably, sounding like someone's mother. Not mine. Mine was only ever concerned with the state of your soul. I think she marked up sins on some kind of celestial score-sheet. And she could sense a sin a mile off. Mind you, she thought most things people do were sinful, so it was always a pretty safe bet to assume I was doing something she disapproved of. And as about the only thing she did approve of was prayer, she could be damned certain I wasn't doing any of that.

Anyway, I probably should lay off the smokes while I feel this bad. Not a good idea to throw up over the witch. I turned to Zacuto.

"What the hell did you do?" I asked him. Felt for the mark through my shirt, which by rights ought to've been smouldering at least. Nada. Not even warm.

"I banished her through the key of Solomon," he answered. "You yourself were my physical link. The mark, it pains you?"

You could say that. "Feels like I've been branded," I complained.

"Residual magic energy," said the ghost. "Contact with the other mark should disperse it."

Oh, thanks. Since Emilia has the other mark, halfway across the city. And much as I'd like to go and make plenty of contact, I've got too many things to do before it's even going to be likely. I rubbed my chest ineffectually.

At that moment, the rain began again. Tatiana Dimitrovna sighed. "This is your father's house?" I nodded. "May I ask why you didn't ring the bell?"

"Demon got in the way," I said.

She stepped up to the door and remedied this. I heard the familiar chime deep inside. Presently my father appeared, showing no sign that he'd heard anything unusual. Shrieking demons outside his front door, and he doesn't turn a hair.

Glad he still *has* hair, by the way. Means I probably won't lose mine when I get to his age. Vanity, da Silva.

Peering out, he began, "Can I help — oh." The *oh* on seeing me. Held a million nuances of meaning.

"Where's Alegria?" I asked.

"She's right here," my father replied. And she came up behind him and smiled at me. Almost conspiratorial, that smile. I was immensely relieved.

"I felt it go," she whispered.

And she's still here. So she really *isn't* the demon's creation. I hadn't thought she was. But it's nice to have your instinct proved right.

Tatiana Dimitrovna was staring at her as if... well, none of the usual clichés work in my case, do they? As if she'd seen a ghost. She was standing right next to one.

"Come in, come in," my father urged. "Don't stand about in the rain. Would've thought you'd learn something in thirty years, Luís."

Seeing as I've spent most of them getting wet on ships, not really. I stood aside to let the witch precede me, and Alegria watched her like a bird looking at a cat. Zacuto, of course, doesn't get wet. And in fact, neither had Tatiana Dimitrovna. She saw me eyeing her, and raised her eyebrows with a smug little smile.

"Better than an umbrella," she murmured. So I'm the only one in the party who *has* gotten rained on. Ah well. The witch looked back at Alegria. "Just when I think you can't surprise me any more, you spring something else on me."

I took off my hat and coat. "Well, I'd hate to think I'm predictable," I said, and hung them up on the rack. Turned to my father and Alegria and made introductions, in English for Tatiana Dimitrovna's benefit. She was smiling slightly, I don't know why. Ghosts learn things after they've died, and languages may be one of them. Or Zacuto may have known English anyway. And Alegria, not being real, or being created by my father's wishes, came out of his head and knows what he knows. And his mother, my grandmother, was English.

"Not that it isn't pleasant to see you again so soon, Luís," said my father, "but what do you want?" He looked pointedly at Zacuto and the witch and bowed slightly. "Not that I'm not delighted to make your acquaintances, too," he added. Without a trace of irony. At least, not one that I could detect.

And so, not the time to bring up Alegria. Anyway, I'm not comfortable discussing her while she's there. I can't view her as a thing, any more than my father does. But she's not the main reason I asked the witch to meet me there.

"Would you show Tatiana Dimitrovna the picture that changed?" And obviously it was only then that he made the connection. He turned to her in astonishment.

"You're the woman in the painting," he exclaimed. She frowned at him. Then at me. I shook my head slightly.

"You'll have to see it first," I said.

"I don't like surprises, Luís," the witch retorted tartly, and I saw my father's surprise at her using my first name. I gestured for her to follow him into the studio. Alegria flinched back as she passed, and shot me a wide-eyed glance. Struck a sympathetic note with me. I smiled, I hope reassuringly. Touched her hand. Cool, paper-smooth. Not remotely human. But a person, nonetheless. I'm sure of that.

"What is she?" she whispered, frightened.

"Just a witch," I said. "Remember the painting."

Alegria nodded. "She could unmake me." Her voice had a tremor in it. She jerked her head at Zacuto. "So could he. So could you, so could Sebastião. But only that woman makes me think she might."

For a witch, Tatiana Dimitrovna's remarkably intolerant of the supernatural. Well, I don't trust most of it myself, I admit. I tend to attack first, before it attacks me. All right, Belphegor was an exception. And look what happened in that case. But at least I trust the ones who've proved themselves. I sighed, and followed in the witch's wake.

Found her and my father looking at the painting, now presumably quiescent.

"How did you come to paint this?" she was enquiring as I came into the studio. His hands were clasped behind his back. That means he's thinking about something. Or at least it used to. Meant he wouldn't even notice anyone else in the room.

"I dreamt it," he replied, proving me wrong. Tatiana Dimitrovna looked up, met my eye. I scratched my cheekbone reflexively. Wishing for a smoke. Involuntarily remembering her body under mine. Get your mind elsewhere, da Silva. I gestured at the picture.

"Were you there?" I asked her. She stared at it with narrowed eyes.

"In a way," she said after a moment. "Inasmuch as I was anywhere. I was… seeing by metaphor, you might say. I don't know whether there are really any physical structures in Hell. I don't know whether its — its inhabitants are as I perceived them, or whether I saw them in demonic forms because that was what I expected. But yes, I recognize this place. This representation. I should think the dream that framed it came from a demon, without question."

I walked up to her and said quietly in her ear, "And Alegria?"

The witch eyed my father speculatively. He was contemplating the painting, his face abstracted. I wondered what she was thinking. Then she shook her head slightly.

"Entirely from your father." I looked round for Alegria. She'd assumed that stillness that I'd first taken for unawareness. As if when no one was looking at her she was — well, turned off, like an electric light.

"What gave him the power to do that?" I asked quietly. "Was it the demon?"

"Not exactly," she replied, turning back to me. "Demons can't really create, you don't need me to tell you that." Tell that to Belphegor. There's one demon that's had a bloody good try. "I think it made him *see*."

"But he didn't see Alegria," I pointed out, rubbing at the burning mark under my shirt. Did no good, of course. "Unless you mean with his mind's eye." She folded her arms, and seemed about to speak.

"Excuse me," interrupted my father, with some asperity. "I'm still here, you know." I turned my head.

"Yes," I said, and stuffed my hands in my pockets. "But unless you can shed some light on the matter, we're no further forward."

"Where, though," Zacuto enquired in a tone of academic enquiry, breaking his silence, "are you heading?"

"I don't *know*," I said in frustration. Don't ask me. I'm just tossing thoughts around to see what happens.

"Ah, but I do," said Tatiana Dimitrovna, and everyone looked at her. She touched my father's arm. "If you, sir, can make things happen by painting them, we may be able to stop Munro from getting what he wants very simply."

My father rubbed his eyes. I know how he feels. "Who's Munro?" he asked plaintively. Óptimo. Now his memory's going. Bad sign. I think I'd rather lose my hair. I'm sure of it. Or maybe it's just Alegria.

"A sorcerer," I told him again. "I told you, remember?"

He blew out his cheeks and tugged at his beard. "Sorcerers, witches, demons," he grumbled. "Whatever next?"

A woman made from paint, I felt like saying.

Zacuto was staring at the witch. "What is your thought, senhora?" She turned to me. Eyes blazing with excitement. Or something.

"If your father can do this…" she said, pressing her fingers to her chin, "perhaps he can paint away Munro's powers."

Paint them away?

Everyone started talking at the same time. Tatiana Dimitrovna clapped her hands. Silence. Could do with a bit of that on board *Isabella*, sometimes.

"How?" my father asked. What we all wanted to know. He pointed at the canvas. "I'm not going to harm anyone. It was bad enough when I — I only *thought* I was."

"Not do him physical harm, no," she said impatiently. "Listen. Symbolism is important here, is it not?"

"We accept the symbolism," Zacuto prompted. "Go on."

"Then painting him *impotent* should — could work," the witch explained.

My father frowned at her. I found I was rubbing my chest again, and stuck my hands in my pockets. "Impotent?" he asked. She shot him an annoyed glance.

"Emasculated," she ground out. "Paint him sexless, master artist. Even if it only works for a little while, it may buy us time." She turned to Zacuto. "As your sending that demon back to Hell has bought us all time."

Am I the only one who thinks there's something wrong here? I glanced curiously at Alegria. *No, she doesn't like it either.*

"You don't know it'll work," I said to the witch. *Da Silva, playing devil's advocate.* She put her hand on my arm.

"No, but it's a chance worth taking." She looked at me strangely. *Imploringly, I realized after a moment. Never seen that expression on her face before. She's still afraid of confronting Munro directly. Even after a trip to hell herself. Então, I can't say I blame her. But being unsure of herself isn't the Tatiana Dimitrovna I know.*

"Well, I'd try it," announced my father unexpectedly, "but there's one problem. I don't know what this Munro character looks like."

Hadn't thought of that, had you, bruxa?

"But *we* know what he looks like," she said. *And she's a sculptress by trade. In the world of the mundane, at least.*

My father turned to me. "Then you can draw her."

"I beg your pardon?" I said, caught off-balance. He crossed to his desk, opened a drawer, and held out a sheet of paper to me.

"Come on," he urged. "You spent most of your childhood drawing, until your mother beat it out of you." His eyes grew distant. Bitter. *Don't go down that road, da Silva.* "Admittedly it was always pictures of ships. You can draw. You've passed it on to José, too."

That's news to me, as well. "Zé draws things?" I asked stupidly, scratching at my eyebrow. He rummaged in the drawer again and brought out a battered sketch-pad. Bemused, I took it from him and discovered a series of drawings of life aboard *Isabella*. *They seemed remarkably good to me. Not that I'm any kind of judge. When did he find time to do them? Zé, who thinks that work is something invented to inconvenience him personally?*

"It's all right, Luís," Tatiana Dimitrovna interrupted, "I can remember him well enough." Her tone was dry. *Naturally she could remember. She'd had an affair with him, or vice versa. I shook the thought away.* The witch picked up the blank paper and a piece of charcoal. Sketched quickly for a few moments.

Came up with a likeness of Munro that was uncannily good. In the face, anyway. Don't know about the rest of it.

"Hmm," my father said grudgingly, "you've done this before." Holding the paper in one hand, he started to copy the face onto a small blank canvas. Then he looked round irritably at his audience. "All right, the show's over. There's nothing to see."

Maybe not. But there's plenty to do. I turned to Tatiana Dimitrovna.

"How did you get on with Susana?"

"She—" Her eyes widened. As if she'd only just remembered something startling. "The child spoke a word."

Meu Deus. So it was true. I don't know whether to be pleased or sorry, though. I rubbed my cheekbone. "What did she say?"

The witch found a scrap of paper in her pocket and uncurled it. *"Kealba,"* she read carefully. Meant nothing to me. But Zacuto thrust his head forward to look.

"It is the Maltese word for dog," he said unexpectedly. I stared at him.

"Are you sure?" asked Tatiana Dimitrovna. He shot us a wry look from under his bushy eyebrows.

"I was a Jew four hundred years ago, *maga.* I know the word for dog in many tongues. Not to mention numerous other terms less polite."

I looked across at my father, already lost in his painting, Alegria at his side. Then back at the witch and the ghost.

"I haven't got the time to go sailing off to Malta," I objected.

"It might not mean that the hallows are in Malta," Zacuto said. "Remember how fraught with obscurity such clues usually are."

Well, that's one way of putting it, I suppose. I suddenly felt very tired. No, weary is a better word. I have a sore head thanks to Inspector Corvo. A bruised shin from a demon's kick. Toothmarks all along my arm. And an invisible burn on my chest courtesy of Zacuto. Not to mention all the bloody things I have to think about. Sometimes I even almost wish I was back with the Venetian. But not quite. Not ever that. At least sometimes I can maintain the illusion that my life's my own now. *Yes, keep on thinking that, da Silva. That's bound to make it all go away.*

"So," said the witch, "a Maltese dog. Does that mean anything?"

"Only in the derogatory sense," Zacuto muttered. He's entitled to harbor a grievance. Given that he was murdered by a mob for nothing more than being a Jew. But sometimes he does go on. And now isn't the time.

Tatiana Dimitrovna looked across at my father. "I'm afraid Munro will be even more set on getting his hands on the hallows, if your father succeeds," she observed, like someone commenting on the weather.

"I thought the idea was to make it easier to stop him," I said. The burning sensation was distracting. I wanted to rub it again. Restrained myself. Knew it wouldn't do any good.

* * *

Harris sniffed the air, and sneezed. *Three nights a month the moon makes me a wolf, come the morning I ain't sure what I am.* His senses were heightened to an unpleasant, almost painful level, and often overlapped in odd ways. He smelled the rain, tasted a storm in the offing, heard the winds heading towards Lisbon. The ozone in the atmosphere made his skin prickle and itch. Mixed in with all this was his extra sense, the one that could detect demons. Which were somewhere close, he knew. *Just can't tell where right now.* And that made his mind crawl and tainted the taste of the weather.

Besides all that, he felt all achy as if he had the flu. *And less'n I pay attention, I end up thinking I'm on four legs instead of two. Which ain't a good idea.*

"Is it still raining?" Pierce asked.

"Yeah," said Harris, finishing his cigarette, "but not too much right now. You wanna go check up on the store?"

"I suppose so." The antiquarian took off his spectacles and contemplated them, then folded them carefully and placed them in his top pocket.

"You see alright without those things?" Harris enquired. Pierce laughed ruefully, and patted the pocket.

"Not really," he admitted. "But I'd rather blunder about a bit than have to wipe the rain off them every five minutes."

"Huh," said Harris in reply, not more than a grunt. *How's that different from taking 'em off and polishing 'em every five minutes?*

"And anyway," the antiquarian added, " I'll have you with me, won't I?" He grinned at Harris unrepentantly.

Who rolled his eyes and said resignedly, "Might as well get this show on the road, then." Pierce hesitated.

"Er — I'll just go and tell Dona Emilia where we're going."

"Sure." Harris retrieved his cap and coat, stared at them for an instant as if unsure what to do with them, then shook himself and put them on. A moment later Pierce reappeared, also hatted and coated.

"All right?" he asked, a little nervously. Touched his nose, where his spectacles weren't, and then wiped his fingers distractedly across his lapel.

"As I'll ever be," said Harris. *Sure he's nervous. Jesus in the jungle, who wouldn't be? This Munro fellow sounds like bad news. And poor old Pierce is the bait in the trap. Bet he's wishing he never sent that telegram.*

He went to scratch his left elbow, which was itching particularly fiercely, and nearly fell over, having momentarily forgotten he was shaped like a man at the moment. He looked up in wolfish embarrassment to see Pierce watching him with an almost indulgent expression on his face, which was mitigated by the

Englishman's myopic squint.

Pierce gave no other sign of having noticed Harris's temporary lapse, though, saying merely, "Let's go, then."

A fine thin rain was falling, little more than a mist, really. Harris and Pierce found themselves skirting gray puddles wherever the ground leveled out. The sloping streets, lopsided alleys and uncounted flights of steps allowed some runoff, but there had been so much rain recently that much of the water had nowhere to run to.

"Guess you feel right at home with all this rain," remarked Harris. *Oops, forgot there that he's lived in Brazil since before I was even a glint in Pa Harris's eye.*

"Why d'you think I left England in the first place?" grumped Pierce, stepping over a puddle and dodging a very tiny child, sex indeterminate, that suddenly appeared from nowhere. "And if I'd known Lisbon was going to turn into London I'd have stayed in Rio."

Bet he wouldn't'a, though. He was hooked on that library the instant he put his foot inside the door.

Harris lit a cigarette, cupping the match against the rain with the ease of long practice. "Don't it rain in Brazil, than? It's a tropical country, last I heard."

"Warm rain," said the antiquarian succinctly, sourly. "And then the sun comes out." He looked upwards resentfully.

While they walked, the mist of rain ceased. Above, though, the sky bulged with thick dark clouds barely holding onto their cargo of water. The shop Pierce had taken over from John Yeoh was only a short walk away. Harris smoked two cigarettes. They acquired the company of a small black-and-white dog which seemed extremely interested in Pierce. *Wonder what he trod in? Huh, maybe it's just nervousness it smells.* Harris sniffed surreptitiously, having learnt from experience that most people don't take kindly to being smelt. *Could tell he's nervous without even looking at him. Hell, could tell it a mile away.*

They rounded a corner, and Pierce stopped so suddenly that Harris nearly ran into him.

"Hey, let me know if you're—" he began, and then the glutinous copper scent of congealed blood hit him. Blood that was cooling in a corpse, settling down in the body under the pull of gravity and nothing more. And he knew where it was.

"The door's open," said Pierce in a worried voice.

Been dead a couple hours, whoever it is. Harris swallowed, not because he was squeamish. Quite the opposite: the rich smell, the iron taste, were making him salivate. He swore silently, and caught Pierce's arm. The

Englishman's eyes widened at the expression on his face.

"Blood," Harris said. "Someone's dead in there."

Pierce blanched. "Caracol?" he whispered.

"You wait here," Harris told him. "I'll go see." Pierce nodded, moistening his lips anxiously with his tongue. "And don't let that goddamned dog follow me."

Usually he had to work to suppress his wolf-instincts when he was in human shape. *Twice in one day. Get to be a habit at this rate.* But he let his perceptions expand for a few seconds before he entered the shop. He didn't want to encounter anything unexpected. Though he knew there was nobody alive inside the shop, that didn't necessarily mean there was no one there. Or that there were no booby-traps, supernatural or otherwise.

Mechanical and insensitive, the clocks ticked on, registering the passage of time that had stopped for Caracol. Harris followed his nose and found the old man's body, lying broken-backed on the floor. A little blood had run out of the corpse's nose and mouth. There was nothing to show how he came to be lying there, or how he had met his death.

Though I guess it's safe to say he didn't trip and fall.

*   *   *

Sir Robert Munro, in a very ill temper, stalked up and down his hotel room. Rather, as befits someone of his importance, it is a suite, so there is plenty of room to pace. His familiar, in the small shape of a monkey, the least conspicuous form it can manage, squatted on top of the wardrobe and watched him nervously.

If Munro regrets the casual murder of Caracol, he gives no sign of it. Pilgrims returned from hell, the demon knows, those that find a way back, that is, fall into two categories. This is not something that it has had any chance to observe at first hand, since Munro is its first mortal master and this is its own first trip out of hell, it is a fact which it learned like a catechism a long, long time ago, though not really very long in the life of a demon.

Munro falls into the first category, those whose souls belonged in hell before they ever went there, those who cleave to it in mutual recognition. He has its powers, certainly, even hell is bound by rules and must grant the pilgrim what he wants, but they will drive him insane in the long run as he tries to use them too soon. And this kind of man always does.

The demon does not know Tatiana Dimitrovna any more than she herself knows that her own father made the same pilgrimage as she has just completed, but would recognize her as the other type, the ones with sufficient darkness or potential for darkness in their souls to enter hell but with enough free will to renounce it. These are dangerous souls. They have the powers of hell but will not bow to its dictates, their heads are not turned by the sudden rush of potential.

There cannot be a third type of pilgrim, runs the credo, for those wholly of the light would be unable to pass the portal. But then there has never been a mortal soul whose ties to the light are inviolable, who has not, at one time or another, embraced or at least flirted with the dark, no matter how briefly.

And the gates of hell are not barred to the likes of these. The gates of hell are always open. And the dark is always as ready to reclaim as to claim.

On its own level, the demon is aware, too, of others of its kind. It senses Mouffi, which it does not fully understand, it is like an adult human trying to comprehend the thought processes of a fetus. It was aware of Belphegor's banishment. It feels the shattering echoes of demon deaths, resonating after seven months, they will still echo after seven years, seventy times seven, the destruction of hell's princes is no small thing.

In a small mirror that a casual observer would take for a shaving-mirror, something like a firework sparkled. Munro ceased his pacing and inspected the glass, and a smile of nasty triumph spread over his face.

"Pierce," he murmured. "And a werewolf. How interesting." He turned to the demon, which feared his anger, but when it saw his expression, it feared his pleasure even more. "Go," he said to his familiar, and the demon did his bidding.

*   *   *

Fighting a strong impulse to flee — *you ain't a wolf now, no one can tell, nobody's gonna point a finger at you and accuse you, nobody's gonna come after you with silver bullets, so give yourself a break* — Harris stood over Caracol's body and tried to make sense of the layers and layers of odors in the shop. The majority were merely human, evoking fleeting impressions of their owners that would let him recognize them instantly if he ever saw them. But there were a few that puzzled him, obviously a few people who were only passing for human had investigated Pierce's books in the past months.

Hell, I dunno why I'm so surprised. I'm standing here, ain't I? And I ain't human. Stands to reason that those kinda folks'd be interested in old Pierce's stock. Probably can't get into the library even if they knew about it. Still, most of 'em seem pretty harmless, 'cepting just the one and jumping Jesus, that's nasty.

He sniffed audibly, but he was using the sum of his senses in harmony as he did in wolf-shape to give him a rounded impression of whatever had left the taint. Except that they weren't, in this case. *Knows how to hide its tracks pretty goddamned well, this son-of-a-bitch.*

But Harris, being not only werewolf but also human, however he might argue to the contrary, could get quite a lot from even so small and well-concealed a residue. Not that it was much use, since he could hardly convey what he sensed to the police. *Wish I could.* Caracol's death angered him because it was pointless. Someone had just come in here and casually killed the old man for no reason. He growled impatiently.

Come on, there's a reason. Even if you don't get it, there's a reason. Come on, think. What do we know? Old boy was deaf as a post. Couldn't hear squat. So someone asks him something, he just shrugs, right? Huh, no, not every time. He knew how to lipread. Leastways Pierce said he could. Couldn't read mine, and why? 'Cause I don't speak Portuguese worth a damn.

As the implication of this hit him, a little late, he turned on his heels and broke into a trot, cannoning into Pierce just inside the door.

"Your man Munro," he began, and then a demon exploded out of the air in a mephitic cloud of psychic stinking evil and grabbed at the antiquarian, who swore in fright and dodged, showing a turn of speed Harris had certainly never suspected him of. He stumbled backwards and the demon's arm whistled over his head, and that was an accident, thought Harris, but he had no time to think.

The first time he'd encountered a demon, he'd not been able to move a muscle to fight it. Not out of fear, at least he didn't think so, he'd simply been completely paralyzed when he tried to approach it. The second time, he had been able to fight at least, although ultimately it hadn't done much good.

Now, however, he had no choice, and apparently nothing to prevent him, either. He flung himself at the ugly stinking thing, snarling, and mentally at least he was more than half wolf as he did so.

It was taller than Harris's human form, and covered in coarse black hair, its arms and legs long and thin with more joints in them than a human's, etiolated fingers tapering to deadly-looking claws. Eyes clustered all over its head, and it was those that Harris went for.

His first spring had the advantage of surprise, and he bore it to the floor with a resounding crash. He snapped his teeth in its face before realizing he didn't have jaws, at least not the kind of dentition that could harm it much like that. Still he felt one eyeball burst gelidly in his mouth with a wet crunch, and spat convulsively. The demon screeched and slashed at him with its long pointed fingers, narrowly missing his face. Harris jerked his head back, and it threw him off with a mighty heave.

He thudded into a bookcase with an impact that hurt his back, and had to scramble out of the way in a hurry as it came after him, enraged. A wild kick connected with its skinny leg, the sound of the crack making him wince, and the demon skittered out of range of his boot, hissing at him in pain and fury.

Then it turned and went for Pierce again, apparently deciding that it didn't want to take any more damage from Harris. Who went after it instinctively, trying to grab it before it reached the Englishman. Pierce seemed rooted to the spot, apparently incapable of movement, a sensation Harris remembered. If he'd had the time he would have sympathized. His fingers slid off its greasy fur, disgusting sensation, but he'd deflected it from the antiquarian. He wished there was something in the shop he could hit it with. But there wasn't. *Not unless you throw the book at it,* a tiny and hysterical part of his mind chittered.

Panting, he stationed himself in front of Pierce and tried to look threatening. But he was tiring, and the demon knew it as well as he did. It crouched in front of him, a momentary impasse, thick liquid still leaking from one of its eyes.

Harris whirled round, seized the Englishman by the arm, and ran, his thoughts a melée in his head.

Don't get it, how could that thing get in, shitfire, he didn't invite it, goddamn it, he never invited me in either, must be the store don't count as part of his home, if'n I ever get outa this I'm gonna get me a knife like the skipper, not that I can carry silver, is it following? He glanced over his shoulder to check and promptly cannoned into a gaggle of black-clad matrons who had just rounded the corner, gossiping.

The effect was rather like a fox blundering into a henhouse. Harris came to a halt with a virulent, though thankfully unspoken, curse. Not that the ladies were likely to understand such language, at least not in English.

And the demon, which had easily followed them on its long thin legs, wrapped its arms round the horrified Pierce and disappeared. Leaving Harris marooned alone in the midst of an angry crowd of squawking and flapping that made him feel he was being mobbed by a flock of large and irate crows.

Losing what little Portuguese he'd managed to get into his head, he stood helplessly amongst them, shrugging his shoulders in what he hoped was a placatory way and saying, over and over, "Sorry." Though whether he was apologizing to them or to Pierce he wasn't at all sure.

One of them, at least, understood that. "You big ape," she shrieked. "What you doing? You late for something?"

He shook his head mutely. *No, not now. Too late, is what. Too late to help poor old Pierce, anyways.* And he remembered a useful word, at last.

"Desculpe," he said, excuse me, and fled, rightfully assuming that none of them was capable of giving chase. Already short of wind, he managed to get round the next corner before he had to stop again, his breath tearing his lungs. He was furious with himself. But he knew one thing. He had to get Pierce back from wherever the demon had taken him. And that would take more tracking skills than a mere werewolf had at his disposal.

And now I gotta find the skipper again. Tell him I did my best for poor old Pierce. Just so happens, best wasn't good enough. Goddamn it.

It never even occurred to him that the women he'd bumped into, who had witnessed a tall redhaired man running from what turned out to be the scene of a murder, would later tell that fact to the police.

*   *   *

Zé, charged with escorting Ana and her daughter to São Rafael, did so with some reluctance. He would rather have gone in search of Sílvia. But, he realized, of course the library was only a short distance from the orphanage, in fact *home* wasn't that far away, and technically he was on shore leave. Although *shore leave* had an increasing tendency to translate into *getting involved with the supernatural,* at least where his father was concerned.

His father would possibly have been surprised at how much Zé had managed to piece together. He'd not been ten years old that rainy night in Venice five years before when his father had come in with a blood-soaked towel clasped over his face. Zé was used to nocturnal comings and goings in those days, he knew very well his father's job involved him in things that weren't always legal, and he'd seen him the worse for wear more than once. Though he'd never been this badly injured before. And Zé, in fact, enjoyed a certain cachet among his peers as the son of Della Quercia's fixer, as some people called him.

That night Caterina's bad dreams had woken Zé up, she was only four and a half and had tugged him awake with incomprehensible nightmare babbling. He'd carried her in to their mother for better comfort than he could offer, but hadn't been able to sleep again.

And when his father came in, he'd listened at the door.

Actually he hadn't learnt very much from that episode of eavesdropping, except for the intriguing fact that Della Quercia had died a good quarter-hour before he finally lay down and expired, and even that he hadn't been sure he heard right.

It wasn't until he joined *Isabella* and made the acquaintance of the ship's doctor, who had introduced him to dime novels and shilling shockers — ostensibly to improve his English — that he began to have an inkling of the world his father had become involved with.

The joke was, the cheap gothic tales were actually right, in substance if not in detail. Ghosts did exist, and witches, and sorcerers, and demons, and werewolves. Even vampires, if the Russian witch (countess, he corrected himself, another stalwart of O'Rourke's library) was telling the truth, and he'd been sure they were the figment of someone's imagination. Sr. Bram Stoker's, to be precise.

Life, Zé was discovering, as most fourteen-year-olds do eventually, is a lot more complicated than he had originally thought.

He looked across at Ana speculatively, but he was thinking of Sílvia and wondering what it would be like to kiss a girl. The thought was no longer disgusting, as it would have been a year ago. But it was, in entirely different ways, disturbing and disconcerting.

9

"IF YOU DON'T STOP SCRATCHING THAT," SAID TATIANA DIMITROVNA THREATENINGLY, "I will tie your hands behind your back." I jerked my hand away from my chest and glared at her.

"If you and my father would let me smoke, I'd have something to do with my hands," I retorted. Two can play at that game.

"If you were to go home, senhor capitão," Zacuto pointed out, more than a little impatiently, "you could scratch everything that itches, smoke all you like, and free your mind for more constructive thoughts." It was about the fourth time he'd said it, or something like it. I looked from one of them to the other, and scratched my eyebrow instead. What is this, a conspiracy?

"He's right, Luís," said the witch. "You aren't needed here, so go."

They're not needed either, right? —*And you want them along, do you, da Silva?* I should do what Zacuto says while I have the chance. Before something else pops out of thin air intent on killing me. Before someone else turns up with more bloody riddles. Before — well, before my imagination overheats, for one thing.

I ran a hand through my hair. "How will you get back?" I asked Zacuto. He inclined his head to Tatiana Dimitrovna.

"No doubt the senhora can act as my anchor," he suggested.

"Yes, of course." She gestured at the door. We'd left my father and Alegria in the studio. "Until the painting is finished, we — I mean, I — can do nothing about Munro."

Zacuto sighed. "Little as I relish the inaction, you are right, senhora. But I should still like to examine the medallion of Belphegor."

Meu Deus, I'd forgotten all about that. And it's what we came here to get in the first place. "It's in the studio," I told him, moving towards the door. He held out a hand as if he could stop me physically. I think he sometimes forgets he's a ghost.

"Then there will be time enough when you are gone," he said, in a tone I know well. And so does anyone who's ever had a parent or a teacher. It means *no arguing*.

Faced with such determined opposition, I bowed to the inevitable and went. Who am I to argue with a ghost and a witch?

Oddly enough, as the door closed behind me, I felt peaceful. Probably has something to do with not currently being on my way to do something unpleasant. Quite the contrary. To see Emilia. Or make contact, as Zacuto put it. I found my hand stealing to the mark again, and restrained it with some difficulty. It burned and it chafed against my shirt. Damn it, it hurt. And I still couldn't feel it with my fingertips. Bet I couldn't see it, either.

Another advantage. I don't have Zacuto tagging along. So I can use public transport.

There are more ghosts on trams and funiculars than you might expect. And trains too, I suppose, though I rarely use them. But I suppose people are as likely to die en route from one place to another as they are when they're in — well, one place or another. People who're alive instinctively seem to avoid the phantoms. Have a look next time. The last seat to get taken, chances are there's a ghost sitting in it. But it'll *always* be the last seat to get taken.

I sat next to a steamy window and lit a cheroot. Amused myself by watching passengers avoiding the shade of an enormously fat man who'd most likely died of apoplexy. A small diversion, yes. But better than trying to stare out of the window. I was so busy with it that I took no notice of the man who came and sat next to me. Well, I knew there was someone there, of course. But I don't have an eye that side to look out of the corner of.

"Excuse me, senhor," I heard a bass voice say. "Would your name be Captain da Silva?" I turned my head sharply. My seat-mate was an African. An unremarkable, rather thin man, not especially dark-skinned, wearing a tweed overcoat that smelt of rain and a bowler hat a size too small for him. He had a faint Mozambique accent.

"Who wants to know?" I asked, blowing out smoke.

The tram was noisy with conversation, but his voice rumbled beneath it. So, soft as it was, it was easy to hear.

"I am known as Leão," he replied. "I've been wanting to meet you for some time."

No, I'm not surprised. I'm past being surprised by things like complete strangers accosting me in trams and saying they want to make my acquaintance. I raised an eyebrow at him.

"I take it you don't want to discuss a cargo for my ship," I said dryly. The man who called himself Leão laughed. Can't say he looks much like a lion.

But John Yeoh might say different. You can't tell much from appearances. I don't consider I look like a paladin. I look like what I am. Rather battered, forty-four years old, a slightly-used sea-captain with one eye and a headache. All right, perhaps you can't see the headache.

"No, senhor capitão, I don't," he rumbled. "I do want to tell you that if you need my help, you may call on me." I frowned at him, and took another drag on my cheroot. Need his help?

"You're a sorcerer of some kind, than," I guessed. Perceptive, da Silva. He nodded, and ducked to one side as a woman jostled past with her shopping.

"The term shaman is more accurate," said Leão didactically, "but it is, in the end, only a word. A label." I gave my cheekbone a scratch. Doubt whether it's semantics he wants to discuss, either. I gave a non-committal grunt.

"Mm. And why do you think I should need your help?"

He looked down his nose at me like a schoolmaster whose pupil has given the wrong answer. "Sometimes we all need help," he said. Óptimo. Truisms, now. Care to elaborate? "But you should know, if you do not already, that a very great evil has come to this city. Greater than the one you faced last year."

He sits there and springs that on me. I dropped the end of my cheroot and ground it out with my toe. What did he know about what'd happened last year? None of us is likely to've shouted it from the rooftops. Unless Paciência — No. Paciência be seen talking to an African? She'd sooner be seen dancing the can-can in the middle of the Rossio.

I turned and looked straight at him. He stared back expressionlessly.

"Last year?" I repeated. "This'll be the sorcerers' grapevine in action, will it?" They've told me more than once that there's some kind of communication channel they can tap into. I've no idea how it works. Though I should imagine it's not much like the telephone. For God's sake, it could be bloody crystal balls for all I know.

Leão was still eyeing me in that schoolmasterish way. "I have heard that you resist your powers," he said in a disapproving tone. And who gave him the right to do that?

"I didn't ask for them," I muttered, fingering the scar on my cheekbone.

"And what has that to do with anything?"

Quite a lot, if you believe in free will. Which I have to. If I thought my life was mapped out before it even began, I'd have to say why bother? But I can't believe that's the case. What would be the point?

"Sr. Leão—" I began.

"Just Leão will do."

"What the hell d'you want?"

"Nothing," he said, and smiled, showing a gold tooth. "Not to be disappointed, perhaps." And what did that mean?

I got to my feet. Had to get off at the next stop. He moved his legs to the side and looked up at me.

"And are you?" I asked.

"No," said Leão.

The tram banged to a halt, and I alighted. Stared after it as it rattled away. Wondering what the hell that was about. Now it's African shamans dropping out of the woodwork. As if I don't have enough on my plate.

Not that I don't appreciate his offer of help, but he didn't even leave a business card. And I don't know how to use the sorcerers' grapevine.

What's more, I'm damned if I want to know how.

The skies opened, and the rain began to pour down again.

"Stupid bloody weather," I grumbled, and splashed up the hill towards home.

To be accosted just as I got there by a panting and disheveled Harris. Bareheaded. He'd lost his cap. His red hair was plastered to his scalp. The rain had turned it almost black.

"Skipper," he gasped, and then lost it. Crimson in the face, he took several deep ragged breaths. I shook myself out of the momentary paralysis he'd inflicted on me, and opened the door.

"Get inside, Harris," I told him. "What the hell's happened?"

"It's Pierce," he got out between gasps. "Demon — took him. And — old boy in his shop — dead. Murdered — I reckon. Gotta be — Munro."

Oh *merda*. And just when I thought things were coming under control. Should know by now that the instant I start thinking I've got a breathing space, everything falls apart. Punishment for complacency, da Silva. And I'll have to postpone dealing with the mark, too. I rubbed it, irritably. Not Harris's fault.

Well, at least it looks as if his leg is better now.

I closed the door. Harris leaned against the wall, getting his breath back. You don't improve your wind on a ship a hundred and fifty feet by thirty. Not even if you did laps round the deck. Something I've never caught Harris doing.

Not much point offering him a brandy, but I did anyway. He shook his head. Could do with one myself, that's for sure.

"Talk to me, Harris."

He made a disgusted face, and wiped sweat off his brow with his sleeve.

Although it probably just spread it around a bit.

"It grabbed him," he said, "and disappeared. Jesus, skipper, I did my best." I know. It's not his business to go off fighting demons. It's mine. There, I admit it. "Did it some damage. Just not enough, I guess. But I can't even track him. Need a witch or something for that."

And I left Tatiana Dimitrovna at my father's. Damn it.

Which became academic a moment later. I opened the door of the office, looking for Emilia, and found her closeted with a brace of 'em. One of whom'll make Harris happy. The other, not so much. Luzia's here. So is her mother.

"That's good work, Harris," I remarked, taking out my cheroots. "You wish for a witch and you get the matched set."

Harris looked over my shoulder and gave a sort of relieved growl, Paciência and Luzia both turned round, with the expected expressions on their faces, and Emilia gave me a wink. I managed a rather strained smile in return. The burning pain of the mark wasn't getting any better. In fact I fancied it seemed to be pulling towards Emilia. The instant I thought that, she touched her breast with her fingertips. Making me wish with sudden and compelling urgency that I could do the same thing. Sometimes just the sight of Emilia drives out everything else just for a moment.

"We'd better adjourn to somewhere a little larger," she suggested, and reached for her stick to help pull herself to her feet.

Since the office is like a third-class railway carriage when there are only two people in it, that seems like a good idea.

"What brings you here, Dona Paciência?" I asked, striking a match and putting it to the end of my cheroot. She frowned at me, and shot a withering glance at Harris. No, she doesn't like her daughter walking out with a werewolf.

"Luzia thought *he* was in some danger," she replied. I raised an eyebrow at Luzia, who turned pink. She'd been right, at that.

I'd rather have let Harris tell the story, but of course Paciência doesn't understand English. And I think I've heard enough of Harris trying to speak Portuguese to last me a lifetime. And anyway he was too busy staring at Luzia to put together anything coherent. As for her, she never took her eyes off him the whole time. Yes, I know. I'm not making *any* comments on that.

"Sr. Harris," said Emilia urgently when I was done. He turned to look at her. I found I was rubbing my chest again, and scratched my cheekbone instead. "I think you had better go to the library as soon as possible."

"Huh?" exclaimed Harris. "The library?"

She sighed, the way she does when she thinks someone's being obtuse. *What have you missed, da Silva?*

"If you left poor Sr. Caracol without calling the police, and those women tell someone they saw you running away —"

"Son of a bitch," muttered Harris, then colored. "Beg your pardon, ladies." Luzia put a hand over her mouth, but I was sure she was trying not to giggle.

Paciência may not have understood that last exchange, but she was on the job, though. She turned to me. "Ask your man if he has anything belonging to Sr. Pierce."

I did as I was told, and Harris nodded. "There's these." And he took Pierce's spectacles out of his pocket. One of the lenses was broken.

We all stared at them. Somehow that broken lens made everything real.

* * *

Inspector Corvo, rain dripping off the brim of his hat, also down his neck and off his nose, identified himself to the officer standing guard sensibly just inside the door of Pierce's shop. Though the man looked more like a peasant than a policeman, not that Corvo thought that farmers were waterproof, simply that they'd be accustomed to bad weather.

It was nice, he thought, not without irony, to view a corpse that was actually intact for once. Though it would, of course, be much nicer not to have to view corpses at all. And it wasn't that this death was straightforward, either.

That would be too much to hope for, wouldn't it?

But for the fact that nothing had taken bites out of the body, it had more in common with Aranho's death than anything else. Insomuch as you considered the smashed spine and the shattered skull. But impacts forceful enough to cause that much damage should at least have spattered his brains around the place, thus reducing the value of many of Pierce's rare books.

And there'll not be a fingerprint on him, Corvo predicted morosely. He looked around the shop. He knew perfectly well who it belonged to, and where *was* Sr. Montague Pierce?

His gut feeling said the perpetrator of this murder was human. Not the monstrous thing that had stalked him the night before. Pierce's assistant was dead, and Pierce was missing, but there was no reason for the bookseller to kill his assistant.

However, his neighbors complained about a strange man banging on his door in the middle of the night and yelling, possibly in English. The neighbors were not linguists. And then there was the story of the tall redhaired man seen running from the crime scene by no fewer than five elderly women ("Six and a half feet tall, and built like an elephant"), who'd apologized to them in English. Corvo was inclined to trust the old ladies over the neighbors, at least one of the latter had been so drunk he could've been seeing Adamastor the Titan and sworn he was an Englishman, but you could always rely on a grandmother to twitch a metaphorical curtain and remember every little detail, even if it wasn't to do with the depth of the dust in her daughter-in-law's home.

More, the tall man had been a sailor.

Ricardo Corvo decided he'd delayed his return visit to Captain da Silva long enough. He got to his feet, holding onto a bookcase because nobody was looking at him, and told the guard that he was done.

"Very good, Inspector," said the man dourly, and Corvo thought how much happier he'd look behind a plough-ox. Or, in this weather, under a tree with a jug of wine while his son trudged behind the beast in the sucking mud.

*   *   *

Present, but not in any material or corporeal sense, Mouffi drifts. The demon-remnant, though much grown from its small beginnings, is still frustrated by its inability to influence matters in any significant way. But it is both puzzled and fascinated by what else is going on, both in the mundane world and in the place where it exists, the astral plane some might call it, or the ether. It is that channel where sorcerers and witches, as well as demons, sense significant developments, not so much a way of communication as a shared awareness.

Mouffi is so annoyed by what has been happening with Susana that it almost seems too much of an effort to try to keep the child apt for possession. True, its sole successful effort at influencing events is centered in her, and she is, by now, more like an infant whose age is measured in months rather than in weeks or days. But first Mouffi was cosying up to her, and then a rather nasty charm charged up a barrier round her that stung the demon-fragment all over like nettles and wasps and scorpions and made a hasty retreat necessary. Then the charm was removed again. And Mouffi hardly had time to register that than the child disappeared from its perception altogether.

But there was so much else going on. Mouffi had especially enjoyed the strange chimera of Belphegor's that had caused such consternation among the mortals with its apparently random killings. Its parent-demon's banishment had been particularly delightful, too. Though that meant the creation was dormant for now, demons are not known for solidarity with their own kind. They may not have invented the concept of schadenfreude (or maybe they did, at that) but it is something very close to their nature. Belphegor's downfall at the hands of a ghost, of all things, caused a black joy to course through the consciousness that was Mouffi.

And now not just one sorcerer back from Hell, but two, how delicious is that? On the one hand, a man who embraced all the delights on offer, and what a wonderfully tainted thing he is now, hell's own creature, whether he knows it or not.

On the other hand, a soul ripe for corruption, just now balancing precariously on the cusp between good and evil, will she control the powers of hell or will they control her in the end, as they must almost inevitably. Her fall will be splendid to witness, especially — especially! as it could drag down another soul with it. The soul of the man who killed great Malphas, of whom Mouffi is all that remains.

The one-eyed captain. The paladin.

* * *

Harris looks pretty sick. Not too difficult to guess why. If he's in a police cell when he goes wolf, his future won't look rosy. Or long.

"Go now," I told him, taking Emilia's hand in mine. Luzia, seeing it, shot a defiant glance at her mother and went to Harris.

"Be careful, Ed," she said, and gave him a kiss on the cheek. He managed a nervous smile, and grabbed her hand.

"You can count on it," he assured her, and took his leave.

Her mother hadn't commented. Amazing. Now she picked up Pierce's spectacles and turned them over in her hands.

"Can you find him?" Emilia asked. The witch smiled grimly.

"If he is on this plane," she said. "If he is in this time. If he is in this life." And that felt like a blow to the stomach. Obrigadinho, Paciência, for saying what we're all thinking but don't want to hear said out loud.

She held the spectacles loosely in her left hand. With her right, she pulled the pendant round her neck out of her blouse, then over her head. Held it over the spectacles. Closed her eyes and began to mouth silently. I almost wish I could lip-read when she starts doing that.

But do you really want to know what she's saying, da Silva? No, I don't. She can keep her secret knowledge stored up in her mind.

Slowly, the pendant stone began to rotate. Well, I know there's not much difference to her between finding a person and finding an umbrella. Her way's certainly easier than sending a werewolf to sniff something out. Although, stripped to its essentials, it's much the same thing.

Mind you, it's not as easy as you might think. Given that the answers she gets are always cryptic. Whatever the spirits are who answer her questions, they're too fond of word games for my liking. But then it's pretty typical. You won't find any prophecies written in straightforward language, either. Oh no. It all has to be done in riddles and gnomic utterances. If you ask me it's just another kind of oneupmanship.

Emilia and Paciência are well on top of that kind of thing, though. Especially Emilia. How she does it — well, I was going to say it's a mystery to me, but there's nothing mysterious about it. All you need is an encyclopedic knowledge of classical mythology and a brain like a card-index. I learnt some of it at school, of course. Also had to read the *Lusíadas*. If you want obscurity, Camões is your man. But it was all a long time ago, and I've forgotten most of it.

This time, though, the pendant didn't stop. Its movement stuttered. It reversed. Swung wildly around. I saw sweat trickling down Paciência's face. Her eyelids fluttered, and she looked deathly pale.

I was still holding Emilia's hand, perched on the arm of her chair. She squeezed my hand tightly. I glanced down at her, but her eyes were fixed on the witch.

Whose hand was shaking violently. And then she gave a terrible moan, and Luzia jumped to her feet, shouting words I couldn't make out. Words in no language I know or even recognize. You know what I mean. Once you've heard someone speaking it, you know what it sounds like even if you don't understand a word of it.

At the same time, the mark over my heart gave a sudden agonizing throb that made me inhale sharply. I pressed my free hand against it as hard as I could. Didn't do any good, of course. Emilia looked up at me, worried.

But then Paciência drew in a long hooting breath as if she'd been holding it for a long time and her eyes snapped open. The pendant was still again, and so was her hand. She put Pierce's spectacles to one side, a strange pained expression on her face. Hung the chain on the back of her chair. Perhaps it's still too charged up with magic. Like my burning mark. I removed my hand from it and paid attention to lighting a cheroot.

Emilia turned her attention to Paciência. "Are you all right?"

Yes, good idea to check up on the witch first. But she was staring at her daughter. "What did you do?" she asked dangerously.

Luzia rounded on her, eyes blazing. "You lost control," she snapped. "You did."

She's learnt how to stand up to her mother, then. Something I never did. Emilia's grip tightened on my hand again. What, she expects me to step between two quarrelling witches? I'd rather have teeth extracted. By O'Rourke.

Paciência looked down at her hands. Her shoulders drooped. "And so I did," she admitted. A miracle. "There is something very dire in the vicinity. It is blocking my spells."

Dire. That's one way of describing Munro. Incidentally, I couldn't help noticing that there was nothing resembling a *thank you* in what she said to Luzia. Not that I'm going to say anything. Believe me, Paciência's one person you don't want mad at you. Leery, da Silva? Absolutely. I don't even want her attention anywhere near me in this mood. But unfortunately I don't have any choice about that. I took the cheroot out of my mouth and said, "We have plans for that."

"What d'you mean, plans?" asked the witch, sternly. Making me feel as though I was still at school. I explained about my father and his paintings.

She got up, a little unsteadily, from the chair, an odd expression on her face. Half-angry, half-worried.

"What?" I said.

"I don't know," she replied. Picked up her pendant and looked at it thoughtfully before putting the chain back over her head. "This painting magic — I have no idea how it works. And all magic is a double-edged sword."

That's something she's said before. I don't think witches and sorcerers like anyone else working magic. Probably think it's poaching on their territory. Or something. I, on the other hand, would offload my other-worldly talents in a minute. If anyone was stupid enough to want 'em. But then it's not stupidity that makes magicians want more power. It's the power itself. Which makes 'em stupid, of course. I rubbed the mark on my chest. It was still burning like fury.

"The main thing is *if* it works," said Emilia, getting to the heart of things as usual. But even she sounded dubious. "Why *is* your Russian witch so reluctant?" She isn't mine. But that was a thought I didn't voice. There's some saying about protesting too much. I knocked ash off the end of my cheroot, and shrugged.

"She knows what Munro can do." And so do I. But I'm not the one who's going to have to go up against him.

"I thought that was why she went to — you know," she said. I looked down at her, with a strong urge to stroke her hair. Felt eyes on me: Luzia. I met her gaze. Caught a strange yearning expression on her face. Gone the moment I saw it.

"What language was that?" I asked curiously.

"Aramaic," she said.

I'm not even going to ask.

The witch cleared her throat. "I am sorry," she said. Although not to Luzia. "I sensed the sea, so he may be near the docks."

"The docks," I repeated. With a waterfront of nearly twenty miles that's not a whole lot of use. Paciência shook her head.

"Other than that, I cannot help. I cannot track him." She closed her eyes wearily.

"I can," whispered Luzia to me.

I turned my head, startled. Luzia shot a glance at her mother to make sure her eyes were still closed. Apparently she was under the impression that this made her deaf as well. A common misapprehension. I've suffered the consequences of it myself in the past. She opened her mouth to speak, but then there was a knock at the door and Joana came in.

Disgruntled is the only way to describe her expression. "Excuse me," she said to me. "There's a policeman come to see you, senhor capitão," *policeman* in the tone reserved for — I'd guess — *night-soil collector*, "and that telephone contraption rang too, but there was no one alive at the other end."

What a strange way to put it. I blew out smoke and raised an eyebrow at her. And why hadn't I heard either of these things?

"Did you say anything?" I asked her. Since she's about a hundred times less comfortable with the telephone than I am. And that little speech used up more words than she usually speaks all day.

"Of course, senhor." Indignantly. All right, maybe not quite as uncomfortable as I thought. "I said, *Is anybody there?* but all I hear is a hissing noise. *Sssss,*" she added, helpfully. Just in case I didn't know what it sounded like.

"All right, Joana," I said with a sigh and a glance at Luzia. "The policeman. Is it Inspector Corvo?"

"Corvo, yes, that was the name," Joana affirmed, disapprovingly. Still looking rather as if there was a nasty smell under her nose. I stubbed out my cheroot.

"Better show him in, then."

The inspector looks rather more composed than the last time I saw him. Though he still wears his suit the way I wear a suit. It looks as if he'd slept in it. I, no doubt, look rather more the worse for wear.

His eyes went to the cut on my head. And so they damn well should.

"Good day, Captain da Silva," he said, urbanely. As if he hadn't nearly put a bullet in my brain the night before. "Senhora," to Emilia. Bowed to Luzia and her mother, and stared at the gathering as if trying to figure out what a sea-captain might be doing in a roomful of women. "Am I interrupting something?"

Yes, as a matter of fact. But there's not much I can do about it at the moment. I turned to Luzia. "Do it, if you can."

She nodded. Gave a small smile and started being solicitous to her mother. Though I'm pretty sure she'd rather have left her there, slumped in the chair. But if she's found the courage to talk back to Paciência, she can afford to be magnanimous, I suppose. If you can talk back to Paciência you can talk back to anyone.

"Perhaps Inspector Corvo would be more comfortable in the office," suggested Emilia. Away from all these women, she didn't add.

"Yes," I agreed. Stroked her hair briefly. Regretfully. And got to my feet, suppressing a groan at various aches and pains. Falling to bits, da Silva. "Shall we?" I said politely to the inspector, who nodded back.

"As you wish," he said.

Most of my life I've managed to avoid the police. Apart from a couple of drunken episodes when I was much younger. When I had to skirt round the edges of the law for the Venetian I just made damned sure I didn't get caught. Easy enough if you know what you're doing.

At least I can talk to Inspector Corvo with a clear conscience. Though what more I can tell him than I said last night, I don't know. Have to wait and see how the conversation goes, won't we? And I must remember that I haven't heard about Caracol's death yet.

A situation which Corvo quickly remedied.

"Do you know a man who goes by the name of Caracol?" he asked, taking out his cigarettes and offering me one. I declined. Pulled out a cheroot instead.

"Caracol, yes," I said, striking a match. "He helps Sr. Pierce in his bookshop." I lit Corvo's cigarette, then my cheroot. Always be polite to the constabulary.

"He's dead," Corvo told me, and blew a smoke-ring. Show-off.

"Dead?" I said, raising my eyebrows. "Was he murdered?"

"Why do you ask?"

I grinned. "Because you're asking." Inspector Carrion-crow. Who gave me a rueful smile.

"Why do I get the impression I'd never win an argument with you?" he asked. I removed the cheroot from my mouth and contemplated it. Then I looked up at him and took all the good humor out of my voice.

"Because you wouldn't." I tapped the eyepatch. "I won this argument. Try not to lose any, after that." He looked taken aback. Da Silva has teeth, after all. I showed them to him, then asked, "What do you want, Inspector?"

He tapped ash off the end of his cigarette. His fingers were nicotine yellow. After a moment, he said, "Caracol was killed by — by being smashed into the floor, or the wall," he said. "Like Aranho Alves was apparently dropped from a great height. Similar, but not the same. I think Caracol was killed by a man. However strangely. Would you know anything about a tall redhaired man seen running away from Sr. Pierce's shop?"

Glad I've already talked to Harris. I leaned back in my chair and looked levelly at the inspector. "My second mate fits that description," I told him, and added, "You met him last night," enjoying his expression.

"He was the—"

"The werewolf, yes. He didn't kill Caracol."

Corvo blew out smoke. Sat back and crossed his legs. "I suppose you know who did," he said grumpily.

"Yes," I replied, deadpan. "An Englishman called Sir Robert Munro. Though you'll never prove it."

"No?" murmured the inspector. "You'd be surprised."

Probably not, to be truthful. But in this case — "He'll buy himself off. He's a politician. He'll have fifty people willing to swear he was celebrating Mass at the time."

"And why," Corvo enquired, "would an English politician kill an elderly shop assistant in Lisbon?"

Good question. "I think he just lost his temper," I said. "Caracol was deaf, you know. And sometimes he liked to play on that. You know, me deaf peasant, no understand, that sort of thing. If Munro asked him something, it would've looked as if Caracol was ignoring him." And someone like Munro doesn't stand for being ignored by peons.

The inspector took another drag on his cigarette. "I've seen people killed for less," he agreed, nodding glumly. "But what did Munro want?"

"A book?" I hazarded, pressing my hand against the burning mark again. It didn't get any easier. The inspector gave me what I think is called an old-fashioned look.

"Must've been a very special book," he observed.

You might say that. Since it contains spells that could bring the world to an end. I scratched my eyebrow. "Do you know what kind of books Pierce sells?"

He eyed me sourly through a cloud of smoke. "I suppose you're going to tell me it's books of spells and suchlike."

"There, see," I said. "I didn't need to tell you."

I never really thought about it before, but Pierce's trade isn't exactly whiter than white. He was getting hold of grimoires for the Venetian before I even met him. Either of them. And you only use those for one thing. Unlike guns, even drugs. Which you might argue could be used for the good of mankind.

Corvo sat and smoked. I would've bet money he was thinking the same thing as I was. Finally he said, "There's no evidence against this Munro."

"Find some?" I suggested. He laughed mirthlessly.

"Are you suggesting the police are in the habit of fabricating evidence?"

"All the time," I said, and ground out my cheroot in the ashtray.

* * *

Zé was bored. Books held no great fascination for him, and neither did babies. Other than that, though, São Rafael didn't have much to offer.

He was disproportionately pleased, therefore, when the door swung open to admit a sweating and disheveled Harris.

Who slammed the door shut behind him and leaned against it, panting. His face was wet, whether with rain or sweat Zé couldn't tell.

"Sr. Harris," he exclaimed, jumping to his feet, and then, in alarm at Harris's expression, "What's the matter?"

Still leaning against the door, Harris took several deep breaths, then ran his hand over his face and said, succinctly, "Cops."

"*Meganhas?*" Zé squeaked, and then had a coughing fit to cover up his cracking voice.

Not that Harris noticed. "We've all gotten so used to coming here when there's demons about," he said, "we musta forgot that cops ain't the bad guys and this place won't keep 'em out. Leastways," he added dubiously, "I don't think they're the bad guys."

Zé had his voice under control now, he hoped, and growled out "Are they following you?" Harris sniffed.

"Not yet," he said. "Least I don't think so. But I ain't gonna be safe here." He looked around, evaluating escape routes, which were in short supply. Eventually he flung himself down into a chair, but there was a temporary look about his posture.

"But what did you *do?*" asked Zé, wide-eyed, visions of werewolf depredations filling his head, although he couldn't imagine Harris-wolf behaving like that. But he was still partly in thrall to the dime novel.

"Nothing, goddamn it," snarled Harris, half-rising from his seat and scowling threateningly at Zé. "And I oughta box your ears for thinking it. What're you doing here, anyhow? You suddenly developed a taste for literature?"

"No," said Zé indignantly, beating a strategic retreat behind a desk. "I had to bring them." He nodded at Ana, who was sitting by one of the rain-streaked windows. Realized belatedly that she was feeding the baby, and turned beet-red with embarrassment. Harris chuckled, which didn't make things any better, and Zé scowled at him.

"She ain't worried about it, Zé, why should you be?"

"I don't know, it just seems…" He groped for a word, staring at the floor. "Indecent," he finally muttered.

Harris hooted with laughter. "Listen to you, you sound like my Auntie Judy who was so prim and proper she put bloomers on the joanna."

"What?" asked Zé, gaping at him in total incomprehension. It sounded like English, but didn't seem to make any sense at all.

"Covered up the legs of the piano," Harris translated. Which wasn't much more illuminating. Not having moved in the right sort of circles, Zé had never heard of this particular cliché of the Victorian age, and didn't quite understand it.

"Huh," he said sullenly. But he glanced back, defiantly, at Ana. Who, having finished, was now wiping little Susana's face with a cloth. She smiled vaguely at him, and he smiled back, more confused than ever.

And Susana burped loudly, filling the room with a milky odor that made Zé wrinkle his nose, and then said, *"Tanit."*

Zé and Harris both jumped as if they'd been shot, then Zé grabbed a sheet of paper and scribbled the word on it. He looked over to Ana and the baby. If last time was any guide, Susana would start crying about—

Now. Right on cue, she let out a lusty yell. Ana sighed audibly and rocked the child in her arms. She looked sternly across at Zé and Harris.

Wiped a hand across her brow.

"Don't *ever* have children," she said, and there was a measureless weariness in her voice. Then she yawned.

"Skipper needs that word," Harris muttered to Zé, who looked helplessly at Ana. No help to be had there.

"I'm supposed to stay with her. Perhaps—" But Harris was too old a hand to be caught like that. He got to his feet. The chair scraped along the floor with a noise like nails down a blackboard. He winked at Zé.

"Enjoy the view," he said.

"Wait, where are you going?"

"I ain't gonna skulk in here," said Harris. "There's no point. The cops want me, they'll find me easy enough. That Corvo fellow knows what's what. I'll be okay if'n I can get to talk to him. 'Sides, I can't even have a smoke in here, and that's something I surely need right now. You keep your ears peeled for whatever the nipper says next."

And then he was gone. Zé stared at the closed door in annoyance. Oh well, he thought dully, things can't get any worse.

Then the door opened again, admitting wind, rain, and a priest. But it was only Fr Pereira, and he was all right. The dumpy cleric flapped his umbrella outside, then quickly shut the door behind him. Seeing Zé, he looked surprised, then turned his head quickly to scan all round the library, as if looking for something. Ana crossed herself dutifully and lowered her eyes as his gaze passed her. Susana, luckily, had stopped crying.

"José?" said Fr Pereira, with a puzzled frown. "What brings you here?" He waddled over to where Zé was sitting and lowered himself into the chair recently vacated by Harris. It was taking a lot of punishment that day.

"Why is everyone so surprised?" Zé complained. "I do know how to read, you know. Father," he added quickly, for politeness. He moved a book around the table top.

Fr Pereira hid a smile. "I do know," he said gravely. "But you *aren't* here for the books, are you?"

"Well, no," Zé admitted. "I'm here with Dona Ana." He lowered his voice, confidentially. Fr Pereira was in on a lot of the less conventional aspects of Lisbon life, in fact it was he who had introduced Zé's father to the library — not to mention being his source for holy water — so it was safe to talk to him. "There's a sorcerer after the baby."

"Why?" asked the priest, leaning back in the chair, which creaked dangerously. Zé liked that, in a funny sort of way. He didn't mess about with stupid questions, the way a lot of grownups did. He went straight to the heart of the matter.

"She's in a prophecy. The baby. Susana," he explained. "She's supposed to say four words that give him the key to something, something that could give him power. And he's already got too much."

The priest looked curiously at the baby, who was now fast asleep, one tiny hand clutching her mother's index finger. "What words?"

"Well, she just said *tanit,*" said Zé, "and a while ago she said *kealba.*" The priest raised his eyebrows.

"Tanit?" he repeated.

Ana interrupted. "She said *lupo* as well." Both Zé and Fr Pereira stared at her, and she quailed slightly.

"Wolf?" said Zé, unable to stop himself thinking of Harris. "When did she say that? Why didn't you tell us?"

"Last night," said Ana in a small voice.

"How very strange," remarked the priest. "As you say, that's the Italian word for wolf. Tanit was the Phoenician goddess of Carthage, her name means serpent-lady. I don't know what, or who, *kealba* might mean, but it's obviously a word." He sighed. "What has your father gotten himself involved with now?"

"It's not his fault," said Zé defensively, and Fr Pereira smiled. Zé had a strong suspicion that the priest would've tried to ruffle his hair if he'd been near enough.

"I know," Fr Pereira agreed. "It's his task."

Whether that was meant to make Zé feel better, he didn't know. He knew one thing, though: it didn't. Because with Susana spouting words like water out of a fountain, he had to tell his father quickly. And he didn't know how to ask the priest to stay and mind Ana. Although that was the only alternative he could think of.

"Er—" he began. But Fr Pereira had, apparently, read his mind.

"Run along and tell him, José," he said, in an avuncular sort of way. "I'll keep an eye on these two ladies."

Zé still had enough energy to take this instruction literally, and he was going at full tilt when he ran into Luzia on the corner of the square.

She grabbed him by the arm. He hated it when people did that. But all annoyance flew away at her anguished words.

"Ed's been arrested," she gasped. "We have to do something."

*   *   *

It calms him, painting. You can't paint if your mind is in turmoil, at least sane men can't, if any artist is completely sane, surely anyone with such limitless imagination must be at least partly mad to be able to tell lies for a living.

Luís would say that includes priests as well, came the irrelevant thought. But they believe the lies. And politicians make other people believe their lies. Artists, writers, our lies are benevolent. Most of them, at any rate, he added.

In the liquid light that the rain filters through the big window, the picture takes shape at the end of his brush, charcoal bones fleshing out with paint, a portrait of a man in late middle age, in robust health apparently, though he has been told this is an illusion, the body may be healthy but the soul is sick.

He has not painted, as the Russian woman suggested, a nude, not because he is uncomfortable with the idea, an artist is probably the last person who would be, but because symbolism is all-important to this endeavor. The symbolism is, in any case, obvious: the draped classical figure holds an empty flask, its final drip is drying on the barren ground.

This essential central image being complete, now the artist in him is playing, engaged upon embellishing the picture with more symbolism, an empty scabbard discarded on the ground, a tideless sea, a mule in a field.

And Alegria watches, content just to be there, if a woman made out of canvas and paint can be said to be content. He is happy that she is there, and so, if she reflects his moods, then she too is happy.

In the next room, the ghost and the witch are poring over a medallion that looks like bronze but is no more mundane metal than the Judas tree is natural flora.

Only Tatiana Dimitrovna, who has been to Hell, has the knowledge and the sight to recognize it for what it is. And perhaps only a ghost, a thing not of the physical world but manifested in it, can understand its power. Or at least fear it as it needs to be feared. Like the Judas tree, it is very dangerous to him. If Zacuto had pores, skin, flesh, breath, he would be sweating.

"Can it be destroyed?" he asked, eyeing the thing as a man would a scorpion or a poisonous snake.

"Not in this world," the witch replied, "not truly. And it would not be a good idea. This thing is... a door. Not a portal like the one created by a Judas tree, but the door at the end of a corridor, a passage that only the demon that used it can pass through. There will be an identical door somewhere in hell. Destroying both of them would destroy the demon's access to this world — destroying only one would make its access easier."

"Then the demon can come through at any time," said the ghost, frowning.

Tatiana Dimitrovna shook her head. "Your banishment was not wasted. It should hold it back for a while at least. We should probably remove the medallion from this house, though, and put it somewhere more, shall we say, difficult for the demon?"

Zacuto smiled, his teeth flashing white in his beard. "I am guessing you mean — perhaps in a church?"

The witch laughed. "Old man," she said, "your mind is almost as devious as mine." Zacuto was not sure whether this was a compliment or not.

"I may not have been to hell," he retorted, "but I have had over four hundred years to hone my talents."

They looked at each other, an unexpected empathy flowing between them. Rain flowed down the window, its thrumming a beat as incessant as the sea, will it ever stop?

"Do you suppose he has finished the picture of Munro yet?" Tatiana Dimitrovna asked after a moment.

"We should go and see," Zacuto replied. "The paint-woman is too afraid of you to come and find us."

"Yes, she is, isn't she?" mused the witch. "I wonder why that is."

"You should know," he said with a reprise of his former acerbity. "As I know. You are too real, senhora. You have touched the roots of the world. If you survive it, you will be the strongest of us all."

"If I survive it?" she asked sharply, but the ghost made no reply. After a moment, Tatiana realized he wasn't going to.

* * *

In retrospect, it probably hadn't been the smartest thing in the world to break that policeman's nose.

I panicked. Hellfire, who wouldn't? Way those fellows was looking at me, I thought they was looking to kill me for sure. Makes me jumpy, daytime at full moon. Shoulda toned it down a bit. Poking a cop in the snoot, that's just plain dumb.

Harris eased himself into a more comfortable position on the bunk, wincing as broken ribs grated together. *Going wolf'll heal that if I get outa here. 'Course if I go wolf in here some smartass'll start melting down the spoons. Next thing you know, bang, no more Ed Harris.*

When he thought of all the times as a new werewolf that he'd wished devoutly for an ending courtesy of someone with a silver bullet, only to have the prospect looming now when he actually wanted to carry on living, it almost made him laugh.

Everybody pretended not to speak or understand any English at all — *yeah, and I believe in the tooth fairy* — so Harris sat on the bunk in a tiny green-walled cell that stank of carbolic and urine, and tried to remember his Portuguese lessons.

Joke's on you now, Ed my boy. Yeah, but never thought my life was gonna depend on it. How long till moonrise? Hours. Forget about it. Use your goddamn brain. It can't be difficult. Seven words in English.

Right. I want. Quero. *To speak.* Falar. *With Inspector Corvo.* Com o Inspector Corvo. *There. See. That wasn't difficult, was it? May not be proper grammar, but who the hell cares?*

He tested it by banging on the cell door and yelling it at the top of his voice until someone came and told him, by the tone, to put a cork in it. He shouted it again. And again. And again, until he was hoarse and anxiety was bringing on the tugging of the moon hours early. He rested his head against the cold metal door in despair.

Get him here soon, for Godsakes. Or it's gonna be too late for Mrs. Harris's little boy.

*   *   *

And not too far distant as the crow flies — the winged sort, not the eponymous inspector — another prisoner.

Pierce was not in a cell, as such, though he had a jailer. It was currently in the form of a small monkey, although there was something murderous in its eyes that made him studiously avoid looking at it, after the first awful glance. He was glad he'd lost his spectacles and therefore couldn't see it clearly.

He told himself not to worry, but that was a fairly fruitless exercise. The antiquarian believed he'd grown a little more courage since his first direct encounter with this world last year, but it still didn't mean he could confront a demon with equanimity. Even a minor one.

Instead he surveyed his prison, also not a terribly productive thing to be doing. He didn't know where he was, except that from the watery, vaguely sewery stink he imagined he was probably near the docks.

Much good that piece of information did him.

The demon's very presence was debilitating. It was difficult to prevent his gaze from sneaking to the creature. Difficult to think straight.

But a revelation came to him then. He didn't need to think. He just needed to stay sane until da Silva found him.

This room was just a room. Ten feet square, or thereabouts. Brick walls, whitewashed, but a long time ago. Crusted with nitrate deposits, mottled with mold. Wooden floor. Big, thick planks or beams like railroad sleepers. Same sort of thing covering the window. Tarred at some time, the smell of pitch still lingered. Also, a vague faint smell of spices. Warehouse, it added up to.

What could he do to take his mind off his frightful jailer? Count the bricks in the walls. Yes, that would be productive. Sing what snatches of Wagner he could recall. That would probably make the demon eat him, double-quick. Especially since all that came to mind was *The Ride of the Valkyries*. Recite mathematical formulas. Of which his knowledge stopped at the twelve times table. The idea is to *stay* sane, Pierce, he told himself sternly, not drive *yourself* out of your mind.

What was the stupid prophecy that had started all the trouble? "Bloody Johanna Kundrie," he muttered, only to spider-crawl across the room in panic as the demon's head whipped round towards him with a horrible squawk. Pierce echoed the sound, in his own fashion.

"You command me," it gibbered. Its voice echoed, as off huge empty halls.

"What?" Pierce quavered, trying to burrow into the wall behind him.

"The prophet's name binds me to speak," the monkey-thing chittered, reaching out a long-fingered hand to him.

"Johanna Kundrie?" he asked querulously, trying not to flinch.

"Three times is the charm, mortal," it said.

Pierce swallowed. His mouth tasted like old boots. "Johanna Kundrie," he repeated, more firmly this time.

And the demon began to speak, no, to chant. A formal recital, it was, and the antiquarian listened open-mouthed and terrified that Munro would choose this moment to come in and interrupt the creature.

"*By the coming together of the hallows shall the wounded king be made whole.*

"*By the silver dish whose key lies on the island of the knights.*

"*By the broken sword whose key lies in the city destroyed by the sons of Romulus.*

"*By the chalice whose key lies on the island of Aphrodite.*

"*And by the bleeding lance whose key lies in the city of the dead under the volcano.*

"*And the key to all the hallows lies with the child in the city of Ulysses who is born to speak the four words of power.*"

In separate corners of the room, the demon cringed, and Pierce cringed, both mortally afraid of the man who had brought them here, both now bound together by a secret, the words of the prophecy that even Munro had not heard in full from the mouth of his familiar.

But even in his terror, Pierce identified the places. Malta. Carthage. Cyprus. And, probably, Pompeii. Or Herculaneum.

And he rested his forehead against his knees in anguish. Now he knew this, how could he withhold his knowledge from Munro?

The demon's delicate spider-touch on his ankle made him jerk his head up. "What?" he blurted out, as though talking to a human colleague.

"I did not ask to be bound to him," whispered the demon. "He is not my master. I still seek a master." It looked hopefully at Pierce, who knew better than to meet its eyes.

"I can't be your master," he told it, his voice shaking despite his best efforts.

"I know," it said, a little wistfully, he thought. "I am bound to him, though not by my own will. Thus I can reveal certain things to those who know how to ask." It squirmed around, Pierce studiously avoiding looking into its eyes. He shook his head, obscurely regretful.

"I'm sorry," he muttered.

"Break the spell," implored the demon, staring round the room wide-eyed. "Field another candidate for the king. Find the hallows. Free me. Free your mortal world too. That one means ill to all. To you, to us. To everything."

"Help me, then," Pierce said.

"I have given all the help I can," the monkey-thing told him. "Now — he calls me. Human, do not resist him. And do not let him suspect I have spoken to you."

Sweat crawling in his hair, and not sure whether these two things were simultaneously possible, Pierce nonetheless pledged his word to the demon.

"I won't," he promised.

*   *   *

Safira Martins stepped out into the rainy afternoon with a moué of distaste at the weather. She stepped back into the lee of the hotel and snapped her fingers imperiously at the doorman, a model of a major-domo. He in turn summoned a cab and accepted her tip with a hauteur that matched her own, yet he was a hotel employee and she was a prostitute.

She settled herself back into the creaking leather seat, wrinkling her nose at the odors of damp, mold within the cab, sodden clothes and sweat from the driver, the slightly more wholesome smell of wet horse. Taking a cab at all was a bit of a luxury for her, although she earned more than enough to pay for it, but in weather like this is was really more of a necessity. Safira examined the hem of her skirt with distaste. Despite all her best efforts, it was still mud-spotted.

If all the gentlemen paid her this well she would take cabs everywhere. Hell, if they all paid her this well she could retire. It was very civil of him, she thought, to be so generous in the light of his own failure. Such things happened to men his age, it was a fact of life which Safira took as a bit of relief when it happened, although of course she was always sympathetic to her afflicted clients. Except the ones who decided it was her fault, of course.

Strangely enough, though, this particular gentleman had seemed almost pleased.

Ah well, she thought, relaxing as best she could into the swaying of the cab, she wasn't paid to *understand* men. It wasn't really part of the job description.

And in his suite, Sir Robert Munro poured himself a whisky from his private bottle, the hotel had no malt like this, and smiled. The smile made his familiar quail and wonder what new torment the man had dreamt up this time.

Munro, however, had no present plans to pull wings off flies. He knew the power of metaphor as well as the next sorcerer, and whatever odd magic had managed to penetrate his defenses and render him impotent had done him a favor that overcame the biggest stumbling block in his quest to become the new Fisher King.

Whyever had he thought, up to now, that the wound had to be a physical one?

*   *   *

"I don't like it," said Paciência for the twelfth time. And she wasn't referring to my cheroot. She gave me a very black look. Blames me for introducing Harris to her daughter, as if I'd made them attracted to each other. "Why would she need him for her spell?"

Confidence, perhaps? I blew out smoke, to her continued disapproval. She may be Emilia's friend, but my God, she's a prickly woman, and she loves putting people down. Including her own daughter. Especially, it seems to me, her own daughter. But then I suppose my own made me suspicious of mothers in general. And I had to put thousands of miles between us to escape. What confuses this relationship is that Paciência's younger than I am. In physical years, at least. Most of the time she treats me like a fourteen-year-old.

Right now I'm more captivated by that stray tendril of hair on Emilia's forehead. By the line of her neck. And the curve of her breast. And — And we're waiting here for Luzia to track Pierce down. Damn it. I took a drag on my cheroot and crossed my legs. Carefully. Emilia glanced at me sideways, looked down, and put a hand over her mouth to hide a smile. Suddenly, I wanted to laugh. Paciência glared at us.

And then I heard the front door bang open. Didn't even have time to get to my feet before Zé burst in, closely followed by Luzia.

"Sr. Harris's been arrested!" he shouted. Luzia's face was pale and sweaty. I thought she was going to faint, and pushed myself quickly upright. But she shook her head, one hand pressed to her side.

"Stitch," she explained, breathlessly.

I shot a regretful glance at Emilia, and stopped my own hand from rubbing at the burning mark on my chest. "Looks like a return meeting with Inspector Corvo, then," I said, turning my head to look out of the window.

"Still raining," Zé told me helpfully. Which I could see for myself.

"Yes, and what are you doing here?" I asked him, finishing my cheroot.

He looked alarmed. "Fr Pereira's with them," he said hastily. "Susana's said more words. And we know what they mean." We? He went on before I could ask. "She said *Tanit*, and Fr Pereira says it's a snake-woman, a goddess of something, and Dona Ana said she said *lupo* last night. So if we can find out what a *kealba* is—"

"Dog," I told him. "Sr. Zacuto knew that one. The Maltese word for dog." Then something hit me. "You said serpent, snake-woman?" Zé nodded. That's what John Yeoh called Tatiana Dimitrovna. Not to mention that Yeoh's own Chinese name meant Faithful Dog. And the wolf... well, we're on our way to rescue the wolf.

What in God's name will the fourth word be?

* * *

Fr Pereira had won Ana over very quickly. Unlike a lot of priests, he didn't disapprove of women in principle. And he liked children. In fact, it was simpler to say he liked *people*. Which, in turn, made *them* like *him*.

He hadn't asked Ana the baby's age. Sometimes it proved to be an awkward question, you could see the mother's often rather rudimentary knowledge of mathematics flash before her eyes, and Fr Pereira didn't like embarrassing people unnecessarily. Sin it might be, but people produced babies all the time without the benefit of the marriage sacrament, and he didn't think God was really going to get too hot under his metaphorical collar about it, not with so many much greater things to worry about. Little Susana looked to be about six months old, too young to articulate words, certainly, but if there was a prophecy of some kind at work, anything was possible.

Baby Susana, anyway, was much like any other in that she enjoyed games that involved pulling fingers and making silly noises, and Fr Pereira endeared himself to both mother and daughter by proving adept at these.

Finally she lay back and looked up at the adults with a very knowing expression on her little face, and said the final word, *"leeondahri."*

Which, as Fr Pereira knew well, was the Greek for *lion*.

10

I NEVER KNEW THERE WERE SO MANY POLICE STATIONS IN LISBON. And I never will know what kind of logic applies when it comes to deciding which one of them to shove a prisoner in. For God's sake, if you arrest someone in the Alfama, where's the sense in taking him all the way to the Rossio to throw him in a cell? I tried four before I even got anyone to admit to having heard of Harris, but as to where I might find Inspector Corvo, I can't even guess. From the stonewalling I got, you'd think he didn't even exist. I know he exists, all right. Since he nearly blew my head off.

Anyway the whole saga was officialdom at its worst. And it got worse when I finally managed to track Harris down. The sort that makes you want to commit murder yourself. Preferably the smug bastard sitting in front of you. It didn't help, of course, that my werewolf had broken an officer's nose. Resisting arrest, as they put it. It's so typically Harris that I'm almost inclined to believe it. But even he wouldn't be so stupid as to be the one who throws the first punch. At least, I'm reasonably sure he wouldn't. Even if he does have a very short fuse around the full moon.

So here I am, bogged down in bureaucracy until I'm ready to emulate Harris and wade in with my fists. What is it about putting someone in charge of an office that instantly makes him want to throw a spanner into everything? Or is it just that this type of job attracts the kind of man who enjoys obstructing people? It may be good to see someone enjoying what he does. But not this much. *Try counting to ten. Or a hundred might be more effective.*

Finally I managed to persuade the minion to let me speak to someone higher up the food chain. Who in turn let me see Harris. Not that I thought that would be much use to either of us. He'd still be in the cell. I'd still be minus a werewolf. And the day crawls on towards moonrise. What you might call stalemate.

If they'd let me in the back to start with I would've known Harris was there. I heard him all the way down the corridor. Hell, you could've heard him in Cascais. Banging on the door and yelling for Inspector Corvo.

"Nice to see your language lessons have had some effect," I said round the door. Wasted on him. He looks a complete wreck. *Oh yes, and what do you think you'd see if* you *looked in a mirror, da Silva?*

"Jesus, am I glad to see you, skipper," he exclaimed. "You happen to know what time it is? Bastards took my watch."

"It's hours to moonrise, and you know that better than I do." I stuck my hands in my pockets and glared at him. "Next time, do me a favor, don't break bones. It's going to cost me a fortune in bribes if we can't find Corvo."

"They started it," said Harris sullenly. "I got at least two broken ribs here. Hurts like a son of a bitch."

Maybe, but he'll heal tonight. I fingered the scabby cut on my head. Wondered where to go from here.

"They charge you with anything?" I asked. Apart from mutilating the Portuguese language, that is. He shook his head.

"Nope."

That's a good sign. I hope.

"Captain da Silva," said Corvo's voice from behind me. "I didn't expect to have the pleasure of meeting you again so soon."

Pleasure. Not quite how I would've put it. But what the hell. He was holding out his hand, so I shook it. Keep on the right side of the constabulary.

"Inspector," I said.

"And this is Sr. Harris," he remarked, narrowing his eyes. "We've met before, the senhor capitão tells me, but I must say I wouldn't have recognized you."

Harris grunted uncomprehendingly. "Hope you're planning on letting me outta here, Inspector. Skipper'll tell you I ain't the man you want."

Corvo followed this with some difficulty. You could almost see his brain working. After a moment he said, in careful English, "Yes, Sr. Harris, we have no reason to hold you. I apologize for the inconvenience."

Well, now I've got the werewolf back. Trouble is, what do I do with him now?

Luzia at least had no doubts. She flung herself at Harris so violently that he almost went over. Quite a feat, that. He stared at me over her head with a bemused expression on his face. I lit a cheroot and let them get on with it.

After a few moments I cleared my throat pointedly and said, "Now can we get on with finding Pierce?"

"I'll need somewhere to lie down," said Luzia, her voice muffled by Harris's shirt. How is that going to help find missing people?

"Lie down?" I repeated. She disengaged from Harris.

"I'm going to ride a cat," she explained. Although the explanation made no sense. Luzia turned to face me. Touched her forehead. "With my mind."

"She can, too," said Harris proudly. He had a silly grin plastered over his face. Meu Deus, maybe he really *is* in love.

So, back home, then. I sighed. How much longer before I can get this damned mark defused, or whatever you call it.

"Come on, then," I said. "Let's get on with it."

Because the sooner we find Pierce, the sooner we can try and free him. I have to admit, though, that I have no idea how to get him out of Munro's clutches.

One thing's certain, though. It won't be nearly as easy as springing Harris.

*　*　*

After what seemed like a very long time, although time is not a natural concept to demons, Mouffi found a trace of the child. There was a trail to follow, faint and barely discernible, but a trail nonetheless. The demon-fragment had invested too much in Susana to give up now, and pursued the scent as far as it could. Which was not very far. The infant was out of its reach, protected by the wards of São Rafael.

Yet Mouffi remembers penetrating this place, in mouse-shape, when its parent Malphas, if parent is the right word, was still alive. If alive is the right word.

When Malphas was slain, it was all Mouffi could manage to maintain the mouse-shape. Now, however, the fragment got an unpleasant shock when it tried to repeat the change. Unpleasant at first, anyway.

It found it was no longer able to shrink into a mouse. And that meant it couldn't get into the library. It was simply too big. But after a moment of frustration the truth sank in, and Mouffi realized with an increasing sense of exultation that this meant it was growing. At last. In size, and therefore in power.

And that also implied that it could get inside the library by other means. São Rafael, after all, protects its contents first and foremost, and by extension those who use them. But it is not a dwelling-place, and so is subject to different rules.

In the plane of existence where Mouffi's true being exists, there is currently a strange ownerless creature, as lost as a bag lady, the odd construct put together by the demon Belphegor in imitation of the painter's woman of pigment and canvas, although it is in fact made from things much more dire, including the corpses it feasted on while tied to the painting. But it has no mind as such, no place where thoughts generate, no sense of self, only an emptiness.

Mouffi may be neither very big nor very powerful at the moment, but it is perfectly capable of filling a void. And the construct, which had lain immobile as a puppet without a puppeteer, was suddenly animated. Not activated, not yet. But aware.

It was a body, something Mouffi was heartily sick of being without. Grotesque, yes, but since when has a demon cared about appearances?

And oh, the sensations. The tastes and smells and savors. Things which the construct, being driven by artificial urges and not sentient, had not been capable of benefiting from. Or even of using. And therefore still rich and fresh, as if preserved in an ice-house.

The demon-fragment was like a child given free rein in a sweet-shop. So much to sample and explore. So much to save for later. Essences of victims. Their thoughts, the tastes of their souls. And among all that, traces which Mouffi recognizes. The taste of a werewolf, whose soul Malphas captured before being slain. And the taste of Malphas's killer, too.

This body is something a small remnant of a demon can enjoy inhabiting. At least until it regains access to the child.

*   *   *

Luzia is *cat*. A big bruiser of a tabby, this time, with a ripped ear and two inches missing since long ago from the end of its tail. She is steering it towards the docks, because that is their best guess as to Pierce's whereabouts. This animal, though, is less biddable than the last one. And anyway she knows a cat is not quite suitable for her present quest.

However there is no particular reason, as far as she knows, why she shouldn't be able to switch, to jump, as it were, from one mind to another.

Tomcat is distracted by juicy rat-smells, being a hunter rather than the more pampered pet Luzia occupied last time. And it is rat that Luzia wants. Tomcat is too solitary, but she knows that rats have something like a hive-mind, well, not mind exactly, not even consciousness to be precise, call it a shared awareness, a universal sense.

Of course, she will have to be careful when she swaps hosts. She does *not* want to end up a supper for the cat that brought her here.

Her concentration lapsed for an instant. Tomcat has found a victim. The animal's spring disoriented her momentarily, but she let it break the rat's back. Its companions skittered away. That part of her which had become cat wanted to linger and torment it, but Luzia wasn't having any of that. She made the cat kill the rat, and then gathered herself together and *jumped*.

Rat-mind feels very different from cat. Smaller, of course, but less timid, more feral than she had expected. Rat does not think of itself as victim, despite the nearness of cat, but as predator. And rat's mind is not an island, it does not have defined edges. A thousand other rat-awarenesses mesh into it, spreading over most of the city.

All the other rats shun one old warehouse in the Rua Moçambique. There is about it a taint, a wrongness. Nothing to scavenge, or not enough to tempt rats. Luzia senses it as a kind of poison cloud, and rats are well-acquainted with poison. Which makes her pretty sure that this is the place she is looking for.

Should she try, though, to overcome rat's reluctance to investigate more closely, or is she certain enough to go back to the others and tell them her conclusions?

Pride and curiosity won over caution. Luzia had no intention of going back and admitting that she had lost her courage at the crucial point. Especially not to her mother. But how to persuade rat, shunning the black cloud of whatever-it-was? Food worked with cats. Food was an imperative. She imagined cheese, old cheese, reeking and delicious, but rat only twitched its whiskers and made no sign of being persuaded. Picturing cat right behind, however, worked a treat. For all its bravado, rat was not stupid.

It scampered down an alley at the back of the warehouse and through a gaping door that looked to Luzia as though it had been standing open for a very long time. She directed it to stairs, reasoning that a prisoner would be more secure on an upper floor.

But now the rat balked, managing to convey that the poison-mist-thing was actually in this building, and it would rather take its chances with the cat Luzia had imagined behind it. Luzia felt rat-terror as an almost tangible thing, and knew she had to yield the point. It was infecting her own mind with an unreasoning urge to flee, and her control was beginning to slip.

She released the rat-mind, and felt herself plummeting back into her own body as if from a great height.

* * *

Pierce, to preserve his dignity, climbed to his feet, using the wall for support. This was no place for an antiquarian of fifty-five. He ran his hands over his beard and combed his disordered hair with his fingers. Neither of these things had any effect on his appearance, but they made him feel marginally better. His collar was wrecked, but he re-fastened it, and knotted his tie back round his neck, tugged his cuffs down, and dusted himself off as best he could.

Then he leaned against the wall next to the shuttered window, less for the cool damp air that penetrated than for the solidity of the bricks at his back. The shutter, big heavy thing though it was, rattled ponderously, less stable than it looked.

He folded his arms so that Munro, when he came, wouldn't see his hands shaking.

Thinking about the things he'd faced and survived last year gave him a little courage, but the Englishman wasn't truly afraid until Munro came through the door. Which was worse, he found, than being closeted with the demon.

Not that there was anything discernably evil about his old customer's appearance, even if Pierce had had his spectacles. But Munro was smiling at a man he'd imprisoned, here they were in a disused warehouse, itself a strange enough thing to find in a busy port, and they both knew that Pierce had been transported here by a demon. The memory of that trip still brought nausea climbing up his throat.

"Well, Mr. Pierce, I imagine you know what I want," the politician said pleasantly.

The antiquarian tried to summon up indignation but could manage only querulousness. "I demand to know why you brought me here."

"Oh, dear, dear, dear, no." Munro shook his head in pained disapproval. "You promised me the *Book of Souls*. You are never in your shop. Not a way for a tradesman to make a profit, I might point out." He seated himself comfortably on the air, like a man in an armchair, and crossed his legs. Pierce tried to ignore the burst of irritation he felt at the word *tradesman*.

"You killed poor old Caracol," he accused. Munro smirked at him.

"He deserved it," he said casually. Callously. And that made Pierce so indignant that he threw caution to the winds.

"Nobody deserves to be murdered," except perhaps you, he thought, and felt sweat break out afresh in fear that Munro could read his mind, but carried on recklessly. "And who gave you the right to set yourself up as some kind of judge?"

"This," said Munro, flicking his forefinger in Pierce's direction, and the antiquarian gasped as a line of pain ran down his cheek. He felt blood trickle into his beard, and put up a hand to touch the wound. "And this," Munro added, with another gesture. Pierce felt the cut close up, and though his fingers came away bloody from his face, the flesh he touched was smooth and unwounded.

He stared at Munro. "You've got a funny way of trying to make people do what you want," he remarked. The politician raised his eyebrows.

"The mouse has grown some teeth." He took a cigar case from his jacket and slid one out. It looked the size of a frankfurter sausage to Pierce, who loathed ostentation of this sort. He kept his inclination to sneer under wraps, though. His legs were shaking.

Munro spent some time snipping off the end of his torpedo and setting light to it, both cigar-cutter and lighter being made of gold. Pierce refused to be impressed, privately he thought it all right for a Brazilian to show off a bit as they were naturally flamboyant people, but found it distasteful, as an Englishman, in an Englishman.

He folded his arms again and asked, "So why did you bring me here?"

Through a cloud of smoke, the sorcerer said, "So that you can tell me where the *Book of Souls* is, of course."

"I can't imagine what you need with the *Book of Souls* now," Pierce retorted, more sharply than he had intended. He flinched involuntarily, but there was no further show of temper from his smiling captor.

"You don't understand very much about sorcerers, then, do you?" he observed. "Or the nature of power."

But Pierce did. Only he wasn't stupid enough to say so. He raised his eyebrows. "What can the book teach you that you don't already know?"

The politician smiled nastily, and Pierce gritted his teeth against the implicit threat. "Secrets," he said. "Secrets. The spell of mastery over the four elements. The spell of immortality. The spell of the perfect man."

"The Eidolon?" queried Pierce. "Someone tried that here, last year. Didn't do *him* much good," he couldn't resist adding. Munro narrowed his eyes and looked at him curiously.

"Would that be the former owner of the book you photographed?"

Pierce nodded. No harm in telling him that. "He came to a bad end," he informed Munro, not without satisfaction. The sorcerer's nostrils flared.

"Obviously he was careless," he said lightly. Careless, Pierce thought, no, the only thing he did wrong was to go up against da Silva. "Where is the *Book of Souls*, Pierce?"

Again, the antiquarian had no qualms about singing like a bird. "It's in the library of São Rafael, where you can't get at it."

Munro's face darkened. "Are you threatening me?"

"Of course not," said Pierce with nervous haste. "It's a place that protects its books." He felt sweat running down his ribs, and suddenly realized that the room had grown excessively stuffy. Vaguely, he wondered why. A moment later he realized it was due solely to Munro's anger. His heart began to beat faster, and he swallowed nervously.

"Someone will let me in," he remarked, confidently. "How do I get there?"

"That's just it," Pierce faltered. "I can't tell you. I mean I really, literally, am not able to. You just have to know where you're going, and I wouldn't if I tried to take you there, physically I couldn't. The knowledge would've gone from my mind. I don't know how it works. But it does."

Thoughtfully, Munro contemplated his cigar. "Then you will have to fetch it for me, will you not?" Pierce tried to think of an excuse. Any excuse. "Unfortunately," the other man went on, "I don't trust you to do that." He replaced the cigar in his mouth and inhaled deeply, then took it out and let the smoke trickle out through his lips. "Any suggestions?"

"N—no," said Pierce, taken by surprise.

"Well then," Munro said, getting to his feet, "I'll just have to leave you here until you come up with something, will I not?"

* * *

Some people you come across give you the impression that they always know exactly what they're doing. That they're in control. It's all an act. I'm sure of it. I still believe in free will, mind you. But that's a sign that no one's in control. The world's a place of complete anarchy. Despite anyone's best efforts to tell you otherwise. If you doubt it, just think back to any important choice you've ever had to make. Right or wrong. And imagine what your life would've been like if you'd made the other choice. Don't tell me that's not random. And that's anarchy.

Rambling, da Silva. Sign of old age. What triggered that thought is simply the sheer number of people I suddenly have to keep track of. It's a lot simpler on board ship. There, I have officers to delegate to, not that I'm the world champion at that, and a number of people who're there to do one specific thing. A cook. A sailmaker. A doctor. And so on. Not anarchy. A nice orderly chain of command that falls apart the instant I set foot on shore. Well, no. That fell apart the day I began seeing ghosts, to be more accurate.

So here I am sitting in the parlor. With Emilia. Key of Solomon still burning away like fury but nothing I can do about it. Not with Harris here too, anxiously watching over Luzia. I almost said like a hen with one chick. But it'd have to be a large carnivorous hen that turns into a wolf every full moon. Luzia seems asleep, but we all know she isn't. Her mind is off roving. And so Harris isn't with us either.

And that's only the people I can *see*.

Being careful of Inspector Corvo's souvenir, I rubbed a hand over my face. It felt grubby, as if I'd forgotten to shave. Which I hadn't. Scratched futilely at the mark through my shirt. Also felt as though there was grit under my eyepatch, so I took the damn thing off and dragged my fingers over the sweaty place it covered. Still feels strange. Sometimes I do think a glass eye'd be more comfortable, something Emilia keeps on at me for as well. But most people prefer dealing with an eyepatch than a three-inch scar. And I've no wish to join the freak show.

Except that you already have, haven't you, da Silva?

Paciência, to everyone's relief and bewilderment, had gone shopping. Probably to get new twigs for her broomstick. One tiny blessing, then. But everyone else seems to be dispersed to the four points of the compass. Tatiana Dimitrovna and Zacuto with my father. Ana and Susana in São Rafael with Father Pereira. Pierce in Munro's clutches. And Zé, God only knows where he's got to. Is it always this complicated when you start getting involved with magicians? And what do you mean, start? It's been five years, and not one single thing in all that time has been simple.

Live with it. It's not going to go away.

Harris was chain-smoking, and I was almost matching him. We'd made a small cloud in the room. Only Emilia was doing something useful. Of those of us who were awake, that is. Doing the books, thank God. I was watching her. It's better than watching Harris, by a long way. Watched the light falling on her hair.

The light. I glanced out of the window. Saw that the rain had stopped. Amazing. Not only that, but the sun was trying to shine. A pale shaft of light through a gap in the clouds. Harris saw the direction of my gaze, and raised his eyebrows at me.

"Thought it was never gonna stop," he muttered, but looked sour at the angle of the sun. Of course that would be what he'd notice first. At least at this time of the month.

At the same moment, Luzia's eyes snapped open and she sucked in a long wheezing breath. Harris's head whipped round. He had an arm under her shoulders before she could stir. I replaced my eyepatch hastily. Fortunately she wasn't looking in my direction. She coughed a few times, and then sat up, Harris supporting her.

"Rua Moçambique," she gasped. *"Um depósito deserto.* Gomes e Capa."

I got to my feet, found a bottle, and poured her a brandy. Handed it silently to Harris, who put it to her lips. Luzia took a big gulp that would've floored most girls her age, and he took the glass away.

"Are you all right? Did you see him?" Harris asked her. She shook her head.

"I am fine, Ed," she said in English. "No, I did not see 'im. But I felt—" She paused, and blinked, then went on in Portuguese. "We felt. That is, all of them — something terrible there. I think it must've been the sorcerer."

"Not a demon?" I asked, fiddling with the eyepatch. I'd got it off-center, or something. It was more noticeable than usual, anyway.

"I don't think so. The rats just pictured it as a sort of poison cloud. Perhaps it was his aura… It's difficult to describe how rats see. Or sense. They're different to a cat. So many of them, it complicates things." She took the glass from Harris's hand and finished the brandy in one swallow. I hope Paciência doesn't nose that out. I don't even have to ask whether she'd approve. And I really don't want to be turned into a toad. I gave Harris a quick translation of what Luzia'd just said, since he was looking blank.

"So now what?" enquired Emilia, looking up from the accounts. That wayward tendril of hair has fallen over her face again. I walked over to her. "I hope you aren't all going to go charging off like a herd of bears."

No, I'm not quite that reckless. Or that stupid. "We'll have to wait for Tatiana Dimitrovna." I pushed the hair off her forehead. I've been thinking about what to do. That's why the Russian witch went to hell, isn't it? To get the strength to stand against Munro. Emilia touched my hand, and I caught her fingers.

"And how long will she be?" asked Harris, lighting another cigarette.

"Not long, I hope." In other words, I've no idea. I'm not entirely sure what she and Zacuto are doing at my father's, anyway. Apart from looking at the medallion Belphegor left, and how long does that take? I suppose it depends on what they decide to do with it. Have to hope they don't want to go and throw it into a volcano.

Emilia squeezed my hand. "Listen, I don't want to be a wet blanket, but what are you going to do when you get there, even *with* a witch?"

"That'll be up to her," I said, fighting an urge to bury my face in her hair. But she never says anything without a good reason. "What are you thinking, love?"

She released my hand and closed the ledger in front of her. "That you might need a back-up plan. For instance, what if Munro knows how to do what Sr. Yeoh does, move in and out of time? You'd never find Sr. Pierce."

I put my hand on her shoulder and nodded slowly. I'm reasonably certain Yeoh is unique, but you never know. I'm also optimistic that my father can paint some of his power away. Even if it's only temporary.

"So what do you recommend as Plan B?" I asked.

"The bait that tempted him to Sr. Pierce's shop in the first place," she said. "The photographs of the *Book of Souls*."

"You mean a swap?" The prospect of Munro getting his hands on the information in the *Book of Souls* turned my blood cold.

"*No*," she admonished. "Too dangerous. That's what we *offer* him. But I'm sure between us we can come up with a way to offer him an exchange without actually doing it."

"Thought we kinda wanted that to be our ace in the hole," objected Harris, taking a drag from his cigarette.

"What is ass in the 'ole?" enquired Luzia.

Interlude while I translate Harrisian into Portuguese for the werewolf's girlfriend.

"It depends," I went on when that was done, "on which he wants more. The *Book of Souls*, or the hallows."

"I think we can assume the hallows," said Emilia. She looked up at me worriedly. "Is Susana safe in São Rafael?"

I squeezed her shoulder. "As anywhere." Which says everything and nothing. Just like a politician. But we can't put her anywhere else at the moment. I wondered about Zacuto's old room in the wall. Must remember to ask him about that.

At that point Luzia looked out of the window and blurted out a word a well-brought-up young lady shouldn't even have known.

"It's my mother," she explained, coloring.

On the whole I was glad that Paciência insisted on taking Luzia away with her. She'd found Pierce for us, but I'd rather she was out of harm's way when we go after him. After all, she's only nineteen. And still only an apprentice witch, no matter how skilful. And besides, I don't want to give her mother any reason to be mad at me.

And with her out of the way I'll have Harris's full attention again. Which

I'm sure I'm going to need. Ha. I wonder why.

Thank God Tatiana Dimitrovna and Zacuto turned up shortly after they'd left, as well. I didn't get a chance to ask Zacuto about his hideaway, because Harris had the jitters.

"We should go now," he growled. I looked at the sky.

"You're not going to go wolf on me early tonight, are you?" I asked. The Russian witch was staring at him mistrustfully. Harris didn't seem to notice. Water off a werewolf's back, perhaps. I rubbed my cheekbone.

"Shoulda thought you'd prefer it," he said, pulling on one of his earlobes. "But I was thinking we oughta go look at this place in daylight. Figure out the lay of the land. Luzia did say it's deserted, right?"

"Oh, you got that, did you?" I lit a cheroot. Helps me think. *Of course it does, da Silva.* "Do we have time to get there before moonrise?"

"Uh-huh," he grunted. I took that to mean yes. "If we go now."

Docklands are pretty much the same the world over. They have the same vile stink. Look more or less similar. And they all attract rats. The human kind as well. Away from the working bits, the seafront and the wharves, the bustle of getting cargo on and off the ships, they're not very nice places.

Full of ghosts, of course. The drowned and the murdered. But that's what I see anyway. People who met violent ends. The untimely dead. Of which Lisbon has more than its share because of the earthquake, of course. Earthquakes don't just move the land. They shake the sea as well, and that means *big* waves. Which is what happened to the city in 1755. Bit rough to survive your house falling on top of you or catching fire in the aftermath, only to be drowned by the mother of all tidal waves. One of nature's little jokes. Soon as humans start thinking they've tamed it, up pops a flood or a volcano and proves the opposite.

As a sailor, of course, I never even imagine we can tame the elements. I've got a healthy respect for them. So far, it's worked.

Anyway, this evening. Or late afternoon. I never know when one becomes the other. Too used to thinking in terms of watches. End of the first dog, beginning of the second. Harris is so jumpy and agitated I doubt if anyone would have a chance to creep up on us before he'd have them pinned to the nearest wall. There weren't many people around anyway. Yes, I know you don't see the ones waiting to ambush you.

Tatiana Dimitrovna, I was amused to notice, was using something like her raincoat magic to keep her skirts clean as we walked through the filthy streets. She saw me watching her, and smiled slightly.

"What, a witch isn't allowed a little vanity?" she laughed quietly. "Or even to save on her cleaning bills?"

I raised my eyebrows. "Did I say anything?"

"Ssh," said Harris peremptorily. "Trying to listen here, folks."

And then we turned a corner, and there it was. GOMES E CAPA painted in big peeling letters on the grimy façade. That unmistakable air of no one at home. Harris eyed it with distaste. A small ghost walked through him. Looked like a Lascar. Other ghosts flitted around, agitated. Which usually only means one thing, of course.

"Anything?" I asked in a low voice.

"Stinks of demons," Harris said, wrinkling his nose, although he's usually at pains to explain that he doesn't really *smell* them, as such. Not what I'd wanted to hear. What I'd expected, though. On the other hand, it was possibly an indication that Munro had been around.

"Sr. Pierce?" Zacuto enquired.

"Dunno," replied Harris. "Demon-stink's covering anything else. Someone's gonna have to go in."

"I'll go," Zacuto volunteered. Sensible. Being a ghost, no one's going to hear him coming. Also being a ghost, no one can hit him over the head with a crowbar.

So here we are. A witch, a werewolf, and da Silva. Standing in the street outside, trying to look inconspicuous in case anyone came by. Well, to blend in, which is really quite easy considering where we are. Not looking inconspicuous, but obvious. After all, I'm a ship's master, here's one of my officers. Who could have better business in the heart of docklands? I looked at Tatiana Dimitrovna, who seemed to've read my mind.

"No one will see me unless I want them to, Luís." she said, gesturing at the deserted street, "but if you prefer, I can cast a glamor that makes me look like someone with as much right to be here as both of you."

I nodded, and took out my cheroots. Nice not to have to be trying to strike matches in the rain. But there hasn't been a drop now for several hours. A minor miracle, given what it's been like lately. Wonder if the weather's being messed up by demons, like it was last year. But there were a lot more of 'em around last June. Perhaps it was Zacuto banishing Belphegor that made the sun come out. Yes, and I'm Signor Enrico Caruso.

Unlike John Yeoh, Zacuto can't slip in and out of time at random. But he *is* a ghost, and not anchored in it like someone alive. So he can manipulate it to a certain extent. Don't ask me to explain. I don't pretend to understand how it works. Anyway, he'd only been gone about five minutes before he reappeared. Or rather, he put his head round the half-open door — this from someone who can walk through a wall if he wants — and looked furtively up and down the empty street. Then he scuttled over to where we were standing. He might just as well put on a cloak and a big black hat and hold a smoking bomb in his hand.

Just as well no one was looking.

The ghost had a worried expression on his long face, which wiped the grin at his performance off *my* face. I threw the end of my cheroot into the greasy water running along the gutter, and asked, "What is it?"

"I cannot sense anything in there," he said, shaking his head, "alive or otherwise. It is as if the whole building is… a dead zone. That is, let me tell you, a most uncomfortable feeling, even for a ghost."

A dead zone? I glanced at Tatiana Dimitrovna. Who looks just the same as ever. If she's casting an illusion, she hasn't included us in it. Probably just as well. Might be a little disconcerting, depending on her definition of someone with a right to be here. A crewman? A shipping agent? A stevedore? A whore?

But she shrugged. "I will need to see for myself, I think."

Decision time, da Silva.

"We go in," I said.

Dead zone it may be to Zacuto, but it's bloody oppressive. I felt sweat run down my temple. The air is heavy and dull and almost difficult to breathe. It's not like the sensation you sometimes get when someone's working magic. That feels alive. Energized. This, though — I can see exactly what the ghost means.

The first floor was mainly taken up by storage space. It was completely empty. Not even a packing case. A few dusty small rooms, also empty. No evidence of rats. No sign of poisoned bait on the floors. No sound, no stink. And believe me, I know the odor of rats. The smell was musty and mildewy, that acrid odor that catches in your throat like a fishhook and makes you cough. The floorboards, though, were splintery, dry and dusty. Place feels as though it hasn't been used for years. And how likely is that in a port this busy?

"Upstairs, skipper?" Harris asked hoarsely, touching my arm and pointing. The huge heavy silence deadened his voice, and he spoke quietly. But echoes whispered and ran round the unseen walls. Or maybe they weren't echoes, at that.

I stared up the shadowy staircase. Then back into the dim warehouse space. The lantern Harris carried was making everything around us darker by contrast. The small enclosed circle of light it gave us took on a faintly menacing air. As if it was denying us knowledge by illuminating only a small space. Denying us the greater truth by showing us the smaller details. Sounds a lot like religion, then.

"How long have you got, Harris?" I asked. He shrugged, setting the light swinging gently so our shadows bellied like sails in a high wind.

"Maybe an hour," he said morosely. It may be my imagination, but his voice is beginning to sound less human so close to moonrise.

"Can you see in the dark yet?"

He knew what I was getting at. "Yeah. Here," he held out the lantern to me. I took it in my right hand and, needing some security, drew my knife with my left. Harris and Zacuto both flinched back from it. The witch, however, raised her eyebrows and smiled. I looked round at all three of them. Felt, suddenly, almost like laughing. I've let myself be conditioned simply by being human. *Clever, da Silva.*

"So I'm the only one who needs the light," I said. And the only one that's human, too. If I still am. "Tatiana Dimitrovna, Sr. Zacuto, follow me. Harris, you're rear guard. Let's go."

The bottom stair creaked as I put my foot on it. Of course it did. Just as long as none of them give way, I don't mind. I started to climb, steadily, knife extended, lantern held up at eye level. Could always smash it into anything — or anyone — coming down to attack. It could be a someone. Never rule anything out. Especially when you haven't got a clue what you might be fighting any minute now.

The sense of oppression increased, pressing in, beating at us. Getting my breath became slightly difficult. Each time I inhaled, the mark on my chest pulled and chafed like a burn. I felt as if we were sharing space with huge unseen creatures which were using up the air faster than it could blow in from outside. Sweat trickled out of my eyebrows. Into my eye. Down behind the eyepatch. And also down my sides. The back of my hair felt saturated. And yet it's so cold my breath makes clouds when I exhale.

We managed to get to the top of the stairs without being attacked by winged demons. And why that particular image came into my mind I don't know. I shook it off, annoyed. Plenty of other things to concentrate on here. Like finding Pierce. That's what we came for, after all. But it's pretty obvious that we're expected. I went cautiously on, knife extended.

There's something very strange about the layout of this upper floor. I can't see any further in front than the lantern showed me, of course, but this corridor seems a lot longer than it should be. We must've been walking for a good five minutes, and we haven't even come across a door yet. Hell, we could've walked to the Baixa by now.

As soon as I realized this, I stopped. Turned to Tatiana Dimitrovna. The lantern gave her face witchy shadows.

"Where are we?" I asked her bluntly. She gave a light puzzled frown, and then her eyes narrowed and her face went hard.

"Oh, very clever," she whispered. "We're in a loop." Sweat ran down my face. I wiped it away, still looking at her.

Harris came warily into the light. "A loop?"

"A loop in time," said Zacuto. "Then in all probability we have not moved far from the top of the stairs. That is a powerful glamor, madam. Can you break it?"

She nodded, grimly. "Once you recognize it, you can break it."

"I know," the ghost agreed, a little tartly. Always annoying when someone explains something you already know.

Tatiana Dimitrovna said something sharply in Russian, and the air suddenly seemed to exhale. Grew less oppressive just for a second. But what replaced it was worse. It was sheer unreasoning terror, an overwhelming fear that had no source. No logic. No cause. No explanation. No more than a child's night-time panic does.

I was, quite suddenly and simply, frightened of the dark. I gripped the handle of my knife tightly, my hand suddenly slippery with sweat. Looked at Harris. Saw white all round the pupils of his eyes. He was breathing heavily, swinging his head from side to side. The witch was very still. She had her eyes closed and looked as though she was concentrating. Zacuto, scowling fiercely, watched *her*.

"What is it?" I asked him, and wasn't surprised that my voice was shaking. I bent down and put the lantern on the floor. Just in case.

"Negotium perambulans in tenebris," he whispered.

"Talk English," growled Harris, nervously wiping his face with his hand. The ghost obliged him, but not with an answer that I liked very much.

"The terror that walks in darkness." Zacuto bared his teeth. "I feel it too. And why should *I* fear? I cannot be harmed."

But perhaps he can. Had he forgotten the Judas tree, the portal to hell that nearly dragged him down? I was about to say so, too. Put him more on his guard. I got as far as opening my mouth to speak. And I heard a rattling sound, like someone shaking a box of pebbles, that made my blood run even colder.

"Now!" snapped Tatiana Dimitrovna suddenly, making me jump. My heart started to pound. I raised my knife. "Show yourself!"

And it did. And it wasn't a someone as I'd thought it might be, it was a something. Or rather, a whole pack of somethings.

"Sweet jumping Jesus Christ," said Harris. Well, at least now I could see what we were afraid of. With good reason, I might say.

If they resembled anything, it was cats. But cats as big as mastiffs, that walked upright on their hind legs. Not that they were walking. They bounded towards us, hissing and snarling, stinking of carrion. Hooked claws as long as my fingers on their handlike paws. All with different pelts, brindle, tabby, calico, piebald, tiger-striped, leopard-spotted. The tails were naked, ending with clattering bone like rattlesnakes'. Meu Deus, how many of 'em *are* there?

Their faces were the worst. Cat-shaped, cats' pricked ears, hissing mouths full of needle-fangs like furious cats'. But with forked tongues, flickering in and out. And human eyes, pain-haunted, the eyes of souls in torment. Eyes I couldn't look at, seeing only a person there. *And these aren't people, da Silva.* And then they were on us.

The one thing in my head as I yelled some inarticulate kind of battle cry — don't ask me where that came from — and charged them was that I'm the only person armed here. With that thought I knew I had to act fast. I sliced my knife furiously down at the first snarling cat-thing, a kind of tabby. The blade bit sideways where neck meets shoulder and sliced down through the torso, almost cutting it in two. I jerked it out, dodged dying claws flexing in and out, and went for a second on the backswing, a striped beast. It jumped back, no matter, my momentum carried me pivoting round to sever a black-and-white head. Its blood fountained out, splattering the wall in a swath of red that looked black in the flickering lamplight.

I noticed in passing that Tatiana Dimitrovna had found herself a weapon. She must've magicked it up. It looked like a quarterstaff and I heard it make contact with hell-cat skull, a crunching blow that cut off a yowl in mid-note. Good. I spitted another of the creatures, a jet-black one this time. As it went down, screaming, I saw Harris snap the spine of a ginger-furred beast and pounce on another. Never saw a sign of Zacuto but I'm sure he wasn't off carving scrimshaw.

One of the cat-things landed on my back. I staggered under its weight, swearing with fright, but the impetus drove me forward into the tiger-beast I'd missed earlier. It fell backwards, hissing, and the Russian witch broke its skull with her staff. Then the weight vanished from my back and I whirled round to see Harris fling a tortoiseshell-coated hell-cat against the wall.

Bones crunched at the impact and the dead thing slid to the floor. I sensed movement on my blind side and drove my knife straight down without looking before turning to see I'd pinned the last of them, a brindled creature, to the floor. It screeched and struggled, trying to climb up the blade, and I jerked my hand away from its flailing claws.

The knife stuck in its body briefly, lifting it off the ground. I tugged it free, and the dying cat-thing slithered sideways into the lantern, knocking it over. Burning oil flooded over the floor, and the creature burst into flames. Harris dodged the blaze, cursing, skidded in the oil, and crashed to the floor. His coat-sleeve was on fire, and he quickly rolled over onto his arm to put it out. I grabbed his other arm and hauled him to his feet.

"Where's Pierce?" he yelled. The fire bit into the tinder-dry floorboards, spreading like, well, wildfire. We fled from it. All animals together, really.

"This way," shouted Zacuto, forgetting to pretend to run, and zipped down the corridor, Harris close behind. The ghost disappeared through a door, and Harris started trying to open it by charging it and banging it with his shoulder. All that did was hurt his shoulder. He winced, growled a curse, and tried again. The fire crackled behind us, eating into the floorboards, turning them to charcoal as I watched. I realized that I was still holding my knife, and sheathed it quickly. Cleaning the blade'll have to wait until we're not in imminent danger of being roasted.

"Stand back," Tatiana Dimitrovna commanded, and pointed at the door. It swung open, and we all crowded through. The flames were hot on my back, and their light threw our shadows into the room.

Pierce was sitting on the floor under the window. The shutter banged loose above him. His fingertips were bleeding, but he seemed mostly undamaged. He looked up at us.

"What kept you?" he asked, scrambling to his feet. "I was beginning to think I'd have to go out that way, and the water isn't what you'd call inviting."

Harris muttered a curse and tapped my shoulder. I turned my head to see the door of the room engulfed in flames. I looked back at Pierce.

"Looks like we're going to have to do it anyway," I said.

And then Harris started to scream.

At the same instant the full moon cleared the clouds and threw its cold light through the window. He fell to the floor, groaning in pain, arms and legs thrashing like someone having a fit. I was momentarily transfixed as he seemed to grow extra knees and elbows and the bones of his skull shifted under his skin. The hair on the backs of his hands thickened, his fingers fused together, his nails thrust out and coarsened into claws. Across his back his coat-seams ripped apart.

Then a burning beam crashed out of the ceiling behind me, showering sparks and flame, and Tatiana Dimitrovna was beating out little fires on my shoulders. I was suddenly struck by a mad urge to kiss her, and fought it down.

"Get them out," she cried, over the roar and crackle of the flames.

"Pierce, get his feet," I shouted, and my memory did a flip-flop to last June. I'm pretty sure it's not part of the job description for an antiquarian to help me carry people around. Or, in this case, chuck werewolves out of windows.

I've lifted Harris-wolf before, but trying to pick him up in mid-change was like trying to hold a sackful of angry bear cubs. You couldn't get hold of a bit that kept still, and he kept trying to bite. The Englishman wasn't actually much help. I didn't know what Munro might've done to his hands, but it's not that. He's just not particularly strong. Well, all he lifts most of the time are books. And I mean one at a time, not piles of 'em.

Finally we managed to heave the convulsing werewolf onto the window-sill, and pushed him over. Tatiana Dimitrovna dived, but upwards, and arrowed into the sky.

"Go," said Zacuto, terror in his eyes. The deep-down terror of a soul that's already been burned once.

"Come on, Pierce." I gave him a shove in the back. The heat behind me was now so intense that I thought the only thing stopping me from bursting into flames was the sweat that soaked my clothes. Pierce turned a frightened white face to me, saw the extent of the fire, and jumped.

Right behind him, I scrambled over the windowsill, and the burning lintel broke and smashed onto my shoulders, sending me plummeting after him into the foul water in the dock thirty feet below.

It was cold and stinking as my feet hit. I remembered to suck in a deep breath before I went under, which nearly made me gag, and I seemed to go down a long, long way before hitting bottom. Something raked my leg, but I hardly noticed it, and then I was coming up again, buoyed up by the filthy water.

By some chance I broke surface right next to Harris, completely wolf now. He looked at me out of his yellow eyes, then swam towards the floundering Pierce.

Who was floundering, of course, because he doesn't know how to swim. Harris-wolf seized his collar in his jaws and started to drag him back to shore.

Between us we got him onto dry land, and watched Gomes e Capa going up in flames. Pierce shivered.

"Pity you couldn't put it out," I remarked to Tatiana Dimitrovna. Who was, of course, still dry. She made a disgusted face.

"By the time I thought of it, the fire was too big," she said ruefully. Harris chose that moment to shake himself and shower everyone with sewage-flavored water.

"Watch it!" Pierce admonished him.

"Don't worry," said the witch, and added a few words in Russian. All our clothes steamed briefly, and dried. Pierce sniffed his sleeve tentatively.

"Clever," he complimented her. "You even got rid of the smell."

"Good trick if you ever want to set up a laundry business," I said. My right leg hurt. Oh yes. I remembered catching it on something underwater. "Hope you managed to dry out my smokes as well," I added, pulling up my trouser-leg. Not too badly damaged, a shallow gouge on my shin leaking blood. I fished out my handkerchief, which had also been miraculously cleaned. Tied it round my leg. *Got off lightly there, da Silva.* God only knows what kind of rubbish is on the bottom of the dock.

"We should move away from here," observed Zacuto. "Firefighters might wonder what our purpose is, if we linger."

I nodded absently, and took out my cheroots. Dry and undamaged. Nice work, Tatiana Dimitrovna. Since she can't stand the things. I turned to Pierce. "Are you all right?" I asked. "What did Munro do to your hands?"

He looked at his fingers and smiled nervously. "He didn't harm me, skipper. I did this opening that bloody shutter."

The thing must've weighed half a ton. My opinion of him rose several points. I raised an eyebrow and grinned.

"We'll have you fighting demons before you know it," I said, finding matches dry too and striking one for my cheroot.

"Not if I can help it," he replied, but didn't appear displeased.

A growl at my side made me glance down. "Harris?" I said. "Are *you* all right?" The wolf nodded.

"Go−n' now," he articulated carefully. I slapped him cheerfully on the flank. He gave me a sideways look in return with such a wealth of meaning in it that it made me laugh.

"Off you go, then," I told him. He loped off into the night. Tatiana Dimitrovna stared after him, shaking her head.

"I still do not understand that werewolf," she said frankly.

Makes two of us. I exhaled smoke and scratched at the mark again. Now I'm not in danger of being burnt myself, it's back in force. Zacuto cleared his throat, or rather, made a noise that sounded like a man clearing his throat.

"The Professor's right," said Pierce, looking at him. "And listen, I've got something important to tell you." I nodded, and started walking.

"Come on then." First café or bar I find, I'm going in. I think we all need a drink. "Tell me on the way. What does Munro want? The book?"

The antiquarian ploughed oblivious through a group of ghosts wearing robes rather like Zacuto's. "Yes," he said, with a strange eagerness. "He wants the book. But his demon, his familiar... spoke to me." That with a shudder. "It told me some more of the prophecy, because I said Johanna Kundrie's name."

"It did what!" exclaimed Tatiana Dimitrovna in disbelief. "Just like that?" Her eyebrows were almost in her hairline. We turned a corner, and suddenly the ghosts were outnumbered by the living. People had taken to the streets with the change in the weather.

Pierce nodded. "It said it was bound by the name. But I think it was looking for an excuse. It doesn't like working for Munro."

"Doesn't... like?" echoed Zacuto, severely. "You make it sound like a person."

"Well, it had a personality," Pierce said. "But it also told me we need to get a rival Fisher King candidate. And it told me where the hallows are." I paused at the door of the bar I'd been about to go into.

"You mean it gave you some riddles, and you spent your time up there working 'em out?" I pushed the door open and went in.

"No, they weren't riddles," he said, following me. "Not even cryptic. City of the dead under the volcano, that sort of thing."

"Pompeii?" I hazarded, finding a table. Even I can figure that one out. The place wasn't too crowded yet, and a waiter came bustling up almost at once. Try to get served in a couple of hours' time, though, see how far you get. I ordered coffee and brandy. The waiter didn't bat an eyelid at the witch, so I suppose she looked like someone else to him.

Pierce sat down wearily, and nodded. I reminded myself he's older than he looks. "Pompeii, Cyprus, Malta, Tunis," he said.

I took the cheroot out of my mouth and looked sourly at him. "At least they're all in the same bit of the Mediterranean."

"That's not all," said the antiquarian. "When Munro showed up, he said something that made me think."

More than usual? Doesn't his brain ever get tired? I covered a yawn with my hand, and stubbed out my cheroot in the ashtray. The waiter brought the drinks and took it away, replacing it rather efficiently with a clean one.

"What did he say?" I prompted Pierce, who seemed to've gone into a trance.

He picked up the coffee and blew on it. "Well, I asked him what he wanted with the *Book of Souls*, what with all the power he already had, and he said something like, immortality and power over the elements."

"Earth, air, fire, water," observed Zacuto, apparently addressing the second element. I lit another cheroot. Using the third. Took a sip of the coffee.

"And?" I enquired. The coffee tasted like mud. I drank the brandy instead. Not a great improvement.

Spectacle-less, Pierce couldn't take them off and polish them. Should've brought them with me. He rubbed his nose instead. Peered rather owlishly at me. "It, ah, occurred to me that the old symbols for the four elements, the ones they use as suits of the tarot, are remarkably similar to the, er, Grail Hallows."

Zacuto leaned forward, eyes sparking with interest. "Indeed," he agreed. "The sword is a symbol of air, the cup obviously signifies water, a disk or coin stands for the earth, and a wand for fire." Pierce turned to him, smiling, and picked up his cup again.

"Yes," he said. "A sword, a cup, a dish, a spear." He sipped the coffee, and grimaced. The witch was watching him intently, too. I noticed that she'd drunk her brandy first. "And in the right places too. That's why bringing them together can heal the land and the king."

"But it would be a passive power," the old scholar's ghost went on. I sighed. They're off again. Put those two together and they'll theorize till doomsday. I glanced at Tatiana Dimitrovna, but she was riveted as well. So I drank the brandy the waiter'd put in front of Zacuto. He wasn't going to need it. Obviously he wasn't going to need the coffee either, but you have to draw the line somewhere.

"He wouldn't be content with that," Pierce said, putting the coffee down almost untouched. "If he wants the *Book of Souls* for power over the elements, he means—"

"The power of earthquakes, tornadoes, volcanoes and tsunamis," interrupted Tatiana Dimitrovna. "Gentlemen, if you have this book, you must destroy it."

This ought to be interesting. I sat back in my chair and rubbed at the mark surreptitiously, then took out my cheroots. Zacuto and Pierce exchanged a guilty glance like a pair of schoolboys caught stealing apples.

"It's not quite as simple as that," Pierce said.

"The book itself was destroyed last year," the ghost told her.

"We knew we might have to do that," the antiquarian augmented, "so I photographed the pages. That's what Munro wants. He knows we don't have the real book."

Relief flooded into her face. I wondered why. "Then he doesn't know much about facsimiles," she exclaimed. "I *knew* he didn't understand the point of a golem."

She'd lost me. "Explain," I said, pointing the unlit cheroot at her. Because I don't, either. Apparently.

"The only way humans can create other humans is by giving birth to them," she snapped. "The only way you can duplicate a book of spells is by having a sorcerer copy it out by hand. Artificial copies don't work, Luís. That's what artificial *means*. Imitation. He can't work spells from a photographed page."

I saw a flaw in this at once. Or so I thought. I lit the cheroot, and signaled to the waiter. "Couldn't Munro copy it from the photographs?"

"No," she explained patiently. "It would only be a copy of an imitation, not of the real thing. A grimoire isn't like a novel, you see. When you write down a spell, part of your power goes onto the page. It's... live. You can't make a living thing out of a dead one. That's why you can't truly raise the dead."

"What about zombies?" objected Pierce. She turned to him.

"Have you ever seen a zombie, Mr. Pierce?" He shook his head. "They're not alive," she went on, looking down at her untouched coffee. "They're poor decaying pieces of meat re-animated by a very simple basic bit of magic that has to be constantly renewed. Any fool can make a zombie. Not many people can keep one animated for more than a couple of days. It takes far more skill and knowledge to animate a golem, but even a golem isn't a person." I noticed she didn't say anything at all about Alegria. "Raising the likes of him," she nodded at Zacuto, "that takes a rare talent. But he's still dead. No offence, sir."

"None taken," said the old scholar, sounding amused. "It's no more than the truth."

11

INSPECTOR CORVO EYED HIS BOSS WITH A JAUNDICED EXPRESSION. He considered it a bit of an imposition to be quizzed about his caseload when his time could be much more productively occupied in trying to reduce it. But that wasn't his main reason for resenting this interview. Corvo was in the minority in not raking in bribes left, right and center — a minority of one, he suspected — and his superior officer, Ribeiro, was rumored to be the most venal of the whole bunch of them. So hearing the man imply that he, Corvo, had been lining his pockets was adding insult to injury. In Corvo's opinion, at least.

Ribeiro also smoked a pipe. The rituals of pipe-smokers irritated the inspector intensely, who suspected them of pretension at the very least. And the fact that his boss had changed from a short pipe to a great monstrosity with a curved stem not long after Corvo began his correspondence with Sr. Holmes in England had not escaped his notice. Obviously Ribeiro considered he looked like Sr. Holmes, with his ascetic face and hawklike profile. Neither he nor Corvo had met the English detective, of course, but even Corvo had to admit that his boss bore a slight resemblance to the pictures he'd seen.

It was the only thing they shared. Intuition was not something that Ribeiro ever showed any evidence of possessing. And Corvo could take some comfort from the fact that his superior wouldn't be able to speak with Sr. Holmes, or even write to him for that matter, not ever having bothered to learn English. Unless, of course, the famous detective spoke Portuguese. Corvo had never tested that issue.

Now, however, Ribeiro was standing by the window in his immaculately-cut suit that probably cost twice Corvo's monthly salary and demanding to know why the inspector had failed to hang on to the Werewolf of Lisbon.

Which, he reflected mordantly, was about the only amusing thing about the situation. Since the man who'd been in the cell had really been, so to speak, a werewolf of Lisbon.

"Well, it's perfectly obvious to me that all the murders were committed by the same person," Ribeiro was saying pompously in his overbred voice.

Corvo, who knew better than to argue, stared back and replied woodenly, "It's certainly a possibility, sir."

"Then why complicate matters with this Englishman, this—" Ribeiro looked down at the blotter on his desk, which, being pristine white, was conspicuously lacking in any trace of his ever having actually blotted anything with it. A small piece of paper was tucked into one leather corner. "—Sir Robert Munro," he read.

"We have to follow every lead, sir," Corvo pointed out. He suspected that Munro had been the man who had disturbed Pierce's neighbors' slumbers. Both that and the furious nature of Caracol's murder showed evidence of a hair-trigger temper.

On a woman, Ribeiro's expression would have been described as a pout. "I still don't understand why you released the sailor," he said petulantly. Corvo sighed, but silently.

"He had an alibi, sir," he explained, patiently, for the fourth time. Which wasn't strictly true, since the doctor hadn't been able to say when Caracol had died, at least not with any degree of accuracy. A four-hour period wasn't really much use to anyone. "And no motive. And no evidence at the murder scene."

Such considerations obviously didn't cut much ice with Ribeiro, who said irritably, "Maybe, but at least you had a suspect in custody." He looked narrowly at Corvo, obviously not quite ready to accuse him outright of taking backhanders. "Until that damn fellow with the eyepatch turned up, that is."

Inspector Corvo, not willing to climb back into an unprofitable argument that he'd already had four times, merely returned the gaze. "Perhaps I could go back to trying to find another suspect for you, sir?"

His boss shot him a slightly suspicious glance but apparently found nothing to object to in Corvo's bland expression. "Oh, very well," he said at last, flapping his hand dismissively, "get on with it."

"Thank you, sir," said Corvo, who could grovel with the best of them when required, and beat a hasty retreat.

When he got back to his office, however, he found himself unable to settle down to his work. He smoked three cigarettes in quick succession, stared out of the window for a while, noted the rain had stopped, and abruptly stood up and collected his hat and coat.

There was, predictably, no sign of Santos, so he didn't bother to tell anyone where he was going. Actually he wasn't entirely sure where he was going. Only that he'd felt a certain... connection with something that had tried to hunt him down, and that there was a strange feeling accompanying that connection that if he followed the trail he might catch the murdering creature unawares.

The question of what he'd be able to achieve if he caught it didn't enter his head, Inspector Corvo has no experience of demons, their presence does not automatically occur to him as an explanation when tricksy things are at large or nefarious deeds afoot, and so the idea that he might be walking into a trap is, unfortunately, excluded from his thoughts.

*   *   *

His heart racing, Zé sidled round to the back of the orphanage, where the door to the kitchen stood open as he'd expected. He pushed it carefully, putting his head cautiously round and peering in.

The kitchen was in darkness, the only illumination provided by the full moon shining in through the windows and painting everything in black and white. Stacks of clean dishes stood draining, everything else was stowed neatly away. The stone floor had evidently been scrubbed, as had all the tables. It smelled of soap and disinfectant, and only faintly of food.

"Sílvia?" he called softly.

"I'm here," came her voice from shadows on the other side of the door, making him jump. "Zé?" she added, belatedly, "is that you?"

"Yes," he hissed. "You all right?"

She joined him. She, too, smelled of soap, but not, fortunately, of disinfectant. "I brought my English homework." This being the subterfuge they had come up with when he'd sneaked in earlier to speak to her.

"Come on, then," he said, wondering if he could — should? take her hand. She disposed of that dilemma by catching hold of his. Which felt very strange at first. Nice, though, he decided.

"Where are we going?" she whispered.

"I told you," he said, grinning at her in the moonlight. "Somewhere no one'll find us." He led her down the alley in the direction of São Rafael. "It's sort of a magic place."

"What do you mean?" Sílvia asked. "Is it warded, or something like that?"

He knew the sort of lessons some of the pupils were having, so he wasn't surprised to hear her ask the question. "Something like that," he replied, blithely. "It's not far." She smiled back, and hitched the strap of her satchel up on her shoulder with her free hand, and he remembered his manners. "Let me carry that."

"All right," said Sílvia, and handed it over.

They walked along, not too furtively. Dr Bosque's régime was not despotic, the worst Sílvia was facing was floor-scrubbing duty, and that was only if she got caught. She knew from acquaintances outside the orphanage, though, that going for a walk with a boy was usually considered, if not a hanging offence, at least a thrashing one by most parents.

"What's it like," she asked him, "being a sailor?" Zé made a face.

"Tough," he said. "Boring. Working the ship and doing schoolwork as well." He didn't want to talk about his day-to-day life. Which he enjoyed, mostly, but wasn't about to admit it. "Come on, down here."

She peered down the alley with interest, if a bit dubiously. "Are you sure?"

"It opens up at the end," Zé explained. "There's a sort of piazza where we can sit and not bother anyone in the library. And no one'll ever find us."

"The library?" she asked, smiling, but let him lead her into the sudden darkness. A few moments later they emerged into the courtyard outside São Rafael. The moon silvered it, the wet wooden bench, the pots full of dripping geraniums, the damp wheelbarrow a gardener had left.

Zé surveyed the scene crossly, and wrinkled his nose. "It's a bit wet," he said.

"Zé," said Sílvia in a small voice, and there was something in it that chilled his blood. "What's that?"

* * *

Be nice to have a bit of a rest now. But of course that's the last thing I'm going to get. At least we've got Pierce back in one piece, though even without that I still need to get to get to São Rafael. Fr Pereira's been stuck there for hours with Susana and her mother. And he's got a job he's supposed to be doing. Though I suppose he'd call it a vocation. Oh, and you don't have a job too, da Silva? What, for instance, am I going to put in *Isabella's* hold next? Especially if I have to go sailing off to Malta and all the rest of it. Which is looking increasingly likely.

The first thing to do is stash Pierce in the library where Munro can't get at him. I hope. I'm sure Pierce won't object to house arrest in São Rafael. If you do have to be cooped up, some place you like being is the best one. He might even make himself useful, now we've got a bit more to work with. Equation: Pierce plus books equals information. Factor in Zacuto and you've got it squared.

Trouble is, I'm still not sure what to get them looking for. Or whether they've already found it. What I don't understand is how it all fits together. Or am I just being exceptionally stupid at the moment? Way my head feels, I'm not really surprised.

No, my first thought was right, I'm sure of it. There's one piece of the puzzle missing. And that's Pierce and Zacuto's specialty.

Dosing everyone with brandy seems to've had the desired effect, anyway. If you can call this stuff brandy. Chances are that fat fellow behind the bar brews it in his bathtub. Probably while he's still in it, with his socks on. That's what gives it its color.

I dragged my hand down my face, clearing grit out of my eye on the way down. Stubbed out my cheroot and looked round at the entourage. I always think we look like a circus troupe when you collect together more than three people in this business. Ladies and gentlemen, will you welcome the Witch from the Russian Steppes. The four-hundred-year-old ghost. Sr. Harris the Wolf-Man from America. The Man out of Time. Teresa, the Brazilian Swordswoman.

Who the ringmaster might be, though, I don't know. It's not me, that's for sure. I'm part of the circus. But I'd like to know who's making me jump through hoops. Or maybe I wouldn't. I scratched my cheekbone and looked round at the others.

"Time to make a move." Pierce looked worriedly back at me. Yes, he's part of the troupe. Sr. Mnemonic, the Man of a Million Words.

"Munro must know about the fire by now. D'you think he—?"

"He'd be a damn fool to try," I said grimly. We may look like the da Silva Circus, but two sorcerers ought to be a match for an English politician. And failing that, I always have my knife if it comes down to slicing supernatural minions into chouriço.

"Let's get on with it, then," sighed Pierce, and pushed himself wearily to his feet. His face seems to've grown more lines since we got him out of the warehouse. For the first time since I've known him, he's looking his age.

Makes me damn glad I can't see what *I* look like.

We've only been in this bar for half an hour or so, but it's gone from being half-empty to bursting at the seams. We worked our way through the throng and out into the moonlit street. Luckily the patrons were too busy drinking to notice Zacuto walking through the odd outstretched arm or leg. Hell, he could've walked through the wall for all the attention they paid him.

Tatiana Dimitrovna looked up at the moon. Is she still worrying about Harris? Apparently not. As I realized when she spoke.

"If Munro's power is linked to the moon," she said thoughtfully, "it will probably not be the waxing one, but the waning, making him strongest at the dark of the moon. At the moment he may be least powerful, even if the painting proves less successful than we hoped. But we really have no way of telling for sure."

So why mention it at all? I know perfectly well. She's talking to cover the fact that she's as nervous and uncertain as the rest of us.

"Why would you conclude his power is under the influence of the moon?" Zacuto asked curiously.

"Because much of mine is, too," she replied, her mouth twisting. "Remember, we have both been on the same pilgrimage."

The old scholar fiddled with his beard. "True," he said. "But is your power not subject to the same limitations?"

"No." She shook her head. "I draw that part of my strength from the waxing moon, and the full. So mine will decline as he becomes stronger."

"Does it give you any insights into what he'll do next?" enquired Pierce.

"None at all," she said. "I understand the lure of power, of course. All sorcerers do. But contrary to popular belief, most of us really don't want ultimate power. We don't want to rule the world. Although," she added with a rueful smile, "we'd probably make a better job of it than some of the current incumbents."

Matter of opinion. Who would you be happier turning your back on, a politician or a witch? Nothing much in it, if you ask me. I lit a cheroot and kept my opinion to myself. Pierce fell into step beside me.

At the corner of the alley that leads to São Rafael, Zacuto's shade — that is, the specter of his death, because that was where the mob killed him — stands guard unseen by his actual ghost. Who has passed it many times and never known it's there. I haven't told him. I don't know if it's possible to spook a ghost, but it'd give me the creeps in his boots. It makes no sign that it can see him, either. This time, though, I thought as we passed that it seemed disturbed, and reached automatically for my knife.

Seeing the movement, the witch touched my arm and mouthed *What is it?*

"Probably nothing," I said. "But keep alert."

She smiled fleetingly, and murmured, "I have been alert all my life."

I raised an eyebrow at her. "I'll go first." It's a very narrow alley. "Don't straggle out too far. Pierce, stay close to Sr. Zacuto."

"Aye aye, skipper," he whispered, tightly.

Turning the corner, I ran smack into Inspector Corvo. Didn't know who it was at first. Too dark. We both jumped back in surprise. He brought up his gun, and I seized his wrist and pulled him back into the moonlight.

"If you shoot me again," I said, "I'll start thinking you've got something against me."

"What are you doing here?" he asked peremptorily. I raised an eyebrow.

"I might ask you the same question."

"Indeed," said the inspector, drily. "But which one of us is the policeman?"

Not the best way to get my co-operation. I dropped his arm and snapped, "I'm looking for Fr Pereira, how about you?"

He rubbed his wrist. "Actually, I'm tracking that… thing that attacked me." Tracking it? What does he propose to do if he meets it again? "Well, *tracking* is a bit too precise. I have a feeling it's near here."

"A feeling?" I repeated.

Corvo laughed, not humorously. "I've lost a lot of preconceived ideas in the last couple of days, Captain da Silva. But I'm still a policeman. Is there any way of, of capturing that thing and bringing it to justice?"

Behind me, Tatiana Dimitrovna whispered, "What's going on?"

Over my shoulder, I explained, "The inspector wants to know if there's any way of capturing the thing that's been hunting him."

"I don't know," she said. "I don't see anything to bind yet."

To bind. It all comes back to slavery. Or at least the vocabulary of slavery. I wonder why.

And then I heard Zé's voice, shouting angrily, "Leave her alone!" But there was an edge of panic in it that made me push Inspector Corvo roughly to one side and take off as fast as I could run. *Worry about manhandling the cops later, da Silva.*

The first thing I saw was Zé, brandishing a gardener's fork in a very martial fashion. Standing protectively in front of a rather pretty girl about his age. She was holding a garden trowel as if it was a sword. I thought I recognized her from the orphanage, and that clinched it. Good work, Teresa.

And they were confronting Belphegor's monstrous, murderous creation. But Zacuto banished Belphegor. Then the mark on my chest gave one sudden thunderous pulse that made me gasp. The thing turned its head, and I realized the creature was subtly different. Something about its expression.

It had a mind. There was awareness in its eyes. But it wasn't anything like human intelligence. Something had slid into this empty thing and given it a kind of reality. Solidity, perhaps.

So perhaps now it can be killed.

I drew a deep breath. I'm past the stage of asking *why me*. But why me? Every bloody time? "Zé, get out of the way," I shouted, and charged straight at it. It dodged my knife-stroke easily, skipping nimbly to one side with a lot more agility than the last time. When it had dodged, but more... ponderously, if you know what I mean. Whatever was in it had made it smarter, too. Not that *that* was a difficult thing to achieve.

But I can be sneaky, too. I stuck out a foot and tripped it, and it staggered into a group of flowerpots and fell over. I went after it, but it was too quick for me, rolling neatly to its feet and aiming a punch at me with its human arm. I ducked and slashed at its legs, and it scuttled backwards, bent low.

Pierce came out of the shadows and hit it over the head with a pot of geraniums. Not a very big pot, granted. But it shattered satisfactorily. The thing whirled round, dazed and angry, swinging its arm backwards and knocking Pierce over. I raised the knife again and swung at it. And then I heard Zé shout, "It's Mouffi!"

The thing stopped in its tracks, and I stopped too and gaped at it. And then I recognized it, too. Don't ask me how. Something in its eyes, perhaps.

Tatiana Dimitrovna, thinking very fast, realized she had its name, and chanted a sentence in Russian. It whipped its head round to her, and strained against the spell until its eyes bulged. But she's been to Hell, and she bound it.

I lowered the knife cautiously, but didn't sheathe it. Not a chance. Inspector Corvo emerged from the alley, gun in hand. Fat lot of good that'll do him, unless he's got silver bullets. Still for all I know he might. And if it makes him feel better, I can't really object. As long as he doesn't point it in my direction.

A drop of sweat ran down from my eyebrow. I brushed it away and said to him, "She's bound it, if you want it."

Corvo eyed the snarling, struggling thing doubtfully. "Would a cell hold it?" he asked, and I translated for the witch's benefit.

"Any room could hold it now," she said. "It can't escape unless I release it." I looked at the inspector, who nodded.

"I got that," he said, and then switched to English. "What can I tell my boss? What can I say it is?" he asked Tatiana Dimitrovna.

She looked at it speculatively. "I think you'll find that people see what they are capable of seeing. It'll look human to your boss, I expect."

"It will?" said Corvo, dubiously. "Are you sure?" The witch raised her eyebrows.

"Unless he's got more imagination than most policemen," she replied. The inspector croaked a laugh that sounded like his namesake.

"I'd rather not have it myself," he observed. "But you couldn't ever accuse Ribeiro of having any imagination at all."

"What are you going to do with it?" asked Pierce. He was rubbing his elbow, but looked pleased with himself. The inspector shrugged, eloquently.

"Take it to the police station, I suppose," he said. "How do we move it?"

"Just speak its name," Tatiana Dimitrovna told him. "Mouffi." It glared at her. She looked at me. "How did it come by a name like that, anyway?"

I made an I-don't-know face, and pulled out my cheroots right-handed. I'm not going to put my knife away *just* yet.

"I've no idea," I said. "Zé, how did you recognize it?" Zé jumped. He'd been whispering with the girl. His girlfriend? Meu Deus. Now *that* makes me feel old.

"I don't know," he answered. "It just came to me."

"Mouffi," said Inspector Corvo experimentally. The thing's head swiveled reluctantly in his direction, and he blinked. His Adam's apple went up and down. He evidently doesn't take to the idea. Don't blame him one bit. "Come here." It took three jerky steps in his direction. Corvo almost succeeded in not flinching. He turned to Tatiana Dimitrovna. "Isn't there some kind of talisman or something I can use?" he asked her.

"Do you have silver ammunition in your pistol?" she enquired. He nodded. "That is as good a talisman as any."

"Very well," he said. "Mouffi, if it means anything to you, you're under arrest for murder. Come with me."

The thing turned its head and shot me a look of pure venom. Then followed the inspector, moving so reluctantly that it looked as if it was wading through treacle.

"Will your spell really hold it indefinitely?" I asked the witch in a low voice, and took a drag on my cheroot.

"Yes, of course," she answered, though I hadn't really been questioning her competence. Then she lowered her voice too. "Munro could break it. So could some demons. But Munro doesn't know anything about it, and I don't see any demons in the vicinity, do you?"

"No," I said. Although Harris could tell me if there are any around. I clamped the cheroot between my teeth and put my knife away. Can't say I like it. Putting the inspector in charge of Mouffi. He's not exactly experienced in these matters. But who am I to argue? I have to assume the witch knows what she's talking about.

I turned to Zé, who'd resumed his tête-à-tête with the girl, and barked his name so that he jumped guiltily.

"Er, this is Sílvia," he ventured in a vain attempt to deflect me. What he thought I was going to do, I don't know. I've got better things to do than tick him off for chatting up girls. Better sense, too. What I *was* tempted to do was tease him.

"Are you all right, Sílvia?" I asked her. She was looking a little white around the gills, but managed a shaky smile.

"I think so," she said, and the smile grew wider. "You're Zé's father, aren't you, senhor? Captain da Silva."

Fame. Or notoriety. I nodded. Zé jumped back in with both feet.

"We, we came here to—"

"Zé, I'm talking to Sílvia." He shut up. I tried very hard not to smile. The cheroot helped. A little.

"What *was* that thing?" she asked. Still holding her trowel defensively. Saw me looking at it, and only then seemed to realize it was in her hand. With a small embarrassed grin, she stooped and put it on the ground.

"It was—" I began, then stopped. Damned if I know. I scratched uselessly at the mark on my chest. Key of Solomon? Bloody nuisance, more like, right now. "I don't actually know what it was," I admitted.

Zacuto looked sternly down his long nose at her. "Do you really want to know, *menina?*" But she refused to be intimidated.

"I — Yes," she replied. "I mean, we do have magic lessons. Are you a ghost?" she asked suddenly, peering at him.

The old scholar blinked, taken aback. Not many people manage to do that to him. And he's not used to being rumbled. Pierce smirked, and Zacuto shot him a sideways glance.

"Yes, *criança,*" he said, a bit petulantly, demoting her. "I died in 1506. And *that* was a creation of the demon Belphegor. Mainly. Does that answer your question?" He didn't touch on Mouffi, I noticed. I don't fully understand Mouffi myself. Except that it's what Harris calls a royal pain in the ass.

If that was meant to slap Sílvia down, though, it didn't work. She turned to Tatiana Dimitrovna and said excitedly in English, "Are you a witch?"

Meu Deus, all these questions. She's worse than Zé. And that's saying something. No wonder they seem to be getting on so well.

Tatiana Dimitrovna smiled and answered, "Yes, I am. That was a clever spell you worked on the ghost, girl. What was it, Seeing At Night?" Sílvia shook her head.

"My teacher calls it *o folego da virgem,*" she said, and bit the tip of her tongue in thought. "Maiden's Breath. It shows the true nature of things."

"Ah yes," said the witch approvingly. I sighed, and threw away the end of my cheroot. They're behaving like Pierce and Zacuto. Witches, talking shop.

"Excuse me, ladies," I interrupted. They gave me an identical look, and I put up my hands defensively. "Library," I said. Pointed at São Rafael.

"Why didn't anyone come out?" wondered Zé as I went to the door. "We must've been making a lot of noise."

Another question I can't answer. Though I suppose you could theorize. I pushed it open, and found Fr Pereira beside it, peering out of the window like a nosy neighbor. He turned to me, eyebrows raised.

"I thought I heard something," he explained. "What have you been battling against this time, my son?"

"Oh, the usual," I replied, standing to one side to let the others come in. "And it's pleasant to see you again, too." Fr Pereira smiled. "We came to relieve you."

The priest glanced towards Ana, who was peacefully asleep in a chair. Likewise Susana, in a nest of blankets. I walked quietly over to her.

"You should know that the little one said another word," he murmured. "Perhaps you'll tell me what's going on, some time?"

"What was the word?" I asked, looking down at the sleeping infant. From what Teresa says — from what I recall with Zé, if not Cat so much — that doesn't happen very often.

"The Greek for lion, *leeondahri*," he said, with a preoccupied nod to Zacuto and Pierce, who'd followed me in. No doubt deep in some academic discussion. Zé pulled Sílvia in behind them. Holding her hand. When did all this happen?

"Lion," I repeated.

"I have to go," said Fr Pereira quietly. "Will you enlighten me, Luís, when you have the time?"

"When I have the time," I promised. Yes, as if that'll be in the foreseeable future. Underhand, da Silva.

So. Wolf, dog, serpent-woman, and lion. Harris, Yeoh, Tatiana Dimitrovna and...? Well, now it's no surprise at all that a man called Leão spoke to me earlier. And offered me his help. I pulled out a chair and sank into it, smothering a yawn. Now that I'm here, what *am* I going to do with mother and daughter?

"Sr. Zacuto," I said. He turned his head. "Is Susana safe here, or would she be better off in your room in the walls?"

He considered the question. "Since you ask," he said after a moment, "she might well be safer there. But it would not be very comfortable for her mother."

Pierce, eyeing Ana sprawled awkwardly in her chair, remarked, "She doesn't look very comfortable there." Which was undeniable.

"The senhora condessa said that taking Susana out of time was a bad idea," Zé piped up, raising his head from whatever he and Sílvia had found to look at. Look, a sudden interest in books. How extraordinary.

"What countess?" I asked, baffled. He nodded at Tatiana Dimitrovna. "You're a countess?" I said to her.

She made a deprecating wave. "In that my father was a count before the Tsar exiled him, yes. Technically speaking. But not of any practical use."

I'd say otherwise. Most people seem tremendously impressed by that sort of thing, apart from communists, of course. Especially in England. But perhaps witches don't want to attract that kind of clientele. I'm not so fussy. If it offers me a cargo, I'll take its money whether it's a duke or a dustman. So to speak.

"Why shouldn't we hide Susana in a pocket of time?" I enquired, scratching my cheekbone. The witch sighed, and found a chair for herself. She was walking as if her back hurt.

"The child is too young," she explained. "Taking her out of time... well, she's not anchored yet. If we took her out of time, she never would be."

"Anchored?" queried Pierce. "You mean she'd be like John Yeoh? Wouldn't that be a useful talent to have?"

"No, no," said the witch. "Not like Mr. Yeoh. His talent is unique, as far as I know. He has a stronger anchor than anyone. He is like this place," she gestured around at the library, "it goes very deep."

"Then *what?*" asked Zé impatiently. Who had obviously been eavesdropping for all he was worth.

Tatiana Dimitrovna frowned in thought. "What would probably happen," she said slowly, "is that she wouldn't grow naturally. I'm not sure what the exact effect would be, whether she'd age faster or slower than normal."

I rubbed my chin. "She's already growing faster than normal," I said. "Look at her, Tatiana Dimitrovna. How old would you say she is?"

The witch did as I said, and shrugged her shoulders. "I don't have much experience of babies," she said tartly.

"Guess."

"Six months?"

"She's less than one month old," I told her. She looked back at the sleeping baby in shock, and put a hand to her chin.

"*Boizhe moi,*" she exclaimed. "Now I wonder what's causing that?"

"Can't you tell?" Zé blurted out. She smiled at him.

"I'm not omnipotent," she said, kindly. Nice of her to admit it. "Though I could probably find out with a spell."

Everyone looked at Susana for a moment. Then Sílvia said brightly, "She's human." And everyone transferred attention to her. She went pink. "Well, everyone knows Dona Ana was… raped." Lowered her voice. "By a demon. Although I don't believe that bit."

"Susana's father was possessed at the time," I told her. Realizing what I'd forgotten as soon as I said it. Possessed.

By Mouffi. Meu Deus.

"I think I'm beginning to change my mind," said Tatiana Dimitrovna. Took a little cloth bag from her pocket. Bright-patterned fabric. Tied with a ribbon. "I think we should probably give this back to her, too."

Sílvia looked at it with great interest. "Is that the charm Dr Bosque got from Sr. Leão?" she asked.

And that gave me the unpleasant sensation of puzzle pieces falling into place. It's a bit like having a chair pulled away from under you when you're on the point of sitting in it.

Coincidence? Don't make me laugh.

The witch tucked the bag among Susana's blankets. "Yes, it is," she said shortly.

"A protection spell," Zacuto remarked. "And a powerful one."

"Against demons, yes," agreed Tatiana Dimitrovna. "But it will betray her presence to Munro, so take it out of her bedding if you leave this place."

Now why do I have the feeling I'm missing something here? But any questions I might've been going to ask were blown away by Zé.

He looked up from the book he and Sílvia had been leafing through, and asked, "What was the name of that woman who made the prophecy?"

"Johanna Kundrie," Pierce supplied.

"Did you know she's buried here, in Lisbon?" said Zé.

I put my head in my hands and groaned.

*   *   *

The trail that led from the warehouse was so blatant an old blind man could've followed it. And that in itself would have made Harris instantly suspicious if he'd been in human shape. But wolves are not noted for subtlety, even the ones that spend most of their time shaped like men, and so he followed the bait with no suspicion at all.

He killed a cat that got in his way, a surly belligerent tabby with a ripped ear which obviously thought he was some kind of big dog that would back down when challenged.

Harris-wolf was in no mood to back down. He badly wanted to bite someone. The cat wasn't really enough, though it had relieved some of the confused anger the hell-cats in the warehouse had caused. Harris-wolf couldn't put it into words, but his human self had been disturbed by their eyes. He'd had no time to come to terms with that before he went wolf. But it was mainly anger at himself that drove him.

By now he was coming to know the city very well, at least the backstreets and the alleys, anywhere he could pass unseen. As wolf, he possessed a powerful glamor that prevented casual witnesses from seeing his true nature — sometimes, when necessary, from seeing him at all — but it wouldn't work in a crowded street. Sometimes some devil tempted him to try it, just to see the looks on people's faces, but luckily never quite strongly enough for him to act on it.

This trail, however, was leading him into populous areas. Harris-wolf slunk behind some trash-cans in a side street and looked out at the passers-by. Looked, of course, being the least of what he did, he used all his senses to build up a complex image of smell and noise and taste that was much more rounded than just seeing what was in front of him.

From that picture he knew that as the night drew on the people would go away. He knew that instinctively as well, but that knowledge got woven into the tapestry of his senses, just one part of a whole that was more than the sum of its parts.

And the trail wasn't going to go cold in a few hours. Harris-wolf tuned it out, so that it wasn't the uppermost layer in his perceptions any more, and started sorting through the others for something else to hunt in the meantime.

*   *   *

Sir Robert Munro's demon-familiar watched its master warily, wondering if he could tell, somehow, of its betrayal. Strictly speaking, the demon didn't consider it as a betrayal because it had been under a geas that took precedent over Munro's ownership. But it doubted that sophistry would cut much ice with the baronet.

It could sense, though, that something was interfering with Munro's power.

Something it didn't understand at all, not the hot raging powers of hell or the cold calculating ones of sorcery, which together had made its master almost invincible, but another kind entirely. Which had sneaked in through all his defenses and barriers. The effects were patchy, and physical as well as magical. The demon had been highly amused, though it was careful to hide that fact, by Munro's failure with the prostitute. Also amusing, the fact that he had been obliged to take a taxi to Gomes e Capa and not travel by his preferred method.

Not so amusing, his all-too-predictable need to take it out on his familiar. The demon had found, since it had been with Munro, that it didn't need to have done something its master disapproved of to earn the sorcerous equivalent of a whipping.

Munro was staring fixedly at a small glass globe. It fit into the palm of his hand, like a pocket version of a gypsy fortune-teller's crystal ball. Archaic as it was, this was the best way to watch someone following a trail. Since Munro had no way of knowing who or what would eventually follow the trail he'd left, the scrying-glass was linked to the trail itself.

He was pleased with what he'd caught, though. A werewolf. And most probably, since it was rather unlikely there were two of them in Lisbon, the one which had been with Pierce when he'd had the demon snatch him.

His lip curled as he thought of Pierce. He had to assume that the antiquarian must have perished in the fire which had razed the warehouse to the ground, but it was devilish odd that the building should catch fire at that time, and especially after all the rain. So perhaps he'd escaped after all. Especially given the werewolf. Munro smiled, nastily. He rather liked the idea of having a werewolf in his service.

But what was the wretched beast doing, skulking in that alleyway? It didn't appear to be interested in the trash cans.

"Come on, you stupid creature," whispered Munro. "Come and meet your new master."

*   *   *

"How much of this prophecy do we have?" I asked, smothering a yawn. I really don't want to add sneaking into a cemetery to my list of things to do. Although I'm pretty damn sure it's going to come to that in the end. Otherwise why would Zé have conveniently come up with that piece of information? Zé, who never reads anything unless he has to. Except for the rubbish he gets from O'Rourke, of course.

"Much of it," said Zacuto. Ghosts don't get tired, of course, but even he looks as though he's drooping a bit. "We know that Susana is the child because she has said the four words. And they give us clues to the location of the hallows."

"Which were confirmed by what the demon said to me," added Pierce. "But why a dog, a wolf, a serpent-lady and a lion? Are they guardians of the hallows?"

I scratched my cheekbone. Thought it was obvious. Maybe it only is to me. "They're the people we need to collect the hallows."

Zé bounced excitedly in his chair. "Sr. Yeoh has a Chinese name that means Faithful Dog," he exclaimed, "and Sr. Harris is obviously—"

"But who can the other two be?" Pierce broke in. He tried to push absent spectacles up, and ended up rubbing his nose instead. He had dark shadows under his eyes. The broken spectacles were in his pocket. Too distracting, he said.

"Apparently I am the serpent," said Tatiana Dimitrovna, rather bleakly. I don't think she likes the idea very much. Or maybe she doesn't like the idea of being chosen. Welcome to the club, senhora condessa. "According to Sr. Yeoh, anyway."

And Sílvia said, caught up in the moment, "Sr. Leão."

"Yes." I turned to her. "Do you know where he lives?"

"No, but Dr Bosque does."

Which can, I hope, wait until morning. I'm just about worn out. Had quite enough for day. Getting too old for this sort of thing, da Silva. I started to push myself to my feet. Framed some kind of *let's call it a night* speech. And Pierce interrupted again.

"There's one other thing," he said. He would.

"What's that?" enquired Zé. Likewise.

I sank back into the chair and gave the mark an impatient rub through my shirt. Surprised I haven't worn it away by now.

"The demon said," the antiquarian pointed out, "that we have to find our own candidate for the Fisher King."

Everyone, for some reason, looked at me. "Oh no," I said, firmly. "That's one thing you can't pin on me. I'm the paladin, remember?"

"Yes, but—" Pierce began.

"No but," I stopped him. "If it comes to being chosen, choose someone else." Or find out who's lined up for that particular job. Because I'm King Neptune if there isn't already a potential Fisher King among us.

Zacuto knew that, too. "It is not a question of choosing, but of finding the one who has been chosen."

"And how are we supposed to find that out?" asked Tatiana Dimitrovna.

"There will be a way," replied the ghost, with certainty. "Since I need no sleep, I will endeavor to find it. I think," he added with a glance in my direction, "that we can be quite sure it is not Captain da Silva."

"*Thank* you," I said.

"It's just as well," observed Pierce with a smile.

"Why is that?" the witch enquired.

"Well," the antiquarian murmured, "I certainly wouldn't like to be the one to attempt to stab the skipper in the groin."

* * *

I sat on the bed and took off my shoes and my eyepatch. Anything else seemed too big an effort. I lay back where I was. Must've fallen asleep, because I awoke with a start to find Emilia leaning over me, tracing the outline of the Key of Solomon. She'd had time to unbutton my shirt, so I must've dropped off for a moment.

"Forward woman," I muttered, looking at her.

"These marks have been screaming at each other all day," she said. That's one way of putting it, I suppose.

"I've got some residual magic sloshing around inside me," I explained. "Take it up with Sr. Zacuto."

"Some other time," said Emilia, firmly.

When the marks finally came together, I saw, like a bolt of lightning, all the ghosts of Lisbon in one volcanic moment. I think they were trying to tell me something, but I was too overwhelmed to make out what it was.

* * *

Restless, Luzia lay in her bed staring at the moon. On wolf-nights, she'd taken to leaving the curtains undrawn. There was a quality in the moonlight that suggested Harris to her. Light evoked werewolf, and so the moon moved tides in her as well. She felt linked to him, though she had no communication, just the fact that the same moon shone on both of them. And on clear nights like this she felt even closer.

She hadn't told her mother about the rats. Cats were just about acceptable, being legitimate witches' familiars as well as among the few creatures Paciência had time for, but rats, she knew, would be quite beyond the pale. Might as well go all the way and ride a cockroach, once you started on rats.

But she didn't really care very much what her mother thought, even through all the years when she'd pretended she did. And right now she was preoccupied. Something perilous in the moonlight, tonight. Not something which was of the moonlight itself, but something present in it, as Harris was. As she was.

I am lying in bed unable to sleep because I'm worrying about a werewolf, she thought. How bizarre is that? But he's all right, she told herself a moment later, the police let him go before it was time to change.

Somehow that wasn't any comfort at all.

Luzia got out of bed and padded barefoot over the smooth boards, avoiding the creaking ones without a thought, to the window, and opened it quietly. Cool air flowed in, still with a damp feel to it from all the rain. She closed her eyes on the brightly-lit garden, let her other senses expand. She heard the sighing of the wind and small rustlings of nocturnal creatures in the undergrowth. Smelled the odors of the garden, wet earth, a promise of spring. And faintly, over everything, the salt tang of the sea.

Leaning on the windowsill, she sighed, still agitated inside. And the idea that had been nagging at her took shape and insistent words.

Go and see if he's all right.

As she had worked out how to ride animals' minds independently of any teacher, she had no idea of the spell's limitations, or even whether there were any. But she was still sensible enough to consider the dangers, and hoped the extra ingredient she added to the mixture, caution, would be sufficient.

Stop dithering around and just do it, she told herself. Pushed herself away from the windowsill and returned to her bed.

She lay down, cleared her mind, wrapping fear and worry and anxiety and all those negative things in black paper and putting them in boxes, and sent her thoughts winging after the rag-eared tabby cat she'd occupied earlier. Chaos and nausea engulfed her, and she had time to whisper a horrified curse before she landed—

In a mind that was shaped like a wolf's, thought and saw like a wolf. But ultimately, wasn't a wolf.

The *why* of how she'd found herself in Harris's mind could wait. Something *was* wrong. Her feeling of unease coalesced into real alarm.

He was following a trail, she perceived, which had been laid for just that purpose. Not to ensnare him specifically, but he'd been the one to put his foot in its jaws, his neck in the noose, and now it was tightening.

But how was she to tell him it was a trap? How could she get through to him? On some level she couldn't get through to him when he was shaped like a man, but she was smart enough to know that came with being human. She certainly communicated better with him than she ever had with her mother. Who was given to sighing in exasperation at Luzia's father, "I'll

never understand men." This from a sorceress. Luzia thought that was a bit
rich.

Luzia brought herself sternly back to reality, if reality is the right term
for occupying the mind of a werewolf who just happened to be her lover
when he was human.

The only way to do it, she realized, was to forget he was Ed altogether and
treat his mind like any other animal's. As a thing driven by instinct.

But what would distract a werewolf from the hunt? She tried the food-
illusion, and it diverted him for all of thirty seconds. The fear-compulsion
might work, but she was too confused and disoriented to remember what he
might be afraid of.

And by the time she realized, it was almost too late, and there was
something unimaginably dangerous much too close.

No time for subtlety, then. All she could do was scream silently with all
her senses, *He has silver bullets in his gun and he is ROUND THAT CORNER!*

Harris-wolf, in full pursuit of his goal and very close to it, suddenly scented
the cold clean taint of silver in the air and skidded to a halt, his sense of self-
preservation kicking in. He was unaware of the passenger in his mind, but his
instincts never failed. They knew the smell of danger, whether it was real or
artificial was a nuance lost on him.

He only knew it was there. And it made him sneeze. Luzia gave a silent
sigh of relief. Trying to control the wolf was like trying to drive a carriage with
the horses galloping in different directions. But she was going to have to stay
in his mind until the moon went away, she could sense the throbbing
magnetism of the trail.

You will not, she insisted. *There's nothing there for you but the man with
the gun and the silver that will kill you. Go hunt something less dangerous.*
Harris-wolf grumbled, but complied, and Luzia concentrated on putting as
much distance between wolf and siren-trail as possible.

* * *

Julia, who seemed to Leão to thrive on about two hours' sleep a night,
went silently down the stairs in the morning darkness. She was neither
sorceress nor shaman, but she had her own talents, and she had sensed the
new arrival. As she and Leão considered themselves under a kind of low-grade
siege — on the purely mundane level, they were in the country illegally — she
looked carefully up and down the alley before emerging from behind a door
that looked like the back entrance to a storage facility.

She covered the werewolf, which was man-shaped but unmistakable, with the blanket she'd brought, propped the door open with a brick, and chanted a few words under her breath before climbing back upstairs.

"There's a werewolf in the alley," she said to Leão when he came blearily out of the bedroom, yawning and shivering in the cold air.

"So," replied the shaman, apparently unsurprised. "It begins." He rubbed his eyes, and Julia went into the kitchen to make breakfast.

Leão waited until he heard the door downstairs give its characteristic creak, by which time the sky had lightened perceptibly into a reluctant January dawn, then walked down to see what was what.

Jesus God Almighty doing the soft-shoe shuffle, don't it ever get better? Harris, suffering from the worst wolf-hangover he'd ever had, was none too pleased to wake up butt-naked in an alley he didn't even recognize, but felt too sick to be angry. *Even with this army of stevedores throwing cargo containers around in my head.*

He blessed the kind soul who'd provided the blanket, and headed for the propped-open door like a drowning man grabbing for a lifebelt. The blanket was even big enough to cover him completely, like a cloak.

Just to round off the whole delightful experience, he trod on a sharp stone which made him hop and curse until he found that it jarred his head too much. *Oh momma. You bottle this and sell it to the temperance folks, nobody'd ever drink again.* He pushed the door cautiously open, and limped inside, blinking as his eyes adjusted. The only light fell through shuttered windows high up in the wall behind him.

"Fecha a porta," said a man's voice, very deep, from somewhere above, startling him severely. Harris squinted into the dimness, wolf-senses alarmed out of functioning for a moment, and saw nothing. He obeyed the command instinctively, removing the brick and closing the door carefully before he even realized it had been in Portuguese.

Man, any other time I'd be mighty pleased about that. But his head hurt too much for any kind of pleasure in this small breakthrough.

"Who's there?" he called softly.

Footsteps on the stair, and a brown-skinned man came into view. Harris blinked in surprise, though he didn't know why. *Ain't as if a port this busy ain't full to busting with folks any color you care to mention. 'Cepting maybe green folks, ain't seen many of them lately, though it wouldn't hardly surprise me these days. Might be it's the pajamas. That you don't see too often in the streets, gotta admit.*

"Chamo-me Leão," said the pajama-ed man. *"E o senhor?"*

Got that, too. "Harris. Edward Harris." He touched the blanket. *Thank you* had been one of the first words he'd actually managed to memorise.

"Obrigado."

"De nada," said the other. *Know that one as well. Dunno how long I can keep this up, though. Guess the old guy don't speak English.*

The man called Leão beckoned, which was unmistakable. Harris nodded, and limped towards the staircase. *Goddamn, that hurt.* He looked down, saw a smear of blood on the floorboard. *Shitfire, what the hell'd I tread on? As if it ain't bad enough waking up God-knows-where and lucky I ain't ended up with frostbite.*

On the dark bare stairs his residual wolf-perception finally came back to him, leaving him sure-footed except for the stab of pain every time he put his weight on his left foot. He sniffed, silently and surreptitiously. The man in front of him smelled almost wholly unfamiliar, a mixture of almost-recognizable human and odors and essences that were outside both Harris's cultural frame of reference and his lupine experience.

At the top of the stairs, a landing, bare boards still, not even linoleum. The whole place had a fusty scent to it. *Smells unoccupied. Different than the other place though. That was just plain nasty. This feels kinda welcoming, even if it is empty. And if that don't make no sense at all I dunno what does.*

Leão waited for Harris to join him, then smiled encouragingly and knocked on the peeling paint of the door that faced them. *That's a signal for sure. Who's behind the door?* A moment later he pushed it open and gestured for Harris to precede him.

Got nothing to lose, I guess. Harris went in and nearly bumped into a tall thin woman with midnight-black skin, who didn't smell human at all, although she smelled of blood. *What's that about?* He jumped back, startled, and sensed Leão behind also jumping back to avoid having his toes trodden on by getting on for two hundred fifty pounds of werewolf. *Like a buncha goddamn dominoes. Oh brother. What've I gotten myself into now?*

"Venha cá," she said in a harsh voice. *"Tem fome?"*

Yeah, ravenous. Harris nodded, still surprised at this sudden miraculous burst of linguistic competence, and the ebony-black woman smiled slightly without parting her lips. *What is she? If'n I was still wolf, might be I could tell. Or maybe not. She ain't no demon, anyhow, so I guess that makes everything just dandy.*

He decided, adventurously, to test his Portuguese and try asking her name. *"Como se chama a senhora?"* he said slowly.

"Julia," she replied. *Goddamn, it worked. Could be I really am getting the hang of it. Well, I'll be.* Then she turned to Leão and asked him something, in a doubtful tone. Harris frowned, positive he'd heard that wrong.

Sounded like she asked him if the wolf drinks blood. Which made sense, partly. *Except that she ain't hardly gonna have any just lying about the place, now is she? Maybe I ain't that good at the lingo after all.*

Leão laughed, and tested Harris's knowledge of verbs, saying what he remembered meant *He's a man at the moment.*

In reply to that Julia said something in a very tart voice that certainly wasn't Portuguese. *And now I'm completely confused.*

She turned to Harris. She was as tall as he was. "You are far away from home," she remarked, in English to his surprise and rather to his annoyance. But he nodded. *Not quite sure what I count as home these days, but yeah. Wherever it is, I ain't near to it.* He was visited by a sudden awful suspicion that somehow he wasn't even in Lisbon any more, but shoved it down. *Feet'd hurt more, at least.*

The thin woman who didn't smell human led him into a tiny, hot kitchen, which suddenly became very crowded. The heat came from a little stove that seemed far too small for such tropical intensity. Harris began to sweat under his blanket, and looked round uneasily for Leão, but he hadn't followed.

Can't figure out what it is with her. He kept feeling he should be worried, but he wasn't. "Ma'am," he said. "I mean, senhora."

"Julia will do," she told him in her crow's voice. She turned with a strange angular grace and opened a chest by the shuttered window, and a cloud of vapor billowed out as if the inside was very cold. *Handy bit of magic, there. Old João'd appreciate something like that.*

He was even more impressed when she took out an enormous piece of steak from the chest and slapped it into a frying pan.

* * *

When I woke up, I lay still for a moment waiting for about a hundred aches and pains to kick in. They didn't. Puzzled, I opened my eye and stared at the ceiling. Not complaining, mind you. I pulled my left hand out carefully from under Emilia. It hadn't even gone to sleep. Felt my head for Inspector Corvo's handiwork. No scabs. No tender bruise.

Must be some useful side-effect from the Key of Solomon. Makes a change for any magic to work in my favor. I investigated my shin. That was all healed up, too. And my arm. Bruises, where I remembered them, were also gone.

I touched the scar on my face, but that was still there. Hadn't really expected anything else. *Lying, da Silva.* My heart had done a stupid little leap when I found everything else healed up. But I never heard of any magic to make a missing eye grow back. But still hoping, evidently.

Emilia felt me moving around checking my non-existent bruises, and came awake.

"What is it?" she mumbled.

"Key of Solomon doing tricks," I said.

She pulled the covers up, and snuggled her head in them. I put my arm round her again. "What sort of tricks?"

"Healing ones," I replied. "Did it do anything to you?"

"Not apart from the firework display," she said indistinctly. I raised my eyebrows. Firework display? "What do you mean, healing?" she asked after a moment. Did she have the same irrational hope as I'd had?

"Less battered than when I went to bed," I explained.

"Probably clearing the decks for another round," she grumbled. Which made me laugh. It wasn't very funny. But it was exactly what I was thinking.

There was no sign of Harris, though. That's worrying. Yes, I know he's old enough to take care of himself. And, God knows, big enough. But he'd lost his clothes by changing when and where he did, and I should think that rather cuts down on your options. Waking up stark naked in an alley somewhere must limit you a bit. Still, as Emilia pointed out, it's probably happened before. And Harris is nothing if not resourceful.

I don't have time to worry about Harris right now, though. If he doesn't show up we'll have to call on one of the witches to find him. That's one thing we've no shortage of. Best use of my time now is to find Leão. Until Zacuto and Pierce come up with any more information.

Pleasant morning. For a change. Sun shining, clear sky that sort of washed blue that reminds me of azulejos. I even managed to have breakfast with my family. And that's a nice change, too. *Make the most of it, da Silva.*

The instant the sun comes out, of course, the washing-lines do as well. God only knows what all the housewives do with their laundry when it's raining. Mind you, it's not just the sheets that get an airing. *Alfacinhas* are outdoorsy people. They won't sit indoors when there's a perfectly good street to gossip in or a café to sit outside. So the living almost outnumber the dead, this morning. Although the living are mostly still carrying umbrellas, just in case the blue sky is all a big, sneaky trick. The shades, of course, don't care.

Which makes me think of the vision I had last night. Nothing happens by accident when you're dealing with the supernatural. If there's one thing the last five years've taught me, it's that. But for the life of me I can't figure out why I should see the dead of Lisbon.

Unless, of course, it was just reinforcing the unpleasant conviction that I'm going to have to go and raise one of 'em.

In which case, wouldn't you call it overkill?

The fierce little woman Dr. Bosque usually refers to as Cerberus, though her real name is Graça, answered the door at the orphanage. I wondered briefly whether Sílvia'd managed to sneak back in without being caught. But that triggered the greater wonder of Zé finding himself a girlfriend. Opens up whole new vistas of things to worry about. Ha. Better get him back to sea as soon as possible.

Teresa Batista came down the stairs as I was being interrogated by Sra. Cerberus, and I looked at her over the little woman's head and raised my eyebrows. Now there's an interesting relationship. She went from helping her father to ensnare my soul to being something like my friend. Though friend isn't quite the right word. There's too much else involved. *Admit it, da Silva, you find her attractive.*

She smiled openly enough, though, and said "How nice to see you," without a hint of irony. Graça, her authority usurped, stood to one side to let me pass and then stumped off like a self-important pigeon.

"I came to see Dr Bosque," I told Teresa. And that's an unlikely partnership. But they seem happy enough. And God knows Teresa deserves a relationship a little less intense than living with her father's obsession for over twenty years.

"He's in the office," she said, stepping lightly off the bottom stair and putting a hand on my arm. "Luís, what's going on?"

I ran a hand through my hair. "Too much," I replied. "Honestly, Teresa, I think it'd take half a day to fill you in."

"I know about the prophecy," she said. "Zé told me."

Zé, it appears, has been blabbing to half of Lisbon. I'll have to have a word with him about that. Or, rather, a few. In which the particular ones *keep your mouth shut* will figure prominently.

12

PART OF PIERCE DESPISED HIMSELF FOR SKULKING IN THE LIBRARY. But he knew himself well enough to recognize that it was vanity that made him want to appear braver than he was. And anything that could avoid a repeat of the journey he'd made in the soul-shriveling company of Munro's demon was something he embraced whole-heartedly.

He spent a lot of time in São Rafael anyway, almost enough to change its metaphysical status into a proper dwelling. However, channels were still open, and when he fell asleep once more with his head pillowed on a book, his dreams were not inviolate.

Munro's familiar, though a minor demon, had powers enough to capitalize on the unexpected link it had developed with the antiquarian. It couldn't bring him dreams, or even change them. But it could go into them.

Pierce was one of those people who claim not to dream very often, when the truth is that he simply didn't remember the majority of them, everybody dreams, but in any case we are not concerned with the very mundane dreams of a middle-aged antiquarian, which were never even invaded by any manifestations related to the sometimes odd books and documents that passed through his hands from time to time.

In this dream he was sitting on a bench in the Alta da Santa Catarina, looking out over the city and admiring a sky that resembled the aurora borealis. Not that he had ever traveled far enough north to view the Northern Lights in person, but he had always wanted to, having been fascinated by accounts he had read since he was a boy.

There were two elderly men sitting on the bench with him, an unlikely occurrence since an awake Pierce would have moved. One had a kind of squashed-in-looking face, the other was dark and cadaverous. They were poring over a newspaper which the thin one was reading aloud to his friend. He read out a story about a witch's husband who wanted to learn how to fly like his wife, but got the spell wrong and ended up stuck in the chimney.

Pierce could understand him perfectly well, but when he looked over the nearer man's shoulder at the newspaper it was just a page full of meaningless black squiggles. In the dream Pierce wondered if that meant he was dead, somewhere he had heard or read that you lose the ability to read after you die, but that couldn't be true, he knew a ghost that could read, although he couldn't remember the name, it was on the tip of his tongue—

He suddenly realized that there was someone sitting on the other side of him, as well. Annoyed, he turned to face the newcomer. It was a man with an anonymous face, a complete stranger, but why did he have the strange sensation that he knew him?

"Don't worry about it," said the newcomer, in a friendly tone. "We have met, but I looked rather different at the time."

"When was that?" enquired Pierce. "I don't recall."

"Well, we... traveled together," said the other, smiling. "And we had a conversation a little later."

The sense of familiarity nagged at him. He frowned. "Why don't I remember?" he asked plaintively.

"It really doesn't matter," his companion insisted, in a reassuring tone. "I came here to tell you something important."

On his other side, the old men had fallen silent. Or maybe they'd gone. Pierce could no more remove his attention from the newcomer than an iron nail can deny the magnet. Why did he have the feeling that he ought to be afraid?

"What did you want to tell me?"

"I would greatly like to leave my current employer," the man told him. "And since I have the means to speak to you, you can help me achieve that."

"Oh," said Pierce, knowing as he spoke that he must sound like a complete moron. "How?" he went on quickly, with an attempt at interested intelligence.

"It's very simple," replied his companion, with another of his pleasant smiles. "Just get the witch to say a word for me."

"Which one?" wondered Pierce. "I know at least three."

The man raised his eyebrows. "The most powerful one, of course." He paused, and then spoke a word Pierce did not understand and couldn't, later, repeat, although he knew how to write it down. That knowledge was burned into his brain.

"Do I need to write it?" he asked, nonetheless.

"No, not until you have the witch with you," the other said. "Once you write it, all knowledge of it will vanish from your mind."

This seemed perfectly logical to Pierce, who nodded his head and promptly woke up with a crick in his neck and a sore back from sleeping bent over. To find pale January sunlight slanting in through the library windows.

"What a very strange dream," he said aloud.

*   *   *

Watching Dr Bosque prevaricate. First he took off his thick pebble-lensed spectacles and squinted at them critically. Then breathed on one lens. Polished it industriously with a handkerchief. He should really exchange notes with Pierce.

"Did you experience any trauma in your right eye when you lost the left?"

I blinked at him. "What?" It was hardly the answer to my question. Which had concerned Leão. He smiled disarmingly.

"I'm sorry, I was curious," he said. Doesn't sound sorry to me at all. Sounds like a man pursuing an interest. "But sometimes people who lose one eye also lose the sight of the other. A sort of sympathetic trauma, you might say."

Well, he might. As I was pretty much out of things at the time, I really don't know. Not something I want to discuss right now. I shook my head. "Why?"

"Interest," he explained. Shrugged his shoulders. "Research. Pushing back the boundaries of medical science." And I know anything to do with sight does interest him. With his spectacles like the bottoms of a couple of bottles. Not to mention his amulet. I scratched my cheekbone reflexively. Glad I don't have to avoid scabs and bruises any more.

"I asked you about Leão," I reminded him.

He put his spectacles back on. "Yes, you did, didn't you. It's not really my secret to give away, though."

All this makes me feel like strangling him. "I wouldn't ask," I said severely, "if it wasn't important." He fiddled with the pen on his desk.

"Can't you get someone else to do it?"

Give me strength. "He's the lion in the prophecy," I explained. Again. "Plus he *offered* me his help."

The doctor sighed. Put the pen down. Picked up a penknife instead. Makes me tired just looking at him. I leaned back in the chair and crossed my legs. Obviously not going to get out of here in the next few minutes. *Patience is a virtue, da Silva. Sit back and be patient.*

At last he said, "I suppose I could take you to him." Finally. Though how that's different to his conscience from telling me the man's address, I don't know. "He's not here legally," the doctor went on. As if I'm going to give the game away. "If anyone found out where he lives, he'd be deported. And if he had to go back home he'd probably be executed. I gather it's something political. Nothing to do with his being a shaman."

"I'm hardly likely to tell anyone," I said testily. "Why don't you bring him to me, if you're worried?"

Teresa's lover peered at me through his lenses. They make his eyes huge and owlish. "I suppose that might be all right." But he still sounded doubtful. I looked pointedly at the clock on the wall. Lost on him, of course.

"Whatever works," I said. "Let's just go?"

So here I am killing time in a *botequim* while the doctor's off to the lion's den. Packed with dock workers and less legitimate tradesmen. One of the lowest dives I've ever visited, I must say. At least in recent years. Well, I'm respectable now. Or something like that.

This, though, is the sort of place where you have to order something strong enough to kill anything else that comes in the glass. Which means brandy. At this hour. Which means it's bound to be vile. And it is.

Nobody took much notice of me. Times like this it's quite useful to look a bit on the villainous side. I smoked, and pretended to read today's *Diário*.

Dr Bosque doesn't want me to know where Leão lives, but I can get a pretty good idea from where I am right now. Can narrow it down to a couple of streets, anyway.

I had to smoke fairly continuously to take away the taste of the liquid in my glass. And hope he comes back soon. I'm not paying money for any more of that stuff. Brandy? My backside it is. I know there's drinkable aguardente in the world. There's some at home. Some in my cabin. Even Jorge Coelho in London manages to keep a stock. But I've never met it in a bar. And if they serve it in restaurants, I can't afford to eat in them.

By the time the doctor came back I was bored and impatient. Kept on mulling things over in my mind and coming back to the same conclusion. Or up against the same brick wall. *No surprises, then, da Silva.*

He came coughing through the smoke, not looking as out of place as he ought to. True, his suit's a bit too good for the surroundings. Então, *any* suit'd be too good for these surroundings. And he doesn't look remotely like a stevedore. But what he does look is confident. Pierce, coming in here, would be diffident and timid, and the bullies would home in on him. Dr Bosque, though, shorter and a lot slighter than I am, they left alone.

"It's all right," he announced, flapping his hand ineffectively to try and disperse the smoke. "Leão says come along. He's got something of yours, apparently." I raised an eyebrow, and got to my feet. Stubbed out my cheroot in the overflowing ashtray. Something of mine?

"And what's that?" I asked.

"A werewolf, he said," Dr Bosque answered blandly. I followed him. Couldn't keep a smile off my face. Trust Harris.

Leão's home — hideaway? was well-concealed, but exactly where I'd guessed it might be. Though I expect he has it well-protected. From anything and everything. Like São Rafael, I bet you wouldn't find it if you weren't welcome there. And expected. So I suppose this whole rigmarole was necessary.

Tableau in the parlor, for want of a better word. Room full of second-hand furniture, impersonal and plain. Harris, wearing a blanket. Leão, as I saw him on the tram, a man you wouldn't take a second glance at. And a tall woman who makes me think of darkness. Not just because of her skin, either. Leão may be able to walk around the streets unnoticed, but she couldn't. Heads would turn. I'm reasonably certain she'd frighten the horses. She was introduced as Julia. But I'd be surprised if that was her real name.

"Good day, Captain da Silva," said Leão in his deep voice, slow as magma in the earth's core. "How may I be of assistance?" Sounds just like a clerk.

Sail to Cyprus with me and help me recover a mystical artifact to heal a wounded king whose identity we don't even know yet. Yes. I can just see myself asking him that. I saw Harris hide a smile. He must've understood. And be thinking the same thing as I was. I scratched my eyebrow.

"As I recall, you offered your help," I replied. "Which I can't believe is a coincidence." I saw that Julia had lit a cigarette, so I took out my cheroots. "You're the shaman, Sr. Leão. Why did you think I'd need help?"

His eyes glinted in his brown face. His mouth curved very slightly. "Things fall apart if no one watches over them," he observed. True. If oblique.

I struck a match and lit my cheroot. "Go on," I encouraged him.

"I think these lands are in need of someone to do that," Leão said.

"What do you mean by these lands?" Dr Bosque asked. Julia laughed harshly.

"Just like a white man, making boundaries all the time," she said contemptuously, and blew a perfect smoke-ring.

"Not these, Julia, you know that," Leão admonished her, and added something in a language I've never heard before. Then he turned to me. "More or less, the continent you call Europe. The people who share a similar culture."

Which was more or less what Zacuto'd said on the subject. But he'd been speculating. Leão, apparently, knows.

"Why would you want to help, then?" I asked, rubbing the scar on my cheekbone and noting that Harris was watching Julia suspiciously. As a wolf might watch another predator.

"Because if I went home, I wouldn't last five minutes," said Leão. "And I can't just sit back and watch while the world unravels."

I must say that his choice of words isn't very comforting. Falls apart. Unravels. And I get the impression that he means it literally. Sorcerers tend to do that. Talk portentiously, I mean. Or shamans, in his case. *Well, and why should you be surprised, da Silva?*

We could do this wary dance all day. I haven't got the patience. Or the time. Or the debating skills.

"There's a prophecy," I explained, exhaling smoke in a sigh, "that says we need a lion, a wolf, a snake, and a dog. To heal a wound. I have the others — that's the wolf," I indicated Harris, who'd got at least part of that. "I take it that you're the lion."

Julia's breath hissed between her teeth. "Man, I told you," she snapped. "You mess with these people, they use you up and spit you out."

Leão turned to her. "Not messing," he said gently. "You heard the man. There's a prophecy."

"Ha," snorted Julia.

"Hey, ma'am," Harris broke in. I don't know how much he understood of the conversation. But he can read a tone of voice as well as anyone. "Don't go getting your... getting aereated. The skipper won't let anything happen to your lion-man there."

Don't make promises you can't keep, Harris. Especially on my behalf.

The shaman looked at him questioningly, which led to a translation from Julia.

"Your people trust you," he said to me when she'd finished. "And you yourself have been chosen, in a different way." I eyed him sourly, and took a drag on my cheroot.

"Chosen," I repeated. Drafted, more like. He picked up on my disgusted tone. Well, he'd need to be deaf not to.

"None of us asked for this, Captain da Silva," he said in his deep slow voice. Makes everything he says sound impressive, I must admit. No more palatable, though. "So my role was foretold by a prophecy. Yours is no less important for being random."

Random. That's all I need. Being picked out like a toy from a bran-tub.

Ha. *Can't have it both ways, da Silva.* Either you have free will, or you don't.

"He don't know nothing," said Julia contemptuously. Leão frowned at her.

"You are always too quick to pass judgment," he said, but his tone was very mild. "The captain was chosen because he is worthy. Knowledge is not mandatory." Well, that's nice to know. Since most of the time I feel I'm blundering around in the dark. Still, I don't particularly like people talking about me as if I'm not there. But I like this topic even less.

I stood up and put my cheroot out in Julia's ashtray. She smells of blood and earth and gunpowder, and when she looked up at me her eyes glowed hot and yellow for a split second. So briefly I'm not entirely sure it wasn't my imagination.

"Sr. Leão—" I began. He tilted his head up.

"Call on me when the time comes," he said simply.

Meu Deus, I wish it was that easy.

Harris, clothed courtesy of a visit by Dr Bosque to the Seamen's Mission and grumbling that the pullover was itchy, made himself scarce. Obviously embarrassed about changing when and where he did. Not that it was his fault.

And I headed home, via São Rafael. Which I found empty, much to my surprise. Would've expected Pierce at least to be there. He's been a little twitchy since encountering Munro's demon. Tatiana Dimitrovna said that after it snatched him it would've taken a shortcut through hell. So it's not really surprising.

Outside, the courtyard's just as peaceful. Only ghosts, drifting in the slanting sunlight that's just beginning to light one corner. Someone had removed the smashed flowerpots. I wondered how Inspector Corvo was doing with Mouffi's latest incarnation. And whether you really can confine something like that in a police cell. I felt one of the benches with the palm of my hand, very tempted to sit there for five minutes. Alone and doing nothing. But the wood was still damp, and time was pressing. I sighed, and headed for home.

A few minutes later I sensed someone following me. And not supernatural, either. Years of dealing with the Venetian's associates, frequenting places where no sane man goes unarmed, have given me sharp instincts. But I can deal with a human threat. Mostly.

Today I don't have my gun on me. It isn't something I pick up as a matter of course. At least not here. And my knife is a little conspicuous to be carrying in broad daylight. Also, any knife escalates the situation. Takes it a level further than bare hands. Means that someone *will* get hurt. That's why I started carrying one big enough to make sure it's more likely to be the other fellow.

On the other hand, sometimes it's the best way to make the other fellow suddenly discover that discretion's the better part of valor.

How do you want to play this, da Silva?

First of all, reconnaissance. I slipped into a deep doorway that concealed me from the corner of the alley. I'll see him before he sees me.

Except there were two of them. Hired muscle. Neither showing a weapon. I found myself grinning wolfishly to myself. Two men I can take.

One of them turned to the other and said something in a low voice, but they kept on coming. I stepped out of the doorway and asked amiably, "Looking for something, gentlemen?"

The taller of the two laughed nastily. "Yes, you," he said. "If you're da Silva."

Still grinning, I tapped the eyepatch. "Can't really disguise it."

He frowned, slightly puzzled, and I pivoted round and belted his companion in the gut. Who went down gasping like a stranded fish. That should make him lose interest for a while. I heard the big one coming and ducked without looking. His fist swung harmlessly over my head, but mine connected with his jaw. His head snapped back, and I aimed a kick at his crotch. But his mate'd recovered more quickly than I expected, and he grabbed me from behind. His meaty forearm went round my neck.

I jerked my head back as hard as I could and was rewarded with a crack, a yelp and a curse. Felt his grip relax and grabbed his wrist, brought his arm down, twisted out of his way and snapped it sharply up backwards. Heard it break. He doubled over with a scream, clutching at his new elbow, and I kicked his legs from under him. He crashed to the ground again.

At that point the other man landed a punch on the side of my head that made it echo, so I swung round and elbowed him solidly in the chest. He staggered, tried to seize my arm, missed, flailed his fist wildly again. I dodged low, punched him in the groin and brought my knee up to meet his face as it came down, with a satisfying crunch.

That one won't be answering questions for a while. His breath was coming in great whooping sobs, and he curled on the ground cradling his family jewels. I turned to the other one, who struggled to his feet, on the point of bolting.

"Don't even think about it," I said savagely, wiping sweat out of my eyebrows.

"You're a fucking madman," he complained. "You broke my arm!" I bared my teeth at him, and examined my knuckles.

"I'll break your bloody head if you don't tell me who sent you," I told him.

"Englishman," he replied, sullen, fingering a split lip. "Smarmy type. Rich. Wants to talk to you." No surprises there, then.

"Well, tell him to come into the twentieth century and use a telephone next time." I grinned savagely. Mindless violence. Just the thing to relieve tension.

"You must be joking," the thug mumbled. "Catch me going back without what he wants?" And getting beaten up won't exactly enhance his reputation on the streets.

I turned my back on them and walked away. Amateurs. The fight left me on a high. Felt I could do anything. I lit a cheroot and tossed the match through the ghost of a fat man with a disapproving expression on his face.

Now comes the part where Munro sends a demon. Or maybe not. Why'd he send that pair? I can think of two reasons. One, he can't command demons any more. Which means my father's painting did work.

Or two, the demon itself wouldn't come after me. Which is a bit more worrying.

*   *   *

When I got home, still feeling rather pleased with myself, I found Pierce drinking tea in my parlor. Together with a very intense-looking Tatiana Dimitrovna. The English tend to forget it was us who introduced them to tea. Even when they call it *cha*. Which is Portuguese. But then the Russians drink it, as well. With jam, or so I've heard. Both nations can keep it, as far as I'm concerned.

"Tea, skipper?" Pierce asked me politely as I came in.

"Meu Deus, no," I said. "Isn't there any coffee?" My mouth tastes like the bottom of an aviary. I went in search of strong coffee.

Better find out what's eating the witch. Though eating is probably the wrong word to use when there's a werewolf around. Even one that wouldn't take it literally. But he's the only werewolf I know with that kind of sensibility.

So I sat down, lit a cheroot, and looked enquiringly a the pair of them. It was Pierce who spoke first. Not, of course, without removing his spectacles and polishing them industriously. He must have had a spare pair hidden somewhere.

"Had an odd dream, skipper," he said, in a strained sort of voice. And proceeded to tell me about it.

"It was Munro's demon," Tatiana Dimitrovna said when he was done. I tapped ash off the end of my cheroot and scratched my eyebrow.

"So what does the word do?" I enquired, patiently.

She frowned. Pursed her lips. "I think it will bind the demon to me. Make it my familiar instead of Munro's." And that was something I knew she didn't want.

"Wouldn't that be terribly useful?" Pierce asked, leaning forward in his chair. "We could have our very own spy in the enemy camp."

"Maybe," I said. I think I'm with Tatiana Dimitrovna on this one.

But she shook her head. Not to refuse the demon, but to disagree with me.

"I have to accept this, I think," she said. "You must write the word, Mr. Pierce, but not here, in Luís's home. We should go to my hotel."

I smiled wryly. That'll be the one with the portal into hell in the basement. Or wherever she put my desk.

Pierce directed a rather panicky stare at me and said imploringly, "Will you come, skipper?"

"Best if you do, I think," the witch agreed. I shrugged. Nothing else to do. At least, not until Zacuto re-appears.

"Where's Zacuto gotten to?" I asked Pierce. He seemed relieved to be asked something unrelated to the topic of demons.

"The Professor? He took Ana and the baby to his old place." Means I'll have to go in search of him. Later. I nodded. Disposed of my cheroot, and took a mouthful of coffee.

"Did he find anything?"

"Don't think so," muttered the antiquarian, drinking tea. His hand was shaking slightly.

Something I need to know before we go. "Tatiana Dimitrovna," I said. She turned to me, black eyes flat and opaque.

"When will you feel able to be less formal?" she snapped.

Well, I could've replied *when I stop wanting to take you to bed*. But even I could see there was a lot more behind the question than the question itself, if you know what I mean.

"I'm sorry," I said, and she blinked in surprise. *Da Silva, apologising?* Stranger things have happened.

"What were you going to ask?" she enquired in a gentler tone.

"Will you check the wards on the house?"

"Of course." The witch smiled. A little strained, true, but it was a smile. Of sorts. "Any particular reason?"

"Yes," I said, finishing my coffee. "Munro sent a couple of clowns to fetch me. I just want to make sure my family's safe."

"What happened to the clowns?" Pierce wanted to know. I raised an eyebrow at him, but he seems immune to the da Silva stare now.

"They sort of lost interest after I slapped them a bit," I said, but he wasn't deterred. He took off his spectacles, but carried on looking at me.

"Slapped them a bit?" he echoed. Back off, Pierce, I'm not going to provide the details for your entertainment.

"That's not the point, anyway." I frowned. "I'm guessing my father's painting must've had some effect."

"Yes, I see," said Tatiana Dimitrovna, nodding. "Be quiet for a moment, then, both of you." She closed her eyes, then seemed to glow for an instant. I exchanged a glance with Pierce, wondering if he'd seen it too. Eyebrows near his hairline suggested he had. In the silence, I heard the telephone bell ring.

The witch opened her eyes and nodded again.

"Yes?" I asked.

"Yes," she confirmed. "Hedge-witchery, but very competent."

I must've looked doubtful, or something, because she went on didactically, "Hedge-witchery can be just as powerful as the powers Munro and I can command." Just like Zacuto in lecture mode. Well, an octave higher, maybe. And without the beard, of course. "Since they are rooted in the earth, which is one of the four elements, as fire is. Powers of hell being rooted in fire. Not more or less powerful, just different."

Elements. Munro wants power over all four elements, he says. I scratched my cheekbone thoughtfully.

"And the others?" Pierce enquired, obviously thinking the same as I was. "Water and air?"

She shot me a strange look. "Seamanship is one manifestation of mastery of the power of water. Heaven gives the power of air. Every sorcerer, every witch, has a little of each. Usually one dominates, though rarely air. Gentlemen, do you want a seminar on sorcery, or shall we go and get me a familiar?"

"Are you sure you want to do that?" I asked her.

"I do *not* want to do it, Luís," she said tartly. "But like you, I recognize necessity when it is staring me in the face." She sighed, then went on in a gentler voice, "Your family is safe. Anyone wishing them ill would not even find the street."

Relieved, I got to my feet and moved towards the door. Which put her on my blind side. "Skipper," I heard Pierce say quietly, so turned back.

Tatiana Dimitrovna had leant forward and put her head in her hands.

The antiquarian raised his eyebrows at me. Damn it. I grimaced, and stepped to her side. Put a hand on her shoulder and squeezed. Felt her take a deep breath.

"Tatiana," I said softly. "Are you all right?"

She raised her head. Touched my hand briefly, and nodded. "Let's go."

While they found their hats and coats, I put my head round the office door. Emilia looked up from the telephone, which she'd just put back on its stand. She was smiling, but in a doubtful sort of way. As if she wasn't quite sure whether she ought to be smiling.

"What is it?" I asked.

"That was Sr. Williams," she said. "He wants you to take *Isabella* to Cyprus."

And I don't even want to think about that now.

So here's a small detachment of the da Silva circus walking down the hill in the sunshine to find a cab. Decidedly warm for January, now. Pierce's spectacles spent even more time than normal sliding down his nose. I saw that his face was beaded with sweat. Even the back of his hair was wet. Hell, it's not that warm.

"She won't let it harm you," I told him. He smiled wanly.

"I know," he said. "It's not that."

I raised my eyebrow at him, but he didn't elaborate.

* * *

"He did *what?*" bellowed Inspector Corvo, a tiny sane part of him still managing to be astonished that he was actually, after all these years, raising his voice. But mostly the anger had taken possession of him entirely. He couldn't remember ever having been so furious in his entire life. It felt as if his head was going to burst.

Santos, an officer not known for his perspicacity, eyed him warily, he is unable to remember ever having seen his boss angry at all, but that is only because it normally manifests itself as sarcasm and irony, two things he is incapable of recognizing, and he has to admit while cringing that Corvo's fury is pretty impressive.

"Released that big ugly woman, sir," he said in a small voice. Corvo whirled round, making him flinch, and slammed his fist against the wall, Santos has just enough imagination to picture the next blow landing on his head. He took advantage of Corvo's back, and slunk away.

Too furious to think, Corvo flung open the door to Ribeiro's office. His boss looked up in surprise, and his eyes grew wide as he took in the inspector's expression.

"What in hell's name were you thinking of?" he roared, and Ribeiro was too astonished to summon up any anger of his own, let alone outrage at this invasion of his office. All he could manage was to sound mildly affronted.

"That poor half-witted cow couldn't kill anything," he protested. "Whatever made you arrest her?"

"María Almeida, Mercedes Domingo, Rita Golfinho, Aranho Alvares," snapped the inspector. Ribeiro blinked.

"Who are they?" he asked uncomprehendingly.

For a moment, Corvo was incapable of speech. And in that second, caution woke and he put a curb on his tongue that was about to call his superior something unforgivable.

When he answered, it was in a marginally quieter, more controlled voice.

"The murder victims," he said sadly. "Just the people she killed."

Ribeiro, showing good sense for once in his life, chose not to bawl Corvo out for insubordination. "Why?" he asked instead. "Why do you think she killed them?"

The inspector brought out the believable explanation. "Because she's a homicidal maniac," he told Ribeiro. "And now she's out there again."

He went back to his office and opened the drawer, took out the gun with its complement of silver bullets, slipped it into his pocket, and left the building.

*   *   *

Pierce, nervous and twitchy, sat down at the desk in Tatiana Dimitrovna's hotel room. Took a sheet of hotel notepaper from the leather folder. Picked up the pen, examined the nib, dipped it in the ink. I wanted a smoke. I rubbed my scar instead, sticking my finger under the eyepatch because no one was looking at me. The witch was watching Pierce intently, and Pierce had all his attention on the paper.

His hand was moving very slowly, as if pressing against some kind of resistance. The letters he wrote were like nothing I've ever seen. I hadn't really expected to be able to read it, of course.

As soon as he'd finished, Tatiana Dimitrovna blurted out a string of equally meaningless syllables, as if unable to stop herself. And the writing vanished from the paper before Pierce'd even had time to put the pen down.

Where the word had been, the paper began to smoulder, and then burst into flames. Pierce jerked his hand away. The pen fell to the desk, spattering ink on the wood.

The witch drew in a sharp breath, and said another word. One I thought I almost recognized. There was a sudden odor of carnations in the room. A flower scent I don't like. Then an implosion. That's the only word for it. Air sucked inwards, somehow. And the demon appeared.

It was a harmless-looking thing. But that doesn't fool anyone. Something like a cross between a small monkey and a dog, blue in color. Its eyes too clever and cunning, though. And red, too. Bit of a giveaway, that. It looked at Pierce, still seated at the desk. The antiquarian flinched, but the demon grinned and nodded to him. If the grin was meant to be friendly there were far too many teeth in it to be remotely convincing.

"It's under an obligation to you now, Pierce," I muttered to him. "Don't forget that."

He nodded, but his eyes were wide and mesmerised. Like a rabbit confronted by a fox. Transfixed.

"Mistress," said the demon in a low but blaring voice, if you can imagine that effect. It set my teeth on edge. I rubbed my jaw, hard.

"I know your name," Tatiana Dimitrovna said to it. "You gave it to me freely?"

"Freely," it agreed, showing all its teeth again. Pierce gave a shudder. "I am yours to command." It shot her a glance, sly and obsequious. "Give me a task, mistress."

The witch looked at me, and there was such immense pain and regret in it that I wanted to put my arms round her.

"Go back to Munro, then," she said. "Pretend you are still his creature. Be our eyes and ears in the presence of our enemy. But first, tell me how he fares." Sorcerers always seem to think they have to talk to demons like that. Part of the mystique.

"He is weakened, Mistress," the demon offered. "He still has some powers, but many are beyond his reach for the present."

"Go on," said Tatiana Dimitrovna.

It licked its black lips with a mottled tongue. I saw Pierce close his eyes and swallow convulsively. The thing had no effect on me. Obviously it was a pretty minor demon. I smiled grimly to myself. Munro may have taken a trip to hell and been rewarded with its powers. But they evidently didn't think he merited anything very spectacular in the way of familiars.

Ha. Even hell doesn't trust him. *How does that make* you *feel, da Silva?*

Not that great.

* * *

Still inside the clumsy creation of Belphegor — though it had been able to make some improvements, at least the thing was a bit more symmetrical now — Mouffi went to ground to regroup its forces. In a manner of speaking. Constrained by its name, there wasn't much it could do against the witch who had bound it.

But it could go in search of its other enemies. If this body was not very good at stealth, it was extremely good at mayhem, and might get a few blows in first before someone shouted its name, if it was lucky. The rudimentary senses the construct had been given wanted blood, and though Mouffi was perfectly capable of controlling something so simple, right at this moment it felt no inclination to do so.

Mouffi, in truth, was one very seriously pissed-off demon-fragment. And it blamed most of that on the one-eyed captain who had killed its parent the year before.

* * *

Though irritated by the temporary loss of some of his powers, Sir Robert Munro did not let it distress him too much. He was convinced his sudden impotence made him a certainty for kingship, and the powers of the Grail Hallows would bring back his own fourfold and more, for the whole was certain to be much, much more than the sum of the parts in this case. Even if he had to travel to collect them by mundane means.

His latest trick had been delightfully successful, though. He hadn't really expected that the two pieces of street scum he'd hired would succeed in bringing da Silva to him. But he'd come through nicely with the violent potential Munro had recognized. He was surprised at the amount of damage the captain had inflicted on them, though. Somehow he hadn't expected that. Da Silva was evidently less squeamish than most do-gooders.

But the small spy-imp he'd attached to the taller thug was now firmly in place, summoned by its carrier's blood and hovering like an invisible insect half a foot above the captain's head, too tiny to detect unless anyone knew it was there. They had only a brief half-life, these things, but it would last long enough for his purposes.

And without it he would never have known that his familiar had been turned. He toyed with the pleasant notion of killing it slowly when it returned, but eventually decided that feeding the witch with false information would be better. Longer-lasting. And ultimately sweeter.

* * *

It had been over six months, as mortals measure time, since Zacuto had visited his erstwhile dwelling in the wall of a house destroyed in the earthquake. Unlike human habitations, though, it could not grow dusty and stale, and the air inside stayed constantly fresh and at a consistently pleasant temperature.

However, it is not a place that offers much comfort for humans, so Zacuto felt obliged to apologize to Ana for this fact.

"Senhor, to tell you the truth I'm so fed up with all these magical things," she said tiredly. "If I could even sleep, it might be better, but Susana — And look how *big* she is!" Ana frowned at the infant, and added in a rueful tone, "I'm afraid I'm not a very good mother. I'm fond of her, I suppose—" this a bit dubiously — "but most of the time she's just a nuisance."

"That's quite understandable, menina," Zacuto murmured. Even when he'd been alive he'd thought it particularly stupid to assume that every woman would miraculously become some kind of maternal paragon the instant she gave birth. And this girl had been raped, after all. It was a wonder she didn't actually hate baby Susana.

Ana sat at the table in one of the chairs, neither of which really existed, and cradled her head on her arms. After a few moments her breathing went deep and even.

Zacuto looked at Susana, who unlike her mother seemed bright-eyed and alert. He had very little recollection of his own family, knew vaguely that he'd had a wife and children, although neither their names nor their fates had survived the mists of death.

The ghost couldn't feel regret the way mortal men can, just a remote unformed longing hardly strong enough to be called an emotion. Although he had, since being raised by da Silva, begun to form attachments to these people, a thought that both amazed and amused him. He'd thought ghosts incapable of change, but not only that, Zacuto had learned so much from the library that he imagined he must now be Portugal's most eclectically-learned scholar.

It was not knowledge from books, however, that told him how much it was safe to let Susana grow while her mother slept. It was instinct. And he was sad for them both.

He had to judge it finely. He had seen the results of bringing on growth too soon, tiny withered children with wizened faces that wasted and died of old age before they reached their teens. Down the ages, people had called such unfortunates changelings, but Zacuto knew they were no such thing.

Real changelings are quite different. And much, much nastier.

Looking at the little baby face, he thought he would have liked to touch it, but that was something he couldn't do. But he knew things about Susana that not even her doctor could. He had, after all, been a healer long before he had been anything else. Dead, for one thing. A ghost. A scholar in esoteric disciplines. The child had already been damaged by the accelerated growth, but that had happened when she was less than the size of her mother's fist. He could sense something amiss internally. But apart from that, she was healthy. No other ill-effects that he could find.

Zacuto sighed. There is no one here to see or hear how well he imitates life, but old habits are hard to break, just as old donkeys find it difficult to learn language, and such little subterfuges are second nature to him now.

And, in fact, sometimes no word, or thought, or gesture is as expressive as a good sigh. Or as satisfying. Even if you have no breath to expel or even lungs to expel it from.

*   *   *

This light which falls into the studio, the brittle sunlight of early spring, has very little in it that is yellow, though sunlight moves through a spectrum of yellow as the year turns. But this is one of the rarest, this light like water, clear and sparkling, it gives everything a clarity quite unlike any other, as if it is a special kind of lens.

To take advantage of it, Sebastião da Silva still spends all the daylight hours in his studio, not that January is generous enough to grant him very many of those. To compensate, some of the pictures he has been working on border on the impressionistic in their brushwork, although this is almost completely contrary to everything he has painted before. But there is something strangely liberating in abandoning the meticulous, at least temporarily.

He is still painting his dreams, and they are still vivid, but now they are powerless to change anything. He can't say how he knows this, only that it is a truth. Whether he could ever paint with power again, he doesn't contemplate, the question is too perilous.

For Alegria is still here, and as the days go by he becomes both more and less confident that he will be able to enjoy her company for a long time. On the one hand, as time goes on, and she is still here each morning when he wakes, he sees continuity conspire with need to make her more real; but on the other, he imagines that is the very thing that puts her increasingly at risk. He may not be privy to all the details, but he has no illusions that his son's involvement with the supernatural is full of dangers he doesn't even understand and cannot even imagine.

* * *

I took Pierce with me to consult Zacuto. Didn't think he'd want to pass time with Tatiana Dimitrovna. Even if the Russian witch had shown any indication of wanting his company. Which she hadn't.

Last time I came up here. Last summer. Demon weather. The city was full of them for a while. Couldn't go round a corner without something breaking open the sky and coming screaming down at you bent on mayhem. Batista used to summon the bloody things as casually as picking up a telephone. More casually than I pick up a telephone, to be quite honest. Don't like the damn things. Telephones, that is. I know, useful, march of progress and all that. But I still don't like not being able to see who I'm talking to.

First time I came up here, too, someone shot Harris with a silver bullet. Only winged him, luckily. Though when he became human-shaped again he couldn't sit down very easily. I looked round automatically, saw only ghosts.

There's an odd feeling in the air. Not quite as if I'm being watched, it's not as identifiable as that. I felt in my pockets in sudden suspicion. Found nothing that shouldn't be there. Found my cheroots, though, so I took one out and lit up.

"What's up, skipper?" Pierce asked. Showing unusual perspicacity. I shook my head.

"Nothing," I said. "At least, I don't think so."

Same ghosts in Zacuto's street. Winter, summer, seasons don't affect 'em. Sometimes the sight of ghosts cuts so deep into me that my heart feels as if it's about to stop. They're the simplest memento mori of all. Right up there with skulls and bones as a reminder of mortality. But even sadder. Reduced to a wavering piece of spectral cinematography, a captured moment. The moment being the one they died. But sometimes even photographs have the same effect. A frozen piece of time. In a photograph, no one ages, but meu Deus, they remind me of time passing.

Snap out of it, da Silva. If you'd been meant to be introspective you'd be wearing a hat like Pierce's. Or Father Pereira's.

I located the door and knocked the way John Yeoh had shown me. A moment later Zacuto peered out.

"Oh, it's you," he said. I blew some smoke at him and raised my eyebrows. Who did he expect?

"Have we come at an inconvenient time?" I asked. Only a little sarcastically.

"Time is the least inconvenient thing here," he retorted, "as well you know." And I put my hand on the Key of Solomon, expecting it to make some sign of recognition. It didn't. The ghost stood to one side. "Come in."

The first thing we noticed was Susana. How big she'd grown. Now she looks about a year old. What is she, two, three weeks?

"My God," Pierce blurted out, taking off his spectacles and pointing them at the child for emphasis. "Is it, ah, *safe* for her to grow so fast?"

Zacuto looked at Susana. "She has grown naturally. We have been out of time." He glanced at me. Yes, I remember. "But you are quite right, more would not be safe at the present time."

Ana, I now saw, was asleep at the table. "She'll have a hell of a crick in her neck, then," I remarked. Not to mention a hell of a shock.

"We had better wake her," Zacuto said, ignoring me.

"I'll do it," volunteered Pierce, and walked quietly over to her. Touched her gently on the shoulder. She turned her head, looking very young in sleep. Well, damn it, she is young. Nineteen. Then she woke up, saw Susana, and gave a little scream.

"Mary Mother of God," she squeaked, and crossed herself. Good thing that old wives' tale isn't true. Or, if it is, good thing that Zacuto's a Jew.

"It is quite all right, child," he murmured reassuringly. "She is well, and you are well, and the world is as you left it."

To tell the truth, I'm not sure she believed that. Because I certainly don't. Economical with the truth, you might say, our Sr. Zacuto.

I didn't make any comment, of course. Instead I asked, "Have you had any luck with the prophecy?"

He turned his head to me, and there was something curiously weary in the way he moved. Which, when you think about it, is impossible.

"No, I fear not," he said, and his voice definitely sounded tired. "I think I will have to ask you to call the ghost of Johanna Kundrie."

And why am I not surprised?

Pierce looked up from Ana. He still had his hand on her shoulder in a paternal kind of way. "I'll take the Professor back to the library, if you like." I raised an eyebrow. Pierce, volunteering for dangerous duty. He shrugged, not at all offended. "It's with the witch now."

Maybe, but it's at large in the world. Have to say this for him, he can still manage to surprise me sometimes. I rubbed the back of my neck.

"What about Ana?" I asked Zacuto.

"You tell me, senhor capitão," he said. "What of Munro?"

Good question. "I'm not sure," I answered, slowly. Not sure whether we've drawn his teeth. Or how many of them we might've drawn. "Tatiana Dimitrovna has his familiar now."

Zacuto looked thoughtful, and fingered his beard. "I would like to be able to take Susana back into the world. This seems to be the best opportunity." He glanced at Pierce, who nodded. Da Silva is obviously superfluous. "Go."

"I'll leave you to it, then," I said. I want to get this over quickly. As I think I might've mentioned once or twice, I don't like raising ghosts. And a seer? Probably won't be as hard as summoning a sorcerer who doesn't want to answer. But God knows what a prophetess will be like. If she's not outright insane she'll probably be speaking in tongues.

The grave was where Zé had said it was. Or rather, his guidebook. I took a quick look round. Don't particularly want any funerals disrupting the proceedings. And funny thing about cemeteries, people keep wanting to bury their dead in them.

But there was no sign of funereal processions. Just a few people paying their respects. Or salving their consciences, depending on your point of view.

I took the flask of holy water out of my pocket. I'm not going to cut myself for a sibyl. Only magicians need the power of blood as a rule. And I'm fed up with leaking amounts of mine all over the place. On the whole I prefer to keep it inside me, where it belongs. Not that I always have a lot of say in the matter.

"Johanna Kundrie," I muttered, and sprinkled the water on her grave.

Nothing happened for a moment. And then two hands shot up out of the earth, startling me badly. I jumped back with a curse and nearly fell over a tombstone. The hands were followed by the rest of her body. Damned fortune-tellers. Always wanting to put on a show.

Face covered by a veil, Johanna Kundrie rose out of the earth, and the soil cascaded off her leaving no marks or stains. As if that's likely. I stuck my hands in my pockets and watched her, one eyebrow raised.

"Very impressive, senhora profeta," I said drily when she was done. She raised her head, gathering her veil back with both hands at the same time.

What was it Pierce called her? Loathly damsel, was it? Well, she's not repulsive. Or grotesque. But she's definitely odd. Looks like a man in a dress. Tall. Large, coarse features. A nose you could break rocks with. Hands and feet pretty big, too. Perhaps she is a man, at that. Was a man.

Her voice, though, when she spoke, was a high clear soprano, with something of the opera singer in it. You could imagine her holding listeners transfixed with nothing but that voice. She looked around, eyes wide, one hand poised dramatically at her throat. Make that melodramatically.

"Why have you called me?" she asked. Even her harsh German accent sounded mesmerising, in that voice. I raised both eyebrows, this time.

"To ask a question." Of course. Why else do people raise ghosts? Come to that, why should I think a prophetess should be exempt from asking stupid questions?

She narrowed her eyes and peered at me, with a shortsighted sort of squint like Pierce's. "You have blue eyes."

Eyes. *Going to argue the point, da Silva?*

"I don't think—"

"I see many of you," she explained. If you can call it that. "A boy, a man. You were not always as you are today."

"Goes for most people," I said, scratching my scar. No, I don't want to be drawn into conversation with her. Just want to ask my question. "Do you remember making a prophecy about the wounded king?"

The ghost looked down at her hands, and she stroked her arms. "One hundred years after the victory of the bear over the man from Cyrnos."

"That's the one." I could do with a smoke. But not a good idea. Some ghosts seem to find it narcotic. And I don't want a drugged sibyl on my hands. She's strange enough already.

"I do not know the answers. The words, only. The things that form the prophecies. I do not know who the bear is, or why he prevailed." She ran her hands down her legs, smoothing the skirt. Ghosts seem solid enough to themselves. It's other people who can't touch them.

"Do you know how to identify the king?" I asked her shortly. Getting a bit impatient there, are we?

"The king is maimed," she told me slowly in her high clear voice, as if speaking to an idiot. Hell, maybe I am an idiot to her. "Sterile. Or wounded. Like a tree in winter."

"What if there were two?"

Johanna Kundrie stared at me. Her eyes were very pale gray, almost colorless. "The painted woman knows the true king, and the king will be in her care," she said, and I felt my jaw drop.

And a voice from behind me said, "So you're a necromancer as well." A voice I recognized. Meu Deus. Munro. I turned slowly.

"Tell him to go away," the ghost ordered, petulantly. "He's all dark and slippery."

I wish I could. But Munro's pointing a gun at me. So I don't really think it'd have much effect. I folded my arms across my chest. *As if that'll do any good, da Silva.*

"What d'you want?" I asked. His nostrils flared.

"For you to start by showing me a bit of respect," he snarled.

"Or what?" I said, raising my eyebrow. "You'll shoot me?"

He smiled spitefully. "I'm going to shoot you anyway, da Silva. You can make things easier or more difficult for yourself." I felt sweat start to crawl in my hair. But I laughed. "Who is the painted woman?" he demanded.

"How the hell should I know?" I snapped back, and couldn't resist adding, "You know more about painted women than I do."

The sorcerer curled his lip. "You have an awfully smart mouth for a man at the wrong end of a gun," he remarked. I shrugged my shoulders. Wondered if I could jump him. "Don't try it," he advised me.

"He's been to hell," remarked Johanna Kundrie, in a conversational tone. "All burned up."

"Shut up, you silly bitch," snarled Munro. Unfortunately he didn't take his eyes off me. So much for spectral distractions. Have to try for another sort, then.

She looked at him contemptuously. "You cannot touch me, empty man," she crooned. Munro's face grew red. And darkened from there. Interesting effect. At least in someone not threatening to shoot me, it would be.

"Tell me what you meant about your father's painting," he ordered. Which threw me completely.

"What?" was all I managed as a comeback. Not my best effort.

"You said it must have had some effect on me. What did you mean?"

Yes, I said that. But I didn't say it to him. I was talking to Pierce and Tatiana Dimitrovna. My stomach clenched. He must have some way of spying on me. And he knows about my father. How much?

"You bastard," I said. Munro smiled, and it made my back crawl. Sweat trickled down my face and into my eye. I didn't move.

"Superior firepower," he replied, smugly.

"Is that why you killed Caracol?" I asked. "Because you could?" He didn't even bother replying. Johanna Kundrie chose that moment to pipe up again.

"Send me back," she demanded. "He makes my skin go crawly."

The Englishman gestured with the gun. "Do as she says," he snapped. "She's getting on my nerves."

"Tough," I observed. "I hope she haunts you the rest of your life after you shoot me."

"Put the gun down," said Inspector Corvo from behind him. "Turn round with your hands above your head. You're under arrest."

Munro pointed his gun at my head. "I don't think so." I ducked, instinctively. And, probably, ineffectively.

"Mouffi, stop him," Corvo shouted.

The misshapen thing lunged between us as Munro fired. It had to obey Corvo. But it chose its own way, knocking me backwards with a blow like a sledgehammer. I was airborne for a second, then crashed into a tomb. And in the instant before I lost consciousness, I heard another gunshot and saw Corvo stagger and fall, a red stain spreading over his chest.

I wasn't out for very long. Luckily. I woke with a foul taste in my mouth and staggered to my feet, fumbling for my knife. My legs felt like rubber.

Inspector Corvo was lying on his back not far away, and Mouffi was crouching over him holding his arm like a chicken drumstick. I pointed the knife at it, and it retreated a couple of paces, glowering. There was no sign of Johanna Kundrie's ghost.

"Touch him and you won't have a head any more," I said as menacingly as I could manage, and spat to clear my mouth. No to very much effect.

"Where is the harm?" the creature asked me sulkily. "This body is hungry, and the human is dying."

Merda. I knelt down beside Corvo, who was breathing in the bubbling sucking way that means a lung's damaged. Pulled his shirt away from the wound. There was an awful lot of blood, and it was still welling out. And how do you put a tourniquet on a chest wound?

He had a scarf draped round his neck. I pulled it off and balled it up one-handed. Stuffed it into the hole and leant on it. It turned crimson very quickly. Didn't do much good that I could see. *Neither does swearing, either, da Silva, so shut up.*

"You, Mouffi." I pointed the knife at it. "Can you do anything about this?"

It shrugged. At least I think that was what it was trying to do. "Perhaps." A big red tongue came out and licked its lips. "You could order me to."

"Do it, then," I snapped.

"It is not that simple," Mouffi said. "You have to make a commitment, Luís da Silva." I took a deep breath. Gritted my teeth.

"The only promise I'll make is killing you, unless you get to the point."

The creature smiled nervously. "You have to embrace the darkness," it said, sounding half scared, half-eager. "You are too clean. It is a two-way thing, a geas. You know this."

Yes, I know it. It's why Tatiana Dimitrovna didn't want a familiar. It's why Zacuto ended up having to exorcise me last year. But Corvo's going to die without it.

Well. *No choice, da Silva.* I suppose Zacuto can always do it again. I looked at Mouffi, loitering just out of reach of my knife. Failing that, I can kill it.

If Munro harms my father, I'll kill *him*.

"Do it, Mouffi," I said harshly. "I order you. Heal him. If you can." I sat back on my heels, feeling sick. My hand was covered with Corvo's blood. Mouffi moved forward and placed its own hands on the inspector's chest. I could hear his bubbling breath becoming fainter.

"Cannot heal completely," it warned me. "Can stop bleeding. Cannot replace blood." It licked its lips again. Not from nervousness. More like appetite. Nasty creature. I nodded my head, watching closely. "Move away."

I took my hand away and leaned back. "Get on with it."

Without warning, Mouffi plunged a hand into the wound. I didn't even have time to speak before it withdrew again. Dropped Munro's bullet on the ground. Then it drew both its hands together over Corvo's chest. He gave a deep groan and sucked in a rattling breath. But the deadly bubbling had stopped. Mouffi removed its hands.

"All I can do," it said. Backed away as I moved to examine the inspector. I realized I still had my knife in my hand, and sheathed it.

The wound was still ugly but Corvo's breathing was easier. And as Mouffi had promised, it had stopped bleeding. Now he's got a chance. If I can get him to a doctor.

Given the choice between the two doctors I know wouldn't ask too many questions, I'll take Dr Bosque any day. An added bonus. The orphanage is closer than *Isabella*.

As I debated the best way to get him there, Corvo's eyes opened.

"*Porra,*" he said weakly. "That hurts."

13

I JUST MANAGED TO STOP MYSELF FROM ASKING *ARE YOU ALL RIGHT?* The instinct to say stupid things is very strong. Especially at times of crisis. Instead, I got my arm under his shoulders and said "Can you sit up?"

Not much of an improvement, really, da Silva.

As I helped him up I caught sight of Mouffi a little distance away. Licking the blood off its hands. Watching it curiously was the ghost of Johanna Kundrie. She met my eye and said regretfully in her sweet voice, "Stained now. All dirty, like spreading ink."

You know, I can see why she infuriates Munro so much.

"Mouffi," I called. "Can you move him?" I turned my head to indicate Corvo. He'd closed his eyes again. His face was gray. A color I've seen before. In dying men. His breath sounds ragged.

"Not the way you mean," it replied. "Not enough power. Need to grow," its voice was frustrated. "Your fault, Luís da Silva. You killed Malphas. My… parent died at your hands."

Óptimo. I'm being admonished by an infant demon. "Never mind that now," I said impatiently. "I need to get him to a doctor."

Mouffi looked sulky. "This body is strong," it pointed out after a moment.

"Then help me get him up." Of course I could carry him on my own. But that wouldn't do his wound much good. Wouldn't do me much good, either. Being slammed into a stone tomb at about thirty miles an hour isn't something I'd recommend.

Johanna Kundrie's ghost was still watching. "No more prophecies," she ventured. I eyed her sourly.

"Do you want to go back to your grave?"

"Yes," she replied. "Sleeping among the worms. Better place for dead people than cluttering up the world."

Not quite the way I'd've put it. Since they clutter up my world considerably. "Go back, then, Johanna Kundrie," I said.

The ghost wavered. Became transparent. And finally disappeared. I turned to Mouffi again. "Come on."

Wonder if it has some kind of don't-look-at-me glamor, like Harris? That'd be handy. Don't want to trigger hysterics in nervous bystanders. All that blood could be a bit alarming. Luckily the orphanage isn't too far. Which is just as well, since I think I'd have a job getting Corvo there on my own.

As it was, I was soaked with sweat and damned sore by the time we got there. Not to mention furious with worry at what Munro might be up to.

And that's not the only thing on my mind. What the hell am I supposed to do with Mouffi, now I've bound it to me? Yes, bound is the word. We're tied together by a bond I can't break, even though I made it in the first place.

Great work, da Silva. Now you have a slave. And that makes me, as far as I'm concerned, no better than the Venetian. Because the really funny thing about slavery is that the owner is worse off than the slave, in the long run.

My back feels like a bar of hot iron. Headache throbbing at every step under Corvo's weight. And that sense of time racing by. Damn it.

At the door, Mouffi hesitated. "Let me go," it said nervously.

I'm happy to do that, but why? I looked at Corvo and knew I might be here a long while. So I turned to the demon-spawn and asked, "Can you defeat Munro?" Hoping that we've weakened him enough.

But it shook its head. "The sorcerer cannot access many of his powers, it is true." It stared hungrily at the inspector. I glared back. Just try it. "But he has a magical box around him that keeps him from harm."

Wouldn't you just know it.

"Go to Tatiana Dimitrovna, then," I said. Paused. "You can manage that?"

"Yes," it replied, apparently affronted.

"Tell her to take my father and Alegria to São Rafael." Mouffi hesitated. "Oh. I suppose I have to command you, do I?"

It looked at me narrowly. "Yes, Luís da Silva, you do. You are my master now."

And thank you for reminding me of that.

"All right, damn you," I said. Which was, of course, superfluous. "I command you. Now bugger off and do it."

Mouffi vanished, and Corvo sagged against me so suddenly that I almost dropped him. I swore, and yanked hard at the bell-pull in retaliation.

Somewhat to my surprise, it was Sílvia who answered the door. She gave a breathy squeak at the sight of Inspector Corvo. Opened her eyes and mouth very wide, and crossed herself.

"He's been shot," I said quickly.

Smart girl, she blurted out, "I'll get the senhor doutor," and bolted, skirts flying round her long legs. I got Corvo through the door, half-dragging, half-carrying him. Deposited him onto a chair. Leaned against the wall. Bloody hell, that hurt my back. Then had to leap forward with a curse and grab him as he began to slide sideways, and both of us nearly landed on the floor. Must've looked like a music-hall drunk act.

Dr Bosque and a couple of his boys appeared a moment later, trailed by Sílvia.

"Captain da Silva, what on earth is going on?" demanded the doctor. "Sílvia says you've got a man with—" He broke off and stopped blustering. Became the bush surgeon, or whatever he'd been in Mozambique. Corvo was whisked away efficiently, leaving me with Sílvia.

I sat down on the chair vacated by the inspector and sighed. Closed my eye for a moment. Opened it to find her bending over me.

"Are you hurt too?" she asked anxiously.

"Just bruised," I said. "Got caught last night, did you?"

Sílvia went pink, but met my gaze and grinned. "Yes." Obviously worth it, then. I marveled again at the idea of Zé having a girlfriend. *Have to get used to it, da Silva. It's not going to go away.*

* * *

Munro, his face red with exertion and fury, slowed to a walk when he was sure he wasn't being followed. He'd been caught wrong-footed, and he knew it. The truth was, he'd been relying on his power for so long that suddenly losing a lot of it had seriously affected his ability to function in the world. He had to rein himself in temporarily, he realized. Use the power he had access to, however small. The *Book of Souls* would have to wait, and so, unfortunately, would da Silva.

Retrieving the hallows had to be his first priority now.

Intellectually he knew that, but he hated leaving loose ends. And there was nothing wrong with his instincts. Which were telling him that da Silva's father, the painter, was important. He didn't believe in coincidences — most of the time he made his own coincidences — and the question of a painting and of a painted woman were much too close for him to ignore.

The January sun warmed his neck. He stood still on a street-corner for a few minutes until his breathing slowed and the sweat on his face evaporated. Then he hailed a cab and directed the driver to his brother-in-law's office. From there, armed with Sebastião da Silva's address, he went to find out what part paint had been given to play.

A man vain enough to desire his own portrait would have no trouble in gaining admittance to an artist's studio.

*   *   *

Tatiana Dimitrovna lay back on her bed, the curtains in her room drawn to give a dim twilight. She felt scratched and raw inside, and her bones ached as if she had a dose of influenza. The headache was the worst she'd had since her father had let her persuade him to teach her a shape-changing spell before she was really old enough. It pounded in her skull, and until she'd drawn the curtains, it had shattered her vision into bright shards like broken mirror-glass.

Sorcerous headaches were bad enough, but if you cured them by more magic, you were setting yourself up for a worse one later. And Tatiana Dimitrovna really didn't want any worse pain than this.

The witch turned over onto her side and put an arm over her temple, but the weight pressing down increased the headache. She cursed half-heartedly, not having the energy for any really virulent swearing.

And then something tapped on the window.

"Go away," she muttered, but without any binding force. The tapping came again. Sighing deeply, she got to her feet and drew one of the curtains, shading her eyes from the sun that slanted in with her other hand.

Outside, on the tiny ornate wrought-iron balcony, the ugly creature called Mouffi. Tatiana Dimitrovna eyed it with a grimace. Though it was not so misshapen as before, a lack of symmetry always offends the human sense of perception. But that was not the main reason for her dislike of the demon-fragment, of course. She knew its true nature, and that was cause for far more than mere distaste.

"Luís da Silva desires your help," it said through the glass.

Oh, not now, she thought wearily. But she spoke a word to make the headache disappear, and opened the window. "Come on in, then."

Mouffi hopped in and stood, hunched and awkward, in front of her. It smelled of stale blood, putrid and coppery. "The man Munro threatens his father," it said, in the sulky tone of a creature under geas, and the witch's heart stuttered.

He's bound it, she thought. *Dear God, does he know what that means?* She picked up her coat and shrugged into it. *Let's worry about that later.*

"What does he need me to do?"

It looked down at its hands, found something interesting, and stuck a finger in its mouth to suck before replying.

"Take them to the sanctuary."

"The sanctuary?" she asked, retrieving her hat and moving to the mirror to position it, one eye on the creature.

"Library," said Mouffi with a shudder.

She thought uncharitably that any one of a number of people could have done this, but supposed she should be pleased that he'd asked her. And then she looked at Mouffi, saw through the strange construct that was its current body to the deep dreadful malice and hunger for revenge within, and she was suddenly so afraid for him that she went cold all over.

Which, for someone who had been to hell, was a sensation so unlikely that it made her worried all over again.

*   *   *

Warmed unseasonally by the unexpected sunshine that slanted through the windows, the church was stuffier than the hundreds of burning candles should have made it. Hurrying to finish up and get out into the fresh air, guilty at that urge with the vague thought that it was disrespectful, the sacristan knocked a silver chalice to the floor in his haste. It rolled away behind the altar.

He fought off an urge to curse, crossed himself quickly just in case God had noticed, and bent ponderously to retrieve the fallen vessel. It had rolled further than he'd thought, however, and he ended up on hands and knees. As he reached for the chalice his other hand encountered something hard and circular that felt like some sort of big coin.

Both were in his hands as he hauled himself to his feet. He replaced the chalice without much thought and squinted astigmatically at arm's length to see the coin, a medallion he supposed it should be called, it had some kind of design on it which he couldn't make out. It went into his pocket, the things people dropped in church, you really wouldn't believe some of them.

And there it remained, forgotten, until he finished his duties and set off home, thinking more about his lunch than anything else. It was, after all, a long time since breakfast, and there was a lot of sacristan to fuel.

Like most people, he rarely looked up as he walked along. And so he failed to see the demon burst out of the sky. Although, to be fair, one reason for that was that Belphegor was trying to be quiet. Being deprived of its portal hadn't robbed it of its cunning, as it would have some lesser demons.

Belphegor, in demonic form, stalked the sacristan for a while just for the sheer pleasure of being able to do it, and then materialized in front of the man. Who stammered out a prayer, holding out his crucifix in a trembling hand, then, finding it had no effect, gibbered with terror for a few final moments before the demon devoured his soul, nicely seasoned with fear, then collapsed onto the cobbles.

Malice satisfied for the moment, Belphegor gave the demonic equivalent of an eructation, and then became aware of something familiar close by. It turned its head to see the construct which it had made, but what had happened to it?

The construct groveled in front of the demon, which told it rather impatiently to get up. There was now an essence inside it that felt demonic, in a sort of sad, crippled, tiny way: What was it? And the outer form of the thing itself seemed... different, too.

What are you? Belphegor asked, but the reply, *Mouffi*, meant nothing. *Explain*, commanded the demon.

Mouffi, desiring to eat, starving in fact, scented the congealing blood in the sacristan's corpse and salivated. Its hunger was almost strong enough to overcome its fear of Belphegor. Almost, but not quite.

A fragment of Malphas, it replied, *split off before Malphas was slain.* The demon was intrigued. A fragment, able to exist independently after the death of its maker? Fascinated as ever by acts of creation and procreation, Belphegor examined Mouffi carefully.

You are *a demon*, it decided finally. *Not just a remnant. You have* grown, *you have life. Child of Malphas, this is delightful.*

Then may this body feed? Mouffi asked diffidently, eyeing the dead man on the ground and drooling. Its saliva spotted his clothes.

Remove the meat to some place more secluded, instructed Belphegor. *I desire more speech with you.*

No one, at least no human person, could see the demon if it didn't desire to be seen, but Mouffi had a physical body. And of course the cadaver was large and substantial. It removed its meal to a nearby rooftop and began to gnaw at the soft flesh of the face while Belphegor watched. The demon had made this body, but Mouffi seemed to have improved it somewhat during its occupation. Belphegor approved of that.

Since it had been some considerable time since the construct had eaten, there wasn't a great deal left of the sacristan's corpse by the time Mouffi was sated. It wiped at the blood on its face, then licked its smeared hands like an inefficient cat.

You should clean the body better if you are to pass as human, Belphegor advised. *Mortals are always suspicious of bloodstains.* Mouffi, admonished, scrubbed at the blood with a piece torn from the dead man's clothes.

Is that satisfactory, great one? it enquired.

Yes, replied Belphegor, a little impatiently. *Now, tell me more about your* growing. *What could you do when you were a mere fragment? What can you do now?*

Mouffi bared its teeth in the nearest it could get to a smile, not having learned the use of small irrelevant muscles. For a fragment, it had actually accomplished a great deal over the past few months. And having all the memories of a full-grown demon, it knew which of these would be of greatest interest to Belphegor.

I have the mortal called Luís da Silva, it said smugly. *He had to bind me, to save the life of another human.*

And that was the best news the demon Belphegor had heard since the portal had been re-opened.

*   *   *

"I am sorry, but Sr. da Silva is not at home," said the small neat woman who had opened the door, in careful English softened by her Portuguese accent, something that irritated Munro beyond reason.

The politician kept his expression pleasant with an effort, though, and even managed a smile. "I would hate to have had a wasted journey," he remarked, deriving small malicious pleasure out of the sentence structure as her eyes flickered momentarily. "Might I be permitted to view some of the maestro's work?"

Sra. Reinaldo paused to sort this out, her lips moving as she worked her way through it, then said abruptly, "Come in."

"Thank you," he murmured politely, and followed her through the hall into Sebastião da Silva's studio.

Like most Englishmen, Munro had little appreciation of art. He thought the Pre-Raphaelites decadent and the Impressionists a waste of paint. The only paintings he had any time at all for were good solid portraits that looked like their subjects.

He was confronted by one of himself.

After the initial shock — the symbolism in the picture was not wasted on him — he thought fast. It was what he was good at, as a politician: lying on his feet.

"That's mine." He indicated it. "I'd like to take it with me."

The woman compared him with the painting, moving her head to look from man to picture, and nodded. Munro smiled smugly.

"No," she said, which wiped the smirk off his face. "I am sorry. But Sr. da Silva is not here. You must come back later."

Munro snarled inwardly, seeing that she was going to be completely intransigent. But he knew when to capitulate.

"Then that is what I'll do," he replied, ranting inside against the stupidity of servants. "Can you tell me when he'll be back?"

"I do not think he will stay out late," said the housekeeper. Which translated, Munro well knew, as *I don't know.* He sighed, frustrated, and took his leave. He was not, however, particularly annoyed at his failure. The painting was safe enough where it was, for now.

Besides, he had no idea what to do with the picture in order to break the spell. He wouldn't dare destroy it. And how else could its magic be unmade?

Outside, he contemplated the house for a moment, consolidating his thoughts. He hadn't identified the painted woman. The picture of himself had thrown him off-track, driving it completely from his mind. Munro shook his sleek head and called for his familiar before remembering it was the witch's creature now.

But a demon came anyway. Although it wasn't the servile thing that had been bound to him. It was a fully-fledged mighty creature, one from the higher echelons of hell, a thing of tremendous power: Belphegor.

It appeared to him in the guise of a young girl.

Of course Munro knew what manner of thing it was the instant he saw it, although his knowledge of demons wasn't great enough to identify it by name. Nor did he know that it had been drawn to him as irresistibly as blowflies to dung and corpses by the rich corrupt stench of his putrefying soul.

"Sir Robert Munro," it said, and though it sounded like a young girl, he could hear its voice echoing down the ages, iron and implacable.

"I am at your service," he replied, not really knowing quite how very true that was. It smiled, because it knew precisely.

"Yet I have come to do *you* a service," the demon told him.

He glanced round quickly. No one was watching, unless Sebastião da Silva's housekeeper was hidden behind a net curtain, that was what women of a certain class and age did, was it not, but all a spy would have seen was a middle-aged man talking with a beggar girl. She wasn't really clean enough to be a whore, although if he'd been himself he would have been tempted by her, the curve of her small breast under the thin cotton dress needing a hand upon it.

But she wasn't a girl, she was a demon, and he knew better, even if he had been himself. And yet he still looked at her — at it — as if it were human.

"What service?" he asked, curious.

"To offer you my aid," replied the demon. Its face was open and ingenuous. "Since much of your power has been leached away."

Corrupt and power-hungry as he was, Munro was still wary about looking a gift demon in the mouth. And venal enough to know that everything had a price.

"Why would you do that?" he demanded. "What's in it for you?"

Belphegor regarded the politician, masking the contempt it felt for him with the ease of long practice. This one was no great gain for hell, he had been theirs before he even contemplated making his pilgrimage there. But he could be the key to something much better. If Mouffi faltered, or wasn't strong enough to hold, or if da Silva knew enough to sever the ties that had been made. Belphegor knows the usefulness of having several irons in the fire, it is sometimes called insurance, though this is not the kind of policy underwritten by Lloyd's of London, no bells will be rung if the vessel founders.

"I would have thought the answers to both those questions were obvious," it said to Munro, a little tartly.

The politician frowned, but in annoyance rather than ignorance. "I'd rather have my own power back." He eyed the demon speculatively. "Can't you tell me how to undo that painting?" he asked petulantly.

But Belphegor only laughed. Mortals, seeking answers to everything. Sorcerers, wanting to control everything. "Art is a power beyond even ours to destroy," it explained, pausing to drink in another taste of Munro's essence like a man savouring a fine cigar. "Not even the painter can do that now. Once created, art and music live in the minds of all those who witness them. It will last as long as their memories."

"But—" began Munro. The demon interrupted him.

"No, think on the hallows you seek, sorcerer. They can give you more power than you ever dreamed of."

Which was probably not true, on second thought. This human's lust for power apparently knew no bounds.

And that could only be to Belphegor's advantage.

"Well," said Munro, staring at the demon, "you can do one thing to begin with. Keep the police off my back."

The expression that crossed its face at that demon sat very oddly on the features of a sixteen-year-old girl. Although it fit a demon's visage very well.

"I think not," it replied. "Do not waste any more time in this city. Things here are irrelevant. Set out for Aphrodite's isle."

Munro looked mulish. "I intend to kill that damned man da Silva first," he snarled, and then cried out in pain as the demon gripped his wrist and the bones of his arm, radius and ulna, ground together beneath his flesh.

"That is not permitted," said Belphegor, sternly. "We have plans for the captain. We do not want him dead." It released its grip.

"What then?" The politician rubbed his wrist.

"We want him, Sir Robert Munro," the demon said, and its wide innocent brown eyes burned hot and yellow for a second. "We want to possess the paladin's soul. War is coming, such a war as the world has never seen. Such potential for apocalypse."

"War?" asked Munro.

It smiled, and the tip of its tongue flicked out and moistened its lips briefly. "We want him on *our* side when that comes to pass." The smile grew wider. "Besides," Belphegor went on, "you can let him do all the work of collecting the hallows for you. He has the company of four, already. All you have to do is wait at the place of the chalice. Oh, and one other thing."

"What's that?"

"You will need to kill the current Fisher King in order to succeed him."

* * *

Police have been and gone. Took away Munro's description, not that I hold out much hope of seeing him in a courtroom any time soon. The words *politician* and *bribery* go together too well. Corvo's still in Dr Bosque's infirmary, though. Better off there, if you ask me. For one thing, the orphanage is officially a dwelling, as far as demons and the like are concerned. Means he's safer there than in hospital. For another, I'd trust Dr Bosque over some quack I don't know. Over some quacks I do know, to be honest.

He insisted on giving me the once-over after he'd sewn Corvo back together, having seen me wince as I got up from the chair I'd been sitting in. Sitting and not leaning back. Though the wince was more from the Key of Solomon than from impacting with the tomb Mouffi'd thrown me against. The mark is resisting Mouffi. I have no idea if it's strong enough to break the binding. But it feels as if there's something biting my heart.

"Your back's as black as the ace of spades," Dr Bosque informed me graphically. A detail I could've done without, obrigadinho. "But you haven't broken any bones, as far as I can tell." Nice to know. Not much help. He walked round his desk, and I put my shirt back on. "You could put arnica on it, but you'd need to buy it by the pint."

"Thanks," I said drily, doing up buttons. I'll prescribe myself some brandy later. The drinkable kind.

Difficult to get moving again. *Good God, da Silva, it's only a bruise. And you're forty-four, not ninety-four. It'll feel better in a while.* Except that it doesn't, not really. Bloody Mouffi. Bloody Munro.

I got myself to São Rafael eventually, although what I really wanted to do was go home. And sleep for about a week. Yes, all right, on my front. But to see, first, if Emilia's mark could help at all.

Never thought this place would end up as a sort of sanctuary for all and sundry. Well, I never thought it'd need to be. But Pierce spends half his time here. Zacuto, of course, haunts it in both senses of the word. And now it seems to have acquired semi-permanent residents in the shape of Ana and her daughter.

But no sign of Tatiana Dimitrovna and my father. Damn it.

"Skipper," exclaimed Pierce worriedly as I walked, or rather limped, in. Started to get to his feet. I waved him down and sank into a chair. Leaned my forearms on the table. "What the devil happened to you?"

Entirely too much. Do you want the long answer, Pierce, or the short one? Well, that's the short one. I shook my head.

"I'm all right," I said. "I think." Turned to the ghost. "Sr. Zacuto, I had to… ah… make a commitment to—"

He interrupted me, scowling horribly. "I can see it. Sit up." I did as I was told. Don't argue with your seniors.

"What?" asked Pierce.

Zacuto held up a finger at him, and he subsided. Then he brought his hand down slowly sideways in front of me. He looked like a man searching for the hidden wires in a music-hall magic act. I felt a sharp tug from the mark, and the gnawing sensation vanished. Much to my relief. I'd been starting to think it was physical.

"Not deeply rooted," the old ghost growled, severely. "But don't make a habit of it. Demons remember routes as readily as people do."

Então, I've met plenty who don't. People, I mean, not demons. Though I've met enough of those to last a lifetime. But I take the point.

"I don't suppose you can do anything for my back," I said. He narrowed his eyes. He doesn't have much of a sense of humor. Though why I expect a ghost to have one at all, I don't know. I don't suppose dying gives you much reason for belly-laughs.

"Got a backache, skipper?" Pierce enquired sympathetically. I turned my head to him. Slowly. You can practically hear me creaking.

"You'd have backache too if a demon'd thrown you into a stone wall." The antiquarian took off his spectacles and stared owlishly at me.

"Magical healing, like every other kind of magic, is a two-edged sword," said Zacuto sternly. Which remark didn't surprise me one bit.

"Don't worry, I wasn't really serious." Only about half. All right, three-quarters. I looked across at Ana. "How is she?"

She was watching Susana staggering around unsteadily. Adventurous little person. Her mother just looked bemused.

"Difficult to tell," said Pierce, dryly.

I heard the door open at that point and turned slowly in my chair. Last thing we want is some scholar wanting to come and *work* here. But it was Tatiana Dimitrovna. Followed, much to my relief, by my father. And Alegria, of course. Apparently you can't pry them apart, now. They come as a pair.

My father stopped just inside the door and stared around, mouth open. The first sight of São Rafael's interior tends to get people that way.

But it was nothing to Alegria's reaction. Although in her case it wasn't the library that had done the captivating.

She advanced on Susana, her eyes wide and shining, a kind of ecstasy on her face. I suppose she'd never seen a baby before. Dropped to her knees in front of the child and held out her hand. Susana, who had been trying to stuff her own fist in her mouth, lost interest in that and lurched towards her.

"She's the key," breathed Alegria. "And the lock. The puzzle, and the solution." My scalp prickled. Susana lost her balance and tumbled forward. Alegria caught her.

"What do you mean?" I heard my father say.

Alegria looked up at him with a smile of sheer delight.

"She's the Fisher King," she said.

You could've heard, as Harris might've said, a fly fart in the silence that followed. Then everyone started talking at once.

Me, I didn't doubt it for a minute. Hell, if a da Silva can be a paladin, a little girl can be the land's symbolic parent. Why not? As Zacuto says, the story's as old as the land. Taken over by whatever religion happens to be on the up. And most cultures look to kings rather than queens. Unless they're republican, of course. Or, for most of the last century, English.

The discussion petered out, and everybody looked in my direction. As if I have all the answers. Though, in this case, I do have an answer.

"Johanna Kundrie said, *The painted woman knows the true king,*" I told them. Of course, they don't even know I've spoken to the sibyl's ghost.

"She's not wounded," Tatiana Dimitrovna pointed out, turning to look curiously at little Susana. "Is she?"

"Some damage was done in the womb," said Zacuto. "She will grow up barren, unable to bear children."

Ana picked up her daughter and held her in her lap.

"But she's so little," Pierce protested.

"Is someone going to tell me what's going on?" asked my father.

By the time everyone had been brought up to date I felt too stiff to move. Like most groups of people, they then decided to have a debate about the current topic. Never figured out why they do that. You can't undo something that's already happened. So why the hell go on and hold a discussion about it?

The human condition, da Silva. Live with it.

I lived with it for about two minutes, and then got fed up and interrupted them. "Can we get on with it?"

Pierce looked round, relocating his spectacles. "Pardon, skipper?" I scratched my scar and wished for a smoke.

"We need to leave as soon as possible," I said. "Munro can still get there before us."

"What, you think he may still have the power to, ah, fly?" he asked dubiously.

"No, but he does have the power to take a steamship," I replied.

Tatiana Dimitrovna raised her head. Her eyes were shadowed. "It doesn't matter, Luís," she said softly, in the tone of someone with bad news to give. "I can take *Isabella* a faster route than he's capable of."

Well, I don't think I like the sound of that very much.

"You must collect the hallows in the correct order," Zacuto instructed while I was contemplating the witch's promise. Does she mean through hell, with her new powers? Or just out of time, the way we did before?

"Yes, earth, air, fire, water," put in Pierce. My God, they're at it again.

"Yes, clockwise from the south." The antiquarian was nodding. He pushed his chair back. The legs screeched on the floor, and Tatiana Dimitrovna winced. Pierce crossed to one of the study desks, piled high with paper and books. "I've got it all written down," he explained, catching my eye. I raised an eyebrow at him.

Normally I would've got up and gone over to join him. Instead I let him do the walking this time. I'm not entirely sure I can move.

He was holding, of all things, a map. I couldn't help a grin. "I do know how to find Cyprus," I said, mildly. "And Malta, Tunis, and Italy, come to that." Pierce colored, and took his spectacles off. Only teasing.

"The map's for me," he explained, squinting at it. "The symbol for earth is the dish, and that's Malta."

Malta, that was the dog. "John Yeoh," I said, wondering how he'd react to yet another strange task da Silva's found for him. "How will we find it when we get there?"

"They will know," Zacuto put in, with an air of finality. "Their roles are foretold. All four will know."

Foretold. I sighed. There it goes again. Pierce moved his finger on the map, tapped it with his spectacles.

"Second place is Carthage. Ah, Tunis, now, of course. That's where the sword is. The symbol of air."

Tatiana Dimitrovna shuddered visibly. "I can hear it now," she said, quietly and unexpectedly. And inexplicably. Hear the sword? Well, she's a witch. *You should be used to that sort of thing by now, da Silva.*

"What comes after air?" I asked, then answered my own question. "Pompeii. Fire." Couldn't be anything else. "Harris. What does he have to find?"

"The lance," supplied Zacuto. "And the chalice in Cyprus." Pierce nodded.

"Water. Your lion-man, skipper."

"Hardly mine," I said, running a hand through my hair. Feeling sweaty and sore. Tatiana Dimitrovna looked in my direction, her own face strained.

"Would you like a pain-killing charm?" she asked, warning, "It'll give you a headache later, though."

"Yes," I replied quickly. Not the time for stoicism. I'll put up with a headache if I can think straight now. Right at this moment it's an effort to keep my mind on this topic. On any topic. And I really don't want to miss anything.

The witch walked over to me and put her hand on my back, very gently. Although I felt myself tense up involuntarily the moment before it touched. Seconds later, the aching eased. I blew out a long breath.

"Better?" I turned my head to look at her, and nodded. She removed her hand, and went back to her chair.

"Thank you," I said, and meant it. She looked very strained. After a minute I asked her, "Do you know what Munro's up to?"

She closed her eyes. "Not now," she said a moment later. "The less I have to do with that demon, the better."

I thought about suggesting that she ask Zacuto to do something about that for her. But she's a big girl. And she knows more about these things than I do. Me, I prefer killing 'em. It's less complicated.

Why haven't I killed Mouffi, then? I have no idea. Perhaps because Corvo would've died without it. But then I'm pretty sure Munro would've shot both of us if Mouffi hadn't been there. Well, he'd said he was going to. Wish Corvo had a sensible deputy to get the creature arrested again. Not that sticking it in a cell worked very well last time they tried it. Which is strange, now I come to think about it. How *did* it manage to escape?

Então, I don't really have time to think about it. I have to get *Isabella* ready for a voyage. And make room for a few more passengers than we're used to carrying. It's all the same even if we're sailing through hell, or whatever Tatiana Dimitrovna has in mind. Don't particularly fancy running into the Flying Dutchman, mind you. Though we could probably compare notes.

About time I paid a visit to my ship, anyway. Ashley is so efficient it sometimes hurts to watch him. But I can't leave him in charge indefinitely. He might start thinking he's indispensable. Can't have that.

"What about Susana?" I asked quietly. While on the topic of finding berths for passengers. Ana, hearing the child's name, looked up and met my gaze pleadingly. Though what exactly she wanted I didn't know. For life to be normal, perhaps. Something I wish myself, sometimes. Not that my life has ever been normal. Or straightforward. What is normal, anyway? I have no idea what I'd have ended up doing if I hadn't run off to sea at fourteen. Having an artist for a father isn't as if there's a family business to join. Well, maybe it is. But I don't suppose I'd have enjoyed it any more than he did while my mother was around to color everything dour with religion. And *she* wanted me to be a priest. You can imagine what I think of *that* idea.

"She will have to go with you," Zacuto said. "Everything I have read indicates that the… the monarch must go to the hallows, not the other way round."

Which sounds bass-ackwards, as Harris calls it, to me. As if the hallows are more important than the king. Perhaps they are, at that. This symbolism stuff gets a bit too complicated for me sometimes. I don't see the point of it.

"But who's going to look after her?" Pierce asked, frowning, and rubbed his beard. "According to the skipper, Johanna Kundrie said the 'painted woman' was to take care of her." He lowered his voice, although we were talking in English for Tatiana Dimitrovna's benefit. "Can we take her away from her mother?"

From all I've seen, Ana would be delighted at that. I didn't say so, though. Glanced at her. She and my father were both watching Alegria playing with Ana. She seemed to be in her element. I raised my eyebrows, and Pierce and Zacuto turned their heads as well.

"The painted woman seems to be doing all right," I remarked.

"Yes, she does, doesn't she?" said Pierce.

I looked at Tatiana Dimitrovna, who had been so quiet I thought she'd fallen asleep. I wondered whether she was alright. Well, *alright* is pushing it a bit. I doubt whether anyone in her shoes could ever be alright.

She had her eyes closed. Looked terribly tired, leaning on her hands.

Hell with it.

"Sr. Zacuto," I said, switching to Portuguese in case she was still awake, "can you exorcise her the way you did me?"

He shot her a glance that wasn't without sympathy, and replied quietly. "Only if she asks me herself."

I raised an eyebrow. "You didn't wait for me to ask you, last year," I pointed out.

"That was because if I had not acted then, it would have been too late," he said severely. "You had been meddling with a great power of hell. This little demon of the witch's, it poses a far lesser threat. Years might pass without her soul being claimed or corrupted through association with it. And I do not think she will wish to keep it after this business is done."

Depends how useful it is to her, doesn't it?

I scratched at my cheekbone, more for something to do with my hands than any good reason like an itch. I'd kill for a smoke. But the panic-stricken look that comes into Pierce's eyes at the very thought of lighting matches anywhere near books would make me feel as if I was kicking a puppy.

* * *

She'd known something had changed the instant she woke up. Her empathic sense threatened to overwhelm her before she damped it down, the strange talent she acquired at the same time as the Key of Solomon.

Emilia refuses to read — doesn't need to read — her husband's emotions, thinking if he has any secrets he hasn't told her, he's entitled to keep them. But she watched him kill Aldo Della Quercia who'd been about to rape her, and she kept that secret even from her own father. It might've made him like Luís better, but the old man would've turned him in all the same. So she knows all about secrets.

It wasn't until she went out into the street en route to Williams's office, though, that she realized what had happened. She staggered as the shock of it hit her, glad for once of her walking-stick, and almost screamed at the kindly neighbor who caught her arm and warned her that the cobblestones were still slippery, she should be extra careful with her poor leg, all that rain, we thought it was never going to stop, next thing would've been old Noah sailing up the Tagus in his ark.

Closing her eyes for a second, she stopped herself from crying out with an effort. Because now she wasn't just reading emotions. She was reading minds. For a moment it had been like a vast crowd all shouting at the tops of their voices, and then some automatic defense kicked in and reduced them to a sort of mental hum.

At the same time, she realizes that mind-reading isn't the right word, she can't hear thoughts in words, she is perceiving reality. A reality made up of the emotions she has been able to sense since last summer, of the dreams and hopes and desires and essences that make up a whole soul. She does not see the shapes of souls as John Yeoh can, this is more, it is deeper, she knows them, their nature, their depth.

Breathing heavily, she waited in the street, leaning more against the wall than on her stick, fighting to control this new way of — this new sense, it is as if she has grown a new organ, maybe there is a third eye somewhere, on her forehead perhaps, though it feels more as if it is in her heart. For a brief and horrible instant she hated the world Luís had plunged into, which was even more disorienting, as a world without these things would also be a world without him, and that was too much to bear.

There was sweat beading on her upper lip, and she hoped she wasn't going to faint. She didn't feel light-headed, not at all, it was more like the weight of all the souls in the world pressing in on her. She transferred her balance back to her stick so she could wipe the moisture away with her hand. Which was, she noticed crossly, trembling.

All this had taken only seconds, she realized. Pull yourself together, she told herself sternly. Taking a deep steadying breath, and turned to continue on her way.

Bumped into a tall black woman with an inner fire like a volcano.

Emilia suppressed a squeak of shock and stared up at her. No, she realized, it wasn't a woman at all, it just looked like one. But it posed no threat to her. Quite the contrary, and sighed with relief. Nice to meet something unhuman that meant her no ill. She knew that thought was unfair, to Harris if no one else.

"Who are you?" she asked, changing the question just in time from *what are you?* Human or other, she was the most striking-looking woman Emilia had ever seen. Her street clothes were no disguise. She looked so incongruous and exotic Emilia couldn't understand why people weren't staring at her. But no one was taking any more notice of her than they did of any stranger.

"I am Julia," she responded, as though that was the only answer required. "And you are the one-eyed man's woman."

It was, Emilia reflected, a rather bald way of putting it. But essentially true, nonetheless. "Luís da Silva," she said. "His name's Luís da Silva."

"I know," Julia replied. "What is it makes people follow him? His wolf. Now Leão, too. I need to understand. So I figure, ask his woman." Her eyes glowed like molten gold, but it was no threat. Emilia smiled, and Julia looked taken aback for a second.

"Perhaps it's something only humans can understand," Emilia suggested gently.

Julia's hands went into claws for a split second. Emilia saw her nails slide in and out. If she'd blinked, she would have missed it.

"You know what I am?" she asked. Feral, predator, feline, registered in Emilia's new sense. She drew a deep breath.

"Are you a lion, too?" she hazarded. Julia laughed bitterly.

"I am a leopard," she explained. "That is why we exiled from home. Lion and leopard, not allowed to love. They call it miscegenation. So Leão kill my leopard-body to disguise me. Cannot return. We leave our home for ever. You understand what that means?"

"Oh yes," said Emilia, the Venetian. Understanding, too, Julia's fear of losing her Leão. "But why did you really come to me?" She let her new sense probe, but encountered only confusion. And Julia didn't reply.

Emilia shifted her weight to a more comfortable stance. Or a less uncomfortable one. Her leg was beginning to ache. But she knew it was important to give Julia time. She was already late. A little longer would make no difference. Five minutes, half an hour. However long it takes.

At length the leopard-woman's face softened slightly. "I think I come to protect you," she said, to Emilia's surprise, and also, apparently, to her own. "When they sail away—" She frowned. "Something here, in the city. Something dangerous to you."

"To me?" Emilia murmured.

"Mis-shaped thing," Julia went on, her hot yellow gaze far away. "Not born in this world. Not born in hell. But with a demon for a soul. Bad thing. It mean you harm, you and yours." She put her long hand on Emilia's arm. Emilia had never seen a black-skinned hand so close before, but it was the size she noticed, not the color. Yet the touch was soft, and so she let herself forget claws. She put her own hand over it, and smiled.

"Thank you," she said quietly. Julia narrowed her eyes.

"Leão tell me this has to be," she told Emilia. "Save the world, or something. And I thinking, Why bother? Only be another big bad come along tomorrow." She shrugged. A half-feral cat, slinking along the street, suddenly saw her. Unlike the neighbors and passers-by, it knew what it was seeing, and backed off with a hiss like a steam-engine. Julia bared her teeth for a split second, showing a flash of fang, not quite hissing herself.

"It's always worth fighting evil," said Emilia, no longer resentful, knowing it for truth. "Because if we do nothing, it wins." She shifted her weight again.

"Maybe so," the leopard-woman responded. "Too subtle for cats, this talk of good and evil. But humans do things for love. And I — Part of me human."

A hot pulse surged through Emilia, and she suddenly longed, as she did through lonely nights when he was away, for her husband. "You do love Leão, then," she said softly, and surprised her yearning's mirror on Julia's face.

"Always," came the reply. "To the world ending, and after. Like you. We are the same. That is why I come."

Part of Emilia, a buried part, still thought she ought to be frightened, but that was the last thing she felt. Ignoring the ache in her leg, she smiled reassuringly again, seeing without even needing to use her new senses that Julia was in need of reassurance. Even though the tall woman could probably have broken her in half with one blow, leopard or not.

"Am I in danger now?" she asked. "Because I really have to get to a meeting." Otherwise there might not be a voyage for you to worry about, she added silently.

"Meeting?" echoed Julia, as though the word was one she didn't understand. Emilia, used to this, explained.

"You could come with me," she suggested. But Julia shook her head.

"White man think you crazy," she said. "You got problems enough without me." And this was so true Emilia felt her cheeks heat up. "You go," Julia added. "I think I know when you in danger. Something tell me."

When Julia was gone, Emilia went back indoors and made a telephone call to Williams's office to apologize in advance for her lateness. She got the sniffy clerk, who deigned to inform her that Sr. Williams had an unexpected visitor and would have to postpone the meeting until the afternoon. Relieved at being saved an uncomfortable wait, Emilia prolonged the contact uncharacteristically by asking whom the shipping agent had changed his schedule for.

The clerk, as unimpressed by politicians as by women in business, replied disdainfully, "Just his brother-in-law, senhora."

Her heart was pounding wildly as she replaced the receiver. "*Dio mio,*" she whispered. If she'd been on time she might have walked right into him. So she already had something to thank Julia for.

She was relieved, a moment later, to hear the clattering and rumpus that announced Zé's return home. The boy was incapable of doing anything quietly, but this time she welcomed it.

As she heard him pass the door, she called out his name. A moment later his head appeared, his normally cheerful face wearing a suspicious expression. Emilia hid a smile, and hid his essence from her new sense. Spying on her son wouldn't be fair. Although she had to admit she was tempted, especially as he has a girlfriend now.

"I just got off watch," he announced, which meant *It's not fair to ask me to do anything right now, but you're my mother and I know you're going to do it anyway.*

"Have you had anything to eat?" she enquired, knowing it was a silly question. Zé would eat everything you put in front of him and then go in search of a snack. He nodded, and then frowned slightly. Then the rest of him followed his head round the door.

"Are you all right?" he asked, surprising her. She touched the bridge of her nose.

"Just a little tired," she said. "And I've got to hike over to Sr. Williams's later. Will you go and find your father for me? I think he's in São Rafael."

Zé brightened. The task wasn't so onerous after all. And the library is handy for the orphanage, too.

"And then?" He stuffed his hands in his pockets and bounced a little where he stood, heels and toes, heels and toes.

"Tell him—" She broke off. Tell him what? That she'd woken up with the power to read minds? That a leopard-woman had offered her protection? That Mouffi was still at large? None of those things was pressingly urgent. They were just excuses, she realized. And though she wished very much for Luís's reassuring solidity, he was needed elsewhere now.

But there was one thing he needed to know.

"Tell him what?" Zé perched on the edge of the desk. His mother looked up at him and sighed. Assuming the sigh was nothing to do with him, he ignored it. He crossed his legs and took hold of the uppermost knee, looking at her over his shoulder.

"That Munro was with Sr. Williams when I telephoned him just now," she said. Zé's mouth dropped open.

"He *was?*" he exclaimed. "What do you think he was doing?"

Emilia shook her head and bit her lower lip thoughtfully. "I don't know. I don't think Sr. Williams likes him very much, so it's not a social call."

"I'll tell him." Zé pushed himself off the desk and grinned. "Anything else?"

"Not at the moment," said Emilia, and her son made himself scarce before she could come up with something.

*   *   *

Williams returned to his desk after seeing Munro out and glared at the closed door of his office, intensely annoyed with his departed visitor. Not only had his brother-in-law interrupted the shipping agent's busy schedule, he'd also deprived him of the pleasure of looking at Emilia da Silva for half an hour.

Not that Williams harbored any impure thoughts about Emilia. He was a married man, and an Englishman, and if his marriage wasn't blissfully happy, it was certainly fairly content. It was just that all his other clients, suppliers and associates were men, mostly dour, usually Portuguese, and always businesslike; Emilia was a breath of fresh air and easy on the eye, and given the choice between having to spend time watching Sir Robert Munro or Emilia for half an hour, no one would voluntarily opt for the former.

But the most annoying thing of all was the fellow's presumption. Williams ground his teeth, picked up his fountain-pen crossly and uncapped it, then drew a hangman doodle on his blotter. Thinking that his grand-panjandrum status ought to make everyone else jump the moment he said frog. And he wasn't even that grand a panjandrum. He scowled at the figure he'd just drawn, and gave it a top hat.

"Bloody Pooh-Bah," muttered Williams. Trying to trade on his non-existent political clout was one thing. When the man tried to smarm a favor out of him on the basis of being family it was nepotism of the worst sort. If there was such a thing as a good sort. It wasn't even as if he'd ever been on particularly good terms with his sister. The beastly girl had spent his childhood tormenting him from the lofty superiority of being three years his senior. And she'd grown up just as disagreeable, as far as he was concerned. They had deserved each other.

He snarled, blew out air explosively between his lips, and rearranged some of the paperwork on his desk. Sent him off with a flea in his ear, he thought. Damn the man. Williams glanced at his diary, a copy of the one his clerk had in the outer office. Now all his appointments would be thrown out for the rest of the day, unless he cut some of his meetings short. Not all of them were with people who could be telephoned. Most captains, for a start. They hadn't figured out a way to run telephone wires to ships yet.

The shipping agent pulled out his watch, a heavy old-fashioned silver thing that had belonged to his father, and stared at it for a moment until he was brought back to the present by a knock at the door.

"Come in," he called, and his clerk opened the door and announced Sra.da Silva. Who came in looking bothered and tired. Very much how Williams himself felt. He smiled at her, pleased to see her at last, and moved a bill of lading to cover the doodle on his blotter. Although he wasn't embarrassed by it. He thought it would probably amuse her. That was another nice thing about her, her sense of humor. His own wife hadn't had much of one to begin with, and she'd lost it almost entirely since her miscarriage.

"Sr. Williams," she smiled back, and sat down with an almost-concealed sigh of relief. Propped her stick on the edge of his desk with an automatic movement. "I hope the delay hasn't been too inconvenient."

"My dear lady," he said, "it is I who should be apologizing to you. But one has to try and accommodate one's family, however trying they are."

"Family?" queried Emilia, with a perfect simulation of polite curiosity. She didn't want to get the clerk's unguarded tongue into trouble, little though she cared for the man.

Williams flapped his hand dismissively, and shook his head. "My insufferable brother-in-law," he explained. "Wanted me to arrange him a passage to Cyprus. As if he can't go and book himself a ticket on a passenger ship. I suppose he thinks it's beneath his dignity. He has an exaggerated sense of his own importance. Can't imagine how he thinks being a British cabinet minister would cut much ice here."

"Cyprus?" Emilia echoed, feeling her heart give an unpleasant little jump, but unable to resist relishing the utter bizarreness of hearing the English idiom translated literally into Portuguese, and saving it to repeat to Luís later. "That's a coincidence."

The shipping agent looked shocked.

"Goodness, I wouldn't dream of imposing him on your husband, my dear Sra. da Silva. Indeed, I wouldn't subject anyone I know to that. The man's a pompous ass. Oh, but you met him, didn't you? Heaven only knows why he wants to go to Cyprus."

"Maybe Aphrodite's birthplace holds an irresistible fascination for him," murmured Emilia, and Williams gave a snort of laughter. He suppressed it quickly, but there was a twinkle remaining in his eye.

"Well now," he said, drawing a manila folder towards him, "since the wretched man has completely ruined my schedule, shall we get down to business?"

"By all means," agreed Emilia, and leaned to one side to pick up the document case she had brought with her.

* * *

Zé, whistling cheerfully, but not a tune anyone could ever recognize, like his father he is tone-deaf, took the steps of the stone stair two at a time. He was probably incapable of climbing any stair sedately, but this one led to the orphanage. Well, eventually it would, there was just the minor detail of finding his father first, he was bound to be in São Rafael, though. Planning what to do next. How to deal with Sir Robert Munro. He wondered whether he'd be able to help, the way he had last summer. His mind skipped over the unpleasant part of that, being held prisoner underground hadn't been particularly constructive, and concentrated on the good bits.

He wasn't looking where he was going, since the automatic map drawn in his head was guiding his footsteps. Broken steps were avoided, cracked stones skirted, and loose cobbles jumped. And thinking equally about Sílvia and supernatural goings-on, he wasn't aware he was being followed, either.

Mouffi remembered that Zé knew its name, and so regretfully it wouldn't be able to harm him. But Mouffi now had a powerful ally who might be persuaded to do something about that. In that hope, the infant demon in its misshapen body moved silently after the boy. There were other possibilities, of course. The girl, whom he seemed to care about. The boy's little sister. Even his mother. All might be vulnerable, if not to Mouffi, then to Belphegor.

It, in turn, was not aware that its ties to Zé's father had been severed. Its perception lacked that level of sensitivity.

Without even knowing that he'd had a follower, Zé wasn't aware when he lost it at the barrier of São Rafael. Mouffi moved off in disgust, in search of mischief. Its physical body was fed. It needed stimulation.

If anyone had noticed Mouffi, its appearance would probably have caused consternation, if not outright panic. Not its true shape, the flawed construct made by Belphegor, that was not remembered, or else it didn't register in the first place. To most people it just looked like a big ugly woman, not worth a second glance.

But Mouffi had recently fed, and its face was still smeared red despite its best efforts at cleaning, which hadn't been that effective. The front of its clothing, though, had been soaked through, and was now crusted with dried blood, and the smell was starting to become offensive.

However, the only person who could have brought the creature to human justice is lying unconscious in the orphanage, stable for now. But Ricardo Corvo is in no shape to apprehend a mortal felon, let alone a demon-fragment inhabiting a body that devours human flesh.

14

"HOW LONG WILL IT TAKE?" I ASKED TATIANA DIMITROVNA.

"A day, a night, and a day," she replied. Sounds like a litany. For all I know that's exactly what it is.

That's all she can tell me, though. Not what it's going to be like. Which is just as important. I should tell my crew what I'm taking them into. I stuck a finger under my eyepatch and gave the scar a scratch.

There lies my ship. My beautiful *Isabella*. Time was, there'd be a forest of masts as far as the eye can see. But now, sailing ships are in the minority. Wooden ships in an even smaller one. The world wants to keep on going faster, and it's leaving me behind.

Not if I can help it.

We lingered on shore for a moment. This time of year, the docks don't smell too bad. It's when the temperature hits ninety degrees in August that you really don't want to loiter. Harris says it really makes you understand the term *high summer*. That's an English pun that doesn't work in Portuguese, of course, and why am I thinking about linguistics at a time like this? *Do you really need to ask, da Silva?*

"Will it be like what we did with John Yeoh?"

The witch shook her head. "I don't think so. We won't be taking her out of time... just somewhere else. Where ships' ghosts are, perhaps." I raised an eyebrow.

"Ships' ghosts?" Seen plenty of them. Of course ships have ghosts. Ask any sailor if a ship has a spirit. I'm not sure whether a motor-car or a train would, though. A ship's spirit isn't created by the people on board her, but by what she is. And those mechanical contrivances are just metal things that run on wheels.

"You can see them?"

I nodded, and said "Yes." I never told her I could see peoples' ghosts. It's not something I share with many people. But she knows anyway.

She gave a short laugh. "Well, don't look too closely at any we might meet there. You might see something you'd rather not."

And with that cryptic remark she shaded her eyes and looked upwards at the mainmast. Or pretended to.

"Well," I said, "let's get on with it."

She put her hand down and shot me a sideways glance, but didn't comment. Nice of her. Seeing that I'm the one prevaricating. I gave her a grin that was more of a grimace, and took out a cheroot. A shrieking seagull swooped after the match I threw away, hoping it was edible. Can't blame them for trying, I suppose. But the world would be a better place without seagulls, if you ask me. Certainly a cleaner one. Harris calls them shit-hawks. Good description. Bloody things.

Ashley gave me a naval kind of salute as I went by, and said formally, "Captain." Well, he's English. You have to make allowances.

"Carry on, Mr. Ashley," I responded, and caught Harris's eye. He nodded slightly, a grim expression on his face, and jerked his head enquiringly towards John Yeoh.

Yeoh was smoking an off-duty cigarette and talking to João, *Isabella*'s cook. I tried not to smile. He's probably still trying to persuade him to expand his culinary repertoire. Personally, I like Chinese food. But there'd probably be a mutiny if Yeoh had his way. At least among the more conservatively-minded section of the crew, and I don't just mean the English. Ha. At least the Italians would eat noodles. Looks enough like spaghetti to convince them it's edible, *and you're prevaricating again, da Silva.* I shook my head at Harris. Don't want Yeoh just yet.

It's pretty cramped in my cabin with three people, especially when one of them's Harris.

"We set to go now, skipper?" he asked, touching his cap politely to Tatiana Dimitrovna. "Ma'am."

"Just about," I said, and heard him draw a deep breath.

"Good," he replied, shortly. "Waiting's getting on my nerves." He looked at the witch, eyebrows raised. "Gonna whistle up a wind for us?"

She smiled, but there wasn't much humor in it. "Something like that."

I disposed of my cheroot in the ashtray, scratched my cheekbone absently, and looked across at Harris.

"How much does the crew know about all this?" Though they'd have to be blind, deaf and stupid not to've noticed something these past five years. He raised his eyebrows.

"They ain't dumb," he said. Quite. "They know about me, for starters."

"Yes, all right, tell me something I don't know, Harris." Fact is, *Isabella*'s crew is sort of perversely proud of having a werewolf on board. I don't know what happened to the superstitiousness of sailors. They seem to enjoy it.

"Yeah, sorry." He doesn't sound particularly sorry. "Some of 'em figured that Yeoh did something to that phantom-*Isabella* ship that was following us from London. And a' course, there was those ghost-pirates came on board when we had that box for that English guy Arkright, not to mention that wizard you had to fight. So I guess they're pretty much up to speed with all that stuff. You gonna talk to 'em?" I nodded.

"Can't tell 'em much about it, though."

With a sigh, I got to my feet and stared out at the brawling seagulls. Saw the reflections of Harris and the witch exchange a glance behind me, though I couldn't make out their expressions. Tried not to look at my own reflection. I know what I look like. Seeing it when I shave is enough. I don't want to see my father's image staring back at me. Well, barring the beard and the nearly white hair. Oh, and the fact that he's got two eyes as well. But you know what I mean.

"It might not seem all that different," offered Tatiana Dimitrovna, encouragingly. Nice try. Didn't work. But I suppose I appreciate the effort. I turned back round with another sigh, and sat down again, expecting to wince. Scratched my cheekbone.

"How long will that charm of yours last?" I asked her. The last thing I want is to be struck down by the grandfather of all backaches the minute I get up on my hind legs to talk to the crew. Doesn't do much for the skipper's image if he's creaking around like the Old Man of the Sea.

"Until you go to sleep," she replied. "It — how can I explain this? It draws energy from your mind while it's active, while you're awake. You'll probably have a headache in the morning. It isn't a cure for your injuries."

Might've known you couldn't cure things properly with magic. I suppose I was lucky that Mouffi managed to do so much for Corvo. If you can call it luck. It was for Corvo, sure. I smothered a yawn, and lit another cheroot. My cabin. I can smoke in here if I want to. Yes, I can see the witch flapping her hand to clear it.

"Harris, get Ashley in here, will you," I said. "Then I'd better have a word with Yeoh. Have you said anything to him?"

"Bits and pieces," he replied, lighting a cigarette, which made Tatiana Dimitrovna roll her eyes heavenwards. I tried not to smile. Better not to antagonize the witch too much. "Figured you better be the one to tell him he's been prophesied. You're better at it than I am." Thanks, Harris. He grinned suddenly. "'Sides, you're the skipper."

"Yes," I agreed, grinning back. "I am, aren't I. So you'd better buzz off before I bounce that one right back at you."

Tatiana Dimitrovna watched him go. Obviously still suspicious of the werewolf. At least she's stopped looking at him as if he's a specimen in a jar.

"I just don't understand how he keeps his humanity," she said, shaking her head. Crossly. I think she feels someone's not playing by the rules. Not Harris. Someone else. I inhaled some smoke, enjoying the flavor, then blew it out again.

"Well, I'm glad he does," I said. "Otherwise I might not be here." And Zé might not be here, either.

"It doesn't make—" Sense, I suppose she was about to say, but a knock interrupted her. I raised my eyebrows. What, was Ashley lurking outside the door waiting for Harris to emerge?

"Come in," I called, and the man himself appeared. Gave the witch a formal bow and stood stiffly to attention.

"Captain. Ma'am."

You know what? I'm irritated, I missed lunch again, and I'm not in the mood to humor stiff-upper-lip British Empire. Hell, we did better than they did in the voyages of discovery line, if you want to argue the point. I dragged a hand over my face and scowled at him.

"Get that broomstick out of your backside and sit down, Ashley," I snapped. "We haven't got the time for all this buggering around."

Ashley, looking as though I'd accused him of farting in church, sat down suddenly, his face dark red, and cleared his throat.

"Honestly, sir, you could remember there's a lady present," he muttered. Tatiana Dimitrovna smiled, but hid it behind her hand.

"Ashley, I need your brain," I said, ignoring his blathering. He shut up at once and looked at me shrewdly with his greenish eyes. Ashley is alright, really. He just wishes he'd been one of Admiral Nelson's officers, I think. But he must think I'm alright, too. He's been with *Isabella* since long before I became her owner. *Tactful expression, that, da Silva.* Became her owner. See, I can euphemise as well as the English. Must have rubbed off from associating too closely with Pierce. Not that he's your typical Englishman.

Hell, I've been *Isabella*'s captain for nearly eleven years now. Which means Ashley's been one of my officers for ten. Dear God, where does the time go?

Now he looked at me narrowly, then smiled. Only a tiny curve of the lips, true. But I don't think I've ever seen him crack a smile before. Don't think I knew he could.

"What do you need me to do, captain?" he asked.

I blew out smoke and said, "What you do best. Keep this ship running."

"Ah." He nodded to Tatiana Dimitrovna. "I assume from the lady's presence that we'll be sailing into... strange waters."

The witch nodded, watching him curiously. She'd not had very much contact with him on our voyage from London. "Very strange waters, Mr. Ashley. Very strange indeed."

"But not uncharted, I take it?" he said.

"Not in one sense," replied the witch, shaking her head slowly. "Though we will not need charts, it's true. Not as such."

He pursed his lips, and turned back to me. I raised an eyebrow and suppressed an urge to scratch my scar. "Sir, would you like me to speak to the crew?"

"You know me better than that, Ashley," I said. "But you can make sure they're all present for me to talk to." He has a mind like a directory. I'm betting he knows exactly where each man is at this precise moment. And probably what he's doing, as well.

* * *

Here is Anibale Ribeiro, who fancies he resembles the famous English detective Sr. Holmes, sitting on his bony backside in a comfortable chair in his pleasant airy office that looks over the city like a miradouro. On his desk, a delicate porcelain cup and saucer that lately contained tea from Ceylon, and a matching plate which shows that the police chief has recently also consumed at least one flaky pastry from the *pastelaria* down the road.

Also on the desk is a fat, dogeared manila folder which is the cause of Ribeiro's pained expression, despite the pastries which must have been delicious he looks like a man who has been presented with a plate of dogshit. The offending folder is Inspector Corvo's case file on the murders of María Almeida, Mercedes Domingo, Rita Golfinho and Aranho Alvares, and Corvo's notes, to his boss, form conclusive evidence not of anyone's guilt but of the unfortunate inspector's descent into complete insanity.

Ribeiro is still not convinced that the anonymous woman Corvo arrested could have killed anyone, the female is obviously a mongol or some such, but the inspector's outburst of temper now makes sense to him, as far as the ravings of a madman follow any logical rules. It is obvious to Ribeiro now that

Corvo has been losing his marbles for some considerable time.

And as for the suggestion that the man who shot him, not to mention killing the old man in the bookshop, was a Minister of State in the British government, well, really. Ribeiro, a political animal to the tips of his well-manicured fingers, tut-tutted over that, it was quite beyond the pale to suggest such a man capable of murder.

Yet there was an eye-witness to Corvo's shooting. And try as he might, Ribeiro couldn't get round that.

Unless, of course, this Captain da Silva had shot the inspector himself. He had managed to get the suspect in the Caracol murder released, after all. Ribeiro conveniently ignored the fact that any sensible murderer would have left Corvo to finish bleeding to death where he fell, rather than go to all the trouble of carrying him to a doctor to get him patched up.

Anyway, most sailors, in Ribeiro's view, are thugs and ruffians. It stands to reason that the people in charge of them must be tarred with the same brush, they need to be pretty much capable of murder to keep the brutes in line.

He sent for Santos, Corvo's deputy, at least nominally, for Santos was Ribeiro's appointee in the first place, anyone with an ounce of political savvy knows the value of planting a man in the enemy camp. Not that Corvo was precisely his enemy, the inspector and the police chief are supposed to be on the same side, but he could be an extremely pointy thorn in his boss's side, and Santos could usually be relied upon to blunt him.

"Find out everything you can about that witness," he instructed him.

"The one-eyed man, sir?" enquired Santos, as if there were a selection of witnesses to choose from. Santos is not stupid, however, whatever Corvo thinks. He knows, in fact, exactly what makes Ribeiro tick, and asking blindingly obvious questions which make the chief feel important and detectively figures high on that list.

"Yes, that's him," Ribeiro confirmed. "I want to find out whether he could've shot Corvo himself. And if so, I want him arrested."

*   *   *

No longer whistling, Zé emerged from the library feeling distinctly disgruntled. He peered up at the sky to judge the time in a way that had become automatic without his even noticing, and grimaced. Sílvia was still in school. He kicked a pebble crossly. Now he had to go all the way back to *Isabella* to find his father. Sometimes it all felt like a big conspiracy.

He detoured slightly to inspect the orphanage, without much hope but unable to resist, and then trotted to the entrance of a narrow plunging alley that hardly seemed wide enough, to him, for a man to walk down. Sr. Harris would get stuck, he thought, and gave a snort of laughter, picturing the second mate wedged between the walls.

A few minutes later he made another small deviation from his route to buy a snack from a woman sitting in a doorway, and not long after that slowed his pace to inspect some interesting shop-windows. In one of them he had previously detected a stuffed crocodile hanging dustily over an eclectic collection of bric-a-brac, and decided that it must be a magical supplies shop. Why shouldn't witches have somewhere to buy stuff for their spells?

The crocodile was still there, its glass eye dim. Zé peered through a bull's-eye pane to make it distort, but this quickly palled as a pastime, and he moved on to the next shop.

Regrettably for any opportunity to play hooky, Zé has a responsible streak. An unfortunate thing for a fourteen-year-old. He sighed gustily, tore himself away from the display, and hurried on his way.

The body that housed Mouffi woke with a start, and the demon-fragment with it. Mouffi, annoyed, realized once more the drawbacks of being corporeal. The thing had been sated and torpid from its meal, and had slept in the thin warmth of the winter sunlight that slanted down to the wooden bench where it sat, snoring like a bag lady.

Mouffi felt a strong desire for a new host. Unfortunately no alternative candidate had presented himself. Or herself. The demon-fragment wasn't fussy. It debated the advantages of leaving this one where it slouched, and becoming disembodied for a while, but the disadvantages outweighed them. Considerably.

Still seated, it sniffed the air, or the body did. Although smell was a part of it, what Mouffi was really doing was both broader and more subtle than any human analogy.

You could, perhaps, say it was scenting souls. And it found Zé not far off, whom it had thought it had lost.

Yet even as Mouffi stalked Zé, the demon-fragment itself was being hunted in turn. By something it could never have imagined.

Her dreams were still filled with lion-colored grass and the hot smell of baked earth, and she still moved with the power and grace of her birth-tribe. But now she lives in this stone city by a colder sea and is no longer capable of leopard, yet sometimes she can still smell the firework stink of the gunshot that severed her from her people.

The weather is tame here, and so too the people, with a few exceptions. Some of them are not tame.

And some of them are not people. As is the case with this great ugly misshapen thing she is stalking.

It is very large, this creature. Julia is not intimidated by size alone. But it feels to her like certain hollow places on the plains, the low-lying muzuku where invisible poison gathers, where any creature unwary enough to crawl into them never draws another breath.

This is enough to make her very, very careful. Demons are universal, the concept is understood by all cultures, although some misunderstand their nature and give them worship. And some might just as well, though they profess and proclaim love and loyalty to their god, their fervour leads them onto the path of evil.

But Julia is not a creature prone to debate or even consider theology. Her world, like that of the leopard she once was, is pretty much a black-and-white place.

Looking up at *Isabella*, Zé scowled and puffed out a disgusted breath. He'd hoped not to be back here until he was due back on watch. He'd hoped to be spending time with Sílvia. Spending time with Sílvia was more fun than running errands. She was smart and nice to look at, and she made him laugh.

He suspected he wasn't going to be doing much laughing for a while.

"Hey, Benjamin," he called, with a wave but without much enthusiasm, as he came on board. "Is my father here?"

"Hey, Zé," replied the big man, gloomily, which alarmed him. Benjamin was a cheerful fellow normally. "The captain here, sure. What you doing back?"

"Need to tell him something. What's up?"

Benjamin spat over the side. "Better ask your pa," he said. "He ain't gonna let you pick shore leave."

"Pick — shore leave?" Zé echoed.

Benjamin gave him a lopsided grin. A year ago, he would probably have ruffled Zé's hair. They both knew this. The breeze plucked at it instead.

"Least he give us fair warning this time," he observed. "We sailing for Malta by way of the seas of Guinee. The witch taking us."

Zé's eyes nearly popped out of his head. "When?"

"Tomorrow morning, early," answered Benjamin. "Captain, he say, anyone not happy, go ashore, you don't lose your pay." He looked past Zé, out into the broad estuary. "Looks like everyone happy."

"I've got to talk to him," said Zé, and bolted below decks.

On the quayside, Mouffi loitered. But for the bloodstains on its clothing and face, you might have taken its form for the world's largest whore. No one was stupid enough to stop and proposition her, though.

Julia, unnoticed, watched the demon-fragment with yellow eyes.

*　*　*

I sat down at my new desk and pulled the ship's log towards me. I must say I'm a little surprised. Not a single one of 'em opted for shore leave. Some of them muttered a bit and crossed themselves, and the odd rabbit's foot and St Christopher charm came out surreptitiously. But when *Isabella* sails into whatever seas the witch takes us to, she'll have her full complement on board.

Plus, of course, a witch, a ghost, a man who is a lion, Susana the Fisher King, her mother, a woman made of paint, my father, and an antiquarian.

"And a partridge in a pear tree," Harris said morosely, perhaps disappointed that we weren't able to squeeze in another witch for him.

Oh, and did I mention that the last two will probably spend the entire voyage throwing up? How the hell I manage to have a father who turns queasy at the sight of water is beyond me. I don't think it's very likely that I inherited seamanship from my mother.

I leaned back in my chair. Carefully. Still no pain, thank you, Tatiana Dimitrovna. Took off my eyepatch. Relief. Rubbed my face and thought about doing nothing for five minutes. *Not a good idea, da Silva.* Don't want to fall asleep just yet. I poured myself a glass of brandy, lit a cheroot, and opened up the ship's log. Not everything that happens gets written down in here, you can be sure of that.

However, I'd hardly finished writing the date when Zé hammered on the door. I knew it was him, of course, even though he's the last person I expected to see. It's not his watch. Thought he'd be with his Sílvia. But no one else makes that much racket.

"Come in before you break the door down, Zé," I yelled. He lost no time, flinging it open and charging in.

"Benjamin told me," he said breathlessly, the words tumbling out. "Are we going to collect—" I interrupted him.

"Zé, what are you doing here?"

He made a disgusted face. "I've been all the way to São Rafael looking for you," he said. Want sympathy? Won't get it from me.

"Exercise is good for you," I told him, taking a drag on my cheroot. He glared at me.

"Huh, and it was all a waste of time."

"What?" I asked, exasperated.

"That man Munro." Zé paused, saw my expression, and hurried on. "He went to see Sr. Williams."

My heart gave a lurch. "Is your mother all right?" An awful thought struck me. "She didn't bump into him, did she?"

"No," said Zé quickly. "She was on her way. She looked a bit tired, though. I think her leg was hurting."

I need to see her. I'm sailing in the morning, of course I have to see her. Writing up the log will have to wait. I looked down at the page. The ink had long dried. I shut the book, and smothered a yawn. Raised my head to see Zé hopping up and down impatiently.

"You can get off now," I told him. "I'm going home."

That got me a grin. "Thanks."

And he vanished before I had time to change my mind. I took a mouthful of brandy. He moves fast enough when he wants to. But ask to do any work and you could mistake him for a snail in a cap. The word *snail* reminded me of Caracol. From there I moved on to Corvo. Wish I'd thought to ask Zé to ask after him. But I should think he'll get a bulletin anyway. If not from Teresa, then from Sílvia.

There are either too many hours in the day, or too few. Or else they're all just too damned full. Seems like I haven't stopped to take a breath since — well, since I walked into Coelho's office in London. I won't say *unsuspectingly*. But whatever I might've been prepared for that day, it sure as hell wasn't all this.

At the moment, though, I'm more concerned about Emilia than anything else. Tatiana Dimitrovna said the house is well-protected. But that's from supernatural threats. And Munro's quite happy to get round that by shooting at it. As I found out today.

Yes, I know I could've gone to the customs house and scrounged the use of their telephone. But it doesn't take me much longer to walk home. *That's a lie, da Silva.* Of course it does. I just don't like telephones.

Besides, the exchange is probably having an off day. *Dia não.* It has more off days than on days, so that's a pretty safe bet.

Of course Emilia was fine when I got home. I spend too much time expecting the worst. And getting it. Being proved wrong is nice for a change.

Being alone in the house is nice, too. When was the last time that happened?

We got round to conversation after a while.

"Munro?" I asked, into her hair. Not a topic I really wanted to broach at that moment. But sometimes you don't have much choice.

"On his way to Cyprus, by now," she said. "Sr. Williams was all ruffled feathers when I finally got to see him."

She always feels so tiny, I want to protect her. I know she isn't fragile. It's a reflex. "We're sailing in the morning," I told her regretfully. Always regretfully.

"How long?" she asked.

"A day, a night, and a day," I answered, in the witch's words. "Which gets us to Malta. After that — I don't know, love." I kissed the top of her head. "I wish I could be sure you'll be all right while I'm away."

To my surprise, she chuckled. "I will, I think," she said. "I seem to have acquired myself a bodyguard."

"A *bodyguard?* What do you mean?" I asked, startled. And she told me about Julia. I knew there was something strange about that woman. *Well, do you ever meet anyone normal, these days, da Silva?*

"She makes me feel safer, anyway," she added.

"Oh, and I don't?" I said. Flippantly. But it gave me a pang of guilt at leaving her. Always leaving her.

Emilia looked up at me. "Of course you do." She saw through me. As usual. "There's something else," she added, and I felt her tense.

"What?"

"This damned mark," she said, with a violence that surprised me. I felt my own mark itching in response, and ignored it.

"Meu Deus, what's happened to it now?"

She didn't reply at once. I held her tighter and felt her breathing. After a moment she sighed deeply and explained. "It decided to get up steam. For a moment it was like all the people of Lisbon shouting in my head. But at least I seemed to know how to damp it down. I hate the wretched thing, Luís. I wish it was gone."

"I know," I said. "I know." But you can't wish these things away. If you could — well, there's no point in that. I've grown so used to seeing ghosts now, I hardly notice them most of the time. And yet when I first started to see them I thought I'd never cope. You should've seen me trying to avoid the stupid things in a crowded street. It wasn't difficult to know what people were thinking. Keep away from the nasty man, children, he's had too much brandy. "It'll get easier," I told Emilia. A bit lame, I know.

"So you keep saying," she grumbled, but the tension went out of her.

Any further discussion was interrupted by the familiar clattering and racket that meant Zé. I let go of Emilia regretfully and raised my eyebrows at her.

"Your son," we said in chorus, and both began to laugh.

The door burst open and he erupted into the room, followed by Sílvia. I turned my head quickly and hunted for my eye-patch. Found it on the floor. Poor girl doesn't need to be confronted by the da Silva scar. Especially after what I landed on her doorstep today.

Zé eyed us censoriously. He had exactly the same expression as Emilia's father used to wear when he caught us kissing. Which made me want to laugh again. It was only there for a moment. Then he blinked and was normal Zé again.

I found my cheroots, and lit up.

"That Mouffi thing is skulking around," he informed me. "We lost it in the alleys, though, didn't we?" Sílvia nodded.

Perhaps Emilia's new friend is about somewhere, as well. I picked up my jacket, with a mental groan.

"I'm just going out for a few minutes," I said. "Won't be long."

"You'd better not," Emilia remarked. "It smells like dinner's nearly ready. You don't want to get Joana mad at you."

I shuddered theatrically. "Rather fight Mouffi."

The sky had grown dark since I came home. The streets held the dusk that makes all cats gray. Above, stars were very bright and clear, and the temperature had dropped sharply. I walked to the end of the street and peered around. No sign of Mouffi.

"Julia?" I called softly. But there was no reply. And I'm certainly not going to call for Mouffi. Let sleeping dogs lie. Or, in this case, demons.

There was no one in sight. No one living, that is. The ghosts are always there. The daytime crowds were gone, but the night shift hadn't come out yet. I sucked in a mouthful of smoke, and turned full circle. Times like this I really miss having two eyes.

A little pool of warm light spilled out from a window that had been behind me, and in it stood a girl. She looked about sixteen. I smiled grimly. Can't smell demons the way Harris does, but I've met this one before.

So much for letting sleeping demons lie. The bastards weren't sleeping. Hell, probably they never do. I drew my knife. And the girl spoke.

"You will not need that, Luís da Silva." It had the sweet voice of a young child.

"Belphegor," I said. Took a drag on my cheroot and blew smoke at it. A passing ghost shied away. The demon took no notice. "What do you want?"

It smiled at me, the pretty face guileless and open, and took a step towards me. I pointed the knife at it, and it stopped, just out of reach. Its eyes gleamed, but not with reflected lamplight. "The question should be, what do *you* want?"

I frowned, looking down at it. I'm not fooled by the sweet innocent exterior. Does it think I've forgotten our last meeting?

"Meaning?" I asked.

"We should not fight," Belphegor said unexpectedly. "When we could be working to our mutual benefit."

Not as long as the sun rises in the east. "I don't think so." I threw the butt of my cheroot at it. The dog-end made a brief glowing arc, passed through the demon, and fell to gutter out on the cobbles.

The demon ignored it. "Hear me out," it suggested. "My masters do not think Sir Robert Munro is the right person to have control of the so-called hallows."

Its masters? I scratched my cheekbone. "I would've thought you lot would approve heartily of him."

Belphegor pouted, like a little girl denied a treat. "He has a heart of darkness, it is true," it agreed. "But he has no imagination. No creativity. No vision, except for his own desires. And no control. We are prepared to help you prevent him from acquiring the items."

Hell, they must be desperate to try something like this. Does this thing think I was born yesterday? "I don't want your help," I told it. I don't like the strings that come attached. No, not strings. Bloody great fetters.

"Think about it," the demon urged.

"I've thought about it all I'm going to," I said, and jabbed the knife-point at it. It skipped back. An expression of pure hatred distorted its pretty features.

"We could make things very difficult for you, if you deny us," it snarled, and there was no sweetness in its voice now.

And that made me burst out laughing. I couldn't help it. Just what in the devil's name makes it think my life is easy?

"You'll have to do better than that." I raised the knife to the level of its chin. "Now bugger off before I use this on you."

It eyed the blade warily. "You would do well not to threaten," it warned. "Have you forgotten our last meeting?"

"*I* haven't," I said. "I thought perhaps you had. Whatever makes you think I'd ever cooperate with the likes of you?"

The demon backed a few paces. "We mean to have your soul, Luís da Silva. One way or another."

I gave a short laugh. Trying for derisive. Not sure I made it. I felt like saying *not even if hell freezes over*, which is a Harris-ism. But it'd probably enjoy informing me that there *is* a frozen hell somewhere. So all I said was "You won't get it."

In the light from the window, the demon's girlish face seemed to ripple and distort for a second. But it remained in that shape. Only the smile it gave me made me recoil. Then it turned on its heel and walked away.

Nice work, da Silva. Now you've got the hosts of hell taking it personally. I put my knife away. Searched for a cheroot. Lit it. My hands, I was relieved to see, were steady. My knees weren't, quite. I swore crossly, and took a few deep breaths to steady myself before going back up the street and opening my front door.

* * *

In the lamplight, the figure of a girl faded back into view. Belphegor was well-pleased with the reaction it had provoked from da Silva, which was exactly as it had expected.

The idea had been planted. And, like the seed of a Judas tree, its roots would grow and multiply and permeate every part of its quarry.

Given the right conditions, of course. That was the only uncertainty. But what was the chase without a chance of failure? Belphegor was not a simple predator, hunting for food, like the body Mouffi wore. It wanted the thrill of the chase.

And then, naturally, it wanted its plan to succeed.

* * *

As I came in, I caught sight of my face in the mirror in the hallway, and wished I hadn't. Study in black and white. I look like Grandfather Death in need of a shave. I turned away, rubbing my hand over my chin. Wondered if I had the energy to do anything about the bristles. Had to smother a yawn, and decided not. Besides, the aroma of dinner was irresistible. And Joana's wrath, if not quite as bad as facing demons, can be considerable.

The next yawn refused to be smothered. I need food. And something to drink. I dragged a hand through my hair, which I don't suppose improved matters, and went to join my family. Plus, of course, Sílvia.

They hadn't waited for the patriarch, of course. None of that sort of nonsense in the da Silva household. Emilia would laugh herself silly at the idea. There was a brief interlude while Caterina, promoted to grown-up dinner when she turned nine, decided I'd been neglecting her and insisted on sitting on my lap. Then Joana brought me some soup.

Well. I'm a ship's master. I can cope with a daughter and a bowl of *caldo verde* at the same time. Only Caterina doesn't think so. Obviously I was devoting too much time to the food and not enough to her. So I lost her off my knee. Which, I have to admit, was a relief. She's getting quite heavy these days. And besides, I need a hand for my glass.

"How's your patient?" I asked Sílvia, who was head to head with Zé. She looked up, apparently startled at being asked a question.

"A lot better," she answered. "Dr Bosque said he should be dead, but he — well, I don't know much about it, but I thought he looked comfortable."

Good. I'm not stupid enough to blame myself for that. Munro was the one who shot him. But I'm still relieved.

* * *

"You did what?" exclaimed Leão in surprise, Julia shrugged. Her eyes seemed very yellow in the lamplight.

"Nobody ever tells the story of the hero's woman," she said. "It don't mean her story isn't worth telling. You go sailing off with that captain, but we're stuck here. It don't mean the evil goes away." She stretched, cat-like, still more inherently feline than Leão, despite having lost her leopard. For she'd been born with it, and he'd had to work long and hard to find the lion, to make it part of himself.

He looked at her fondly. Not liking her getting involved with the world. Though he could hardly argue about that from a position of strength.

But Julia is so much more conspicuous than he is. And she will not be on board a ship, but in a place where she is far more vulnerable.

And she doesn't even like humans.

* * *

When I woke up, I couldn't move. For a moment, the pain in my back was so excruciating that no bits of me wanted to co-operate with my brain.

All right, da Silva. You can kill demons and summon the dead from their graves. Now do something really difficult, like getting out of bed.

I thought about it for a while, then got an elbow underneath me and hauled myself into a sitting position. Sat on the edge of the bed feeling like

Methuselah's older brother. And the headache came charging in.

The witch had warned me. But she hadn't mentioned it'd feel like the hangover to end all hangovers. I know all about hangovers. Haven't had one for years, though. And it's hardly as if I've stopped drinking alcohol.

Ha. Best cure for a hangover is to get up aloft. I don't have that option. Right at this moment I think a flight of stairs'd be beyond me.

Early, and dark. Should really have spent the night on board. Not an option when I can sleep at home. That, I always refused to give up. It even amused the Venetian to humor me over that one thing. He saw it as a weakness, I expect. But it has quite the opposite effect.

Emilia, efficient with robe and walking-stick, came in and put down the tray she was carrying. I could smell coffee. I might live.

She lit the gas. One of these days I must get round to having electric lights installed in this house and move into the twentieth century.

"You're up," said Emilia, a bit unnecessarily. I smiled faintly. Massaged my temples with my fingers and looked at her. Made the aches a bit better.

"Up is not what I feel," I replied.

"What's the matter?" The bed dipped as she sat beside me and held out a cup. She smells of sleep and floral soap.

"Old age, I think," I said grumpily, taking the coffee and drinking most of it in one go. Caffeine, one of the three da Silva drugs of choice.

"Your poor back." I tensed, thinking she was going to touch it, and it felt very tender. But instead she put her fingers on the Key of Solomon. The mark stung, making me suck a breath in sharply. "This thing healed you yesterday."

"Not showing any sign of a repeat performance." But I drained my cup and put it down carefully before slipping my hand inside her robe to touch her own mark. A jolt ran up my fingertips, and I jerked away. But she caught my wrist and put my hand back.

We sat there for a second without moving. I wasn't sure whether anything was happening. Other than the usual reaction of being close to Emilia, that is. My head still hurt. My back still hurt. I decided to kiss her anyway, and put my other hand round the back of her head, in her hair.

After a moment I moved to kiss her neck, and she said a little indistinctly, "We'll just have to join the marks again."

I stopped long enough to say, "What a nuisance. D'you think it'll work?"

"Who cares?" said Emilia.

*   *   *

In the pre-dawn chill over the docks, all sound is muffled by a slight mist, but there is no lack of noise. Enough ships want the early tide that there is a sort of muted bustle, the din of the day but softened, footsteps, voices, creaking of ropes and wood, canvas, pulleys and wheels, shouted orders and curses, plash and suck of water, splash of detritus being thrown overboard.

People, their breath plumes of fog, are moving briskly enough to keep warm in the cold air, and urgently to accomplish their tasks, but perhaps they are unconsciously trying to be a little silent so as not to wake the city, as if the city ever sleeps, as if any city ever sleeps.

Harris, standing at *Isabella*'s rail and smoking, had enjoyed a full night's sleep after his wolf-time and was feeling as chipper as he ever did.

Leastways, I got some energy. Dunno as how I can feel real good about what's gonna happen today. Whatever that is. He spat into the sea and looked sideways to where Tatiana Dimitrovna stood. *She been there all night? Wouldn't surprise me. Maybe I ain't too happy about all this, but when it comes to it, I'm just a passenger. She's the one gonna be doing the work. Guess she won't be feeling too hot either.*

He finished his cigarette and threw the butt over the side, then walked briskly over to the Russian witch.

"Ma'am?" he said politely. After a moment, she stirred.

"Mister Harris," she acknowledged, her accent strong. But she didn't look at him. He wasn't sure what she was looking at. Mist, and darkness.

"You okay, ma'am?" he asked.

This time she turned her head to him. Her eyes looked very flat and black, opaque like pools of ink. There were dark smudges beneath them, as if the ink had run.

"I will be," she said softly. "Thank you for asking."

What's she looking at? Ain't at me. Through me, past me. What's she seeing?

"I get you anything? Smells like João's brewing up."

The witch continued looking through him. "No, thank you. I have to fast."

She ain't in the mood for talking, then. You want your ass kicked, Harris? Then button your lip pronto. He leaned on the rail and watched her out of the sides of his eyes. There was a kind of fascination about her. *And that might be a whole lot to do with being this snake-goddess. Goddamn, wish I knew how this is gonna work.*

"Beg pardon, ma'am. Mind if I ask you something?" She shook her head. "You have any idea how we're gonna collect these things?"

Tatiana Dimitrovna sighed. "No," she said. "Any more that I know how you can be a werewolf and have no control over it yet not be a beast."

Harris opened his mouth and shut it again. Finally he grinned, touched a finger to his cap, and strode off. As he did so, four bells sounded, a little muffled by the lingering mist, and something made him turn to look at the quayside.

And here's the skipper, right on schedule. So all I need to do now is get rid of these goddamned butterflies in my belly.

*   *   *

I can't remember the first time I saw a ship. Or even went on board one. I grew up in one of the world's busiest ports, remember. But the memory of the first one I boarded in earnest is still very clear. Fourteen years old, without much of a clue about what was going on or how anything worked. It just looked like chaos and bedlam to me. I didn't know what to expect.

And some of that's with me now. Which feels very strange. After all, this is the only life I've known for thirty years, and I thought I did know how it all worked. But now I'm about to embark into the unknown. No charts, no compass. No winds of the world in our sails. No stars I know to navigate by. *Por mares nunca de antes navegados.* Camões got *that* right, at least.

Pointless to speculate about what it'll be like. Not a soul aboard knows. Not even Tatiana Dimitrovna.

"Morning, Harris," I said, lighting a cheroot and wincing a little at my aching back. Not sure if there's been any improvement there. But my headache's gone.

"Morning, skipper."

"All the passengers safely stowed?" He nodded. I scratched my cheekbone. "Then I suppose we're ready."

"Good luck," said the werewolf, and I grinned bleakly.

The wind was brisk, but it still took some time to maneuver *Isabella* out of port and towards the open sea. Not too long now, and the wind won't matter. At least, not the one blowing over these seas I know.

And what will the wind be like, on those other seas? A gentle zephyr, or a screaming gale that strips the canvas off any ship foolhardy enough to venture into waters alien to it?

I know which one my money's on. Damn it.

Now the Torre de Belém is behind us. We passed Paço de Arcos and Santo Amaro. Sailed past the place where the Tagus-spirit had barred *Isabella*'s way. The winter sun felt warm on my back. But I'm cold as ice inside.

Out into the Atlantic. Turn to port and head south. The sun warm on my left side now. Tatiana Dimitrovna walking towards me, surefooted as a sailor on the swaying deck. I pulled out my cheroots, and lit one. I think I'd honestly forgotten she doesn't like the smell. She made no comment, however.

"Is it time?" I asked her, and my voice sounded peculiar even to me.

"It's time," she replied. I took a deep breath. Glanced across at Benjamin, who had the helm. He looks reassuringly solid in the thin sunlight.

"What do you want me to do?"

"Find me a ghost-ship, Luís," she said. "I cannot be the guide and the pilot as well as opening the way. Show me where to go."

Not far south, off Cabo Espichel, the sea's full of them, victims of the merciless Atlantic waves. Here, there are fewer. But rarely none, wherever you go. We've been sailing the world's oceans for too long. So it wasn't very long before I found one for her. It was a caravel. Which meant that it'd gone down in sight of home, its voyage either hardly begun or almost over. Cruel, whichever way. But that's the sea for you.

"There." I pointed with my cheroot. She pulled my arm down.

"Don't attract their attention. I don't think they see us, but don't take chances. Steer towards the ship."

I gave the order to alter course. Benjamin swung the wheel.

"Now what?" I asked. The witch turned her head to me. Her face was very pale. Her eyes looked enormous.

"Can you see the ship's name?"

That's what telescopes are for. "*Alcântara,*" I read.

Tatiana Dimitrovna repeated the name, and the sound of her voice made the back of my neck prickle. I rubbed it uncomfortably. The witch's voice echoed across the waves like a drumbeat. My mouth was suddenly dry. I couldn't look away from the *Alcântara*. She was changing as I watched. Or we were moving into her realm. I scratched my cheekbone. *Nervous, da Silva?* As Harris says, you bet your ass I am. Or as the saying goes, *Quem tem cu tem medo.* Anyone who has a backside can be afraid.

From a ghost-ship, a hazy shimmering thing, she gradually grew solid. Her tattered sails snapped in the wind and became opaque, her weathered timbers creaked and lost their transparency. So she'd been at the end of her voyage when she went down, then. I wondered vaguely where she'd been, what she'd discovered, what she'd never brought home.

Isabella neared the dead vessel, and now I could see great gaping holes in her sides. The water must've poured in, sending her to the bottom very quickly. But the caravel rode the waves still, and I heard the sea sloshing about inside her. The doomed *Alcântara* remained afloat because she didn't exist.

I swallowed. I didn't want to get any closer.

But that seems to be how it works. I took a rather shaky drag from my cheroot. Now I can see the men on the deck of the other ship. Not men, not really. They gave no sign they could see *Isabella*. Something to be grateful for, then.

"Don't look at them," warned Tatiana Dimitrovna, putting a hand on my arm. "Don't meet their eyes."

Not my plan. *"Can* they see us?"

"I'm not sure. But when we pass through, they will be able to."

I flicked ash overboard. Looked sideways at the *Alcântara*. "What about the men?" I asked quietly.

"Only you can see that ship until we pass through, Luís," the witch explained, sounding a little impatient. "And possibly her captain can see us." Now there's an idea I don't like. But she didn't elaborate. "After that we need not approach another vessel so closely until we need to return to our own seas."

"Can't you see it?"

"No," she said shortly. Is it satisfying to be able to do something the witch can't? No. Not a bit. I'd rather be without these skills altogether. I sucked in smoke rather morosely, and expelled it on a slow breath.

We were so close, now, that the crew of the caravel could've boarded us. Or we them. If the *Alcântara* had been real, of course. I shook off the memory of Rodrigues's drowned men climbing out of the sea, and tried not to look at the other ship. Then a nasty thought struck me. I turned to the witch again.

"We don't have to pass through it, or anything like that, do we?"

Tatiana Dimitrovna shook her head. "Nothing like that." Good.

"Hold your course," I called to Benjamin. "Steady." Although that last comment was probably meant for me, rather than the helmsman.

There seemed to be no obvious division between the ocean I know and the unknown waters ahead. I suppose I'd had some idea that it'd be like going through a gateway. That the air would be different, or the clouds in the sky. None of this happened.

But I knew, all the same. Felt a jolt as the two ships passed each other. As if something in my head had snapped. I flinched, looked up involuntarily. And the spectral captain of the *Alcântara* caught my gaze, and held it.

A low deadly peal like thunder rumbled across the sea. I had time to see a fair-bearded man, his face gaunt with despair, his eyes blazing. Saw his hair start to darken, his features change. A scar ran across the left side of his face and closed his eye. My heart skipped a beat.

And then Tatiana Dimitrovna dragged my head round and slapped my face hard enough to make my teeth rattle, shouting my name angrily.

"Come back," she screamed, and went to hit me again. I grabbed her wrist,

"Hey," I exclaimed. "Any more and I'll think you're enjoying it." Her eyes blazed. I wanted to kiss her. *Perverse, da Silva.*

"Don't you ever listen?" she yelled, furiously. "What part of *don't meet their eyes* did you not understand?"

I found I was still holding the dead end of my cheroot, and pitched it into the water. We'd cleared the other vessel. Its still black wake spread behind it like spilled oil.

"You didn't say why," I said, watching the *Alcântara* recede astern. Knew as I spoke that it was a pretty feeble comeback, and grimaced.

"I didn't know what would happen!" she snapped back. "But I did tell you before about the metaphysics of being the captain of a ship, didn't I?"

The captain is the ship. Symbolism. I hate it.

"What would've happened?" I asked, contrite.

She wasn't going to let me off the hook. "You saw what was happening! He was changing places with you — the *ships* were changing places! Do you want to spend the rest of eternity like that? Because *I* certainly don't!"

We glared at each other. I backed down first. I was, after all, the one in the wrong.

"I'm sorry," I said, letting out a long breath. "I wasn't thinking."

"No, you weren't, were you?"

"Have we crossed over?" came Pierce's voice from behind me. "Because suddenly I'm not seasick any more."

Óptimo. So I suppose now we'll get the whole pack of them coming up on deck to take the air now. I turned to Pierce. Relieved that he'd showed up and interrupted us, anyway.

"Yes," I replied, rubbing a hand over my face. "Yes, we have."

He took off his spectacles and stared around at the empty sea and the *Alcântara* dwindling in the distance, rubbing the lenses absently on his coatsleeve.

"Remarkable," he said. "Quite remarkable."

One way of putting it. Unless he was referring to not being seasick. Which was remarkable enough for him, I suppose. I turned back to the witch.

"Tatiana." She was still glowering. I still thought I'd like to kiss her. *Come on, I have apologized. And you don't often enjoy that. Da Silva, admitting he's in the wrong.*

"Don't ever do anything like that again," she said in a low, intense voice. Advice I probably don't need. I may do stupid things sometimes, but at least I learn from my mistakes. I raised an eyebrow and shook my head at her. Her expression softened slightly. I gave her a rueful smile and felt for my cheroots.

Found Zé at my elbow, staring at the speck in the distance that was the *Alcântara*. And that said something about the speed we were making.

"Did you see that!" he demanded, his voice on the squeaky side and not even appearing to notice. "That ship had *holes* you could drive a *carriage* through!"

"It's just a ghost, Zé," I said, hunting for matches. "Like Sr. Zacuto." Only bigger. And a lot more dangerous.

"Where are we?" he asked, switching to English and looking past me to the witch. She shrugged helplessly.

"I don't know," she said. "A place of ghosts. Limbo. A sea of passage."

"Beyond the baths of all the western stars," Pierce put in, unexpectedly, and colored as everyone turned to look at him. "Er, Tennyson," he explained, pushing his descending spectacles up. *"Ulysses."*

Ulysses. Lisbon's founder, according to some people. Johanna Kundrie, for one. I sighed. Finally located a box of matches. One thing's certain. Everyone's going to be asking the same question. We ought to have an answer.

Still, Tatiana Dimitrovna's *sea of passage* is as good as any.

I set light to my cheroot, shielding the match from the stiffening breeze. Looked up automatically to check that the canvas was all right. Then stared out to sea. Now that the spectral *Alcântara* had disappeared, there was nothing remarkable in sight. We were in the open sea. Above us, sky. That was it.

Oddly disappointing, really. *Well, what the hell did you expect, da Silva? Sea-serpents and mermaids?*

"Perhaps," said Zacuto's voice, who had also crept up on my blind side, "this is where all legends are real. The imaginary lands. Where the unreal has substance."

Which is a bit fanciful for Zacuto. I turned to see the wind stirring his hair, his robe. A convincing illusion, but why did he think it was necessary?

Pierce laughed suddenly, and put out his hand. "Is it true, Professor?"

The ghost clasped his hand. Didn't pass through it. I nearly dropped my cheroot. Zacuto's teeth flashed in a smile, white against his beard. Tatiana Dimitrovna stared at him with frank curiosity. Ha. Does that mean he's become solid, or that the rest of us have become insubstantial? I really don't like the second alternative. The back of my neck crawled.

"Hope that doesn't mean we're going to run into harpies and — and

Scylla and Charybdis," I said over a mouthful of smoke. Bad enough having to do this in the first place without the trip turning into the *Lusíadas*.

Though when you think about it, my whole life's done that. Without the good bits of having a bunch of gods on my side.

"None of us knows what's going to happen," muttered Tatiana Dimitrovna, and wiped a hand over her forehead.

"Are you all right?" Zé asked her. She gave him a rather strained smile.

"It was — rather tiring," she admitted. "Thank you for asking," she added, giving me a pointed sideways glance.

I drew in a mouthful of smoke and said, "Can't you have a rest now?"

She shook her head, smothering a yawn. "I don't think so. And neither can you, Luís." Zé looked at me questioningly.

"You said you didn't know how this would work," I pointed out.

"That was then," she said sharply. "This is now. You don't know exactly what a storm is going to be like, how you're going to have to tackle it, until you've sailed into it, do you?"

Well, I have a general idea. But I'll allow her the analogy.

"So you're, ah, feeling your way as we go?" asked Pierce. He turned to Zacuto. "Professor, do you have any ideas?"

The ghost, who appeared to be enjoying his altered state, looked round from the railing. "I have never been on any kind of sea voyage before," he explained. "Aside from having to wait four hundred years after my death to enjoy the experience, I do not know what to expect, or how it will differ from such a voyage in the material world."

Pierce took his spectacles off and fiddled with them. Gave a rueful smile. "If it comes to that," he said, "I've never been able to enjoy a voyage in the material world. Since I've spent all the ones I've taken wishing I was dead. So I don't know, either. But I meant in terms of the senhora bruxa's control of this reality." If it is reality. He turned to Tatiana Dimitrovna. "Are you actually, ah, manipulating our passage?"

"More unconsciously, I think," she replied, after a pause. She doesn't sound too sure. "Just as Luís is controlling the ship."

That's news to me. Must be something to do with this metaphysical business. Which I don't really understand.

Frowning, I leaned carefully against the rail. Sideways. My bruises were giving me a sort of dull constant backache that flared up if I made any sudden movements. Wonder how this works, really, this being one with my ship. I tried to sense *Isabella* around me, timber and canvas and rope, tar and hemp and metal. A hundred and fifty feet from bow to stern, thirty wide.

Draft of fourteen. A hundred and ten to the top of the mainmast. That space a world enclosed by sea and air and wind, powered by the elements.

Other than the normal sense I have of *Isabella*, how to handle her and steer her, navigate and lengthen or shorten sail, knowledge of how she'll react to the weather and the sea, nothing. But perhaps that's all the witch means, anyway. Perhaps "being" the ship is just that knowledge. Instinct and judgment.

I brought my attention back to the present to find Zacuto smiling at me. Of course, he knows what I'm thinking. He nodded.

"Not wholly metaphysical after all, Captain da Silva," he observed.

"No," I agreed. Is what we do always an extension of our selves, then? Now that *does* sound a bit too metaphysical. *Not the time or the place for it, da Silva.*

Although if sailing a ship through the seas where myths are true and ghosts can touch you isn't the place for it, I don't know what is.

15

I'VE PASSED BY THE MALTESE ISLANDS DOZENS OF TIMES. Rarely made landfall there. The Venetian did no trade with anyone there. And he didn't like the English, anyway. Not that he particularly liked anybody very much, except himself.

A day, a night, and a day. The wind is steady, the sea calm. Above us, clear skies. Seems like a perfect day for a sea voyage. *Isabella*, I'd say, is running at about eighteen knots, but what does that signify in these waters? For all I know she could be standing still, and the sea the thing that's moving. The witch can tell me nothing. The ghost can tell me nothing. The ghost, in fact, is spending most of his time enjoying the fact that he can touch things, and is not much use to anyone at the moment.

All I can do is carry on.

One thing I'd put money on, though. It's not going to stay like this, quiet and calm and sunny. That's be too easy. And if one thing's constant in my life these days, it's the conspicuous absence of easy.

But what might happen, I've no idea. Well, that's not quite true. I think I've got entirely too many ideas. That's the trouble. Too much imagination. And there was I under the impression I've never been a fanciful person.

Although you don't need an imagination to get spooked, here. Wherever here is. This isn't the Atlantic, at least not the one I know. Or I rather hope it isn't. Trafalgar is bad enough when all I see is its ghosts.

Better not to think of things like that. I lit a cheroot. There's not much else to do but think and smoke. Unless I'm doing something without knowing. My link with *Isabella*.

Think of something else, da Silva.

And that's the best way I know to keep my mind on the same damned tack.

In desperation, I walked over to where Pierce was standing. I don't mean that the way it sounds. I needed someone to talk to who wasn't Tatiana Dimitrovna. Or Zacuto, who had just moved away from Pierce. Someone human, is what I mean, I suppose. And I'm not in the mood to make small talk with my father, if I ever could. I haven't known him long enough as an adult, and I'm sure *he* thinks I'm still fourteen years old.

Pierce took off his spectacles and gave me a shrewd glance. "Feeling a bit superfluous, skipper?" I glared at him, but he'd put his finger on it. Yes, I was feeling superfluous. I blew out smoke, and the wind caught it and snatched it rapidly away.

"That about sums it up," I agreed.

He wiped the spectacles on his sleeve. "Damn things keep getting covered in salt," he muttered irritably, then squinted through the lenses with great concentration and put them back on. Looked seriously back at me. "Better not let it lull you into a false sense of security," he advised, and I raised my eyebrows.

"You think it's too quiet, as well?"

The antiquarian nodded. "Seems these things have a habit of sneaking up on you when you're not looking."

"And biting you in the ass," came Harris's voice from my left. I turned my head to look at him. Reflex. I know what Harris looks like.

"Yes, thank you, Harris," I said sternly, but I couldn't help grinning at the same time. Bit of light relief never does any harm. And God knows I can use some light relief.

"You any idea where we are?" he asked. I scratched my cheekbone, wondering how to answer him.

"Between the devil and the deep blue sea," said Pierce unexpectedly, and Benjamin, at the helm, crossed himself quickly. Harris looked startled.

"Jesus," he exclaimed, "don't say things like that." The werewolf is superstitious. Somehow that struck me as funny.

"You asked," I pointed out.

Pierce gestured with his spectacles. "Have you noticed?" he enquired, and Harris gave him a blank look. "No birds."

"Huh," he muttered, and took out his cigarettes. "What was you looking for, an albatross?" He shielded his match from the wind.

I pitched the remains of my cheroot over the side, and it blew away. "Got any explanation for that, Pierce?"

"Me?" he asked in surprise. Got him there. Still, I expect he's read more books than the rest of us put together. Except perhaps Zacuto, who doesn't have to sleep.

"Maybe there ain't no such thing as birds' ghosts," Harris suggested. He's probably right. I've never seen a spectral bird, though some dogs have ghosts. Hardly be much fun to have the ghost of the chicken you're having for supper clucking in the kitchen.

"I think I'd be more worried about harpies and rocs," said Pierce moodily, taking off his spectacles again. And thank you for that thought. I scowled at him, but he seems immune to the da Silva scowl by now.

"Can we stop all this Odyssean stuff?" I asked. "Bad enough to have this Fisher King business going on."

"Yeah, Prof, put a cork in it," Harris chimed in.

We all stared out to sea, falling silent at the same time. And back came all that gloomy speculation about sailing in these waters. I sighed, and turned to look for Tatiana Dimitrovna. Found her gone.

And then eight bells went, taking me completely unawares. *Great sense of what's going on, there, da Silva.* I looked at the sun in disbelief, then pulled out my watch to check again. How could it be noon already? But then, I don't suppose the passage of time has all that much significance on this voyage.

John Yeoh appeared for the afternoon watch, and I saw Benjamin slap hands with McCulloch and give over the helm to him. I put my timepiece away and rubbed my scar reflectively. Is time going faster? Is that how this works?

"I'm off for some grub," said Harris suddenly. "I'm hungrier'n a bear on short commons. I sure hope old João's cooked up something I can get my teeth into." He shot me a suspicious sideways glance, as if he thought I'd been conspiring with the cook to force-feed him *bacalhau*, then turned to Pierce. "You wanta come with?"

"Yes," replied the antiquarian, looking a little shocked, at the absence of seasickness I suppose. "I could eat a whale."

"Probably have to," said Harris darkly, with another quick look in my direction. I raised an eyebrow at him.

I found I was feeling pretty hungry myself, but I wanted to sound out our resident expert on time before I went for something to eat. Harris and Pierce headed below, and I turned to *Isabella*'s third mate.

"Sr. Yeoh."

He looked round, an amused expression on his face. Damn it, does everyone know what I'm thinking?

"Before you ask, senhor capitão," he said, "I don't know for sure. But it seems likely. Surely these waters must work to a set of rules, just as much as the physical world does." With a few exceptions, I thought, but didn't say anything.

Still, it makes sense to me. I nodded, and hunted for my cheroots. Found them in a different pocket. How did that happen? No matter. Just da Silva going senile. I smiled wryly. Wish that was all I had to worry about.

"Have you seen Tatiana Dimitrovna?" I asked him. He shook his head. I looked around and spotted Felipe. Told him to go and see if she was in her cabin. Hers, Ana's, Susana's, Alegria's. Only way to fit all these passengers in. Ashley's solution even means I don't have to share. Though I suppose I'd have given my bunk to my father, if I'd had to. I'm not that selfish. But hell, I *am* the captain.

Fat lot of good it does me. I feel more helpless in this calm sea running before this fresh wind, under this fine clear sky, on this blue day, than I think I've ever felt in my entire life. At least with demons you can fight back. At least with human beings you can fight back. Damn it. I blew out smoke in frustration.

Felipe came back with the information that Tatiana Dimitrovna was eating lunch with Harris and Pierce. The thought of that was too good to miss, so I went below to join them. Found most of the guests digging in, with the witch casting sideways glances at Harris. Presumably in the hope of catching him in something wolflike. Lunch was *rojões*, which is pork. Well, most of the pig except its squeal, as João says, the way he makes it. (He's from the north.) So I expect Harris was content.

Sailing in strange waters doesn't seem to have diminished anyone's appetite. Quite the opposite. Even my father was shoveling down the food as if he hadn't eaten for a week. I looked for Alegria, but didn't see her. I don't even know *whether* she needs to eat. There's a lot about Alegria that puzzles me. Or she might just be keeping Ana company. Who is probably a little nervous about sitting down to eat with a crowd of men.

Which started me off thinking about this Fisher King business again. I groaned inwardly, and concentrated on my meal.

I'd just finished eating when Felipe appeared at my elbow with a very strange look on his face. "Sr. Ashley's compliments, sir, and could you come at once?"

"On my way," I replied with a sigh, and got reluctantly to my feet. My back told me it didn't like sudden movements. I told it to shut the hell up.

Ashley was standing by the rail, hands clasped behind his back, and staring due east. Two bells sounded as I walked across to join him. He turned at the sound of my footsteps and acknowledged me with bleak formality.

"Captain." He pointed. "Is that what I think it is?"

Of course it would affect him. I nodded.

"Trafalgar," I said.

He doesn't know I see ghosts. So he doesn't know I see this every time I have to head for the Straits of Gibraltar.

But not like this.

The ghosts of the French and Spanish fleet, like the specter of the *Alcântara*, appeared as solid as Zacuto. I didn't use my telescope. It's bad enough when they're phantoms, and you can see through them. And at this rate we'll get closer soon enough.

"There don't seem to be nearly enough ships," he observed.

"That's because you're only seeing the ships that died here," I told him, scratching my eyebrow. It's not the vessels themselves that are the worst of this. Although the burnt ones are pretty bad: all sailors fear fire. But I didn't tell him anything. He'll see soon enough.

Others had seen, too. I heard Yeoh shouting at the men on watch to get back to their tasks. There were plenty who were off watch, though.

And there were our passengers. Some of whom really shouldn't see this. Just have to hope they have the sense to stay below.

A pall of smoke hung over the ghost ships. It looked as solid and real as they did. Not the smoke from wood alone. It came from pitch and tar and human bodies. Thick and greasy and blackish-brown. The smoke from the battle, all those broadsides, roundshot, grapeshot, seemed to separate out from it like vinegar and oil. Less meaty, and lighter in color.

The smoke blotted out the sky as we drew nearer. The sea, too, was invisible, hidden by a debris of broken spars and shattered masts, half-floating shredded canvas, and corpses. Surrounding this, all around for fifty yards and more, the water was red, flecked with soot, and ringed with a fatty scum.

Thank God the ghostly aftermath of Trafalgar had no smell. Because all the rest of it was much too real.

What I don't understand was why we're seeing it at all. There's no sign of the land that should be there. Only this empty sea filled with an enormous horrible specter of burned and broken ships and men.

Beside me, a grim-faced Ashley was keeping tally. I believe the British lost no ships at all, and of men a fraction of the thousands of French and Spanish dead. But this sight would chill any sailor's blood. And the ghostly bodies bobbing in the sea were unrecognizable as either Spaniards, French or British. Only a few had simply drowned. Most were shot to pieces, or burned to overcooked meat. Dismembered limbs floated among the debris.

As we passed by a charred hulk destroyed to the waterline, still smoking, still burning deep inside, I looked away hastily. I'd seen movement on board. And I hadn't forgotten what nearly happened with the *Alcântara*.

Isabella ploughed through the dead. Apparently we had no choice but to take this course. There was no going round the carnage. No avoiding the sight.

Everyone on board was silent now. No one spoke. Caps came off. Rosaries clicked. Ashley, always formal, saluted. I felt the wind in my hair, and it was suddenly deathly cold. The back of my neck prickled. We passed another hulk, like a floating heap of broken wood, trailing the tattered remnants of a Spanish flag. Hardly recognizable as a ship at all.

Behind me I heard Benjamin's mellow tenor start to sing, "Eternal Father, strong to save, whose arm doth bind the restless wave." It's an English hymn. I don't know the words, but apparently quite a lot of the men did. Including Pierce, who was standing on my left. I hadn't even sensed him arrive, but I turned now and saw his face was wet with tears.

By the time they got to the last "For those in peril on the sea" even Harris was singing, and that's not something you want to hear sober.

And then we were past the last poor shattered vessel, and the whole horror was behind us. Not a man looked back. The crowd dispersed in silence. I found a cheroot, and lit it with a sense of relief. Ashley walked away, stiff-backed.

"Poor buggers," said Pierce. His voice shook. "You don't ever need to ask me why I'm a pacifist."

I didn't know he was. But this isn't the time to say so. Tact, da Silva. Instead, I turned to Tatiana Dimitrovna. Hadn't seen her arrive, either. Well, I only have one eye, and it isn't in the back of my head.

"Is that what you see every time you sail past Trafalgar?" she asked me in a husky voice before I could speak.

"Not in such detail," I answered, scratching my cheekbone. My voice didn't sound all that steady, either. "But why did we see it at all? I thought—"

"Some events," said Zacuto from behind me. What, are they all queueing up to jump out at me? "Some events resonate through all times and all realities. This sea-battle—" He cleared his throat. Looks rather green around the gills. Probably the burnt-out ships remind him of his own death. "Is one such. It is too momentous to be forgotten."

Nothing I've seen is as terrible as Trafalgar, though I expect the Grand Banks in the north Atlantic where the SS *Titanic* went down is pretty bad. Not that a sailing ship's got any reason to go up there and play dodge the iceberg. Makes no sense. South with the trades is the best way to cross the

Atlantic if you're under sail.

But no doubt we'll meet more, this trip. A day, a night, and a day. I looked at the sky. Change that first bit to half a day.

For now, though, *Isabella* flew on. And *flew* is probably the only word.

Of course, I spent the time worrying what was going to happen next.

* * *

Caught in the strange limbo which always surrounds her for a few days after *Isabella* has sailed, Emilia stares through the office window onto the now-familiar scene of the narrow sloping cobbled street outside, the peeling white house opposite with its ridiculously tiny wrought-iron balconies stuffed full of potted plants and festooned with washing, and the insouciant tabby cat which sometimes pretends to live with her, and finds nothing to engage her in either ship's accounts or her own craftsmanship.

Thin, pale yellow late January sun mellows the street outside. Sometimes, when winter rain drifts over the city, or even the occasional cloudy day intrudes in summer, you can see this part of town for what it is, none too prosperous despite the air of geniality, even gaiety, that usually imbues. The walls, after all, are flaking and crusted here and there with nitrate deposits or the slime and stain from a leaky drain, the red roofs are ragged and some of them have holes in them, indeed some have collapsed altogether, from above they look as if a giant foot has stepped on them, that of the Titan Adamastor maybe. And in summer, there is no denying it, the smell of drains is prone to intrude, in fact intrude is too mild a word, some days it can reach out and grab you and mug you like a robber in the street.

Yet Emilia, born in a colder and wetter place that nonetheless need not hang its head in shame at the quality of the stenches it can produce, has grown fond of noisy dirty Lisbon. But, though the streets are drier and more precipitous, it is just as empty as Venice when her husband is away. In the old days he would be gone for months at a time, bound for India or Ceylon or Macau, Singapore or Shanghai. They have been married nearly twenty years, what a thing, but have been apart longer than they have spent together. And still, every time he sails away, she fears it is the last time, such is the lot of sailors' wives ever since humankind first made the interesting discovery that wood floats on water and decided to embark on it.

Usually she can lose herself in her work. But right now there is something else niggling at her quite apart from the empty ache for her husband which always presents itself. A sense of unfinished business.

With a sigh, she put down the pen she'd been pretending to write with, retrieved her walking-stick, and pushed herself to her feet with its aid and that of her desk. Her leg is not too bad today, just a vague distant ache, so she will not have to use the crutch she hates so fervently. Thank heaven for small mercies.

She could hear Joana clattering outside, who cleans, cooks and helps out willingly enough but makes almost as much of a racket about it as Zé, always supposing Zé would pick up a mop, such a bizarre image that Emilia had to laugh. Her son, who has a girlfriend, heavens above, where did the time go. She looked at her hands, almost expecting to see brown spots and the crinkly skin of age, but how silly, she is only just thirty-nine, which is not old at all, although some of her contemporaries are bent already into the stooped blackness of old age, perhaps having had only two children has something to do with it.

Emilia shook her head to clear it of such wool-gathering, and made her way to the door. As usual the first step is the worst, and then walking grows easier.

"Olá, Joana," she called, opening the door. "I'm going out for a while, can you mind the telephone?"

There was no reply, but she hadn't really expected one. Joana has always been on the taciturn side, and as for anything as ambitious as holding a conversation, Emilia only knew she could because she'd seen it happen. Once.

A sudden, but momentary, flood of apprehension burst over her as she put her hand out to open the front door, and she stopped for a second. Don't be silly, she told herself, it's broad daylight... and besides, you have a bodyguard. She smiled. She didn't know why she trusted Julia so implicitly, but she did.

Once in the street, whose combination of cobbles and short bursts of stone steps had horrified her at first, but which she had soon grown used to and hardly thought about any more, she greeted neighbors as she passed. In the back of her mind was a funny sort of vaguely guilt-like sensation, as if some part of her thought she was playing truant. But she pushed it down. This was business, anyway. Of a sort.

After a few minutes she became aware of a presence just behind her, and found a use for her new perceptions after all. She smiled to herself and said, without turning or checking her pace, *"Bom dia,* Julia."

Julia took a stride to bring her abreast of Emilia and fell into step beside her, a courtesy she appreciated from someone with legs so much longer, and that worked properly. Exotic as usual, her strange long angular beauty cannot be constrained by European dress, by skirts and coats and shoes, she towers over her by nearly a foot. They made an odd pair, Emilia thought, as they walked along the sunlit street.

It took them less than twenty minutes to reach the orphanage, during which time Emilia found Julia less inclined to talk than Joana. She didn't worry about this. Julia was not at all concerned today. Which presumably meant that Mouffi was far away.

At the door, Julia faded away into the shadows so smartly Emilia hardly noticed she was gone until she was out of sight.

It was Teresa Batista who answered the door to her knock, somewhat to Emilia's surprise, but Sra. Cerberus's absence at least meant less delay. Teresa smiled on seeing Emilia, and invited her in.

"What brings you to visit us, Sra. da Silva?"

"I came to ask after your patient," Emilia explained, following the younger woman into the sunlit entrance hall.

"The inspector?" enquired Teresa, raising her black eyebrows. "I didn't realize you knew him."

"Well, I don't, really," replied Emilia. "I've met him. But I don't suppose he has anyone else to ask after him."

"No, he has that not-married look, doesn't he?" Teresa smiled, as if recalling something. "Listen, sit down a minute, and I'll go and ask Inácio."

Relieved at being able to sit, Emilia lowered herself into one of the chairs and massaged her thigh, hard, with her knuckles. She jumped slightly when someone called her name, and looked up to see Sílvia. I might've known she'd show up, she thought with amusement, and couldn't help admiring her son's taste.

"Sílvia," she greeted her. *"Como está?"* The question was a little superfluous, since the girl's eyes were a little red, a little swollen. Sílvia, however, shrugged, and attempted a smile. It wasn't wholly successful, but Emilia gave her marks for trying.

"Alright, I suppose. Thank you for asking," she answered, then added in a rush, "Is it dangerous, where they're going?"

"O carissima," Emilia said, lapsing into Italian in a sudden rush of sympathy, after all the girl is the same age as she was when she first met Luís, if not younger, "All sea voyages are dangerous." You'll have to learn to live with it, poor child, she added silently, if you're going to have any kind of relationship with my son. She resisted a momentary reprehensible impulse to read Sílvia, and patted the girl's hand. Dr Bosque, whatever his shortcomings in the world of accounts, had a real talent for bringing out the best in his young charges. As far as Emilia could see, there wasn't a bad

apple among them.

Dr Bosque himself appeared a moment later, beaming and squinting at her through his thick spectacles.

"My dear Sra. da Silva," he said, rubbing his hands together and sounding genuinely pleased to see her. "How very thoughtful of you to come to see my patient. Would you like to come through?"

Sílvia offered Emilia her hand, who took it so as not to hurt her feelings. "Thank you," she murmured.

The doctor turned to Sílvia, with an attempt at looking stern. "Shouldn't you be in class?" he asked, mildly.

"Yes, Sr. doutor," replied the girl, and made herself scarce with alacrity.

"Pleasant child," remarked Emilia. "How is the inspector?"

"Well." Dr Bosque gave her a rather puzzled smile. "He's remarkably well, all things considered. He should be dead, he really should, with a wound like that. But he woke up this morning, demanding food." He rapped at a door. "Of course, he's very weak, still. It'll be a long hard road. But I think he'll recover."

The door was opened by a stout woman with a face like a cow, clad in a nurse's uniform. "Sr. doutor?" she asked in a booming whisper.

"Dona Linda," he replied, and Emilia had to stuff a knuckle into her mouth to stop herself from laughing, since *linda* means *beautiful* in Portuguese.

I'm getting as bad as Luís, she thought, and the thought was comforting, as if it brought him nearer, at least in spirit. She dragged herself back to reality, and followed Dr Bosque into the room. It presented a temporary air, a couple of days before it might have been a store cupboard or something of that nature.

She couldn't help a slight gasp when she saw Corvo, though. His eyes were closed, and she'd never seen anyone quite so white in the face. The shock made her relax her mental shields for a split second, and the inspector's thoughts and emotions and fears and memories beat at her in a single overwhelming wave.

Emilia staggered a bit, glad she could blame it on her leg, and Dr Bosque caught her elbow, his face contrite. The portly nurse, showing presence of mind if not a particularly impressive turn of speed, dragged a chair to her, and she sat down quickly with a murmur of thanks.

She accepted a glass of water from the woman and sipped it. It tasted vaguely dusty, as if it had been sitting around for a while, but she hardly noticed. She was watching the man on the bed. He was breathing evenly, and Emilia could see no trace of fever, no sweat on his brow, no tossing and turning, she knows what it is like, her mind flips back despite all her efforts to the weeks after her husband lost his eye.

Then the patient opened his eyes. Dr Bosque and the nurse became briskly efficient, but Corvo was focused on Emilia. She thought he looked as though he wanted to say something, but how could he possibly add anything to what she already knew from him? Although, of course, he didn't know that.

Corvo muttered something, but she couldn't hear what it was. The doctor bent closer, but she could still see him looking at her.

"Don't try to speak," Dr Bosque said.

"Mouffi," whispered the inspector, and this time she heard him. She nodded. She knew. "Tell Captain da Silva."

"Yes," Emilia told him. There was no choice but to lie. She'd seen his dream. Seen Mouffi stalking him, besieging him, trying to break in, overcome his barriers. The demon-fragment couldn't touch him, but there was something else there, behind it in the shadows, never seen but overwhelming. And Emilia didn't know, because Corvo himself didn't know, how long he could hold out. Which meant only one thing.

Somehow she was going to have to defeat it herself.

*   *   *

The last time I felt so completely useless was thirty-odd years ago when I was. Useless, that is. When I'd just signed on a tea clipper called the *Inês De Castro* and set out down the Tagus for the first time in my life. Now there was a ship that could go fast, though not as fast as *Isabella* this present trip. It's a long while since I thought of her. Nobody likes to be reminded of a time before competence. On the other hand, perhaps it's character-building. Ha. My character doesn't need any more building, thank you very much.

What it needs right now is a rest. Normally I enjoy the still peaceful night of the middle watch in fine weather. *Isabella* skimming over the waves, the air and darkness full of ship-sounds and the humming of the wind in canvas. Now, though, nearing six bells, I'm worn out with worry and I want my bunk.

Not going to get it, though, da Silva. The witch and I have to stay awake. For a day, a night, and a day.

I leant on the rail and looked at the swathes of phosphorescence in the sea. It looks like a real ocean. I blew out smoke and almost wished something would happen. Almost.

And so the night passed. Dawn came up like lava and fire in the east, so at least we *are* still sailing east. Couldn't have told it from the stars. No constellations I know. No moon. What drives these strange tides, if there's no moon?

The day that followed was uneventful, too. We drove on through the waters faster than any ship ever built. Or the seas moved under us and we were still. I don't know. We saw no other sights like Trafalgar. Very few ghost-ships at all.

"How will we know when we get to Malta?" I asked the witch, who appeared to be watching some of the men in the rigging. She gave a start, which meant she'd been dozing on her feet. Glad I'm not the only one.

"I suppose we'll see ships from the Great Siege," she replied, a bit dubiously. Obviously hoping it wouldn't be another Trafalgar.

"The Siege," I repeated, scratching my eyebrow. History's not one of my strong points. And I've spent five years learning to ignore ghosts, not seek the damned things out. I yawned. She glared at me, then smothered one of her own.

"Don't do that," she said crossly. "Surely you know it's catching."

My eye wanted to droop and close, and I shook myself irritably and got moving. Coffee. I need coffee.

Which was how most of the day passed. Almost falling asleep and waking myself up with caffeine. I'd be able to keep awake better if I had something to do. God knows I've been up for longer than this through bad weather, but there's no time to think in a hundred-foot sea or a hurricane, let alone sleep. At this rate I'll have to resort to getting Harris to sing again. I'm not serious. He sounds like a wounded bull.

Tatiana Dimitrovna, for all her casual talk of the siege of Malta, doesn't know any more about it than I do. So I had to tackle Zacuto. Who baffled me with so many statistics that I glazed over even more, but didn't enlighten me.

"You are trying to analyse this in too much detail," he told me sternly. "When I was alive, Captain da Silva, we had no microscopes to view animalculi invisible to the naked eye, yet in those days I was a physician and an herbalist and did well enough with the knowledge that I had. Now I know better, of course I wish that I had had modern medical knowledge to call upon. But I had to make the best of what I had."

Everyone is still telling me to rely on fate or something similar. But damn it, I feel manipulated enough.

"Might help if I had a bit more of a bloody clue what's going on," I grumbled. I feel like a tram. Running on rails set down by someone else. I need more control. Sailing a ship is child's play compared to this.

Irritated, I lit another cheroot and stamped off down to my cabin. The one place where I could be sure of a little privacy. And I was wrong about that, too. Of course.

It was just shy of seven bells in the afternoon watch. I yawned until my jaw cracked, took off my cap and threw it on the bunk. Followed it with my coat. And the knife I've been wearing for about thirty hours straight. I flexed my shoulders gratefully. Dragged the eyepatch off over my head. My hair was damp and lank, nasty to touch. My beard feels three days old. And I, not to mince words, feel like shit.

I poured myself a brandy. Probably a bad idea, given I haven't slept, but what the hell. Wondered whether to take my boots off as well, and decided against it. Too much effort. I sat down in my nice padded leather chair. Sighed at how comfortable it is. Lit a cheroot and leaned back, stretching out my legs.

You'll go to sleep, da Silva.

Right now I just can't bring myself to care. In a minute I'll write up the log. That'll keep me awake a while longer. I must've closed my eye momentarily. No, be honest. I fell asleep. But I think it was only for a second.

But I woke up to see a knight sitting the other side of my desk. Complete with chain mail and tunic with Maltese cross on the front. I let out a startled curse, and reached over my shoulder for my knife.

Which was lying on my bunk, along with my coat and cap. *Merda.* There's an armored knight with a bloody great sword lying across his lap sitting in front of me, and I'm in my shirtsleeves with nothing in my hands but a pen and a cheroot. Well, could've been worse. I might've taken my boots off, too.

If he'd been real I could either set fire to his beard or stick the nib in his hand. The pen is mightier than the sword, according to Pierce. Not in my book. I'll take the sword any day. In this case, though, I haven't been given the choice. Haven't been given any kind of choice, come to that. If he wants to run me through there's nothing to stop him.

Yet as I looked at him, he gave a flicker of recognition. He was weary and worn out from long fighting, too. Wanted his bed. Then the moment passed, and his lined face took on an implacable expression. I sighed, and put down my pen.

"So," I said resignedly, "I suppose you'll be Jean de la Valette?" One thing I *had* gotten from Zacuto — about the only thing — and that's the name of the commander of the Knights of St John during the siege.

He stared at me coldly, looking singularly unimpressed. The state of da Silva's probably not very impressive at the moment. Well, tough. He'll have to put up with it. I raised my eyebrows, and took a drag from my cheroot. My back chose that moment to send a twinge of agony through me. Nice reminder of frail humanity.

"I am, yes," the knight replied. "I was. Grand Master of the Order of St John and presently the guardian of the Maltese islands."

"The guardian," I repeated blankly. Brain's not working very fast today. I looked at his sword, then back up to his face. "And what d'you want me to do?" Because there's bound to be something. And I don't expect I'll enjoy it.

"Nothing," he said, proving me wrong. "I am here to examine your motives, and decide whether you can be permitted to make landfall." He paused. I inhaled some more smoke. "We know what you are, Luís da Silva. I am not sure you do."

And what's that supposed to mean? I made a face. Blew out the smoke explosively. "Paladin. So I'm told."

Valette flared his nostrils and moved the sword slightly on his lap. "But do you know what that means?" I shrugged.

"A champion."

"It signifies very much more than that," he snapped, "as I suspect you know very well. You are too intelligent not to, however much you deny it. But let that pass for the moment. We are more concerned at *whose* champion."

I paused with the cheroot halfway to my mouth. "What the hell's that supposed to mean?" I demanded.

"Many powers are interested in you," the knight informed me, frowning. "And all coins have two sides."

And all ghosts talk in bloody riddles. A little less cryptic, a little more informative would be nice. "What?" I said, inanely.

He stared at me intently, and stroked his short gray beard. "You have in you a real capacity for darkness, Luís da Silva." This makes me unique? He went on before I could say anything. "You may think your motives are good, but even good people do evil things for the best of reasons. It is very easy to slip over the edge from righteous justice to wrath, fortitude to pride and on to hubris." Narrowing his eyes. "Sins can be very close to virtues. You love your wife, yet you lust after other women."

Throw that in my face. "I'm a man," I retorted. "I'm fallible. That's what humans do, or have you been dead too long to remember?" I scratched my cheekbone. A thought struck me. "And besides, aren't you lot big on resisting temptation?"

Valette didn't like that. He looked as though he'd just found half a weevil in his rations. He looked at me as though I was the weevil. "And you're apostate as well," he remarked, with distaste. *Nice work, da Silva.* Why not remind a fanatical Christian of that?

As if religion has anything to do with it, anyway. I stubbed out my cheroot and said heatedly, "You know, I'm sick and tired of the likes of you coming along and criticizing me. I do the best I can." I drew a deep breath. "You were a soldier, damn it. You should know what having to make snap decisions is like."

Looking down his nose, he asked, "Do you the stand by the 'snap decision' that had you kill Aldo Della Quercia?" I stared at him, open-mouthed.

"He'd just shot me!"

"You could have disarmed him," the knight said, unimpressed. Easy for him to say. "You knew how to fight a murderer. He had only ever fought women and the weak. Yet you appointed yourself his executioner." I picked up my glass and drank some brandy.

"I paid for that," I pointed out. For nineteen years.

"With service to his brother." Valette's eyes were cold, and so was his voice. "Do you really think that counts?"

I've had about enough of this. "Look," I began, hotly. Pushed back my chair and got to my feet. He gripped his sword-hilt.

"Sit down," he ordered.

"No." I felt for my cheroots, holding his gaze. Thinks he can outstare me, does he? I pointed a cheroot at him, angry. "You listen to me, Grand Master. You said you know what I am. If you know that, you know what Sir Robert Munro is. You think *my* motives are suspect? Have a look at him. And then think about what might happen if he succeeds." I struck a match, and lit up, without looking away.

Valette narrowed his eyes. "That, unfortunately, is why we are going to have to let you pass. I would argue further against it, myself, did I think it would have any effect. But I am only one voice, though not the only dissenting one."

"Do you mean to say," I said incredulously, raising my eyebrows, "that you were going to let us through all along?"

"By no means," replied the knight. He whipped up the sword and the point was under my chin before I could even flinch. Ghost he may have been, but the blade was real enough. I felt it nick my skin, and a tiny trickle of blood run down my neck. I swallowed. Valette's voice rang like iron. "Had you offered violence, Luís da Silva, I would have had to respond in kind, and paladin or no, ally or no, your head would now be sundered from your body."

He removed the sword-tip from my neck. He sounded so certain of that that I did sit down again, and drained my glass quickly. Mopped the blood with a handkerchief. Didn't drop my gaze. Is that so damned sinful?

"Why don't you go and harass Munro?" I asked irritably, wondering if the cut would need holy water.

"The man Munro is traveling by mundane means," Valette said. "You chose to come by this route. Do not be surprised by its hazards." Rising to his feet, he added, "You may not believe it, Luís da Silva, but you passed the test. You are permitted to make landfall in Grand Harbor."

And with that he vanished into thin air.

*   *   *

Emilia knew very well that defeating Mouffi wasn't going to be easy, and for a moment despair threatened to overwhelm her. All she had was a woman who had once been a leopard, and probably could be again if she could find the way. Paciência wasn't powerful enough to tackle a demon, even a fragment of one. Luzia might be, but she was too inexperienced. And right now, Emilia wasn't certain that Julia could kill Mouffi, let alone whatever demon seemed to be sponsoring it. Belphegor, she supposed. At least she knew its name.

But she knew someone who might be able to.

As Dr Bosque shut the door quietly on Inspector Corvo's room, she asked him, "Is Teresa free?" The doctor pulled out his watch and held it close to his face, squinting at it through his thick lenses. She caught, involuntarily, a pang of his terrible anxiety and fear of blindness, and flinched in sympathy.

"Yes," he said. "She hasn't got a class at the moment." He put the watch away, and raised his eyebrows questioningly. "Why?"

"Oh, I just wanted to ask her something."

The doctor looked wistful, and the thought *she needs more friends her own age* leaked out. Emilia clamped down firmly on her extra sense. She didn't want to keep on reading stray thoughts like this.

"I expect she's in the gymnasium," he guessed. "I'll take you. How's your leg feeling now, by the way? Better?"

"A little, thank you," said Emilia.

"Well, the gymnasium's not upstairs, you'll be pleased to hear." He offered his arm. "It's this way."

She took his arm. With some people it is always easier to accept help gratefully, even if you don't want it, and Dr Bosque is one of these. Emilia doesn't mind, not really, he is too nice to hurt his feelings. Although if he were a business rival it would be all too easy to take advantage of him, and that, she reflected, was a very unkind thought.

At the end of the passage, which smelt of floor-polish and that institutional odor of boiled cabbage that even the best institutions can't seem to avoid, he pushed a door open and excused himself, leaving Emilia to slip through the gap.

The gymnasium was larger than she expected, lit obliquely by the sun slanting through its long windows, and equipped with racks of weights, vaulting-horses, and other implements of torture whose purpose she wasn't even curious about.

Teresa was at the far side, a fencing epée in her right hand, and clad rather surprisingly in a pair of pants and a shirt with the sleeves rolled up, an outfit that Emilia thought suited her rather well, though it would scandalize the neighbors if she went out like that, just look at the brazen hussy, well what do you expect from a *brasileira*, she's not married to the doctor you know, yes, I do, who knows what the world is coming to, the things women wear these days, they're no better than they should be, any of them.

Engrossed in her exercising, Teresa didn't notice Emilia, who watched in fascination. She had been subconsciously expecting some kind of fencing exercise. But the routine was fast and furious and looked more like some kind of martial dance than anything. Aside from the epée in Teresa's hand, it bore very little resemblance to any fencing Emilia had ever seen, and she suspected it was something the younger woman had dreamed up. It was too fast to follow, but there were kicks and punches, leaps and somersaults, as well as sword-thrusts, sweeps and wrist action that turned the blade into a blur.

She finished by running at a vaulting-horse, using her left hand to spring off it into the air where her long legs made a scissors-movement almost too quick to see, flipped over and landed squarely on both feet, knees bent, and up into the *en garde* position.

Emilia burst into spontaneous applause, and Teresa noticed her for the first time. She smiled in apparently genuine pleasure, waved, racked her sword, picked up a towel, and walked across the room wiping her face.

"That was extraordinary," said Emilia, sincerely.

"Thank you." Teresa grinned broadly, her teeth a white contrast to her skin. Obviously one or more of her forebears had indulged in a little dallying with a slave.

"But what on earth was it?"

"It's something I invented." She scowled briefly. "Stupid men won't fence with me. Think it's unseemly for me to want to. So until the kids get a lot better I had to come up with something to keep me from turning into an elephant."

Privately, Emilia doubted whether this was possible or even likely, but she smiled back and confessed, "I do have an ulterior motive. Last year, when we all worked together—" She broke off and put a hand to her mouth.

"It's all right," Teresa assured her, and Emilia felt her reassurance like a wave of heat from her skin. Or maybe it was just heat from her skin. Her face was shiny with sweat. She continued rather wryly, "I *have* come to terms with my father being a megalomaniac who nearly caused the world to come to an end, you know. More or less."

"Well, I need to ask you for your help again," said Emilia.

Teresa mopped her sweating face once more, and replacement beads of moisture immediately appeared. "Go ahead."

"Do you remember the Roman sword, the gladius?" Teresa nodded.

"Yes, what about it?"

Emilia took a deep breath and asked in a rush, "Do you think you could kill a demon with it?"

*   *   *

Malta is a rocky island the color of straw and sand. The rocks are the same pale drab shade as the buildings, the fortifications, the rooftops, the roads. I took *Isabella* through the harbor mouth with the world's wind and tide, and all the heights and the vast bastions were completely lined with the ghosts of thousands of cold-eyed knights. They let me pass, but they didn't like it. The weight of all that dislike and suspicion was immense.

The sun dropped below the fortifications, and all the dull stone glowed briefly before giving itself over to evening. From the deck I heard muted murmurs of astonishment at our landfall. Whether at the speed of our passage, or because we'd actually made it to Malta, I don't know. And I was too tired to care.

When we docked I delegated everything to Ashley and called a council of war. Not in my cabin, it's crowded with three people, especially if one of them's Harris. I assembled them all together in the mess.

"You look like crap, skipper," remarked Harris cheerfully. I shot him a dirty look.

"Thanks very much for the vote of confidence," I said. "Now listen. None of us knows what's going to happen, how this works. Unless anyone's had any interesting insights?" Shaking of heads. I raised an eyebrow at Zacuto, but he just looked at John Yeoh, who shrugged his shoulders.

Expressive stuff, body language.

Tatiana Dimitrovna interrupted. "Luís." I turned to her questioningly. "We can't make any plans. We don't know enough."

"I know, damn it," I said in irritation. "But I need to do something." And had to cover a yawn swiftly with my hand.

"Sleep. That's what you need to do," she told me in a stern voice. Sighed. "And so do I."

Sensible advice. I expect I will sleep. Even with the thought of all those hostile knights. Hell, look at me, I'm nearly asleep now.

"Senhor capitão," said Yeoh, "don't fight it. Let it go for now. In this case, we all have to wait and see."

Wait and see. The most dispiriting words I can think of. But there's no enemy to take the fight to. Not even a fight. Unless those knights decide to anything. And then I'll be, to speak Harrisian, up shit creek without a paddle.

Come to think of it, that's a much more dispiriting thought. Since you'd think we're all supposed to be on the same side. What are they afraid of? Me? That's a laugh. At this moment I don't think I could beat my nine-year-old daughter in a fight.

"Go to bed, Luís," my father ordered.

I bowed to the inevitable, and went.

Normally I never remember having dreams. Or if I do they're mostly mundane things. I suppose my life's bizarre enough that the average nightmare couldn't compete. I've had to face some things a lot worse than nightmares.

That night, though, I had what Harris calls a doozy.

The smell of candles was the first thing I noticed. You know how a whole bank of them smells when you go into a church. Hot, smoky, waxy. And yes, hot has a smell. It made me think of the room on the top floor of the Venetian's palazzo, where he'd summoned the demon that took him. That took my eye. I shook off the memory.

Everything was black, though. I couldn't *see* the candles. Though they felt near enough to singe my hair. I realized belatedly that I was blindfolded. A moment after I came to this conclusion, someone untied the blindfold and left me blinking at a blazing chandelier directly in front of me. I felt the heat where my eyepatch usually covers the scar on my face, and reached up. Didn't have it on. How odd. Even for a dream.

And then, of course, I realized it wasn't a dream at all. Although I'm pretty sure it wasn't precisely reality, either. The chandelier began to rise into the air, revealing a room full of stern-faced knights. My heart lurched unpleasantly. They were all in chain mail and tunics, but bare-headed. I was in shirtsleeves, and felt distinctly under-dressed. I was standing behind a railing facing three knights sitting behind a high desk. On either side, several rows of them in wooden pews. Looks suspiciously like a court. *All right, da Silva, you've worked out what it is.* As to where it is, it's either a place like São Rafael, or it's a place like the seas we sailed to get to Malta.

Either way, it's not somewhere I want to be. I turned my head. I was flanked by more knights, and a crowd of them stood silently behind me. I swallowed, and rubbed the back of my neck. Felt a strong urge to turn and run like hell, but I don't know where to. Couldn't fight them. There were about a hundred of them, and only one of me. Besides, every single one of 'em looks bigger than me. And every single one of 'em has a bloody great sword. And I expect they're all as fast as Valette. What's this about? Your big boss agreed to let us land.

"What the hell's going on?" I asked.

It was the knight on the left of the trio on the bench who answered. "We do not agree with the decision to let your ship dock here." His voice was flat and made my back hair stand on end. Well, they are dead. I presume. "We intend to make our own investigation."

Óptimo. Renegade knights. Just the thing to help our quest along. I folded my arms and tried to ignore my back, which had decided to start aching again. Pretty much proves I'm not dreaming. "And then what?"

"We will pass judgment, of course." Of course. Silly question, da Silva. I scratched the scar on my face and wished for a smoke.

"This tribunal is now in session," rasped the knight who was sitting on the right-hand side, abruptly, and banged a gavel on the desk, making me jump. Nerves shot to hell as well as everything else, by the looks of it.

"Wait a moment!" I interrupted. "Pass judgment — what judgment?"

The knight who'd first spoken sighed audibly and scowled. The one in the middle hasn't spoken yet. Maybe he's the judge. Yes, he looks like the sort to enjoy a good hanging. Hell, they all do. "If we decide in your favor," said the knight to port, "you may proceed. If not, you will have to leave. Is that simple enough for you, captain?"

I exhaled through my mouth. "It'll have to do." At least this lot aren't waving their swords around and threatening to separate my head and body. Maybe they'll be open to reason.

Yes, and I'm King João the Pious. Ha. This bunch probably wouldn't even let *him* in. I wondered rather mordantly if I should be asking for a lawyer.

"Luís José Alexandre Fernandes da Silva," the knight addressed me formally. And I got rid of most of that mouthful when I was fourteen. "I am Alessandro Laparelli. My fellow arbiters are Garcia Marcado and Philippe Gilbert. What is your purpose here in Malta?"

What's the purpose of this bloody charade? I glared at them and wiped sweat out of my eyebrows. The room was hot and airless, Windowless, too. Something about it made me think we were underground. A long way underground. "Oh, for God's sake, you know why I'm here," I said irritably. "Can we just get on with it?" Whatever it is.

Marcado, the knight in the center, spoke for the first time. His voice sounded like the rattle of old bones. "This tribunal has not been summoned for your convenience," he informed me coldly. "You are the accused here. And we have the power to prevent your ship from coming to land. Ever again." Arctic water trickled down my back. "Be advised, da Silva. Treat us with courtesy and honor and we will do the same to you. And do not take the Lord's name in vain again. We ask again. What is your purpose in Malta?"

"To—" My voice came out hoarse, and I cleared my throat. "To collect one of the Grail Hallows. The silver dish." I don't ignore warnings like that. I'm not stupid. Pig-headed sometimes, I grant you. But not stupid. Whatever else I might be.

"Why do you seek the Hallows?" Gilbert asked. He looked older than the other two, but his face was even harder. It could've been carved from granite.

My palms were sweating. I wiped them down my pants. "To stop a sorcerer called Sir Robert Munro from getting hold of them."

They conferred briefly.

"We admit this," said Laparelli after a moment. "Munro is not a fit person."

Finally. But they showed no sign of coming to any other conclusions. I felt sweat trickling down my temple, and wiped it away.

At last Marcado looked up. "Now we need to determine your fitness for the task."

"He is not fit," announced Gilbert, flatly. I fought down a surge of anger. "He has summoned demons. He is a murderer. He was the henchman of a black sorcerer at least as bad as this Munro. He is a blasphemer and an apostate."

"Now just a minute," I began indignantly, but Marcado stared at me and I shut up instantly. You don't need to warn me more than once.

Laparelli held up a hand. "Let him answer the charges." He inclined his head to me. "Captain da Silva?"

"You have summoned demons," Marcado said in a stony voice. "For what purpose?"

My mouth was dry. "To protect my family." Some of the charges I can refute. I clenched my hands on the rail in front of me. "And I've killed a few, as well," I added. The tribunal seemed unimpressed.

"And the men you killed?" I beg your pardon, *men?* One of them was already dead... *Don't think it, da Silva, say it.*

"I cut the Venetian's throat to free him from a demon he'd called. After it killed him," I said tightly. "I stabbed his brother to stop him raping a fifteen-year-old crippled girl." Emilia. I winced at a sudden suffocating dread of never seeing her again.

"Your wife," murmured Laparelli. I nodded. All for Emilia. Killed mad Aldo, became his brother's slave. Laparelli turned back to his colleagues. "The charges may be true. But justified. I believe the Grand Master was right to let him pass."

"Apostasy is never justified," snapped Gilbert through thin lips. I was beginning to dislike him a lot.

The other knight frowned at him. I wiped sweat from my eye. "But he has been given skills to use. There are powers beyond those we know, Philippe."

"Dangerous in his hands." He would've enjoyed burning heretics, this fellow. Has that real inquisitor's zeal.

"Dangerous in anyone's hands," Laparelli pointed out.

What, am I supposed to let them argue it out between themselves?

"Da Silva," said Marcado, making me jump again. I turned my head so that I could meet his eye. "You are a necromancer."

I grimaced. Hate the word. "I didn't ask for it." I hate what it means. What it makes me. "But yes, I am."

"Have you ever used the power for personal gain?"

"Dear God, no." Gilbert glowered, and pointed a finger at me. I scowled back.

"See, even now he blasphemes."

"Let that pass," Marcado instructed him. "Such carelessness of speech is the way of this new century. It is of little matter." Gilbert opened his mouth, but the other knight held up a hand to quiet him. Not before time. He subsided, but fulminated in silence. "We are addressing graver matters here."

And then I remembered something. Remembered being in Tatiana Dimitrovna's bedroom when she came back from hell. *And this is a fine time to remember the rest of it, da Silva.* "Do you know the Russian witch?" I blurted out. Three heads turned to me, Gilbert looking even more eager to sling someone on a pyre. Preferably me.

"And is consorting with witches also to be condoned?" he asked bitterly.

Laparelli raised his eyebrows. "There is hope yet for the woman, as you well know." Gilbert fell silent again.

"What of her?" Marcado enquired. I scratched my scar, mainly for something to do with my hand. It still feels strange to be out in public without the eyepatch. Well, sort of in public.

"She went to Hell."

"This we know." He wasn't giving any concessions. I fought down anger again. Don't these people ever consider that they could drive someone to the dark side like this? Or drive you to drink, anyway.

"I was there when she got back," I said, keeping my voice level with an effort. Sweat trickled down my ribs. I wiped more off my upper lip. "I told her I thought I'd have to go and get her. And she said I don't have enough darkness."

Gilbert made a furious gesture. "You would trust the word of a witch, a devil-worshipper?"

"She's not a devil-worshipper," I retorted, angrily, at the same time as Laparelli said "Who would know better?"

"Silence, all of you," ordered Marcado in a voice like a thunderclap. He turned to Gilbert. "I think more of the man on trial here, maître Gilbert, for defending her at his own risk, than I do of you at this moment. A prosecutor should not allow his feelings to govern him as you are doing. Da Silva, the woman spoke the truth, but our concern is not your present condition but your potential value to our enemies. Men can change, it is part of being human. Part of the burden of free will that comes with mortality."

Free will? "It's not a burden," I said. "Having it taken away, that's when things get hard to stand."

A wintry smile came to his face. I stared back. That means nothing good. Or I really am João the Pious.

"We find the case not proven either way," he decided, and banged his gavel on the desk. "Therefore we will move for trial by combat."

"What?" I shouted, forgetting caution. Laparelli and Gilbert got to their feet and came down from the bench. They keep doing this to me. Changing the bloody rules.

"You may walk away," Marcado told me. "But if you shirk the trial, we will bar you from these islands."

I gripped the rail, and bared my teeth at him. I'll give him free will. "I'm staying, you bastard," I said grimly. Bring 'em all on. All right, da Silva has gone mad. *What the hell am I doing?*

"Let our champion stand," ordered Marcado, and a knight got to his feet somewhere on my left. I turned and looked at him, and started to laugh. Somewhere deep inside, my own laughter scared me.

He wasn't the tallest man in the hall, but he had four inches on me. Like all the knights he'd been constructed out of solid muscle. Unlike the rest of them, though, he was alive. Possibly German, his blond hair suggested.

"I am Joachim Schneider," he announced, confirming it, and bowed. I just stared at him, still shaken by laughter.

"The contest is unfair," said Laparelli's voice from behind me. I turned my head. "You have to challenge," he added in an undertone. And why am I surprised no one told me that? He addressed the bench. "The contestants should be equal in arms."

Marcado nodded to Schneider, who handed his sword to a man beside him and stripped off his mail. Handed it to the man and took the weapon back. Laparelli held out his own sword to me. I looked at it blankly. I know next to nothing about what to do with it. I'll probably need both hands just to lift it, and I'm not a weakling.

"Take it," Marcado instructed me. I wrapped my left hand round the hilt. There was room for my right as well. I lifted the blade. It wasn't as heavy as I expected, and very well-balanced. Sweat slid down my face.

"There is still inequality," observed Laparelli. Yes. This Schneider knows what he's doing, and I don't. Marcado inclined his head again at the German.

Who handed his sword back to the man holding his armor, put his hand to his face, and gouged out his own left eye.

"Merda," I whispered incredulously, and Schneider seized back his sword and came at me.

16

DIVERTING YOUR OPPONENT'S ATTENTION IS ALWAYS A GOOD IDEA IN A FIGHT. All right, consider mine diverted. I couldn't stop looking at his bloody, empty eyesocket. And it didn't even seem to slow him down. He came barreling at me, swung the sword in a roundhouse sweep that I managed to parry, sending out a shower of sparks and a noise like a hammer on an anvil. The impact jarred both my arms right up to my shoulders. The bastard's as strong as he looks. Unfortunately. Because that's all he needs. There's no finesse about fighting with these things. All you have to do is keep on whacking until you wear your opponent down.

I dodged his next effort, ducking under the swinging blade and damn nearly getting a shave into the bargain, used my own momentum to swipe the sword I held in his direction. He parried it easily, and I staggered back with the force of the blow, trying to blink sweat out of my eye. I was already getting short of breath. This bloody blade weighs about a ton now.

And then someone shouted "Stop." It was a voice I know. Schneider whirled, blade whipping round, an inch from cutting my arm off. I backed out of range hastily, something blurred between me and the knight, and John Yeoh stood in front of him with his arm outstretched. The knight put up his sword and turned his blood-streaked face to Marcado.

Still wary, I let the point of the blade I was holding droop to the ground. One of the knights handed Schneider a cloth. He took it without a word and held it to his head. It reddened quickly. I looked away, wincing.

"Meu Deus," I said to Yeoh, wiping sweat off my face with my sleeve, "am I glad to see you."

He looked round at the ranks of knights, a little bemused, but addressed Marcado confidently. "Do your rules not permit the challenged party to appoint a champion?"

"Yeoh—" He shook his head slightly.

"That is correct." The arbiter looked at me. "Is this your wish, da Silva?"

Before I could answer, Yeoh said, "My captain does not have the resources to beat your champion." He smiled. "But I do."

Which is true. He can move in and out of time. So when the blade or the club or the bullet reaches him, he's not there. Plus he has some very fancy footwork.

"And who are you?" Marcado asked.

"Some call me the Faithful Dog," Yeoh replied with a thin smile. And a flutter of sound rushed round the hall, like mice in a basement.

"You did not mention the dog," muttered Laparelli, at my shoulder. I scratched my scar, watching Schneider. I know how much that had to hurt. He hadn't even made a sound.

"You didn't give me much chance," I said, mildly enough.

Marcado banged his gavel on the desk. All the knights turned to look at him. "The dog has shown his loyalty. The prophecy is fulfilled. Give him the dish."

Well, I hope getting the other hallows is that easy. Relatively speaking, of course. Can't say I cared much for my part in it.

*   *   *

"You mean all you needed to do was *ask* for it?" exclaimed Tatiana Dimitrovna, blinking in disbelief.

"Well, no, it was a *little* more complicated than that," I said, taking a deep breath of smoke on board. It was Yeoh's offer to stand in for me that did the trick. The dog had been true to his nature. Faithful to — his master.

That's the part that worries me. I'm not his master, not in that sense. At least I really hope I'm not.

"I think you are reading too much into it," the witch remarked. "These are all your people, your crew, your friends. We are loyal to you, but not because of any obligation. Because we want to. You're the captain — the paladin. That's what it all boils down to. A leader worth following."

Normally this kind of talk makes me uncomfortable. But it was soothing to the soul after Valette and then the tribunal sitting there implying I'm not worthy of anything. That's the trouble with people like that. The ones who see only black and white. They won't give you credit for anything. My mother was like that. Apart from the sitting-in-spectral-judgment part, of course.

"One thing's certain," I said. Tapped ash in the direction of the ashtray, and missed. On my new desk, too.

"What's that?" she asked.

"The next one won't be anything like this." I swept the ash off the desk into my palm, and tipped it into the ashtray.

She gave me a twisted smile. "Take that as a given," said Tatiana Dimitrovna, whose task it was.

* * *

Teresa Batista hefted the iron sword in her hand. She had used it before, but had no conscious memory of the event. Her hand remembered it, though. A brutal tool.

"Cold iron," she said thoughtfully, turning it this way and that so that the sunlight caught it. It didn't gleam, as Emilia had noted before, not in the same way as Luís's knife did, but somehow absorbed the yellow light, flattened it, and reflected it back sullenly, like water under a gray sky. "An older magic than silver."

"Older?" questioned Emilia, thinking of ancient coins and jewelry.

"Cruder, then," Teresa amended. She held the sword at arm's length, her other hand on her hip, perfectly balanced. Despite having changed into a conventional skirt and blouse, the pose looked natural. Competent. Confident. "How are we going to do this?"

Emilia stared out of the window, feeling Teresa's eagerness, her own doubt. "I don't know," she said. "I suppose I was hoping you'd have some suggestions."

"Ah," replied Teresa. She bent her elbow, bringing the blade upright in front of her face like a salute, then dropped her arm so that the point was towards the floor. "Then I suggest we involve Luzia. She'll be teaching a class this afternoon."

An army of women, thought Emilia. Well, why not? When the men are off to war, it's the women who have to keep things going. Why shouldn't we fight back? But Luzia is very young. And her mother is Emilia's friend.

Not that that would be any reason for Paciência not to turn her into a toad, if anything happened to Luzia.

"Isn't she a bit young?"

Teresa shook her head. "Luzia may be young, but she's very powerful. And she's smart, too." She sat down, and put the *gladius* across her lap. The blade that had killed Malphas, Mouffi's progenitor.

From the corner Julia, who had been silent until now, looking as out-of-place in the little room as the leopard she had once been (too bright, too dark), snorted and said, "You making things too complicated."

Both the others looked enquiringly at her. She flashed her white teeth in a smile that was just a little bit too feral to be friendly, and picked up a packet of cigarettes from the table beside her. "Simple," she repeated. "All you need, a little bait."

I don't think I'm going to like this, thought Emilia, watching her take out a cigarette with her long thin fingers — claws had extruded from them, she'd seen it — and light it. "And what's the bait?"

Julia didn't reply immediately, and a clock ticked into the silence. Then she blew a smoke-ring, contemplated her cigarette with satisfaction, and said, "What this thing want. A better home than that great ugly monster it got now." She looked slyly at Teresa. "Body like yours, maybe." Emilia raised her eyebrows in surprise.

Of course Julia had no way of knowing how much Teresa hated the idea of letting demons in. Or anywhere near her. Her father had summoned them as casually as picking up the telephone, (more readily than Luís picks up a telephone, thought Emilia with an inward smile), and each one contacted had left a foul deposit on his soul like a snail's track until there wasn't much of Francisco Domingues Batista left, by the time she killed him. Teresa swallowed, and stroked the blade on her lap.

"I still think it'd be a good idea to have a witch around. For insurance."

"Witch can be more liability than asset," Julia argued. "Unless she got enormous power." She blew another smoke-ring.

"Does Luzia have that kind of power?" asked Emilia.

"She will," said Teresa, still apparently concentrating on the sword. "Remember, I lived with a sorcerer for—" *Too long,* Emilia caught the thought like a shout "—many years. I know how it feels, like rock heated by the sun until it's too hot to touch. My father was powerful. But Luzia — Luzia feels like molten metal in a furnace."

"You don't need to do it if you don't want to, Teresa," Emilia pointed out. "It's hanging round Inspector Corvo while he's asleep." The wounded man's awful pallor came into her mind. "Poor man."

"No," said Teresa, picturing the same thing, "we have to get it away from him." Her face was grim. "He's not strong enough to resist for long." She raised the gladius thoughtfully a few inches off her lap. Emilia saw her knuckles whiten for an instant. "It'll come to me. It'll recognize my father's blood."

Let's just hope that Belphegor doesn't decide to tag along for the ride as well, then, thought Emilia. Her fingers went to her breast, and she touched the mark, the Key of Solomon, through her blouse and wondered whether that could be put to use. She would have to ask Luzia. Oh, she thought, I must have agreed to involving her, then. I wonder when that happened?

"What you going to do, then?" Julia enquired, and took another long drag on her cigarette. "You got a plan yet?"

"Sort of," Emilia answered slowly, formulating her ideas as she spoke. "Let's assume that Mouffi will be lurking somewhere near the orphanage tonight. Teresa. If you attract its attention somehow—"

"Blood," said Teresa succinctly.

"Oh. Yes. While it's distracted Julia will have a chance to attack it, pin it down perhaps." She bit her lip. "It's very big. If it's too much for the two of you, Luzia might be able to weaken it or something."

But Teresa was shaking her head. "No, you've got it back to front. We should get Luzia to put a spell on it first. That way we might actually stand a chance of killing it."

This seemed like cheating to Emilia, but she knew enough about demons by now to realize that cheating was a *good* idea.

"Killing the body won't kill Mouffi, though," she pointed out.

"It sure put a crimp in its prowling," Julia observed, which made Emilia laugh. It sounded like the sort of thing Harris would say. Perhaps shape-shifters all have the same sense of humor, who knows?

"Let's do it," said Teresa. "I'll have a chat with Luzia after her class."

* * *

The Fisher King is dying. He has been dying for a long time. In his case the wound is nothing visible, but a cancer that is slowly spreading through him.

He has lived on this sunny island for many years, ever since the pain became too much to bear without the healing power of the chalice. Some might say he is neglecting his duties, but what are the duties of the *roi pêcheur*, wounded king, *roi mehaigné*, save to be wounded? The infirmity defines him, without it he would simply be an old man on a mountain.

A question he has asked a thousand times is, *Can the king be cured and still retain his kingship? Can the land of which he is the symbol and more than the symbol ever be cured, ever know peace and harmony?* He thinks it is doubtful. The British administration has subdued this island, as it had throughout the pink-mapped world, but below the surface of all those places tribal and nationalistic and religious differences fester, ready to burst out again.

You can paint over the cracks with so-called civilization, he thought, but if the foundations are rotten the edifice will fall down sooner or later.

As an Englishman he believes that the British Empire is a good and benevolent thing, indeed he spent many years of his previous life fighting to maintain it, but the longer perspective of the Fisher King sees it as something temporary, because good intentions never make much difference in the long run.

This morning the pain is bearable, and so though the air is chilly he takes a chair out to sit in the sun. There will not be many more days to enjoy the sensations of sun and wind on his face, the resiny scent of the pine trees, or the view from his eyrie. Small pleasures, all, but the only ones left to him, now. He catches sight of his hands with a start of horror, their aged appearance always catches him unawares, these thin wrinkled gloves of bones.

Major-General Sir Douglas Scott tucks the unpleasant things under the blanket on his lap and closes his eyes. Soon he is dozing in the bright winter sunlight, his breathing harsh even in sleep, as if each breath is drawn in pain, a thin aged man with a deeply lined face.

It was there that Nikos found him. Nikos is not his real name, but the guardian of the chalice chooses to wear the appearance, and the none-too-well-cured sheepskin vest, of a Greek peasant, and the Fisher King is content to indulge him.

Nikos hated to wake the old man, but the news couldn't wait. He touched him gently on the shoulder with one huge hand, and Scott awoke with a ragged indrawn breath, opening his pale blue eyes abruptly. "Nikos?"

"I'm sorry to wake you," he murmured, patting his arm. "But there is something you should know."

The old soldier fumbled for his spectacles, and put them on, blinking at Nikos. "What might that be?"

"A new king has been chosen."

Scott exhaled, but it was a sound of relief rather than otherwise,

"Finally," he sighed, and managed a smile. Then noticed the other's expression. "What is it, Nikos?"

"The king is coming here," Nikos told him.

"And?" Nikos's face was strained. But the news had to be told.

"And so is a usurper, my liege," he said, with a grimace. "The signs of their opposition are — not good."

The information was of little significance to a dying man, Sir Douglas Scott thought. But to the present king, in whose metaphysical charge a large part of the world lay, it was just another thing to worry about.

* * *

And heading towards that island, Aphrodite's birthplace, Ophioussa, though its reputation for being snake-infested was little deserved, the subject of this concern in a comfortable cabin aboard the most modern passenger vessel he can find.

Not for Sir Robert Munro — whose title, unlike Scott's, he has done nothing to earn — the cold sea air and the salt spray. He has no intention of leaving his luxurious berth for the duration of the voyage. There are stewards to bring him food and wine, and as for passing the time, well, he has plans for that as well.

Though unable to travel by a faster route, by no means all his powers have been stripped from him. He gave no second thought to a charm against seasickness, which is more difficult than it sounds, having to do with equilibrium and not merely nausea.

Now he poured himself a glass of champagne and regarded the demon imprisoned inside a pentagram on the cabin floor. It had once been his familiar. Now it glared at him balefully, giving off a sulphur stink of fear.

"She sent you to spy on me," observed Munro, pleasantly. He found this highly amusing. "But I could use you to do the same." Not that he really cared any more what da Silva and his merry men — and women — were up to.

The demon was in its natural form, or perhaps natural is not quite the right word to use here: it wore the shape it returned to when not appearing in a guise not its own. It was about the size of a large dog, vaguely man-shaped, and blue. One of its arms appeared to be broken, and it was cradling it in the crook of the other. At some stage it had fouled itself, and a yellowish-green stain tracked down its legs. It was also incredibly ugly, with warty skin and upward-pointing tusks protruding between its lips. But its eyes looked human, and they were fearful.

"I am not your familiar any more," it quavered. Munro burst out laughing.

"As if that makes a difference!" He sipped from his glass. "I know your name, you stupid creature."

Hunched over its wounded arm, the demon cowered. "Master —"

"Oh, shut up," Munro told it. "You're only here so you don't go blabbing to the witch. Not that you can tell her anything."

"I won't tell," it whimpered, attempting obsequiousness. The baronet picked up a silver-headed cane from the floor and casually smacked it against the side of the creature's head, where it left an angry-looking welt. A tear trickled out of one of its eyes, but it made no sound.

"I told you to be quiet," snapped the baronet. "You have two choices, quiet or dead. Take your pick."

It looked at him, and put a claw to its lips. The gesture was so reminiscent of one of his late wife's that Munro started to laugh again.

*   *   *

This may sound an odd thing for me to say. But I wanted to get back on dry land again. Or perhaps I mean on solid ground. After a passage on seas not of this world, and wherever the hell the knights' court was, I need a good strong shot of reality.

So I went ashore and walked away from the clamor and bustle of the docks up through the fortifications of Valletta. Ghosts clustering round the bastions. Thin, transparent things. In a way I was glad to see them. They belong to the normal world. They're the familiar kind of shades I've learnt to live with these last five years. Not the terrible solidity of Trafalgar's phantoms, or the vengeful implacable knights.

According to Pierce, all these bastions and ramparts and fortifications I don't even know the names of were built after the siege. Seems a pretty prime example of shutting the stable door after the horse has buggered off, if you ask me.

Good place to get a bit of peace and quiet, though. I made my way to the top, which tested my wind a bit. But the view was quite spectacular, if you like that sort of thing. I suppose I do. I sat and smoked and looked at it for a few minutes, thinking of nothing at all.

And then I realized there was someone sitting next to me. *Good work, da Silva. Away with the fairies again.*

I turned to see that it was a girl of about fifteen. Or something that looked like one. What a surprise. I sighed. This is all I need just now.

"Belphegor," I said, resignedly.

The demon smiled, and it could've been one of Dr Bosque's charges, or any girl you'd pass in the street. Bright brown eyes. Dark curly hair. Fresh complexion. And so on.

"The knights don't think very much of you, do they?" it asked. I raised an eyebrow at it, and rubbed the scar on my cheekbone with my thumb. "Did it make you angry?"

"What do you think?" I retorted. Its smile grew broader.

"You should expect it," Belphegor said, smoothing the skirt in its lap just like a real girl. "They don't like you refusing to toe the line. People like that think that no one who doesn't share their faith can be any good."

"I know." I blew smoke at it. Unfortunately demons don't melt away at the smell of tobacco. "Don't much care what they think."

"Oh, now that's a fib," the demon chuckled, wagging a finger at me. "They hurt your feelings, didn't they? Apart from nearly cutting your head off," it added. I glared angrily at it, and it shrugged its shoulders. "What, I can't be right just because of what I am? You're thinking just like the knights."

"And I suppose you're really misunderstood and maligned and just want people to like you?" I said sarcastically. Belphegor laughed.

"I like you," it remarked. "I really wish we were on the same side, Luís da Silva." I eyed it sourly, and pointed my cheroot at it.

"What are you doing here, Belphegor?"

"Tsk." It put its head on one side. Coquettishly. Meu Deus. "You know perfectly well. I offered you my aid back in Lisbon. I don't give up so easily."

"You're wasting your time." I finished off my cheroot, and dropped the butt on the ground. Crushed it with my toe.

"Can't blame me for trying," said Belphegor cheerfully. "If you change your mind, you know what to do."

"I am not," I told it firmly, "going to change my mind."

It got to its feet. "Men can change." Looked down at me with a strange expression on its face. "It's part of being human."

Which is almost exactly what Garcia Marcado said to me at the tribunal.

What the hell am I supposed to make of that?

*   *   *

Tatiana Dimitrovna also went ashore, but she wandered along the quayside, idly trying to make order out of chaos. Big modern ships, creations of the new age of steam, jostled for space with sailing vessels like *Isabella* and brightly-colored fishing boats, each with a pair of painted eyes on its prow. She paused to watch one of these little craft come in, back from an early-morning trip with its glistening cargo, surrounded by a crowd of brawling seagulls.

After a moment she felt eyes on her, and turned to see an ancient woman clad in severe black watching her intently. Her face, framed by a headscarf that turned her into a Mohammedan woman, was wrinkled up like a ball of crumpled paper. She looked about two hundred years old. But her eyes were black and bright and shrewd.

The witch knew that most Maltese spoke English as well as their own strange Arabic-sounding tongue, so she asked politely, "Can I help you, little mother?", the Russian-style diminutive slipping out quite involuntarily.

"Tanit, you are Tanit," said the old woman in a soft lilting voice. Tatiana Dimitrovna's heart gave a great thump.

"What?" she whispered. "Little mother, what did you say?" But the crone put a finger to her thin lips.

"Hush." She pushed back her sleeve and showed the witch the symbol tattooed there. A triangle surmounted by a circle, with a horizontal line between them, and from each end of this bar, a small vertical line pointing upward. "Some of us still worship the old gods." With a secret smile, she checked that Tatiana Dimitrovna had seen the sign, then covered it up once more, patting her wrist carefully to make sure her sleeve was back in place. "Serpent Lady."

Afraid she was about to curtsey or something equally embarrassing, the witch seized her elbow and muttered a quick spell of *look-over-there*.

"I'm not—" she began. But the ancient woman smiled knowingly. Tatiana Dimitrovna checked herself with a grimace. "Not yet," she amended.

"You are the mother," insisted her accoster.

The Russian witch narrowed her eyes at this. Maternal was one thing she'd never felt. Would never feel. "No."

"Accept the sacrifice," the old woman went on, relentlessly. "The sacrifice of the firstborn." She pulled away from Tatiana's suddenly relaxed grip. Relaxed in shock. And walked away swiftly, leaving the witch staring after her, angry and apprehensive.

Whatever that was about, she thought furiously, I'll have no part of it. She'd done many selfish things during her life, but oddly enough her trip to hell seemed to have excised a good deal of that egotism. Or maybe the increase of her powers had done that.

An uncomfortable part of her, however, wondered if she had any choice. And she fought that down as well, understanding at last da Silva's revulsion at being forced down a certain route against his will.

*   *   *

No reason to linger on Malta, then. In fact, every reason to get the hell out of the place as soon as possible. Just in case the knights have any more nasty schemes up their sleeves.

Isabella was sailing on the noon tide, and I went in search of the witch. I presume we'll have to do the same thing as we went through with the *Alcântara*. I can live without that, frankly.

I found Tatiana Dimitrovna talking to Zacuto. Pierce, presumably, was below decks feeling sorry for himself. The sea was a little choppy, the wind strong and veering southeast. The Russian witch looked preoccupied. I was feeling rather more cheerful, myself. We had, after all, retrieved the first of the hallows. It's not much to look at, just a plain silver dish, a little battered. Nothing magical about it, according to Zacuto. At least not yet. And I'm happier to be out in the open sea again with no chance of bumping into the Flying Dutchman or the ship made from dead men's nails. Until we cross over again, of course.

Zacuto spotted me first. "Captain da Silva." He seems unhappy too. Is it only me? I looked from one to the other of them, and scratched at my eyebrow. The scar was itching. Strange. It doesn't do that much, these days.

"What's the matter?" I asked. But the ghost simply turned his head to Tatiana Dimitrovna. She was bare-headed, and the wind whipped stray hairs about her face.

"I'm not sure." She brushed ineffectually at the hair. "It's probably not significant." Bite your tongue, woman.

"We know Tanit was worshipped in Malta and Sicily as well as Carthage," Zacuto broke in impatiently, apparently continuing a conversation I hadn't been in on. "The influence could have *leaked* across somehow—"

"A woman on the quayside called me Tanit," she interrupted, putting a hand on my arm. I stared at her in surprise. "She said I was the mother. And she told me to accept the sacrifice of the firstborn."

"Firstborn?" I echoed, thinking of Zé. "What—"

"Her worshipers practised child sacrifice," added Zacuto, as if it needed explanation. I turned to him.

"Yes, thank you, I got that." I took a deep breath. "What — what age?"

Tatiana Dimitrovna squeezed my arm. "Very young children. Babies. Don't worry about your boy, Luís. He's practically grown-up."

I gave a rather twisted smile. Da Silva is getting pretty damned predictable these days. Must be my age. And of course she's right about Zé. "What about Susana, then?"

Zacuto didn't reply at once. He stared out to sea, looking at the waves growing little tips of white. "She is the king," he said at last. As if that's a reason.

"It worries me," the witch blurted out with surprising frankness. "Surely each of these... quests should be self-contained." She took her hand from my arm, and thumped her fist hard and angrily on the rail.

"We do not know that," sighed Zacuto. "Maybe one leads thus to the next. We do not know much about any of the artifacts, who guards them, how to retrieve them."

Make that, we don't know *anything*.

Tatiana Dimitrovna said harshly, "I don't relish being the avatar of a goddess that people sacrificed children to." I raised an eyebrow at Zacuto. Nicely qualified, Tatiana. I bet she didn't even notice the emphasis.

Patting pockets in search of my smokes, a thought struck me. Something I remembered. "Sr. Zacuto."

"Senhor capitão?"

"You told me that the way we see the Fisher King depends on whether we see the fishing or the kingship as more important." I found my cheroots, and took one out.

"Indeed," he replied. "Or even the wounding, which appeared to hold the key in the case of the man Munro." The witch frowned.

"Your point being?" she asked, with some asperity. Quite understandable, as this must sound like one of Pierce and Zacuto's academic chats. I shielded a match from the wind. Lit my cheroot. Threw the spent match over the side.

"Well," I said, "perhaps in this case it depends on whether we see the goddess or the sword as more important."

She thought about this, and her face cleared. "I see," she said finally. "Yes, I take your point. Or maybe which aspect of the goddess I choose to accept."

"Argued like a metaphysicist," murmured Zacuto, with a smile. I glared at him.

The witch shook herself, and drew a deep breath. "Were you looking for me, Luís?" she asked briskly.

"Yes, I was." I took a drag on my cheroot, and blew smoke out. The wind whipped it away. "When do we need to start looking for ghost-ships?" *I*, when do *I* need, don't mince words, da Silva. Tatiana Dimitrovna gave me a blank look.

"What?" Then she laughed, but a bit grimly. "Luís, how far is Carth—Tunis?"

I rubbed the back of my neck. "About two hundred miles, why?"

"Then you may like to consider traveling by the seas you know rather than spending a day, a night, and a day in the other realm."

Ah. Yes. Damn.

But on the other hand, what a relief.

Isabella made landfall the following morning. There's been a ship-canal open for around ten years now that takes you right to the city of Tunis. You can still dock at Goletta, the old port, but Tunis is about ten miles nearer to ancient Carthage. All right, there's a tram. You want to travel ten miles on a tram? I don't. Bad enough that I'll probably have to get on a horse to get to the site of Carthage. Or, God forbid, a camel. I rode a camel last year for the first time in my life. And, I hope, the last.

I've given this expedition some thought. Came to the conclusion that it'd better be just me and the witch. Much as I'd like to take Harris, those remarks about leakage worry me a little. Besides, it's his watch.

The weather was cloudy and mild. Looked a little like rain. I wasted some time and money in discussions with port authorities. All right, that's a euphemism. I haggled. In a mixture of French and Arabic. The officials, like petty bureaucrats everywhere, like to suck up to their bosses so they insist on talking French. Which might be comprehensible if only you could penetrate the accent. It's like trying to understand a Glaswegian talking English. And my French isn't that good in the first place. Still, money is a pretty universal language. I even managed to beat them down a bit on the bribes I had to pay.

Those crew not on watch headed for the souks, or so they pretended. I changed into mufti. I'm not entirely sure why. Left *Isabella* in Harris's capable hands, or should that be paws? And shouldered through the sea of beggars demanding baksheesh, hawkers brandishing cheap trinkets and boys thrusting dirty pictures in my face. Tatiana Dimitrovna followed me, fending them off with her umbrella, which made me smile. Thinking fleetingly of another woman, another umbrella.

Luckily I was spared having to ride any kind of animal, and I should think she was as pleased as I was. I don't know if you can ride a camel side-saddle. Though knowing her she'd hike up her skirt and sit astride. I put the image of Tatiana hiking up her skirt out of my mind. There were more kinds of conveyance for hire than you'd ever need, ranging from carts harnessed to donkeys with open sores on their flanks to carriages and even motor-cars. Though looking up towards the hill where Carthage had once stood, I doubted whether an automobile could make it. Mind you, I had my doubts about those donkeys, as well.

I asked the witch, who looked a bit ruefully down at her smart costume. Don't know why. She can charm her clothes clean, after all. Anyway she opted for a pony-trap driven by a wizened but dapper little man who came up to my chest. I know it's vanity, but I enjoy places where I feel tall. So I haggled with the top of his fez for a while until we came up with a mutually satisfactory figure. He handed Tatiana Dimitrovna politely on board, still complaining that fares like that would drive him out of business and force his children to beg in the streets.

It was a longish drive. And I'd given away the fact that I speak Arabic.

So the driver kept up a non-stop monologue interspersed from time to time with rapid questions to make sure I was still listening. All the way.

"I think my ears are worn out," I muttered to the witch as he drove off.

Pierce had warned me that the place would probably be teeming with archeologists. It wasn't. It was teeming with ghosts. There weren't many people there at all. The shades were another matter. There must've been hundreds of the damn things. And a lot of 'em had obviously died when the city was sacked.

Of real relics from the past, there wasn't much to see. Broken columns. Bits of statues. Heaps of stones. How the fellows digging this lot up know what it all is, is beyond me. Practice, I suppose. After all, an archaeologist probably doesn't know one end of a sextant from the other. The last one I met probably didn't know one end of a *ship* from the other.

But to me this place looks like piles of rubbish overgrown by cactus and scrub, with the odd aloe spike sticking up for variety. I set out across the dusty packed earth.

"Where are you going?" Tatiana Dimitrovna asked me.

"Away from the ghosts," I said shortly. There were too many of them. Wears me down, after a while. I walked away, heading for the edge, leaving the dig behind. Heading for a less populated bit, if there is one. Heard the witch following me. A clatter of stones and a mumbled French curse. I smiled to myself. Cursing in French, now *that* I can do.

At last I found a place where the ghosts of destroyed Carthage clustered less thickly, and found a piece of shattered column to sit down and have a smoke. I sat looking at the view and enjoying the taste of the cheroot for a few minutes. I was sweating slightly, although the air probably wasn't any more than fifty degrees. Damp under the arms but not hot enough for the eyepatch to be uncomfortable. I leant forward, elbows on knees. A position that eased my back a bit. My bruises were making their presence felt. Obviously they'd decided I wasn't paying them enough attention. I finished my cheroot and dropped the end onto the dusty ground.

After a while Tatiana Dimitrovna sat down next to me. The stone I was sitting on wasn't that large, and so her leg was touching mine.

"You're warm," I remarked, idly. She sighed. I turned my head to look at her, and suddenly found myself out of breath.

The witch had taken off her hat, and was fanning herself with it. Her face was flushed, her lips parted, and her hair was coming loose from its pins. She met my gaze quite expressionlessly. Tucked a strand back behind her ear. For a moment I couldn't move. I could hear the blood thundering in my ears, could feel it rushing—

Tatiana Dimitrovna put her left hand on my thigh. Turned my face to hers with her right. I tangled my fingers in her hair and kissed her, felt her mouth open and her tongue, and stopped thinking.

The kiss went on for a long time. Then I felt her change. It didn't matter. My hands moving from her hair encountered bared shoulders, fine thin fabric, a nipple rising hard into my palm. She pulled me off the column, and we tumbled to the ground, panting. Rolled a couple of times. If my back complained, I didn't notice. Ended up with Tanit on top of me, the gown rumpled up round her waist, and I don't think I could've stopped then if I'd wanted to.

Except that Punic goddesses don't have any experience of undoing buttons. We lost a bit of momentum while she fumbled, and I thought *hallows* and then *Emilia*, and pushed her away roughly. *"Merda,"* I muttered. It didn't begin to cover it.

"What's wrong?" she whispered.

I got onto my knees. Pushed myself back to sit on the broken column, breathing heavily and damned uncomfortable. A moment later, a hand on my shoulder. I tensed. Cursed silently. Didn't look round.

"Tatiana—" It came out less forceful than I'd hoped.

"Luís," she said, and it was the witch's voice. "Luís, look." I turned, apprehensive. But it was Tatiana, thank God. A bit disheveled and holding a sword-hilt in her right hand. The blade was snapped off three inches from the guard. In her left she had a plain leather scabbard, presumably containing the remainder of the weapon.

A broken sword. *Oh bloody hell. How's that for symbolism, then, da Silva, you idiot?*

* * *

In the event, of course, nothing ever goes exactly as planned. Emilia, walking-stick in one hand, Luzia's arm supporting the other, peers round a corner to see the big ugly Mouffi-woman keeping vigil in deep shadow at the side of the orphanage, quite oblivious to the quartet of watchers. She could also see that Luzia's face was shiny with sweat at the effort of her spell. But it was working splendidly. Mouffi seems completely unaware of their presence.

And then a voice breathed "What are you doing?" in her ear, and she stifled a startled squeak with an effort. Her stick jerked across the cobbles, but luckily it has a rubber tip and makes no sound. Luzia's hand tightened on her arm.

"Sílvia," she whispered back furiously, "you nearly gave me a heart attack."

"Sorry. Are you going after that thing, then?"

"Ssh!" hissed Luzia furiously, and Sílvia subsided, finger to her lips.

Mouffi's head swiveled round. And round. Until it was facing backwards over the shoulders of the body it wore. Emilia moved back, and slipped. Sílvia caught her other arm, but the walking-stick skidded out of her grasp and clattered to the ground. They all froze, holding their breath. Emilia could see the whites of the girl's eyes all round her pupils. After a moment the demon-fragment brought its body's attention back to the window it had been watching.

"Did you *see* that?" demanded Sílvia in a tiny incredulous whisper. "Her *head*—"

Teresa clamped a hand over her mouth, but it was too late. Mouffi turned from the window, and Luzia gave a low moan of pain as her spell shattered abruptly. She fell to her knees, dragging Emilia down with her, who banged her hip painfully on the cobblestones.

At the same moment Julia sprang at Mouffi. The chiaroscuro of the waning moon strobed her leopard-like, and her momentum sent Mouffi crashing to the ground. Teresa let go of Sílvia and flung herself into the fray, sword raised.

Biting her lip to stop herself from swearing, Emilia crawled to Luzia. Sílvia had the young witch's head in her lap and was wiping the blood trickling from her nose with a handkerchief. Emilia nodded, though no one was looking at her, and groped for her stick. On her feet she'd feel a bit more in control.

Julia and Mouffi rolled on the ground, Julia — Emilia presumed — doing the snarling. She was trying to get a hold on Mouffi's throat. Teresa bounced round, unable to get in a blow without impaling Julia.

Watching them, Emilia found her stick by feel and hauled herself to her feet. Her bruised hip sent a stab of agony through her. It was the left one. Now she'd have to use the damned crutches for a few days, with both sides out of commission.

"What an interesting spectacle," said a voice from beside her, and she whirled with a start.

To see herself.

"*Porca madonna*," she breathed, reverting to her native language in shock. "You must be Belphegor." She leant against the wall and tightened her grip on her walking-stick, clamping down her extra sense firmly. She did *not* want to read this creature's thoughts, even supposing that was possible.

The demon smiled. "I mean you no harm," it said, and though Emilia cannot know how she sounds to others, we all sound more substantial inside our own heads, she knows it is exactly like her voice.

She crossed herself, more in reflex than anything. "You—"

"Contrary to popular belief," Belphegor remarked acidly, "we do not crumble to dust at humans' holy signs."

Teresa, unable to find an opening, turned at the sound of two identical voices, and stared in shock. *"Bosta,"* she exclaimed. "Sra. da Silva?"

Emilia raised her eyebrows. "I think you might call me Emilia," she said drily. "That's Belphegor."

"No, I'm not," the demon protested indignantly, in her voice, and pointed at Emilia. "That's the demon. Kill it while you have the chance!" Teresa looked from one to the other, uncertain, gladius drooping slightly in her hand.

"Never mind that now!" shouted Emilia to her. "Help Julia."

She and Teresa both stared at the brawling heap that was Julia and Mouffi.

"How?" asked Teresa, reasonably enough.

Sílvia looked up from Luzia, balled a fist, and made a throwing motion at the combatants. There was an explosion like a firework, complete with yellow and orange sparks, and the two flew apart, Mouffi slamming into the wall, Julia merely staggering backwards. A strong smell of ozone filled the air.

With a feral smile, Teresa pivoted gracefully and cut off Mouffi's head.

And Emilia pulled the flask of holy water out of her pocket, tugged the cork out, and flung the contents in Belphegor's face.

The demon yowled with pain and covered its steaming features with its hands. It was sizzling like hot oil in a frying-pan.

"Not impressed by holy things?" panted Emilia, heart pounding fiercely in reaction. "How did you like that one?"

Belphegor started to grow in stature, and removed its hands from its face. It still looked like a woman, though any resemblance to Emilia was gone, she was relieved to see. But the skin was blistered and peeling, the eyes like hot coals.

Yelling some kind of incoherent Brazilian war-cry, Teresa raised the gladius and charged. Julia sprang up from Mouffi's body, snarling. Luzia and Sílvia, standing hand-in-hand, raised their outer palms towards the demon, and Emilia, supporting herself against the wall, raised her walking-stick threateningly.

Faced with this army, Belphegor apparently decided that discretion was the better part of valor. *"Bagasci,"* it spat, which only Emilia understood. And turned tail.

"By God," Teresa said, looking after it somewhat incredulously, "we did it." She walked back and stared down at the decapitated corpse. "I thought these things were supposed to dissolve when they're dead."

"It must be too — too solid," guessed Emilia, wondering vaguely why the sight of a headless body wasn't turning her sick. "It was sort of alive before Mouffi went into it. But it's just what we want, isn't it?"

"How so?" Julia asked roughly, yellow eyes gleaming, leopard still leaking out of her aura. Even if she couldn't change completely, she came pretty close, Emilia thought.

"Well, it did kill all those people." She leaned on her stick, feeling suddenly tired. Her bruised hip throbbed. "Now they can write 'case closed' or whatever they do on the file. Whoever's taken over from Inspector Corvo."

"Someone ought to fetch the police, then," Luzia pointed out. The girls weren't upset, either. Strange.

"Don't look at me," said Julia, shrugging her shoulders. "They going to want to know who chopped off its head."

Luzia started to cough, and Sílvia patted her hand, looking worried. "Are you all right?" Emilia asked, and the young witch nodded.

"I'll have hell's own headache, though," she said ruefully.

Teresa wrapped the gladius up in the piece of canvas they'd used to conceal it on the streets, and handed it back to Emilia. "I'll get the police. You'd better hide that away somewhere." She blinked, apparently realising how abrupt she sounded. "If you don't mind," she added, and Emilia nodded with a smile.

"I'm sure I can find a home for it," she murmured. "Now we'd better get out of here, don't you think?"

*   *   *

Zacuto pursed his lips together. His dark eyes were twinkling. Somewhere in the undergrowth, I'm sure he's struggling not to smile.

I don't think it's very funny. Nor does Tatiana Dimitrovna. But the damned ghost seems to find it hilarious.

"Sacred marriage," he said gravely. "Symbolically it could be very significant. Sexual union with the mother goddess—"

"Now just hang on a minute!" I interrupted him, feeling my face heat up. "There wasn't any union." Though it was a pretty close-run thing. I ran a hand through my hair, then rubbed it over my face in embarrassment.

"Well, I wouldn't mind," observed the witch sardonically, "except that I wasn't there, so I didn't even get to enjoy it." She gave me a sidelong look, but her face was white and strained. I guessed that being possessed by the goddess wasn't a great deal of fun. Not much to choose between gods and demons on that score, then.

"Whatever the method," said Zacuto, sternly, bringing us back to the matter in hand, "we now possess two of the hallows. And acquiring both has been relatively easy." All very well for him to say. He wasn't at the sharp end on either occasion. I took out my cheroots, put one in my mouth, and searched for matches.

"D'you think getting the others'll be a problem, then?" I asked around the unlit cheroot. The ghost eyed me unblinkingly.

"I think we ought to be sure we are prepared for trouble."

I raised my eyebrows. You could say I'm always prepared for trouble. I always expect it, anyway. Pessimistic, who, me? I lit the cheroot and stared at the teeming, dirty, noisy spectacle of the docks. The troubles that the sea brings, I can deal with. The other kinds, I'm just never sure about. Although I seem to have coped all right up to now.

Brings a little spice to life, da Silva. Ha. That kind of spice I can do without. Cheerfully.

Isabella is strangely empty. Evidently the souks of Tunis have a greater draw than I thought. For the passengers, I mean. I'm under no illusions that most of the off-duty crew are haggling in a market.

But what the hell. Just because I don't want to go rooting round a labyrinth of filthy back-streets looking at cheap trinkets and getting pawed by hawkers and urchins doesn't mean it's not someone else's idea of an interesting afternoon.

To be honest, I'm not being fair to my father. Just as he did in Malta, the instant we docked he took off with his paints and Alegria. If that's not one and the same thing. He came back with a folder full of watercolors.

Então, Tatiana and I came back with a broken sword.

* * *

Something different about the witch. Goddamned if I can put my finger on it, though, not like she's glowing or anything. So why do think she oughta be?

Harris watched Tatiana Dimitrovna leaning on the rail, fascinated despite himself. The witch, immaculate as usual, had an air of preoccupation, of abstraction, that made her normal aloofness even more remote.

She's probably astral-projecting, down in the deep blue sea with the fishes. He took out his cigarettes, and lit one.

Isabella was waiting for the tide, only. Unlike a normal voyage, there was no cargo to deal with. So Yeoh had the present watch mainly on make-work, maintenance and mucking-out, as far as Harris could see. João had taken a couple of hands with him to the market, ostensibly to take on fresh vegetables. *Least that's what he says,* Harris thought darkly, suspecting the cook of prospecting for the weirder kind of sea-creatures to add to the pot.

But these idle thoughts were just that, idle. *I'm watching the witch 'cause it's my turn next. Jesus, just for Chrissake ask her!*

Tatiana Dimitrovna turned and became aware that Harris was watching her. *She sure is a good-looking woman. Don't blame the skipper one bit for fancying her, not that he'd ever do anything about it.*

He pitched his dog-end over the rail, and walked across to her, touching a finger to his cap. "Ma'am," he said, politely. "Can I ask you something?"

"Of course," she replied with a slight frown, her Russian accent sounding stronger than normal, outlandish.

And she still looks at me like I'm one of the attractions in the menagerie. Well, hellfire, maybe I am at that. "What happened?" he asked, bluntly.

"Nothing," said the witch quickly, coloring. Harris blinked.

"Huh?" *What's that about?* "I mean, how'd you get the sword? Did you turn into—" He stopped. "Sorry," he growled. "I just — Well, it's my turn next, ain't it? I kinda hoped you could let me know what to expect."

She looked down at her hands and shuddered. "I think — the goddess possessed me," she explained, softly.

Aw Jesus. "I'm sorry," muttered Harris, a shudder running down his back. He looked away and pretended to be interested in the seagulls.

The witch raised her head and smiled wanly. "Yes, I suppose you do understand," she said, passing a hand over her brow. "But you — you remember what happens when you're a wolf. I don't remember a thing."

Something she ain't telling me. Something I ain't gonna learn from her, anyhow. It don't take no intuition to see that.

"Was it broke when you found it? The sword?" She shook her head.

"I don't know." In her lap, or what would have been her lap if she'd been sitting down, her fingers were twined together. "I suppose so. I woke up, and the two bits of it were in my hands. And time — time missing."

When she woke up. "Did it send you to sleep?"

"No, I don't think so." Tatiana Dimitrovna sounded more hesitant than he had ever heard her. *Usually seems pretty sure of herself. Musta been a real doozy of a possession.* "I think — elsewhere," she explained, if that was an explanation.

Elsewhere. Goddamn what does she mean? Harris looked at the witch closely, not sure what he was searching for. "Where could *elsewhere* be?" he wondered, not really expecting an answer. He didn't get one.

Abruptly Tatiana Dimitrovna's face distorted, and she drew in her breath in a sharp gasp. *"Boizhe moi!"* she exclaimed.

"What's the—" She clutched Harris's arm. He broke off. *Goddamn, that hurt!*

"Quickly, I must get off the ship. Come with me, *now.*" And she took off at a run, Harris following after a second's hesitation.

Quite a turn of speed. Never know quite how ladies manage to run in their long skirts and those little bitty boots. He shook off a thought of Luzia. *What'n the hell's she up to now?*

The witch stopped on the quayside, so suddenly that Harris nearly cannoned into her. She muttered a few words, and he was startled to be suddenly enclosed in a dome of solid air, like a bell-jar, but infinitesimally thin.

"What—" he began.

"Ssh," she hushed him. "It's only a concealing spell. I'll need your strength, Mr. Harris. Don't be alarmed, but I have to summon a demon, and I must do it now."

If I say 'what' again I'm gonna sound like a phonograph with a stuck needle. But, what? "Uh," was what he came out with. *And that's an improvement?*

"It's my familiar," Tatiana Dimitrovna explained. "I didn't want it, but— ! So just bear with me, please."

Harris nodded. *Sure, I'll hush up.* But he felt more than a little apprehensive. He had good reason to dislike demons.

He was aware of it before it appeared, with the odd extra sense he thought came from his wolf-ness. It wasn't anything like smell, as taste and vision and hearing are nothing like smell, but it made him sneeze.

And then the demon materialized on the ground in front of them, a cringing blue thing that looked malformed. It was shaking slightly, and making a piteous keening noise. A drop of clear fluid fell to the cobbles, and then another, before Harris realized what he was seeing.

Shitfire, it's crying. He took in the creature's injuries in shock. It had been tortured, obviously, none of that was accidental. *Yeah, would've killed it myself if'n it came at me. But, goddamnit, cleanly.*

One of its arms was broken for sure, it seemed to have an extra elbow, and so were the fingers of its other hand. Its warty skin was discolored, which might just have been its own brindle coloring but looked too much like bruises to think it was natural. There were a number of round burns that could only have come from a lighted cigar being pressed into its flesh. One of the tusks that protruded from its mouth had been snapped off, one eye was swollen shut. It squatted on the cobblestones and sobbed.

Jesus, it looks like it's gone ten rounds with a coupla homicidal water buffaloes. He spat into the sea. "Who the fu— er, hell did that to it?" he asked in disgust.

"Munro." Tatiana Dimitrovna squatted down beside it and put a hand out to touch it. Harris almost grabbed her wrist to stop her.

Bad idea, bad idea. It's a demon, for godsakes. The creature whimpered as it felt her fingers, and she grimaced as if touching it hurt. But she stroked its head gently, and after a moment its keening quieted.

"Mistress?" it faltered, the word coming out mushy over the broken tusk.

"It's safe now," the witch said gently. "I won't let him harm you any more. Mister Harris, can you pick it up?"

"Pick it up?" he echoed, not understanding. She showed him her palm. It was red and blistered. The demon whimpered, and she resumed stroking it.

"I can't," she explained. *Yeah, 'cause she's human. Been to hell and all but she's still human. And I ain't. I can hold it and no harm. Goddamnit.*

He squatted beside the demon, and it flinched away.

"Hey, okay, little feller, take it easy," Harris said, as if to a frightened animal. *Can't believe I'm doing this.* "Gotta take you—" He turned to the witch. "Where *are* we taking it?"

"To someone who can help it," she replied, stonily.

She knows people who can mend demons. Jesus in the doldrums, she knows a demon veterinarian.

"Take you to a demon doctor," he told it. It looked plaintively at the witch.

"It's all right," she said reassuringly. "Let him help you."

Harris lifted the creature, and it snuggled against his shirt. It was very hot. *Goddamn, the little sucker's heavy.* He felt sweat pop out on his forehead with the effort as he managed to straighten his legs. *Witch couldn't have gotten it off the ground, less'n she could magic it. And I guess she woulda done that already if'n she could.*

"Okay, Bonzo," he grunted. "Let's get this show on the road. Lead on, ma'am."

She led him away from the quayside towards the labyrinth of the old town. *Hope it's not too far, my arms're aching already. And I bet I got demon goop on my shirt. Ugh.*

By the time Tatiana Dimitrovna halted, which was only about five minutes later, he felt sure his arms were going to come out of their sockets.

The witch ducked into a stall selling hookahs. They ranged from miniature decorative things to monumental pipes nearly as tall as Harris. *Jesus, wonder what in the hell you cook up in those things. Hold enough hashish to knock out an elephant.* She dissolved the barrier round them with a gesture, and a thousand sounds and stinks that Harris hadn't realized the spell had shielded him from burst in on him.

A small boy wearing a nightshirt too big for him appeared from some nether regions, and looked at the group with wide eyes.

"Is the *moghrebi* here?" Tatiana Dimitrovna asked. The child nodded, and fled. A few moments later a woman appeared, Arabic in appearance but in western dress. She was also exceedingly pretty, but Harris was too intent on his burden to appreciate it. So he failed, as well, to notice that she wasn't human, but her disguise was, admittedly, very good.

"'Scuse me," he ventured, "but can I put this critter down yet? Weighs a coupla tons."

But she merely beckoned to him. Harris glanced at the witch, who nodded, and followed her down a dark incense-perfumed corridor. At the end she opened a door.

He went through close on her heels, expecting an alchemist's den full of dark and dust and spiders. But he emerged into a bright airy tiled courtyard with a fountain playing in the center.

Should know never to expect the obvious after coming up to three years with the skipper. He smiled, wryly. *Jesus, three years. Never thought I'd ever get a berth for more'n one voyage again, after Riga.*

Since he had also, subconsciously, been expecting some kind of Arabian Nights figure, the dapper little man sitting by the fountain came as even more of a shock. He caught a whiff of something so genteel he didn't recognize it for a minute, then grinned. *This feller must be keeping the pomade industry in business all on his own,* he thought, eyeing the other's gleaming coiffure, *pity about the five o'clock shadow.* He grimaced reflexively, becoming aware of bristles on his own chin.

The man bowed his head gravely and said something in French, to Harris's disgust. *Oh great. Just beginning to get a handle on Portuguese and they throw a frog in the mix.* He shook his head helplessly, and the Frenchman rolled his eyes heavenwards and gave an ostentatious sigh.

"Put 'im down 'ere," he said, with a sweeping gesture.

"On the floor?" asked Harris. The little demon clung to him.

"*Qu'est-ce que vous voulez?* What do you want, a feather bed?" snapped the other, testily.

And screw you, too, friend. Harris, instead, advanced to the fountain, scowling. Sat down on the edge at a small distance from the man and tried to ease the demon into his lap. It resisted, clutching at his coat.

"Come on, Bonzo," he coaxed. "This here's the demon doctor." This earned him a fulminating stare, but whatever the Frenchman had been about to say went unvoiced as Tatiana Dimitrovna came into the courtyard. His antagonism vanished at once. He preened. Bounced to his feet and went to embrace her.

"Ma chère sorcière."

Harris eyed them in a jaundiced sort of way. *Go on, get all cosy with Monsewer Sourpuss. Might get him to lighten up a bit.*

On his lap, the demon squirmed. He patted its head absently. Its body heat felt like he was holding the world's largest hot-water bottle. *Yeah, that'd warm up your bed, right enough.*

"Don't like him," it muttered indistinctly, and Harris jumped slightly. *Almost forgot the thing could talk.*

"You and me both, pal," he said quietly. "But I guess the witch knows what she's about. Gotta trust her on this one."

On cue, Tatiana Dimitrovna turned to him, looking apologetic. She indicated the Frenchman. "This is Paul Thierry."

"Edward Harris," grunted the werewolf.

"Mister 'Arris," Thierry said, with apparent politeness but without warmth. He glanced at the woman, who hadn't said a word. "What 'as 'appen to this demon?"

"You're supposed to be the doc," Harris retorted, grumpily. "Though I don't reckon much to your bedside manner."

Unexpectedly, Thierry laughed. "I am not the doctor, Mister 'Arris. But there is not much reason to be gentle with demons."

"Yeah, well." Harris wasn't inclined to yield on this one. "Bonzo here could do with a bit of sympathy."

"I 'ave never seen a *loup-garou* give a care to a demon before," remarked Thierry. "But you are not the common kind of *loup-garou*, are you?"

Depends what you mean by common. "Guess not. But if you ain't the doc, who is?" He looked up to see that the woman had come silently to stand by him. *Holy shit, I didn't even notice. What's the matter with me?* She looked down at him with deep dark eyes.

And he realized that although she must be the demon physician, he really didn't have a clue as to what she really was.

"She cannot talk. She was cursed," Tatiana murmured to him. "Paul has to speak for her."

"But what is she?" Harris asked, unaware that his hand was still stroking the demon like an injured dog.

"She is a djinn," said Thierry.

17

"HELL'S BELLS," BLURTED HARRIS BEFORE HE COULD STOP HIMSELF, "what did she come out of, a lamp or a bottle?"

Tatiana Dimitrovna put a hand over her mouth. "Ssh!" she hissed around a startled laugh, "she'll hear you." But Thierry shook his head.

"She won't. She only 'ears me."

"What was the curse?" Harris asked, interested. The Frenchman shook his head a second time.

"This is neither the time nor the place," he said austerely. "Now, this demon."

Harris raised an eyebrow at his tone. *Ah well. Can't say I won't be glad to get shot of it.* "Okay, Bonzo. Time to get you fixed up."

At that, the demon stretched up, its claws digging into his thighs. It was as heavy as a full-grown wolf in his lap. Harris winced. "You helped me," it announced, slurring the words a little. "I will help you, if I can." And it whispered its name into his ear.

The silent woman, no, the djinn, reached out her hands to it, but she didn't attempt to lift it out of his lap. *Might've known* that *wasn't gonna happen any time soon.* He sighed, resigning himself to supporting its weight for a while longer, and turned his attention to the healer. *What's she gonna do?* he wondered.

But there wasn't much to see. All she did was put her hands on the little demon's head and close her eyes. The creature shuddered, and then Harris did see something. Saw the livid bruises lighten and the burns fade away, the crooked arm straighten, the broken fingers knit, and the swollen flesh subside.

"She cannot make 'is tooth grow back," explained Thierry, touching one of his own incisors with a finger.

"Have to call you One-Tusk, then, won't we, Bonzo?" Harris said to it. The demon bounced to the ground, using him as a starting block — *look out with the claws, goddamnit!* — and turned to Tatiana Dimitrovna.

"Mistress, will you release me?" it requested, lisping over its broken tusk. Harris wiped his hands along his thighs and examined his clothes surreptitiously.

"You don't fear that Munro will snare you again?" the witch asked. She was holding one hand tightly in the other, Harris noticed. He could see how red it was. *Jesus on a railroad train, that's got to hurt. Needs a blast of holy water, I guess.*

"He doesn't have the power any more," it said contemptuously. "He only snared me with a trick." It looked slyly up at her. "You could kill him."

The witch smiled grimly. "I could," she agreed. "And maybe I'll have to. And maybe someone else will get there first, or he'll drown in the sea. If you are confident you don't need my protection, demon, I will release you."

"Yes," it insisted, and she made a pass with her unburned hand. The demon vanished, leaving a faint smell, like fish and sulphur, in the air.

"Payment?" Tatiana Dimitrovna asked.

"Non," said Thierry. "She works towards redemption." *Redemption for what?* "I will show you out."

Once back in the bedlam of the souk, the witch turned to Harris. "We had better hurry," she observed. He nodded. Someone tugged at his sleeve, someone else at his jacket. Which was, as he'd feared, stained with demon goop. *Can't think what else to call it. Bet it won't wash out, neither.* He grimaced at the thought of paying for a new one.

"One a those *we-ain't-here* spells'd go down good," he remarked, shaking a persistent beggar off his arm. The beggar got a whiff of the demon goop, and recoiled. *Oh, so it is kinda handy for something.*

"What about your own glamor?" asked the witch. Harris pulled a face.

"Don't work any too good just after full moon."

She took a deep breath that sounded a bit ragged to him, as if she hurt. "Well, there's one thing you won't have about your person," she said, "and that's holy water." *And here we are in a country full of mosques.*

Obviously the same thought was with the witch. She turned her hands in a quick gesture, and the hawkers suddenly lost interest. *Oh yeah. Guess the biggie she did at the quay was to shield old Bonzo rather than us. We don't rate more'n a little bitty spell.*

They hurried through the narrow alleys. *She sure can shift quick when she has a mind to.* "What about the curse?" he enquired, after a while. The witch looked at him with a small frown. "The djinn?"

"Oh," said Tatiana Dimitrovna. "Yes. The story is that she killed another of her kind, so she is working off the penance. She has to heal any supernatural creature that comes to her, good or evil. For oh, something like a hundred years."

Tough one. "And where does Monsewer Frog come in?"

"He's just a conduit." She stepped round a particularly noisome puddle, holding her skirt above her ankles, then gave Harris a nasty smile. "I knew him in Marseille. He used to hang around any warlock or sorceress he could find, trying to get them to teach him magic. As if he thought it could rub off on him. He's got no talent for it at all. And it's a penal sentence, really, being the djinn's… interpreter."

"How's that?" But she didn't answer, and after a moment he realized she wasn't going to. *Must be secret witchy stuff. Don't push it.* He shrugged. *Don't really want to know.* Instead, he said, "That critter told me its name."

The witch looked at him, eyebrows raised. "Well," she remarked. "Well. It must have thought you might need it."

Don't much like the sound of that. "Ma'am, do you think I will?"

"I don't know, Mr. Harris. But you may have heard your captain observing that there are no such things as coincidences."

* * *

The Bay of Naples. We sailed here on the real sea, as we did the last leg. Though we'll have to pass through to that other ocean to get from here to Cyprus. And there sits Vesuvius, the sleeping dragon that laid waste the town of Pompeii. Looming. Last woke up seven years ago. I'm not looking forward to meeting its ghosts. Some time I'd like to visit a town that hasn't been devastated by man or nature. And that's being naive, da Silva.

Come to think of it, there aren't too many of those, anyway.

I know Naples quite well, or I used to. The Venetian used to do quite a lot of business there. Mind you, I'd never claim to understand the Neapolitans. There's something mad about them that may have something to do with living under the volcano. People, like Ashley for instance, tend to lump all the Italians together. But I was based in Venice for nineteen years, and I can tell you northerners and southerners don't have much in common.

Mind you, when people talk about Mediterranean peoples, they somehow include us Portuguese in there too. Which either shows they know bugger all about geography, or they think we caught it from Spain. It all makes as much sense as saying that all Americans are the same, if you ask me. And we're all just bloody foreigners to the English.

And why am I daydreaming about racial traits, anyway? Prevarication, it's called. I seem to do it when I'm afraid.

It's Harris's turn to go and do his bit. Part of me, well, a lot of me, to be honest, thinks he's quite capable of getting the spear on his own. He doesn't need his hand held. He doesn't want the skipper breathing down his neck. Besides, aren't we seeing a pattern here? Da Silva is with Yeoh in Malta, and nearly gets chopped into little bits. With Tatiana Dimitrovna in Carthage, and — Well, you get the idea.

Fact is, though, I can't let him go alone, however much I'd like to. It may be his task to get the spear, but I suppose the overall task is mine. Damn it. I'm the captain. And anyway, he might need someone to watch his back.

Who the hell am I trying to fool? It's this bloody destiny thing again. So I'm not going with Harris as some mystical metaphysical leader. Nor as the Fisher King's champion. I'm going because he's my friend.

Feel better, da Silva? Not much.

Our passage from Tunis to Naples took about the same length of time as a voyage through those other seas. Only a lot more restful. I'm delighted not to spend any more time than I have to wherever they may be. And so is everyone else, except perhaps Zacuto. Oh, and my father and Pierce, of course.

So I, at least, managed to have a good night's sleep.

Harris, on the other hand, looks like a bear with a hangover. He came on deck scowling and bad-tempered, and I told him to go and drink large amounts of coffee. Didn't seem to have much effect., though. I asked him what was the matter, and he shrugged and said "Wolf-dreams."

"Well, come on, Harris. We've got a train to catch. It's going to be quite a hike to get where we want to be."

"It would be," he muttered gloomily. That's the old Harris I used to know, before Luzia came on the scene. The man who can define the word lugubrious without opening his mouth.

I have to confess I'm not that fascinated by ruins. Rather like museums. Rooms full of lots of broken pots. You've seen one, you've seen them all. So all the times I've been in Naples, I never was interested enough to take a side trip up to Pompeii, even supposing I'd had the time. No, not even to see the dirty frescoes.

And now, of course, all I see is ghosts. These cities of death almost take me back to the days when I was first seeing shades. When I found them impossible to ignore.

They died under a cloud of burning ash, Pierce was eager to enlighten me.

He was so enthusiastic about it I'd half-expected him to want to tag along. He would've given me a blow-by-blow account of the eruption if I'd given him any sign of encouragement. All I'd asked him was whether he had any clues about where to look for the spear.

Not that we'll need any, I'm sure. It'll find us. As Zacuto says, metaphysically the hallows *want* to be together.

Doesn't prevent the damn things from playing their bloody games first, though.

There's more standing of Pompeii than I expected. From what Pierce had said, I'd expected it to be flattened. You can see the layout of the town, straight rutted streets, wide piazzas, broken columns, hollow shops, headless statues, shattered houses, all silent, all empty. Except for the ghosts. And Vesuvius looming, like the threat of doom. I wouldn't want to live in a town with that hanging over me. As the Neapolitans do. Mad, like I said.

"Any thoughts?" I asked Harris, getting my cheroots out. Harris shook his head and looked gloomy. I felt like shaking mine, to get rid of the ghosts. Only I knew it wouldn't. The place was worse than Lisbon's earthquake, London's fire. The sack of Carthage and Malta's siege.

But get things in perspective, da Silva. I struck a match, and the noise it made almost made me jump. It's not as bad as Trafalgar. And they're only shades, after all. Less than magic-lantern slides. Everyone else forgot them a long time ago.

Perhaps that's why I see them. Just so they don't get completely forgotten. That time doesn't pass them by. What a strange thought. I lit my cheroot and threw the match away.

We'd come into a wide piazza of skewed stones. Archways and columns like broken teeth. The remains of a colonnade along one side. A palm tree and a couple of cypresses growing up through one of the ruined buildings.

"Quiet, ain't it?" remarked Harris. And he's right. No birdsong. No people. No wind whispering over the stones. No insects, even. The sky a great blue dome of silence. Oppressive. I felt a drop of sweat trickle down my face, though I wasn't hot. Far from it. I blew out smoke. It hung in the still air for a moment before dispersing.

"I hope it's not the calm before the storm," I said quietly, but the words echoed off the hollow stones in an odd sort of way. I clamped the cheroot between my teeth and drew my knife. Harris raised his eyebrows.

"Trouble?" he enquired.

"Count on it." I turned round in a slow circle. Saw nothing but the shades. "Can't you feel anything?"

"Place gives me the creeps, but that's all." Then he suddenly doubled over with a gasp. I started towards him. He straightened instantly, but I saw his eyes gleam yellow for a split second.

And that, for some reason, scared me worse than anything.

"Harris." I said, urgently. He blinked. "Don't go all wolf on me, now."

"Can't," he ground out. Sounded in pain. "Doesn't work outside of full moon." He put his hand against a column and leaned on it. His face looked pinched. Hollow. His eyes faded into yellow again, then back to normal. Breath hissed between his teeth.

My back started to prickle, and I did another slow turn, wishing I had the full optical complement. Again, nothing. Nada. Then why do I feel there's something very close, and very dire?

Easy. Because they were hidden by the ghosts.

Roman soldiers. One of the most efficient bunches of fighters the world's ever seen. And if we're looking for a spear, every single damned man of them has one in his hand.

Então, I don't know what the hell you'd do if you suddenly saw Julius Caesar's crack troops coming towards you. What my mind said was run. What I did was say "Oh *merda*," and put my knife away. Very quickly.

"Don't suppose they're here for a military tattoo," muttered Harris. His voice was strained and tight.

One of the soldiers stepped forward. He had a deeply scarred face and a fancier helmet than the others. Centurion? Is that the head soldier? And does it matter? He gave a fist-to-chest sort of salute. Beside me, Harris grunted as if someone had hit him, and I turned my head to check. No one had. I looked back at the centurion.

"And who the devil are you?" I asked.

"My name is not important," he said, austerely. He had wintry gray eyes. Not very Italian-looking. But then, blue eyes aren't exactly a Portuguese trait. Perhaps this fellow had an English grandmother too. And why am I thinking about heredity at a time like this? "You come in search of the spear?"

No, we were passing by and were struck by an overwhelming desire to look at some ancient ruins.

I nodded. *Keep it casual, da Silva.* The less aggressive you look, the less of a threat they'll take you for. Oh yes. As if you can fool this bunch. The supernatural bush telegraph's been humming for weeks, and you think you can pretend anything?

Beside me Harris fell to his knees. I heard him grunt, "Now would be a good time for some help," but couldn't spare him any attention.

"You both seek the spear," announced the centurion. "Only one of you may claim it."

"He's with me," I assured him.

"No." The Roman soldier looked from one to the other of us. "He is not with you."

A low growl from Harris made my neck hair prickle, and I turned. His eyes were true wolf-eyes now, yellow and feral. His lips were drawn back from his teeth. And I realized something, though I don't know what put the notion in my head.

Harris-wolf is a wolf-body with Harris inside it. His mind, his thoughts. This is the opposite. It's a man with a wolf in its head. Harris isn't there anymore.

And that was the final straw. I was suddenly, furiously angry. Vesuvius up there had competition at blowing its top. What right do all these guardians, powers, whatever the hell they are, what right do they have to play these *stupid* games?

Breathless with fury, I took a step towards the centurion. Felt the blood thundering in my head. "You," I said. He almost stepped back. "The whole bloody pack of you. I'm sick to death of it." I felt my fists clenching. Need to hit something. Not quite far enough gone to make it a fully-armed Roman soldier, though. I unclenched my left hand with an effort and ran it through my hair. Pointed a finger at him. "Meu Deus! If you lot are the forces of good—" I'd hate to see the opposition, I was going to say. But I *have* seen 'em. "Can't you work *with* me for once?" The centurion's face was impassive. "All right!" I shouted. "I've had enough of your stupid bloody games! *Vai para a puta que te pariu!*"

And I turned my back on the lot of them and started to walk away. The centurion's voice stopped me.

"You may think you can walk away," he said, "but you cannot. The wolf will be true to its nature, and so will you."

Which was when Harris jumped me. And when I say jumped, I'm not speaking figuratively. There was a wolf in his mind, and he did what wolves do. He sprang. I tried to dodge, and aimed a punch at him, but wasn't quite quick enough. My fist glanced off the side of his head, and then I was on my back with Harris half on top of me. I kneed him hard in the thigh and rolled away, rolled to my feet, fast as I could.

Have to get his over quickly. I can take Harris but only if I act before he uses his weight. He's got at least fifty pounds on me and more inches than I like. Luckily the wolf isn't thinking like a man. He came at me crouching low and growling, and I punched him in the face with all my weight behind it.

Harris staggered sideways, and I tripped him up. Or so I thought. He recovered with wolf-reflexes and bounded back upright, fists windmilling, caught me in the chest with a wild swing. I skidded, got my balance back. Made a strategic retreat.

With a snarl, he charged at me, and this time I dodged him easily, let his momentum carry him past me. What are the damned soldiers doing? Can't spare the time to look. Panting, I went after Harris and he swiveled as I grabbed him, flailing his arms, dislodging my grip.

"Harris!" I shouted, but he didn't hear me. Couldn't. There's nobody home. I swung my fist back and hit him in the jaw hard enough to make him grunt.

He blinked twice and shook his head. Then he picked me up as if I weighed no more than Zé and threw me bodily over a low wall to land, luckily, on grass.

Swearing, I lurched back to my feet as Harris came tearing after me. The centurion, unexpectedly between us, observed, "You could kill it with one knife-thrust."

"I don't kill my friends," I panted.

"That is not your friend," he said, and stood to one side to show me Harris's wolf-face. Nothing human in it. No hope of getting him back? There has to be. I backed away, wondering what the hell to do next.

And a small blue creature popped out of the air and seized Harris round the neck, stopping him in his tracks.

There was a *zing* of metal as the centurion drew his sword and advanced on them.

"Hey," I exclaimed, barring his way. "What d'you think you're doing?"

"The wolf must not be compromised." He looked severely at me. "Stand aside."

My knife is no match for a Roman gladius. I'm going to regret this. My hand's already sore from repeated contact with Harrisian bone. But there's no alternative.

I gathered up all my anger and focused it. Whacked a right in his eye to distract him, then pounded him in the face with my left fist. His head snapped back. He was real enough that I felt his nose break, and blood began to pour from his nostrils.

"That's what I call being true to my nature," I yelled at him, rubbing my knuckles. Feels like they're broken too. *Merda.*

The centurion looked at me, his expression unreadable. "Just so," he said, neutrally.

I stared at him for a second, then turned to look for Harris. He was sitting on the low wall, one hand covering his ear, a small demon squatting at his feet and a spear lying across his knees. Inexplicably, he was stroking the little creature's head. I scratched my scar bemusedly. I don't know which part of this picture I should be gaping at.

"Skipper," said Harris, feeling his jaw gently, "this here's Bonzo."

"Bonzo?" I echoed, wincing at bruises on top of bruises and examining the knuckles of my left hand ruefully.

"Well, it ain't his real name, of course." Harris looked sheepish. "He's Countess Tatiana's, really, but he seems to've kinda latched onto me." He took his hand away from his ear, revealing a bloodstained handkerchief. "Wish you coulda found another way to bring me round, fella," he muttered, and replaced it.

"It bit you?" Seems such an undemonlike thing to do. Biting someone in the ear. I shook my head, and took out my cheroots. Badly in need of a smoke. I wiped sweat out of my eye, and hunted for a match.

"Oh, well done," remarked a voice from my left. I turned without surprise to see Belphegor in its little-girl disguise, applauding. "Now you have three of the hallows. *Very* good!"

"And you wonder why we oppose you," snapped the centurion, acidly. "Seeing what you consort with." I turned angrily to him.

"I'm not the one doing the consorting," I retorted. Ever thought of that? "I didn't ask it to come." And what about Harris's familiar, then? I suppose that doesn't count as high as a prince of hell. I lit my cheroot. Wiped sweat out of my eye.

"Nonetheless, it is here." The Roman soldier's voice was wintry. The kind of winter they have in Siberia. He seems quite oblivious of the blood on his face. His broken nose. "What is your interest in this matter, demon?"

Belphegor smiled sweetly, and did a little twirl just like the child it isn't. "Luís da Silva is our candidate for Fisher King, *centurion.*"

"I'm nothing of the kind," I said hotly. "You can't pick me if I refuse to do it."

"We can pick anybody we like." The demon looked at Harris, who gripped the spear. The little familiar clutched his leg, obviously terrified of Belphegor. "We could pick him."

"A werewolf?" The centurion raised one eyebrow scornfully and curled his lip. "He is only here for the spear."

"Which he seems to have in his possession, centurion," Belphegor pointed out. "So your business in this place is at an end."

"And why don't you bugger off, too?" I suggested, pointing my cheroot at it.

"Or what?" The demon's features flowed and changed. "You may be a slayer of demons, Luís da Silva, but I doubt you could kill anything that looks like your wife."

It doesn't know how much I want to kill it just for doing that?

"Think again," I said, and took my knife out. Harris got up from the wall and leveled the spear at it.

"And you haven't forgotten this little old pig-sticker?" he asked, baring his teeth.

The demon looked from one to the other of us. It no longer looked like Emilia, but thin, witchy. "Bored now," it announced, and vanished.

"Shitfire," said Harris.

Couldn't've put it better myself.

* * *

With all the unaccustomed passengers, the 'prentices had been the first to be turfed out of their cabin. Zé, however, taking advantage of the captain's absence to indulge in the benefits of a spot of freelance nepotism, had borrowed his father's cabin to do his homework.

It was a bore and a chore, and if he'd realized there was going to be so much studying involved he'd have chosen a different career. Although, he reflected glumly, you don't seem to be able to escape school whatever you do. Even Sílvia had to have lessons, and she didn't even have parents to make her study.

He dipped his pen in the inkwell and stopped himself at the very last minute from doodling on the blotter. The borrowing of the captain's cabin was not officially sanctioned. In other words, if his father found out he'd get more than a tongue-lashing.

And nothing would give the game away faster than unfamiliar doodles right under his nose.

Zé drew a circle in the corner of the page he was writing on, and then a triangle beneath it, so the circle was sitting on its top point. He contemplated this figure, and the separated the circle and triangle with a horizontal line. Added a little vertical line to each end. Chewed the end of his pen and considered a little shading to make it three-dimensional, but decided against it.

* * *

The centurion had to let us leave. He's only an agent of the prophecy. Has even less say in the matter than we do. Harris balanced the spear over his shoulder and we walked away from the soldiers.

"Like to know how I'm gonna get this goddamn thing on the train," he grumbled.

"I expect you'll manage," I said, and blew out smoke. People see what they expect to see. Not a two-hundred-and-fifty-pound werewolf carrying a spear, but a big redhaired man with — a walking stick?

"You whaled me pretty good back there," he remarked, and I turned my head to him, eyebrow raised.

"You remember?"

"Hell, no." He grinned wryly. "My face feels like Gentleman Jim Corbett's been pounding on it, is all. You sure can hit hard, skipper."

"You shouldn't have such a bloody solid head," I retorted, scratching under my eyepatch. "Anyway, you threw me over a wall."

"Jesus, did I?" He took out his cigarettes. "Guess that just about makes us even, then." I looked at him sideways.

"So tell me about this demon. Bonzo. Why Bonzo?"

"Why not?" said Harris. "Got a match?"

"Here." I handed him the box. His paw dwarfed it. "Well?"

Harris shrugged. "Not much to tell. That a — Munro'd been beating on the poor little critter. Your witch got me to carry it to the veterinarian. Who was a djinn. Seeing as how I can." He broke off to light his gasper.

His ear. I'd forgotten. A human ear, demon-bitten, would be suppurating by now. But the vet? A djinn? I shook my head, amused. Can't leave him alone for five minutes. It followed me home, papaí, can I keep it?

So Harris has found himself a familiar. And given that the centurion seemed to want a fight to the death, I'm pretty damned glad about it. I finished my cheroot and threw away the end. Stuck my hands in my pockets. Harris started whistling. I told him to stop. His whistling's almost as bad as his singing.

We'd reached the outskirts of the ruins, now. Pompeii's suburbs. And da Silva has gotten complacent. I didn't even notice the mist until we were almost in it. But then I stopped pretty smartish. Can't be anything good.

"Stop a minute," I said, holding out my hand.

"That's odd," He agreed with my unspoken thought. "Don't like it. Could those Roman soldiers—?"

"No." They were only guardians. As Belphegor pointed out, their task was over. "Can you feel anything?"

He got a look of concentration on his face, but shook his head a moment later. "No demons, skipper."

Then I started to hear a confused shouting, screams. Crashing noises. The sound of a mob. I frowned. Turned to Harris, and stopped in shock. The broken house behind him had grown, not whole, but less ruined. As if earthquake-damaged, but not devastated. Above, the sky grew dark. The temperature rose, the sky grew oppressive. I felt sweat break out on my face. Smelled sulphur. And fire. A hot wind started to blow. People ran by us in twos and threes, panic on their faces. People wearing tunics, togas. The citizens of Pompeii. Whose ghosts filled the ruins with their fright and fear.

"*Merda,*" I breathed. "Harris, the volcano—"

And behind him I saw Vesuvius blow its top with a noise like the end of the world. A column of churning fire shot miles into the air and turned into a billowing enormous cloud of black smoke. It obscured the volcano's summit, blacked out the sky, and roared down the mountainside faster than anything I've ever seen. Faster than anything can travel. Faster than a galloping horse, a train. Eighty, ninety miles an hour.

"Christ in a locomotive!" exclaimed Harris, rooted to the spot. Mouth agape, cigarette stuck to his lower lip.

"Can your demon get us out of here?" I yelled over the noise of the eruption. The roasting gale blew in my face, tugging at my hair. "Otherwise we're going to get fried!"

He shouted something that must've been the familiar's name. The blue demon appeared instantly this time and its human-looking eyes widened in very human-looking shock.

"Cut a portal with the spear!" it shrieked.

"What?" But I got it. I grabbed Harris's arm.

"In the mist," I shouted. "Cut a hole in the mist."

Once he'd got the idea, he didn't waste time. The billowing, bellowing cloud-avalanche thundered towards us. Harris extended the spear firmly and drew the point up, across, down, back. An opening appeared. He seized the demon by the arm and we tumbled through. Fell for a vertiginous moment. Crashed to the ground. More damned bruises.

The eruption scene vanished. The mist dispersed. Harris's cigarette was still in his mouth. He took it out and looked at it.

"What the fuck was that?" he demanded, indignantly.

"Last nasty little trick, I suppose," I said wearily, clambering to my feet and extending a hand. "Come on, let's get back to *Isabella.*" Before some other resident warlock decides it's open season on da Silva.

"No argument from me there, skipper." I hauled him to his feet. Harris dusted himself off and turned to the demon, which was squatting on top of a tumbled stone column, watching us. "Thanks, Bonzo."

"Nada," it chirped. Winked at me, and disappeared.

That's all I need. A familiar demon that behaves like Zé.

*   *   *

It was a shockingly dirty place, Pierce thought, worse than Rio's slums. Steep narrow noisome alleys festooned with grimy washing: the filthy air ingrained its dirt into everything it came in contact with. In places the stench was bad enough to make him want to tie a handkerchief over his nose and mouth, and it was only January. Hordes of screaming half-naked children with smeared grubby faces descended on anyone unwise enough to set foot on shore, tugging at one's clothes, screeching like strange birds. Harpies, perhaps. Pierce spoke passable Italian but heaven only knew what impenetrable patois passed among these denizens.

Then there were the beggars and panhandlers, the pedlars, hawkers and whores, the bone-thin cats with their loud plaintive cries, the skinny stray dogs which all on their own could ensure that the streets were impassable, and that was before all the other dirt. You really couldn't tell whether some of the streets were paved or not, everything is coated with a layer of slimy mud that made him fear for the soles of his shoes.

And yet the noise is not entirely cacophony, frequently a voice lifts in song rather than a fishwife's scream, birds trill from their cages, someone picks out a tune on a guitar so plangently that it might be a harp. And many of the young women are beautiful, even the ones in rags, they have a grace that makes their poverty almost irrelevant.

But having once noted all this, you then tread in dogshit once more and remember that all those girls will eventually turn into their mothers. Having ventured ashore when *Isabella* docked, Pierce wasn't sure it was worth it even to have his stomach settle for a little while. The resolve lasted all of half an hour.

His second desperate attempt to escape from the terrible motion of the ship proved more successful, however, since this time he was accompanied by Zacuto. No one could tell by looking at him that the old scholar was a ghost, but the children, who were by far the most importunate of the nuisances, sensed something and gave him a wide berth. Which was fine by Pierce.

So, comparatively unmolested, the two academics made their way to more salubrious areas and stopped to patronize a surprisingly empty bar which provided them with surprisingly Brazilian coffee. Zacuto, of course, couldn't drink it, which meant Pierce had to ingest twice as much espresso as he really wanted, but it was worth it.

"Won't be long now," he remarked, taking off his spectacles and polishing them. Zacuto inclined his head and smiled gently into his beard. As a ghost, of course, his perspective on things was slightly different to Pierce's.

"I have no doubt that the captain and Sr. Harris will be successful," he assured the Englishman, answering the question that hadn't been asked. But even without being able to read minds, he would have known that one.

The antiquarian smiled too, replaced his spectacles, and stirred his coffee with a spoon that was almost as big as the cup.

"I know," he murmured. "The hallows, ah, *need* to be together. But that doesn't guarantee they will be. Prophecies notwithstanding. There's a lot of, of *may* and *might* about that prophecy." He picked the cup up, testing its temperature.

"There always is," commented the ghost. "Prophecies are, by their nature, never complete certainties."

Pierce took a sip of coffee and looked at the ghost over the rim of the cup. "I don't know whether I should advise you to tell the captain that, or not."

Zacuto pursed his lips, then carefully pretended to drink coffee while Pierce admired the co-ordination of levitating cup and ghostly movement.

"Captain da Silva is... pulled in many directions," the old scholar said finally, thoughtfully. "I had not realized how difficult it would be for him. Which is my shortcoming, not his." Pierce blinked in surprise at this admission, and pushed his descending spectacles back into place, hoping for more information. But Zacuto merely completed his coffee-drinking illusion by replacing the cup delicately on its saucer.

"What did you make of the, ah, tribunal?" Pierce asked, finishing his own coffee. "The knights. What were they up to?"

"It is part of the imbalance. You should drink this coffee, too." Zacuto gestured at the cup. The Englishman nodded, and switched cups deftly.

"The imbalance?" he enquired. The ghost made a sniffing sound.

"Light and dark," he said. "Good and evil. Right and wrong. None of these are absolutes, despite what their adherents may claim. Ill things may be done for good motives. Equally, good may come out of a malicious act. I do not know why the captain was given the ability to see ghosts. Or fight evil, though that is evidently what he wants to do without any larger role. Therefore I am not sure where his path will take him. And neither, it seems, do other powers. The uncertainty leads to imbalance."

Fascinated, Pierce kept his mouth shut. Zacuto was not usually so forthcoming. He drank the second espresso without taking his eyes off the ghost's face.

However, that appeared to be the sum of it. Pierce waited. Took off his spectacles again and rubbed the lenses on his sleeve. But the oracle had dried up.

"Mightn't it be a good thing?" he ventured. The old scholar looked up, surprised.

"How so?"

"Er — well, confusion to your enemies, and all that." He realized he was babbling, and replaced his spectacles on his nose. "I mean, if one side doesn't know, neither does the other. Or is that too Manichean?"

"That," said Zacuto, "is a very interesting point." He saw how intently Pierce was watching him. "And one that I will have to give some thought to."

Pleased with himself, Pierce nodded. He even allowed himself a smirk. It wasn't often he succeeded in silencing the ghost.

*   *   *

The harbormaster said, "There's a bad storm coming." He's a wizened little fellow who looks as if someone left him out in the rain, and he shrank. He turned to me. "You might want to wait her out."

We should be where storms don't affect us by that time. Not that I can tell him that. "I'm on a tight schedule," I told him. "But thanks for the warning."

He shrugged. "Always the damn same. Schedules and contracts and business. You're old enough to know the sea doesn't mix with those sorts of things."

Thank you for that, Methuselah. Though if age was measured in aches and pains, you could add twenty years onto me. I don't like being thrown around the place very much. And it seems to be the fashion these days. Seems everything I land on is harder than I am.

However, the harbormaster's right. My father and Pierce may have a rough time of it for a while.

And after that, it'll be me having the rough time. *Não me diga.*

So, south we go, a stiff breeze up and *Isabella* running before it. I may never feel the same again at the beginning of a voyage. Setting out, casting off, raising anchor. A new venture. But sailing this way, there's only uncertainty.

We found, that is I found, a ghost ship without any difficulty, a poor broken schooner. And I remembered not to meet anyone's eyes. But if I thought the other place would be the calm voyage it was before, I was wrong. *Isabella* sailed unsuspecting into a maelstrom of wind and water under a sky livid with lightning.

"Shorten sail!" I yelled, struck in the face by gallons of seawater as a wave sluiced right over the deck.

"All hands!" bellowed Ashley, almost simultaneously, and in seconds the rigging was alive with men working frantically. *Isabella* bucked and heeled, canvas snapped with a noise like a monstrous whip cracking, and the air was full of salt water and the bellowing of the storm.

They're a good crew, of course. My ship was never in danger of losing any of her sails, for which I was grateful. Soon we were running before the gale, riding the big sea as if it was a calm day in the Mediterranean. I sent Zé to check up on the passengers, then went below myself to change my clothes and get my oilskins. That first wave had soaked me to the skin. And the days are gone when I don't mind wet things drying on me. Besides, I'm the captain.

It only occurred to me then, when I was in my cabin rubbing a towel over my hair, to wonder if this other ocean mirrored the real world at all. Storms there, storms here. Well. Difference here is, we have to ride it for less time. So there is some advantage, after all.

We ran before the storm all the rest of the day, and most of the night. But by morning it had blown itself out, and I put some more canvas up. Not that it makes a lot of difference here. The voyage takes as long as it takes. But maybe seamanship still counts. Maybe an unwary captain wouldn't ever get to leave. *Not a good area for speculation, da Silva.*

Frankly, I'm more concerned with what happens after we get to Cyprus.

Towards the end of the afternoon watch on the second day I found my father beside me. Hadn't seen him come up.

"Sorry I haven't had any time to talk to you," I said to him. "How are you enjoying your sea trip?"

"No need to apologize," he replied. "I know you've been busy. And," he laughed shortly, "it's strange enough for me even being on a ship, let alone being — wherever we are."

Don't ask me to explain wherever we are, old man. "It's not something *I've* ever done before." I lit a cheroot. "I know about as much about it as you do."

He leaned on the rail. "Not true. You've been doing this for some time. I don't mean this," he gestured around vaguely, "but dealing with, with the supernatural."

I sighed. Took the cheroot out of my mouth and inspected it. It didn't offer me any inspiration. "Yes," was all I could think of to reply. Lame, I know.

"Never thought—" He stopped. "Never believed in it. Had to change my whole way of looking at the world. At my age." He looked at me shrewdly. "Much as you did, I suppose."

"You could say that." I scratched the scar on my cheekbone.

"You never did tell me how that happened."

"No," I said, thinking of the way the Venetian's eyes had changed and how much it had been like Harris's in Pompeii. Five years ago I might not have been able to avoid killing Harris. I shook myself. *"Àguas passadas."* Old history.

My father smiled thinly. Accepted that I wasn't going to tell him. He changed the subject. Answered the question I'd asked him earlier. "Without seasickness, this is really quite pleasant. Sailing, I mean. But I don't suppose you see it that way."

Given that I'll never venture into these waters again if I can help it, you could say that. "It's a little different for me."

"A lot of responsibility," he said. "You would have surprised your mother, Luís."

That made me want to spit over the side. The thought of my mother. I took a drag on my cheroot instead. "She'd've found something to criticize."

"Yes," my father agreed, wistfully. "I suppose she would."

"How's Alegria?" I asked. Which wasn't very tactful, was it, da Silva? To be honest, I was surprised to see him without her.

But he didn't seem to mind. "She's very well, I think. She's with Susana. They get on better than the child does with her mother." He looked disapproving. Perhaps it reminds him of my mother's lack of maternal instincts. Though it seems very different to me. Even I can see that Ana is fond of her daughter. She just doesn't seem to know what to do with her, and this whole Fisher King business has put her in awe of Susana. Whereas my mother never showed any sign of even liking me. The only thing she ever gave any devotion to was the church. Religion, or rather the rituals and the trappings of it. I don't think she even liked God very much.

I shook off these unpleasant memories. *Àguas passadas,* again. Brooding on the past, not like me. Perhaps it's fear of the future that does it.

But I still never know what to say to my father. Although the silences are getting less uncomfortable. So I suppose that's an improvement.

"It's that damn prophecy." I scratched my eyebrow in frustration. My father looked at me intently.

"You should talk to Leão," he said unexpectedly.

"What?"

"Leão. I think he's worried about his part in this."

He's worried? I'll tell you one thing. When he goes to collect the chalice, I'm going to stand *well* back.

However, my father's right. I've hardly gone out of my way to have a conversation with him. And all right, I may have a ship to run, but I admit I've been using that as an excuse. Since when we're in these seas, I'm hardly needed. Except when the wind got up, of course. I threw the end of my cheroot over the side.

"You're absolutely right," I agreed, and he blinked in surprise. It's probably the first time in his life he's heard me admit I'm wrong. I grinned at the thought. "And I need to talk to him before we get to Cyprus."

Leão, it appears, has been getting pally with Zé. I found the pair of them sitting together on the fo'c'sle head, deep in conversation. The shaman had abandoned his European clothes for a robe that made him look much more impressive. More like a man with power. And don't forget that, da Silva, when he comes to get the chalice.

"Captain da Silva." He gave me an intense look that made my back prickle for an instant.

"Sr. Leão," I replied. "I've been neglecting you."

"There is no need to apologize," he said, echoing my father, with a white smile. "You have had more than enough to occupy your time, this voyage." He gestured around at the empty sea. "I never even saw the ocean until I had cause to flee across it. And now you take me on stranger tides than I ever thought to travel by."

Stranger tides. Yes.

The strange tides released us that evening outside the port of Limasol. I stared at all the other ships in harbor, wondering where Munro was. If any of these vessels had brought him here. And what he intended to do.

And hoping, of course, that I get through the night without any bloody tribunals, tests, trials or any other mystical hoop-la.

"There aren't any knights of Cyprus, are there?" I asked Zacuto, suspiciously.

"Not that I am aware of," he answered with a small smile. But it was a smile.

In the morning I woke to someone banging on the door. Zé, without a doubt, judging from the amount of noise.

"Come in," I shouted. My bruises had come home to roost, and I don't feel like moving. Of course if there's clamor and rumpus outside, I'm going to have to. I groaned silently, and Zé came barging in.

"It's seven *bells*," he announced, disapprovingly. In the *I'm-up-but-you're-not* sense. I sat up and rubbed my eye. Everything ached. The aches had invited all their friends to stay.

"Zé, when you've been thrown over a wall and dropped from a height, then you can tell me I should be up with the lark." I lit a cheroot. My left hand was sore, too. I investigated and found more bruises on my knuckles. Harris's rock-hard jawbone. Ha.

"Huh, thought it was old age." Cheeky little brat. "Let's see your bruises, then."

"How about these?" I made a fist and showed it to him. "You tell me you came charging in here and you didn't bring me any coffee?" Need to get mobile. I stretched my arms out in front of me. My shoulders creaked. At least it felt like it.

"I'll get you some. But Sr. Leão is prowling round and looking like he thinks he'll miss his train."

I rotated my shoulders. Muscles protested. I sighed, and rotated them the other way. "Has he said anything?"

"No," Zé answered, "but if he had a pocket-watch he'd be looking at it."

"All right," I said in resignation. "Get me some coffee and I'll be up shortly."

Shortly, that's a good one, da Silva. I clambered out of bed like — well, like a man who's been thrown over a wall and dropped from a height. Stripped off my nightshirt. Even that hurt. Had a rather cursory wash, during which Zé returned with my coffee. And, with uncharacteristic forethought, hot water for shaving as well. So he got to see the bruises after all.

"Ouch," he commented. "That had to hurt,"

"It does," I grumbled. "Hand me that towel."

He obliged, and asked, "What happens when you've got all four of the thingies?"

"I've no idea."

"Did you know your bruises show exactly where your knife goes down your back?"

I pointed my shaving-brush at him and said menacingly, "Are you still here?"

He got the message.

The man who invented the safety-razor gets my vote for biggest contribution to mankind's wellbeing. People say you don't get as good a shave as you do with a straight razor. I suppose it's true. But I know which I prefer when I'm on board a ship.

It means a clean, shaved, rested and coffee'd da Silva is ready for action by the start of the forenoon watch. I collected the hallows people. Assembled them on deck. John Yeoh with the dish, Tatiana Dimitrovna with the broken sword, Harris with the spear, and Leão. Ana and Alegria together brought Susana. Which means my father's along for the ride. And I get the scholars' double-act too, Zacuto and a green-looking Pierce. The only reason I didn't get Zé as well was because I put my foot down.

Another outing for the da Silva circus. I eyed the throng rather sourly. My God, I'll have to hire a charabanc.

As it happened, though, I didn't need to. Tatiana Dimitrovna put a hand on my arm as if she thought I was about to make a speech or something.

"I know how to get us there," she said, smiling triumphantly. Wherever *there* is. "Or rather, Mr. Harris does."

"Harris?" I repeated, turning to look at him. He shook his head, don't ask me.

"The spear," explained the witch. "As you did in Pompeii. Open a portal."

Well, I'll be damned. It's actually got a use.

Eyebrows raised, he held out the spear he was holding and looked at it. "Here?" he asked, doubtfully.

"Anywhere, I think." Ha. Nice to be sure, Tatiana.

Harris shrugged. "Okay. You're the boss." Extended the spear, holding it two-handed. The tip shook. Bloody long thing to try and balance.

"Can you feel anything?" Pierce asked curiously, fascination winning out over sea-sickness. "Any resistance?"

Bringing the point slowly up, Harris frowned. "Yeah," he answered thoughtfully. "It's kinda like cutting through — through cotton candy."

He made the four cuts clockwise, as he had before. By instinct, I suppose. Or maybe just because he's right-handed. Through the gap he created I could see a mountainside, thick with pine trees. Hell, I could *smell* the pine trees. And feel the icy freshness of the mountain air. This done, Harris turned to the witch.

"The other hole closed behind us," he pointed out. "How we gonna get back?"

"Same way," she said. "If it closes. It may not. It's possible the other one closed because of the instability the other side." Instability. That's one way of putting it. A monstrous great fiery cloud about a million degrees in temperature rushing down the mountain. Yes, you could call that unstable.

"All right," Pierce interrupted. Leão shifted impatiently. I took out my cheroots. "Then how do we close it?"

"Let's take things one at a time," I suggested, looking at the shaman over the flaring match. "Come on, Harris. We'll go first, just in case."

I stepped carefully through the portal, and still nearly fell over. The transition between gently swaying deck and stony mountainside, plus a ten-inch drop, was awkward.

"Mind your step," I advised Harris.

When we were all through, the opening blinked shut.

"Well, that answers your question, Mr. Harris," remarked Tatiana Dimitrovna.

"Ssh." I held up a finger. Everyone shushed. I heard birdsong, high and clear. The whisper of wind in the pine trees. A bloody cold wind. Somewhere close by, a goat bleated. A bell tinkled. And a little further off, a dog barked once.

Down below I could see rooftops through the conifers. Half a dozen, no more. I turned round slowly. Wary, but not enough to draw my knife. A little way up the hill, a white wall showed among the straight tree-trunks. There didn't seem to be much in the way of roads. We were standing on a narrow path that wasn't much more than a sheep-track.

"Munro's going to have a bit of a job getting up here," remarked Pierce, with a smirk. I laughed humorlessly.

"Don't count on it," I said. "Up or down? Leão?"

Someone had given the shaman a pea-jacket to cover his robe, but his bare feet had to be cold. Though come to think of it he hadn't been that keen on shoes in Lisbon. So he was probably doing all right. He breathed out deeply, puffing out a breath as smoky as mine. And I had a cheroot on the go.

"Something is wrong," he rumbled in his deep voice.

And a second later a new voice asked, "Which of you is the lion?" He answered himself. "Ah, I see."

*   *   *

A little further down the mountain, Sir Douglas Scott is roused from his doze by an unfamiliar voice and opens his eyes to see a stranger, a fleshy man with the sleek well-fed look of the thoughtlessly rich. The Fisher King curls his lip, though he knows the man has come to kill him, this is a breed of Englishman he despises, an abuser of his power and position and thus, he thought bitterly, a politician.

"You will be the usurper, then," he observes, his old voice, usually so thin, taking on a strength which surprises him.

Sir Robert Munro allowed himself a sneer. This frail old fool in his faded clothes, his threadbare blanket, is the symbol of Europe? No wonder Europe is in such a parlous state.

"You have no power," he said contemptuously.

"None the likes of you can see," retorted Scott. He'd had no patience with his political mentors when he was in the Army, it was why he'd never risen above the rank of Major-General while less able men were promoted over him. He was damned if he was going to have any truck with this specimen.

Munro was standing with his back to the sun, but he looked more like an ageing gigolo than the angel of death.

"I don't understand," he said, frowning at the old soldier. "You could have had all that. Elemental power."

"It doesn't work like that," Scott murmured. The man's a fool! "If you don't understand that, you misunderstand the entire nature of the Fisher King. The power is essentially passive. Try to use it otherwise, and balance will be destroyed."

"I don't believe you," Munro snapped, looking at the old man's faded gray eyes. "There is no point to power if you don't use it."

Scott eyed him wearily, hoping that the true heir would arrive soon. The other man's aura felt hot and red, like a forest fire. Out of control. "You would think that," he said in a tired voice. "Your kind always does."

His adversary's face reddened. A vein throbbed in his temple. The heat radiated off him. "I know all about power."

"About its misuse," agreed Scott.

"You are very mouthy for a man in your position." Munro took his revolver from his pocket, and the old soldier began to laugh, wheezily.

"And you are entirely predictable," he managed to say. Munro, enraged, pointed the gun at him. "Oh, please. Do you really think you can threaten me with that thing?"

The baronet's face distorted with fury. Scott refused to flinch. "I should just shoot you and have done with it."

"And then what?" asked Scott. "You think the burden passes automatically to you if you kill me?"

"No," Munro snarled. "I think I should kill you because *you won't shut your mouth!"* His voice rose to a shout. In the chair, Scott merely smiled.

"Your power is not so very great now, is it?"

"Shut up!" screamed Munro, and hit him across the face with the barrel of the gun. The old man's thin skin broke, and blood trailed down his cheek from the cut.

Too accustomed to the abuse of power, Munro did not understand why the Fisher King felt no fear.

*   *   *

Meu Deus, he makes Harris look small. I glanced at Leão, stunned by the sheer size of the man coming down the mountain. Beside me, the shaman gave a low growl.

"Wait," I said quietly to him. Put out a hand to hold him back. "Who are you?" He must be six foot six if he's an inch. And built like a — Well, he could squash Leão.

He could squash me, too. Bad idea, da Silva. I started up the track.

"Who am I?" repeated the giant, thoughtfully. "I have had many names. Cuchulainn. Herakles. Gilgamesh. At present, I am merely the guardian of the healing chalice."

I looked at his enormous hands. "You know about the prophecy?"

"That the lion must come and be true to his nature," he said, nodding his huge head. "As I am to mine."

My classical education had been interrupted a long time ago. I didn't make the connection until it was too late.

Leão pushed past me. "I think I have to do this, captain."

"No—" I made a grab for him, but he dodged. Launched himself towards the guardian. In mid-air for an instant, I thought he blurred into a big cat shape, but when he landed on the man, he was only human, and terribly small in comparison. But the guardian staggered backwards under his momentum and fell to the ground.

"Skipper—" shouted Pierce urgently from somewhere behind me. I didn't have a chance to turn and look at him. "Herakles killed the Nemean lion, it was one of his labors—" Yes, trust Pierce to come up with the classical reference.

The guardian put his huge arms around Leão and began to squeeze. I saw his great muscles straining. "Stop that!" I drew my knife and started towards them. Heard Leão wheezing. Put the blade at the big man's throat. "Let him go," I told him, "or you'll regret it."

He threw himself backwards from the knife and surged to his feet, still clutching Leão in a death-grip.

"Are you offering to fight me in his stead?" He sounds amused. Well, who can blame him? I eyed him sourly.

"Looks like it," I said. *Of all the damn silly schemes you've come up with, da Silva, this one wins the first prize.*

"And who are you?" he asked, easing the pressure on Leão. I scratched my eyebrow and grimaced.

"They tell me I'm a paladin." Shrugged my shoulders. "Let's find out if it's true."

"Let me help," a low voice insisted, in my ear. I don't have time for this now.

"Oh, go away, Belphegor," I said irritably, without turning.

The giant guardian dumped Leão on the ground. He fell to his knees, coughing. "Come, then... paladin."

"Hey, big fellow," called Harris. "You don't think we're gonna let the skipper do this alone, do you?" I turned. They were all right behind me. There was no sign of Belphegor. Perhaps it's really gone back to hell.

"We have skills you may not suspect," Yeoh put in.

"And the rest of the hallows," added Tatiana. Though quite how much of a threat that is, I'm not sure. We can cut our way back with the spear. But we don't know what the dish and the broken sword can do. If anything.

He bowed his head with a great sigh. Seemed about to speak. Then his eyes widened in alarm. I looked quickly around. Just in case there was a dragon coming up the path behind me. Jumpy, da Silva?

"All hangs in the balance," exclaimed the guardian, starting to run down the hill. "You, lion-man, are worthy of the chalice. Bring the other hallows, bring the child, and follow me! We may yet be in time."

There was such urgency in his voice that we did as we were told without question. But in my experience, an expression like *We may yet be in time* usually means, *We're already too late.*

18

SOMEONE ELSE DOING THE LEADING FOR A CHANGE. I LIKE THAT, I
THINK. Well, no, I don't, to be truthful. It's just another way of not being in
control. But I suppose now's not the time to debate the chain of command. At
least this fellow didn't hang around wasting time debating the state of the da
Silva soul.

We crashed down the hillside in his wake. I was still clutching my knife. Big
fellow didn't say anything about needing to put it away. And seems to me it'd
be a bad idea anyway. I saw the look in his eyes.

I wish I knew what the devil it is we're charging after. So does Harris,
who muttered breathlessly, "What'n hell're we chasing?"

"Search me," I shot back, and he gave one of his barking laughs.

Didn't have to wait very long to find out. We bypassed the village I'd
seen. Raced round the back of a house standing a little apart from the others.
The guardian stopped at a door in the white wall and punched it with his
fist. Which made me wince, but the door burst off its hinges with a crash and
his knuckles didn't even look bruised. *Nice trick if you can do it,* I thought
manically, and exchanged a glance with Harris.

A heartbeat later, I was through the door. Saw a pleasant courtyard
furnished with potted plants. And a chair with an elderly man sitting in it. His
head was bleeding, and Sir Robert Munro was standing beside him, with a
gun in his hand.

"Here you are," he said silkily. "Have you brought my hallows?"

"My liege, are you all right?" asked the guardian, ignoring him and
stepping forward. Stupid question. Stupid idea. I grabbed his arm. It felt like
skin over stone. He shook my hand away, like swatting a fly.

"He'll shoot—" I got out. And Munro did. I saw a spray of blood fan out
from the guardian's chest, and he staggered back. Munro shot him again,
and I went for him, low and more frightened than I've ever been of any

demon. Heard the crash as the big man fell to the ground. Meu Deus, how appallingly easy to kill a hero.

I was six feet from Munro when he brought his gun round and pointed it straight at my face. I nearly fell over trying to stop before he shot me. He's out of reach. Damn it. I eyed the distance between us.

"Don't try it," he advised me. "Or you'll be dead as well."

"He's not dead," said the old man in the chair.

He's not singing comic songs, either. "You're the Fisher King?" I asked him. He nodded. The blood on his face wasn't moving. It was a while since Munro'd hit him, then.

"Douglas Scott," he said. Voice calm as if he was shaking my hand in the street. The English stiff upper lip in action.

"Ah... Luís da Silva," I introduced myself. And assorted retinue.

"Shut up, both of you," spat Munro. "This isn't a blasted garden party. That bugger's not dead, you say?"

"It is not so easy to kill a hero," Scott remarked. I'm glad to be wrong, then.

"I don't much care. As long as he stays down." I turned my head to look at him. Couldn't see much else than that bloody great black hole at the end of the gun-barrel. I moistened my lips. Raised one eyebrow. Knew my hands were shaking.

"So what are you going to do now?" I asked him. At least my voice is steady. "Shoot me — then what?"

"Oh, I'll think of something." He smiled. About the most purely nasty expression I've ever seen on a human face. "Drop the knife."

"Why should I?" I retorted. "You'll shoot me anyway." His finger tightened on the trigger. Be told, da Silva. I bent my knees and put the knife on the ground. Didn't take my eye off him. Don't know why. Not much I can do about it if he does pull the trigger. Sweat started trickling down my face.

"Kick it over here." Munro was enjoying this. He's the only one. I gritted my teeth. Did what he told me. "You people. If any one of you moves without my permission, I'll shoot this bloody interfering dago. Now, I want the hallows here."

Scott's eyes widened slightly, and he gave the smallest of smiles. Munro's done something wrong. What? Calling for the hallows? Why? Would they heal this old man? I looked at him closely, but got no clues. Was a bit preoccupied. You might say.

"How can we bring them if we're not supposed to move?" Tatiana Dimitrovna enquired, acidly. Munro's smile widened.

"And the little witch as well. Are you warming his bed now? Does he know you're a whore?" I clenched my fists. My nails dug into my hands. "Well, you can be the first. Bring the sword here. Any sign of any magic, and I'll blow his bloody head off."

"Your magic will not work here," the Fisher King interrupted, "any more than this warlock's does."

"Be quiet," Munro snapped. "Come on, witch." I heard her footsteps. "Stop there." But couldn't see her. "Now slide it over to me. Blade first."

The two bits of the sword slid into view. "Happy?" she snarled.

"Kick it to me, da Silva." I glared at him, but complied. "Witch, get back. Now you, Chinky. Do the same with the dish."

He stopped Yeoh behind me as well, too far from him to try anything. "I cannot reach him," he whispered. I shrugged my shoulders as unnoticeably as I could. Yeoh slid the dish viciously across the paving stones. It came to rest against the hilt of the sword with a clang.

"Temper, temper," Munro murmured. "Go back, now." I heard Yeoh retreat. What the hell can I do? "Bring me the chalice, now, you, negro."

"I am sorry," said Leão from behind me. "I failed."

"You didn't," I said, wishing I could wipe some of the sweat off my face. He pushed the chalice past my feet. I wondered fleetingly whether it was possible to kick it at Munro. Damn stupid thought. Shows how far gone I am. I clutched at my temper, trying to subdue it. *Cool heads are better in crises, da Silva.*

"What are you waiting for?" Munro demanded. "Go on, get back. Now you — Ginger. Don't get too close. I don't want any funny business with that thing."

Harris was too far behind for me to hear what he said. But I knew as he spoke what he was up to. I could've wished he'd done it sooner. But maybe he thought he needed to be as close as Munro would let him. My heart gave an enormous lurch, and began to pound.

And the little blue demon, Tatiana's familiar, Harris's pet, popped into existence and clutched at Munro's head with all four limbs.

"Skipper, take the spear!" Harris shouted.

"No," I said. "I refuse to be an archetype." I took two quick steps, seized Munro's wrist and tried to wrench the gun out of it. He fought like a madman, the snarling demon still attached to his face. The bastard kicked me painfully on the shin, and I swore. Any kind of residual doubts I had about hitting a man so much older than me had pretty much gone when he pointed the gun at me, so I knocked him to the ground and banged his hand against the paving stones. He lost his grip on the gun, and tore the demon loose from his head. His face was bleeding.

With difficulty, I restrained an urge to smash his head on the ground. Pinned him down instead, breathing hard, shaking with anger and reaction. He tried to throw me off, and I put my hand round his throat.

"Luís—" I heard Tatiana say, from a long distance away.

"Give me one reason why I shouldn't kill you," I said. Munro glared murderously up at me, but said nothing. I wiped sweat off my face with my free hand.

"Look at the hallows!" exclaimed Pierce.

Leaving my hand where it was, leaning on it so he choked a bit, I turned to look. If he doesn't get the message that I'll crush his windpipe if he moves, he'll soon find out.

Little Susana was sitting on the old king's lap. At his feet the four hallows had — changed. I don't quite know how to describe it. They seemed to have become more real. More solid. As if everything else around them, trees, earth, us, were less substantial than the hallows.

"You can use them to heal Nikos," said Scott, gesturing to the fallen guardian. Zacuto was squatting beside him. The nearest thing we have to a doctor.

"Can't we heal you, sir?" Pierce asked him. Bit of English fellow-feeling there.

"No. I am dying." Everyone looked in Munro's direction. "No, not by his hand. He is only a sorcerer who cannot even command the element he has passed through."

"Fire?" Tatiana asked. Scott nodded.

"The grail to heal Nikos; the sword to disunite and reunite." Susana gripped his forefinger with one tiny hand. He looked down at her and smiled. "This little one is the heir, as you recognized," he said softly. "But the hallows cannot heal her yet, not until she reaches puberty. So you should heal Nikos. He has been my... friend for many years."

"How very touching," sneered a voice I recognized. I turned my head to see Belphegor standing over Munro. It was wearing the semi-mechanical demon guise I'd seen outside my father's house. "You disappoint me, Luís da Silva." Then it said something to Munro in a language I didn't recognize. But Tatiana Dimitrovna did, and so did Zacuto. Munro's eyes widened.

"Kill it!" shouted Zacuto, and "Kill Munro," the witch screamed.

"*Venite*, Belphegor, I invite you in," gabbled Munro. And the thing happened that I'd seen once before. The demon sank into, was absorbed by, the body of the man. It killed him. This time I felt him die under my hand, felt the last rattling breath leave his body. Saw his eyes turn red.

At that, I let go of his throat and lunged for my knife. Felt, rather than saw, Munro's body lurch to its feet. Swiveled awkwardly in a half-crouch and rose to face it.

"It is time," said the Fisher King calmly. I haven't the time to ask him what he means. Harris yelled something incoherent and scythed the spear at the possessed man. Who leapt nimbly into the air letting the blade swish harmlessly beneath his feet.

"Hey!" barked Harris, indignantly.

Munro — Belphegor — landed, caught his balance, grabbed the shaft just behind the head and drove it hard into Harris's midsection. He went down gasping for breath and swearing. The demon threw the spear down contemptuously.

Whatever Belphegor intended, and with this particular demon it's not always the obvious, possessing Munro did one thing for me. Removed any inhibitions about killing him.

Because, like the Venetian, he's already dead. And it's all down to da Silva again, because Harris is on the ground gasping like a landed codfish and everyone else was rooted to the spot. Demons do that to most people.

Inhabiting Munro, I realized a moment later, limited Belphegor's fighting skills. An elderly politician's body simply isn't as flexible as the demon's girl-form. It could make him stronger and faster, sure. But it couldn't make him do back-flips.

I lunged at it with my knife. Munro's body dodged. His eyes glowed red as coals. As he backed, he scooped up the scabbard with one hand and tipped the sword-blade out of it.

Oh *merda*. How could I have forgotten the Venetian's death-grip on my knife, his fingers nearly severed? Munro was dead, and couldn't feel pain. And Belphegor didn't care. I saw blood start to flow sluggishly down the man's arms.

But instead of coming at me with two feet of razor-sharp metal, he turned and swung the blade at the Fisher King. It sheared his head from his shoulders with one reaping stroke. Susana shuddered as if someone had hit her, and blood fountained over her. I saw Alegria snatch the child from the dead man's lap as she began to scream. Ana, not to be outdone, joined in.

The sword-blade fell to the ground with a clang, spattering a fine spray of blood over the paving stones. I didn't see where Scott's head went. Or have time to look at his ghost boiling up out of his body. I slashed at Munro furiously. The point of the knife grazed his face as he swayed to avoid it, and I snatched it back before he could grab hold of that as well.

Wounding it won't do any good. It would have to be a killing blow. And even that wouldn't kill Belphegor. Seems you can only kill the bloody things when they're in their own shape.

Munro skipped backwards, dodging my knife with a daintiness that was quite grotesque. Apparently it doesn't want to fight. What does it want? Stand still, damn you.

"Belphegor," I panted, "what the hell are you doing?"

"This man wanted to be king," answered the demon in Munro's voice. Only it wasn't quite Munro's voice. There was a hollow timbre to it that left anyone who heard it in no doubt that he was dead.

"He wanted the power of the hallows." I wiped sweat off my face with my sleeve. The demon attempted to smile, but it didn't have full control of the facial muscles and the smile didn't quite work.

"Oh, he has much more than that, now."

"Only a demon could think that." *Kill it, da Silva. Don't hold a conversation with it.*

Belphegor had another try at a smile. It wasn't any better than the first one. "And what do you propose to do, then, *mortal?*" it asked pointedly.

I took a deep breath. Laid the flat of the knife-blade across the palm of my right hand and felt its reassuring weight. The tip was stained with Munro's blood. I was careful not to touch that. "Kill you, of course."

"Skipper," wheezed Harris, "be careful." He was halfway to his feet. Munro's body swiveled gracefully on one heel and kicked him halfway across the courtyard. Harris crashed into a flowerpot about the size of a madeira wine barrel, smashing the terracotta, and lay still.

"That," I said to the demon, "was about the stupidest thing you could've done." And I charged it again, fed-up and angry.

But it's too bloody fast. I can't even land a blow. Ducks under my arm, comes up inside, aims a fist at me, I dodge. Try to skewer it, it's spun out of reach again, foot in the air to kick me under the chin.

Dropping the knife, I seized the flying foot in both hands, damn that hurt! Gave it a twist and flung it to the ground. Sweat stung my eye. Scooped up my knife, taking too much time. Belphegor bounced back to Munro's feet like an india-rubber toy. Came in low and tried to punch me in the groin. I turned fast, caught the blow on my thigh, felt like the kick of a mule. Drove the knife into its neck, but it moved its head to the side. Flesh-wound again. Munro grunted. No, I'd done more damage than I thought. Nicked the artery perhaps. But blood flows too slowly from an animate corpse.

It stepped back, squatted down, and leapt at me too fast for me to bring the knife up again. We crashed to the ground, but I twisted sideways, bruises screaming at me. Still got the wind knocked out of me. Munro landed awkwardly, and I heard something crack, hoped it was a major bone. He couldn't get up with a broken femur. I moved before he could, got my right elbow under me, hand, onto my feet without too much of a stagger.

And Tatiana Dimitrovna stepped forward quickly, put Munro's gun to his head, and pulled the trigger.

Belphegor screeched like an express train and yanked itself out of Munro's body almost as fast as one. A kind of semi-formed, semi-transparent cloud sucked out from the corpse, and vanished. The body left behind desiccated, flesh shrinking away, skin flaking like burnt paper and blowing off the bones. Then the skeleton itself crumbled into fine dust and blew away.

Tatiana Dimitrovna, still holding the gun, remarked, "Idiot demon."

Have to agree with her on that one. I looked at her, then down at the blowing dust. Cleaned the blood off my knife. Put it back in its sheath. "Thank you," I said. "What took you so long?"

She grimaced. "It has a strong fear-geas, that demon. I had to work round it. Did you not feel it?" I lit a much-needed cheroot and sucked smoke in gratefully. Grateful, in another sense, that I still could.

"Met that one too often to notice." I limped over to where Harris was lying in a pile of earth and potsherds. He groaned, coming round. I squatted beside him. My left knee cracked, then the right. Full house. Damn it. Da Silva's falling to pieces. "You all right, Harris?" Define *all right*. Alive? Undamaged?

He spat. "Yeah, I guess so. Feels like I've been kicked by a goddamn carthorse. Twice." He looked round. "You kill it, skipper?"

"Not this time." I nodded at Tatiana with a wry grin. His eyes widened as he took in the gun she was holding. He gave a grunt of laughter.

"Poetic justice, huh?"

"For Munro, maybe," I agreed, darkly. Took a drag of my cheroot.

"The demon?" He knows better than to name it. Smart werewolf.

I pushed myself to my feet. The bruise on my thigh throbbed painfully at me. "It'll be back." Sure as Christmas comes in December. Harris phrased it better.

"Yeah," he said gloomily. "Sure as a bear craps in the woods."

There was a kind of subdued cacophony going on. And guess who'll have to sort that out. Calm things down. Pat ruffled feathers. And all that sort of thing.

Alegria, bless her, had calmed Ana down. Thing of paint and imagination she may be, but she does being human better than a lot of humans I've met. Though to be fair, Ana can be forgiven for having hysterics. It's not every day a demon-possessed politician decapitates someone right next to you.

"I don't get it," said Harris, bending with a grimace of pain to look at the sword-blade. "How'd he do that? I thought these goddamned things were supposed to be — well, good." Zacuto moved to join him. As usual, the ghost had an explanation.

"The grail hallows are all double-edged," he said, in full didactic mode. "Like all magic," he added with only a fleeting glance at the witch. Quite right too. It's not as if he doesn't practise magic himself. Hell, he wouldn't be here without magic. And how, if Scott was right, is he even still here? I hadn't given much thought to it when he'd said other magic doesn't work around the hallows. Or whatever it was he did say. Since I had other things on my mind at the time.

"He told us to heal — Nikos, was it?" I asked, looking at the fallen giant and expelling smoke. "Any ideas how to do that?"

"Oh, yes." Zacuto sounded a little impatient. "That was why he had to die. For balance."

"That must have been what he meant," Pierce interrupted. "When he said it was time."

"A sacrifice?" Tatiana Dimitrovna sounded doubtful. The ghost turned to her.

"This is old magic, senhora," he reminded her. "Very old. And the older it is, the more elemental it is. The more likely to be blood magic." He eyed her closely. "As you should know from your experience of the goddess Tanit."

She winced. I'm also entitled to wince from *my* experience of the goddess Tanit. It hadn't been blood sacrifice on her mind on that occasion. I scratched my cheekbone instead.

"I thought the old king had to die to pass... whatever it is on to Susana," I said. *Something* had certainly happened to her at his death.

"Yes, of course," Zacuto agreed. "The passing of the kingship. He told us he was dying, and I at least could see it was true. He chose to make the sacrifice." The ghost looked narrowly at me. I blew out smoke. Wondered what the look meant. I don't see shades until the person is dead. No thanks. "He also told us, if you recall, that Susana cannot be healed yet."

"Until she reaches puberty," remembered Tatiana. "And then, one presumes, another sacrifice will need to be made."

The old scholar nodded. "At that time, another sacrifice may present itself. Until then, there is no point in speculation. Now, please, let us carry out the late king's wishes."

"The king is dead, long live the king," muttered Pierce. Susana chose to agree by letting loose a hiccup and a penetrating scream that made everyone jump. That child certainly has a pair of lungs. If she weren't the Fisher King she'd probably grow up to be an opera singer.

The chalice was still standing by the chair where the old king's body was slumped. Where his new ghost shimmered. Someone had pulled the blanket up to cover the headless corpse. Some drops of his blood had splattered into the inside of the cup. They appeared to be still liquid. Why am I not surprised?

"Leão," I said. The shaman, who was standing a little way off, raised his head.

"Yes, Captain?"

"You should do this." I glanced at Zacuto, who nodded.

"Yes, senhor, the chalice is in your charge now."

"Very well." Leão gestured downwards. "I was considering the old man's words. The sword to disunite and reunite."

I walked over to see what he was looking at. Scott's head lay half-concealed behind a flower-pot. There's something very disturbing about severed heads. Well, they give me the creeps, anyway. I frowned.

"He can't have meant we could heal him?" I said. Examined the end of my cheroot. Not enough for another drag. I disposed of it in the flowerpot.

"No, indeed," Zacuto agreed. "That would not be possible, even with something as powerful as the hallows. I think he was acting for our benefit. As a king should." We looked blankly at him. He smiled in that smug way he has when he's worked something out ahead of the rest of us. Which is most of the time. "We would find a decapitated corpse difficult to explain, no? He gave us the knowledge to spare us that problem."

"Well, that was damn decent of him," said Pierce after a pause. He was avoiding looking at the head. His face had a greenish tinge. "But shouldn't we, ah, heal poor old Nikos first?"

Leão nodded. "Yes, indeed." He bent down and picked up the chalice, grunting almost inaudibly. As if it was tremendously heavy. The antiquarian followed him over to the huge prone figure of Nikos. I watched them, feeling slightly guilty that I hadn't gone to check on him. Bit of resentment there, da Silva? Against the regular pedigree sort of hero? I smiled wryly, and followed them across the courtyard. Pierce is right, of course.

"What d'you suppose?" he asked, taking off his spectacles and wiping the lenses absently against his waistcoat. "Rub it on, or drink it?"

For answer, Leão upended the chalice over Nikos's wounds. I suppose the guardian of the chalice instinctively knows how to use it. Two drops of the old king's blood fell on them, and they absorbed it like dry earth soaking up rainwater. And then the bullets that had struck him just popped out of their holes. The angry wounds scabbed over. The scabs dried and shrank, then fell off, leaving two round pink scars behind.

"Goddamn, that was easy," remarked Harris, adding a moment later, "He ain't waking up, though."

"Maybe he's sleeping it off," Pierce suggested.

Well, if you ask me he can stay asleep until we're gone.

Tatiana Dimitrovna picked up the sword-blade rather gingerly, and started to wipe Munro's blood from the broken end using a corner of Scott's blanket. I eyed the shrouded corpse and Scott's drifting ghost without enthusiasm. *Delegate, da Silva. You're the captain.*

"Harris," I said resignedly, "give me a hand."

Together we lifted the old king's body carefully, more out of a desire not to get covered in his blood than of reverence. We only take care with the dead to avoid upsetting the living. Far as I'm concerned, when it's dead, it's dead. The soul's gone wherever it goes, and what's left is meat. Perhaps literally, to Harris. Though I'm sure he would only eat a human body as a last resort. Damn it, he's fastidious about rats, never mind anything else.

When we'd put Scott's body on the ground I glanced at Harris and raised an eyebrow. He gave me an amused sort of glance and went over to where the head lay.

"Don't worry, skipper, it won't bite," he remarked, cheerfully. And that's all *he* knows.

"No, it probably won't, now," I agreed. He looked startled, but bent down and picked it up in both hands.

"Heavier than you'd think." Yes, they always are. I nodded.

He put the head in position, and the hovering ghost seemed to pay closer attention. Tatiana Dimitrovna brought the sword-blade over and laid it on his chest. The shade fluttered agitatedly. Is it trying to tell me something? I cast around for ideas.

"Better get the hilt as well," I suggested, scratching my eyebrow.

She did so, and knelt carefully beside the body. "Do you think I should put them toge—" The broken ends of the blade clicked together of their own accord, and pulsed for an instant with a light like the sun. I turned my head away, closing my eye and shading it with my hand as well. And I should think everyone else did too. When I opened it again, Scott's body was whole, and so was the sword.

A sharp metallic cracking sound made me whip round, hand hovering over my shoulder. I blinked in surprise. The dish, Yeoh's charge, had cracked down the center and lay in two pieces by Scott's chair.

Zacuto chuckled. "Entirely appropriate," he remarked with something like satisfaction. "Come on, captain," he added at my puzzled look, "you realized the significance of the broken sword. The wounded king is now female, the sword is inappropriate."

And the witch started to laugh too, but she didn't sound that amused. "Tell that to Tanit," she said dryly.

*   *   *

After we released the captured souls last year I felt much the same. We just won a war but nobody knows. But this time there's a bit more to it than just putting an over-ambitious sorcerer out of business. Well, when I say out of business, I mean dead, of course.

Quite apart from this whole Fisher King business. I'm getting more than a little fed up with every damn supernatural bigwig in the ether getting into a lather about me. I'm not even going to enter the debate. I see ghosts. Fine. No, not fine, obviously. But that, I can live with. I don't like it, but I can live with. Hell, I've got no choice. However, that's it. I'm not the Fisher King's champion. I'm not anyone's champion. Except Emilia's. That's the way things stay. And you think I'm turning my back on my responsibilities, that's tough. Running *Isabella* is quite enough for me.

I know, of course, that one day little Susana will be old enough to do whatever it is the Fisher King does. Given her strange rate of growth, it probably won't be fourteen years. She already looks like a two-year-old. But until then, who knows. I don't understand her tie to the land. I do know that the old king's disease was incurable. And that the land itself isn't in a good state. If the German Kaiser doesn't declare war on someone this year or the next, someone'll declare war on Germany instead.

According to Zacuto, who is the nearest thing we have to an expert, the hallows stay with their new custodians. Harris, for one, wasn't particularly happy about that. But the things aren't real, at least not in a physical sense. He doesn't have to cart around a great long stick with a point on the end. Which is what he was worried about. After all, where would he put it when he goes wolf? He didn't appreciate my suggestion.

When *Isabella's* official business in Cyprus was done, we actually sailed most of the way back to Lisbon on the other sea. I'm more comfortable with it than I was, though I don't want to make a habit of it. Not that I can, without a witch who's been to hell to guide me. I did insist on returning to the world's oceans well before Trafalgar, though.

I'm going to have to be creative with the dates in the log on this one. And more than the dates.

It was mainly, I admit, because I wanted to be back with Emilia. It's not that I don't trust myself around Tatiana Dimitrovna. I am just about old enough to keep myself under control. And oddly enough I trust her better now than I ever did before. Only, I don't think it's fair on either of us to be near each other at the moment. She says she's going back to London. By her own methods. London's not that far, but it'll do. I worried about what to say to Emilia about her. Until I decided that the only thing I could tell her was what I always tell her. The truth. Obvious, da Silva. What were you using for brains?

And of course when I saw her it was all easy. I won't say I forgot about Tatiana Dimitrovna, but I lost the lust spell. No, I said I was going to be honest. I know it wasn't a spell. It was me. Us. The Russian witch and Luís da Silva. I don't deny there's something between us. Even Munro saw it, and he was hardly the most sensitive of souls.

I watched the dawn lightening the sky over Lisbon through the open shutters with Emilia in my arms. How I miss this. How I value it. And how I want to stay here. Sometimes, at times like this, I wish I could retire and never have to go to sea again. But then I think of the best days on board *Isabella*. Skimming over the ocean with all the canvas taut above me, the air full of the indescribable sound of the wind, the sun warming me. I am my ship every bit as much as the witches and the ghosts tell me. The sea is in my blood as much as Emilia is.

She brought me back to dry land, then said, "You said that man Munro left a golem behind in London to take his place."

"That's what the witch said," I answered absently, enjoying the smell of her hair and skin against skin.

"And he's a politician."

"Mm-hm," I mumbled, not feeling particularly eloquent. She started to shake, and I realized that she was laughing. I opened my eye and said, "What?"

"Oh, Luís," she got out between giggles, "Whoever is going to be able to tell the difference?"

That was all it took to set me laughing as well. I buried my face in her hair and hugged her tighter, and we clung together, cackling like loons.

Outside, over the red rooftops, the sun came up.

ALSO BY CHICO KIDD

Demon Weather (Da Silva Tales, #1) (Fantasy) The adventures of Captain Da Silva, who has lost an eye and gained the power to see ghosts. A rollicking, rip-roaring read.

The Printer's Devil (Historical Fantasy) A demon summoned long ago by a heartbroken lover in Cromwellian England, now reawakened by a curious scholarly researcher. Who will pay the price?

www.ingramcontent.com/pod-product-compliance
Lightning Source LLC
Chambersburg PA
CBHW030349030726
47497CB00002B/247